Summer Reads Box Set

Volume #1

Summer Secrets

Golden Lies

Don't Say A Word

BARBARA FREETHY

BARBARA
FREETHY
—BOOKS—

Fog City Publishing

SUMMER SECRETS

SUMMER SECRETS - BLURB

#1 New York Times Bestselling author Barbara Freethy presents a powerful contemporary novel—the story of three unique sisters ... the secrets that bind them for life ... and the summer that will set them free.

Eight years ago, the three McKenna sisters—Kate, Ashley, and Caroline—had their fifteen minutes of fame. Driven by their ambitious father, they won an around-the-world sailing race as teenagers. But something happened out on the stormy, turbulent sea they could never forget ...

Now Tyler Jamison has come to Castleton, a picturesque island off the coast of Washington State, asking questions about the famous McKennas. But even as the sisters close ranks against the tenacious reporter, the past threatens to drown them in its wake. It will take Caroline's willingness to right a wrong, Ashley's struggle to face her greatest fears, and Kate's attempt to embrace life—and love—again to finally calm the winds and stop the rain.

PROLOGUE

SHIP'S LOG, Moon Dancer, July 10

Wind: 40 knots, gusting to 65 knots
Sea Conditions: rough, choppy, wild
Weather Forecast: rain, thunder, lightning

Kate McKenna's fingers tightened around the pen in her hand as the Moon Dancer surfed up one wave and down the next. The ship's log told nothing of their real journey, revealed none of the hardships, the secrets, the heartbreak, the danger they now faced. She wanted to write it down, but she couldn't. Her father's instructions were explicit: Nothing but the facts.

She couldn't write that she was worried, but she was. The weather was turning, the barometer dropping. A big storm was coming. If they changed course, they would lose valuable time, and her father would not consider that option. They were currently in second place—second place and heading straight into the fury of the sea. She could hear the winds beginning to howl. She feared there would be hell to pay this night. Everyone's nerves were on edge. Arguments could be heard in every corner of the boat. She wanted to make it all go away. She wanted to take her sisters and go home, but home was at the other end of the ocean.

"Kate, get up here!" someone yelled.

She ran up on deck, shocked to the core by the intensity of the storm. The spray blew so hard it almost took the skin off her face. She had to move, had to help her father reef down the sails to the storm jib. But all she could do was stare at the oncoming wave. It must be forty feet high and growing. Any second it would crash over their boat. How on earth would they survive?

And, if they didn't, would anyone ever know the true story of their race around the world?

CHAPTER ONE

EIGHT YEARS LATER...

"The wind blew and the waves crashed as the mighty dragon sank into the sea to hide in the dark depths of the ocean until the next sailor came too close to the baby dragons. The End."

Kate McKenna smiled at the enraptured looks on the faces before her. Ranging in age from three to ten, the children sat on thick, plump cushions on the floor in a corner of her store, Fantasia. They came three times a week to hear her read stories or tell tales. At first they were chatty and restless, but once the story took hold, they were hers completely. Although it wasn't the most profitable part of her book-store business, it was by far the most enjoyable.

"Tell us another one," the little girl sitting next to her pleaded.

"One more," the other children chorused.

Kate was tempted to give in, but the clock on the wall read five minutes to six, and she was eager to close on time this Friday night. It had been a long, busy week, and she had inventory to unpack before the weekend tourist crowds descended. "That's all for today," she said, getting to her feet. Although the children protested, the group gradually drifted from the store, a few mothers making purchases on their way out the door.

"Great story," Theresa Delantoni said. "Did you make that up as you went along, or did you read it somewhere?"

"A little of both," Kate told her assistant. "My dad used to tell us stories about dragons that lived under the sea. One time we were sailing just outside the Caribbean, and the sea suddenly seemed to catch fire. Dragons, I thought, just like my father said. It turned out to be phosphorus algae. But my sisters and I preferred the fire-breathing dragon story."

"A romantic at heart."

"It's a weakness, I admit."

"Speaking of romance..." Theresa's cheeks dimpled into an excited smile, "it's my anniversary, and I have to leave now. I promised I wouldn't be late, because our baby sitter can only give us two hours." Theresa took her purse out of the drawer behind the counter. "I hate to leave you with all those boxes to unpack."

"But you will." Kate followed her to the door. "Don't think twice. You deserve a night off with that darling husband of yours."

Theresa blushed. "Thanks. After eight years of marriage and two babies who need a lot of attention, sometimes I forget how lucky I am."

"You are lucky."

"And you are great with kids. You should think about having some of your own."

"It's easy to be great for an hour."

"Brrr," Theresa said as they walked out of the store together. She stopped to zip up her sweater. "The wind is picking up."

"Out of the southwest," Kate said automatically, her experienced nautical eye already gauging the knots to be between twelve and fifteen. "There's a storm coming. It should be here by six o'clock. Take an umbrella with you."

"You're better than the weather report," Theresa said with a laugh. "Don't stay too late, now. People will start to suspect you don't have a life."

Kate made a face at her friend. "I have a fine life." Theresa was halfway to her car and didn't bother to reply. "I have a great life," Kate repeated. After all, she lived in Castleton, one of the most beautiful spots in the world, a large island off the coast of Washington State, one of the several hundred islands that made up the archipelago known as the San Juans.

Her bookstore at the northern end of Pacific Avenue had an incredible view of the deep blue waters of Puget Sound. It was one of the interesting, quaint shops that ran down a two-mile cobblestone strip to Rose Harbor, a busy marina that filled every July with boats in town for the annual Castleton Invitational Sailboat Races.

Castleton was known for its rugged beauty, its fir and evergreen-covered hillsides and more than one hundred miles of driftwood-strewn beaches. Most of the island traffic came via the Washington State Ferry, although boaters were plentiful, and small private planes could land at the Castleton Airport.

The unpredictable southwesterly winds created swirling, dangerous currents along many of the beaches and had driven a few boats to ground on their way to shelter in the harbor. But the winds didn't stop the boats from coming or the sailors from congregating. Tales of sails and storms could be overheard in every restaurant, café, and business in town. There were more boat slips in the marina than there were parking spaces downtown. The lives of Castleton's residents weren't just by the sea, they were about the sea.

Kate loved her view of the waterfront—loved the one from her house in the hills even better—but more than anything she appreciated the fact that the view didn't change every day. Maybe some would call that boring, but she found it comforting.

The wind lifted the hair off the back of her neck, changing that feeling of comfort to one of uneasiness. Wind in her life had meant change. Her father, Duncan McKenna, a sailing man from the top of his head to the tips of his toes, always relished the wind's arrival. Kate could remember many a time when he had jumped to his feet at the first hint of a breeze. A smile would spread across his weather-beaten cheeks as he'd stand on the deck of their boat, pumping his fist triumphantly in the air, his eyes focused on the distant horizon. The wind's up, Katie girl, he'd say. It's time to go.

And they'd go—wherever the wind took them. They'd sail with it, into it, against it. They'd lash out in anger when it blew too hard, then cry in frustration when it vanished completely. Her life had been formed, shaped and controlled by the wind. She'd thought of it as a friend; she'd thought of it as a monster. Well, no more.

She had a home now, an address, a mailbox, a garden. She might live by the water, but she didn't live on it. The wind meant nothing more to her than an extra sweater and a bowl of soup for dinner. It didn't mean that her life was about to change. Why couldn't she believe that?

Because of the boats.

They'd been sailing into the harbor for the past week, every day a few more, each one bigger, brighter and better than the last. There was an energy in the air, a sense of excitement, purpose, adventure. In just a few days the race would begin, and next Saturday the biggest and brightest would race around the island in the Castleton Invitational. Two days later, the boats would be off again, racing to San Francisco and then on to Hawaii for the Pacific Cup. The sailors would battle the elements and one another. In the end, only one would be victorious.

Kate didn't appreciate the direction of her thoughts. She didn't want to think about the boats or the damn race. Ten days. It would all be over in ten days, she reminded herself as she walked back into the store and shut the door firmly behind her. She could handle the pleasure cruisers, the fishermen, the tourists interested in whale watching; what she couldn't handle were the racers, the fanatical sailors who lived to battle the ocean, to conquer new seas. She knew those men and women too well. Once, she'd been one of them.

The door to her store opened, accompanied by a melodious jangle from the wind chimes that hung outside. A man entered, dressed in khaki pants and a navy blue polo shirt. He had the look of a man on business. There was energy in his movements, a gleam in his deep blue eyes, and an impression of power and purpose in his stance. As he ran an impatient hand through his dark brown hair, Kate felt her pulse quicken. Strangers came into her store all the time asking for books, directions, information about the island, but none of those strangers had given her heart such a jump start. Maybe Theresa was right. She definitely needed to get out more.

"Hello." His voice had a bit of a drawl to it. The South? Texas? She wasn't sure where he'd come from, but she had a feeling it had been a long journey.

"Hello," she said. "Can I help you?"

"I certainly hope so."

"I'm betting you need directions, not a book."

He gave her a curious smile. "Now, why would you bet that?"

"You don't look like an armchair adventurer."

"You can tell that just by looking?"

She shrugged. "What can I say? I'm good."

"Not that good. I don't need directions."

"Oh. A book about sailing, then?"

"Wrong again."

Kate studied him thoughtfully. He hadn't stood still since he walked into the store, shifting his feet, tapping his fingers on the counter. He looked like a man who couldn't stop running even when he was tired. Hardly one to settle into a recliner with a good book.

However, she couldn't refute the fact that he had come into the bookstore of his own free will, so he must have had a reason.

"I know." She snapped her fingers. "Gift book. You need a book for Aunt Sally or Cousin Mary, or maybe the girlfriend whose birthday you forgot."

He laughed. "No Aunt Sally. No Cousin Mary. And, regretfully, no girlfriend."

Kate had to bite back the incredulous *really* that threatened to push past her lips. She settled for "Interesting. So what do you want?"

"I'm looking for someone."

"Aren't we all?"

"You're very quick."

He was quick, too, and it had been awhile since she'd flirted with a man. Not that she was flirting; she was just being friendly. "So, who are you looking for?'

He hesitated, and it was the small pause that made Kate tense. That and the way his gaze settled on her face. It had been eight years since someone had come looking for her. It wasn't likely this man was here for that reason, though. What were the odds? A million to one.

"A woman," he said slowly.

Kate licked her lips, trying not to turn away from the long, deep look he was giving her.

"I think I've found her," he added.

So much for odds.

"It's you, isn't it? Kate McKenna?" He smiled with satisfaction. "The oldest sister in the fearsome foursome that raced around the world in a sailboat. I recognize you from the photographs."

"Who wants to know?"

"Tyler Jamison." He stuck out his hand.

Kate gave his hand a brief shake. "What do you want?"

"A story."

"You're a reporter?" She had to admit she was surprised. She'd once been able to spot a reporter from a block away. She'd gotten complacent. That would have to change right now. "I can't imagine why you'd be looking for me. That race was a long time ago."

"Eight years. That would make you twenty-eight, right?"

Kate walked over to the door and turned the sign to *Closed*. If only she'd done it five minutes earlier, she would have missed this man. Not that he wouldn't have come back in the morning. He had a look of stubborn persistence about him. She suspected that he was a man who usually got what he wanted.

"I'd like to do a follow-up story on what's become of one of the most interesting sailing crews in ocean-racing history," Tyler continued. "It would tie in nicely with the upcoming sailboat races."

"I don't race anymore, but I'm sure I can find you some interesting racers to talk to. Take Morgan Hunt, for instance. He raced in the Sydney to Hobart last year and could tell you tales that would curl your toes."

"I'll keep that in mind. But I'd like to start with you and your sisters. Your father, too."

Duncan McKenna would love the publicity, adore being in the spotlight, but Lord only knew what he'd say once his tongue got going, especially if his tongue had been loosened by a few pints of beer, which would no doubt be the case.

"My father loves to talk about the past," Kate said, "but just like those fishermen whose stories of catches grow bigger by the year, so do my father's stories about that race. You can't believe a thing he says."

"What about you? You'd tell me the real story, wouldn't you?"

"Sure." She gave him what she hoped was a casual shrug. "Let's see. We sailed forever, it seemed. Some days were windy; some were hot. The wind ran fast, then slow. One week turned into the next with more of the same. The food was terrible. The seas were treacherous. The stars were always fantastic. That's about it."

"Short and succinct. Surely you can do better than that, Miss McKenna. A woman who appreciates books should be able to tell a better story."

"I sell books; I don't write them. Besides, there were a dozen news stories about the race in the weeks that followed our return. Everything that needed to be said was said. If you're interested, I'm sure you could find them on the Internet or in the library." She paused. "Do you write for a sailing magazine?"

"I'm a freelancer. I go where the story takes me."

Kate frowned. This was great. Just great. Another man who went with the wind. Why did they always stir up trouble in her life? "Well, there's no story here. We're all very boring. I run this bookstore, not exactly a hotbed of commerce, as you can see." She swept her hand around the room, forcing him to look at the cozy chairs by the window, the neatly stacked shelves of mysteries, fiction, fantasy, romance, children's books and, of course, the ever-popular books on seafaring.

Although she was trying to downplay the bookstore, she couldn't stop the sense of pride that ran through her as she looked around the room that she had decorated, remembering the care she'd taken with the children's corner now brightened by posters and stuffed animals. She'd turned the bookstore into a home away from home, a place of delicious escape. It hadn't been easy to build a business from nothing. But somehow she'd done it.

"It's nice," Tyler said. "From sailboat racer to bookstore owner. Sounds like an interesting journey. Tell me more."

She'd walked right into that one. "It's not interesting at all. Trust me."

"You're avoiding my questions. Why?"

"I'm not avoiding anything," she said with a laugh that even to her own ears sounded nervous. "It's like this—I was barely out of my awkward teenage years during that trip. I'm an adult now. I don't particularly want to rehash that time in my life. It was no big deal."

"It was a huge deal. Most people who win ocean races are seasoned sailors, sponsored by big corporations, sailing million-dollar boats. But the McKenna family beat them all. I can't understand why you don't want to talk about it. It must have been the biggest and best thing that ever happened to you."

"We had fifteen minutes of fame a long time ago. And our race was different. It wasn't filled with racing syndicates but with amateur sailors who had a passion for sailing and a longing for adventure. The racing world has changed. No one cares what happened to us."

"I do."

"Why?" Something about him didn't ring true. He seemed too confident, too purposeful to be after a fluff story. "Why do you care?"

"I like to write about adventurers, ordinary people who accomplish extraordinary things. And I'm fascinated by the thought of three girls and their father alone on the ocean, battling not only the other racers but the wind, the icebergs, fifty-foot waves. I've read some accounts of the trip, especially the harrowing details of the terrible storm during the second-to-last leg of the race. I can't imagine what you must have gone through."

There was a passion in his voice that bespoke a genuine interest, but why now? Why after all these years? Why this man—who had appeared out of nowhere and didn't seem to work for anyone? Why him?

"You look familiar," she said, studying the sharply drawn lines of his face. "Where have I seen you before?"

"I just have one of those faces. An average, everyday Joe." He paused. "So, what do you say? Will you talk to me? Or do I need to track down your sisters, Ashley and Caroline?"

Kate couldn't let him talk to Ashley or Caroline. She couldn't let this go any further. She had to get rid of him. But how?

"You're stalling," Tyler said. "I can see the wheels turning in your head."

"Don't be silly. I'm just busy. I have boxes to unpack before tomorrow, so I'm afraid we'll have to do this some other time."

The phone behind the counter rang, and she reached for it immediately, grateful for the interruption. "Fantasia," she said cheerfully. Her heart sank as she heard a familiar voice on the other end of the line. Will Jenkins ran the Oyster Bar on the waterfront, her father's favorite hangout. "How bad is he?" The answer put her heart into another nosedive. "I'll be right there. Yes, I know. Thanks, Will."

"Trouble?" Tyler inquired as she hung up the phone.

"No." She opened the drawer and pulled out her purse and keys. "I have to go. And so do you."

"You look upset."

"I'm fine." She opened the door, the breeze once again sending goose bumps down her arms. There was change in the air. She could feel it all around her.

"You don't look fine. Is someone hurt?" Tyler waited while she locked the door behind him. "Can I help?"

Kate told herself not to be taken in by the concern in his eyes. He was a reporter. He just wanted a story. "No one can help. You should go home. Back to wherever you came from."

"Thanks, but I think I'll stay a while. With all these sailors in town, I'm sure someone around here will talk to me."

"Suit yourself."

Kate hurried to her car, which she kept parked in back of her store.

Tyler Jamison was a problem she hadn't anticipated, but right now she had a more pressing matter to deal with. She turned on the ignition and let out the brake. Her small Volkswagen Jetta shook with another gust of wind. Her father always said if you can't own the wind, you have to ride it out. She had a feeling this was going to be one wild ride.

"Get me another beer," Duncan McKenna demanded as he put his fist down on top of the bar. He'd meant to slam it down hard, make the glasses jump, but he was too tired. "There was a time when a man could get a beer around here, Will."

The bartender finished drying off a glass at the other end of the bar. "You've had your limit, Duncan. You'll get no more from me tonight. You need to go home and sleep it off."

Sleep it off? He couldn't sleep. Hadn't for years. Oh, he dropped off now and then once the liquor took hold of his mind and gave him a blessed few hours of peace. But that didn't happen often, especially lately...

"Dammit, Will, I need a drink. I need one bad." He could hear the desperation in his voice, but he couldn't stop it. The need had been building in him all day, growing fiercer with each boat that sailed into the harbor, each dream of a journey, of a race to be sailed and to be won. That had been his world. God, how he missed it, missed the pitch of the waves, the power of the wind, the thrill of the race. Missed the pounding of his heart, the spine-tingling, palm sweating moments when all would be won or all would be lost. What a rush his life had been.

"I need a drink," he repeated.

Will walked down the length of the bar and gave him a hard look. "It won't do you no good, Duncan. I called Kate, and she's on her way."

"Why the hell did you call her?"

"Because you need a ride. You've been in here all day."

"I can get myself home." Duncan tried to stand up, but the room spun around, so he sat back down and held on to the edge of the bar for dear life.

"Sure you can," Will said dryly. "Just sit there. Don't try to leave."

"I'll do what I want," Duncan snapped. "I've been around the world upside down and backward. I won the goddamn Winston Around-the-World Challenge. No one thought we could do it. But we did, me and my girls." He paused and let out a weary sigh. "We were the best, Will. The very best. My girls got heart, just like their old man. They don't quit. I don't quit. McKennas don't quit."

"Yeah, yeah, I know."

And he did know because he'd heard it all before. Will was only a few years younger than Duncan, but he'd been tending bar for more than twenty years. Duncan couldn't understand how a man could be happy staying in one place for so long. Twenty years ago, Will had had hair on his head, a flat stomach, and girls lining up three-deep to flirt with him. Now he was bald, soft in the middle, and married to a librarian. Hell of a life he'd made for himself.

Will walked away to serve another customer at the end of the bar. Duncan turned his head and saw a woman sitting at a nearby table. As she moved, her hair caught the light, and he lost his breath at the glorious, fiery shade of red. Eleanor, he thought impossibly. His beloved Nora had hair the same color, and deep blue eyes that a man could drown in. He'd gone overboard the first time he'd seen her standing on the docks in a summer dress that showed off her long legs. His gut twisted in pain at the memory. Eleven years she'd been gone, but he still missed her. His heart felt as heavy as a stone. He wanted a drink. He wanted oblivion. He wanted—so many things.

"Dad?"

He tried to focus, but he couldn't see clearly. It's the alcohol, he told himself, but when he wiped the back of his hand across his eyes, it came away wet.

"Are you all right?" Kate asked with concern on her face.

Kate had the look of Nora in her eyes, but her hair was blond, her skin a golden brown and free of the beautiful freckles that had kissed Nora's nose. Kate's face was stronger, too, her jaw as stubborn as his own. There were other differences as well. Nora's love had never wavered. But Kate's...

"The boats are coming, Katie girl. There's a wind brewing. You know what that means? You know where we should be?"

"Not today," Kate replied.

"You never want to sail anymore. I don't know why." He shook his head, trying to concentrate, but his head felt thick, his brain slow. "What happened to us, Katie?"

"Let's go home."

Home? Where was home? He'd had to sell the Moon Dancer. It had almost broken his heart, selling his beloved boat. Now he lived in a small old sailboat. He'd wanted to call the boat Nora, but he couldn't quite bring himself to paint his wife's name on the side. Nora wouldn't have been proud of this boat or of him. Kate wasn't proud of him, either.

"I'm sorry, Katie. You know how sorry I am?"

"You're always sorry when you drink." Kate put out her hand to him. "Let's go home."

"I can't go now. I'm telling Will here about our big race."

"He's heard it before. I'm sorry, Will," Kate said.

"It's no problem," Will replied.

"What are you apologizing for?" Duncan demanded. "I ain't done nothing. And I'm your father. You don't apologize for me." He got to his feet, wanting to remind her that he was bigger and stronger and older than her, but the sudden motion caused him to sway unsteadily. Before he knew it, Kate had a hand on his arm. He wanted to shrug her away. In fact, he would do just that as soon as he caught his breath, got his bearings.

"Need some help?" a man asked.

Before Duncan could answer, Kate said, "What are you doing here?"

"I was thirsty."

"Can't blame a man for being thirsty, Katie girl," Duncan said, feeling more weary by the second. "I gotta sit down."

The man grabbed Duncan's other arm as he started to slip out of Kate's grasp.

"Your car?" he asked.

"I don't want to go home," Duncan complained. "I want another drink."

"The alcohol is going to kill you, Dad," Kate told him as she and the man managed to walk him out of the bar and into the parking lot.

"Better the alcohol than the loneliness," Duncan murmured. Kate pushed him into the front seat of her car. His eyes closed and he drifted away. He was finally able to sleep.

Kate saw her father slump sideways in his seat. For a moment she felt a surge of panic that he wasn't just sleeping, that something was happening to him, that he was sick or—no, she couldn't think the word, much less say it. Her father was strong as an ox. He wasn't even that old, barely sixty. He was just drunk. A terrible, lousy drunk. A terrible, lousy father for that matter. Why was she worried about losing him when it was so apparent that she'd lost him a long time ago?

"You'll need help getting him out of the car," Tyler said, interrupting her thoughts.

She'd almost forgotten he was standing there. "You've gotten yourself quite a headline, haven't you? 'Victorious sailor turns into worthless drunk.'"

"Is that how you think of your father?"

"No, but it's probably what you'll say."

"How do you know what I'll say?"

"I've been interviewed before, had my words twisted."

"Is that where your resistance comes from?" he asked with a thoughtful expression on his face. "I'm not interested in embarrassing you, Miss McKenna. I just want an interesting story. Fame, success, adventure—those are things that change people's lives forever. Most people never experience even one of those, much less all three, the way you did."

Kate didn't know what to say. She needed time to think, to figure out the best way to handle this man Maybe if she told him just enough, he would go away. But what would be enough? Would he start digging? And if he did, what would he find?

"I need to take care of my father," she said. "Maybe tomorrow, if you want to stop by the bookstore, we can talk."

"Why the change of heart?" He sent her a skeptical look.

"You don't look like someone who gives up."

"That's true." Tyler tipped his head toward the car. "Will your father be all right? I could follow you home, help you get him into the house."

"No, thank you."

"Where is home, anyway? I don't think you said."

"I don't think I did." Kate got into her car and shut the door. "I don't know what to do about that man," she muttered, glancing over at her father. Duncan's response was a very unhelpful snort. She'd have to take care of Tyler Jamison herself.

Tyler stared down the road long after Kate's taillights had disappeared. What had seemed so simple had suddenly taken on new and disturbing dimensions. The first was Kate herself. She wasn't what he'd expected. For some reason, he'd thought tomboy, tough girl, overachiever, but she hadn't looked all that tough in black pants and a clingy T-shirt that matched her light blue eyes. Her blond hair had fallen loosely around her shoulders, and she'd moved with a feminine grace, spoken with a soft voice. She had a great smile, too, he thought, the kind that invited you to come in and stay awhile, the same way her friendly little bookstore invited customers to stop in and browse. Not that she'd been all that friendly when she'd discovered he was a reporter. Despite her casual manner, he'd sensed a wall going up between them with every question that he asked.

Tyler reached into his pocket and pulled out a folded piece of paper. It was a magazine cover from eight years ago. Three blond, sunburned girls stood on the deck of a sailboat, holding an enormous silver trophy in their hands, their proud, beaming father in the background. The McKennas had conquered the world's toughest oceans. But were there secrets behind those smiles? Was there another story of their trip, one that hadn't been printed? Tyler suspected the answer to both questions was yes.

In fact, if one looked closely at the picture, only Duncan looked really happy. The girls appeared shell-shocked. It was the only word he could think of to describe their expressions. Maybe he was reading more than was there. He'd spent most of his life living by the facts and only the facts, but this story was different. This story was personal.

Kate McKenna hadn't wanted to talk to him. As she said, it was an old story, so why the resistance? She was hiding something. A drunken father—not the biggest secret in the world. There had to be something more. Tyler had a hunch he knew what that something was.

He folded the magazine cover, slipped it into his pocket and took out his cell phone. He punched in a familiar number, then waited.

"Jamison residence." Shelly Thompson, Mark's private nurse, answered the phone in her no-nonsense voice.

"Shelly. It's Tyler. How's Mark doing today?"

"Not good. He tried to stand, but his legs couldn't support his weight. He's very depressed."

Tyler let out a sigh filled with frustration, helplessness and anger, emotions that swamped him every time he thought about his younger brother who had once been such an accomplished athlete. "Can I talk to him?"

"He's asleep. Do you want me to wake him?"

"No. But when he gets up, tell him I found the McKenna sisters." Tyler ended the call, slipping the phone back into his pocket. The McKenna sisters might be good at keeping secrets, but he was even better at uncovering them.

CHAPTER TWO

ASHLEY MCKENNA TAPPED her foot nervously on the dock that bobbed beneath her feet. The swells grew larger with each passing minute as storm clouds came in from the west. "We need to do this soon," she told the man on the deck of the boat she was about to photograph. "We're losing the light."

"We've got one more guy to get in the picture. He should be here any second. Hang on."

Hang on. Sure she could do that. As a photographer, she was used to waiting patiently for the right shot. But not when she was standing so close to the water, not when she could see the waves beginning to churn. She sent a longing look behind her. She'd much rather be on solid ground than standing out here in her impractical high heels with her skirt blowing up around her legs like a Marilyn Monroe photo. For the hundredth time she wished she'd had time to change, but she'd rushed from shooting the ribbon cutting of the new maritime museum to this assignment, photographing the crews and boats entered in the Castleton Invitational.

Water splashed over the side of the dock, and she took a hasty step backward. She felt small and vulnerable on this bobbing piece of wood with a storm blowing in. The sea had often made her feel that way. Her father had always told her to look the ocean right in the eye, never back down, never give up, never give in. There was a time when those brave, fighting words had given her courage. Then she'd learned through hard experience that the ocean didn't back down or give in, either. That if it was man or woman against nature, nature would win.

Ashley shivered as she glanced at the boat, watching the men scurry back and forth, checking the sails and completing the chores necessary to settle in for the night. A strong gust of wind blew strands of her long blond hair across her face. Setting her camera bag on the dock, she knelt down and dug into her purse for an elastic band.

She should have cut her hair years ago. In fact, she considered chopping it off every six weeks, but she never quite got up the nerve. As a result, her hair dipped down to her waist. It made her look too young, and it was often tangled, but in a small way it made her feel closer to her mother. Ashley had inherited her mother's red streaks, making her more of a strawberry blonde than her sisters. But it wasn't just the color that reminded her of Nora McKenna, it was the memories of her mother brushing her hair every night, one hundred strokes exactly. Those nights had been a long time ago, but she still missed them. Sentimental tears blurred her vision.

She told herself to stop being so emotional. She was an adult now, twenty-six years old, an independent woman with a career. It was time to grow up, to stop being sensitive. Her sisters certainly didn't cry at every Hallmark commercial. They didn't wax sentimental about family moments from a lifetime ago. And she shouldn't, either.

As Ashley pulled the elastic band out of her purse, the dock rolled, and she had to put one hand down on the wood to steady herself. She made the mistake of looking at the gap between the dock and the boat, at the greenish-blue water rising up and down, up and down. The sight was mesmerizing. She wanted to look away, but she couldn't.

How many times had she stared at the water? How many times had it been her friend as she played with the dolphins and swam in the waves? Those were the times to remember, she told herself desperately. Not the other times, when the waves grew as high as skyscrapers, when the water threatened to swallow everything within its reach. Her body began to sway. She was afraid to move, afraid to get sucked into that terrible vortex where nothing ever came back.

"Ashley? Ashley? Is that you?"

She heard her name called from a great distance, but when she looked up she found a man standing right next to her. Faded blue jeans covered a pair of long, lean legs and a navy muscle T-shirt hung loosely around his waist. As her gaze traveled up his body, she told herself to look away before she got to the dimple in the chin, the slightly crooked nose broken by a football when he was twelve years old, and the sandy-colored hair streaked with blond highlights that he'd never had to pay a dime for. Unfortunately, she couldn't stop herself from meeting his gold-flecked brown eyes.

"Sean," she murmured.

"Ashley," he said, watching as she slowly got to her feet.

Even in her heels, Sean Amberson towered over her, six foot four inches of solid male. He was broader across the chest now, and his upper arms rippled with muscles honed by years of building and sailing boats. She cleared her throat, trying to calm the sudden racing of her pulse. It was bad enough the wind was blowing; now she had Sean to deal with as well. She'd known he'd come back again. His parents still lived on the island, still ran the boat-building business that would one day go to Sean. But knowing he would come home and seeing him in the flesh were two very different things.

"When did you get back?" she forced herself to ask.

"Yesterday. Did you miss me?"

"I—" Ashley shrugged helplessly. "It's been a long time."

"Almost two years since my last visit, and I think you managed to dodge me the entire week I was here."

"I don't remember."

"Sure you do. You developed a sudden and very contagious case of the flu, as I recall. Wouldn't even open your door. I had to yell at you from the hallway of your apartment building. The time before that, you claimed you had poison ivy, and the time before that—"

"Stop it. I can't help it if I'm sick when you happen to come to town." She refused to admit she'd been hiding out in her apartment on any of those occasions. The wind blew her hair in front of her face, and she remembered the elastic band in her hand. She quickly pulled her hair into a ponytail, acutely aware of his very long and intent stare.

"I'm glad you didn't cut your hair," he said. "It's still... incredible."

Ashley swallowed hard, the husky note in his voice stirring up unwanted emotions. She'd loved this man once, loved him more than anyone or anything. But it was over. It had been over for more years than he'd been gone. She just wished he'd go away again, because it was easier when he wasn't around. She could almost forget. She could almost move on.

"So is this just a family weekend visit?" she asked, hoping it wouldn't be longer than that.

"Not exactly. I'm racing in the Castleton."

"You can't be serious. You said you'd never race."

"Never is a long time. I just finished refurbishing Stan Baker's boat, the Freedom Rider. He asked me to race it with him in the Castleton and on to Hawaii. I thought it was about time I raced in one of the boats I helped build."

She was more than a little surprised. "You're not a racer."

"Who says I can't be?" he challenged.

"You can't race, Sean. Your parents would die."

"My parents won't die, but I suppose it's possible I might." His gaze bored into hers, searching for an answer she couldn't give him.

"Why risk it?" she asked instead.

"Because I'm..." He shook his head. "I'm restless. I can't settle in anywhere. College didn't work out. The jobs I've had never seem to last."

"You always have your family business. I've heard your father say he wants you to come home and run the business." Not that she wanted that to happen. If Sean ever came home for good, she'd have to leave. This island wasn't big enough for the both of them. Sean took up too much space. He'd always made her feel small—it wasn't just his height but his personality. He was a man in constant motion, impatient, energized, restless. He made her tense; he made her a little bit crazy. Make that a lot crazy.

"I'm sure you'd prefer that I stay far away," he said.

"I don't care what you do."

"Dammit, Ashley." He slapped his hand against his jeans in a gesture of frustration. "Don't say that. Don't pretend. Don't act like we never meant anything to each other."

"What we had was over a long time ago."

"Yeah, so you said."

"You can't possibly still care," she murmured.

He stared at her for a long minute, then shook his head. "Of course I don't still care."

It was the answer she wanted, but it still hurt. Not that she'd let him see that. "I didn't think so," she said. "You probably have a girlfriend, don't you?"

"More than one. What about you? Dating anyone these days?"

"Sure," she lied, knowing that the last date she'd gone on had been at least six months ago.

"You'll have to introduce us. Is he a local guy?"

"Uh." She shifted her camera bag on her shoulder, relieved when a man ran by her and jumped onto the boat she was supposed to photo-graph, and she didn't have to answer. "Are you the last one?" she called to the man.

"Yes. We just need one minute," he replied.

"You're photographing the crews for the Castleton?" Sean asked.

She nodded. "I wish they'd hurry up."

"My mom said a bunch of your photographs are displayed in the Main Street Gallery."

"Janine is a friend. They're not that good."

"I bet they are. I remember when your mom gave you your first camera. You were hooked. You wouldn't go anywhere without that thing, and you were always snapping shots of me doing something stupid."

"Which was fairly often," she said, thinking back to those carefree days before everything had gotten so complicated. "But you rarely stood still long enough for me to get a good picture."

He grinned, and for a brief moment he was her best friend in the world again, the boy who'd started kindergarten with her, who'd joined her in food fights, backyard picnics, and neighborhood ball games. He'd been her first dance, her first kiss, her first promise of love. And now—now he was nothing. They couldn't be together, and she couldn't tell him why.

His grin faded, and their eyes met in a long, poignant moment of desire and regret.

"God, Ash," he murmured. "I told myself I wouldn't do this, wouldn't try to talk to you about what happened. I told myself I was only beating a dead horse. But, dammit, it's still here, whatever this thing is between us. I can feel it right now."

"It's just the—the wind," she said desperately. "It makes me edgy."

As she finished speaking, the dock took a big roll, sending her stumbling. She grabbed Sean's arm like a lifeline, terrified of ending up in the water.

"Easy," he said.

"I have to get out of here." But she couldn't let go of Sean's arm. What if she fell? The water would be cold. It would make her heart stop. It would rush over her head. She'd have to fight to get back to the surface. Her clothes would drag her down.

"Ashley," Sean said sharply. "What the hell is wrong with you?"

She sent him a blank look. "What?"

"You're white as a sheet."

His words slowly sank in. She realized she was letting him see a side of herself she didn't want anyone to see. "I'm okay." She took a deep breath and forced herself to let go of his arm. "I just felt dizzy for a minute. I guess I didn't eat enough today."

"You don't look like you eat much any day. You're thin as a rail."

Ashley didn't comment, her attention drawn to the crew member on the boat waving her over. "Are you ready?" she asked.

"Yes, but we've changed our minds on the angle. We'd like to have you shoot from onboard, not from the dock. Get the pier in the background and the banner for the race."

Ashley stiffened. She had already shot three boats and their crews from the safety of the docks. It was a good shot. She didn't need to get on the boat. "I think it's better from here."

"No, we want you onboard. Come on." He extended his hand.

Ashley looked from his hand to the water that separated the boat from the dock. It was only a foot or two, barely anything. She wouldn't slip or fall. She couldn't. It was perfectly safe. But the swells were lifting the boat and pushing it farther away. What if the line got loose? What if she couldn't get back?

Feelings of panic swamped her. Her breath came faster. Her hands tingled. But she couldn't let on. No one could know. No one could ever know.

"It's getting dark. The clouds are rolling in," Sean said as he watched her measure the distance between the boat and the dock. "Maybe you should wait until tomorrow."

"It's too dark," she told the man on the boat. "We'll have to reschedule. I'm sorry, but I know you wouldn't be happy with the photos in this kind of light. I'll come by tomorrow. We'll do it then."

"Hey, wait a second," the man called after her, but Ashley had already begun walking down the dock, and she didn't stop until she reached solid ground.

She didn't realize Sean had followed her until she stopped abruptly and he barreled into the back of her.

"Sorry," he said.

"It's fine. I'm fine."

"No, you're not. It's still with you, isn't it?"

"I don't know what you're talking about." She looked away from his probing gaze.

"I'm talking about the fear on your face when you considered getting on that boat. I saw it before, when you first got back from the race. I wish you'd tell me what happened to make you so afraid."

"Nothing happened. I just got tired of living on a boat. So tired I can't stand the thought of getting on another one."

"Even after all this time?" he asked, a skeptical note in his voice. "It's been eight years."

"I know how long it's been," she snapped as she looked back at him. "I have to go. I have to talk to Caroline. I'm worried about her."

"What's going on with your baby sister?"

Ashley hesitated, not one to share family business, but talking about Caroline was preferable to talking about herself or her irrational fears. "It seems that Caroline is dating Mike Stanaway."

Sean raised an eyebrow. "He's at least ten years older than her. Maybe fifteen. Not to mention... Well, let's just say he has some problems."

"That's why I need to talk to her. Not that she'll listen, but I have to try."

"I could go with you," Sean offered.

"No," she said abruptly. "You know how defensive Caroline can be when she feels she's being ambushed. I'll see you around."

Ashley walked away, wondering if he'd call her back, but he didn't. As she headed toward Caroline's salon, her thoughts weren't on her sister but on the man she'd left behind. She wondered why it never got any easier to walk away from him. Lord knew she'd had enough practice. For a brief second, she was tempted to look back, to see if he was still standing there, still watching her, still wanting her—the way she still wanted him.

"Phone for you, Caroline," the receptionist at Noel's Hair Salon said. "Line one."

"Just a second." Caroline squeezed the last bit of color out of the plastic bottle and looked at her client in the mirror. "We'll let this sit for a while. Can I get you a magazine?"

"I brought a book," Peggy Marsh replied. "And take your time. This is the first bit of peace and quiet I've had all week. The kids have been driving me crazy. Take my advice, Caroline; do not rush into the marriage and children thing. Enjoy this time of your life."

"I'll keep that in mind." Caroline certainly wasn't pushing for marriage or kids. She was twenty-four years old and had plenty of time to do both. Someday when she was ready. Right now she had her job as stylist at Noel's Salon and a small apartment in a building just a few blocks away. She was happy. Most of the time. Sort of.

It was probably the wind that was making her restless. She was like her father in that regard. A good stiff breeze always got her itchy to go somewhere. But she couldn't go anywhere. She had another haircut in ten minutes.

She walked over to the reception desk and picked up the phone. "Hello."

"It's me, Kate."

"What's up?" Caroline couldn't help tensing at the sound of her older sister's voice. She had things she needed to talk to Kate about, but now wasn't the time or the place. Not that she knew when that time or place would be.

"It's Dad," Kate said with a weary note in her voice.

"Where is he?"

"Sleeping on my couch. I was lucky to get him this far. He really tied one on today. Will called me to come and pick him up."

"It's hard for him with all the boats coming to town. It makes him want to be out there with the other racers. He misses the life he used to have."

"And that's an excuse for drinking himself into oblivion? How can you defend him?"

"Someone has to," Caroline snapped. Kate had always been hard on their father. She didn't understand him. She never had.

There was a pause on the other end of the phone.

"Look, Caroline, that's not really why I'm calling. Although it's a lot easier to defend Dad when you aren't the one constantly called to come and pick him up from some bar. I'm sorry if I'm a little out of patience, but I'm just sick of it."

"Hey, they can call me anytime. But everyone knows you're in charge."

"I never said that."

"Oh, please, Kate. You've always been in charge."

"Fine. Whatever. We have another problem."

"What? I have a haircut to do." Caroline looked up as the front door to the salon opened and a man walked in. He must be her seven o'clock appointment.

"A reporter came into the store today," Kate said. "His name is Tyler Jamison. He wants to do a story on us—a where-are-they-now piece."

Caroline didn't know what to say. The reporters had stopped coming around years ago, and they'd all begun to breathe easier. Lulled into a false sense of security, she realized now. "What did you tell him?"

"That we had nothing to say. That there was no story."

"Did he believe you?"

"I don't know. He seems very persistent. I just wanted to warn you not to talk to him if he comes around. Don't let yourself get taken in."

The way you usually do.

Caroline could hear the unspoken words as clearly as if Kate had said them out loud. "As if I would," she said, once again feeling defensive. "Ashley is the one you should warn. She's so nervous all the time. There's no telling what she'd say."

"I left her a message to call me, but if you see her first, let her know."

"I will." Caroline paused, wishing there was something else to say. When had it become so difficult to talk to Kate? They'd once been close. Kate had been her idol, her big sister, the one who told incredible stories, made her laugh, made her feel safe when the world outside got too scary. But things had changed. There was too much they couldn't talk about. It was easier to speak of nothing than worry about crossing a line that wasn't supposed to be crossed.

Caroline hung up the phone and walked back to her station. "Sisters," she murmured, meeting Peggy's gaze in the mirror.

Peggy nodded. "You love 'em and you hate 'em."

"Exactly. I have another client, so why don't you move into this seat, and I'll put the hot lights on you. We'll see if we can't speed this process up a bit." Caroline moved Peggy to the station next to hers.

She adjusted the octopus-style lights and said, "Let me know if it gets too hot."

"I love your color," Peggy said.

"You do? I did some experimenting." Caroline glanced at her reflection. Her hair was dark blond with brown streaks that were emphasized by a short, spiky cut and a lot of mousse.

"You look hip," Peggy said wistfully. "I haven't been hip in a while."

"Kate thinks I should go back to my natural color."

"Which is what?"

"I don't remember," Caroline said with a laugh.

"Caroline, your client is here," the receptionist, Erica Connors, interrupted, tipping her head toward the man leafing through a magazine in the waiting area. "A hunk," Erica mouthed silently.

Caroline had to admit the guy was exceptionally good-looking, not in a pretty-boy sense, but in a mountain-climbing, ocean-racing kind of way. When he stood up, she saw that he was well over six feet tall, and as he walked toward her she got the full benefit of his sexy smile.

"Caroline?" he asked.

"Yes."

"I need a haircut."

"You've come to the right place." She motioned him toward the chair Peggy had just vacated. "Can I get you a cold drink or some coffee?"

"No, thanks." He sat down in her chair, and she looked at him in the mirror. His face was well-defined, with a square forehead, a strong jaw, intelligent eyes, and thick, black lashes that were wasted on a man.

"What do you think?" he asked.

"Uh, what?"

"About my hair? How short should I go?"

His hair, right. She was supposed to be concentrating on his hair, which actually was fairly spectacular—dark brown, thick, naturally curly she suspected as she ran her fingers through the strands. It was already well styled. In fact, it didn't look like it needed much more than a trim, if that.

"A quarter inch," she said, meeting his gaze in the mirror. "Unless you had something else in mind? A buzz cut, perhaps." She laughed at his wary expression. "Just kidding. I had you worried there for a second, didn't I?"

"For a second."

"Shampoo first?"

"If you want to just wet it down, that's fine."

"Whatever you like." She pulled out a plastic cover-up to protect his clothes and used the spray bottle to wet down his hair. "So, where are you from? You've got a touch of the South in your voice."

"Good ear. Texas."

"You're a long way from home. Are you here for the races?"

"As a matter of fact, I am. What about you? Are you a native?"

"I was born here." She ran a comb through his hair and picked up her scissors.

"Have you lived anywhere else?" he asked.

Caroline didn't know how to answer that question. Did sailing across several oceans count as actually living somewhere else? "I've been around. Are you crewing for someone?"

"I haven't firmed up my plans yet."

"Waiting for the best offer?"

"You could say that. Have you done any racing yourself?"

"Some."

"But you're not involved this year?"

"No, I have other things I'm more interested in right now." She trimmed his hair, then pulled up strands of hair so she could measure the cut. "How does that look?" she asked, meeting his gaze in the mirror.

"Perfect."

"Mousse, gel, blow-dry?"

"No to all three."

"A natural kind of guy. Or you're just cheap."

"It's raining outside," he said with a grin.

"Then you're a smart guy." Caroline pulled off the cover-up and shook out the loose hair. "You can pay Erica at the desk," she said as he stood up.

"Maybe I could buy you a drink, hear more about your racing experience."

A date with a fascinating stranger? She'd be crazy to say no. In fact, every instinct in her body told her to say yes. Especially since Mike had already canceled their plans for the evening, and she didn't particularly want to be alone.

"I'd like to show off my haircut," he said persuasively.

God, his smile was hot! Reason warred with impulse. "I have to finish a highlight. It will be at least another thirty minutes."

"I can meet you. I saw a bar down by the wharf."

"How about some food instead? There's a terrific seafood restaurant a few blocks from here called the Castaway. It's on Gilmore Street. When you leave here, turn left at the next corner and go down about four blocks."

"Sounds good. An hour?"

"Sure."

"Good. I'll see you there."

"See you there," she repeated softly, as he handed Erica a twenty and told her to keep the change. Caroline was still staring when he went through the door, caught up in genuine appreciation of his nice ass. It wasn't until Peggy began to cough that she turned away. She forced herself not to say a word until she heard the door close behind him.

Erica let out a whoop and jumped up from her desk. "You got yourself a real hottie there, Caroline," she said with her usual twenty-year-old candor.

"He's all right."

"Honey, he's better than all right," Peggy put in. "If I wasn't married, with enough stretch marks to make a map of Washington on my hips, I'd have gone for him myself."

"Did you see his ass?" Erica asked.

"I wouldn't mind getting my hands on those abs," Peggy added.

Caroline groaned. "You are both terrible. Why do I suddenly feel like we're twelve and at a slumber party?"

"Hey, it's not like a gorgeous stranger walks in here every day of the week," Erica said. "Usually it's cranky old ladies or middle-aged marrieds, present company excluded, of course."

Peggy laughed. "Believe me, at this moment, with my head covered in tinfoil, I'm happy that the only name you called me was middle-aged married. But you look great, Caroline. It's no wonder he went for you."

"Do you think so? The skirt isn't too short?" Caroline looked at her reflection in the mirror. Her black skirt was as mini as they came, her stomach bared by a short, cropped, purple V-necked top that would have showed off some generous cleavage if she had any. Unfortunately, Kate was the only one of the sisters with more than a boyish bosom.

"You look terrific," Peggy assured her.

"I look like I've been at work all day."

"A little lipstick, some blush, you'll be good as new."

They both turned as the door to the salon opened once again. For a moment she thought he might have come back. "Oh, it's just you," Caroline said, as her sister Ashley walked into the room. Normally, Caroline got along much better with Ashley than with Kate, but at the moment she wasn't particularly interested in talking to either of her sisters.

"Gee, thanks. Who did you think I was?" Ashley asked.

"A hottie," Erica said irrepressibly. "This incredible man came in to get his hair cut, and he made a move on Caroline. She's going to meet him for dinner as soon as Peggy's hair is done baking."

"Thanks for sharing," Caroline said with an annoyed look in Erica's direction.

"Who is this guy?" Ashley asked, her brows knitting into a frown. "Does he have a name?"

It was only then that Caroline realized she didn't know his name. Had he said it? She tended to think of her clients by their appointment time or what they were having done. But he must have said his name. What was it?

"You don't know his name?" Ashley asked when she didn't reply. "And you're having dinner with him? How can you go out with him if you don't know his name?" Ashley's lips tightened. "I don't like the sound of this at all."

"I know his name. I just don't remember it. For heaven's sake, Ashley, I'm not sixteen. It's just dinner in a public place."

"But he's a stranger."

"You worry too much."

"And you don't worry enough. It's raining out there, too."

Caroline realized her sister's agitation had more to do with the storm than with her. "Are you okay?"

"I'm fine," Ashley said evasively. "I came to check on you."

"Fine here, too."

"Well, good. Why don't you cancel your date and have dinner with Kate and me instead?"

"Kate has Dad on her couch."

"Oh."

"Don't say anything," Caroline warned her.

"I wasn't going to. What could I say, anyway?" Silence fell between them as they both avoided a subject neither wanted to cover. "Did you want anything else?" Caroline prodded.

"Yes. Rumor has it you're dating Mike Stanaway."

"So what if I am?"

"He's too old for you. And isn't he still married?"

"He's separated."

"Caroline—"

"Ashley, I have work to finish. You don't have anything to worry about. Mike and I are just friends. Trust me."

"Are you sure?"

"Positive. Now, I really need to finish Peggy's hair."

"I guess I'll see you later," Ashley said after a moment. "But I think you should be careful about meeting this strange guy."

"He's not strange. He's just a stranger."

Ashley didn't look convinced as she said good-bye to her sister and dashed out of the salon into the rain.

"He's not a stranger, exactly. I have his name written right here," Erica said triumphantly, holding up the appointment book. "Tyler Jamison. Now you know who he is."

Caroline's stomach flipped over. Tyler Jamison? Wasn't that the name of the reporter Kate had warned her about? Don't let yourself get taken in. Kate's voice rang through her head. Caroline frowned. She hated it when her sister was right.

"Yeah, now I know who he is," she said heavily. And she also knew exactly what she had to do.

CHAPTER THREE

"So what was it about me that made you think I was the most gullible? Because I'm the youngest? Because I have a reputation of being an airhead? What was it exactly?" Caroline set her purple purse on the table in front of Tyler, then sat down across from him in the lounge of the Castaway.

"You've spoken to your sister." Tyler took a drink from his frosted beer glass. He'd had a feeling Caroline would catch on to him sooner rather than later. But he'd taken a shot, and in the end he'd gotten what he wanted. She was sitting across from him. Mad as hell, maybe, but definitely within conversational distance. "Can I get you a drink?"

"No."

"Are you sure?" he asked as a waiter came up to take her drink order. "Our table won't be ready for a few minutes."

"Fine. I'll have a mineral water," Caroline said, forcing a tight smile as she said hello to the waiter. "Hi, Bobby. How are you?"

"Great," Bobby said. "No wine for you tonight?"

"Just the mineral water." She turned back to Tyler. "And I won't be staying for dinner."

Tyler hoped he could change her mind. "Why don't we start over? I'm Tyler Jamison."

"What do you want?" Caroline asked. "And why didn't you just tell me who you were when you came into the salon? I knew your hair didn't really need cutting, but I thought you were one of those types who has to have his hair perfect at all times."

Tyler put a self-conscious hand to his head, aware that he hadn't even looked at his hair since walking four blocks to the restaurant in the wind and rain.

"I can see I was wrong about that," Caroline said.

Tyler smiled. "Listen, I probably should have introduced myself, but you were busy, and your sister gave me the cold shoulder earlier, so I thought it might be better if we had a chance to speak in private. I did give my name to the receptionist at the salon. I didn't realize you weren't aware who I was." Actually, he had realized early on in their conversation but had decided to see how far he could take it.

Caroline appeared somewhat mollified, but she still had her arms crossed defiantly in front of her. "Fine. What is it you want to know?"

"I'd like to write a follow-up story about your family and the race, what happened then, what's happening now. I'd put the photograph of the three of you holding the Winston trophy right next to a photograph of the three of you today. Show where you are in your lives now, how the race may have changed you, that kind of thing. Where-are-they-now pieces are quite popular these days."

"I'm sure Kate told you we weren't interested."

"I thought you might have a different opinion. And I didn't think you'd want your older sister to speak for you."

Caroline sat up straighter in her seat. Tyler could see he'd hit a nerve with that one. Caroline was not about to let Kate speak for her, that was quite clear. He had a feeling this sister was his way into the family.

"I speak for myself," she replied. "But, that said, I can't imagine what you'd write about us that would be at all interesting. We're not exactly living a wild and crazy life here on Castleton Island."

"True, but I'd like to know how hard or how easy it was to go from sailboat racer to hair stylist."

Caroline gave him a wide, toothy grin that made her look young, fresh, full of life. "That sounds like a headline that will sell about ten copies. Tell me something. Are you even a good reporter?"

"I've done all right," he said, biting back a smile. "And the value of the article would, of course, depend on how forthcoming you and your sisters are with the interesting details that people want to know."

"I barely remember the details now. Our journey was well documented in the logs we showed to the press at the end of the race."

"I've seen them—a page-turning discussion of the fish world, a little about your struggles with a geometry correspondence class, Ashley's reluctance to put a worm on a fishhook, and Kate's fascination with the brightness of the stars and planets as seen from each of the different hemispheres. Incredibly juicy stuff."

"Hey, I told you we were boring. Even when we were racing, there were a lot of days at sea where nothing happened. You've heard the expression *in the doldrums*? We got stuck in them for days. Just lying there waiting and praying for a wisp of wind to get us on our way. Sometimes I wanted to scream or pull out a paddle and start rowing. Once Kate and I did that just to be funny. Dad wasn't amused. Thought we were breaking the rule about not using anything other than our sails."

"You and Kate, huh? Are you two the closest?"

"We're sisters."

"That's not what I asked." He paused. "I haven't met Ashley yet. What's she like?"

"Quiet, pretty, sensitive. But I didn't come down here to tell you that."

"Why did you come?"

"Because I said I would. And because I didn't want you to think I was an idiot. I'm not. I was just distracted earlier. Otherwise, I would have seen right through you." Caroline lifted her chin in the air, the gesture filled with bravado.

Tyler nodded approvingly. "I understand, and I like your style." But he thought her words had an edge of desperation to them, as if she wanted to make sure he understood that she was smart and capable. He had a feeling Caroline had been trying to prove herself for some time.

"I don't care if you like me or you don't. That's the end of our discussion. I'm not interested in a story, and my sisters aren't, either."

Tyler considered her words, then leaned forward in his chair. "You know, Miss McKenna, you and your sister are awfully secretive for no apparent reason. Most people who win races love to talk about them."

"So go talk to them."

"Can't. My curiosity is piqued."

"Curiosity killed the cat."

"Hmm, what should I make of that?"

"It's just an expression." She paused as the waiter set down her mineral water. "I really can't stay," she said when they were alone again.

"Why don't you have your drink and give me the opportunity to change your mind?"

"That won't happen. I'm not as gullible as some people seem to think."

"Like Kate," he said, taking a wild guess.

"I didn't say that."

"You didn't have to. You're the baby sister. Did Kate try to boss you around when you were at sea?"

Caroline rolled her eyes. "She bosses me wherever we are."

"But on a boat, in close quarters, I would imagine not everyone gets to be chief."

"Daddy was the chief."

"Daddy," he murmured, taking another sip of his beer. "I met him earlier, you know—your father. He was three sheets to the wind."

"His favorite place to be." Caroline picked up her glass, running her finger around the edge. "But he's a good man. He did his best by us. And he did accomplish an amazing feat. People forget that nowadays."

Tyler put his elbows on the table and leaned in, sensing he'd just gotten the opening he needed. "They won't forget if you let me tell the story again, and not just that story, but the one you're living now. Your father could have it all back, the glory days of his life. What's the harm in that?" Caroline didn't reply right away, and he could see the indecision in her eyes. "This could be a good thing for you and your family."

Before she could answer, a loud group of men entered the lounge, their voices high and filled with energy.

"Damn," Caroline muttered, looking past him. "Just what I need."

Tyler followed her gaze to the four men sitting down at a table near the door. "Friends of yours?"

"Kiwis," she said.

Tyler raised an eyebrow. "Are we talking fruit here?"

"New Zealanders."

"Ah. And we don't like Kiwis?"

"My father is an Aussie. There's a long-standing rivalry between Aussies and Kiwis in ocean racing," she explained, tensing even further as one of the men approached their table.

"Caroline," he said in a loud, boisterous voice. "Just the person I was looking for. Did you hear who's coming to town?"

"Do I care?"

"You should. Or at least your father should."

"What are you talking about?"

"The Moon Dancer is a last-minute entry in the race. She should be here by Monday."

Tyler watched Caroline's face pale as the news registered. The Moon Dancer was the name of the McKennas' boat. Now it was back, apparently with a different owner. He didn't know the significance of this news, but it seemed to disturb Caroline.

"That's not possible," she said.

"Oh, but it is, and guess who bought it?" The man paused dramatically. "Good old K.C. Wales. I can't wait to see Duncan's face when he finds out his nemesis is coming to town on his boat."

"He won't care a bit."

The sailor laughed. "Yeah, sure. See you around."

"That's your boat he was talking about, right?" Tyler asked as the man left.

"What?" Caroline sent him a blank look.

"Your boat. The Moon Dancer. The one you sailed around the world."

"Yes, it was our boat," Caroline said slowly. "I can't believe that K.C. bought it, or that he's bringing it here. My dad will go crazy when he sees her. Kate, too. And Ashley..." Caroline shook her head. "This is bad, very bad."

"Why?'

"A lot of memories. I should tell my father and my sisters." She started to get up, then sat back down in her seat. "I don't want to tell them."

"Why not?"

"Because it will hurt. I don't have the stomach for it."

He raised an eyebrow. "Three ear piercings, a tattoo on your shoulder, a naval ring, and you don't have the stomach for a little pain?"

"Not that kind of pain." She frowned at the mineral water in front of her. "I need a real drink."

"I'll get you one." He put up his hand to motion for the waiter.

"No. Wait, never mind," she said hurriedly. Tyler put down his hand.

"I'd rather eat instead. I wonder when our table will be ready."

"I can check."

"I'll do that. Is it under your name or an alias?"

"My name." He watched her walk away. She was careful not to go near the bar, but he did see her fling a somewhat desperate look in that direction. Was Caroline a drinker? She'd said she'd wanted a drink, but then changed her mind. And the waiter had seemed surprised she'd ordered a mineral water. Not that it meant anything, but her behavior was a bit off, he thought. As a reporter, he'd become very good at paying attention to the details. It wasn't what a subject said or did that was important but what they didn't say or didn't do.

With an alcoholic father, it was certainly possible that Caroline had her own problems with alcohol. He made a mental note to check it out. Mark would definitely want that information. Tyler raised his beer glass to his lips. He had a feeling things were about to get interesting.

Kate opened her door just before nine o'clock that night to find Caroline on the porch. It was a little surprising, since none of her family was prone to dropping in, to suddenly have Ashley in the kitchen making tea, Duncan in the living room sleeping it off, and Caroline on her doorstep looking guilty about something. "You talked to him, didn't you?"

"He didn't tell me his name right away," Caroline said defensively as she entered the hallway. "Where's Dad?"

"Can't you hear the snoring?"

Caroline peeked into the living room where their father lay sprawled on his back amid Kate's fluffy sofa cushions. "He looks tired. And his face is all red."

Kate followed her younger sister's gaze and saw exactly what Caroline saw and more, not just the weary lines, or the red face, but the thin translucent skin on his arms and hands, the lack of meat on his bones. Their father had always been big and stronger than most, but he was fading away like an old photograph, and she didn't know how to make it stop.

"We should do something for him," Caroline said, echoing Kate's thoughts.

"Like what?"

"I don't know, something. He looks pathetic. I don't like seeing him like this."

Duncan had always been Caroline's hero, even when he was at his most unheroic. Most of the time, Kate tried to protect Caroline from seeing moments such as these. Perhaps that had been a mistake. But she was so used to being the big sister she couldn't stop the nurturing instincts from kicking into gear.

"Come into the kitchen. Ashley brought over her chocolate cookies, and she's making tea."

"That sounds good. I'm still hungry."

"You mean he didn't buy you dinner?" Kate asked wryly as she followed Caroline down the hall and into the kitchen.

"Who didn't buy you dinner?" Ashley asked from the kitchen counter where she was pouring tea into a cup. "Hi, Caroline. Do you want some tea?"

"Just cookies." Caroline grabbed one off the plate on the counter and took a seat at the kitchen table. One bite brought a squeal of delight. "These are heaven. I swear, if you weren't a photographer, you could be a chef."

"All I can make are cookies and tea," Ashley said. "Not exactly chef material."

"Don't forget your famous blueberry pancakes or your turkey stuffing," Kate reminded Ashley. "You're always too humble."

"Makes a change from you," Caroline said.

Kate made a face at Caroline, who stuck her tongue out in response. They both burst out laughing. Kate was amazed how good the sound made her feel. It had been awhile since she'd had both her sisters together in one place.

Ashley handed Kate a cup of tea, then sat down at the table. "So who didn't buy you dinner, Caroline? It wasn't that strange man you were going to meet, was it?"

"You knew?" Kate asked in surprise. "You knew she was meeting Tyler Jamison, and you didn't stop her?"

"Tyler Jamison? The reporter you just told me about?" Ashley asked in confusion. "That's who Caroline met for dinner?"

"Exactly."

"But why?"

"I have no idea. I told her to stay away from him."

"Okay, both of you, breathe," Caroline said. "Yes, I met the reporter for dinner, and yes, I did eat, but as you know I can always eat more. Before you ask, I didn't tell him anything. So chill out. We have bigger fish to fry. The Moon Dancer was sold to K.C. Wales. He's planning to race her in the Castleton, then on to Hawaii. They should be here by Monday."

Ashley put a hand to her heart. "K.C. Wales? Oh, dear."

"Dad will freak." Caroline picked up another cookie. "You'll have to tell him, Kate."

"Why me?"

"You're the oldest, the most responsible, the most understanding."

"Since when?" Kate asked. "According to you, I'm bossy, opinionated, and critical."

"That, too," Caroline said. "But I'm Dad's baby, and you know he never takes anything I say seriously. And Ashley can't do it because... well, she just can't do it."

"I could do it," Ashley said defensively, then quickly added, "But it would come better from you, Kate. You always know the right thing to say."

Once again, both sisters looked to her for the answer to their problem. They'd played out this scene many times before—Caroline eating chocolate, Ashley biting her fingernails while she paced. As before, she wanted to say something reassuring. She wanted to give them the answers they were looking for, but words were difficult to find.

Her mother would have known what to say. She'd understood each of them and had passed on special pieces of herself: sensitivity to Ashley, passion to Caroline, and loyalty to Kate. It was that loyalty they needed now. Kate had promised her mother that she would protect her sisters and look out for her father, and she'd do it now, just as she had done before.

"It's funny how life goes merrily along and then, boom, the past comes back and bites you in the butt," Caroline said.

"I wonder if the Moon Dancer still looks the same," Ashley said quietly. "I wonder if Mom's curtains are hanging in the master cabin."

"What I wonder is why K.C. bought the boat," Kate said. "He must know that Dad will hate him for it."

"I doubt he cares," Caroline replied. "He was always more interested in winning than in friendship."

"Not always." Kate shook her head, confused by the turn of events. K.C. had once been a family friend, then an enemy. What was he now?

"Did I tell you that Sean is back, too?" Ashley asked. "I saw him down at the docks. He says he's going to race in the Castleton. Now that I know the Moon Dancer is in the race, I have an even worse feeling about it. Look, I've got goose bumps," she said, extending her arms.

"You're too thin—that's why you have goose bumps," Caroline retorted. "And you knew Sean would come back again. His family is here."

"I know, but I'm not ready to deal with him."

"You'll never be ready."

"Okay, let's put Sean aside for the moment," Kate cut in, knowing that Ashley and Caroline had never seen eye to eye on that subject. "What did you tell Tyler Jamison about us, Caroline?"

"I told him to leave us alone. But—"

Kate groaned. "Please don't let there be a *but*."

"He might be able to do us some good. Dad would love to be in the spotlight again. It would give him a reason to get up in the morning. It could turn his life around."

"It could turn his life upside down. Are you actually telling me you think that an article about us is a good idea?" Kate didn't give Caroline a chance to respond. "What do you think Dad will tell Tyler? What do you think he remembers about the race? About the storm? What do you think will come out when he's wasted out of his mind? It's crazy."

"She's right," Ashley said. "We can't let a reporter into our lives. There are too many people who could be affected, like Sean. I knew the wind would bring trouble. I just knew it."

"So did I," Kate agreed.

"Well, I didn't. I thought it was a grand wind and a great storm while it lasted," Caroline said. "You two have forgotten how to live. We used to be brave. We used to be adventurous. Kate, you used to climb to the top of the sail without any fear. Ashley, you used to dive to the bottom of the sea. What happened to us?"

"You know what happened," Kate said pointedly.

"I'm not sure I do, not really. We've never talked—"

"And we're not going to talk now," Kate interrupted. "We can't. There's too much at stake. We have lives to live, maybe not wild and adventurous, but good solid lives, the kind Mom wanted us to have."

"I want more than good and solid. And you should want more, too," Caroline muttered.

Maybe she did once in a while, Kate thought, not that she'd admit that to her baby sister. But Tyler Jamison's appearance in her bookstore had sent an unexpected burst of adrenaline through her bloodstream. And she'd enjoyed the heady rush far more than she should have.

"I wonder why this reporter came to town now?" Ashley mused. "It's not the tenth anniversary of the race. Why is he interested in us? It seems like he came out of nowhere for no reason. And who does he write for, anyway?"

"He's a freelancer, or so he said," Kate replied. "He told me that there is a lot of interest in sailboat racing, and because we don't fit the traditional mold of a racing syndicate, we're of even more interest to the general public. It makes some sense. I know short biographies are popular right now, but I still don't have a good feeling about this. My instincts tell me that he came looking for something in particular."

"I agree," Caroline said. "The fact that he didn't tell me who he was, that he asked me out to dinner without revealing his identity, goes along with the idea that he's playing some sort of game. He's good at the game, too. He's very charming."

And attractive, Kate thought. But it didn't matter. Charm and good looks would not destroy her family. He'd have to come up with something more than that.

"If none of us talk, there won't be a story," she said decisively. "We have to stick together, protect one another, the way we used to do. Remember?" Kate walked over to the table and took each of her sister's hands in hers.

"We're not kids anymore," Caroline complained, but she still slipped her other hand into Ashley's completing the circle they'd always formed.

"All for one," Kate said.

"And one for all," Ashley and Caroline repeated. A reassuring squeeze went from hand to hand.

Their unity had gotten them past a lot of hardships. With any luck it would get them past one very persistent reporter.

It was past ten that night when Tyler finally picked up the phone to call his brother. He knew it wasn't too late to call. Mark had always been a night owl. Catch him in the morning, and he was a grumpy bear. But, after nine o'clock at night, he was ready to party—at least in the old days. Mark's life had changed drastically since the car accident a month earlier.

Tyler could still remember getting the call. He'd been in a hotel room in London covering a summit meeting. The phone had rung in the middle of the night and he'd known, even before he answered it, that bad news was coming. Those first words had stopped his heart: Your brother has been in an accident. You should come as soon as possible.

His immediate reaction had been a silent, desperate prayer: Please let him be all right. Then he'd asked about Mark's eight-year-old daughter, Amelia, and Mark's wife, Susan. Amelia had made it. Susan had died on the way to the hospital. And Mark was in surgery to save his life.

The time it took to get from London to San Antonio, Texas, had been the longest hours of Tyler's life. He'd made a million promises to God along the way, using every bargaining chip he could think of to plead for his brother's life. Amelia would need her father to help her get over the tragedy of her mother's death. Mark had to survive to take care of his child. And Tyler couldn't lose his brother. Not when they'd just begun to get close again. So he'd begged God for a miracle and promised he would do anything and everything he could to protect Mark and Amelia from any further pain. He would make himself responsible for them. He hadn't known then just how far that promise would take him.

"Hello?" Mark said, his voice corning over the phone.

"How's it going, little brother?" Tyler deliberately put a cheerful note in his voice, trying to sound casual, as if this was any other conversation they'd had over the years.

"Not so good," Mark replied, making no effort to aid in the pretense of normalcy.

"What's wrong?"

"What isn't wrong? Do you have any news? Shelly said you found the McKenna sisters. Did you talk to any of them?"

"Yes, I spoke to two of them—Kate, the oldest, and Caroline, the youngest. Kate runs a bookstore and appears to run the family, too. She's smart, responsible, wary, doesn't let her thoughts show. Caroline is a firecracker, impulsive, headstrong, wants to be taken seriously and doesn't like big sister calling the shots. I still have to track down Ashley."

"Did they tell you anything?"

"Not yet. They're not particularly interested in a follow-up story. In fact, they're more secretive than I expected. I also met their father, Duncan. He was bombed out of his mind. Kate was called to take care of him, and I got the feeling this was definitely not the first time. I think it's likely he has a drinking problem."

"He's not important. I don't care about him. It's his daughters. One of them..." Mark's voice caught on a sob of emotion. "Amelia is all I have left. I promised Susan. She was dying, Tyler, and she knew it. I can still see the fear in her eyes. She was afraid, not for herself but for me and for Amelia."

"I know," Tyler said tightly. "You won't lose Amelia. Trust me."

"I do trust you. But it's a hell of a big problem even for you, big brother."

And he'd been a hell of a big brother, Tyler thought, as a shaft of pain ran through him. He'd missed a lot of years of his brother's life. "Go to sleep," he said gruffly. "I'll call you as soon as I know anything. And I won't give up. No matter what the McKenna sisters throw in my path.

CHAPTER FOUR

KATE STARED at the blanket tossed haphazardly on the living room floor. Her father was gone. She'd planned on offering him a cup of coffee, some breakfast, and a stern warning not to speak to Tyler Jamison. But Duncan had already left. He'd always been one to get up with the sun, hangover or not. He was probably on his way to his boat or maybe to the Oyster Bar for a Bloody Mary.

As she picked up the blanket, she caught a whiff of her father's aftershave. The musky scent reminded her of childhood, the scent forever linked to her father, to childish hugs and Daddy's strong arms. He'd once been her hero, her protector, the man who stood taller than all the rest. She remembered sitting on the floor by his feet listening to him tell stories about his adventures. His words would sweep her away. She could smell the sea and feel the splash of the waves, and she would shiver with the imagined wind. She couldn't have stopped listening if she had tried, and she'd never tried, because having her father at home was always special. He was gone a lot in her early childhood, running fishing boats, charters, whatever he could do to make a living. His frequent absences had made his rare presence that much more special, a time to be treasured, as her mother often said.

But those times of treasuring had created a man who took for granted the devotion of his family, Kate thought now. And once her mother had passed on, the responsibility of taking care of Duncan had fallen to her, the eldest child. She'd cooked and cleaned and mothered her sisters and tried to make sure her father's life always ran smoothly. She'd supported his every decision, including the one that had taken them to sea for three long years, always believing in her heart that Daddy knew best.

As a grown woman, she realized that Daddy hadn't known best for a very long time, and somewhere along the way their roles had reversed. Duncan had become the child, and she had become the parent. It was not the role she craved. And she couldn't help but wish for the impossible, that he would wake up one day and be the father she craved, the kind of man who would listen and advise, who would laugh with her and come to her bookstore and tell her he was proud of her. But he had never been that kind of father. Proud of her, yes, but only when it came to sailing. The rest of her life—her interests, her emotions, her ambitions—had never been of concern to him. If it didn't touch his life, he just didn't care that much.

Sometimes she hated him for not caring. But most of the time she loved him. He was her father, and she could still hear her mother's voice in her head: Your father is the most special man in the world. You are a very lucky little girl.

Maybe she just hadn't figured out the special part yet. She sighed as she took the blanket into the laundry room and tossed it in the pile to be washed. As for lucky, well, she could use a little luck right now, because she had a feeling her father was the least of her problems. No doubt that reporter would be waiting for her when she got to the bookstore. And she needed to figure out how to handle him.

As she returned to the kitchen, her eye caught on the laptop computer on the counter. She hadn't had a chance to look last night, but maybe she should make the time now.

Taking the computer over to the kitchen table, she got it started, then poured herself a cup of coffee. When she was logged on to the Internet, she quickly did a search on the name Tyler Jamison. If he was a reporter, he'd no doubt published some stories somewhere, and she was more than a little curious as to where.

The answer wasn't long in coming, but it was long in detail. The results jumped out at her.

Tyler Jamison reporting from Somalia for Time magazine...

An in-depth look at India's Kashmir region by Tyler Jamison...

Japan's new royalty, Tyler Jamison, U.S. News and World Report...

Kate's jaw dropped farther with each entry. It couldn't be the same man. A foreign correspondent, a man who covered war, whose words had been printed in every national magazine—that kind of reporter didn't write about sailboat races in Puget Sound. Something was definitely wrong.

Either Tyler Jamison wasn't really Tyler Jamison, or he'd come to Castleton for another reason.

Maybe there was a photograph of him somewhere, she thought, hastily clicking on each of the entries and scanning the articles for a picture. She had barely started when the doorbell rang. Her nerves tensed as she went to answer it, suspecting the worst, and her instincts were right on the money.

Tyler Jamison wore jeans and a short-sleeved polo shirt. His eyes didn't look nearly as tired as they had the day before, and he'd obviously showered only a short time earlier, as his dark hair was still damp and there was a glow to his cleanly shaven face. Or maybe it was just the glow that came from his eyes. He really had incredible eyes, a much darker blue than her own. They reminded her of the deep waters of the ocean. She just hoped he wouldn't prove as dangerous or as deadly as the sea.

"Good morning. Can I interest you in some bagels?" He held out the white paper bag in his hand. "I don't know about you, but I always think better on a full stomach."

"Were you hoping to bribe me with food?"

"Did it work?"

"Come in," she said, waving him in. "How did you find me?"

"The island isn't that big, Kate, and everyone knows you. You don't mind if I call you Kate, do you?"

"Would it matter?"

He smiled in reply. "Are you ready for your interview? You did tell me we could talk today."

"I said you should come by the store, not my house."

"We'll have more privacy here." Tyler walked into the living room and glanced around.

She knew what he saw—a comfortable, warm room, with pastel colors, puffy white couches, throw rugs that warmed up the hardwood floor, and small lamps on every table. This was her haven, her home, and she'd make no apologies for the decor. Her years on a sailboat had left her with a distinct longing for a place of her own that didn't rock with the waves or blow in the wind, a house she could make a home, with a garden and trees, with roots that went deep into the ground.

"Landscapes," Tyler mused, surprising her with his words.

Kate followed his glance to the pictures of hillsides and meadows, flowers and trees on the walls. "You don't like landscapes?"

"They're okay. But where's the sea, the lighthouses, the boats?"

"Just a few miles down the road."

"No reason to put them on the wall?"

"None whatsoever." She met his gaze head-on. "Do you find that surprising?"

Tyler nodded. "Among other things. Are you going to talk to me, Kate?"

"I might." She still didn't know what to do about him. She'd dreamed about him last night, the first time in a long time a man's face that wasn't Jeremy's had appeared in her dreams. But she didn't want this man in her dreams, or in her house for that matter.

Tyler walked over to the mantle and studied the portrait hanging over the fireplace. It was Kate's favorite picture of the McKenna women, her mother and her sisters and herself. They'd had the portrait painted for her father's birthday when Kate was fourteen years old, Ashley twelve and Caroline ten. She could still see her father unwrapping the portrait, the love, joy, and pride lighting up his eyes when he saw it. He'd jumped to his feet, grabbed her mother in a huge bear hug, and swung her around until she was dizzy. Next he'd picked up Kate and spun her, then done the same with each of her sisters. There had been so much laughter that day, so much love.

"Your mother?" Tyler asked, drawing her attention back to him.

"Yes."

"You look like her."

"I've always thought Ashley looked the most like her."

"I haven't met Ashley yet."

And it was going to stay that way, if Kate had her wish.

"What happened to your mother?" Tyler asked.

"She died of cancer when I was seventeen years old."

"I'm sorry."

"So am I."

"Was she a sailor?"

"Yes, but she didn't like sailing far from home. A spin around the islands was enough for her. She was an artist, a dreamer. She used to design sails, not for money, just for friends. She was more of an armchair adventurer than anything else." Kate let out a small sigh, feeling a wave of longing and nostalgia that never seemed to go away completely. It had been years since her mother's death, but she still missed her. "I wish she could have seen my bookstore. I think she would have liked it." She stopped abruptly, remembering whom she was talking to.

"Don't stop now. You're on a roll." Tyler sent her a curious look. "We don't have to be adversaries. I'm not sure why, but I get the feeling that you don't want me here. In fact, I believe you'd like to send me away as quickly as possible. I just don't know why."

"What are you really after?" she asked, deciding it was time to turn the tables. "You don't write stories about ocean racers, not even world-class ones. You write about wars and international economies. You've had bylines in every national magazine. And I think somewhere along the way you've won a journalistic award or two."

His eyes narrowed with a glint of admiration. "You did some checking."

"Is that a problem? Do you have something to hide?"

"Not at all. I'm just not used to being on the other side of the research."

"So, tell me, Mr. Jamison, why would a man comfortable in the hottest spots of the world want to recreate an old story that wasn't that exciting to begin with?"

"Again, I think you underestimate the level of interest in your experience. But, to answer your question, I wanted a change of pace. It's been an intense few years for me. After a while there's only so much blood and carnage you can absorb without going a little crazy."

"I can imagine," she murmured.

"No, you can't."

The grimness on his face bespoke of things she probably couldn't imagine. "I'm sorry. I didn't mean to make it sound--"

"Why don't we talk about you?" He moved closer, invading her personal space, making her feel very aware of herself as a woman. She hadn't spent much time on men or relationships in the past few years, keeping herself busy with family, friends, her home, and her business. It seemed to be enough most days. But not today, not with this man standing so close, his warm breath brushing her cheek, his lips within kissing distance.

Kate cleared her throat, feeling distinctly warm and foolish as she took a step backwards. Tyler Jamison wasn't interested in her. He was after a story, and he wasn't above using his appeal to get it. She'd have to be careful. She sat down on the edge of the couch and waved her hand toward a nearby chair.

"What do you want to know about me?" she asked as he took a seat.

"When did your family decide to race around the world?"

"It wasn't a family decision. My father decided for us. After my mom died, we were at loose ends. My dad wasn't good at homework and carpools, so he decided to take us to sea. He'd always been a sailor. He was in the navy in his early years, raced as a younger man, then settled down to running charters around Puget Sound once he married my mother. He always felt more comfortable on water than on land. He had itchy feet. My mother was the only person who could keep him in one place. Once she was gone, he couldn't settle down."

"Sounds like he loved her."

"He did. Very much. He was different with her. She understood him in a way that I've certainly never been able to."

"So you took to the sea. What happened next?"

"At first we just sailed. That lasted about six months. Then a short race came up, and we joined in. After our first win, my dad wanted another and another. It became a fever. He filled up our future with big dreams of big races. We were somewhat limited, because our boat wasn't as sleek or powerful as the boats used by the racing syndicates. But my dad was determined to win an around-the-world race. The Winston came up in one of the off years between the Whitbread and America's Cup. It was a different kind of race, one for both amateurs and professionals; the class level of the boats made sure of that. The crews were limited to no more than six. There was more time built into the race and into the layovers."

"But there were only four of you. Why not fill out the crew with a couple of hefty guys?"

She smiled at the familiar criticism. So many people had suggested that they take on additional crew members. The initial reports of the race had all predicted that the McKennas would finish last, if they finished at all.

"We were good at what we did," she said. "I think we proved we were quite capable of winning without two hefty guys."

"Good point. What happened to the boat after you came home? It's my understanding that it's now owned by someone else."

"Yes. We sold it when we returned home."

"Why?"

Kate thought for a moment, wondering how she could answer that without drawing additional questions. "That part of our life was over," she said finally. "We needed the money for other things."

"What other things?"

"Just things."

Tyler tapped his foot against the floor. "Okay. Tell me this, how will you feel when you see your boat come sailing back into the harbor on Monday?"

"How do you know about that?" she asked sharply, then remembered he'd had dinner with her sister. "That's right. You were out with Caroline last night."

"Yes."

"Why did you ask her out?"

"I thought she'd be more forthcoming than you."

"And was she?"

"You know she wasn't. She was as evasive as you are, although a bit more colorful in her language."

Kate could believe that. Caroline had always loved a good swear word. "What else do you want to know?" she asked, checking her watch. "I have to get to the bookstore."

"Did you ever want to quit the race?"

"Yes. But my father was determined, obsessed with getting to the finish line. Once we began, nothing and no one could stop him."

"I guess that's how you win races."

"I guess." She hadn't let herself think about the race in a very long time. There were too many emotions wrapped up in that part of her life: incredible joy, horrific pain. Standing up abruptly, she said, "We're done."

"We're just beginning," Tyler said as he also stood up.

"If you want more information, go to the library."

"I thought we were getting along, breaking the ice." His soft smile was meant to take the edge off her mood, but it wasn't enough. She'd started to feel the pain again. She couldn't go back there. She wouldn't go back there.

Tyler reached out and touched the side of her face with his hand. The heat burned through her skin, the intimate gesture startling her.

"What put that look of enormous hurt into your eyes?" he asked softly, his gaze intent on hers.

"Nothing. You're imagining things." She wanted to look away from him, but she couldn't seem to break the connection between them. "You're staring at me."

"You're staring at me," he murmured.

And she was, dammit. Why now? Why did her sleeping libido have to suddenly wake up now?

"Was it a man?" Tyler asked.

"What?" Caught up in her physical reaction to him, she'd completely lost the thread of their conversation.

"Was it a man who hurt you?"

"No," she said quickly.

"Did something happen to one of your sisters while you were racing?"

"Why would you ask that?"

"Because you're their protector. And anything that hurts them hurts you. Am I right?"

She was relieved that the conversation had turned to her sisters. "I'm the oldest," she replied. "I do what I have to do."

"I can understand that."

"Good. Don't go after my sisters, Tyler. That would be a big mistake."

Tyler sent her a long, measuring look. "I believe it would be."

"Then we understand each other." She turned to escort him out of the room, but he caught her by the arm.

"Not so fast."

It wasn't fear that drove the shiver down her spine but an undeniable attraction, and Kate couldn't afford an attraction to this man. She couldn't let herself like him or trust him. She had family to protect, not to mention her heart.

"We're not done," he added.

"Yes, we are. I don't trust you. I don't believe you're here for a simple story."

"And I don't believe nothing happened during your race. I think you're hiding something."

"Believe what you want. I don't have anything to gain by talking to you."

"You may have nothing to gain, but I suspect that you have something to lose."

He had no idea how much. And she desperately hoped he would never find out. Before she could reply, the doorbell rang once again. Her house had never been this busy, but she was grateful for the distraction. She pulled her arm away from his hand. "I need to get that." Opening the door, she found Ashley on the doorstep.

Ashley's eyes were wild, her long hair tangled and falling around her face and shoulders. "I can't do it, Kate. I can't get on the damn boat. The wind has died down, but I still feel a breeze, and it's too much." Ashley's words tumbled out in a rush as she stepped into the hallway. "If I don't photograph all the crews, Mr. Conway will give the assignment to someone else, and I really need the money. But I can't get on the damn boat. What's wrong with me? Why do I have to be so afraid all the time?" She waved her hand in frustration, the action sending her purse flying to the ground, the contents spilling on the floor. "Dammit. I can't do anything right."

"Oh, Ash," Kate said, putting a calming hand on her sister's arm. "It's going to be fine."

"No, it's not." Ashley stopped abruptly as Tyler squatted down to collect the things that had spilled from her purse. "Who are you?"

"Tyler Jamison," he said as he stood up and handed Ashley her purse back. "You must be Ashley."

"The reporter?" Ashley looked from Tyler to Kate in confusion. "You're talking to the reporter, but you said—"

Kate cut Ashley off with a warning glance. "I said that he was very persistent, and he is."

"Right. I'm sorry I interrupted you."

"Oh, this must have come out of your purse, too," Tyler said, handing Ashley a small bottle of pills.

"Thank you," Ashley said hastily, sticking the pills in her purse. "I should go."

"You don't have to go. Mr. Jamison was just leaving." Kate sent Tyler a pointed look, willing him to just leave. She needed to deal with Ashley in private.

"All right. I'll go," Tyler said. "It was nice to meet you, Ashley. I'll talk to you later, Kate."

"Sure, whatever." Kate shut the door behind him and turned to her sister. "Now then, tell me again why you're so upset."

"One of the boat crews is insisting that I photograph them from the deck of the boat. I've made up two excuses already, and I'm going to lose the assignment if I don't take their picture the way they want it." She shook her head in frustration. "It gets harder every day, Kate. I lived on a boat for three years, and now I can't get on one for twenty seconds. It's stupid. I thought the fear would have gone away by now, but it's worse than it was eight years ago. It's as if every day the fear pushes me back another step. I used to be able to go out on the Sound, remember? When we first got back, I went on some day trips. I was nervous, but I made it. But each time I went out got shorter and shorter. Now I can't even get on a damn boat."

Kate saw the frustration and pain in Ashley's eyes and wanted so badly to make it all right again, but Ashley's fears ran deep, probably deeper than Kate even realized. She'd told herself in recent months that Ashley was doing better, that she was fine. It was easier to believe they were all okay now, to pretend that the past no longer had the power to hurt. But it was clear that Ashley wasn't better, and pretending otherwise would only make it worse. "Do you want me to go with you?" Kate asked. "Maybe it would help."

"I can't ask you to do that," Ashley said, but there was a plea in her eyes that told Kate not to give up too easily.

"I want to do it. I want to help you. It will be fine, you'll see. We'll go together and you'll snap their pictures, and it will be over before you know it. Not nearly as bad as a root canal, I promise."

"I'm such an idiot."

"No, you're not."

Ashley drew in a deep breath and let it out. "You know, just telling you about it actually makes me feel like I can do it."

"You can do it. Remember, the boat isn't going anywhere."

"I know. My fear is ridiculous. Even if the boat got loose, I could swim back."

"You could sail back."

Ashley gave her a reluctant smile. "Yeah, I could do that, too." She paused. "What did you say to the reporter?"

"As little as possible. I don't trust him, Ash. He's got a hidden agenda, but I don't know what it is."

"It's been so long. I didn't think anyone... What are we going to do?"

"Check him out at the same time he's checking us out. I already did a brief search on the Internet. He's been all over the world, covering major stories."

"That doesn't sound good."

"No, it doesn't. I'd like to find out why he has developed a sudden interest in ocean racing."

"If he's been all over the world, maybe we ran into him before and just don't remember?"

Kate thought about the rugged, dark-haired man who had just left her house and knew deep in her soul that if she'd ever met him before, she would have remembered. "If our paths crossed, I don't think we knew it. But it might be interesting to find out what Mr. Jamison was doing eight years ago."

"Do you think you can?"

"I'm sure going to try."

"I'd like to look at news articles that appeared eight years ago in reference to the McKenna family's racing victory," Tyler told the librarian. Castleton's library was little more than a two-story Victorian house, but since the McKennas were local, he figured he might get lucky.

"Oh, well, that's easy," the librarian replied. "We photocopied and laminated every article we could find, seeing as how the McKennas are hometown heroes. We were so proud of them, you know. They were amazing."

Tyler nodded. "That's what I understand." He followed the librarian into the next room.

"This is where we keep everything on sailing. And this is the

McKenna shelf," she added, pointing to several notebooks. "Do you mind if I ask why you're so interested? It was a long time ago."

"I'm writing an article on ocean racing featuring famous crews. A where-are-they-now piece."

"Well, they're all right here," she said with a gleam in her eye. "And all quite single. Are you single, Mr...?"

"Jamison. Tyler Jamison. And, yes, I'm single."

If the woman asking him had been less than seventy years old, he might have felt awkward, but she was clearly not asking for herself.

"Really? A handsome man like you—what are the girls thinking? Why, if I were twenty years younger, I'd go after you myself."

"I would count myself lucky."

"Oh, you're a charmer, you are. Well, I'll leave you to your reading. Let me know if you need anything. My name is Sheryl Martin, and I'll be here until we close at five."

"Thank you." Tyler pulled out the first notebook and sat down at a nearby table. He'd already read through several articles on the race that he'd found on the Internet, but most of those articles had been about the race itself: winners of each leg, time handicaps, and weather conditions. Nothing that helped his cause.

He turned to the first page. The headline stated FIVE RACERS LOST AT SEA.

Tyler had read a little about the storm but hadn't thought much about it since the McKennas had come through unscathed. Now he wondered if that storm had caused some trauma. Ashley seemed to have a surprising fear of the water. His mind darted back to the bottle of pills that had fallen from her purse. The label had read Xanax, which he knew to be an anti-anxiety medication.

Tyler skimmed the article, but there was no mention made of the McKennas or the Moon Dancer. Instead, the article focused on a boat that had capsized, losing all but one of her entire crew to the raging sea. Turning the page, he found more reports on the storm, quotes from some of the sailors.

"The winds were screaming. It was a scene from hell."

"The waves were three stories high. I couldn't tell if I was on the boat or in the water."

"There were Maydays and distress calls everywhere. Flares popping up all over the place, like the Fourth of July. We were no longer racing. We were simply trying to survive."

Tyler wanted a quote from one of the McKennas. He wanted to know what they had been thinking, what they had been feeling. It sounded terrifying. Certainly something that could bring on a water phobia, maybe even a need to drink, he thought, his mind turning to Caroline and to Duncan. But what about Kate? She didn't have any noticeable vices or inconsistencies. Had the storm or the race itself affected her in some way? He'd have to find out. Mark was counting on him.

He wondered if Kate had somehow connected him to Mark. It seemed unlikely; they didn't share the same last name since Mark's stepfather had adopted him. But she'd obviously been on the Internet. What else had she come up with?

Tyler shook his head. Too many questions, not enough answers. The second notebook focused on the end of the race. There were photos taken of the Moon Dancer's arrival in Castleton, most of which he'd seen before.

It occurred to him that a week had passed between the official end of the race and the McKennas return to Castleton. It must have been a strange few days, anticlimactic for sure, but what else? Had the McKennas simply sailed home, gotten off their boat, and said good-bye to sailing forever? According to Kate, that was the scenario. He studied the girls' faces as they waved from the deck of the boat. They looked weathered, exhausted, and completely overwhelmed. He supposed those were natural responses to a race that had gone on for eleven long months. But he knew something else had happened during those eleven months, something no one wanted to talk about.

Turning the page, he found a photo of Ashley and a young man. The caption: Sean Amberson welcomes home high school sweetheart, Ashley McKenna.

Amberson? Wasn't that the name of one of the men lost at sea?

Tyler flipped back to the article on the storm, tracing the names of the five sailors lost with his finger. The final name was Jeremy Amberson. The brother of Ashley's boyfriend? That was an interesting connection. Sean Amberson sounded like someone who might have insight into the McKenna family, especially Ashley. If he couldn't get answers from the McKenna sisters, maybe he could get them from their friends.

CHAPTER FIVE

"READY?" Kate asked, watching Ashley take a deep breath before boarding the sailboat. "They're waiting for you."

"Thanks for coming with me. I know you should be at work," Ashley said.

"It's fine. Theresa handles the store as well as I do, although I hate to admit that. You know me, control freak to the end."

Ashley nodded, but Kate could tell her sister wasn't listening. Her mind was wrestling with the task ahead of her. It saddened Kate to see her once-courageous sister battling simple and often imagined fears. At one time, Ashley had been so decisive, so eager to explore the unknown. Now there always seemed to be a battle going on between mind and body, between right and wrong, truth and lies.

"Here I go." Ashley squared her shoulders and lifted her chin. She called to one of the crew that she was coming aboard. An eager male came to assist her, stretching out a strong, secure hand for Ashley to take. And she did, stepping onto the boat with just a bit of a stumble.

Kate watched while Ashley went into photographer mode. With the camera in her hand and the vast expanse of water at her back, she seemed able to keep the fear at bay as she instructed them on where to stand and where to look.

While Ashley took care of business, Kate looked around. It was a beautiful day. The stormy night had blown away all the dust, leaving the sky a bright, brilliant blue, and the water glistened like diamonds in the sunlight. There were colors everywhere, from the sails on the boats to the multicolored roses in planters along the waterfront that gave Rose Harbor its name. There was excitement in the air, too. The slips were filling up with boats, the local bars teeming with racers looking for crews.

For a moment, Kate felt a strange sense of yearning that she didn't begin to understand. She'd turned her back on this world a long time ago. And she didn't regret it. She didn't miss the life she'd led. Not for a second. She knew how quickly the magic could go, the wind could change, the race could turn from one of friendly competition to cutthroat obsession. Out in the middle of the ocean anything could happen. The sea could swallow up a boat without anyone knowing. People could disappear.

Kate turned her back on the water and tried to quell the sudden nausea in her stomach. She shouldn't have come down here. She should have stayed safe at home or in the bookstore. God, she was getting as bad as Ashley.

"Kate?"

"Sean," Kate murmured in surprise as he approached. "Ashley said you were back." She slipped her hands into the pockets of her slacks. She always felt awkward around Sean, especially since he'd grown into a man, a man who reminded her of Jeremy.

"What are you doing down here?" he asked.

"I came along with Ashley." Kate tipped her head in Ashley's direction.

He nodded with a pleased smile. "Ah, she got on the boat. I guess the sun brought out her courage."

Kate looked away. His brown eyes were too familiar.

"It's all right. I know I remind you of my brother," he said quietly. "I figure that's why you avoid me."

"I don't mean to," she said, forcing herself to meet his gaze.

"It's just easier if I'm not around."

"Ashley said you came back to race in the Castleton."

"I thought it was about time. So many of these racers remind me of Jeremy—young, reckless, willing to sign on with anyone to go anywhere. Do you remember the first Castleton that Jeremy sailed in?"

"I—I don't know."

"He was fourteen, but he lied and said he was eighteen. By the time my parents found out, he was halfway across Puget Sound. He was fearless. I admired him so much."

"Why are you racing now, Sean?" she asked, searching his eyes for the answer, but she couldn't find one. "Why would you want to do the one thing that will hurt your family even more?"

He thought for a moment. "Because I need to know. I need to feel what Jeremy felt. I don't think I can let him go until I know what he went through, what he experienced, what he saw. I've never been more than a couple of miles offshore. I can't imagine what it would feel like to be two or three days from land."

"It feels lonely and scary. Everything is bigger than you are—the waves, the wind, the sky. I've never felt so helpless, so vulnerable."

"That's not the way Jeremy described it. He talked about how fast the boat rode the waves, how the wind sounded like a song, and how the spray in his face made him feel alive."

Sean's words, actually Jeremy's words, stole the breath from her chest. She remembered Jeremy saying the same things to her. She could still feel the breeze on her neck as his arms crept around her waist and his whispered words ran through her mind: "The wind is playing our song, Kate. Listen."

"I have to go," Kate said quickly. Her sister seemed fine now, and she really didn't want to continue this conversation with Sean. "Could you tell Ashley that I needed to get back to the bookstore?"

"You don't have to run away, Kate. I'll leave."

"It's not you."

"Sure it is. You don't like to talk about Jeremy. No one does." A hint of pain flashed through his eyes. "My father hasn't mentioned his name in years. Sometimes I catch my mother looking at a photo, but as soon as I come in, she hides it away. Maybe that's why I can't let my brother go."

"It's been a long time, Sean."

"I know. Every year I think I'll move on. But changing locations hasn't helped. I've been in more cities than I can count in the last few years. The only place I haven't gone is the middle of the ocean, the place where Jeremy died."

"There aren't any answers out there. There aren't any answers anywhere."

"I know it was an accident, a risk Jeremy was willing to take to do the one thing he loved most. I've heard it all, Kate. But, dammit, it still doesn't make it easier." He ran a hand through his hair in frustration. "I can't let go. Believe me, I've tried."

Kate wished she had an answer for him, and as she watched Sean's gaze turn to Ashley, she realized that he hadn't let go of Ashley, either. There was a naked need on his face that made her ache for him.

"I'm sorry," she murmured.

"You don't have anything to apologize for. It's my problem. I'll deal with it." He walked away with a brisk, impatient stride, as if he were sorry he'd stopped at all and wanted to get away as quickly as possible.

Ashley stepped back onto the dock and rejoined Kate. "I'm done," she said, with a relieved sigh. "I did it."

Kate smiled, happy to see how proud Ashley was of herself. She'd battled one demon and won. "I knew you could."

"Was that Sean I saw?"

"Yeah."

"He looked mad."

"He is mad, and by that I mean crazy. Wanting to race in the Castleton, wanting to follow in Jeremy's footsteps. His parents must be beside themselves. I hope he changes his mind. It's not going to solve or change anything. It certainly won't bring Jeremy back." She paused, giving Ashley a thoughtful look. "He's still in love with you, Ash."

"No, he's not," Ashley said immediately. "He told me he has lots of girlfriends."

"Yeah, that's why he's here alone and wanting to sail to the edge of the world."

"We don't even know each other anymore. Aside from last night's short conversation, it's been years since we talked, spent time together. It's over. And I don't want to talk about him."

"Okay. I have to get to work, anyway."

"Why now?" Ashley asked abruptly.

"Because I've been gone half the day."

"Not work. I mean, why now, why is the reporter here? Why is Sean wanting to crew? Wanting to follow in Jeremy's footsteps? What happened, Kate? Why is it all coming back now?"

She met her sister's questioning gaze. "I wish I knew. Just when you think it's safe to go back into the water..." she wisecracked.

"Hush. You know that movie gave me nightmares for weeks."

"Not me. Out on the open sea, the sharks were only one of our worries."

Kate was reminded of sharks a few hours later when Tyler walked into her bookstore just before closing time. He'd pulled a dark blue sweater over his polo shirt, which should have made him look casual and friendly. But the way he moved, the way he looked at her, reminded her of the sharks that had circled their boat from time to time. They'd come close, then disappear, then pop up again. You could never be truly sure they were gone. You could never be truly sure that they wouldn't attack even if they weren't provoked. She'd learned to respect the sharks as much as she'd respected the sea. She didn't want to respect Tyler, but she had a feeling it would be even worse to underestimate him.

"I'm back," Tyler said, a challenging glint in his eyes as he approached the counter.

"I figured you would be." Kate fiddled with a stack of flyers. "So what do you want now?"

"The pleasure of your company."

"Yeah, right. You have more questions."

"A few."

"Maybe I could find you something more interesting to write about than my family," she suggested, searching her brain for an idea.

"Okay, shoot. What have you got?"

"Micky Davis said he saw a mermaid off the coast of Florida last year."

"After how many drinks?" he challenged. "Nice try, but I don't do alien stories."

Kate thought for another moment. "The owner of the Sally McGee, that's the racing yacht that came in third in our race, just got married for the sixth time, and, get this, the first wife, the third wife, and the sixth wife are all named Sally."

Tyler grinned. "You just made that up."

"I didn't. I swear. He said Sally was a lucky name for him."

"Not if he was married six times."

She smiled back at him. "Good point."

"Tell me about the storm," he said abruptly.

She stiffened. "Last night's storm? Well, I think we got about a half inch of rain."

"You know what storm I mean, the one that almost sent your entire race fleet to the bottom of the sea."

"Why do you want to know about that?"

"Because I do."

"Well," she thought for a moment. "It was terrifying. Huge waves, monster winds. I can't describe it. It was like a freight train bearing down on us. But we battled, and we came through. There's really nothing else to say." Or, at least anything else she wanted to say.

"Did anyone get hurt?"

"Just bumps and bruises, that sort of thing."

"What would you have done out there in the middle of the ocean if someone had been injured?"

"We had a good first aid kit. Dad knew the basics, or at least enough to keep anyone stable until port could be reached."

"Quite a man, your father. And you, too. I'm still baffled as to how three young girls could handle a boat of that size. You're not exactly built like an Amazon."

"My sisters and I were good sailors. We learned to sail the same time we learned to walk. It was second nature to us. Some jobs required more strength than others, but we were extremely fit. My father insisted on fitness even when we were small children. Some kids got bedtime stories, but we got personal training—sit-ups, push-ups, leg lifts, weights."

"Sounds like a slave driver."

"Well, he did tell us a few stories while we were working out."

"Stories about what?"

"Sailing, of course. They were always tales that involved great courage, determination, physical and mental strength. They were meant to inspire us. My father taught us how to use our minds and our bodies to make things happen that seemed impossible. And that's exactly what we did when we raced, we accomplished the impossible."

"Is that a note of admiration in your voice?"

She sighed, wishing she could say no. "I think it might be."

Tyler studied her thoughtfully. "You and your father have a complicated relationship, don't you?"

"That's an understatement."

"And no one in the family races anymore. I can't help but wonder why."

"We lived a lifetime in those eleven months, Tyler, not to mention the two years of sailing that came before the race. It was enough."

"That's the first time you've called me Tyler." He tilted his head. "I think I like it. Makes it seem like we're getting along."

"Well, I wouldn't get carried away unless I start calling you Ty."

"I'll keep that in mind. Now, how about some dinner?"

Kate immediately shook her head. It was hard enough to get through five minutes of conversation with him. She certainly couldn't do dinner. "No."

"Why not?"

"I don't want to have dinner with you because, frankly, I don't want to talk to you and find my innocent statements written up in some magazine in a few months."

"We can go off the record."

"I'm not stupid. There is no off the record with reporters, especially not a reporter who has interviewed Fidel Castro."

Tyler grinned. "More research?"

"You're not hard to find on the Internet. In fact, you've led a very busy life. You don't seem to stay home much. Where is home, by the way?"

"Now, that's the kind of question I'd be happy to answer over dinner."

"I'm still not interested," she said quickly.

"What if I tell you about my tattoo?"

"I don't care about a tattoo."

"It has a woman's name on it."

Kate's eyes widened. She had to admit she was curious. "You actually did that? Tattooed a woman's name on your body? I hope she's still in your life."

He shook his head. "A youthful mistake. I've made a few others, too. If you buy me a drink, I might tell you about them."

"Buy you a drink? I don't think so. You're definitely paying."

"Then we're going to dinner?"

He sounded far too satisfied with the turn of the conversation. "A drink, that's all," she replied firmly.

"All right, I guess I can find someone else to have dinner with." He paused. "Maybe I'll ask Sean."

Sean? How did he know Sean? Not that Sean was a secret or anything. But dammit all; she didn't want Tyler talking about her family all over town. Nor did she want him talking to Sean's parents about either of their sons.

"You don't know Sean," she said.

"I hear he and Ashley were childhood sweethearts. In fact, he was one of the first to greet her when she got off the boat. I saw a photograph of them."

"If that's the best you've got, I think your reputation as an investigative reporter is overrated."

He laughed. "Point taken. Have pity on me and join me for dinner. I obviously need a face-to-face interview."

"Fine, you win. We'll have dinner, and for every question I have to answer about my personal life, you have to do the same."

"Deal. I'll show you my tattoo, you can show me..." His gaze traveled down her face to her chest.

"Nothing," she interrupted, crossing her arms somewhat self-consciously. "I will be showing you nothing."

His smile grew broader. "Too bad. So, what time can you go?"

"An hour. The Fisherman is very good. It's at the end of Main Street. I can meet you there at six o'clock." She waved her hand toward the door. "The sooner you go, the sooner I'll be able to leave."

He moved away from the counter, then paused. "Are you a woman that's always punctual, early even or never punctual, always late?"

"Which would irritate you the most? Never mind. I know."

"You don't know."

"I do," she said with a laugh. "You're type A—intense, driven, ambitious, stubborn, and absolutely always on time. Never early, because you wouldn't want to waste a second waiting, which means a woman who takes an hour in the bathroom would drive you nuts."

"But you're not that kind of woman," he returned. "You're the oldest child, the responsible one. You're smart, determined, protective, and you hate to fail. Being late would seem like a failure to get somewhere on time. I'll see you at six."

She wished she could say he hadn't gotten her right at all, but that would have been a lie.

Tyler smiled to himself as he walked away from the store. He felt good, invigorated, and it wasn't the late afternoon breeze or the beautiful view of the harbor that made him feel alive; it was the woman he'd left behind. He couldn't remember the last time a simple conversation had given him such a charge. He just hoped Kate showed up for dinner. While he might be making a mistake in liking her, he wouldn't make the mistake of trusting her.

His cell phone rang, and he pulled it out of his pocket, not particularly happy to see his brother's number. "Hey, what's up?"

"That's what I want to know. What's going on?" Mark asked, impatience in his voice. "You said you'd call me today."

"The day isn't over yet."

"I can't stand the waiting. Just give me something, please."

"Well, I met Ashley today," Tyler replied. "She's a very tense, uptight woman. And she carries around anti-anxiety medication in her purse. She also seems to have a fear of the water, which is odd, considering the sailing background."

"That's something, I guess," Mark said, hope evident in his voice. "What about Kate?"

"I'm having dinner with her tonight. I wish I could move faster, but if I tip my hand, who knows what will happen?"

"I agree, but you can't move too slowly, Tyler. I got an e-mail from George today. He received a letter from an attorney out of Seattle by the name of Steve Watson. Mr. Watson states quite clearly that he believes George handled a private adoption in Hawaii eight years ago, and he has some questions about the way the matter was managed and the welfare of the child involved."

"Damn. That was fast."

"My thoughts exactly. He's already found George. How long will it take him to find me and Amelia?"

"George won't talk."

"But someone else might. And I'm a single, disabled father without a job. Hell, a job is the least of my worries. I can't even walk. But that doesn't matter, because I'd cut off both legs before I'd give up my daughter. You've got to help us, Tyler. You've got to find out the truth. I need to know which of the McKenna sisters is Amelia's mother."

"I understand," Tyler said in frustration. He just wished Mark hadn't cut corners in the first place.

Mark and Susan hadn't asked many questions when their lawyer,

George Murphy, showed up with a baby girl eight years earlier. They'd been trying for a few years to adopt, and Amelia had looked like a gift from God; a gift they'd paid George Murphy very well for, Tyler thought cynically. If he'd known what his brother was up to, he would have told him to ask more questions, like why there was no signature from the birth mother giving up her rights to the child. The only reason they knew the baby belonged to one of the McKenna girls was because the baby had come with a locket, the name Nora McKenna engraved on the back, the picture inside matching the one he'd seen of Kate's mother. Nora McKenna was definitely Amelia's grandmother. Unfortunately, they still didn't know which of the sisters was Amelia's mother. Duncan had apparently given the baby to a doctor in Hawaii, who had been paid handsomely for his silence. The timing had coincided with the last stop in the race. One of the McKenna sisters had given birth to a baby during that race—but, surprisingly, there was absolutely no record of that birth, no photographs of a pregnant girl onboard the boat, nothing.

"You have to find Amelia's biological mother before she finds me," Mark added. "And once you find her, you have to find a way to discredit her. If this Ashley has prescription medication or mental issues, that could make her an unfit mother, or at least give us some ammunition."

"Ashley may not be the mother."

"But she might be. Until we know for sure, we need to dig up information on each of the women. I must have something to fight with. The more dirt you can get, the better. I'll do whatever I have to do to protect Amelia."

"So will I," Tyler promised. His niece had already lost her mother; he wouldn't let Amelia lose her father, too. They deserved to be together. No matter how they'd started out, they were a family now, and if Tyler had anything to say about it, they would stay that way.

CHAPTER SIX

THE FAMILY PICTURE EVOLVED SLOWLY—FIRST the father, then the mother, the son, the daughter, and finally the dog. Ashley stared at the photograph she was developing in her makeshift darkroom, which also served as the bathroom in her one-bedroom apartment. It had been a good day of work. After she'd left the marina, she'd joined the Haroldsons for their family reunion picnic at Stern Grove. She'd snapped a dozen photographs of the large clan and the individual families who had come from far and wide to spend the weekend together playing volleyball, barbecuing burgers, and laughing a lot. The Haroldsons had treated her like part of the family, and she'd enjoyed herself, too.

Stern Grove was a forested area set deep in the center of the island —no sign of water, just tall trees, thick bushes, and plenty of flowers. It was one of Ashley's favorite spots, and one she'd photographed many times. She'd had a picnic at Stern Grove with Sean once. They must have been eleven or twelve, and their picnic fare had consisted of peanut butter and jelly sandwiches, apples, and Twinkies. She smiled at the memory, wishing all her memories could be so happy and carefree.

Although it wasn't her memories that were the problem these days; it was Sean's presence on the island. She no longer had the luxury of roaming freely without worrying about running into him. She'd already bumped into him twice in as many days. And, with race week coming up, they'd be crossing each other's paths constantly. How on earth was she going to handle him?

The doorbell rang, and she started. What if it was Sean? Her pulse sped up at the thought. She wanted to see him almost as much as she didn't want to see him. But, if it was him, she had to answer the door; she simply could not allow him to go on thinking that she was avoiding him. It made it all seem that much more important. She just had to act casual, as if she didn't care, as if it really was over between them.

Squaring her shoulders, she walked out of the darkroom, closing the door behind her. A quick glance at her small apartment reminded her that it was in its usual state of disarray. Her kitchen table was covered with photographs, her coffee table piled high with more of the same. She liked to think of her space as controlled chaos, but in truth it was more chaos than control. Her attention span had never been particularly long; she was known for starting one thing, getting distracted, and never coming back to it. She picked up the half-eaten sandwich she'd made for lunch and tossed it in the wastebasket as she headed for the door.

"I'm coming," she called. She threw open the door, and her jaw dropped open in surprise, for standing in front of her was the last person she'd ever expected to see—Sean's mother, Naomi Amberson.

Ashley stared at her in dismay. They'd shared a few brief conversations over the years, even conversed about the weather or some island happening, but they hadn't had a private discussion in years, and Ashley didn't particularly want to start now.

"I should have called," Naomi said, holding her purse tightly in both hands. "But I need to speak to you. It's important. May I come in?"

"Of course." Ashley stepped back as Naomi entered the room. A petite brunette, Naomi barely reached five feet. But what she lacked in height, she made up for in the sheer force of her personality. She'd always ruled the Amberson household, despite the fact that her husband and sons topped her by a good twelve inches. She knew what she wanted, and she knew how to get it. And what she wanted always had to do with her family's happiness, which made Ashley uneasy. Why did Naomi need to speak to her now?

"Do you want to sit down? Can I get you a drink?" Ashley asked.

Naomi shook her head. Standing stiffly in the middle of the living room, she looked as uncomfortable as Ashley felt. "I'll get right to the point. Sean has signed on to race in the Castleton. I want you to talk him out of it."

"Me? I can't talk him out of it."

"You're the only one who can."

"Sean and I aren't even friends anymore. He's been gone for years. We barely know each other."

Naomi dismissed that with a shake of her head. "Sean has been in love with you since he was twelve years old."

"But that was a long time ago," Ashley protested, not liking the look in Naomi's eyes. "We had a teenage crush, that's it."

"I know my son. That was never it. But we can argue about that later. Right now, I need you to focus on getting Sean out of that race." Naomi's lips drew together in a tight line. "I can't lose him, Ashley."

"I'm sure he'll be all right," she said tentatively.

"The only way I can be sure is if he doesn't go. If you were a mother, you'd understand how hard it is to watch your child head straight for danger. I can't let him do it. Not without trying to stop him. Will you help me?"

Naomi's pain was so palpable Ashley could feel it coursing straight through her. But she didn't know what to say. Sean wouldn't listen to her.

"You're my only hope," Naomi continued. "His father and I have tried. Sean seems determined to do this, as some sort of quest to retrace Jeremy's path. But I don't want him to go down that path. The sea already took one of my sons; I won't let it take another. You were out there once, Ashley. You saw how horrible it could be. You saw what the sea could do to a boat and a few men who thought they were invincible."

Yes, she had seen all of that. In fact, she still saw it now in her dreams—in her nightmares.

"I don't want to lose Sean. I don't want to spend the next year worrying about whether or not there's a storm blowing his way. I want him on solid ground. I want him to be safe. Please, Ashley, you have to try." She could see the desperation in Naomi's eyes.

"All right. I'll try," she replied. "But don't expect too much."

She should have been late, Kate thought as she pulled into the parking lot next to the Fisherman restaurant exactly on time. She'd wanted to make Tyler wait for her. He thought he had her pegged, and he was right, dammit. Both her watch and the clock in her car read exactly six o'clock. She was embarrassingly punctual.

Stalling, she tilted the rearview mirror and checked her face one last time. With the blush on her cheeks, the light blue shadow on her lids, and the soft pink on her lips, she almost didn't recognize herself. Why on earth had she put on makeup for this guy? This wasn't a date. It wasn't even a friendly dinner. It was a battle. She couldn't let herself forget that, couldn't let herself get lost in a pair of incredible dark blue eyes that reminded her of the waters of the Mediterranean.

Moving the mirror back into place, she wondered if she was doing the right thing. Just because she'd agreed to have dinner with Tyler to head him off from other sources didn't mean he wouldn't go after Sean or Ashley or Caroline tomorrow. In fact, he probably would. Which meant this dinner was a complete waste of time. Of course, if she were honest, she'd have to admit that having dinner with him appealed to her on a personal level. And, obviously, if having dinner with a reporter was appealing, she needed to get out more. She needed to work on a social life. In truth she was a little lonely. It wasn't a crime. People got lonely, especially people who'd been working nonstop the past few years.

Maybe she'd call someone tomorrow. Maybe Neal Davis. He'd asked her out before. And be was nice looking, not to mention responsible, decent, kind... boring. Or maybe it was just his job. There wasn't a lot of excitement in the accounting field. But he did a heck of a job on her books.

No, not Neal. Dating someone who knew her finances wasn't a good idea. Maybe Connor O'Brien, one of the bartenders at the Oyster Bar. No, she couldn't date a bartender. Besides, Connor knew her father and had heard many stories about her. How embarrassing would that be?

Maybe dating an out-of-town stranger was a good idea. Someone who wouldn't be around forever. Not that she was dating Tyler Jamison. Good heavens, where was her mind going?

Kate banged her head gently against the steering wheel, hoping to knock some sense into herself. She was attracted to Tyler, no doubt about it. But she didn't want to be attracted, didn't want little shivers running down her spine. They reminded her of the past, of feelings she didn't want to feel again. Love hurt. It was an irrefutable, inescapable fact of life. She knew that without a doubt. But she also knew that someday she would have to try again, that she wanted the things that came with love, like marriage and children. She just had to find the right man, one who didn't sail into the wind, didn't lead with his heart, didn't do anything remotely dangerous or risky.

Someone who wasn't anything like Jeremy.

Eight years had passed, and Jeremy still had a grip on her heart. It was funny, in an odd way, because Jeremy had never been possessive. He'd been too busy leading his own life to worry about what she was doing, who she was seeing. He'd trusted in their love, figured it would always be there.

Even when her father had taken her to sea, Jeremy had assured her that they'd still be together when she got back. He hadn't worried about anything. He had taken life as it came, and he'd lived every minute of it. He wouldn't want her wasting her time like this. He'd want her to move on. In fact, he was probably looking down on her right now, tilting his head to the right the way he'd always done when her behavior confused him, muttering, "Katie, what are you thinking? Life is going to pass you by while you're making all your plans."

So, she'd stop making so many plans, stop trying to second-guess

Tyler Jamison and his intentions. It was just dinner. She'd survive. And she'd handle whatever came her way. Checking her watch, she was relieved to see a good ten minutes had passed. She was now sociably late. Getting out of her car, she walked into the restaurant, prepared to look like she'd almost forgotten their date.

Kate was disappointed not to find Tyler cooling his heels on one of the nearby benches. She walked into the dining room, a large, airy room with windows overlooking the water. Fishnets hung from the ceiling, poles decorated the walls and photographs of fishermen displaying their prize catches covered every other available space. The room was crowded, but there was no ambitious, handsome reporter at any of the tables.

Tyler could not be late. He wouldn't take the chance that she'd wait for him. She tapped her foot impatiently as she considered her options. It would serve him right if she left. Then again, she'd just be delaying the inevitable. The sooner she steered Tyler Jamison in another direction, the sooner she could get back to her life. Maybe she'd wait a minute—or two.

Tyler was running late, but he couldn't break away from the conversation in the Oyster Bar. He'd gone there to look for Duncan McKenna. Instead he'd run into Ashley's friend, Sean Amberson. They hadn't exchanged more than a few words when a boisterous crowd at a nearby table captured their attention with swaggering stories of a ferocious storm.

"It was a beautiful spinnaker run down the coast," one sailor said.

"Magic conditions," another man added.

"Twenty-four hours later, we had gale force winds of ninety miles per hour and waves eighty feet high."

"I thought we were going to die."

A murmur of admiration broke around the table, and more and more people gathered around the group of sailors talking about their experience in the southern seas. Tyler looked to his right where Sean

Amberson was perched on a bar stool, nursing his way through yet another beer. He was listening to the stories with an odd look in his eyes, as if a part of him wanted to listen and a part of him didn't.

"Sounds like a hell of a trip," Tyler said.

Sean nodded, his face somewhat grim. "My brother Jeremy used to talk about the *Furious Fifties*."

"The what?"

"*Furious Fifties*—the high-latitude zones known for winds gusting to seventy knots. Jeremy said that when you sail through them, you feel like you're flying."

"Are you a racer, too?"

"I'm thinking about it," Sean replied, draining his glass. He set it down on the bar and motioned for the bartender to give him a refill.

Tyler checked his watch. He doubted Kate would wait for him. On the other hand, she was probably late herself; no way would she want to prove him right about her punctuality. But he hated to leave Sean without getting whatever information he could. Maybe it was time to go for the jugular.

"I understand your brother Jeremy was one of the sailors lost in the Winston race," Tyler said.

"That's right," Sean said curtly, now eyeing Tyler somewhat suspiciously. "Who are you, anyway?"

"I'm a reporter. I'm writing a story on sailboat racers. I'm particularly interested in ocean racing and the McKenna family. In fact, I'd like to do a follow-up piece on the sisters and their father."

"Good luck," Sean said, a cynical note in his voice.

"Do I need it?"

"With Duncan, no. With the sisters, yes. They don't talk about the race."

"Why is that?"

Sean shrugged. "Who knows why they do anything?"

"You're a friend of theirs, aren't you? I saw a photograph of you and Ashley taken after the race."

"I used to be." Sean's eyes darkened with something—regret, anger —Tyler couldn't quite tell. "Ashley and I hung out together when we were kids. But when she came back from sailing around the world, it was over. She was a different girl."

"How so?"

"She wouldn't go near the water or boats, for one thing."

"Why not?"

"I don't know. Not much of what she did made sense to me. It doesn't matter anymore. It's all in the past."

Sean didn't sound like a man who was done with the past. Nor did he sound like he was done with Ashley. Which was all well and good, but it didn't help Tyler's search.

Although, he mused, Ashley had been in love with Sean when she left, but changed when she came back. Maybe she was the one who'd gotten pregnant. Maybe by another guy. Feeling alone, afraid, she'd given up the baby. And when she returned home, she couldn't look Sean in the eye, couldn't go back to him without admitting everything that had happened to her. Ashley would have been eighteen when the race ended. As a young girl who'd given up a baby, she could have been traumatized.

It made sense, but he was only speculating. He still had no hard facts and too many questions. For instance, why hide the pregnancy? Not only why, but how? Hadn't anyone seen a pregnant girl on the Moon Dancer? Hadn't anyone taken a photograph? Sure, they were at sea, but there were ports of call throughout the race. That part baffled him.

"Do you think there was someone else?" Tyler asked Sean, returning to the subject at hand.

"What do you mean?" Sean seemed confused by the question.

"Another guy. Someone Ashley met while she was sailing around the world."

"No," Sean said forcefully. "Absolutely not. They were on a boat, the three of them and their dad. There wasn't anyone else around."

"But they stopped along the way, and she was gone a long time."

Sean shook his head. "Something else happened. Something to do with Kate and Jeremy, I think."

"Your brother had a relationship with Kate?" Tyler asked, his pulse jumping with this new information.

Sean nodded. "They were going to get married."

Married? The thought stuck in Tyler's throat. Kate was going to get married? Why hadn't that been in any of the news reports?

"After they got back?"

"Yeah, they'd even set a date for a month after the race. My mother had the church booked and the band picked out. I was going to be the best man." Sean let out a long, heartfelt sigh. "And then that damn storm blew everything to bits."

"Why were they racing on separate boats?" Tyler asked. "It seems like Jeremy would have been a nice addition to the Moon Dancer."

"Duncan wouldn't take Jeremy on as crew. He wanted to win the race with just his family. At least, that's what he said. Duncan and Jeremy rubbed each other the wrong way, even though they were a lot alike. I wish he had taken Jeremy onboard. Then he'd still be alive." Sean set down his glass. "I've got to go. I hope you find what you're looking for."

Tyler hoped so, too. He knew one thing for sure—he now had a lot more questions for Kate.

Kate tapped her fingernails on the bar and stared moodily into her diet cola. Times like this she wished she drank. But her father's nasty habit had cured her of that desire years ago. After her mother died, Duncan's drinking had spun out of control, and it had been left to Kate to make sure her sisters got what they needed while Duncan was partying it up or sleeping it off. She'd thought things would get better when they went to sea. It was one of the reasons why she hadn't fought him on going. Leaving her life and her friends had seemed like a small trade-off if they could find their way back to becoming a family again.

For the most part, life at sea was better. Duncan didn't drink as much when they were racing. He'd let loose when they got to port, but on the ocean he'd managed to keep it together, at least most of the time.

Looking back, she realized now how naive she had been. There had been so many dangers that she hadn't seen, hadn't even imagined. The ocean had toyed with them like a cat plays with a mouse, sucking them into a game they couldn't win, but one they couldn't stop playing, either. Not even now.

There was solid ground under her feet, but sometimes she still felt as if she was moving, as if her world was rocking. She'd turned her backyard into a garden worthy of the cover of a magazine just because it made her feel better to dig her hands into the dirt and hold on. She'd planted roses, foxgloves, hollyhocks, and violets, a cornucopia of colors that wouldn't remind her of the endless blue of the sea and the sky. She'd built a trellis for the roses to climb, and she'd planted several fruit trees with roots deep in the ground. She wished she could be there now, feeling those roots between her fingers. She wanted something to hold on to, something strong and unmoving. Her hand curled around the glass in front of her. It was cool and wet, slippery. A shiver ran down her spine, the memory of hands slipping. She'd tried to hold on. She'd tried desperately to hold on.

"Kate? Are you all right?"

"What?" She looked up in confusion to find the bartender, Keith Brenner, staring at her with concern.

"You look like you're about to break that glass." He tipped his head toward her drink.

Her knuckles were white, her fingers leaving prints on the moist glass as she forced herself to let go. "I was thinking about something else."

"Like the guy you're waiting for?"

"Who said it was a guy?"

"It's Saturday night. You're wearing makeup, looking annoyed, checking your watch. Gotta be a guy. Want to tell your friendly bartender about it?" He gave her a warm, inviting smile. "Just think of me as *Dear Abby*."

Kate rolled her eyes. Keith Brenner was one of the local boys she'd grown up with. "You're a worse gossip than Caroline. I wouldn't tell you what kind of perfume I wear."

"Don't have to. I already know—Shalimar."

Her jaw dropped open in shock. "How do you know that?"

"I was with Jeremy when he bought it for you for Valentine's Day. Frankly, I couldn't believe the kind of cash Jeremy wanted to spend on you. He was crazy."

Jeremy had been crazy, Kate thought, as Keith moved down the bar to help another customer. Crazy in love. And she'd felt the same way.

Jeremy had been bold, daring and impulsive—and he'd brought out those traits in her, encouraging her to dream big, think large, live life. Jeremy had put the sun back in her life after her mother died. He'd always been a good friend, but after her mother passed on, he had become everything. Leaving him behind had been the hardest thing she'd ever done. But Jeremy had promised he'd see her again. Somewhere out there in the middle of the ocean when she least expected it, there he'd be.

And there he'd been.

She smiled, thinking of the first time she'd seen him after two years apart. He'd been standing on the deck of a beautiful sailboat, his brown hair so long he could have pulled it back in a ponytail, an earring in one ear, a tattoo on one arm, both new since the last time she'd seen him. He'd looked like a pirate, a sexy pirate. And she'd fallen in love all over again.

Everyone had told her they were too young to be in love. It was just a crush, a youthful infatuation that would fade with the years.

The years that they wouldn't have.

Kate took a sip of her cola and tried to focus on the present, the future. She'd learned to play *keep away* with her thoughts a long time ago, but sometimes the effort it took was exhausting.

"Drinking in a bar? I'm shocked."

Kate was surprised to hear her father's voice. She looked up to see him standing next to her bar stool. Duncan didn't usually frequent the touristy restaurant bars, preferring the more casual atmosphere of the pubs along the waterfront where the sailors and the fishermen hung out.

"What are you doing here?"

"I have a meeting." He pulled together the edges of a well-worn navy blue sports coat. "What do you think? Your mother used to love this on me."

Which went to show just how old the jacket was. As she took in Duncan's freshly showered and shaved appearance, Kate's stomach muscles tightened. She didn't like the look of this, didn't like it at all. There was a rare sparkle in her father's eyes. He was up to something, probably something she did not want to know about. Still, she had to ask. "Who are you meeting?"

"Rick Beardsley," he said smugly.

"The owner of Summer Seas?" she asked, naming one of the entries in the Castleton Invitational. The Summer Seas had undergone several owners in the last five years, Rick Beardsley being the most recent. Rick had been on the sailing circuit for years and had garnered himself quite a reputation for being a daring, no-holds-barred racer, a man cut from the same cloth as her father.

"The one and only," Duncan replied. "He wants to hire an experienced skipper." Her father stood taller with each word, pride throwing back his shoulders and lifting his chin.

"You?" she asked, feeling a wave of nausea run through her. "You're thinking of racing again?"

"Why not me? I am the best in the world." He grinned as Keith came over to take his order. "Isn't that right, Keith?"

"Whatever you say, Mr. McKenna," Keith replied evenly. "What can I get you?"

"Your best whiskey and a round for everyone here at the bar," Duncan said, waving hello to three lucky tourists. "Whatever you're having," he told them. "I'm celebrating tonight."

Kate sighed as her father moved down the bar to shake the hands of three complete strangers. Duncan had always been one for grand gestures. As for strangers, they were just friends he hadn't met yet.

"Dad," she said when he returned to her side, "you promised me you wouldn't race again."

"Now, Katie girl—"

"Don't you 'Katie girl' me. You promised. We made a deal."

"That promise was made a long time ago. I need to do something. I need this."

"You can't have this," she hissed, dropping her voice down a notch as she realized they were still the center of attention. "Pick something else. Find yourself another hobby. Take up flying. Join the circus. I don't care what you do, as long as you don't race."

He paled, but his eyes had a steel glint in them, a glint she remembered all too well.

"I'm still your father. You don't talk to me like that."

"You haven't been my father for a long time." The words struck him hard. She could tell by the sudden catch of his breath. But she didn't regret them. He'd promised. And now he was breaking that promise, like he'd broken so many others. "Why can't you just do this for me?" she pleaded. "We went through so much..."

"I need to race again. It's important to me. I'm dying inside." He put his hand to his heart in yet another dramatic gesture. "I need to be on the water. I need to feel the wind in my hair, the ocean spray on my face."

"You don't need to race to feel those things. You can just go for a sail."

"I need the excitement, the rush, the speed, the power." For the first time in a long while his eyes were clear and purposeful instead of dull and vague. He'd come alive. "Ah, Katie girl, aren't you tired of dragging me out of bars?"

It was the first time he'd ever acknowledged that she did that.

"I can't go on like I've been going on," he continued. "If I could get out there on the ocean, see the distant horizon, the endless possibilities in front of me, I could breathe again. Haven't I paid enough penance, Katie, or will you be leaving me in purgatory forever?"

"I'm not your jailer. That's your conscience. Or maybe you don't have a conscience. Because if you did, you wouldn't break your promise. You wouldn't race again." She scrambled off her bar stool, her eyes blurring with angry tears. "Do what you want. You always have, and you always will."

Kate hurried out of the bar, wanting to put as much distance between her father and herself as she could. She threw open the door to the restaurant and ran smack into Tyler.

He caught her by the arm. "Kate? What's wrong?"

"You're late," she cried, a little more loudly and more vehemently than was necessary.

His gaze narrowed. "And you're angry," he said slowly. "But I don't think it's at me."

She pulled away from him. "I'm tired, and I'm going home." She headed down the stairs to the parking lot. She fumbled with her keys as she reached her car, dropping them on the ground in her haste to get away.

Tyler picked them up before she could move. "You're not going anywhere until you can see straight," he said.

"I'm fine."

"You're furious. I'm sorry I was late."

"It doesn't matter."

"Tell me what's wrong. I can't imagine my tardiness would piss you off this much."

"I've had it with lies. I've had it with people making promises that they have no intention of keeping. And no one changes. People say they'll change, but they don't. So I give up. I quit. I'm throwing in the towel, putting up the white flag."

"Are you finished?" he asked gently as she ran out of steam.

She frowned. "I don't know yet." She drew in a deep breath. "Sorry, that wasn't about you. It was about my father. He drives me crazy."

Tyler nodded in understanding. "What did he do?"

"He's in there having a meeting." She tipped her head toward the restaurant. "He's trying to get back into racing. Someone actually wants him on his boat."

"Why is that surprising, given your father's track record? From what I've read about him, he was an amazing sailor. I think one of the sailing magazines called him a genius at working the sails, at taking the best advantage of the wind."

She suddenly realized who she was talking to. "He's too old to race," she said, which was only part of the truth. "And that genius quote probably came from my father."

"But he was good, wasn't he?"

"Yes, he was good," she admitted reluctantly. "Sometimes brilliantly good. But that was before, and this is now. And, more importantly, he promised he wouldn't race again."

"Why?"

"It doesn't matter why. And it's none of your business, anyway."

He stared back at her. "All right, I'll drop it. Are you hungry?"

"I'm not going back in there."

"Then we'll go somewhere else. Your pick."

She wavered between wanting to go home and not wanting to be alone with her thoughts and memories.

"Come on, say yes," Tyler prodded. "You can order the most expensive item on the menu and eat until you drop, my treat."

His wheedling smile suddenly reminded her of just who she was dealing with, a man who could probably charm the socks off her, not to mention a few other items of clothing. "I feel like I'm choosing between the devil I know and the devil I don't know," she muttered.

"Is that a yes?" he asked with a grin.

"I'm going to regret this."

"Don't worry. I'll still respect you in the morning."

She smiled as she was meant to, but she knew she had to be careful. She had a lot more to lose than respect.

CHAPTER SEVEN

ASHLEY TRIED to tell herself that it would be impossible to find Sean on a Saturday night. He could be anywhere—a restaurant, a bar, the movies, making out on some woman's couch. The possibilities were limitless. She could only try so hard to find him. She couldn't work miracles. Maybe she'd just wait until tomorrow.

Or she could walk down to the marina and check the family boat that Sean had always been fond of sleeping on.

Indecisive and more than a little reluctant to actually locate Sean, she paused in front of the travel agency on Main Street. The windows were decorated with flyers inviting her to summer in Savannah, wine taste in Santa Barbara, take a ferry ride to Vancouver, or sail on a fancy yacht to San Francisco. None of those places appealed to her. If she went anywhere, it would be somewhere in the middle of the country, someplace where water came out of wells in the ground, where the hills rose up like protective guardians and the endless plains made her feel safe and secure.

Who was she kidding? She wasn't going anywhere. She loved this island, loved the forested hills, the quiet coves, the pretty neighborhoods. This was home. It always had been, and it always would be. She could still remember the first time she'd seen the island after years at sea. A huge weight had slipped from her shoulders when she stepped off the boat and onto solid ground. She'd let out her breath after months of holding it. The island felt safe. The thought had come into her mind and never left. Just as she could never leave.

Unless... What if Sean came back here to live? If she did convince him not to race in the Castleton, that might mean he would stay on the island, take over the family business. What would she do then? She wouldn't be able to avoid him. And avoiding him wasn't even her biggest worry—giving in was more the concern. If he still wanted her, if he tried to kiss her, tried to persuade her they should get back together, how would she keep saying no?

Maybe he wouldn't stay. Maybe he wouldn't race, either. The best scenario was if he just went back to wherever he'd been and stayed there for another eight years.

Turning away from the window, she trudged down the street, avoiding the bars overflowing with Saturday night sailors. She could almost hear their conversations, arguments about which boat was faster, who had the best crew, where the winds would be the strongest. Every one of those sailors would have the most information they could have, the best boat, the most experienced crew, the strongest and bravest men, but none of it would matter in the end. The ocean was the ultimate equalizer. It was Mount Everest in constant motion. Everyone wanted to conquer the sea, but no one could.

As she neared the marina, the noise began to fade and the shadows lengthened. She passed by a couple kissing in a doorway. The man's hands were under the woman's shirt, and they were moving their bodies together in such an intimate way it looked as if they were having sex with their clothes on. Ashley caught herself staring, feeling a rush of warmth course through her body. How long had it been since she'd kissed a man like that, felt passionate, out of control, full of desire?

"Maybe we should tell them to get a room," Sean said, coming up behind her.

She whirled around in surprise, embarrassed to be caught watching. "You startled me."

"Sorry. What are you doing down here?"

"Looking for you. I thought you might be on your boat."

"Now you're scaring me," he said with a smile. "Why on earth would you come looking for me when you usually do everything you can to avoid me?"

"I want to talk to you. Can you sit for a minute?" Ashley walked over to a nearby bench and sat down. Sean took a seat beside her, resting his elbows on his knees as he stared straight ahead.

Ashley crossed her legs, then uncrossed them. She smoothed out the sides of her jeans, then played with the necklace that hung around her neck. Sean didn't say a word. She didn't, either. The silence wasn't comfortable. The tension grew with each passing second.

"Your mother came to see me," Ashley said finally, knowing she had to say something.

"So that's why you came looking for me," he said with a nod.

"She's worried about you. She doesn't want you to race in the Castleton, although I think it's the on-to-Hawaii part of it that really bothers her."

"So she said."

Ashley could tell that Sean wasn't in a particularly flexible frame of mind. Casting him a sideways glance, she was struck by the shadow of beard along his jaw, the lean lines of his face, the strength of his chin. It occurred to her how much he had changed. This wasn't the boy she'd fallen in love with. This was a man, a stranger almost. Their private conversations had ended years ago. The time when she had known his every thought, his every dream, was far in the past. She had no idea what he was thinking now, no idea whatsoever.

"I don't know you anymore," she said softly, not realizing she'd spoken aloud until he turned his head, his eyes dark and somber.

"Did you just figure that out?"

"Maybe I did." The realization fueled the sadness that ran deep within her. The only person who had ever really known her was Sean. Not even in her sisters had she confided some of the things she'd told Sean all those years ago. She'd trusted him. He'd trusted her. And that was the crux of the problem. His trust had been misplaced.

"What do you want, Ash?" Sean muttered, his voice edged with annoyance. "Why did you really come looking for me? I have a hard time believing you're at all concerned about anything I do."

"Your mother was very persuasive. I couldn't say no."

"You can say no to me, but you can't say no to my mother?" he asked with a skeptical look in his eyes. He started to stand up, but Ashley put her hand on his arm, the touch between them shocking in its heat and intensity. Their eyes met for a long, long moment.

"It's still there," he muttered. "You can tell me whatever you want, but I can feel it right now, and so can you."

She dropped her hand, her voice unsteady as she said, "This isn't about us; it's about you. Your safety. Your life. Your future. I don't want you to go chasing after Jeremy. You're never going to be able to catch him. You have to let go."

"He was my brother. I can't let him go."

"Whether you let go or not, he'll still be dead. And whether you sail in his wake won't matter a bit to Jeremy, but it will matter to your parents. They don't want to lose you, too."

"I don't want to hurt my parents, but this is something I have to do, Ash. I was fifteen when you left and sixteen when Jeremy took off. I felt like the two people I cared about the most were somewhere in the world having this incredible life while I was plodding away here in town, going to school, doing my homework. I wasn't living the way you were, the way Jeremy was. Whenever he'd call, my parents and I would crowd around the phone, eager to hear every word that came out of his mouth. And when my dad would hang up the phone, he'd look at my mother with incredible pride in his eyes and say, 'That's our son, Naomi. Isn't he something else?'" Sean paused. "They've never said that about me. Why should they? I haven't done anything exceptional."

"I'm sure they're proud of you."

"How could they be? I dropped out of college halfway through. I've changed jobs as often as I've changed my shirt. I've been drifting. And when they asked me to come back and work in the family business, I said no. Believe me, they're nowhere near proud."

"You're just figuring out what you want to do. There's no crime in that."

"Then why are you trying to stop me from racing?"

"Because I don't think you'll find what you want to do out on the ocean. It's a hard life, and it's lonely. And you've never liked being stuck in small spaces."

"How would you know what I like anymore?"

She looked into his eyes and saw anger, but also truth. Some of the things they knew about each other would never change. "You don't have to prove anything, Sean."

"Don't I?" He paused. "I know why you broke up with me when you got back. You'd had all these incredible adventures, and I was just the small-town guy you'd left behind, who'd never understand what you'd seen, what you'd done. That's why you blew me off."

Ashley tucked her hair behind her ear as she looked away from him. It was all so much more complicated than he realized. "I didn't come back to town thinking any less of you. It was me. I was different. I was the one who had changed, who had done things I wasn't proud of."

"I don't understand."

"I kissed someone else," she said impulsively, not really meaning to say the words, but there they were.

He stared at her in bemusement. "What?"

"I kissed someone else while I was away on that trip."

He cleared his throat. "Okay, well... You were young. We were apart for a long time. Why didn't you tell me? We could have started over. I can't believe you broke up with me because you kissed another guy, someone you were probably never going to see again. Why didn't you trust me?"

She took a deep breath. "It was Jeremy." She looked him straight in the eye so there could be no mistake. "I kissed Jeremy."

Tyler sat back in his chair as the waiter filled their coffee cups. Dinner with Kate had gone surprisingly well. In light of her edgy state, he'd chosen a non-combative approach. They'd discussed the weather, local sports teams, the latest bestsellers, and finally the quality of the Italian pasta they'd just consumed at a tiny restaurant named Piccolo's hidden on one of Castleton's backstreets. He'd enjoyed getting to know her better, which only made his job that much more difficult. He had to start asking questions, but he selfishly didn't want to raise the wall back between them, which in turn made him feel guilty.

He had no business liking Kate. His brother's family was at stake. Kate could be Amelia's mother. She could be the one hunting down his brother, threatening the life Mark had built with his daughter. And even if she wasn't the mother, she was the sister. She'd support Ashley or Caroline to the bitter end. And he'd support Mark. They'd never be on the same side. Never.

Kate set her spoon on the table. "It's time, isn't it?"

"Excuse me?"

"To discuss what you really want to discuss. Despite the fact you've stuffed me full of tortellini, I'm still not interested in an interview. I don't trust you. I don't think you're being completely up front about your intentions."

"I don't trust you, either," Tyler said with a smile. While he didn't trust her, he did admire her spirit. He liked being with a woman who gave as good as she got, who could keep up with the conversation, anticipate the twists and turns before he did. He'd always liked a challenging puzzle, and Kate was certainly that. He still didn't know who she really was, but he damn sure wanted to find out. Before he could say so, a woman stopped by their table. She had her hands full with two small children who had probably put some of the weary lines on her face.

"Kate, I'm sorry to interrupt, but I just wanted to say thank you for the casserole. It was incredible and very much appreciated."

"You're welcome," Kate said, smiling at the children. "Hello, Sammy, Joe. Did you like my noodles?"

"They loved them," the woman answered. "In fact, they want to know why I can't cook like that."

The woman sent Tyler a curious look. Kate intercepted the look and, after a moment's hesitation, said, "This is Tyler Jamison. My friend, Ruth Lewis."

"Nice to meet you," Ruth said, her brown eyes very curious. "Are you here for the race?"

"Yes, I am."

"My husband Larry was going to race, but he had an accident a few days ago."

"I'm sorry," Tyler murmured.

"Oh, he'll be okay. He just won't be able to race until next year. Kate saved me by making me enough dinners to fill my freezer."

"It was nothing. I like to cook," Kate said with a dismissive wave of her hand. "And let me know if you need anything else. Oh, I also picked out a few books for Larry in case he goes crazy waiting for that leg to heal. I'll bring them by tomorrow."

"I can stop by the bookstore and get them."

"It's not a problem."

"Thanks again," Ruth said. "I hope you enjoy Castleton, Mr. Jamison."

"I'm sure I will." Tyler paused, waiting until Ruth and her children had walked out of the dining room. "So you're a good neighbor and a good cook. I'm impressed. Was that a skill you learned after your mother died?"

"Actually before. My grandmother taught me. She used to live with us when I was really small. She'd cook all the meals. I think she and my mother carved out their territories early, and they rarely crossed the lines."

"Your mother's mother or your father's mother?"

"My father's mother. She could make a feast out of nothing. She'd take celery and carrots and onions and turn it into a thick, rich stew. It was like magic."

He leaned forward, captivated by the softness in her voice when she spoke of her grandmother. He had a feeling Kate was a woman who still believed in magic. He wondered if she could possibly rub off on him, but he doubted it. The thick skin he'd grown repelled magic and all other silly sentimental notions.

"My grandmother died when I was eleven," Kate added. "After that, my mom and I split the cooking and, when my mom got sick, it became my job."

"And are you as good a cook or magician as your grandmother?"

"Oh, no, I'm not nearly as good. I've never quite mastered the concept of completely letting the recipe go and making it up as I go along. My grandmother knew instinctively what would work and what wouldn't. I still need a cookbook and a measuring cup."

"What about you?"

"Me? I need a microwave and a frozen dinner. Or a good take-out menu."

Kate laughed, and the warm sound ran through him like a pretty song that he wanted to hear over and over again. She picked up her coffee cup and took a sip. "This is one thing I've never been able to master, a perfect cup of coffee."

"Now, that's something I am good at, as long as you like your coffee strong and black."

"Actually, a little hazelnut and vanilla are my preference."

"That's sissy coffee."

"I don't have anything to prove." Kate sat back in her seat. "Thanks for the dinner. It was a nice break."

"You're welcome. But I'm sure there must be lots of men on this island interested in giving you a break."

"Is that a roundabout way of asking me if I'm seeing someone?"

"Are you?"

She hesitated. "Not that it's any of your business, but no, not at the moment. I do get asked out. Just because I was free tonight does not mean that I'm not usually busy on the weekends."

"I believe you," he said with amusement.

She made a face at him. "Actually, I'm not all that busy," she admitted. "I've even been accused of not having a life."

"Something else we have in common."

Disbelief flashed through her eyes. "That's a stretch. I can't believe you don't have a social life." She paused. "So, what's wrong with you?"

"I don't think there's anything wrong with me."

"There must be, if the girls are turning you down."

"I may have heard a few comments about working too much." Along with not being able to open up, not trusting anyone with personal information, not sharing his thoughts, not putting his heart into the relationship and numerous other complaints. Tyler didn't really understand why the women he'd dated felt they had a reason to complain. He'd never promised to give his heart. He'd never led anyone on. But it didn't matter. Women who started off okay with casual inevitably ended up wanting more, a lot more.

"Travels all the time, doesn't want to commit, here today, gone tomorrow," Kate said with a knowing nod. "Ambitious, competitive, willing to sacrifice anyone and anything for what you want. I know the type. I grew up with one."

"Your father?"

"Yes. He's a charming man, gregarious, fun loving, a storyteller. Most people think he's a terrific guy. Kind of like you, I bet. But my father has a dark side, an obsessive nature, an ambition that knows no bounds." Her blue eyes filled with shadows. "He has a desire to win at all costs."

"And you think I'm like that?" Tyler asked, annoyed by her assessment. She didn't know the first thing about him, didn't know where he'd come from, what he'd been through, what winning even meant to a man who'd lost everything very early in life.

She stared at him for a long moment. "Aren't you?"

"No, but I know someone who is like that. My own father."

"What do you mean?"

He didn't answer right away. Talking about himself had never come easy. And his natural reticence had been increased by his father's constant reminders: No one needs to know who we are, where we come from, what we're doing here. Just keep quiet. Mind your own business, and make sure they mind theirs.

"Tyler?" Kate prodded. "You were saying?"

"Never mind."

"You can't do that. You can't start and not finish."

"You do it all the time," he pointed out.

"Tell me something about yourself. Give me one good reason why I shouldn't walk out the door right now and watch my back where you're concerned."

He couldn't afford to have her walk out the door or start watching her back. He'd have to tell her something, but what?

"Forget it," she said abruptly, reaching for her purse. "I think it's time I went home."

"All right. You win. Put your purse down."

She hesitated, her handbag firmly planted on her lap. "I will after you start talking."

"You know, if you're this demanding on sharing personal information, there may be a reason why you aren't busy on Saturday nights."

"And if you're this secretive, it's no wonder you aren't married or involved in a serious relationship."

"Are we even again?" he asked, feeling ridiculously charged up by their exchange.

"Stalling, stalling, stalling," she said, putting the strap of her purse over one shoulder.

"Fine. What do you want to know?"

"Start with something easy. Tell me about your childhood, your family."

"My family isn't easy."

"Tell me about them anyway. Think of it as a way of gaining my trust. That should give you some motivation."

He debated just how much to tell. Hell, with the way things were going, she probably wouldn't believe him anyway. "Okay. I was born in San Antonio."

"Texas. I knew I heard an accent."

"I lived there until I was twelve. That's when my parents divorced."

"That must have been difficult."

"It was, but it got worse. A few weeks after the separation, my father picked me up from school one day and told me my mother didn't want me anymore. She couldn't handle two boys, and my brother was younger, so I had to go with my dad. I didn't have a change of clothes or a toothbrush. Or a chance to say good-bye."

Tyler's chest tightened at the thought of Mark waiting on the porch for him, hoping to play catch or throw a football or follow his big brother around. With their dad gone and their mother interested in dating, Mark had only had him. And, that day, Tyler hadn't come home to take care of his younger brother. Damn.

"Oh, my God," Kate breathed. "That's awful."

He hated her look of pity. Hated himself even more for sharing something with her that he hadn't shared with anyone else. He didn't know why he had told her. He could have told her anything. She wouldn't have known if it was the truth or not.

"Your mother must have tried to find you," Kate said. "Where did you and your dad go?"

"All over the country." Endless motel rooms, dive apartments, cities that looked the same. "It took me awhile to figure out that we were hiding. My father had these letters, you see, from my mom and my brother. They told me how much they loved me and how someday we'd be together, but for now it was better if we were apart. I stupidly believed the letters were genuine. And more letters and postcards followed those, including a note that told me they had moved to a new house. There was even a goddamn description of the new house. I was completely taken in."

"Oh, Tyler. How could you have known? Your father sounds like he was very clever. And you were just a kid. How could you not believe him?"

"By being smarter. I should have found a way to call home. In the beginning I was angry. I didn't want to call. If they didn't want me, then I didn't want them. But I started to waver with time, started to talk about a visit. That's when my dad pulled out his ace."

"What was that?"

"He told me there was a fire. The house was gone. My mother and brother were killed. We only had each other. And you know what else he did? He made up an obituary. That's how sick and twisted he was. And I bought it," he said in self-disgust. "I was an idiot. I look back now and see that I had countless opportunities to figure things out." He doubted he'd ever be able to forgive himself for being so trusting. "At any rate, by the time my mom caught up with us, six years had passed. I was eighteen years old. I didn't need a mother anymore, and even though she was happy to see me, she didn't really need another kid. She'd gotten remarried. My brother had been officially adopted by his stepfather. My mother had another child, a girl. Life had moved on for all of us."

"That's a terrible story." She gave him a searching look. "You're not lying, are you?"

"I'm telling you the truth."

"About this."

"About this," he agreed.

Kate sat back in her chair. "Well, I don't know what to say."

"Don't say anything. I only told you because I know what it's like to live with a father who's willing to do whatever it takes to get what he wants."

"My dad looks like a saint in comparison."

"It's all in the perspective, isn't it?"

"Where is your mother today?"

"Dallas."

"And your father?"

"He died a couple years ago." Tyler picked up his coffee cup, regretting his confession. "I wonder what they put in this coffee. I don't usually spill my guts like that."

"It's truth serum. That's why I brought you here."

He appreciated the light tease in her voice. She was letting him off the hook instead of going after him when he was down. She wouldn't make a very good reporter, but she might just make a good friend. Not that they were going to be friends, he reminded himself. That wasn't possible.

"It's interesting to me that you picked a career that would take you on the road," she said. "Seems like you would have wanted to settle in one place, put down roots, reconnect with your family, your mother and your brother."

"Is that what you wanted?" he asked, countering her question with one of his own. "Did those years at sea make you yearn for the hard ground under your feet?"

"Absolutely. When I first got back, I'd lie in my bed at night and feel the boat rocking beneath me. It took weeks to get my land legs back, to get comfortable with steadiness."

"And you don't miss the rush of the sea?"

She hesitated. "I should tell you that I don't miss it at all."

"But..." he prodded.

"Maybe a little. I don't miss the racing. But sometimes I miss the wonder of it all, the incredible sunsets, the awesome quiet, the sense of being a part of something so much bigger than we are."

"What don't you miss?"

"The cold, the endless wet, the hard work, putting up the sails, taking them down, fighting the wind, then praying for the slightest breeze, feeling helpless and vulnerable."

"What else do you miss? Or, should I ask, who?"

"What do you mean?" A wary note entered her voice, but Tyler paid no heed.

"Do you miss Jeremy?"

Kate reached for her water glass and took a long sip. Tyler almost regretted his abrupt change of topic. But experience had taught him to get the interviewee comfortable then strike. Whatever answer he or she came up with wasn't as important as the reaction, and judging by Kate's reaction, Jeremy was a very important subject.

"I ran into Sean earlier," Tyler continued. "That's why I was late."

She raised an eyebrow. "You ran into Sean? How convenient."

"Actually, I was looking for your father at the Oyster Bar. I found Sean instead. He told me that you and his brother Jeremy were going to be married after you came home from the race."

Her eyes filled with shadows. "Yes, we were."

"I'm sorry."

"So am I."

"Is that why you don't want to talk about the race—because Jeremy died?"

"It's a good reason, don't you think? I won a big race, but I lost someone I loved very much. Can't you understand that I want to leave it in the past? It has been difficult to move on, but I've managed to get my life together. I don't want to go back to that place. I don't want to talk about it. I want you to drop the article idea and write about someone else. Would you do that for me?" She paused, her gaze pleading with him to let it go.

Tyler wanted to say yes. He wanted to promise her he wouldn't hurt her. He wanted to tell her there would never be a story. But she was asking him to choose between his brother and her, and he couldn't do that.

"Maybe you should go back to that place," he said finally. "Sometimes hindsight makes things clearer. Decisions you made can be reexamined."

Each word he spoke seemed to draw the blood from her face until she was a pale version of herself. Why? What had he said? Was she thinking about a decision she'd made—maybe the decision to give up her baby?

She and Jeremy had been engaged to be married. If anyone was pregnant on that boat, it was probably Kate. Jeremy had died, leaving her alone. Had she felt her life was over? Had she chosen to give away her baby rather than be tormented by the memory of a family that could never be?

"Is there something you wish you'd done differently?" he asked.

For a moment he thought she might answer him, might tell him what he really wanted to know.

Her mouth trembled slightly. Her lips parted, then closed. She got to her feet. "I don't believe in looking back. It's a waste of time. The past is the past. I'm only interested in the present."

"Maybe someone else in your family will be more accommodating."

"There's no story, Tyler. Let it go."

"I can't," he said as he stood up, using his height to remind her that he was in charge of this situation.

She frowned, throwing back her shoulders and lifting up her chin, as if that could give her a few extra inches of courage. He found the gesture strangely appealing. He liked the way she didn't back down. In fact, he was liking way too much about her. He wished they had met under different circumstances. But, then again, different circumstances would not have brought them together.

"How much will this article pay you?" she asked abruptly.

"That depends on how good it is."

"What if I paid you to stop writing it? What would you say to that?"

"I'd say you don't have enough money."

"It can't be worth that much. A couple thousand dollars? You could leave tomorrow, earning the same amount of money for absolutely no work. It's a good offer; you should take it."

He smiled as he gazed into her blue eyes. Innocent eyes, he realized. Eyes that expressed pain and hurt and a discomfort with the whole situation. "And you should realize," he said deliberately, "that offering a bribe to a reporter raises the curiosity level. You obviously have something to hide." He reached out and let his finger drift down the side of her face. "What on earth are you trying so hard to protect? Or maybe it's not a *what*. Maybe it's a *who*. What happened during that race, Kate? What are you so afraid I'm going to find out?"

CHAPTER EIGHT

HE WAS IMPOSSIBLE, Kate fumed, as she strode briskly away from the restaurant. She didn't bother with her car. She needed to walk off the anger and frustration building inside her. She should never have agreed to have dinner with Tyler or thought she could handle him by telling him just a little. A little would never be enough for a man like him. He was ambitious and ruthless, determined to get what he wanted.

Why couldn't she just accept that she had absolutely no way of making stubborn, strong-willed men in her life do what she wanted them to do? Her father had certainly never caved in to her demands. Why should Tyler be any different?

Kate stopped abruptly as three people spilled out of a local bar, stumbling across the sidewalk, obviously having tossed back a few drinks. She recognized one of them, a young man who worked in the marina office.

"Hi, Kate," he said with a cheerful slur. "Your sister is one hell of a good singer."

"What?" she asked, not sure she'd heard him right. He tipped his head toward the bar he'd just left. "Check it out."

Kate stepped inside the doorway of Jake's. The room was smoky, the tables packed with tourists, and the music loud enough to demand attention. Or maybe it was the singer.

Kate's jaw dropped at the sight of Caroline holding a microphone in her hand. Her sister was dressed in a micro-mini denim skirt, knee-high stiletto boots, and a spaghetti-strap top that barely covered her breasts. But it wasn't her looks that took Kate by surprise; it was her voice. Her sister was belting out a pop song as if she'd been doing it all her life. And she wasn't bad. In fact, she was pretty good. Apparently the crowd thought so, too, jumping into brisk applause when the song ended.

"Thank you," Caroline said, her face aglow with excitement. "That was fun. And now more of Deke and the Devils." She waved her hand toward the band behind her, which broke into a fast beat.

Kate watched her sister step down from the stage and move slowly through the crowd, chatting with friends and strangers alike. She seemed to laugh every other minute, as if she'd never had such a good time before. It struck her then how much her sister and her father liked the spotlight. Being the center of attention was their favorite place to be.

Kate frowned as she saw a man approach Caroline. It was Mike Stanaway, and he was forty if he was a day, a rough, bearded man with dark eyes and a grim expression. Ashley had mentioned something about Caroline and Mike, but she'd dismissed it as a rumor. Now she wasn't so sure.

Caroline didn't appear happy to see him. They exchanged a few words. He waved a hand toward the door, but she shook her head. After a moment, he shrugged and walked away. Caroline sat down on a bar stool, then lit up a cigarette. As she took her first puff, she saw Kate. Her smile faded, and a defensive expression swept across her face. For a moment it looked like she was going to hide the cigarette, but then she took another defiant puff, got up, and walked across the room.

"What are you doing here?" she asked.

"I heard you singing."

"That was just a spur-of-the-moment thing. Deke thought it might be fun."

"You were good."

"I was?" Caroline asked, that familiar little sister insecurity in her voice. "Did you really think so?"

"Yes. I can't remember when I last heard you sing. It must have been when we were on the boat."

"Probably." Caroline paused. "Are you going to hang out?"

"No," Kate said with a shake of her head. This wasn't her scene. It was too loud, too chaotic, too young. Her sister would think she was crazy if she said that. After all, she wasn't even thirty yet, but sometimes she felt a lot older. "You shouldn't be smoking, Caroline."

"You're not my mother," Caroline said for probably the thousandth time. In fact, if Kate had a dollar for every time she'd heard those words from either Ashley or Caroline, she'd be a millionaire by now.

"It's bad for you," she persisted.

"Maybe that's why I like it." Caroline coughed at the end of her sentence, making a mockery of her words.

"I can see how much you like it." Kate took the cigarette out of Caroline's hand and walked over to the bar, snuffing it out in a nearby ashtray.

"I'll just light another one."

"We have more important problems than your smoking." Kate pulled her sister over to a quieter corner. "I just met with Tyler Jamison. He's not going to quit digging into our lives. He's been talking to Sean and God knows who else. I don't know what to do."

Caroline looked at her in amazement. "You don't know what to do? You always know what to do."

"I don't this time, all right?" Kate snapped. "I need some help. I need to find a way to distract him."

"Well, that's easy. The best way to distract a man is with sex, or the possibility of sex. In fact, anything to do with sex."

"I'm not going to have sex with him." Kate was shocked her sister would even suggest such a thing.

"He doesn't have to know that. Flirt with him, Kate. Kiss him. Get his mind off the past and on the present and the future."

"That's your advice? Why did I bother to ask?"

"I have no idea why you asked, since you never take my advice. But that doesn't mean it isn't good." Caroline laughed as a young man slipped his arms around her waist and nuzzled her neck from behind.

"When are you going to run away with me?" Curt Walker asked.

"When you let me cut your hair," Caroline said, twisting around in his arms to give him a kiss on the cheek.

"Kiss me on the lips, and I'll let you shave my head," Curt said.

Caroline looked over at Kate. "See how easy it is? You ought to try it. You might even like it."

Kate turned away as her sister gave Curt a flirtatious kiss. Everything was so simple for Caroline, so easy. She walked out of the bar, telling herself firmly there was no way she was going to kiss Tyler Jamison. It was a ridiculous idea. She didn't know why she was even thinking about it. Nor did she understand why her cheeks were suddenly warm and her heart was beating so fast. She didn't want to kiss Tyler. She couldn't want that. And even if she did, it wouldn't work.

Tyler wanted a story. He didn't want her. She'd have to find some other way to distract him. She waved a hand in front of her face, wishing for a cool breeze, but strangely enough there was not a speck of wind tonight. Another bad sign. She would have to be patient, wait Tyler out. He wasn't a man to stay in one place for long—wind or no wind.

Sunday morning had come and gone, and Tyler was getting nowhere fast. He stopped at the edge of the pier, out of breath and out of patience with himself. His run around the town had done little more than raise his pulse; it certainly hadn't brought him the peace or the answers he craved. He needed a different approach, a new plan. Kate wasn't going to tell him anything willingly. That was certainly clear. It was also clear that she was a very good candidate to be Amelia's mother. She'd been engaged to Jeremy, planning to get married, then her fiancé was killed, and she was devastated. Sounded like a good reason to give a baby away. At least the best reason he'd heard so far.

If Kate was Amelia's mother, Mark was in trouble, because as far as he could see, Kate was a good person. She ran her own business, owned a house, took care of her family. She didn't appear to have any overt vices. She was damn near perfect.

He scowled at the thought, knowing that he liked her much more than he should. He needed to stay objective and detached; otherwise, he would have no hope of helping his brother.

The sound of an argument brought his head around. About fifty feet away a couple appeared to be arguing heatedly about something. The man tried to pull the woman into his arms, but she pushed him away with a small cry. Tyler tensed. There was no way he would stand by and watch some jerk hurt a woman. He moved closer, assessing the situation as he did so. The woman's back was to him, but he had a clear view of the man. He was older, forties maybe, a rough beard on his face, a tattoo on his right biceps. He was strong, muscled; a man who would be formidable in a fight.

"I can't do this anymore," he heard the woman say.

"You don't have a choice," the man replied, grabbing her arm once again.

"Just let me go."

"You don't want that, Caroline. You know you don't."

Caroline? Tyler's gaze flew to the woman. Sure enough, he recognized that spiky hair. It was Kate's baby sister. He walked quickly down the path. "Everything all right here?" he called.

The couple split apart. Caroline looked upset. The man appeared wary.

"Tyler," she said warily. "What are you doing down here?"

"Jogging. How about you?"

"Me, too," she said.

He wondered how she could have been running in a pair of flip flops and cut-off shorts, but be refrained from commenting.

"Call me later," the bearded man said. "I'll expect to hear from you."

"Sure, whatever."

"Are you all right?" Tyler asked when they were alone. He didn't like the desperate look in her eyes, and even though she shrugged off his comment, he had the feeling she was far from all right.

"You don't have a cigarette, do you? I could really use a hit right now," she said.

"I don't smoke."

"That figures."

"Who was that guy?" he asked.

She started walking down the path the same way he had come. "A friend."

"He didn't look too friendly. What's his name?" He fell into step alongside her.

"Why do you care?"

"It's the reporter in me."

Caroline stopped and rested her elbows on the rail overlooking the boats. "Mike Stanaway," she said. "And I don't appreciate the third degree or the questioning look. I don't need a big brother. I already have two big sisters butting into my business."

"I understand." He leaned on the railing next to her. "There are a lot of boats in the harbor today. Do you still sail?"

"Sometimes."

"But you don't race?"

"Not anymore."

"You don't miss it?"

"Sometimes," she said, repeating her earlier answer with a smile. "Is this the best you've got?"

"Why don't you and your sisters want to talk to me?"

"I'm talking to you right now. I had dinner with you the other night."

"And we talked about the different kinds of clam chowder. You prefer the white over the red."

"Good, you were listening," she said with a laugh, her mood obviously changing. She took in a breath and stretched her arms over her head. "It is a nice day, isn't it? Why can't I just enjoy a beautiful day without wanting more?"

"More what?"

"I don't know. More something. Do you ever feel like there's a hole in your stomach that you can't fill, no matter what you try to do?"

"Every day about four o'clock."

"I'm not talking about food. I'm talking about life."

"I'm not that philosophical. I'm usually too busy."

"Trying to get from one place to the next," she said. "You're not exactly an island-living kind of guy, are you?"

"I haven't been."

She sent him a curious look. "Does that mean this place is growing on you?"

"I make it a rule not to get too attached to any place," he said. "It makes it easier to leave."

"What if you find somewhere you want to stay?"

"I haven't yet."

"You sound like my father."

Tyler frowned. Kate had made the same comparison the night before, and he hadn't liked it then, either. "Why do you say that?"

"He's a wanderer, a traveling man, a gypsy at heart."

"Your father doesn't seem to have wandered too far in recent years."

"I'm not sure that's completely by choice."

"He stays for the family?" When she didn't reply to that question, he asked another. "What's your father like?"

She thought for a moment. "Daddy is one of a kind. He's bold, brave, crazy, selfish at times, generous at others. He's complicated. He's like an upside-down cake. All the ingredients are there, but they're not in the right order. Does that make sense?"

"It's an interesting description."

"That's Duncan McKenna—interesting. Not always smart, not always right, but always interesting."

"You admire him," Tyler said, reading between the lines.

"He lives over there." Caroline pointed to the marina. "In a small sailboat. When we first came back here, he rented us all an apartment. He lasted three months there, then he bought the boat and left us on our own. He couldn't sleep on land. He still can't."

"So you and your sisters stayed together?"

"For the first year or two. It wasn't easy. We'd lived together on a boat for almost three years, but we were suddenly bumping into each other and tripping over things. We argued all the time. Kate wanted a house. Ashley wanted a job. And I was trying to finish high school, but I didn't really belong there. I was a lot older than the other kids— maybe not in years, but definitely in life experience. I took an early test and got out as quickly as I could. Once I was out of school, Kate got going on her plan to buy the bookstore, and Ashley started taking classes in photography. We eventually split up and got our own places."

"What happened to the family home—the one you lived in before you took off on your three-year adventure?"

"My dad sold the house when we went to sea. He needed the money to finance the trip." She paused. "I wish he hadn't sold it. I think we all would have liked to go back there to live, Kate especially. She loved that house."

"Who lives there now?"

"It has changed owners over the years, but the family who owns it now bought it to use only as a vacation place. It's boarded up in the winter. They usually show up sometime in July. Kate tried to buy it back, but they didn't want to sell. Sometimes I go out there and wander through the yard. It's on a bluff overlooking the water. We used to sit there, the three of us girls and my mom, watching for my dad's boat to sail back into the harbor." She gave a disgusted shake of her head. "That sounds pathetic, doesn't it? I'm not going to spend my life waiting for someone to come home, believe me."

Tyler smiled. "How about Kate? What can you tell me about her and Jeremy?" he asked.

"What did Kate tell you?"

"Not much, just that they were engaged to be married before he died."

"Yes." Caroline looked away. "It was very sad. He was a great guy."

"Must have been tough on Kate."

"I'm not sure she'll ever get over him."

"She loved him that much?" The idea disturbed Tyler more than it should have. It was no business of his whom Kate had loved or how deep that love had gone unless, of course, she was Amelia's mother.

"Kate is an all-or-nothing person. She loves with her whole heart. She doesn't hold anything back, even if people don't always deserve it, like my father." Caroline paused. "And Kate doesn't tolerate anyone messing with the people she loves."

"Is that a warning?"

"I find myself liking you for some unknown reason," Caroline said frankly.

"I like you, too."

She smiled at him. "Coming from a reporter, I'll take that for what it's worth."

"One last question?"

"What?"

"Why wasn't Jeremy sailing on your boat?"

"Because my dad wanted it to be a family venture, and Jeremy wasn't family."

"So he joined the competition."

"He wanted to race. It was his best option."

"But a decision that turned out to be disastrous."

Caroline nodded, and for a moment silence fell between them. Then she said, "Can I ask you something, Tyler?"

"Sure."

"Do you think you can go back?"

"I don't think you can change the past, if that's what you mean."

"Can you change the memories? Can you ever forget things you want to forget?"

Tyler didn't have an answer to that question. He was surprised at the depth of emotion in her voice. His first impression of Caroline had been of a young, reckless woman, perhaps a little flaky, but she was as complicated as the rest of the McKenna clan.

"Never mind," she said. "I'll have to figure it out for myself. That's the problem with life. It's not really a spectator sport."

Maybe life wasn't meant to be a spectator sport, but watching Kate had certainly become Tyler's favorite pastime, he thought later that afternoon as he followed Kate's car up the hill leading away from town. He'd meant to catch her at her bookstore but instead had found her pulling away from the curb in her Volkswagen. She hadn't seemed to notice his car behind hers. If she had, she probably would have tried to dodge him.

His eyes narrowed as she veered away from the street leading to her house. Where was she headed? Neither Ashley nor Caroline lived in this direction. A few blocks later he had his answer when she pulled up in front of two stone gates with a sign that read Castleton Cemetery. She drove through the gates as if she knew exactly where she was going, and Tyler had the terrible feeling he also knew exactly where she was headed.

Kate's stomach began to churn as she drove up the quiet, winding road that led through the cemetery. She hadn't been here in a while. For years she'd come once a week, sometimes two or three times, but lately her visits had dwindled. Caroline would have said, *Thank heavens, you're finally getting on with your life.* Ashley would have said, *It's okay to let go. Jeremy would want you to stop being sad.*

Had she stopped being sad?

Had she finally let go?

Obviously not completely, since she was here now. But she wasn't here because of Jeremy, but because of Tyler.

She hadn't been able to sleep last night, thinking about Tyler, about Jeremy, about her father. God, all these men; they were making her nuts.

Stopping in front of a familiar tree, she turned off the engine and sat for a moment. Then she got out of the car and walked onto the grass. She knelt down by the headstone and read it for the thousandth time, tracing the letters of Jeremy's name with her fingers.

Jeremy had been a loving son and brother, as the headstone read, but he'd been so much more: adventurous, carefree, bold, confident, a man who'd loved the sea, loved life, loved her.

If only she'd done things differently.

How many times had that thought gone through her mind?

Kate sat back on her heels. It was peaceful here, quiet. Jeremy would not have liked it at all. He was a man of action, a man of the water. His dreams had always taken him to the farthest ends of the earth. She'd gone along with him in most of those dreams. He'd made the future sound wonderful. They'd travel for years, see everything they could see. They'd climb pyramids, visit holy temples, hike through rain forests, and when they were done—they'd have kids.

She'd tried to tell him that they would need to make plans, do research, work within a budget. He'd only laughed and told her she worried too much, and she supposed she did. But her worry and his daring had made for a nice balance.

It didn't matter that their dreams now seemed so foolish, so ridiculously young. Maybe they wouldn't have accomplished everything Jeremy wanted them to do, but Kate knew they would have still loved each other. Their connection had been deep and emotional. They'd grown up together, shared an abiding friendship. Jeremy had held her in his arms when her mother died. He'd helped her through the worst experience of her life. Jeremy had been her everything—and she'd been his.

But even as the thought crossed her mind, she knew it wasn't true. Jeremy had had another love—the sea. Just like her father, the ocean had called to Jeremy in a way she never could.

Jeremy wouldn't have wanted to be buried here in the ground. He would have rather had his ashes flung into the wind over a beautiful sea. But Jeremy's parents had wanted him here with his grandparents, with his ancestors. Kate hadn't had the heart to argue with them. It didn't matter anyway. Jeremy wasn't really here. Only his headstone.

Kate stiffened at the sound of footsteps. The hairs on the back of her neck stood straight up. She didn't have to look to know who was behind her. It seemed almost inevitable that he should be here.

"Kate?"

His voice was a warm, rich baritone. It ran through her like fine wine and weakened her resolve.

"Are you following me now?" she asked sharply. Maybe anger could get her past this foolish, dangerous attraction.

"Guilty, but I thought you were going home when you left the bookstore."

"I changed my mine," she replied, plucking at an errant weed with her fingers.

"I realized that too late. Am I intruding?"

"Yes, but you already knew that." Kate finally allowed herself to look at him. She immediately wished she hadn't. Last night she'd tried to convince herself that she was not attracted to him, but dressed in jeans that emphasized his long, lean legs and a rugby shirt that stretched across a very broad chest, he looked as good as she remembered and so very vital, so very alive.

Jeremy's image vanished from her mind. She strained to bring back the laughing, boyish smile, but she couldn't. Because of Tyler.

"You shouldn't have come here," she said harshly, jumping to her feet. "Why can't you just leave me alone?"

He tilted his head, looking somewhat perplexed. "I've been asking myself the same question," he said, surprising her with his answer.

She saw something in his eyes, something that looked like truth, something that told her that he felt something that had nothing to do with a newspaper story. Or did she just want to believe that?

Was he just flirting with her to get a story?

Kate walked down the path toward her car. Tyler immediately followed.

"I have a proposition for you," he said, as she opened her car door.

"I'm not interested."

"Hear me out?"

She shook her head.

He put a hand on her shoulder, forcing her to look at him. "I don't want to like you, either," he said. "I can't seem to stop myself."

"I don't like you," she said quickly.

"Maybe like wasn't the right word, but there's something between us."

"You'll say anything to get a story, won't you?"

"This isn't about the story." He paused, giving her a long look. "Are you still in love with Jeremy?"

Her mouth went dry. How had their conversation gotten so personal? "That's none of your business. I'm going home."

"I'll go with you."

She sighed. "I won't answer any more of your questions."

"Any more? You haven't answered any yet. I just want to spend some time with you, do whatever you're doing." He paused. "What are you going to be doing?"

"Nothing that interesting."

"It might be more interesting if we do it together." He sent her a sexy, charming smile. "We got off on the wrong foot, Kate. Let's start over. I'm Tyler Jamison. Nice to meet you." He extended his hand.

She hesitated and then slid her fingers into his. A jolt of electricity shot through her body. She looked into his eyes and saw the same flash of awareness. Oh, Lord. She was in trouble.

"Let me spend the day with you," Tyler said quietly. "Give us a chance to get to know each other."

Kate could think of a dozen reasons why that wasn't a good idea, but the only answer she could give him was yes—and hope to God that at some point she'd have the strength to say no.

CHAPTER NINE

CAROLINE WALKED into the Oyster Bar and paused, letting her eyes adjust to the dim light. She shouldn't have come, but her feet wouldn't go in another direction. She needed something to fill the gnawing hole in her gut. As she turned toward the bar, her attention was caught by a group of men in a far corner and a very familiar voice.

"Kate was the best at keeping us on course. She could steer by the stars," Duncan said in his big, booming voice. "And she never let herself get distracted. That girl was all purpose all the time. Ashley always had her head in a book or her eyes behind a camera. She was a watcher, she was. And Caroline? Well, what can I say about my baby girl?"

Caroline wondered what he would say about her. She couldn't help but listen, hoping for something that she couldn't even put into words, but she knew it had a lot to do with approval. Duncan always raved about Kate's abilities to do just about anything, and he spoke fondly of Ashley as if she were a gentle creature that just needed to be loved. But what about her? What did he say about her when she wasn't listening? She wanted so badly to know, so she crept forward, hoping he wouldn't see her, because then he would surely shut up.

"That Caroline is a piece of work," one of the other men said. "A born hellion."

Caroline frowned. That wasn't what she wanted to hear. Speak up, Daddy, she silently urged. Tell him what I'm really like. Tell him how fast I was at raising the sails. Tell him how good I was at the wheel, how important I was in winning the race.

"Caroline was a loose cannon. I never knew what that girl was going to do. But I'll say this for her—she always kept us on our toes." Duncan laughed and took off his well-worn navy blue cap.

Caroline turned away in disgust. She'd been a fool to believe she'd hear praise from her father. He'd never been proud of her, and he never would be.

"I will say this, though—she could sing like a pretty bird," Duncan added, halting Caroline in her tracks. "Some nights I'd be alone at the helm, thinking the girls were all asleep, and I'd hear this song drifting across the waves like the sea was singing to me. Caroline sounded so much like her mother then." His voice broke, and he cleared his throat. "Another round for the boys," he called to the bartender.

Caroline blinked back the unexpected moisture in her eyes. She'd never heard him compare her voice to her mother's. At least he'd noticed something about her, something good instead of something bad. That was probably a first. What he never seemed to notice was how alike they were—how comfortable they both felt in dark, smoky bars, how much they'd both loved the sea.

Sailing around the world had been terrifying, but thrilling, too. Maybe she needed to get back out there. What was she doing, spending all her days on this island? It was home, but it wasn't enough. She wanted more, but more what? Nothing seemed to fill the emptiness inside of her. God knows she'd tried filling it with just about everything she could find.

She cast another look at her father, wondering if she should join in their conversation.

"Did I tell you about the time Kate sewed up my hand with a needle and a thread?" Duncan asked his captivated audience. "It was incredible. I'd cut my hand, a huge gash, bloody as hell, dripping all over the deck. Caroline screamed bloody murder, and Ashley looked like she was going to faint, but Kate just calmly went for the first aid kit..."

Caroline sighed as her father's story took off. Another tale about Kate. She was definitely not in the mood to sing praises to her sister. Not that she could blame Kate for being her father's favorite. And it was impossible to hate Kate. She was too damn nice. And Kate had been more of a mother than a big sister to her. She'd taken care of them all, even when they didn't want her to.

"Caroline, can I get you something?" Will asked as she passed by the corner of the bar.

She was about to answer when her cell phone rang. She reached into her purse and pulled out the phone. "Hello?"

"It's me, Ashley. Are you busy? I'd like to talk to you."

"About what?"

"I don't want to do it over the phone. Can you meet me at Kelly's? I'll buy you the greasy fries you like so much."

"This must be serious," Caroline said, not liking the nervous edge in Ashley's voice, although she should be used to it by now. Since they'd stepped off the Moon Dancer eight years ago, Ashley's nerves had grown tighter and tighter until the least little thing seemed to make her anxious. She was terribly afraid that one day Ashley might just snap.

"Where are you?" Ashley asked. "How long will it take you to get here?"

"A few minutes. I'm at the Oyster Bar."

"What are you doing there? It's the middle of the day. You're not drinking, are you?"

"No, but Dad is." She cast one last look at her father, who was so wrapped up in his storytelling that he still hadn't noticed her.

"Maybe you should try to get him to go home," Ashley suggested.

Caroline thought about it for a moment. Deep in her heart she knew that her dad's alcoholism was getting worse by the minute, but she also knew that drinking was the only thing that seemed to make him happy these days. In fact, he looked happier now than she'd seen him in a long time. How could she take that away from him? If she tried, he'd only get angry with her. He wouldn't leave. All she would accomplish was chalking up one more black mark by her name.

"He won't go," she said shortly. "You know he never listens to me."

"I guess not," Ashley replied.

Caroline didn't like the way Ashley agreed with her. Perversely, she'd wanted her sister to tell her that Dad *would* listen to her, that she was probably the only one who could get through to him. But Ashley didn't say that.

"Maybe you should call Kate and let her know," Ashley said instead.

"I'm sure she'll get called soon enough. I'll meet you at Kelly's in a couple of minutes. Make sure you get a double order of fries. I'm starving."

"Leaving?" Will asked as she ended the call.

"Yes."

"Good."

"Why do you say that?" she asked curiously.

"You've been in here a lot lately, Caroline. I don't want you to end up like your dad."

"That won't happen. My dad and I are nothing alike. Just ask him— he'll tell you that."

Ashley tapped her fingernails against the top of the redwood table in their favorite hamburger joint, Kelly's. As she waited for her order, she stared idly at the Rose Harbor Marina spread out before her like a picture postcard. It was a beautiful summer day, with plenty of boats out on the water and tourists strolling along the pier. It was a day to be carefree and happy, to let loose of the worries of everyday life and just enjoy the moment. But she couldn't enjoy this moment because she was worrying about the next moment and the one after that, not to mention the moments she'd shared with Sean the night before. She hadn't handled that well at all.

"Hey there," Caroline said, joining her at the table. "So what's up?"

Ashley didn't reply, waiting until the waitress set down a basket of fries and two diet sodas. Then she said, "I did something stupid last night."

Caroline raised a surprised eyebrow. "Wow. You did something stupid, and you're telling me about it? Oh, wait." Caroline snapped her fingers. "You're telling me about it because you don't want to tell Kate. Am I right? Ooh, this must be bad."

"Sean's mother asked me to talk him out of racing in the Castleton next week," she replied.

"And did you?" Caroline asked as she squirted ketchup into one corner of the basket.

"Yes. I tried to tell him that his family really didn't want him to race and that I thought chasing Jeremy's wake was a bad idea. I emphasized how dangerous it could get out there."

"But Sean doesn't care what his family thinks or whether or not it's dangerous," Caroline said. "Did you really think he would buy that argument, Ashley? The last thing he wants to look like is a wimp, especially in front of you. And you made it sound like you didn't think he was capable of doing what you did. How do you think that made him feel? Don't you know anything about men, Ash?"

Ashley stared at her younger sister in surprise. She obviously didn't know as much about men as her sister did. "I never meant to imply that I thought he was a wimp or a coward or incapable. I just want him to be safe."

"I'm beginning to think being safe is highly overrated." Caroline leaned forward, an odd look in her eyes. "Don't you miss it, Ash? Don't you feel like the years we were racing were the most thrilling years of our life? Look at us now, traveling the same few blocks day after day, seeing the same people, doing the same things at the same time. Don't you ever get bored with this island? Don't you ever want more?"

Did she want more? Was that why there was an ache in her body that never went away, a yearning for something she couldn't have? "Sometimes," she muttered. "But that's beside the point."

"Which is what?"

"Sean and the Castleton."

"It's not your problem. So what if he races? You two aren't a couple anymore. And, look at it this way: He'll be gone. Won't that be easier for you?"

Easier in some ways, harder in others. Since he'd come back to town she'd been intensely aware of his presence on the island, and she'd realized how much energy he brought into her world. Her life was like a black-and-white photograph that burst into full color with Sean's arrival. Seeing him, talking to him, getting so close she could touch him had aroused all the old buried feelings. It would be easier if he left, but she'd miss him again. She'd go through that whole horrible cycle that she'd gone through the last few times he'd come and gone. It was exhausting—this love she had for him, a love that could never be. Maybe that's why she had told him about Jeremy. She'd needed another barrier, another wall to throw up between them.

"I told Sean that I kissed Jeremy," she said abruptly.

"You did what?" Caroline echoed.

"You heard me."

"Why would you tell him that?"

"I wanted to make sure it was really over. I wanted to put something between us that he couldn't forgive."

Caroline muttered something under her breath, then popped a fry in her mouth.

"He just got up and left after I said it," Ashley continued. "Not a word, not a question; he just walked away."

"That was a stupid thing to do," Caroline said flatly. "Because when Sean gets over the shock of it all, he might just come back and ask you where the hell you were when you kissed his brother. Then what are you going to say?"

"I know. I keep screwing things up." She shook her head, feeling frustrated and annoyed with herself. "I just want him gone. I want to get back to my normal little life."

"Then you shouldn't be trying to talk him out of racing."

"But I don't want him to race, Caroline. I don't want him to get hurt. Even though we're not together anymore, I still care about him. I don't want to spend the next few weeks worrying about every storm hitting the Pacific between here and—" Her words were cut off by Caroline's sudden gasp. "What's wrong now?"

"Look," Caroline said, pointing to something in the distance. "Look there, out on the water."

Ashley followed her sister's gaze, and her stomach did a flip-flop as a boat sailed into the harbor. "The Moon Dancer," she breathed. "She's back."

"So, this is the backyard," Tyler mused as he stood in the middle of Kate's overflowing garden.

"This is it," Kate said with a smile and handed him a pair of garden gloves. "You'll need these."

"For what?"

"Weeding, deadheading, planting."

He looked at her as if she were speaking another language, and she couldn't help but laugh, pleased to have thrown him off balance for a change.

"Excuse me?"

"We're going to garden, Tyler. You said you wanted to do whatever I was doing. This is what I'm doing." She led him over to the rosebushes that lined the fence on one side of the property. "Let's start with these." She handed him the shears. "You can use these to cut off the dead blossoms."

"I was thinking more along the lines of having a beer and a burger together, maybe listening to some music," he said with a wistful smile.

"You can always leave," she said. "No one's forcing you to be here."

"I'm staying," he said, picking up some gloves. "But I don't have much experience, so I might need some help."

"No problem."

"And maybe while we're gardening, you can answer some questions."

"I'd be happy to tell you about this garden. Last year I had to put blankets on the roses to protect them from the frost. And then there was the fungus that attacked the fruit trees, the pesticide that killed more than the pests."

"Stop, stop," he said, holding up his hand. "I cannot listen to you talk about fungus. A man has his limits."

She smiled. "Then why don't we talk about you for a change. Tell me about one of your reporting adventures."

"Well, let's see. I jumped out of a plane over Paraguay. Then there was the time I got thrown into a Mexican jail for interviewing the wrong person."

"How did you get out?"

"I bribed the guard."

"Very impressive, unless you're embellishing."

He grinned. "I did bribe the guard and I did jump out of a plane, but if it makes you feel better, I sprained my ankle when I landed."

"It doesn't matter to me at all. Our lives aren't in competition. I don't really care how brave or daring you are."

"You were probably more brave and daring during your ocean-racing days than I've ever been."

She shrugged, disappointed that the conversation had returned to sailboat racing. Tyler was like a dog with a bone; he just didn't quit. "You should get back to work," she said, ignoring his question. "All this chatting isn't getting my roses pruned."

"You're a slave driver."

"Don't make me take out my whip." She put a hand up to ward off what was sure to be a sexy reply. "Forget I said that."

He grinned. "If I must."

Kate knelt on the ground a few feet away from Tyler and spent the next twenty minutes clearing away the weeds threatening to suffocate her hollyhocks. The familiar task should have relaxed her, but she was all too aware of Tyler's very male presence. When he bent over to toss some blossoms into a trash bag, she couldn't help noticing his fairly spectacular ass. Unfortunately, Tyler caught her staring, and she flushed.

"See something you like?" he drawled.

"Just making sure you were doing it right."

"I've never had any complaints."

She rolled her eyes. "You are one cocky—"

"Son of a bitch," he finished. "I know. I've been told that a few times." He sat down on a nearby redwood bench. "You really love this, don't you? Your face is practically glowing. I must admit I haven't met many women in my life who were content with simple pleasures like the joy of weeding a garden."

"What kind of women do you usually meet?"

"The ones I work with are ambitious, determined, ruthless."

"The female version of you."

He tipped his head in acknowledgment. "Possibly."

What about the women you don't work with but see socially?"

"The same."

"So, you like women in power suits?"

"Actually, I prefer them in a lot less clothing than that," he said with a teasing grin.

"Bathing suits, lingerie."

"Sure," he said agreeably. "You must have spent a lot of time in a bathing suit, living on a boat."

"Sometimes, but it wasn't always warm. In fact, we often had to wear heavy weather gear on deck when we were racing. It was not very attractive, as Caroline used to say, but it was necessary."

"I still wonder how three girls and a slightly crazy father could beat the best sailors in the world."

"Slightly crazy?" she asked with a rueful smile. "My father has never been slightly anything."

"How did you do it, Kate?"

"With a lot of hard work, determination, stubbornness and luck. We had a good boat, too. The Moon Dancer did us right." She paused, suddenly curious about Tyler's own background. "Have you ever been sailing?"

"Never."

"Really? How is that possible?"

"I spent a lot of time in the middle of the country. Nobody owned a boat."

"Everybody I know owns a boat," she said with a sigh.

"Is that so bad?"

"It's hard to get away from it when everyone is so involved."

"Then why stay? Why not live somewhere else?"

"This is where I was born. The land is in my blood, my heart. Most of my family, the people I love, are buried in that cemetery on the hill."

"You stay for the people who are gone?"

"No, I stay for myself. Everything I need, everything I want, is here. I know it's not enough for most people, but it is for me. Every time I leave, even for an afternoon or an overnight trip to Seattle, I can't wait to get back. This is home. And I guess I'm a person who needs a home, a place to plant seeds and watch them grow."

"This is an amazing garden," Tyler said, sweeping his hand toward the bounty of flowers, bushes, ferns, berries, and trees. "I've never seen anything like this outside of an arboretum or a magazine cover. You have a green thumb, that's for sure."

"Do you have a house somewhere?" she asked.

"I have a tenth-floor apartment in downtown San Antonio, but I'm rarely there. I'm usually on the road somewhere. It's the only way I know how to live," he said on a somber note.

And the only way he wants to live, Kate thought, intensely aware of how different their lives were, and how different they would always be. She got to her feet. "I'm thirsty. I'll make some lemonade."

He smiled. "I haven't had lemonade in years."

"I like my life, Tyler. Don't make fun of it."

"I wouldn't dare. The truth is, I like it, too." He stood up, blocking her way into the house. He moved in even closer, so close her breasts were almost brushing against his chest.

"You don't like it," she said, cursing the breathless note in her voice, but she could barely speak. Her breasts were tingling. Her heart was racing. And all she could think about was lifting her face to his and pressing her lips against his mouth.

"I do," he said, his mouth covering hers. His lips were warm, coaxing, and she could no more resist kissing him than she could resist taking her next breath. A wave of heat ran through her body, creating a deep ache within her as she pressed closer to him, running her hands up his back, feeling the taut, powerful muscles beneath her fingers. He was a solid man, a man who could sweep a woman off her feet and carry her upstairs and have his way with her.

"Kate, open your mouth," he whispered.

Her lips parted on command, and his tongue swept inside, deepening the intimacy between them. Dazed, she kissed him back with a need that grew more demanding by the minute. She wanted this man, wanted to slip her hands under his shirt, touch his bare chest, slip her legs between his, and get even closer to the hardness pressing against her belly.

"Again," he muttered as he allowed her a small breath.

She should have said no, told him to stop. This was madness. He could ruin her. He could ruin everything. But he tasted good and felt even better, reminding her that she was a woman who hadn't been kissed like this in a very long time—maybe never.

"Let's go inside," he said, lifting his head.

She wanted to say yes. But how could she? This wasn't right—it wasn't anywhere close to right. "I can't." She forced herself out of his arms and put a good two feet between them. "I don't have casual affairs with men who are leaving in the morning."

"I'm not leaving in the morning."

"Close enough."

"Kate—"

"Tyler, listen to me. I'm the kind of person who gets emotional and attached. That's not the kind of woman you want to get involved with, is it? Don't you like things easy and simple and uncomplicated?"

"I used to," he muttered.

"You should go."

He hesitated, then said, "I probably should." He walked toward the back door of her house, then paused, casting one last longing look in her direction that almost made her run into his arms and beg him to take her into the house and make love to her. To hell with the morning or the next day or the day after. She didn't always have to do the right thing, did she? Why couldn't she be reckless and impulsive like some of the other members of her family? Why did she always have to be the good girl?

The kitchen phone began to ring, a reminder that she had responsibilities and people in her life who needed her to do the right thing. "I better get that." She moved past Tyler and into the house, reaching for the telephone on the kitchen wall. "Hello?"

"It's Caroline, Kate. You need to come down to the marina right away."

She didn't like the tense note in her sister's voice. "Why? What's wrong? Is it Dad?"

"It's the Moon Dancer. She's back."

Kate hung up the phone with a shaky hand. She'd known the boat was coming back, hadn't she? So why was she so shocked?

Tyler stood in the doorway, staring at her. "Does your father need another ride home?"

"What? Oh, no." She grabbed her keys off the counter. "I have to go." She urged him down the hall and onto the front porch. "Don't follow me this time," she said, as she ran across the yard to her car.

"You know I will," he called back.

"It's none of your business."

She slammed the car door and pealed out of the driveway. With any luck she could lose him on the way to town.

———

"It's none of our business," Ashley whispered, as Caroline dragged her down the sidewalk leading to the marina. "We should stay out of it."

"None of our business?" Caroline asked in amazement. "K.C. Wales bought our boat and brought it back here to sail right in front of us. I think we're supposed to be involved in this. That's why he's sticking it in our faces."

"We should wait for Kate." Ashley stopped walking. It was the only way to slow Caroline down. "What exactly are we going to do? What are we going to say?"

Caroline tapped her foot impatiently. "I don't know yet."

"Let's think about it for a minute."

"I want to know why K.C. brought the boat back here. I'll just ask him."

"That's not a good plan."

"What's wrong with it?"

That was the problem with Caroline, Ashley thought. She never thought before she acted. "K.C. knows things, remember? There's a reporter in town, remember? We have to be careful. Let's wait for Kate."

"Fine. But if K.C. comes down this path before Kate gets here, I'm asking him what's up. I'm not afraid, even if you are."

It wasn't fear Ashley was feeling right now but uneasiness and maybe a hint of... longing? Was it possible that she wanted to see the Moon Dancer again?

No, that was crazy. That boat had been the site of her worst nightmare. Their home at sea had turned into a living hell. She couldn't possibly want to see it again, so why was she craning her neck, hoping to catch another glimpse?

"I'm calling Dad," Caroline said, taking out her cell phone. "He needs to know. We can't let him be blindsided."

"Maybe he already knows. Kate was going to tell him."

"I don't think she did. She's been so caught up with that reporter."

"Let's wait and ask her."

"It's ringing," Caroline said. "Damn. No answer."

"Would you just take a breath, Caroline? We don't have to talk to Dad yet."

Ashley wasn't up to dealing with her father on top of everything else. Her relationship with Duncan had always been awkward. She didn't have Caroline's faith in her father or Kate's unending loyalty. In fact, sometimes she didn't care for him at all.

Ashley was relieved to see Kate's car pull up in a nearby space.

"You didn't talk to K.C. yet, did you?" Kate asked breathlessly as she stopped in front of them.

"Not yet," Ashley replied.

"Good." Kate cast a quick look over her shoulder. "Tyler is probably on his way here right now. I tried to ditch him, but I don't think I succeeded. He drives very fast."

"Did you tell Dad about K.C. and the Moon Dancer?" Caroline asked Kate.

"No, I meant to, but when I saw Dad last night, I got distracted when he told me that Rick Beardsley had asked him to join his racing crew. Can you believe that?"

"But Dad promised he wouldn't race again," Ashley said, wondering why everything was suddenly off kilter.

"Maybe Dad just wants to move on," Caroline offered. "There's nothing wrong with getting on with our lives. The past is long gone."

"Not that far gone," Kate said, stiffening. "Here comes one person from our past right now."

CHAPTER TEN

K.C. Wales was a tall man, well over six feet. In his younger days, his hair had been sandy brown. Now it was stark white. His dark eyes blazed against his ruddy complexion; his skin bore the weathered look of a longtime sailor. In his mid-sixties, he was still an imposing man, with a wiry strength about him and a sense of purpose. He was followed by another man, who appeared to be in his twenties and looked familiar.

K.C.'s son, David? Kate hadn't seen David in years, but then David had been raised by his mother in California.

Kate felt Ashley and Caroline draw close to her, forming a united front as the men stopped before them. There was instant recognition in K.C.'s eyes, despite the lapse in time since they'd last seen one another.

"Ah, Katie," he said with a pleased nod of his head. "Ashley, Caroline. I hadn't expected that you would be part of my welcoming committee. You're all looking well."

"And we never expected you to come back here, especially in our boat," Kate said.

"The Moon Dancer hasn't been your boat for years," he said evenly.

"You know what I mean. Why did you buy it?" she asked.

"Because it was for sale," he said simply. "I'm sure your father must have seen it listed in the magazines. If he'd wanted it back, he could have bought it."

Kate wasn't about to tell him that her father didn't have the kind of money to buy back a world-class racing yacht. Instead, she said, "He's moved on in his life. I thought you had, too."

"Things change. Life changes. No day is ever the same as the last. You should know that, Katie."

"There are hundreds of better boats, especially if you're racing again."

"But the Moon Dancer is a winner, isn't it, girls?" He paused. "I've been remiss. You remember my son David, don't you?"

Kate turned her head to take a better look at David. Her first impression was of a rebel in blue jeans. With a cigarette hanging out of his mouth and long brown hair, he looked like a punk. He had none of the sophistication of his father. And he was too pale to be a sailor. She wondered what he'd grown up to be. Aside from the few summer vacations he'd spent with his father when they were children, she knew little about him. "Hello," she said.

David just shrugged.

"You look more like Nora than I remember, Katie," K.C. mused, studying her face. "Quiet strength suits you well."

Kate wasn't quite sure how to respond to his compliment, if in fact it was a compliment. Maybe it was a warning that she would need strength.

"Where is your father?" K.C. asked.

"He's around."

"It shouldn't be too difficult to find him. I'll just look in the nearest bar."

Kate wished she could tell K.C. that her father had changed, that he wasn't so easy to predict, but she couldn't. Duncan probably *was* at the nearest bar.

"As much as I'd love to stay and catch up, David and I have a meeting to get to," K.C. said. "We'll talk again. We have things to discuss—unfinished business, you might say."

"I can't imagine what," Kate murmured.

His smile was silky-smooth. "I'm sure you can imagine. As I recall, Katie, you had the best imagination of all the girls."

K.C. and his son moved away before Kate could reply.

"I don't think you had the best imagination," Caroline said after a moment. "I'm very imaginative. And Ashley has seen ghosts and all kinds of supernatural phenomena, so you might have the worst imagination."

"Caroline," Ashley said in frustration, "didn't you just hear what K.C. had to say?"

"He didn't say anything. He just implied things."

"That's what bothers me." Kate watched David and K.C. walk down the path toward the marina office. They passed by Tyler Jamison, who was leaning against a post, watching them. He tipped his head toward her, then walked away.

His quick departure surprised and worried her. Why hadn't he come over? Why hadn't he asked who the two men were? It seemed out of character for him to just leave without saying a word. What was he up to now?

"What are we going to do about K.C.?" Ashley asked, interrupting her thoughts about Tyler. "Do you think he really knows something, or is this just about sticking the Moon Dancer back in our faces?"

"I don't know," Kate replied. "I guess we should speak to Dad, and he probably is down at the bar."

"I can't go," Caroline said abruptly. "I have something else to take care of. I'll catch up with you two later."

"What do you have to do?" Kate asked.

"Stuff," Caroline said, refusing to give any more details before she walked away.

"I wonder if Dad knows about K.C. and the Moon Dancer," Ashley mused.

Kate suddenly saw the truth. "That's why he suddenly has to get back in the game. He wants to race K.C. That's what this is all about. Finally, a connection that makes sense."

"We have to find a way to stop him."

Kate met her sister's eyes. "Yes, we do."

Tyler sat down on a bench by the harbor, staring at the boats before him. He took out his cell phone, then hesitated.

How could he explain to Mark that he needed a shot in the arm, a kick in the butt, a reason to stay in the hunt? Mark wasn't here. He didn't know that Kate was a beautiful woman with a great smile and a big heart, a woman who loved and protected her family. Mark didn't know that Ashley was quiet and vulnerable and looked like she'd lost her best friend. And he didn't know that Caroline was a spunky young woman who seemed more of a confused innocent than a determined troublemaker.

Frankly, Tyler couldn't quite decide which of the girls was the most likely candidate to have given up a child. He had some ammunition to use if it was Caroline or Ashley. With a little creativity, he could probably make a case that Caroline was a reckless, irresponsible party girl with lots of vices and that Ashley was a head case, probably in need of a good psychiatrist. Kate still seemed clean as a whistle. Damn. He did not want Amelia's mother to be Kate. He did not want to have to take her down in any way. How could he? Ten minutes ago he'd wanted to make love to her, and whether or not she was Amelia's mother had been the last thing on his mind.

He punched in Mark's number, and when his brother answered, he said abruptly, "I need to talk to Amelia."

"Why?" Mark asked suspiciously. "What's going on?"

"I just miss her. Is she home?"

"Yeah, she's home," Mark said, a catch in his voice. "She's taking care of me, Ty. She's eight years old, and she's taking care of me. I don't know what I'd do without her."

There it was, the shot in the arm he needed. A moment later, Amelia's sweet, girlish voice came over the phone.

"Hi, Uncle Ty. Where are you?" she asked.

"I'm looking at some boats. What are you doing?"

"I was reading Daddy a story. But now I'm making him a milkshake, because Shelly says he needs milk for his bones to get better."

"You're a good girl."

"I know," she said breezily.

Tyler's heart squeezed again at the familiar note in her voice. Did she sound like Kate—or was that just his imagination?

"I'm going swimming later," Amelia continued. "I can go all the way down and touch the bottom in the deep end now. And yesterday I got all three rings without coming up for air."

"That's terrific."

"Uncle Ty?"

"Yeah?"

"Can I ask you a question?" Amelia's voice dropped down as if she didn't want her father to hear.

"Sure, honey."

"Do you think Mommy can see us from heaven?"

"I know she can."

"Do you think she's mad because Daddy and I didn't go with her?"

His gut clenched at the question. "Oh, no, absolutely not. She wants you to be happy, Amelia. That's all she ever cared about."

"I'm going to take care of Daddy for her."

His heart broke a little bit more. "I know you will. Can I talk to him again?"

"Bye, Uncle Ty."

Tyler drew in a desperately needed breath as he waited for Mark to come on the line. Amelia was strong and courageous. And he had a terrible feeling he knew who she got that strength from.

In a moment Mark's voice came over the line. "Any other news?" he asked tensely.

"Not really. Every time I think I've got it figured out one way, I see another possibility. Has there been any more contact between George and the other lawyer?"

"Yes. George got a registered letter from Mr. Watson basically stating that if he didn't come up with a name and address of the baby's adoptive parents, he was going to make sure that there was a thorough investigation into George's practice."

"Damn. What did George say?"

"Nothing yet. But if this Mr. Watson found George, he might be able to find me, too. You have to figure out which one of the McKenna sisters is the mother. For God's sake, Tyler, I thought you were a hotshot reporter. What's taking so long?"

"What do you want me to do—come out and ask them? Don't you think that will raise some questions? You have to be patient. You have to let me handle this my way."

"Just find her, Tyler. Dig deep. Be the ruthless son of a bitch I know you can be. I need to know who's trying to take my daughter."

"I'll call you when I have more information." Tyler slipped the phone into his pocket and debated his next step.

He knew there was something going on with the McKennas and the two men they'd met on the docks. But what did that have to do with his problem? Probably nothing.

He could follow up on Caroline. He could check out her party-girl reputation at the Oyster Bar, maybe run into Duncan and find out what was up with the infamous K.C. Wales and the Moon Dancer.

Relieved that he had a plan that did not involve Kate, Tyler got to his feet and headed toward the bar.

Duncan felt better than he had in years, and it wasn't just because of the whiskey sliding down his throat; it was the taste of a challenge. In one week he'd be the skipper on the Summer Seas. He couldn't wait to feel the wind in his face, hear the roar of the ocean, smell the fish and the salt. God, he ached for those smells, those sounds, those sights. He'd paid his penance. Katie would just have to understand that a sailing man couldn't stay in port forever. Nora would have understood. She'd always known that he needed the sea almost as much as he needed her. He could hardly believe eight years had passed since he'd sold the Moon Dancer.

Duncan raised his glass to his lips once again. K.C. had come just as he'd expected. It hadn't taken a rocket scientist to figure out that K.C. would buy the Moon Dancer. Maybe the girls would be surprised, but Duncan knew better. He'd known K.C. would come back eventually, and returning in the Moon Dancer would fit K.C.'s sense of drama.

It didn't matter. The boat's return added to the challenge, and Duncan felt exhilarated by the thought of it all. He was living again. He was calling the shots. He'd had plenty of time over the past few years to think. And he knew what he wanted now. A twinge of conscience stabbed him as he recalled the horror in Kate's eyes when he'd told her he was racing again, but he ignored it. He'd suffered enough.

"Mr. McKenna?"

Duncan looked up to see a young man approaching him. "Do I know you?"

"Not yet. I'm Tyler Jamison. I'm a reporter, and I'd like to do a follow-up story on your family's impressive racing victory in the Winston Challenge."

He smiled. A reporter? Perfect. This day was getting better and better. "You've come to the right place."

"Can I buy you a drink?"

"Of course." As Tyler sat down, Duncan saw Kate and Ashley walk into the bar. He frowned in disgust. "Don't tell me that fool bartender called you already. I've only had two drinks."

"What are you doing here?" Kate asked Tyler.

Apparently, his daughter had already met the reporter. Probably tried to steer him away from the family. Well, not this time. A reporter suited his purposes just fine.

"You're interrupting," Duncan said. "Mr.—What was your name?"

"Jamison."

"Mr. Jamison and I are going to have a drink."

"Dad, he's a reporter," Kate protested.

"I know who he is," he said with a grin. "I just don't know what he's drinking."

"I'll have a beer," Tyler said to the nearby waiter. He turned to Kate. "What about you, Kate? Are you staying?"

Kate looked undecided, Ashley even more so.

"Sit or go," Duncan said impatiently. He would have preferred that they go, but he suspected that no matter how uncomfortable Kate felt, she would not leave him alone with the reporter.

"I'll stay," Kate said firmly. "Ashley will stay, too."

Ashley looked like she'd rather do anything else. But then that's the way Ashley looked most of the time, Duncan thought. His middle daughter had always been more of a mystery than the other two, and always so damn sensitive.

"Now, then, what can I tell you?" Duncan asked Tyler as his daughters joined them at the table.

"I'd like to hear about your experience racing around the world."

"That could take awhile, son," he said with a laugh.

"I'll bet." Tyler leaned forward. "I've read a great deal about the race, but what I'd really like to know is how it felt to sail through one of the most terrible storms in ocean-racing history."

"Ever had someone hold your head underwater?" Duncan asked. "I thought God had his hands on our heads that night. The waves got so bad we couldn't tell if we were sailing or if the boat was just filling up with water."

"It must have been terrifying," Tyler commented.

"It was the worst we'd ever been through." Duncan knew there had to be limits to this conversation, but, dammit, some day he wanted to tell the world just how hard it had been to sail through that monster. "But we survived."

"Were you close to the boat that didn't make it?" Tyler asked.

"Who could tell?" Kate said quickly. "We couldn't see past our noses out there."

"But they kept shouting *Mayday* over the radio," Ashley said. "I can still hear their voices filled with panic, begging for help. I don't think I'll ever forget those voices." Her own voice drifted away as if she were sorry she'd joined in the conversation.

Duncan shifted uncomfortably in his seat. He didn't want to talk about those voices; he wanted to talk about the roller-coaster waves and the strength it had taken to keep the boat from going under.

"When did you know that one of the boats had gone down?" Tyler asked Duncan.

"The next day, when it was over."

"I understand one man survived."

"Yes," Duncan answered. It was all a matter of public record, at least that part. He looked up as the door to the bar opened and his onetime friend and nemesis walked into the room. "Well, if that isn't right on cue. There he is now."

Duncan got to his feet, watching the man he had once loved as a brother, then hated as an enemy, walk into the room. K.C. looked good, too good. There was a glint in his eye, a spring in his step. He wanted the challenge as much as Duncan did. Two old gunfighters looking for a last shootout.

"Duncan," K.C. said.

The room grew quiet, as if everyone knew something was coming, but they weren't sure what.

"It's been too long," K.C. said.

"Has it? I haven't noticed."

"You haven't missed me?"

"Not at all," Duncan replied.

"I hope it's not difficult for you to see your boat being sailed by your old friend."

"I hope it won't be difficult for you to lose to your old friend yet again." Duncan felt his temper rise despite his best attempts to stay calm. God, he hated K.C.'s smug, smirking face and that slimy voice of his, pretending to be sophisticated and rich, when they both knew he'd come from nothing, same as Duncan. He didn't understand how Nora could have ever been taken in by this man.

"That's right. I just heard you were racing," K.C. continued. "I'm glad. It's only fitting. After all, the last time we raced in the Castleton, it was against each other. I remember Nora—"

"Leave her out of this." He couldn't stand the sound of Nora's name on this man's lips.

"That would be impossible. Nora was always between us. Just like the Moon Dancer was always between us. She feels good under my hands, Duncan, almost as good as—"

"You son of a bitch." Duncan lunged for K.C. but missed, landing on his knees. He heard K.C.'s mocking laughter and felt a terrible rage. He would make this man pay, if it was the last thing he did.

Kate ran to her father. He pushed her away, his pride stinging more than his body. "I'm fine."

"You were always so predictable," K.C. said, "so easy. I thought things might have changed, but they haven't. I'll see you on the water, old friend." And with a wave he was gone.

"Are you all right?" Kate asked as he got to his feet.

"I just tripped, that's all. What are you looking at?" he asked the other customers, who finally turned away.

"What was he talking about, Dad?" Ashley asked when he returned to the table.

"Nothing. He just likes to shoot off his mouth. Forget about it."

"That won't be easy to do," Kate said slowly. "Is there something you need to tell us about Mom and K.C.?"

"There's something I need to tell you about the boat," Duncan replied. He paused for a moment, sure they wouldn't like what he had to say, but he would say it anyway. "I'm going to win it back."

Kate looked at him in surprise. "What are you talking about?"

"K.C. is going to make a bet, and he'll lose."

"What's the wager?" Tyler asked.

"If I win the Castleton, he gives me back the Moon Dancer."

"Oh, my God," Kate said. "You can't be serious, Dad. What if K.C. doesn't agree?"

"Are you kidding? A chance to beat me? He'll agree."

"What happens if you lose? What does he get?" she asked.

"I won't lose."

"You can't guarantee that."

"I can. Rick Beardsley gave me carte blanche to pick my own racing crew." He looked his daughter straight in the eye. "I want you, Katie girl. You and Ashley and Caroline. I want us to take back what was ours. Say yes."

CHAPTER ELEVEN

"YOU'RE OUT OF YOUR MIND," Kate said, shocked to the core. "I'm not going to race. And neither is Ashley." She glanced at her sister, who looked sick at the thought of it.

"Not even to get back our boat?" Duncan challenged. "It's mine, Katie. I won't have K.C. living my life, sailing my boat. I'm getting it back. I want you girls to help me. We're a family. We stand together."

Kate saw her father turn to Ashley, whose eyes had filled with unimaginable terror. Even Duncan could see it. He opened his mouth to speak, then closed it. He put out a tentative hand to Ashley, but she pushed back her chair.

"I—I can't," Ashley stuttered. She ran out of the bar as if the fires of hell were chasing after her.

Kate could understand the feeling. She wanted to flee, too, but she didn't have the luxury. She couldn't walk out on Duncan—not with Tyler so close, waiting, watching, listening.

Duncan motioned for the waitress to bring him another drink. "You think about it," he said to Kate. "You were always my best sailor. I know I could do this with you at my side. And talk to Caroline. She'll come along. She'll want to help. She always does."

"Because she wants your approval."

"She'll definitely have it, if she comes onboard."

"You knew he was coming back, didn't you?" It suddenly became clear to Kate that Duncan had not been surprised to see K.C.

"Yes." Duncan paused as the waitress set down his drink. "I knew that as soon as he saw the Moon Dancer was for sale, he'd find a way to buy it."

"Because?" Kate was almost afraid to ask, but she couldn't stop the question from breaking through her lips.

"He always wanted it. He couldn't stand that Nora and I built it together."

"So this does have something to do with Mom," she said slowly. "Just like he said. Something happened between the three of you. I remember when he was your best friend. He spent all the holidays with us, then he was gone. Instead of being our favorite uncle, he was someone you didn't even speak to. What happened?" Kate couldn't bring herself to ask if there had been an affair. It sounded so disloyal. Her mother wouldn't have had an affair. She had too much character and integrity, and she had loved Duncan. Kate would have bet her life on it.

"That's between K.C. and me. What you need to be concerned about is someone else sailing our boat."

"Someone else has been sailing our boat for eight years."

"Not this someone."

"You'll have to give me a better reason." She turned to Tyler. "Would you mind giving us some privacy?"

Tyler simply smiled in return. "I don't think so."

"K.C. bought the Moon Dancer to show me up," Duncan said, obviously not caring that a reporter was listening in. "He wants me to think he's the winner and I'm the loser, but he's wrong. And I'm going to prove it."

"Hasn't the time for proving things passed? Haven't you both lost enough?"

"I want my boat back. Our boat. Our home. Think about it. It's the last place we were together, and I mean your beautiful mother, too. We designed and built that boat, decorated it in our own way, spilled sweat, blood, and tears on that deck. I won't have K.C. in it. I won't have him living my life. Help me, Katie."

Kate didn't like the idea of K.C. sailing the Moon Dancer, either. But to race again? To compete for a boat that held so many memories, both bad and good? She couldn't do it. It would be too painful. "I can't."

"Katie, please."

"You'll have to do this one on your own. I really wish you'd forget it. Let K.C. take the Moon Dancer and sail to Hawaii. He'll be gone in a few days, and we can get back to normal."

"Normal? You call this normal—this life we're leading? Hell, Katie, I haven't felt normal in eight years."

Kate watched as he drained his drink. "Maybe it's all the booze. Maybe that's why you don't feel normal."

"Fine. Whatever. Go on, get out of here. You know, Katie, your mother was never so judgmental. So hard. Everything with you is black and white. People are good or they're bad; there's no in-between." His eyes bored into hers with anger and frustration. "You can't stand to be wrong, and you can't stand it when people don't measure up to your lofty standards. Some of us are human. Some of us have weaknesses."

Kate felt incredibly hurt by his harsh words. She wasn't judgmental or hard. And she was human. She cared. She cared too much, if he only knew the truth. "This isn't about right or wrong—"

"I thought you were leaving," Duncan said, cutting her off. "I've got business to discuss with my new friend here." He tipped his head in Tyler's direction.

Kate saw concern in Tyler's eyes, or was it guilt? No, he didn't feel guilty. He'd already told her he didn't waste time on that emotion. This was the opportunity Tyler had been looking for, a chance to get the inside scoop from Duncan. And there was not a damn thing she could do about it. If she protested, it would only make Tyler more suspicious, and Duncan was hell-bent on living out his glory days one more time. Sometimes she wondered why she bothered to protect him. But it wasn't just him, she told herself firmly. That's what she had to remember.

"I'll call you later," Tyler said quietly.

She got to her feet. "Don't bother. I've said all I need to say—to both of you."

Ashley dragged an old duffel bag off the top shelf of her closet. It came down with a layer of dust and a couple shoe boxes. She coughed, sneezed, then nearly burst into tears when an old and terribly familiar smell wafted through the room. It was the smell of the sea, the smell of the boat, the smell of fear. She stared at the duffel bag in dismay. It had been eight years since she'd used it. Too long for the smells to still be there. Was it just her imagination?

Oh, what did it matter? Her life was falling apart.

She couldn't believe her father wanted them to race again. She couldn't believe that K.C. had somehow been involved with her mother. What was that all about? Was it a lie? Or something more? And did she really want to know?

She had to get away. The walls were closing in. Just like before, during that terrible storm, when she'd seen the water slipping in under the door. She'd had the terrible feeling they were already underwater. She wouldn't be able to get out. She wouldn't be able to breathe. She'd die slowly, suffocating, the way she was suffocating now.

"Ashley—open up." She heard a male voice and a pounding on the door. The voice brought her back to reality, and she ran out of her bedroom before the memories could come back.

Sean was at the door. Her jaw dropped in shock. "What are you doing here?"

"I want to know what happened," he said, his eyes determined.

"About what? Are you talking about K.C.? He just showed up with the Moon Dancer. My father wants to race him, and he wants me onboard. It's crazy. I don't know what's happening. Everything is changing."

"What the hell are you talking about?"

Ashley stared at him. "K.C."

"I didn't come here to talk about K.C., but about Jeremy. I'm talking about my brother, and that little bombshell you dropped last night."

It seemed like a million years ago since she had spoken to Sean. Had it only been last night?

"You said you kissed him." Sean planted his hands on his hips. "I want to know why and when and all the rest. So start talking."

"I don't have time," she said, making a quick decision.

"Make time."

"I can't. I'm leaving." She walked into the bedroom and began emptying her drawers into the duffel bag.

"Where are you going?" Sean asked from the doorway.

"Away."

"Why?"

"You always have so many questions for me," she said, pushing her hair out of her face.

"And you never have any answers."

Sean crossed the room as she yanked open another dresser. "Stop it, would you?" He grabbed her by the arm. "Stop packing and talk to me. I want to know what happened between you and my brother. And why you decided to tell me now."

"Let go of me." She tried to free her arm, but he held on tight, so tight she felt trapped. Acute panic set in. "Let go!" she yelled. "I have to get out of here." She finally yanked her arm free.

"Ashley, wait! Where are you going?"

"I don't know." She tossed more clothes into the bag, some falling on the floor, some on the bed, but she didn't care. "I have to get out before I lose what little is left of my mind. If you care at all for me, you'll help me."

"Ash, I don't know what you want me to do."

What did she want him to do? She drew in a deep breath, forcing herself to think. She knew the last ferry had already left the island. If she wanted to leave Castleton, she needed a boat. "I want you to take me to the mainland."

His jaw dropped. "You're willing to get on my boat?"

"I just said that, didn't I?" But could she get on his boat? It was dark now. The water would be black. She wouldn't be able to see the horizon or where she was going.

Sean gave her an uncertain look. "Maybe you should talk to some-one, call Kate or Caroline. You're obviously upset about something."

"Upset? You think I'm upset?" Was that her voice screeching like a maniac? It must be, because Sean was staring at her like she'd gone over the edge. "I'm sorry. I can't do this anymore. It's too much for me." She felt overwhelmed, exhausted, terrified, and almost wished she could cry to release some of the tension, but her eyes were dry. Her tear ducts as empty as everything else.

"Look, I don't understand half of what you said before, but just take it easy, okay? Don't do anything rash. There's always tomorrow, if you still want to go."

"If I don't go now, I'm not sure I will ever go."

"Then that's a good reason to wait."

Ashley sank down on the edge of the bed, feeling defeated.

After a moment Sean sat down next to her. "Do you want to talk about any of it?"

"No." There were too many thoughts crowding her head to make sense of any of them.

"All right, then."

Sean put his arm around her shoulders. Ashley tensed, but when he didn't make another move, she gradually began to relax, taking precious comfort in his embrace. He wasn't asking anything of her. He wasn't demanding that she do something or say something. For the first time in a long time, she felt safe. This was Sean, her first love, her only love, if the truth be told. No one else had ever come close. She'd tried to put her love away, because she didn't deserve him. But he was here, and she was weak. She needed to lean on someone.

"Don't go," she whispered, resting her head on his chest. The beat of his heart was strong and steady. "I know I shouldn't ask."

"It's about time you did," he muttered.

"You must hate me."

He let out a heavy sigh. "I wish I did. It would make it a whole lot easier."

Kate just wanted a closer look. It wasn't a crime, she told herself, as she walked down to the docks. She was human after all, despite her father's earlier criticism, which still stung. She'd tried to work, but sorting inventory at the bookstore hadn't proved a big enough distraction, and there was no way she was going back to the Oyster Bar. She'd had enough of her father, and Tyler, too.

She just wanted a few minutes alone with something that had once been a very important part of her life, the Moon Dancer. They'd come together as a family when they'd first set sail, the close confines of the boat forcing them to talk to one another, to share the workload, to rely on one another for everything from food to survival. They'd learned a lot on the water with only themselves to depend on. When the racing had begun, the experience had taken on a new dimension.

The competition had created an excitement, a rush as they barreled into the wind, trying to go as fast as they could. The ports of call had been filled with parties, celebrations, and tall tales of what had happened during each leg of the race. In the beginning, she had soaked it all up as if she were a hungry sponge. She'd loved being part of it, seeing her father in his element, and Jeremy, too, sharing the same excitement and joy. She should have realized that two such strong men would come into conflict.

Looking back, she could see where the first thread had begun to unravel. Unfortunately, she hadn't noticed that loose thread until everything fell apart.

Shaking her head, Kate moved closer to the siren that called her name. The Moon Dancer sat proudly on the water, bobbing gently with the swells. Her breath caught in her throat. It was a magnificent boat, a lightweight, forty-seven-foot speedster guaranteed to give a spirited yet comfortable ride. Her parents had designed the boat and had it custom-built at a yard in Seattle. Their idea was to use race technology to build a cruiser that could win races. And the Moon Dancer had more than lived up to the challenges they'd put it through. She'd not only won for them, she'd sheltered and protected them.

Kate drew in a breath and slowly let it out, allowing the emotions to sweep through her soul. There was no point in trying to hold them back; they were overflowing. She felt joy at seeing the boat; she also felt incredible sadness for a time in their lives that had been both the worst and the best. Maybe life would always be like that, offering something good, only to counter it with something bad.

"Boo!"

Kate jumped at the sound behind her. She whirled around in surprise to see K.C.'s son, David, laughing at her. "David. You scared me."

He pulled the cigarette out of his mouth and flicked the ashes into the water. "That's what you get for trying to sneak onto my boat. Or do you still think it's yours?"

"I wasn't trying to sneak onto the boat. And I know who owns it."

"I hope so. If not, I can always show you my daddy's pink slip. That's right, my daddy. Not yours, Kate, even though you used to think of him as a second daddy, didn't you? Uncle K.C., isn't that what you called him? Didn't you give him a big fat kiss every time he brought you candy or toys or whatever else you wanted, little princess?"

There was an animosity in David's voice she hadn't expected. "You sound like..."

"What? What do I sound like?"

"Like you hate me." She laughed as if the thought were absurd, but he didn't laugh back, and a chill washed over her body.

"Of course I don't hate you," he said smoothly. "I don't even know you. Isn't that right? We only spoke a few times over the years when I came to visit my father. You were all too busy to hang out with me."

"I didn't think you were interested in hanging out with us."

"Oh, I don't know. I was always curious about the girls who spent more time with my father than I did."

"That wasn't our fault."

"Did I say it was?"

She didn't like the thread of their conversation. "I'm leaving now."

"Don't you want to go onboard?"

"No." Kate shook her head, even though his unexpected invitation had sent her heart racing.

"You're not interested in seeing what the inside looks like?"

"Not really."

He stepped in front of her as she turned to leave. "It's the first time in my life that I got something of yours, instead of the other way around."

Kate frowned, seeing not just anger in his dark brown eyes but also pain. "What are you talking about?"

"I'm talking about holidays and birthdays, Christmas presents that my father gave to you and your sisters instead of to me. He wanted your family, your mother. He wanted your life."

"That's not true. He was a friend, that's all."

"Really? You think that's all he was?"

"Yes." She hated the doubt that once again crossed her mind. First K.C., then her own father, now David. Did they all know something she didn't?

Uncle K.C. had always been around when she was small. So many videos showed him standing by the Christmas tree or laughing with her mother in the kitchen. Then it had changed. Something had happened. She did not want to believe it had anything to do with her mother.

"I thought you were the smart one," David said. "I must have been mistaken."

"You don't know anything. You're just trying to annoy me."

"I might be," he admitted. "Or I might not."

"Why did you and your father come back here? So you could have this little moment of triumph in front of us? So you could say you're better than us? Is that what it's all about?"

David didn't answer right away. Then he said, "I'm not sure." There was a touch of uncertainty in his voice.

"What? Now you're pretending ignorance? I thought you knew everything about the relationship between your family and mine."

"I know more than you, obviously."

"Like what? What do you think you know?"

"My father and your mother had an affair."

His blunt words stole her breath away.

"That's not true." A sense of impending doom lent little strength to her words. "It can't be true."

"You look a little like him—my father."

The implication flashed through her like the sharp edge of a knife. "You are sick."

"Why don't you ask him?"

"I wouldn't believe a word your father said." She walked briskly away from him.

"Then ask Duncan," David called after her.

She didn't have to ask Duncan. She knew who her father was. Didn't she?

CHAPTER TWELVE

K.C. Wales, born Kendrick Charles Wales in San Francisco, California, was the only son of a fisherman and a high school English teacher. Tyler skimmed the data appearing on the screen of his laptop computer. He wasn't sure exactly what he was looking for, but he knew it wasn't in K.C.'s childhood. The connection with the McKenna family had come later. Sure enough, as his fingers flew across the keys, checking various search results, Tyler came up with the sailing connection. K.C. Wales and Duncan McKenna began racing each other in competitions during what had to be the early years of Duncan's marriage. Their rivalry had continued into the Winston Around-the-World Challenge, in which K.C., the skipper of the Betsy Marie, had been the only survivor of the ship that went down in the storm.

Tyler frowned, searching for what happened next. There didn't appear to be any further reports. The man seemed to disappear after the race. Tyler supposed that wasn't unusual for someone who had almost drowned. Then again, K.C. had looked in fine health when he'd confronted Duncan in the Oyster Bar several hours earlier.

Tyler tapped his keyboard impatiently. What he really wanted to know was what K.C. had done between the race and now. He'd tried to get the information from Duncan, but Duncan had been strangely quiet on the subject, despite consuming enough whiskey to float a boat. While Duncan had spewed forth endless tales of racing victories, he'd refused to say anything about the girls or K.C. Finally, Tyler had given up when Duncan called over more of his pals to share tales with.

Giving the bartender a twenty-dollar bill and instructions to make sure Duncan got a cab ride home, Tyler had returned to his hotel, hoping that Kate wouldn't be called out yet again to rescue her father. Not that she'd thank him for getting in the middle, but he was there, no doubt about it. And he was more than a little curious about K.C.

Who was this man? Duncan's friend? His rival? His enemy? Had there been something going on between K.C. and Kate's mother, Nora, as K.C. had implied? And what was K.C.'s motive for bringing the Moon Dancer to Castleton?

"It doesn't matter," Tyler muttered to himself. So what if K.C. had slept with Kate's mother? They weren't the ones who'd given Amelia up for adoption. He had to get his focus back. Rubbing the tense muscles in his neck, he rolled his head back and forth on his shoulders. He closed his eyes, trying to relax and de-stress, but now all he could see in his mind was the hurt look in Kate's eyes when her father had criticized her.

A quiet knock brought his eyes open. The clock read just past nine. He got to his feet and opened the door. Kate stood in the hallway. As always seemed to be the case when he saw her, his body tightened and his heart began to race. It was ridiculous, the way she made him feel tense and uncertain.

He knew what he had to do with her, and it wasn't at all what he wanted to do with her, which was to drag her into the room and make love to her.

Wearing blue jeans and a pale pink sweater, her hair loose about her shoulders, she could have passed for younger than twenty-eight, until one looked closer and saw the tiny lines around her mouth and the shadows under her eyes. She'd lived a long life in those three years at sea. Maybe a longer life since then, as she'd tried to hold the family together.

"Hello," she said with a weary note in her voice. "I bet I'm the last person you expected to see."

"You could say that."

"Can I come in?"

"Sure." He stepped aside and motioned for her to enter.

"It's nice," Kate said, looking around the room.

He followed her gaze. It was a basic hotel room, although the Seascape Inn had provided a nautical-themed wallpaper trim as well as some interesting seascapes on the walls. "It's okay."

Kate nodded, standing awkwardly in the center of the room. "Is the bed comfortable? Sometimes they're so hard in a hotel you can bounce coins off the mattress. Caroline used to do that..." Her voice drifted away. "I didn't come here to talk about hotel rooms."

"Do you want to sit down?" he asked.

She glanced over at the desk where his laptop was open. "Are you researching me?"

"Why are you here, Kate?"

"I need a favor."

Now he was surprised. "What kind of a favor?"

"Information."

"About?"

"K.C. Wales." She walked over to the computer and stared unabashedly at the screen. "I see you're ahead of me." She lifted her gaze to his. "Why are you researching K.C.?"

"Because he's tied to your family in some way. I also find it interesting that he was the sole survivor of the ship that capsized during your race."

"Why is that interesting?"

"Oh, I don't know. A sole survivor might have a different story than everyone else."

"He doesn't remember what happened. He had a severe head injury and amnesia after the tragedy. The last thing he remembered was the start of the race almost eleven months earlier. Everything else was gone."

Tyler straightened, sensing that this was the piece of information he'd been waiting for. "He had amnesia? I thought that only happened in books."

She shrugged. "I'm not a doctor. He was unconscious for several days, and when he woke up he couldn't walk or talk. The doctors said it wasn't surprising that he didn't remember a big chunk of his life, especially the recent memory. What else did you find out about him?"

"Probably nothing you don't already know. What are you looking for?"

She hesitated for a long moment. "I want to find out about K.C. and my mother."

"I don't think that answer will be on the Internet."

"I don't, either." She turned and walked back to him, digging her hands into her pockets. "But you could talk to him. You're a reporter. You'd know how to get that story, wouldn't you?"

"Maybe. What would I get in return?"

She sent him a pleading smile. "My deepest gratitude."

"Try again."

"Forget it. I knew you wouldn't help me. I don't know why I bothered to ask. In fact, I don't even know why I came here."

"If you want to know if K.C. and your mother had a personal relationship, you should ask your father. There's something between those two men, something deep and very intense."

Her eyes lit up with his words. "You saw it, too. It wasn't just me?"

"It wasn't just you."

"I went down to the docks a little while ago to look at our old boat. I ran into K.C.'s son, David. He acted like he hated me. He was clearly jealous of the time I'd spent with his father when I was a kid."

"David didn't live with K.C.?"

Kate shook her head and sat down on the edge of the bed. Tyler took a seat in the desk chair.

"David lived with his mother in San Diego. K.C. and his wife divorced when David was just a little kid, maybe two or three. I never met his mother. But David would come and spend summers here on the island with his father."

"So K.C. used to live here?"

"Part of the year, when he wasn't sailing somewhere. He and my father ran charters for a while or worked for other people."

"Did K.C. come back here to recuperate after the race?"

"No. He was originally airlifted to the hospital in Oahu. After that he went to San Diego to be with David, I guess. I don't know. We didn't keep in touch."

"Why not?" Tyler asked sharply. "Your families were best friends, then that's it? It's over?" There was something she wasn't telling him.

She stared back at him. "My father and K.C. had a falling out long before that race. In fact, I think one of the reasons we entered was so we could beat K.C. and his crew. I can't help wondering now if that falling out had something to do with my mother, which I never considered before. But the last time K.C. was friendly to me or my sisters was just before Mom died." She paused. "I remember he spent a good hour or two with her the day before she passed away, but he didn't stay for the funeral. He said he couldn't handle it or something. I don't remember exactly."

Kate got up and paced restlessly around the room. "I should be talking to Caroline or Ashley, not you."

"Why aren't you talking to them?" he asked curiously.

"Because..." She waved her hand in the air as if the answer would magically appear.

"Because why?"

"David said something to me that is ridiculous. I don't believe him, and it would really upset everyone if I even mentioned it."

"Are you going to tell me? Or make me guess?"

"I shouldn't tell you."

Tyler saw the indecision in her face. "Come on, spill it. It can't have anything to do with whatever you're hiding, or else you wouldn't be here. I already know you well enough to know that. It has to be personal, because you'd protect your family no matter what the cost. But yourself? That's a different story."

"I'm that easy to read?"

"I've been studying you for a while now."

"You're right. It was about me. David said, actually he implied, that

K.C. might be my real father. Isn't that just ridiculous? It can't be true. I am my father's daughter, right? I certainly don't look like K.C. And my father and mother were madly in love with each other, especially when they first got married. There's no way there could have been an affair so early on. But then again..." She paused, sending him a desperate look. "Say something, Tyler. Convince me that I'm right."

"I don't know what to say," he muttered, more than a little surprised by the twist in events. "I guess anything is possible."

"That's not what I wanted to hear."

He shook his head. "I have no idea if K.C. slept with your mother or if he fathered you. It seems to me you have only two choices: ask your father or ask K.C."

"I doubt my father is in any condition to ask, if he continued drinking after I left him earlier."

Tyler tipped his head at her silent question.

"That's what I thought," she said grimly. "And I wouldn't give K.C. the satisfaction of the question. I know he's got something up his sleeve. I could see it in his eyes earlier, but I didn't think it was something like this."

"No, you thought it had something to do with your other secret," Tyler said, taking a wild guess.

She stiffened. "I don't have another secret. I wish you'd let that idea go. At any rate, I have enough to worry about besides you and your questions. I'm afraid your presence here is no longer going to make the top ten on my worry list."

He smiled. "I'm hurt. I thought I was at the top of your list."

Her returning smile was weak at best. "I have to talk to my father, but I really don't want to have that conversation."

"It's your best option, Kate."

"I suppose. To tell you the truth, I don't know how my mother got mixed up with either one of them. She was kind and honest, with tons of integrity, which is why this is so unbelievable. My father wasn't one to lean on, but my mom, she was rock solid. She knew right from wrong, and she always did the right thing."

"And she raised you to do the same." Tyler was beginning to understand how Kate had become so conflicted after her mother's death when she'd been left to temper her father's ambitions.

"My mom tried to raise me right. But I've let her down," she said with a sigh.

"I find that difficult to believe."

"I promised I would take care of my sisters and my father, that I would make sure the family stayed together, but I didn't do that."

He heard the regret in her voice, the blame, and he was moved by the torment in her eyes. He knew what that kind of guilt felt like and how it could eat away at your soul. He didn't want to see that happen to Kate.

"She asked me that last day," Kate continued, her voice somewhat dreamy as she recalled the memory. "I didn't know she was so close to the end. I guess a part of me still thought she'd get better. But she was so thin, and her hair was gone, just little wisps of reddish blond on the top of her bald head." Kate's mouth trembled.

"You don't have to tell me," he said quietly.

She gazed into his eyes with so much pain it almost hurt to look at her. "She took hold of my hand. She could barely lift her arm, but somehow she managed. I can still feel the pressure on my fingers. It was like she was trying to hang on to life through me. And I didn't want to let her go, but I didn't know what to do. She asked me to promise to keep the family together, to watch out for my dad, and to protect my younger sisters. She told me that I had to be the strong one. I had to take her place. And I said yes, I'd do it. She closed her eyes then and she let go." Kate stopped as a tight sob broke through her lips. "I'm sorry," she said quickly, struggling to regain her composure.

"It's okay." He put his arms around her and pulled her against his chest. "It's hard to be strong all the time."

"Sometimes I get tired," she admitted.

"I know. I understand." He stroked her back, hoping she would let herself lean on him for at least a moment.

"You do understand, don't you?" she said, looking up at him. "You're the strong one, too."

"Oldest-child syndrome."

"I want to keep my promise."

"I know you do. And you will. I'm sure of it."

She shook her head. "I wish I could be sure of it. I've already made so many mistakes, Tyler."

"Don't be so hard on yourself, Kate. You were a young girl when you made that promise to your mother. And maybe she shouldn't have asked you."

"It was the least I could do. She suffered so much at the end. I would have promised her anything to ease her mind." Kate took a deep breath, then stepped out of his arms. "Thanks for the shoulder to cry on."

"Anytime." He paused. "I mean that, Kate."

"Thanks. I guess I'll go home and forget about this until tomorrow. I need to talk to my father when he's sober. But even if he is sober—how will I know if he's lying? He's very good at it." She took a breath. "Caroline always tells me I'm the suspicious one, looking over my shoulder, suspecting the worst from people instead of the best. It's because I don't trust myself to know what's the truth and what's not."

"You should have more faith in your instincts."

"I wish it was that easy. Where my father is concerned, I'm often baffled. Even if he tells me the truth, will I believe it? Or will the doubts eat away at me? Will I have to live with something else I can't stand to live with?" She stopped abruptly, realizing what she'd said.

"Something else?" he queried.

"Nothing."

It was definitely something, he thought, as she averted her gaze. What was she having trouble living with? Having given up her baby to a stranger? His stomach churned. Was that what haunted her? But would she protect her own secret so ferociously? Or did the secret belong to someone else—someone she'd promised her mother to protect—Caroline or Ashley.

Or maybe he just wanted it to be one of them.

"I have to go," Kate said. "I shouldn't have come here and dumped all this on you."

"You needed to talk."

"And you were hoping I'd drop something juicy for you to bite into."

"I thought you were starting to trust me."

"I really can't let that happen."

He looked directly into her eyes. "I don't trust easily, either, Kate. My father lied endlessly to me, and I bought most of his sorry stories, I'm sad to say. But you live and you learn, and eventually you figure out who you can trust. You stop making those mistakes."

"Really? You think so? Because I just trusted you by telling you something I don't really want anyone else to know. Was that a mistake?"

He wanted to reassure her, but the words wouldn't come. If he and the McKennas ended up on opposite sides, he would choose his brother.

Disappointment flashed in her eyes. "Well, your silence is enlightening. Thanks for the chat. Good night." The door shut firmly behind her, and Tyler punched his fist against the wall with a muttered curse.

He wanted to help his brother and his niece, not hurt Kate. But she would be hurt as soon as she found out just how far his deception went.

Yanking his wallet out of his pants, he pulled out the photograph of Amelia and stared hard at it. Her sweet, innocent face, blond curls, and blue eyes reminded him of Kate. But Amelia wasn't Kate; she was a child who had already lost her mother and almost her father.

He had to stay strong. He had to protect Amelia. Kate could take care of herself.

"Is there anything I can help you with?" Kate asked a young woman browsing the bestseller rack early Monday morning.

"I'm looking for a good mystery for my father. He doesn't like the mystery to be too easy or the love scenes to be too graphic or for there to be too many female characters. He's a little on the picky side."

"At least he knows what he wants."

"Unfortunately, I don't, and his birthday is today. I'm running out of time."

Kate selected a book from the rack. "This is by Stuart Lawson. He writes about contemporary pirates on the high seas."

"Oh, he would love that," the young woman exclaimed. "He's an avid sailor. In fact, we're here because of the Castleton Invitational."

"I figured," Kate said with a smile. "Most everyone is." She walked behind the counter and rang up the sale, including a complimentary bookmark and store flyer. "We're having a local author book signing all day Sunday, if you're still in town. We have quite a few excellent writers who spend their winters or summers here on the island penning their latest bestsellers. There's a list on the flyer."

"Thanks, that sounds great. Thanks."

As the customer left, Kate glanced around the store, checking to see if anyone else needed assistance, but there were only a few people browsing the shelves. Most people were probably down by the water. Race week had officially begun an hour ago. Today's races were for twelve-foot Beetle Cats. Each day's races would feature a different class of boats. In between the races, the larger sailboats would also make practice runs before the big race around the island on Saturday. And every evening there would be parties and celebrations for the winners.

Race week brought in a tremendous number of tourists. The hotels, inns, and private cottages were booked solid. All the local businesses, including her bookstore, benefitted from the influx of summer money, as they called it.

Kate walked over to the door and stepped onto the sidewalk in front of the store. It was a bright, sunny day, and from her vantage point she could see dozens of colorful sails out on the water. She felt a slight pang at the sight of all those sails, and she didn't understand why. She didn't want to be out there. So why did she feel strangely wistful? Why did the light breeze brushing against her face make her yearn for something when she'd thought she was content with her life? Her father had always said it was impossible to get the sea out of your soul. Maybe he was right.

The door to her bookstore opened behind her, and her assistant, Theresa, stepped out. "What are you looking at?"

"The boats, Kate said, giving her sweater a quick zip as the breeze picked up.

"Do you miss sailing?"

"I never thought I did. But I must admit I have a silly urge to wander down to the water to see who wins."

"So go. Maybe you'll run into that cute reporter again."

Lord, she hoped not. She still couldn't believe she'd confided in Tyler. She should have her head examined. Anyone else would have been a better choice. Although she didn't want either Caroline or Ashley to hear about David's theory until she had a chance to figure it out for herself.

"Kate," Theresa said. "Did you hear me?"

"Something about a cute reporter. But, cute or not, I'm not getting involved with a guy who's only in town for a few days, another week at the most."

"You could just have some fun. Not every relationship has to be serious."

"I'm not in a relationship with anyone, especially him."

"Whatever you say. Why don't you go down to the water, take a break. It's slow right now. I can handle things on my own."

Kate hesitated, knowing it would be better to stay in the store, to concentrate on work, but something was drawing her to the sea, the call of the wind, her father would have said. And she couldn't resist. She walked around to the back of her store and pulled out her bicycle.

It was mid-morning, but Ashley was probably still asleep, Sean thought when he woke up stiff and disoriented from a night spent on her hard couch. Stretching, he swung his feet to the ground and stood up. He only wanted to check on her, he told himself, as he walked toward her bedroom. The door was open, and all was quiet. He paused in the doorway, catching sight of her in bed.

Lord, she was pretty. Her long blond hair spread across the covers like it had been prearranged for a photo session. She wasn't wearing anything sexy; a long-sleeve, gray knit T-shirt could be seen where the covers had slipped off. Still, she was gorgeous, her face like one of the porcelain dolls his mother collected, not a blemish or a wrinkle marring her skin. She looked like an angel.

A deep ache centered in his gut. He wanted her so much it was painful just to look at her. It had always been this way. He couldn't remember a time when he hadn't been fascinated by her, when he hadn't wanted to spend every minute of every day talking to her or looking at her.

It had all started out so innocently. They'd met in kindergarten. He could still remember sitting at her table, watching her color. She'd always liked to color. And she'd been so careful to stay between the lines.

As they grew up, their friendship deepened, despite the fact that they had different personalities. He'd always been active, energized, unable to sit anywhere for very long. Ashley could sit for hours if she had a good book or something to draw on. The rest of the world could be spinning around her in utter chaos, but there was always a peacefulness about her. Maybe it was that peacefulness that had called to him. With Ashley he could relax, he could be himself. He lost some of the nervous energy that made it impossible for him to stay on track.

When she'd gone to sea with her dad and sisters, he'd felt like someone had cut off his right arm. He hadn't realized until that moment that he was in love with her. Oh, sure, they were only fifteen and no one thought it was anything more than a crush or an infatuation, but he'd always known it was more. He'd dated other girls while she was away, but no one had ever made him feel the way she did. And he'd thought she'd felt the same.

He frowned, remembering her recent confession. She had kissed his brother. That was something he hadn't known, something he wished he didn't know now. When had that happened? And why?

It didn't make sense. Jeremy had loved Kate. He wouldn't have fooled around with Ashley. There must have been something else going on. Maybe someone had had too much to drink or something.

Oh, hell, it didn't matter now anyway, he thought, running a hand through his hair. It had been eight years. And he wasn't really all that interested in the past; he was more concerned with the present. He'd held Ashley in his arms last night. She'd turned to him for comfort, and even though he still didn't know exactly what had gotten her so upset, he'd been grateful that whatever it was had driven her back into his arms.

He'd tried to stay away. He'd tried to make a new life for himself. He'd dated every kind of girl he could find. A few had made him laugh. A couple had made him horny. But none had really gotten under his skin the way Ashley had.

Shaking his head, Sean moved farther into the room, wondering if he should wake Ashley or just go. But he didn't want to go. He wanted to talk to her. He wanted her to trust him with whatever was bothering her. He hadn't realized how messed up she was until last night. He'd known there was something going on with her and the water, but there was obviously more that was wrong, and he wanted to know what it was. She'd always been cautious but never so afraid, so fragile. He wanted to help her. He wanted to take care of her. He wanted her to lean on him the way she'd once done.

He sat down on the bed beside her. Ashley moved slightly, murmuring something in her sleep. He put a hand on her shoulder. Her eyes flew open. Startled by his presence, she hit her head on the headboard as she hastened to sit up.

"Easy there," Sean said. "Everything's cool."

She tucked her hair behind her ear in a self- conscious gesture as she came fully awake. "What time is it?"

"Almost eleven. We both slept in."

"You stayed all night? I thought you'd left."

"I slept on the couch. I didn't want to leave you alone in case you decided to take a midnight sail to the mainland.

She flushed, embarrassment in her eyes. "I'm sorry I was such a basket case last night. You must think I'm nuts."

"I think something is bothering you. Would you tell me what it is?"

She looked at him with her heart in her eyes, and he saw the indecision there, the hesitancy. She wanted to talk, but something was stopping her.

"Is it your family? One of your sisters? Your father?" he prodded.

Ashley shook her head. "I'm all right. You should go now."

"You know the reason I came here last night was to talk to you about Jeremy," he said, changing the subject.

She pulled the sheet up over her chest, twisting the material with her fingers. "Right."

"Just tell me one thing. Did you break up with me eight years ago because of this kiss between you and my brother?"

"Not exactly."

"So that wasn't the reason? Then, just out of curiosity, why do you think I would care about a kiss that happened eight years ago, even if it was my brother? Or was it just one more brick to throw at my head to remind me that you never wanted me as much as I wanted you?" He hated to think she would deliberately hurt him like that, but he couldn't discount the possibility.

"No, I didn't say it to hurt you, Sean."

"Then why say it at all? What possible difference could it make now?"

"Maybe I just wanted you to see me for who I really am."

He stared at her for a long moment, absorbing the pain in her eyes. "Do you even know who you are, Ash?"

"I know I'm not that girl you put on a pedestal all those years ago. I've made a lot of mistakes over the years. Kissing Jeremy was just one example. I betrayed you. I betrayed my sister. And I did it out of spite and annoyance and loneliness, and I don't know what else. I hated that race, Sean. It turned my family inside out. My father became this monster competitor, and Kate and Caroline and I got caught up in it, too. When the storms came that summer, it was only a reflection of how messed up I felt inside." She paused. "I'd get this feeling in my body, like claustrophobia. The walls would close in on me. I couldn't focus. The world was spinning, and the air was too thick to breathe. I'd do anything to stop the feeling."

"And Jeremy was part of that anything?" Sean saw the apology in her eyes even before he heard the words.

"Yes."

"Did it ever go further than a kiss?"

"No, absolutely not."

He nodded, insanely relieved. It would have been hard to accept Ashley and Jeremy together under any circumstances, even though it had happened years ago. "So, what's next, Ash? What else do you have to tell me?"

"N-nothing," she stuttered. "That's it."

He didn't believe her, but maybe there had been enough revelations for one morning. "Why don't you get dressed and come with me today?"

"With you where?"

"Wherever we want to go."

She smiled, and all the years, all the anger, all the silence faded away. "You always used to say that."

"Then we'd hop on our bikes and take off down the hill, remember?"

"Of course I remember. I beat you down the hill every single time," she boasted.

"That's because your foot never touched the brake. I can still see your hair flying out behind you."

Her smile turned sad. "God, Sean, where did that girl go?"

"I don't know, but maybe we can find her again. Do you want to try?"

"More than you know."

CHAPTER THIRTEEN

It was a couple of miles to Miramar Point, but Kate made quick time on her bike, finding a spot on a bluff overlooking the Sound that gave her an excellent view of the sailboats competing below.

There were a few other locals with binoculars in hand. One of those locals looked distinctly familiar, wearing a bright red sweater that Kate recognized as the one Caroline had borrowed a month ago from her and never returned. Her sister sat cross-legged on the ground, her attention fixed on the water below. Kate flopped down next to her. "Hey," she said.

Caroline looked at her with surprise. "Kate. You're the last person I expected to see up here."

"The call of the wind," she said with a wry smile.

"You, too? I thought you were immune."

"Not when the breeze picks up. I'm glad you're here. I wanted to talk to you about K.C. and Dad. You took off so fast yesterday I didn't have a chance."

"Did you find out why K.C. bought the boat?"

"No. But I did find out that Dad is going to skipper the Summer Seas. He wants to race against K.C. And here's the kicker—Dad wants us to be his crew. He wants to make a bet on the race with K.C., and if we win, we get the Moon Dancer back."

"Whoa!" Caroline put up her hand. "Did you just say Dad is racing for the Moon Dancer, and he wants us to help?"

"I did. And the worst thing is that he was actually sober when he said it." Kate gazed at the water, but she wasn't seeing the boats, she was seeing the gleam in her father's eye when he'd made his announcement. He'd looked alive, happy, energized—and terribly angry when she hadn't supported the idea. She didn't want to feel guilty at sticking a pin in his happy balloon, but, dammit, she'd changed her life once for him, and she didn't want to do it again.

"It's not completely crazy," Caroline said slowly. "I hate to see someone else sailing our boat. It doesn't feel right."

She frowned at her sister's answer. "Caroline. Snap out of it. Dad isn't fit enough to race. He's old, and he's drunk half the time."

"He still exercises, sometimes," Caroline said defensively.

"Don't be ridiculous. Walking down to the Oyster Bar doesn't count as exercise, nor does stumbling home."

"Just because I have a different opinion than you doesn't mean I'm wrong."

"What is your opinion, exactly?"

"That maybe encouraging Dad to sail again isn't such a bad idea."

"We're not talking about sailing; we're talking about racing. They're two different things, and you know it."

"I know he's not happy, Kate. He hasn't been for a long time. You know what frustrates me the most? I can ask him out to dinner or stop by for a chat, and we always start talking about you. No matter where the conversation begins, it always ends with you, the one who doesn't respect him, the one who doesn't like him, who treats him like a child."

"I don't do that. Or, if I do, it's because he acts like a child."

"The point is, Kate, you're the one whose respect and friendship he wants the most. I could tell him it's fine for him to race. I could even join him. But he wouldn't be happy if you weren't there, too. You're the one. You're it."

"Caroline, I don't think any of that is the point."

"Well, you wouldn't." Caroline took off her sweater. "It's getting warm. So much for the breeze. It seems to have died down as fast as it came up. There will be a lot of disappointed sailors down there."

Kate glanced at her sister, about to say she was more concerned about her father's disappointment, when she was struck by the sight of several dark purple bruises along Caroline's left arm. "What happened to you?" she asked with concern.

Caroline followed her gaze. "Oh, I just banged my arm on something. It's nothing."

"It doesn't look like nothing." Kate didn't like the way Caroline averted her eyes. "Did someone hurt you?"

"I'm fine."

"Was it Mike Stanaway?"

"No." Caroline slipped the sweater over her shoulders, hiding the bruises, but the damage was done.

"Then who?"

"It wasn't a *who*. It was a door. I just banged my arm, that's all. Leave it alone."

"I think I've been leaving you alone for too long. Caroline, you have to tell me if you're in trouble."

"Would you stop being the big sister and let me be an adult?"

"Not when I see that someone has hurt you or that you've hurt yourself. I want to help. Let me help," Kate said in frustration.

"I don't need your help. I've got it under control."

"You call dating an ex-con under control? I heard that Mike hit his wife. That's why she left him."

"That's not why she left," Caroline said quickly. "But, I told you before, Mike didn't hurt me, and I'm not dating him. So drop it."

Kate didn't want to drop it, but pushing Caroline wasn't getting her anywhere. Maybe she'd have a talk with Mike Stanaway instead.

"Tell me more about Dad and this race," Caroline said. "He really gets to pick his own crew? I'm surprised Rick Beardsley doesn't want more say in it."

"That's what Dad said."

"Is Dad going to race to San Francisco and on to Hawaii, or just around the island on Saturday?"

"I didn't even ask him that." The thought had never occurred to her. Was her father leaving Castleton for good?

"So Dad could be gone in a week. That will be weird."

It would be strange without their dad in town. Even though he was often a nuisance, he was still their father, still their checkpoint, still the only parent they had left. "We have to stop him from doing this, Caroline. We both know what a maniac he can be. There are no rules out on the sea, no sense of what's right or wrong, especially where Dad is concerned. For his own protection, we need to take a stand, all of us together. Are you willing to say no to him? That's what I need to know."

"I'm not sure. Maybe if I race with him..." Her voice drifted away.

"He'll like you better? Is that what you were going to say?" she challenged, seeing the truth in her sister's eyes. "Dad loves you, Caroline. I don't know where you got the idea that he doesn't. You're his baby, his princess."

"I'm the one who disappoints him the most. It's okay, Kate. I get it. I've gotten it for a long time. What you don't get is that we can't outrun the past. It's catching up. Every day it's getting closer. Don't you feel it?"

Kate did feel it. Even now she had goose bumps running down her arms. "We set our course a long time ago. We have to stick with it. No uncharted waters, remember?"

"Dad will race no matter what we say."

"We have to try to talk him out of it, Caroline."

"Fine. If you want me to go with you to talk to him, I will."

"Thank you."

For a moment they sat in quiet, looking out at the boats. Then Kate felt Caroline stiffen next to her. "What?" she asked.

Caroline pointed to the water below. "There she is."

Kate squinted against the bright sunlight. Sure enough, there was the familiar bright blue sail with a white dove soaring toward the sky.

"The Moon Dancer," she breathed. "K.C. can't be using the same sails, the same colors. He can't be."

"They wouldn't be in good enough condition," Caroline agreed. "Unless he had them copied."

"Why would he do that? Mom designed those sails. She was so proud of them being one of a kind."

"I don't know why he's doing anything. I'm the younger one, remember? Usually the last to know. And I never had much contact with K.C. when we were kids, just his annoying son."

"You didn't like David?"

"Hell, no. He was an annoying, irritating asshole most of the time."

"I don't remember him being around much."

"That's because you were older. I was the one who got stuck with him when he came to visit. He didn't like us. He was jealous of his dad spending time with us. I remember one time when K.C. brought you one of those snow globes. David was so pissed off he tried to break it when you weren't looking. But I stopped him. So you can thank me now."

"Why didn't you tell me then?" Kate asked curiously.

"I don't remember why. Probably because I wasn't supposed to be in your room."

Kate thought about Caroline's words. They certainly painted David as a person with a grudge—a big enough grudge to make up a lie about K.C. being her real father? Or had he wanted to break her snow globe because even then he'd sensed she was more important to his father than he was? She did not want to believe that was true, but she couldn't stop wondering now that David had put the thought into her head.

"Don't you miss it just a little?" Caroline waved her hand toward the Moon Dancer streaking proudly across the water. "We should be on that boat. She's ours. She doesn't belong with K.C. and his nasty little son."

Kate had to admit it was difficult to watch their boat under someone else's hands. Especially someone who had made their life difficult during their very long race around the world.

Caroline turned to her with the same gleam in her eye that their father had had, and Kate felt every muscle in her body tighten.

"Don't say it," Kate warned. But Caroline wasn't listening.

"I think we should do it, Kate. We should help Dad win her back."

———

Tyler climbed on board the small boat that several people had mentioned belonged to Duncan McKenna. "Hello," he called, hoping he was in the right place. The boat swayed slightly beneath him. It was an odd feeling. He couldn't remember the last time he'd been on the water. His life for the past few years had been airplanes, fast cars, and maybe a train or two in Europe. Boats were foreign to him. Especially sailboats.

He couldn't imagine waiting for the wind to change before you could move. He needed control, a good solid engine that could take him where he wanted to go, wind or no wind.

"Hello, there," he called again. He jogged down the stairs and peered into the empty cabin. The interior was small, with an unmade bunk in one corner, newspapers, magazines, and clothes strewn about. The air was filled with the smell of cigarettes and booze, but there was no sign of Duncan McKenna. Damn. He'd hoped Duncan was still sleeping off what surely must have been a hangover from the night before.

Walking back up the stairs to the deck, he looked around, noting the numerous empty boat slips. Apparently there was some sort of a race going on today.

He sighed, wondering what to do next. He'd already learned a few more details about the McKenna sisters by spending some time at the local bars and cafes. The McKennas were hometown heroes, and people loved to talk about them. He'd heard that Ashley had suffered a collapse several months after returning home from the race, stress and malnutrition, allegedly. But combine that collapse with the anti-anxiety medication he'd seen in her purse, and he could probably make a case for some type of mental breakdown. And then there was Caroline, who'd been picked up a few times for underage drinking and seemed to be a frequent visitor to the bar scene, along with her father.

Which brought him to Duncan, the one who had set the private adoption into motion.

If only Mark had done things the right way, they wouldn't be in this mess now. But Mark and his wife Susan had been desperate for a child, having tried for several years, and they just hadn't wanted to wait a second longer. When the opportunity had presented itself, they'd put a second mortgage on their house and bought themselves a birth certificate and an instant family.

It wasn't completely legal, but, then again, they hadn't stolen the baby. She'd been given up willingly, according to everyone involved. Unfortunately, there were no letters or signed documents to support that assumption. Everything had been done as anonymously as possible. Duncan hadn't wanted anyone to know about the baby. And Mark and Susan hadn't dared to ask any questions that would prevent the child from becoming theirs. For eight years it had all gone smoothly, until three weeks ago when it became clear that one of the McKenna sisters had hired herself an attorney to find her long lost baby.

He wondered now what had triggered that move. What had happened three weeks ago? Maybe that's where he should be looking, instead of so far in the past.

Tyler turned his head as he heard a man singing about beer, broads, and a good boat. It was Duncan—Duncan and a friend. Duncan had one arm flung around the other guy's shoulders, and they staggered slightly as they came down the docks. Two old salts, Tyler thought, for surely there was no better description for the weather-beaten, sunburned men who lived to sail and sailed to live.

"And she's all mine," Duncan wailed.

"All mine," the other man harmonized in an off-key, drunken voice.

Duncan stopped abruptly when he saw Tyler on his boat. "Well, now, who's come to visit but my favorite reporter. Pete, have you met Taylor?"

"Tyler," he corrected.

Duncan pointed to him. "That's right, Tyler. I remember. I bet you think I'm drunk, don't you? Now, Pete here, he's drunk, aren't you, Pete?"

The other man could have been forty or sixty, it was impossible to tell, but he was definitely not sober.

"Pete is my neighbor," Duncan said, dragging Pete down the dock toward the boat next to his. "Help me get him onboard, would you?"

Tyler hopped onto the dock and helped get Pete onto his boat and down the stairs to a cabin very similar to Duncan's. Tyler couldn't help wondering how many good old boys were living on sailboats in the harbor.

"You okay, Pete?" Duncan asked. Pete rolled over on his bunk with a snore. "He's okay."

"What about you?" Tyler asked, as he followed Duncan back up the stairs. He was relieved to see that Duncan walked a straight line fairly easily.

"I'm just dandy," Duncan said, hopping off the boat with a spry step. "I ran into Pete on my way back from a meeting. Couldn't let him wander down here on his own. He's a sad case these days. Lost his wife a few months back and hasn't been the same since."

"I guess you know how that feels."

"That I do, son, that I do," Duncan said with a sigh. "When my Nora died, she about took me with her. I didn't think I could bear to see the sun come up without her by my side."

Tyler was touched by the depth of emotion in Duncan's voice. He sounded very much like a man who had loved his wife deeply—a faithful, loving husband. But had Nora been a faithful, loving wife? "What was she like?" he asked. "Your wife, Nora."

Duncan lifted his face to the sun. "Close your eyes," he said.

"What?"

"Close your eyes," Duncan repeated.

Tyler hesitated, then closed his eyes, wondering what was supposed to happen.

"Feel the heat on your face?" Duncan asked.

Now that he mentioned it, yes. "Sure." There was a warmth on his skin, a light behind his lids, the scent of summer in his nostrils. His senses were heightened with his eyes closed.

"That's what she did for me," Duncan murmured. "She made me feel everything more intensely than I'd ever felt it before."

Tyler opened his eyes and saw Duncan wipe a tear from his cheek, a dramatic, emotional gesture for a crusty, tough old man but a seemingly genuine one. Apparently there was more to the man than he'd first realized. Maybe that's why Kate stuck by him the way she did.

"You coming aboard?" Duncan asked as he climbed onto his boat.

"I would like to speak to you."

"I don't have much time. I've got a race to plan. Things are finally turning around for me."

Tyler could see that. Duncan looked like a different man today—a light in his eyes, an energy in his step. "Have your daughters changed their minds about racing with you?"

"Not yet, but they will. Kate is the stubborn one. Where she goes, the other girls follow. But she'll change her mind. When push comes to shove, she always chooses family."

Duncan sounded confident. Based on past experience? Or just a hopeful wish?

"Why did you sell your boat in the first place?" Tyler asked.

"I needed the cash. And I wanted to make sure the girls had money to live on."

Tyler nodded. "I'd love to see what it's like to sail around the islands. I was wondering if you could take me out sometime."

"You know anything about sailing?"

"Not a damn thing."

Duncan laughed. "No bullshit, huh? I like that. But I can't let you race with me—too much at stake."

"I understand."

"I can take you out on this boat, though. Maybe tomorrow. Come by the Oyster Bar later and we'll talk."

"Great. I'll look forward to it." As Tyler got off the boat, he saw Kate and Caroline making their way down the dock. Kate hesitated when she saw him, then continued forward.

"Tyler," Kate said coolly, obviously not happy to see him with her father. "What are you doing here?"

"Talking to your dad."

Her frown deepened. "Well, I hope you're done, because Caroline and I need to speak to our father."

"He's all yours."

"If you've come to sign on for the race, climb aboard and we'll talk," Duncan said. "Otherwise, I have things to do."

Duncan stood straight and tall, his position on the boat setting him above them. With his shoulders squared and his jaw firm, he appeared very much the master of his destiny, and perhaps theirs as well, Tyler thought, casting a sideways glance at Kate and Caroline.

"We've come to talk you out of this crazy idea," Kate said.

Wrong choice of words, Tyler wanted to tell her, but he didn't have time.

"It's not crazy, and it's not an idea," Duncan snapped. "It's a fact. I'm sailing the Summer Seas. I'm going to win back our boat. I'd like you two to help me. We lost her together. We should get her back together."

"We didn't lose her; we sold her," Kate replied.

"Actually, you two sold her," Caroline interjected. "I don't think I had a say in the matter."

"Caroline, you're not helping," Kate grumbled.

"And you don't speak for me," Caroline retorted. She turned to her father. "Daddy, why is K.C. racing our boat?"

"To show us up, that's why. He wants revenge. And this is his way of getting it. But he won't succeed if we stick together. I need your help. We're family."

Tyler watched Kate's reaction as Duncan played the family card. He could see the indecision in her eyes. She was as loyal as they came. Caroline also watched Kate. Despite Caroline's brashness and bravado, she seemed willing to give Kate the lead.

"We made a promise to one another to move on with our lives. This is moving back, not forward," Kate said.

"I don't see it that way," Duncan replied.

"There is no other way to see it."

"I want the Moon Dancer back. And I'm going to get it, with or without you." And with those words, Duncan disappeared into his cabin.

"Great job, Kate," Caroline said as she blew out a large bubble of pink gum that snapped against her lips.

"What did you want me to do?"

"Not call him crazy for one."

"Racing is crazy."

"You used to love it. Kate was the bravest one of all," Caroline added for Tyler's benefit. "Utterly fearless. I admired her so much."

"I'm still here, Caroline," Kate said with annoyance.

"Not the person you were. That person left a long time ago. I kind of miss her." She paused. "I'll see you around, Kate, and probably you, too, Tyler."

Kate sighed as Caroline left.

"Is she right? Were you once fearless, Kate?" Tyler asked.

"Not fearless, stupid. I believed in the wrong people and the wrong things. Then I grew up. I wish I could say the same for the rest of my family, but you might as well call my father Peter Pan, because he is never going to leave Never Never Land."

Tyler smiled. "I think you're right."

"What are you doing here, anyway? Digging for more dirt?" she asked.

"Don't worry. Your father didn't tell me the location of the family jewels."

"What did he tell you?"

"That I could sail with him tomorrow."

Her jaw dropped in surprised. "What?"

"He said he'd take me out on his boat tomorrow so I could see first-hand what it feels like to sail."

"I'd advise against it."

"I'm sure you would. But why, exactly?"

"Because my father is reckless and unreliable."

"I can't imagine someone would put him in charge of their boat if he didn't have some skill."

"You didn't say anything to my father about K.C., did you?" she asked, looking past him toward her father's boat. "About the possibility that my mother and K.C. had some sort of relationship?"

"No. That's up to you."

"It would make sense—why they started to hate each other," she murmured.

"So you believe it now?"

"I don't know, but I couldn't stop thinking about it last night."

"Just ask him, Kate. Go in there and ask him. What do you have to lose?"

She stared back at him. "Everything. My whole identity, that's what. And he's already angry with me. I don't think it's a good time." She spun on her heel and started walking down the dock.

"Where are you going now?" Tyler asked as he followed her.

"Back to work, I guess."

Her halfhearted reply gave him hope. "I have a better idea."

"I doubt that."

He put his hand on her shoulder, stopping her in her tracks. "It's a beautiful day. How about a picnic on the beach?"

"A picnic on the beach?" she echoed, as if she'd never heard the words before.

"You know, wicker basket, fried chicken, potato salad, blanket, maybe a little wine. I was reading a brochure I found in my hotel room about a beach with a waterfall. I'd like to see it."

She cleared her throat. "I don't think so. Things didn't go very well yesterday when we spent time together."

"Today is another day."

"I don't know, Tyler. There's no point."

"Does there always have to be a point?" he challenged.

"For you, I would think so. You came here for a reason, to write an article. I've already told you I'm not going to help in that regard, so I'm not quite sure why you're still hanging around."

He considered her point. It was something he'd spent a lot of time thinking about, in fact. The suggestion of an article had been the easiest way to get into the McKenna family, but it hadn't played out the way he and Mark had intended. Maybe it was time to change the plan.

"I've actually decided to do as you originally suggested."

"Which is what?" she asked, surprise in her voice.

"Talk to some of the other sailors, find some interesting anecdotes, come up with another story angle." It wasn't completely a lie. He had never actually intended to write an article, only to find out who was Amelia's mother.

"If that's true, then you should be picnicking with someone else."

"Maybe I just want to spend time with you," he said with a smile. "Come on, say yes. It's just a picnic."

Kate didn't answer for a moment, a battle going on in her eyes. Then she said, "You better put together the best picnic basket I've ever seen, which will definitely include potato salad, some kind of fancy Brie cheese, and chocolate. Got it?"

"I got it."

"I need to stop in at the store."

"I'll meet you back there in twenty minutes." He didn't want to give her too much time or she'd surely change her mind.

"I'm fairly sure this is a mistake," Kate said.

"Well, if it is, it will be delicious." Whistling, he headed down the street in search of a delicatessen.

CHAPTER FOURTEEN

"YOUR CHARIOT AWAITS," Tyler said a half hour later as he pulled Kate out of her bookstore and pointed his hand toward the street where he'd rented two bicycles. The picnic basket was strapped somewhat precariously on the back of a sleek, fifteen-speed racer. Tyler supposed he could have chosen something more modest, but, hell, he was a guy, and certain macho tendencies couldn't be denied.

Kate raised an eyebrow when she saw her matching bike. "Are we riding in the Tour de France or pedaling around the island?"

"Too much?"

"You think? These have to be the most expensive rental bikes I've ever seen."

"Probably, but they were also the coolest."

She walked over to the bicycles. "I know all about boys and their toys. Bikes, boats, cars—it's all the same where men are concerned. They want the fastest, the biggest, the best."

"And what do girls want? Surely big and best is a requirement at times."

She smiled. "But speed isn't always a plus. Some things are meant to be enjoyed more slowly."

"I absolutely agree."

"Well." She cleared her throat, a faint blush coloring her cheeks. "I do have my own bike but it pales in comparison to this one."

"It's already paid for, so let's go. You can lead."

"Fine. I just hope you can keep up."

"Don't worry. I have no intention of losing you." He got on his bike and followed her down the street.

Kate rode with a purpose; no meandering, no stopping and looking at the view. She zigged and zagged through the downtown village, cruised along the wharf, then led him through a residential area before turning back toward the water. It was a beautiful summer day, the kind of day Tyler hadn't stopped to enjoy in years.

How long had it been since he'd ridden a bike that wasn't stationary in some twenty-four-hour gym? He couldn't remember. How long had it been since he'd actually stopped and looked at the scenery? Years, probably.

Since that day, more than twenty years ago, when his father had picked him up from school, he'd been on the move, never calling one place home, never making more than casual friends, never letting himself get attached to any place, any person. He supposed he could have stopped sometime in the past fifteen years and made a home for himself, bought some land, put down roots, but the concept was foreign to him. It was easier to go on living the way he'd grown up, reporting on life, watching other people live instead of living himself.

Shit! Way too heavy thoughts for a simple bike ride. What the hell was the matter with him? He didn't psychoanalyze his life. He didn't have the time, the patience or the desire. He was what he was. He didn't need to change. It was just this decadent lazy island lifestyle that made him think of change.

Normal people didn't ride bikes and have picnics on Monday afternoons unless they were on vacation. He wasn't on vacation. He was on a mission, a mission he did not intend to fail. He simply had to get Kate relaxed, catch her off guard and go in for the kill. He did not intend to end this day without a solid lead or maybe, if he was lucky, a definitive answer.

They stopped about fifteen minutes later, walking their bikes over a rough patch of grass that led down to a sandy, secluded beach.

"Hey, where's the waterfall?" he asked, looking around.

Kate pointed to a small stream of water dripping down between two rocks on the far side of the beach.

"'That's it? I'm not impressed."

"It's low tide. When the larger waves hit the other side of those rocks is when you get the waterfall. Disappointed?"

Actually, he wasn't disappointed at all. He liked the intimate atmosphere. The beach was almost deserted—a mother and her toddler at the water's edge, a couple on a blanket down by the rocks and a man throwing a stick to his dog. "Where is everybody? Isn't it summer?"

"They're watching the boats. You can't see them from here."

"Do you want to go somewhere else?"

"No, I like this beach. It's small and quiet, peaceful. We get so many tourists nowadays. I miss the years when nobody came to Castleton."

"That wouldn't be good for your business." He unstrapped the picnic basket and set it down on the ground. "Damn. I forgot a blanket."

"We'll survive." Kate plopped down on the sand and took off her tennis shoes, running her toes in the fine sand. "This is nice."

Nice wasn't the right word. Sexy was. He loved the flash of hot pink polish on her toes; it seemed at odds with her very practical personality and hinted at her passionate side, a side he wanted to see more of. "What is this love affair you have with dirt?" he asked as he knelt down on the ground next to her.

Kate laughed. "I don't know. I just like the feel of the sand. Why don't you take your shoes off?"

"I don't think so."

"Why not? Is something wrong with your feet?"

"No, there's nothing wrong with my feet."

"Then let's see 'em."

"Fine. But if I'm taking off something, so are you."

"I already took off my shoes."

He grinned at her. "I wasn't talking about your shoes."

She shook her head. "You have a one-track mind."

"Well, I am a man."

"So I noticed," she muttered.

"Good."

"Stop flirting and settle down. Get comfortable. Take off your shoes."

Shoes again. He stretched out on the ground and slipped off his tennis shoes. His white socks followed. "Are you happy now?"

"Not even an extra toe. I'm disappointed."

He flopped down on one side, letting the sand trickle through his fingers. "It's cool," he said. "Moist. Does the tide cover the sand completely when it comes in?"

"Only with a storm."

"No chance of that today. Not a cloud in sight."

"A perfect day," she agreed, and for a moment they both watched the water lap against the protected beach in small, rippling currents. "It's amazing how fast it can change, though. One minute there's nothing but blue sky, and the next minute it's totally black and threatening."

"You're remembering, aren't you?" he said after a moment, watching the play of emotions across her face. "Some day in particular?"

She didn't answer for a moment. "Yes."

"It's a bad memory. It makes you sad."

"How do you know that?" she asked, turning to look at him.

"The shadows in your eyes, the way your voice drops down a notch when you talk about the sea." He reached out and stroked the side of her cheek. "Your mouth draws into a grim line as if whatever you're going to say is so distasteful you can barely spit it out."

"You're very observant."

"That's how I make my living."

She caught his wrist and pulled his hand away from her face, but she didn't let go. Instead, she interlaced her fingers with his. "You have strong, capable hands. I like that about you."

"I'm glad there's something you like about me, but I think you're changing the subject. We were talking about storms."

She looked away from him at the water, at the horizon, at the past —he wasn't quite sure what she was seeing. He just knew that her fingers had tightened around his.

"I was washed overboard during the storm," she said finally.

"You were?" He was shocked. "I never heard that. I don't remember reading anything about it."

"My father pulled me back in. There was no official rescue or anything."

"So no need for a report," he said slowly, his mind wrestling with the implications.

"I wasn't the first, the last or the only person to go overboard during that race. It actually happened fairly frequently."

"I thought you wore safety harnesses."

"We did, but I had taken mine off for a minute. It was stupid," she continued rapidly. "A mistake. Anyway, it took me a long time to forget the feeling of water rushing over my head."

Tyler sensed there were still pieces of the story that were missing. But at least she was talking. "That must have been terrifying, Kate."

She tilted her head as she considered his words. "I was dazed at first. I wasn't sure if I was dreaming. It was an odd feeling. Was the boat underwater, or was I? Then I saw the boat drifting away from me. That's when the fear hit. The waves were so high it would completely disappear from my view. I tried to swim, but I got disoriented." She paused, drawing in a long breath and slowly letting it out. He could see the fear in her eyes and knew that her words had taken her back to that place. He was almost sorry he'd asked. "Then my dad managed to get a line out to me, and he pulled me in. He saved my life."

"Is that why you're still saving his?"

She met his gaze, and the truth passed between them. "I guess I am trying to do that. It might be a lost cause, though. I keep throwing lines to him, but he doesn't grab on to them. He doesn't want me to pull him in."

"Maybe he needs to rescue himself."

"Maybe." She drew in a breath and slowly let it out. "Well, this conversation has gotten heavy. How about some food?"

"If you let go of my hand, I might get you some. That is, once the blood starts flowing back to my fingers," he said, flexing his hand as she let go.

"I'm sorry. I didn't realize. So, what's for lunch?"

"Everything you said. Fried chicken, potato salad, Brie, wine and chocolate." He sat up, opened the basket, and began pulling out containers.

"Very good, but I don't think I said wine. I'm not a drinker. My dad drove that desire right out of my head."

"Unlike your baby sister."

"What do you mean?" she asked sharply. "Caroline likes to party, but she's not out of control or anything."

"Sorry. I guess I read her wrong." But he wondered if Kate wasn't protesting a little too much.

"You did read her wrong. I'd know if Caroline had a problem." She paused, worry in her eyes. "I would know, don't you think?"

"You know your sister better than I do."

"Exactly. I'll take one of those mineral waters."

He handed her a bottle of Crystal Geyser. "I'm not a drinker myself," he said. "I like to keep my wits about me. Stay in control. Part of that oldest-child syndrome, I think. Always be the responsible one."

"Is your brother irresponsible?" she asked.

How did he answer that one? And why had he even mentioned his brother? Mark was a dangerous subject. Then again, Tyler wondered if he could gain her sympathy by telling her about the terrible tragedy that had befallen his brother. But if he told her anything, she might one day use it as ammunition against Mark. He couldn't take that chance. "He's more impulsive than I am," he said finally. "Now, what do you want to eat?"

Kate pulled off her sweater and spread it out between them. "We can put the food on this."

"Are you sure? It might get dirty."

"I like dirt, remember? And I have a washing machine."

"You're a very low-maintenance woman, aren't you?"

"I'm used to taking care of myself."

"And other people, too—your sisters, your father, your friends, your customers. Don't you ever get tired?"

"Even if I did, I haven't seen any fairy godmothers hovering about ready to turn my pumpkin into a carriage."

He smiled, liking her wit, her sense of humor, her lack of pretension. "What about handsome princes?"

"Not a one in sight."

"Are you sure about that?"

"You're not suggesting you have one of my glass slippers?" she teased.

He picked up her abandoned tennis shoe. "Will this do?"

"I'm afraid not. There are several dozen women who could wear that shoe and do. It's not one of a kind."

"But you are," he said impulsively, leaning over and kissing her on the lips. Her mouth was cool, moist from the water she'd been sipping. He wanted to linger, wanted to warm those lips, taste her more deeply, but she was already pulling away.

"Why did you do that?" she asked.

"I wanted to," he said simply.

"You make it all seem so easy, the flirting, the kissing. It's second nature to you, isn't it?"

He saw the question in her eyes, heard the hint of insecurity in her voice. "Maybe you just make it harder than it has to be."

She gave him an odd look. "Jeremy used to say the same thing. He thought I worried too much, thought too long, planned too hard." She shrugged. "But that's just me. I can't help it."

"You don't have to change—not as long as you're happy with who you are."

"For the most part, I am. Not that I don't have my faults, and I certainly haven't lived an error-free life, but I try hard. Does that count?"

"Enough to get you a chicken leg." He handed her a drumstick.

"Hmm. This looks good. Jack's Deli?"

"I heard it was the best."

"You heard right." She took a bite and sighed as if she'd just tasted ambrosia. He loved watching her lick her fingers in between bites. Made him want to lean over and take a taste himself.

"You're staring," she said. "I hate it when people watch me eat."

He smiled at that. "It doesn't seem to be stopping you."

She took another bite. "Okay, it doesn't bother me that much, but, if you don't eat, there may not be anything left. I am the fastest eater of the McKenna sisters. Although we're all pretty speedy."

"It must have been fun growing up with sisters." He'd had a good time with Mark when they were little. He'd missed that when he'd become an only child.

"It was wonderful. Even though they often drove me crazy, especially when we lived on the boat together."

"What was that like?"

"Ashley taking our pictures every other minute. Caroline sneaking into the food rations. Card games that went late into the night, flying fish that landed on our deck when we least expected it, dolphins that were so friendly we could swim right along with them." She let out a sigh. "We were a tight group. We got used to having only one another. We didn't need anyone else."

And apparently they'd kept everyone else away, Tyler thought, especially while one of them was pregnant. Otherwise, someone somewhere would have said something about it.

"Sometimes it's hard to let go—even now," Kate continued. "But we have our own lives to live. Caroline reminds me of it often enough. And Ashley has been pulling away lately. With my father wanting to race again, I think I'm the only one trying to keep us together."

"Everyone grows up and sometimes apart. That's the way of families."

"You're right. I've actually been thinking about making some changes in my own life."

"What kind of changes?" he asked with interest.

"Well, when I turned twenty-eight three weeks ago, I looked at all those candles on my cake and thought about the years that had passed.

Maybe it wasn't a midlife crisis, but it was a wake-up call to break out of my little cocoon, take a look around, figure out what I want to do, where I want to be, that kind of thing."

Three weeks ago? She'd had this revelation three weeks ago? The same time that Mark had received the first contact from Steve Watson? Tyler's pulse sped up. It had to be a coincidence. It had to be.

"What kind of things, exactly?" he asked carefully, trying not to sound too eager.

She hesitated, then said lightly, "I signed up for an exercise class, for one."

"That's it?"

"What did you expect?"

"How about a trip or a move, maybe looking up an old friend, someone you hadn't seen in a while?"

She looked at him through narrowed, thoughtful eyes, and he realized that he sounded much too intense for what she probably thought was a casual conversation.

"Sorry," he said quickly. "It's not for me to say how you should change your life. But I thought you meant something on a grander scale than an exercise class."

"I think I'm ready for the potato salad now."

He handed her the container and a fork.

"What about you?" she asked. "Ever had one of those life-changing moments?"

"Not while blowing out the candles on my birthday cake," he replied. "But, yes, I did have one. Fairly recently, in fact."

"What happened?"

He shouldn't tell her. He absolutely should not tell her. He tapped his fingers against his thigh. "My brother was hurt in a car accident," he said shortly. "He could have been killed. And I realized how little time we'd spent together lately. I'd spent years of my life wanting to be with him, and then wasted the opportunity when I had it. I won't let that happen again."

"Is he all right now?"

"He's getting better."

She tilted her head, giving him a thoughtful look. "Why are you here, Tyler? Why aren't you home with your brother?"

Damn. He'd known confiding in her was a mistake. He tried to think of a plausible excuse. "My brother is very interested in sailing and sailboat races. He's the one who first told me about you and your big victory."

"So I have your brother to thank for your intrusion into my life?" she said with a dry smile. "I hope I meet him someday."

He offered a weak smile in return. "It's possible. Hey, aren't you going to share some of that potato salad with me?"

She handed him the container. "Help yourself."

He looked down at the potato salad, then set it back in the basket.

"What's wrong? Why aren't you eating?" Kate asked.

He cupped her face with his hands. "I just realized it wasn't potato salad I wanted."

"What do you—"

He cut off her question with a long, deep, wet kiss that turned into another and another. He liked the way she kissed him back, the way her tongue played with his. She smelled like vanilla, and she tasted even better. He ran his hands down her back, grabbing her by the waist and pulling her up against him. He wanted to feel her soft breasts. He wanted to touch every inch of her.

"Oh, God," she murmured as his mouth moved down the side of her neck. "We have to stop."

"We're just getting started."

"I—this is crazy," she said breathlessly, pulling away from him. "We're on a public beach. Tyler, stop."

He sat back, knowing she was right. He watched her fidget with her blouse and her hair and whatever else seemed out of place. He wanted to tell her to stop. He liked her loose and messy and a little out of control. He liked her passion and her spirit and, well, pretty much everything else about her.

"You're staring again," she said. "And I'm embarrassed."

"Why? We just kissed."

"It felt like more than just a kiss." She darted a quick look at him, then glanced away.

He flopped down onto his back, closing his eyes against the bright sun. She was right. It hadn't felt like a kiss; it had felt like a promise.

"Tyler, can I ask you something?"

"Sure."

Her words didn't come right away. "Are you connected to K.C. in some way? Are you part of a plan to get back at my father? Is this about revenge?"

His eyes flew open, and he sat up. "Why would you think that?" he asked, genuinely surprised at her conclusion.

"You both show up here unexpectedly. You want information about the race. You're going to sail with my father. It all adds up."

"That adds up? How far did you go in math?"

"You didn't answer my question."

"No, I'm not connected to K.C." He was glad he could tell the truth.

"Good." She put her arms around her knees and stared out at the water. "What do you want to do now?"

"Believe me, you don't want to know the answer to that question."

She turned her head to look at him, her gaze drifting down to his mouth. "I really want to kiss you again."

"Then come here," he said softly.

"I can't. I seem to go up in smoke every time you touch me."

"It's one of your most appealing qualities."

She scrambled to her feet. "I need to walk."

"Walk? You need to walk? Now?"

"Exercise would be good."

"I can think of a more interesting form of exercise than walking."

"Come with me," she said. "There's a cave on the other side of those rocks. I'll show it to you."

"Now you're talking." He held out his hand. "Help me up."

A smile curved her lips. "Do you think I'm going to fall for that?"

"Please."

"Fine."

She slipped her hand into his, and, for a moment, he was tempted to pull her back down on the sand and kiss her senseless. But two young children chose that moment to run by him, kicking up sand with their bare feet, and he knew this wasn't the time nor the place.

Once on his feet, he didn't let go of her hand, and, after a momentary resistance, she relaxed, and they walked along the water's edge together. Tyler had never been so aware of the details of his existence than he was at this moment with Kate. All of his senses were engaged. The sand was cool beneath his bare feet, the sun was warm on his head and the woman beside him was soft, feminine, desirable—and he was as hard as a rock. He needed to relax, too, he told himself, but the tension wouldn't go away. All he could think about was how easy it would be to lean over and kiss her again. He picked up the pace.

"Hey, what's the hurry?" Kate asked as she jogged to keep up with him.

"I'll race you to the cave."

"You don't know where it is," she called after him, but he didn't care. He needed to run along the shoreline. He needed to burn off the sexual energy that was making him crazy.

He heard her footsteps behind him, then felt her draw alongside. Damn, she was fast. She flung him a smile and passed him by.

"What the hell was that?" he asked breathlessly when he caught up to her.

"That was a sprint. I beat you."

"I let you win."

"Liar."

He could think of only one way to shut her up. He tackled her. It wasn't pretty, it wasn't coordinated, but it was effective. Because her soft, squirming body was now under his, exactly where he wanted it.

"Tyler, I can't breathe," she gasped.

"I'll have to give you mouth-to-mouth," he said, moving his weight off of her at the same time his mouth came down on hers.

So much for burning off the tension. It was back with a vengeance, and now he was acutely aware of her legs and her thighs and her hips moving beneath his. He wanted to get closer. He wanted to touch her bare skin. He wanted—

"Oh, my God!" he yelled as a blast of cold water hit his legs. He rolled to the side abruptly, realizing his pants were now soaking wet.

Kate laughed. "That's what we call a rogue wave."

"That's what I call bad timing."

"Better than a cold shower."

"You can say that again." The water had definitely cooled off a very important part of his body.

Kate got to her feet. "We'll dry off as we walk. The cave is just up ahead."

He followed her down the beach, now very much aware of how cold and wet he was. But Kate didn't seem bothered at all—probably due to all those years of living on a boat. The cold and wet were second nature to her. A moment later they rounded a curve, and he followed her pointed finger to a cave set into the rocks.

"There it is," she said. "When the tide comes all the way in, it fills completely with water. My mother used to warn me over and over again not to get caught here."

"Did you listen to her warnings?"

"Absolutely. I'm the cautious one, remember?" She walked over to the rocks. "It's still here." She traced the carving of two names.

"Kate and Jeremy," he murmured. "Hard to compete with that."

She looked at him in surprise. "What do you mean?"

"Jeremy is still very much a presence in your life. You go to his grave. You can see your names carved into rocks, probably all over this island. How can anyone compete with that?"

"Do you want to?"

He should say no. His life wasn't going to take place on this island, that was for sure. Once he found Amelia's mother, he'd be gone. Kate would be just a memory. He'd probably forget her in a week. And she'd forget him, too. It wouldn't be like their names would be carved into a rock anywhere.

"Never mind," she said quickly. "I don't know why I asked you that. Anyway, this is the only place that we carved our names." She walked farther down the rocks. "There are lots of other names, as you can see."

"Sean and Ashley, Mark and Connie, Paul and Rita," he murmured. "I guess this was kind of lover's lane, huh?"

"It was a good place to get a kiss. And once you'd gotten one, you carved your name into the rock." She put her hand up as he started to speak. "But we're not going to do that. That kind of permanence probably terrifies you. Let's go back to our picnic. I've worked up another appetite."

So had he, but it wasn't for food. And it wasn't even for a kiss. He cast a somewhat wistful look at the names and hearts scratched into the rocks next to him. For some damn stupid reason, he wanted to put his name there, too. His name right next to Kate's. Something that would last forever.

"That was fun," Kate said, as Tyler took her bike and handed it back to the manager of Bill's Bicycles. "I can't remember when I've spent such a lazy Monday. I feel guilty."

"It's good to play hooky once in a while."

"But now it's back to reality. Unless..."

"Yes?" he asked with a raise of his eyebrow.

"The world's best ice cream parlor is just down the street."

"You can't possibly still be hungry."

"You've found out my biggest secret. I'm a pig."

He laughed. "I'd love some ice cream from the world's best ice cream parlor. Although I think that might be an exaggeration."

"Wait until you taste it. You'll see I'm right." She didn't resist when he took her hand. In fact, she liked it. She liked it all, the kissing, the touching, the laughing. She hadn't had such a good time in years. And, with Tyler, she felt free to be herself. It was nice to be with a man who didn't know everything about her. They didn't have a history, only a present, and the future wasn't important. Tyler would eventually leave, and she would stay. But today they were together.

Maybe that was enough. Maybe she could stop planning, worrying, analyzing for five seconds and just let it all be. It had been working pretty well so far, so well she didn't want it to end. She didn't really care if she had ice cream or not; she just wanted more time with Tyler. Now that he'd agreed to drop the article, she could relax even more. The fact that he'd made that agreement niggled a bit at her brain. It didn't seem entirely logical or probable that a man who had such deter-mined purpose a few days earlier could so quickly change his mind, but she was reluctant to bring the subject back up.

They walked down the street, stopping at the corner as the light in front of the ferry terminal turned red.

"Doesn't it bother you that you can only get off this island at certain times of the day?" Tyler asked.

"Not at all."

"I live ten minutes from an airport that can get me to any country in the world about as fast as I can buy a ticket and board a plane."

"And you find that comforting?"

"I guess I do," he admitted. "I used to feel trapped as a kid. I couldn't get away from my father, couldn't get back to my mother. I spent a lot of time looking desperately at exit signs. Old habits die hard."

"You really had a terrible childhood, didn't you?" She couldn't imagine what he'd gone through.

"Not completely. My father didn't abuse me. He just wanted me with him in the most selfish way possible." He cleared his throat. "But we don't need to talk about him. Hey, isn't that Caroline?"

She followed his gaze to where the ferry was loading. Her sister was with Mike Stanaway. Kate tensed, not liking the way Mike had his hand on Caroline's arm. "What is she doing with him?" Worry gripped her as she watched them board the ferry. "I don't like the look of that. We need to stop her."

"What?"

Kate began walking rapidly down the street, breaking into a run when she realized that the ferry had finished loading and would no doubt pull away any second. Sure enough, it was fifteen feet into the harbor by the time she arrived at the dock. "Damn."

Tyler caught up with her a second later. "What were you going to do, Kate? Pull Caroline off the boat? Isn't she a grown woman? Aren't you being a little overprotective?"

She turned to face him. "Caroline has dark purple bruises all over her arm. I saw them earlier today. She said she banged her arm, but I think she was lying. Rumor has it that Mike's wife left him because of abuse. I'm afraid he might have hurt Caroline."

"Did you ask her about it?"

"She said he didn't do it."

"Maybe you should believe her."

She ignored that. He didn't know Caroline as well as she did. He didn't know how many lies Caroline had told in the past.

She pulled out her cell phone and called Caroline, hoping she had her phone with her.

"Hello?" Caroline said a moment later.

"It's Kate. I just saw you get on the ferry with Mike."

"Are you spying on me?"

Kate ignored the outrage in her sister's voice. "Where are you going?"

"None of your business, Kate. I'm hanging up now."

"When will you be back?"

"When I feel like it."

"But—" Kate's words were met with a click. "She hung up on me."

"I can't say I'm surprised. Are you going to call her back?"

"She'll probably just hang up again. If I tell Caroline not to jump, the first thing she wants to do is jump. I should know that by now." Kate stared after the rapidly disappearing ferry. "I just hope she'll be all right."

"I saw them together yesterday," Tyler said. "They were arguing, but he backed off when I approached them."

"Why didn't you tell me?"

"Because Caroline wasn't upset, Kate. She wasn't scared. She didn't act like she was in trouble."

"Maybe she didn't want you to know." She frowned, hating feeling so out of control. Caroline might be an adult, but she was still her baby sister. "I wish they hadn't left the island. I'd feel better if she was within shouting distance."

"She has her cell phone. She can call you if she needs help."

Kate let out a sigh. "I guess there's nothing more to do."

"Except have some ice cream."

"Except that. Then I really have to get to work. What are you going to do with the rest of the day?"

"I'll probably wander down to the marina, talk to some sailors, figure out a new angle for my story. Unless you have another idea, one that might involve your house, your bedroom, maybe some candles?"

"I don't think so," she said with a smile, knowing he was only teasing. And she was glad that he wasn't serious, because if he had asked her seriously... In fact, if he'd kissed her instead of asking, they might be on the way to her house right now. Talk about acting crazy; apparently Caroline wasn't the only one making foolish decisions right now.

"Well, tomorrow is another day." Tyler put his arm around her shoulders. "You never know what the future will bring."

CHAPTER FIFTEEN

TUESDAY WAS FAR TOO QUIET, Kate thought, as she checked her watch for the sixth time in an hour. It was almost five thirty, and she hadn't heard from anyone—not Caroline, not Ashley, not Duncan, and not even Tyler, who had been her constant shadow the last few days. She wondered if he'd gone sailing with her father. Tyler would love being on the water. She knew that, even if he didn't. The wind rushing, the waves rolling, the boat flying. He'd be hooked. He'd never again be able to say he wasn't a boat person. She almost regretted that fact. It had been nice to know someone different, someone who didn't eat, sleep and breathe sailing.

"I'm leaving," Theresa said, stopping in front of the counter with purse in hand. "I know it's early, but everyone is down at the square for the annual clam chowder cook-off."

"It's fine." Kate smiled at her assistant. "You must be eager to see how well you'll do against your mother-in-law's clam chowder."

"I doubt I'll beat her this year, but one of these days I will. She still doesn't think I cook as well as she does."

"She's wrong. You're a terrific cook."

"But not good enough for her little boy. Just wait till you get married, Kate. Pray for a good mother-in-law, preferably a non-cook, non-homemaker type, who doesn't criticize or interfere. And make sure you also pick a husband who stands up for you and doesn't become Mommy's little boy as soon as she steps into the room."

"Are we talking about me or you?"

Kate gave her a compassionate smile. Theresa's battles with her mother-in-law were nothing new.

"By the way," Theresa continued. "I saw the Moon Dancer when I had lunch at the marina today. She's a beauty. Everyone in town is talking about the boat and your family, wondering how you all feel about it."

Kate hated to hear that, but she'd expected as much. It was one of the reasons why she'd brought a turkey sandwich from home and had her lunch in the back room instead of going into town. "It will all be over on Saturday. I just keep telling myself that."

"Why don't you put out the closed sign and come have some clam chowder with me? We haven't had a customer in more than an hour."

"I'll be down in a bit."

The door shut behind Theresa, and the silence was suddenly deafening. Her cozy store of fantasy felt empty and lonely. Kate sat down at the desk in front of her computer. She clicked on her inventory program first, checking on upcoming releases and pre-orders. She supposed she could have gone through all the titles, but she just didn't feel like it at the moment. In fact, she hadn't felt like working all day. Switching from inventory to the Internet, she pulled up one of her favorite gardening sites and read through the headlines for the latest articles involving introducing toads into your garden, getting rid of unwanted pests, and growing the best vegetables. The toad idea was a new one on her. She was just getting into the article when the door opened.

Her heart jumped into her throat when she saw Tyler. She'd known he would come. In reality, she'd been waiting all day for him. And here he was. But she wouldn't tell him that. She forced herself to stand up slowly and casually, as if she had her mind on other things, as if she hadn't expected him.

"Hi," Tyler said. His voice was low, intimate, as was the look he gave her.

She cleared her throat. "I thought you were out on the water today," she said. She was grateful to have the counter between them. It provided a much needed barrier, as she fought the urge to throw herself in his arms and kiss him until she forgot why getting involved with him was not a good idea.

"Your father begged off," Tyler said. "Apparently he's busy inter-viewing potential crew members. He said Thursday would work better."

"I wouldn't set my heart on it," she told him. "My father isn't known for keeping his promises."

"So what have you been doing all day?"

"Working. What about you? Have you found a new angle for your article?"

"No. Are you sure you won't reconsider? Don't you trust me enough yet to tell me your story? I'm not a bad guy. I won't crucify you."

It wouldn't be up to him, she could have answered. Telling her story would affect far too many lives, and at this point there was nothing to be gained and everything to be lost. She was moving forward with her life. She was making positive changes. Discussing the past with Tyler would not be in any way productive.

"I should introduce you to Mitchell Haley. He competed in the Whitbread ten years ago. I'm sure he has a lot of stories to tell. He actually lives in Seattle, but he usually comes to Castleton for race week. If he's here, I'm sure my father will know where to find him. They're old friends."

"I'll keep that in mind." He took a step closer, resting his arms on the counter between them. "You look good."

"I—uh, thanks." She tucked a piece of hair behind her ear, feeling distinctly uncomfortable with his intimate perusal. She was suddenly very aware of how empty the store was.

"Kate," he said in a husky voice.

"What?" She looked into his eyes and saw them darken with desire. "Tyler. We can't start that all over again."

"Why not?"

She couldn't think of an answer. And it didn't seem like she really needed one. Words were passing back and forth between them, and yet not a one was spoken aloud.

"I was sent here to get you," Tyler said, surprising her.

"By whom?"

"Caroline. She was setting up a clam chowder booth down by the marina."

"Oh." Her baby sister's name brought her back to reality. "I can't believe she sent you. She's been avoiding my calls all day."

"Maybe sent wasn't the right word."

"I didn't think so. What did she say, exactly?"

"That you should stay out of her business or she won't tell you which of the clam chowders Mrs. Rayburn made. Whatever that means."

"Mrs. Rayburn sent ten people to the clinic last year for using bad clams."

He nodded. "Your sister doesn't pull her punches."

"I just hope she's not taking any."

"She looked fine, Kate."

"Some scars aren't visible."

He sent her a curious look. "What does that mean?"

She couldn't begin to tell him. "Nothing. It doesn't mean anything. I'm glad she's fine, and I'll tell her I'm sorry for sticking my nose in her business when I see her later."

"Good, then let's go."

She wavered. She'd spent most of the night tossing and turning in her bed, reviewing all the reasons why she needed to keep her distance from Tyler. Those reasons had nothing to do with his job as a reporter and everything to do with who he was as a man and the way he made her feel.

"You think too much, Kate," he murmured. "It's just a bowl of clam chowder I'm offering you."

"Is that all it is?" She gave a helpless shake of her head. "When you're around, I have trouble remembering my own name," she confessed.

"Kate McKenna," he offered, his expression a bit grim, his voice a little harsh as he said her name.

She frowned. "Why do you suddenly sound angry?"

He stared back at her. "Sorry. Are you coming, Kate?"

Making a quick decision, she reached into a drawer and pulled out her purse. "Let's go." She turned off the lights, changed the sign to *Closed* and locked the door behind them. That's when the wind almost knocked her off her feet. "Where did that come from?" she asked with a shiver.

"The weather turned about an hour ago. You hadn't noticed?"

"I've been inside."

"I'll keep you warm," he said, putting his arm around her shoulders.

That's exactly what she was afraid of.

"Hold on tight," Sean yelled as the wind caught his words and threw them back at her. "This hill will be one hell of a ride."

"It's too steep," Ashley protested, tightening her arms around Sean's waist as he stopped at the top of Sorenson's Hill. So far he'd driven his motorcycle with caution, taking care not to alarm her. Apparently, that was about to change.

"I won't let anything happen to you, Ash," he said. "You can trust me."

She wanted to believe him. She wanted to let it all go, the worries, the fears. She wanted to be that girl again who could soar down a hill with her hair flying out behind her. But he was asking too much of her. Wasn't it enough that they'd spent the last two days together, that they'd explored some of their favorite haunts and gorged themselves on fish and chips? Wasn't it enough that she'd actually agreed to get on the motorcycle with him today? Did she really have to agree to this, too?

He flipped up the visor on his helmet as he glanced back at her.

"Remember what you used to say to me?" he asked her, his eyes warm with understanding. "When we used to ride our bikes down this hill?"

She shook her head.

"Just take your foot off the brake. That's all you have to do."

When she was a kid, she'd lived for speed, but no more. "I really wish I had a brake right now. I'd stop you from doing this."

"I won't do it, if you really don't want me to. But I think there's a part of you that wants a fast ride. Come on, Ash."

"All right. Do it before I change my mind," she said, squeezing her eyes shut.

She heard him laugh, then he revved up the motor, and they were off.

She hugged herself to Sean's body, tightening her legs around the bike, praying they wouldn't lose their balance or hit a big bump. But there was no more time to think. The speed, the wind, the motion of the bike were all terrifying and exhilarating. She felt like she was flying, sailing, racing into the wind on a glorious day.

Within a minute they reached the bottom of the hill, back on even ground, the bike slowing faster than her heart. She opened her eyes to see that the world was still upright. The sun was still shining. Life was good. And she felt better than she had in a long time.

Sean stopped the bike on the side of the deserted road. He got off, threw his helmet onto the ground, and said, "Wasn't that fantastic?"

She took off her helmet with shaky fingers. She wasn't sure she could actually get off the bike. Her legs were shaking. Sean must have read her mind, because he helped her off the bike, put his arms around her, and spun her around in a dizzying hug.

When he finally put her feet back down on the ground, his grin went from ear to ear. She couldn't help but smile back. His joy was contagious.

"Tell me you loved it as much as I did. Tell me."

"I liked it."

"You loved it."

"I was scared out of my mind at first, but then it was like before, better than before. I felt like myself again," she confessed. "I didn't know it was possible to have courage again. It's been so long." Her eyes filled with tears. "You gave it back to me, Sean. I don't know how you did it, but—"

He cut off her words with a kiss, a demanding, hard kiss that was as impatient and reckless as he was—and just the way she wanted to be.

He was in the mood to do something outrageous, Tyler thought. Two hours of clam chowder tasting, chatting with Kate's friends, and listening to local bands had done nothing to quiet the reckless feeling in his gut. He wondered if Kate felt the same way. She'd glance at him, then look away without saying a word. She'd barely touched her food, which was unusual, because in his experience she was not shy about eating. And then there was the way her fingers tapped nervously, or was it impatiently, on the red-checkered tablecloth. He wanted to put his hand over those fingers and pull them to his lips in a silly, old-fashioned kiss.

Maybe it was the small-town party atmosphere that made him feel like a stranger in his own body. Or maybe it was the magic of a summer night. He wasn't a romantic, but he suddenly wanted to tell Kate how beautiful she looked in the deepening twilight, how the music made him want to take her in his arms in a long, slow dance. He drew in a deep breath and let it out, wondering how he could feel so hot when the evening air was decidedly chilly.

"You haven't said a word in a long time," Kate remarked.

"Neither have you."

"Do you want to go back to your hotel?"

"Only if you're going with me."

She quickly looked away. "That's not what I meant. I thought you might be bored. This can't be very exciting for a big-city reporter."

"It's so exciting my heart is beating double-time." He grabbed her restless hand and pressed it against his chest. "Feel that."

"You're definitely still alive," she said somewhat breathlessly as she tried to pull her hand away. "Let me go. People will look. They'll talk."

"And what will they see? What will they say?"

She thought about his questions for a moment, and when she gazed back at him, her expression was somber. "They'll see the local bookstore owner losing her head over a sexy stranger."

"Would that be so bad?"

She ignored his question, getting to her feet. "Do you want to see one of my favorite places on the island?"

"Absolutely. Is it your bedroom?"

She smiled. "No, but nice try. Let's walk back to the store and pick up my car."

"Are you going to tell me where we're going?" he asked, following her down the street.

"What would be the fun in that?" she countered.

After picking up Kate's car, they drove to the other side of the island, to an isolated building out on the bluffs. And it wasn't just any building, but a castle with a drawbridge, towers and turrets.

"What the hell is that?" Tyler asked.

"The Castleton Castle, also known as Frank's Folly. Frank Castleton was one of the original settlers on the island. He built the castle on a whim. At one time he envisioned an entire island filled with castles." Kate gave him a smile. "Fortunately, no one else shared his vision. It's not just a castle; it's also a lighthouse. Do you want to go inside?"

"Sure."

"No one lives here anymore," she said as they got out of the car. "Frank was the only one who actually spent time in the castle. Apparently he'd hoped for a Cinderella to share it with, but as the legend goes, he was more of a toad than a prince."

Tyler followed her across the drawbridge that lay over a dry gully, which he surmised was supposed to be a moat. The huge wooden door opened to Kate's gentle push. It was dark and dusty inside.

"There's a kitchen down here, a small dining area, and a bedroom. But the best room is upstairs." Kate took his hand and led him up a staircase that opened onto one very large, round room. The walls were glass, and the only furniture was a wooden bench window seat that encircled the room. The rising moon sent shafts of light through the windows, creating an atmosphere of dark, romantic intimacy.

"What do you think? Doesn't it feel magical?" Kate asked, doing an impulsive little twirl that reminded him of Amelia.

He chased that thought right out of his mind. The last person he wanted to think about right now was Amelia. At least he was doing one thing Mark had asked him to do; he was sticking close to Kate.

"It does," he agreed, but he had a feeling the magic had more to do with Kate than with the room.

She walked over to the windows. "The Sound is there. You'll be able to see the water when the light goes on."

"There's a light?"

"It's automatic. It comes on around nine o'clock in the summer. But I prefer it like this, the moon dancing around the room, lighting up the shadows."

There was something about her words that gave him pause, and then it clicked. "The Moon Dancer. This is where the name came from, isn't it?"

Kate nodded. "Yes. This was my mom's favorite place. We always came at twilight, just as the moon was coming up. She'd tell us stories about the island. She was born here and knew all the history. Some-times we'd bring a picnic. There are a lot of memories here," she said with a wistful sigh.

"Of both your parents, or just your mother?"

"Just my mom. My dad never came with us. For him, the magic was always out on the water."

"Am I trespassing on sacred female ground, then?"

"I think it will be all right. I sense that despite your outwardly cynical appearance, there is a bit of the dreamer in you."

"I'm about reality, not dreams."

"That's not true. Any man who roams the world in search of stories has to be a dreamer at heart, just like any man who sails across the ocean. You like a big canvas to paint on; so does my father."

"What about you, Kate?" he asked, searching her eyes. "Wasn't there a part of you that enjoyed that trip around the world?"

"Oh, yes, there definitely was," she said, surprising him with her answer. "But it wasn't so much about battling the water that thrilled me; it was that first glimpse of land off in the distance. Was it a mirage born of boredom and loneliness? Was it a deserted island? Would there be people living on that island, lost to the world? Would we be their rescuers? I used to make up stories along the way." She smiled at him. "We never did find anyone on a deserted island, but every time we saw land, I thought it could happen. And when we'd sail into some foreign port, I'd stand on the deck of the Moon Dancer and soak it all in. I loved hearing the different languages, seeing faces of people I'd never seen before and never would again. I remember this little girl on the docks in South Africa. She was begging for food. I'd never seen such poverty in my life. I gave her my sunglasses, and her face lit up like a miracle had just occurred. That's what I miss, Tyler. Those little miracles that you don't expect."

"And yet you're happy to stay here on this island, reading about other people's adventures?"

"Yes, I am. I'm not saying that someday I won't travel again. But for now what means the most to me is predictability, security. Maybe it's just part of getting older. I don't want to be a gypsy. I want to be a part of something that takes root and grows. What I did on the Moon Dancer was enough for me. But I bet you can't say the same. You're still a wanderer. You're still in search of something."

"Possibly," he admitted. "But I'm not sure what it is."

"You'll know when you find it," she said, meeting his gaze.

"Yes," he agreed.

"Are you ready to go?"

"No. I have another idea." He extended his hand to her. "Would you dance with me?"

"There's no music."

"For dreamers like us, that won't be a problem, will it?"

Kate hesitated, then put her hand into his. "I have a hard time letting someone else lead."

He pulled her up against his chest and gazed into her eyes. "Then just take me wherever you want to go."

She cleared her throat, a slight blush washing across her cheeks. "I don't think I can—I need a beat."

"How about if I sing?"

"You can sing?"

"Don't sound so surprised. I'm a man of many talents."

"What do you sing?"

"Frank Sinatra mostly. My dad was a huge fan. Played Frank's songs over and over again." He began to hum a tune, because he couldn't remember the words. But, then again, it was difficult to remember anything with Kate in his arms. Picking up the pace, he moved her rapidly around the room until they were both laughing.

"Oh, my God!" she said breathlessly. "I feel like I should be wearing a chiffon dress with a big skirt that swings around my legs when I spin."

"You should," he said, twirling her again.

She looked at him with sparkling eyes. "This reminds me of one of my favorite movies. There's a scene in *The King and I* where Anna teaches the king how to do a polka. And they go flying around the room, spinning and spinning and spinning."

"Like this?" Tyler asked. He spun her around until they were both too dizzy to do anything but collapse onto the window seat.

Kate held up her hands. "Time out. I need a breather."

"Hey, I'm just getting started."

"You're not a bad dancer," she admitted.

"I still have a few moves I haven't shown you yet." He gave her an exaggerated wink, and she laughed.

"You are terrible. A natural-born flirt." She paused, her expression turning serious. "I can't remember when I've had so much fun."

"Neither can I. It's been awhile, that's for sure."

A charged silence fell between them, the coziness of the room and the darkness of the night drawing a blanket of intimacy around them.

"If we wait a few minutes, we'll have a spotlight to dance under," Kate said somewhat nervously. "When the light comes on, this room will be as bright as day."

"I kind of like the moon shadows." The moonlight had turned her from pretty into beautiful, from an ordinary woman into an angel. He wanted to take her in his arms and make love to her. "Kate," he murmured.

"Tyler," she echoed, as she stroked his cheek with her fingers.

His breath caught at the tender, womanly caress.

"You must have to shave every day," she murmured as her fingers brushed against his jaw. She paused. "I want to kiss you again." She surprised him with her boldness.

"What's stopping you?" he asked, but in her eyes he saw the conflict of duty versus desire.

"Who you are. What you want with me and my family."

"I thought we'd moved past that." He turned his face into her hand and kissed her palm. He looked up and saw the spark of desire in her eyes. It was all the encouragement he needed. Leaning forward, he kissed her on the mouth, slowly, deeply. He didn't want to rush, wanted to take the time to savor the taste of her mouth.

But Kate seemed impatient with the slower approach. She slipped her hands under his shirt, her fingers glancing off his abdomen, running through the hair on his chest. His muscles tightened at every touch.

"Yes," he muttered with encouragement.

"You feel so good, Tyler."

"Say my name again," he ordered.

"Tyler, Tyler, Tyler," she said against his mouth, punctuating each word with a kiss. "Maddening, annoying, frustrating Tyler."

"Don't get carried away, now."

"I want to get carried away," she said with a longing that removed the last of his doubts.

He moved his hands under her sweater. Her skin grew warmer the higher he traveled, until he met up with a lacy bra that thankfully had a clasp in the front. He didn't realize how much he wanted that bra undone until his fingers fumbled with the clasp once, twice, before opening. He cupped her breast with his hand, the softness of her skin sending him over the edge.

He caressed her fullness, brushing his thumb over the taut peak. She was as excited as he was. It wasn't enough to touch her like this. He wanted more, much more. While his hands explored her breasts, his mouth moved from her lips across her cheek and down the side of her neck. God, she was sweet. Sweet and sexy and willing.

Kate tugged at his shirt. "We need to get rid of this."

"My pleasure." He pulled the shirt over his head and tossed it on the floor. He liked the way she looked at him, wanting him with her eyes, but she hadn't touched him again, and he wanted that more than anything. "Kate," he said, willing her to come the rest of the way.

She didn't move for probably the longest minute of his life. Then she slowly lifted the sweater over her head and slipped off her bra. Her hands came up to cover herself, a shyness that he liked but didn't want now.

"Don't." He put his hand on hers. "Let me look at you."

Her hands slowly moved back to her side. "You are one beautiful woman," he murmured.

She stared back at him without moving. "Touch me, Tyler. Put your hands on my breasts, the way you did before. I want to make love to you."

Her words drove a wave of guilt through him. There was trust in her sweet blue eyes. And he didn't deserve that trust.

"Tyler, what are you waiting for?" she asked, her gaze narrowing.

Before he could answer, a shockingly bright light hit the room like a spotlight on center stage. Kate gasped and covered her breasts.

"Oh, my God. I forgot about the light," she said. "It's so bright!"

Shockingly illuminating, Tyler realized, and it had probably just stopped them from making a huge mistake. Tyler handed her the bra and sweater from the bench. "Do you want to put these on?"

She hesitated and then nodded. "I should, shouldn't I?" She put on her bra and pulled her sweater over her head with swift, jerky movements. "I don't know what came over me. I don't usually do stuff like this."

"I'm glad this isn't usual for you. I'm happy it was just for me."

She stared at him. "You stopped, Tyler. Even before the light came on. I saw it in your face. Why?"

He didn't know how to answer that question. There were too many lies between them, so he settled for another. "I don't have anything with me—protection," he said. "I'm guessing you don't either."

"Oh," she said, her voice faltering. "I—I didn't even think."

She got to her feet and looked out at the water that was now lit up by the light. "When you're on the ocean, a light like this can be a savior, the promise of a safe harbor. I never thought I wouldn't be happy to see the light." She turned to him. "I know it was smart to stop. I just kind of wish we hadn't. Because it felt good, and it's been a long time since I felt like that. I wanted to be selfish. It's a family trait, you know." She headed toward the stairway. "Let's go home."

Home? Where was that? he wondered. Logically, he knew his address in San Antonio. That's where his things were, where his friends lived, where his brother and niece made a life. So why was he starting to feel as if this island was home, as if wherever Kate was going was where he wanted to be?

CHAPTER SIXTEEN

KATE DROPPED him off at his hotel without even turning off the engine. She muttered a good-bye and took off as soon as he'd shut the door. It was just as well. This trip wasn't supposed to be about anything but finding Amelia's biological mother. And it was time for him to refocus on his goals.

He felt too wired to even think about going inside to his quiet hotel room. Most people in Castleton apparently felt the same way, Tyler realized, as he walked back through the town square. The food booths were being dismantled, but there were still crowds of people gathered around small tables, talking and laughing. A few people called out hello, people he'd met through Kate or on his own. He'd only been in town a few days, but they were making him feel like part of the community, part of their lives, and it was a nice feeling, almost too nice.

A small island in the Pacific Northwest was not the place to get attached to. There were no earth-shattering news stories here, no need for tough investigative reporting. It was a tourist destination, a place for fishermen and sailors, bikers and hikers, honeymooners and retirees, a place for people to relax, smell the flowers, enjoy life—not a place for him. He liked to be on the go, flying in fast jets over countries whose names he could barely spell. He liked the unpredictable, the never-ending adventure.

Didn't he?

Then why was this scene so appealing? Why did Kate's small house charm him so? Why did he feel so attracted to a woman who had made it clear she was never going to move? Why did he suddenly wonder what it would feel like to have a house of his own and friends who would welcome him home, who would butt into his business and protect him from strangers' questions, who didn't expect anything from him? Why did the idea of one woman, one long-term relationship, one marriage suddenly sound so attractive?

Hell, he was out of his mind. He didn't want any of those things. What he wanted was a drink. Thankfully, the Oyster Bar was just around the corner.

It was fairly crowded for a Tuesday night. Tyler stood for a moment, checking out the room for familiar faces. Sure enough, there were two: Caroline and Duncan sitting at a table in the corner. His eyes narrowed at the sight. He wondered what they were cooking up. There was an intensity to their conversation that was apparent in their body posture, the way they leaned in toward each other, the sharp look on Duncan's face as he said something to Caroline.

Tyler moved closer, unabashedly eavesdropping, but they were too caught up in their conversation to even notice him.

"I want to help you, Daddy," Caroline said. "You know I do. But Kate won't race again, and Ashley can't even get herself on a boat these days."

"You have to convince them, Caroline. I'm counting on you," he said loudly, firmly.

"I'll come with you. I'll race. I'll be your partner. Maybe that will be enough. We can get a good crew. There are plenty of strong, willing sailors around. We don't need Kate or Ashley."

"Of course we need Kate. She's—" He waved his hand in the air as if searching for the right word. "She's the one who makes it all work."

"I can make it all work."

Duncan called to the waiter to bring them two beers.

"I don't want a beer," Caroline said. "Look, why don't you take me out on the practice run tomorrow? You'll see how good I am."

"You haven't sailed in years."

"Neither have you," she argued. "But I've kept in shape. I'm still really strong."

The waiter set down two beers in front of them. Duncan picked his up and drank like a man who hadn't tasted water in a week, but, judging by the empty glass on the table, this was not his first beer. Nor would it probably be his last. As he set down his glass, he saw Tyler and motioned him over.

"There you are, my favorite reporter. What are you drinking?"

"Beer, I guess."

"Will, bring me another for my friend," Duncan called out. "And put it on my tab."

"How's it going, Caroline?" Tyler pulled out an empty chair at their table and sat down.

"Fine," she said with an expression that was not particularly welcoming. "You sure do seem to pop up wherever we are."

"She's upset," Duncan told Tyler. "She wants to race with me, but I need Kate, too."

"I still don't get why," Caroline retorted.

"Well now, honey, I don't want you to get your feelings hurt, but you're kind of a jinx."

Caroline sat upright in her chair. "I am not a jinx. How can you say that?"

"Trouble follows you around like a tail follows a dog." Duncan smiled over at Tyler. "If there was a bucket nearby, Caroline would no doubt step in it. If there was a drink by her elbow, she'd knock it over, accidentally of course." He glanced back at his youngest daughter. "It's okay. You can't help it, and you always try hard."

"I am not that clumsy," she protested.

"Oh, look, there's Rudy." Duncan waved his hand toward his friend. "Hey, Rudy, come over here and sit your sorry ass down."

A big, burly man in his late fifties ambled over to the table. "Who's your friend?" Rudy asked.

"Tyler something," Duncan replied. "He's a reporter looking for some good sailing stories."

"Don't believe a word this bastard has to say," Rudy said, giving Tyler a hearty pat on the back. "Duncan lies so much he's forgotten what the truth looks like."

"That's for sure," Caroline said harshly as she got up. "I'm out of here."

"Hey, you haven't touched your drink," Duncan said. "Push it on over here, would you? I don't want good beer going to waste."

Caroline looked as if she was going to do what he suggested, but when her hand touched the glass she hesitated. She lifted it to her mouth and took a sip. She gave her father a hard, unforgiving look, then tilted her head back and drank the beer down to the last drop. She set the glass down on the table. "See, there are some things I'm good at," she said and turned toward the door.

Tyler wanted to go after her, but Duncan was saying something to him and Rudy put a hand on his arm, and by the time he excused himself and got to the door Caroline had disappeared. She'd had a dangerous, reckless look in her eye, and she was looking for trouble. He wondered if she would find it. He wondered why he was hoping she wouldn't. He'd come to Castleton to discredit the McKenna sisters, or at least the one who was Amelia's mother, and that could be Caroline. But now that he was here, he was finding it more difficult to see any of them as his enemy. He really did need to regroup and get his head together. Because no matter how nice they appeared to be, one of them wanted to take his niece away from his brother, and he couldn't let that happen.

Kate jogged down the sidewalk that ran along the marina early Wednesday morning. She'd almost made a huge mistake the night before, and she was doing penance this morning by putting her body through a punishing workout. Maybe if she got tired enough, she'd stop thinking about Tyler, stop wanting to make love to him, stop acting like a fool.

He'd been the one to call a halt to things. She was the one who'd been caught up in the moment, and it still irked, even after a long, sleepless night. She liked to be in control at all times, especially of herself and her emotions, but there had been a few minutes last night when she had been completely out of control.

What had she been thinking? She barely knew him. And she wasn't sure she could trust him. Her instincts told her he was hiding something. Then again, so was she. It was difficult to call him a liar when he could throw the word right back at her.

But all that aside, Tyler had been charming, fun. He'd made her laugh, made her feel emotions she hadn't felt in a long time—if ever. That traitorous thought brought her jog down to a walk.

Had it ever been that good with Jeremy? Had her senses been so completely involved? Or was it even fair to compare? Time had dimmed so many memories. And she had changed as well. She was a grown woman now. Her needs, her wants, her wishes were different.

Kate paused along the rail, looking out at the water and the boats. She'd been content before Tyler came to town. She'd told herself work and family were enough. She didn't need a man in her life, didn't want all the messy, emotional complications of love, didn't want to have her heart broken again. And she'd almost bought into all of that until Tyler had arrived.

Now she'd had a taste of what she was missing, and that taste had made her want more.

It could hurt, a voice inside her head reminded her. And could she survive another loss? Wouldn't it be better to play it safe?

While she was thinking, she caught a glimpse of a man coming out of the coffee shop down the street. It was Mike Stanaway, the man her sister had been with at the ferry landing on Monday. She'd tried to talk to Caroline about him at the clam chowder cook- off, but her sister had claimed she was too busy to chat and then disappeared.

Maybe this was her opportunity to talk to Mike. While Kate weighed her options, Mike took off at a brisk pace. She broke into a jog to follow him and came down the dock just as he disappeared onto his boat.

Climbing aboard without waiting for an invitation, she called out his name as she went down the stairs into the cabin. She stopped abruptly as she saw Mike offering her sister Caroline a cup of coffee. Caroline was sitting up in bed, wearing a black spaghetti-strap under-shirt. A tangled sheet covered her bottom half.

Her hair was a mess, her makeup smeared as if she'd been crying.

"What are you doing here?" Caroline demanded.

Kate was so stunned by her sister's appearance she could barely speak. "I—I wanted to talk to Mike. I didn't know you were here."

"About me? You wanted to talk to him about me?"

"Get dressed. I'm taking you home." Kate glared at Mike, daring him to try and stop her, but he didn't say a word.

"I'm not twelve, Kate. I'll go home when I want to," Caroline snapped. "And I'd like you to leave."

"What?" Kate asked in shock.

"You heard me. I want you to leave."

"Not without you. I'm not leaving you here with him."

"I'm fine."

"You don't look fine. You look like someone who knocked back a liquor store last night."

Caroline uttered a bitter laugh. "You don't know anything."

"I know this is not a good place for you to be."

"Mike is my friend."

"She's too young for you. What are you doing with her?" Kate demanded of Mike.

"That's her business and mine," he said quietly but firmly.

"I know what I'm doing, Kate. You have to trust me."

"It's him I don't trust," Kate said, tipping her head in Mike's direction.

"He won't hurt me."

"He already has. Look at your arms."

"I told you I banged my arm. For God's sake, Kate, would you just leave? I'll call you later, or I'll come by the bookstore. Just go now.

Go," Caroline added, with a pleading smile. "Trust me to take care of myself."

Kate did not want to leave without her sister, but what could she do? "You better not hurt her," Kate said fiercely. "Because if you do, I will come after you."

Mike didn't reply, just tipped his head in acknowledgment. Kate hesitated, then turned and ran up the stairs. Once on the dock, she stopped, debating her options. If she stayed nearby, she could hear Caroline if she called for help. Would she even call for help? Caroline certainly didn't want her interference. But, if she left, she'd be worrying the rest of the day.

As she paced back and forth on the narrow dock, she saw a man approaching her—K.C. Just when she thought her day couldn't get any worse.

"If you wanted to take a closer look, why didn't you just ask?" K.C. said as he stopped in front of her.

"What are you talking about?"

"I'd be happy to give you a tour, Katie. I'm sure you're curious."

It was then that Kate realized the Moon Dancer was just a few slips down. She'd been so preoccupied with following Mike that she hadn't noticed until now. "I didn't come here to see you or the Moon Dancer." Although now that she was here, maybe she should find out what K.C. was up to.

"Have it your way," he said, walking past her.

"Wait. I did want to ask you something."

K.C. smiled as he turned back to face her. "I thought as much."

"Why are you really here? Why did you buy our boat and have the sails remade in exactly the same design? I'm sure that wasn't a coincidence."

"I bought the Moon Dancer because I wanted it, because your mother and I designed that boat in our heads long before she and Duncan decided to have it built. It was always meant to be mine—like so many other things that Duncan stole from me."

She drew in a shaky breath. "I assume you mean my mother."

"Nora belonged to me. He knew that."

"My mother went where she wanted to go," Kate countered. "And the three of you were friends. I remember you being at every important occasion in our family until my mother died. Why would you have been there if you hated my father so much?"

K.C. sent her a steady, assessing look. "That was because of you, Katie."

Her heart stopped. He couldn't mean what he was implying.

"I thought you were my daughter," he added, confirming her worst fear.

"But it wasn't true." She made sure the words were a statement and not a question, but she was still holding her breath as she waited for his answer.

"No, it wasn't true," he said finally and seemingly with regret. "Nora had told me that all along. But I had reasonable doubt. We'd both slept with her within the same critical period of time."

"I find that hard to believe." She hated the thought of her mother with K.C., with anyone besides her father.

"Nora and I had been dating, but we'd had an argument, a misunderstanding. A few days later Duncan returned from one of his trips. My good friend was back," K.C. said with bitterness. "I was happy to see him. So was Nora. She'd met him a few months earlier. I didn't realize what an impression he'd made on her until he came back. They started seeing each other. The next thing I knew, they were married. I didn't know she was pregnant at the time, but then you were born six weeks too early." He paused for a long moment. "When she told me I wasn't your father, I didn't believe her. I thought she was protecting her marriage, protecting Duncan. I couldn't fight her on it, not without hurting her. So I stayed close, figuring if I couldn't have you, I'd at least see you, spend time with you."

"Give me presents that made your own son jealous," Kate interjected.

K.C. looked at her in surprise. "Excuse me?"

"You didn't realize what effect your actions had on your son? David still believes that you're my father, and that I'm your favorite."

"That's not true. I love him very much. And I never told him there was any possibility I was your father."

"Then he guessed. Whatever happened back then, you need to let go of this old hatred of yours. What's it going to accomplish to beat my father? Will you be happy then?"

K.C. didn't answer right away, then said, "I think I might be. Duncan didn't just cheat me out of the woman I loved. He cheated me in many other ways, including our race around the world."

Kate stiffened and silently begged, *Please don't remember. Please don't remember.*

K.C. watched her closely. "Can you deny that he didn't?"

It was a risky question, one she didn't quite know how to answer, especially since she didn't know what he knew. "That race was over a long time ago."

"I was leading—going into that storm. I should have won that race."

"It's not our fault your boat went down."

He didn't look like he believed her.

"We all need to move on with our lives," she added quickly. "Don't you think it's time to put this thing with my father behind you? How long will you try to make him pay for winning my mother's love?"

"As long as it takes," K.C. said coldly. "You've heard about our bet, Katie?"

"Yes. My father is racing you for the Moon Dancer." She paused, unable to stop herself from throwing gasoline on the fire. "And he'll probably win."

K.C. bristled at her words. "I guess that would depend on his crew. You were always a better sailor than your father. Another reason why I thought you were mine. But, no matter. When your father loses, I'll get something else I want."

Kate knew she would regret asking, but she couldn't stop the words from coming to her lips. "What's that?"

"The portrait of your mother with you and your sisters."

"That's mine," she said tightly, unable to believe what he was saying.

"Technically it belongs to your father, does it not?"

Kate couldn't believe Duncan would have bet the portrait. Or maybe she could. His ego knew no bounds. He probably didn't consider it a risky bet.

Kate turned her head, hearing a commotion behind her. Caroline jumped onto the dock. She scowled when she saw them. "Waiting for me, Kate?"

"K.C. stopped to talk to me," she said, taking advantage of his presence. He might as well be good for something.

"I'm going home," Caroline muttered. "Don't follow me. I'm not in the mood for you or one of your lectures."

Kate let Caroline go, because it was obvious this wasn't the time or the place. At least Caroline was going alone. That was worth something. She turned back to K.C. "You will never get my portrait."

"Who's going to stop me?"

Kate wanted to slap the sneering smile off his face and say she would stop him. But she couldn't quite get the words out of her mouth. That would mean agreeing to join forces with her father and racing again. How could she do that?

"No one will stop me, Katie. You've left your father on his own this time. And we both know he can't do it without you. He never could."

Tyler flipped off the television set in his hotel room and realized he couldn't put off calling his brother for another minute. He should have called yesterday, but he'd felt so conflicted after spending the evening with Kate that he just hadn't had the heart to call Mark. He felt like a wishbone, being pulled in two directions, and it seemed like he was betraying both of them. There was no way they could all win. In the end, someone would be terribly hurt.

Picking up his cell phone, he punched in Mark's number and waited.

"Hello?" A childish voice greeted him.

"Hi, honey. It's Uncle Ty."

"Hi, Uncle Ty."

"How are you, sweetie?"

"I'm fine. Daddy needed some water, so I got it for him. I even put ice in it."

"You're a good helper. But I thought that was Shelly's job."

"She had to go out for a little while. She's not back yet."

"Not back yet?" Tyler wondered where Shelly had gone. Mark was supposed to have twenty-four hour care at all times, especially with Amelia in the house.

"Do you want to talk to Daddy? I think he might be asleep, but I can check."

Tyler felt even more uneasy at the idea of Amelia being in the house with Mark asleep and no Shelly nearby. Amelia was only eight years old, although at the moment she sounded closer to twenty. For the first time, Tyler wondered if he was doing the right thing. Mark would have a long road back to recovery, a road that would require care, money and time. Would Amelia be shortchanged growing up in such a way?

"Are you okay there by yourself?" he asked her.

"I'm not by myself. Daddy's here. He'll wake up if I need him."

"What if you fall or something?"

"Then I'll get up," she told him with simple childish logic.

He couldn't help smiling at her practicality. "I guess you will."

"Daddy and I wrote Mommy a letter, and we put it on the dining room table so she could see it when she's looking down on us. I printed in really big letters, too, so she could read it from heaven."

Tyler's stomach clenched at her words. "That sounds nice."

"Do you want to hear what I wrote?"

Did he want to have his heart ripped out of his chest? "Sure," he said, knowing that was the answer Amelia wanted.

"I'll get it."

Tyler heard her set down the phone and wished he could call her back. He was torturing himself—punishing himself for getting carried away with Kate yesterday, for letting Mark down, even if only in thought, not in action.

"Are you there?" Amelia asked when she returned to the phone.

"I'm here."

"Dear Mommy, we miss you a lot," she read. "We hope you're happy in heaven, but we wish you were here. I sang your song last night to Daddy, and he said I must take after you, because he sings really bad. I'm going to try to be just like you when I grow up."

Tyler's heart twisted with emotion at her simple statement, and he couldn't help wondering for the thousandth time why Mark and Susan hadn't told Amelia she was adopted, maybe not the who, why, where, or whatever, but enough so that Amelia wouldn't be shocked to find out one day that she was not who she thought she was.

"I'm talking to Uncle Ty," Amelia yelled, probably to her father. "Daddy wants to talk to you," she said. "Bye."

"Bye, honey."

"Ty? What's up?" his brother said a moment later. "Why didn't you call me back yesterday? I left you three messages."

"I didn't have anything new to report."

"Well, maybe I had news," Mark snapped. "George got another letter from the investigator, Mr. Watson. He found the doctor in Hawaii who delivered Amelia. He has a signed letter stating that the doctor turned the baby over to George on the exact same date of our adoption. He's getting closer, Tyler. The doctor even has my name listed as the adoptive parent. But there's no signed release by the birth mother or father. George assured me he had one, but he can't seem to find it."

"He never had it, Mark, you know that," Tyler said forcefully. "That's why he charged you so much money for the adoption. That's why he told you to leave Hawaii immediately. And you did it, because you didn't want to ask any more questions."

"Yes, I did it. For Susan," Mark replied. "I loved her so much. I don't know if you can understand that. She was everything to me, and after all those miscarriages, I couldn't stand to see her in any more pain. I'd do it again, if I had to make the choice. I don't care if the birth mother signed the paper or not, she still gave her baby away."

"Or her father did," Tyler said. But did that make sense? Wouldn't one of the girls hate Duncan if he'd stolen her baby and given it away?

No one reacted that way to him, except possibly Ashley, who seemed to be the most distant from her father.

"I'm thinking about leaving town," Mark said, ignoring his comment. "Taking Amelia and disappearing forever."

"You can't do that, Mark. You need medical care. You're rehabilitating. How can you go into hiding? You need a full-time nurse."

"You could help. You're not getting anywhere in Castleton. Why don't you come back here and help me and Amelia disappear?"

Like he and his father had disappeared? Always on the run. No chance to make friends, to feel a part of something, belong somewhere. Did he want that for his niece?

"It's my best chance," Mark added. "It's a big world. We couldn't find you for six years. I don't think it will take that long for Amelia's biological mother to give up."

"It's a terrible life. I don't want it for you, and I sure as hell don't want it for Amelia."

"It's better than giving her up. She's my life. She's all I have left."

"But you don't want to ruin her life."

"I'm not doing that. I'm trying to save us."

"You sound just like Dad." How many times had his father said, I'm trying to save you, Tyler. Save you from a life of pain, living in a home where no one wants you. But his father had been trying to save himself, not his child. Just as Mark was doing now.

"Don't ever compare me to him," Mark said coldly. "And I'll do this with or without your help. I thought you could find something out, but obviously you can't. I'll make other arrangements."

"Don't do anything yet," Tyler said, knowing he was well and truly caught. He couldn't let Mark go off half-cocked. He didn't want to lose contact with his brother again. "Give me more time. I'll find out who it is before Saturday. And we'll make a decision then."

There was a long silence on the other end of the phone.

"I'll think about it, Tyler. But make no mistake—I'll do what I have to do. If they get too close, I'll be gone."

CHAPTER SEVENTEEN

KATE DEBATED what to do next. Torn between anger at her father for betting their portrait and concern for Caroline, Kate wasn't sure which way to go. In the end, she decided to go after her father. It would be smarter to track down Duncan before he went out on the practice run or drank too much to make any sense. She could not allow him to bet their portrait. It was the only picture she had of her mother and her sisters all together. And she wasn't about to let K.C. win it and hang it on his wall, as if they were his family. It was sick.

When Kate arrived at her father's slip on the other side of the marina, she found him on deck talking to Rick Beardsley, the man who had hired him to skipper the Summer Seas in Saturday's race. She'd met Rick a few times over the years. In his early fifties, he was younger than Duncan but close enough in age to remember Duncan at his best. Which must be why Rick had decided to give Duncan another shot at racing glory.

She paused for a moment, watching the two men talk. Her father had on his usual sailing cap, but what really disturbed her was the bright orange-red T-shirt he had on. He'd always claimed it was his lucky shirt, that it reminded him of the color of her mother's hair. She also didn't care for the way he was waving his hands, punctuating each word with obvious vigor. She hadn't seen him look so energized, vital and completely in charge in years.

Was she wrong? Was this what he needed? Was this what they all needed?

"Katie," Duncan called out with a cheerful wave when he spotted her. "Come on up. Say hello to Rick."

She climbed aboard. "Good morning."

"Nice to see you again, Kate. I can't wait to show you my boat this afternoon," Rick said.

"The practice run, you remember," Duncan said quickly, a plea in his eye.

Kate was torn once again between family loyalty and honesty. As usual, the two didn't seem to go together.

"Right," she said, hoping it was a neutral enough word to satisfy both of them.

"I'll see you then," Rick said. "Remember what we discussed," he added to Duncan. "I'd like to see Caroline and Ashley onboard as well."

Duncan nodded. Kate stood motionless and silent until Rick stepped off the boat and was halfway down the dock.

"He thinks I'm racing with you. He thinks we're all racing with you," Kate said slowly, realizing that her father had misled Rick.

"It's a possibility."

"It is not a possibility."

"Katie, I want you with me. You're my daughter. This is a family matter. We're not just racing to race, but to take back what's ours. You must help me."

Her stomach knotted with guilt. He always did know how to push her buttons. "What did you tell Rick?" she asked, trying not to weaken. Someone had to make the tough decisions. Someone had to be logical, practical and unemotional. And that someone had always been her. She was tired of trying to keep things from sinking or drifting away, but, if she didn't do it, who would?

"I told him I'm building a solid crew, one that will win, and that my daughters always support me."

"You don't always deserve that support."

"We all make mistakes. But we don't turn our backs on one another. And there's a lot at stake."

"I know exactly what's at stake. I ran into K.C. a few minutes ago. He told me you bet our portrait on the race. I said that couldn't possibly be true. You know how much that portrait means to us."

Duncan shrugged. "Don't get all bent out of shape. I'm not going to lose."

"You always say that."

"And I haven't lost yet, not to K.C."

That was true. But they both knew there were things they weren't saying. "What if this is the first time? How could you live with the idea of K.C. putting that portrait up as if we were his family?"

"It's what he wanted to wager against the Moon Dancer. I had no other choice."

"You had a lot of choices, including not making a bet at all."

"He won't beat me, Katie. You're worrying for nothing."

"I won't give up that portrait. It's mine." The portrait had hung on her wall for the last eight years, and before that it had hung in the main cabin of the Moon Dancer. It had gone around the world with them, and it was one of the few things they'd taken off the boat before they'd sold it.

"Then sail with me, Katie. You were always the best of the girls. If you sail with me, we won't lose." His voice grew more energized with each word, the passion of his quest clearly visible in his eyes. "Don't you want to feel the wind in your hair, at your back, driving you toward the finish line? Don't you want to hear your heart pounding? Don't you want to feel alive again?"

It was the talk of an addict, an adrenaline junkie. Hearing the need in his voice awakened memories from long ago. Kate could almost hear the wind, feel the spray in her face, see the other competitors in front of her, behind her, and beside her as they raced for the finish line, willing to win, no matter the cost. She was shocked at how easily it came back to her, that thirst for victory, as if it had been biding its time, hiding beneath the surface, until she couldn't hold it back anymore.

"I can see it in your eyes, Katie. You want it as much as I do."

"I don't."

"Say yes," Duncan urged. "Help me right this wrong. K.C. shouldn't have our boat. Your mother would hate knowing he was sailing it."

"Would she?" Kate had to ask. There had been too many secrets between them for too long. Perhaps if she understood this one piece, the others would make more sense.

"Of course she would hate it," Duncan said fiercely. "She was a McKenna. She was proud of that boat, proud of us."

There were so few things about her father that Kate was certain of, but his love for her mother had never been in question. Would she hurt him if she spoke the words running through her brain? He'd hurt her many times, her conscience argued. But this could go deep. Would her mother want her to speak?

"K.C. told me that Mom loved him first," she said, taking a deep breath. "He claims that she slept with him, that he actually thought I was his child for most of my childhood. Did you know about that?"

Duncan's eyes turned cold and hard. "Nora never loved K.C. He lived in a fool's paradise, and he's still there, thinking he can take over my life, my boat, my family."

"That's what this is all about," she said, finally understanding the elusive missing piece of Duncan's ambitious drive and his intense, fierce rivalry with K.C. It had never been about the sailing, not really. It wasn't who was the better sailor; it was who was the better man. "K.C. couldn't accept that Mom loved you," she continued. "For a long time he convinced himself that they had a special secret: me, the daughter no one but the two of them knew about. When he realized that it wasn't true, the pretense at friendship was over."

"I won't let him take over my life, Katie. Your mother chose me." Duncan brought his hand to his chest. "Me. I was the one for her. But, even after we married, K.C. was always around. Nora said, 'Let him be, Duncan. He's lonely. He needs friends.'" Duncan's voice took on a bitter edge. "She had no idea he was trying to destroy me every chance he got."

"How did he do that?"

"He'd sabotage my boat before races or he'd bribe someone to race for him instead of for me. He'd drop hints that I was with some broad when I said I was working, just to make your mother doubt me. I didn't see it at first. I thought they were innocent remarks, but he was playing a game all along. He brought you and the other girls presents when I couldn't afford to give you what you wanted so he could be the big man." Duncan looked her straight in the eye. "He bought that damn portrait, Katie."

"What?" she asked in surprise. "But Mom got it for you, for your birthday."

"He paid for it. Said he wanted to share in the birthday present. He knew I couldn't afford it. So he arranged for you all to have it done while I was away on a fishing charter."

Her heart sank. The portrait was paid for by K.C.? Kate would never be able to look at it in the same way. And her mother had let K.C. do it. Why? Hadn't she realized that the man was still in love with her?

"Why didn't Mom tell him to go?" Kate asked. "Did she know he thought he was my father?"

"She was too softhearted. That's why she let him stay."

"I don't believe it was just that." Perhaps her mother had still felt some love for K.C., some unwillingness to completely break the tie.

"She told him a bunch of times that you weren't his kid, but it wasn't until she was on her deathbed that he finally believed her."

It made sense. Because he'd never been on their side after that.

"That was it for him," Duncan added. "He'd thought he'd have something of Nora after she died, but he wouldn't. You weren't his. You were mine. It broke him. That's why he went after us during the race. He was always in our faces, always trying to bend the rules."

K.C. or her father? Kate asked herself. Sometimes she didn't know who had bent the rules more. It was hard to remember.

"I'm not lying about this, Katie."

She wanted to believe him. But as she'd told Tyler earlier, Duncan had a way of making everyone believe his lies, including himself.

"We can't let him win, Katie." Duncan's voice once again held desperation. "This is probably our last chance. If he even lets us have this chance."

"What does that mean?" She stared at her father in dismay. "What else aren't you telling me?"

"There's a slim chance K.C. knows something."

"About the storm?"

"He's made some comments. I don't know if he's fishing, or if he remembers. I want to race him, Katie. I want you and your sisters to help me. Our family will take back what's ours, making damn sure that K.C. doesn't end up with anything McKenna. Your mother would have wanted it this way. She wanted you to help me keep the family together. Didn't you promise her just that?"

Kate wanted to tell him to go to hell. That it wasn't fair to put this on her. But, on the other hand, she really hated the idea of K.C. sailing their boat. And she hated the thought of him winning their portrait even more.

Now that she realized there had been something between K.C. and her mother, it made all of his other actions—the presents, the friendly pretense—that much more sickening. He'd had a hidden agenda the whole time he was acting like a family friend. He'd waited for Duncan to screw up, maybe even tried to help that along, so he could steal Nora back.

Still, race again? It was an impossible thought. She couldn't go back on the water. She couldn't face the other sailors, the boats, the crowds, the wind. She couldn't put herself out like that, couldn't expose herself to that world again. She knew what men could do in the heat of a race. She knew what she could do.

"I can't," she told him. "I want to move forward, not backward."

"It won't ever be over, not until we take back the Moon Dancer."

"We made a promise, Dad."

Duncan looked her straight in the eye. "I can't keep it."

Her heart sank. "Well, I can."

"Racing is who I am. I'm starving, thirsting, dying for it. Please, I'm begging you. Talk to your sisters, Katie. Together, we can take back what we lost. We won't be free of the past until we do. Say yes."

"I can't."

"Think about it. Don't say no now," he pleaded.

She doubted she'd be able to think of anything else.

She should have stayed at Mike's, Caroline thought, as she faced herself in the bathroom mirror. She didn't want to be alone in her apartment. She didn't want quiet or time to think. Nor did she want to have to look at herself. But she was drawn to the mirror as if it were a car wreck, one she couldn't pass by without turning her head to see the damage. And there was considerable damage.

Her mascara was no longer on her lashes but under her eyes, giving her the appearance of a prizefighter. Her lipstick was long gone. Her hair lay in sweaty strands on her head. She looked as if she'd spent the night having sex and taking drugs, which was no doubt the conclusion Kate had drawn when she'd found her in Mike's bed.

It hurt to know that Kate's opinion of her had only gotten lower. But it was going to get worse, much worse.

Closing her eyes, Caroline took a deep breath. Her head was pounding so hard it was making her sick to her stomach. She'd made a big mistake last night, and it had begun with that one stupid, reckless drink when her father had told her she was a jinx and a klutz and basically not good for much of anything. Damn him. He'd pushed just the right buttons. He'd made her feel bad about herself, insecure, unworthy, the way he'd done so many times before.

She opened her eyes and stared defiantly at the mirror. She was just as good as him, just as good as Kate, just as good as anyone...well, maybe not this morning. Maybe this morning she was only as good as her father, who probably felt as bad as she did.

Bending over, she splashed cold water on her face. Rubbing her cheeks ruthlessly on a terry cloth towel got rid of the rest of her makeup, and the stinging sensation made her feel better. She walked out of the bathroom and stood in the middle of her bedroom, still wearing her low-rise blue jeans and black tank top. She needed to change, to go to work. She didn't feel like doing either.

How would she get through the next five minutes, much less the next few hours? There was so much going on in her head. So many things she wanted... no, needed. The craving started deep in her soul, an itch that couldn't be scratched. She had to do something to stop it. Before she could move, the doorbell rang, followed by a pounding knock and a loud voice that belonged to her oldest sister.

"Would you shut up already?" Caroline snapped as she opened the door. "I'm here. What do you want?"

"I want to come in." Kate walked into the apartment, shutting the door behind her. "I want you to tell me what's going on with you and Mike."

"It's none of your business."

"I'm making it my business."

Caroline flopped down on her secondhand couch. "I'm not in the mood for a lecture."

"I don't care if you're in the mood. Tell me what's going on."

"Nothing."

"Caroline Marie McKenna, you are going to talk to me. I'm not leaving until you do." Kate sat down on the other end of the couch, folding her arms in front of her chest. Caroline knew that stubborn look well. But she preferred this look to one of disappointment, disgust and embarrassment, which were exactly the expressions she'd see as soon as she told Kate what was really going on.

"I'm an adult, Kate. I can see who I want."

"I don't care how old you are. I'm your sister, and I won't stand by and let you make a huge mistake."

"The mistake was made a long time ago."

"Caroline, I love you. But I'm worried and scared. I know this guy is up to no good, even if you can't see it."

"Because he has a snake tattoo and wears an earring?"

"No, because he has a criminal record and a history of drunken brawls. I want more for you. I won't apologize for interfering. You need someone to give you a good kick in the butt. And if I have to be the one, I will do it."

"You're so strong," Caroline said wearily. "Where do you get that from? Dad or Mom? Or maybe both of them? Maybe you got everything, and there just wasn't enough to go around for Ashley and me."

"What are you talking about?"

"I'm talking about why I never measure up. Why I can't seem to do the right thing. Why I need someone to swoop in and rescue me."

"We all need that at times."

"You never do."

"I've had my share of weak moments, Caroline. You know that better than anyone. You were there for most of them." Kate paused, letting her words remind Caroline of all they'd been through together. "I know something's wrong. I won't leave here until I find out what it is."

"I don't know where to start."

"Start with Mike."

"I've told you a dozen times that Mike is just a friend, and that's what he is—a friend." As she finished speaking, her stomach rebelled once again, the nausea overwhelming this time. She ran into the bathroom and threw up until she was shaking. Dimly, she was aware of Kate handing her a towel and helping her into the bedroom and into bed.

"Do you want anything? Do you want me to call Dr. Becker?" Kate asked.

"I don't need a pediatrician. I'm grown up," Caroline grumbled.

"He's a family doctor. Maybe you have the flu."

"I don't have the flu, Kate."

"You can't be sure."

"I'm sure."

"Caroline, I don't want to argue, but—"

"Then don't." Caroline put up her hand. "I'm not sick, at least not in the way you think. Don't you get it? Isn't it clear?"

"Oh, my God! You're not pregnant, are you?"

"No, I'm not pregnant," Caroline said in exasperation.

"Then what?"

"I'm an alcoholic, Kate. Your baby sister is a drunk."

CHAPTER EIGHTEEN

YOUR BABY SISTER IS A DRUNK.

Kate couldn't believe the words ringing through her head. Yet the evidence was right in front of her. In fact, faced with the actual words, she wondered why she hadn't seen it earlier. Or had she?

"I think I've left you speechless for the first time in your life," Caroline said.

"I knew you drank, but I didn't think... I mean, you're not like..."

"Like Dad? He's an alcoholic, too, you know."

Kate sat down on the end of the bed, feeling very tired. Of course she knew their father was an alcoholic. She'd known that for years. But Caroline? She was so young. So full of life. Had all that life and energy come from an endless supply of liquor?

"I'm trying to stop drinking," Caroline continued. "Mike is helping me. He's not my boyfriend. He's my sponsor, the person I can call when I'm feeling desperate. Most people don't realize he's been sober for more than a year because of Alcoholics Anonymous. He took me to my first meeting a few weeks ago. I was doing really good... until last night." She punched the pillow up under her head.

"What happened last night?"

"I went to see Dad at the Oyster Bar. I thought I could handle being in there for a few minutes, but he put a drink down in front of me. I wasn't even going to taste it until..."

"Until what?" Kate prodded. "What did Dad say to you?'

There was a bitter pain in Caroline's eyes when she looked back at her. "He told me he didn't want me to sail with him unless you came along to watch out for me. Apparently I'm a huge jinx."

"That's ridiculous. You're not a jinx. And he'd be lucky to have you."

"He doesn't think so. I don't know why I keep trying. I'm never going to be good enough. I'm never going to be you."

Kate frowned as Caroline slid down in the bed, pulling the covers up over her head the way she used to do when she was a little girl and the world got too scary. The memories suddenly swamped Kate: Caroline curled up just like this in her bedroom in the middle of the day, the day their mom had died. Kate had come into the room to tell her, because her father couldn't do it, and Ashley was too distraught to speak.

Then there were all those times on the boat when it got too much for Caroline, when slipping under the covers and escaping seemed to be the only way out. Sometimes Kate had wanted to do the very same thing. But someone had to be there to pull the covers back, and that someone was her.

She did it now, pulling the blanket off Caroline's head and smoothing down her sister's hair with a loving gesture. "It's going to be all right, Caroline. We'll get through this. I'm going to take care of you."

"You can't make this better," Caroline said dully. "I can't even seem to make it better."

"You should have told me about the drinking."

Caroline looked at her with a truth in her eyes. "You knew, Kate."

Kate began shaking her head. "I didn't think..." But hadn't she sometimes worried about Caroline's drinking, her smoking, her need to let loose? Hadn't those worries started years ago? It all seemed so clear now.

"Last night was the first time I drank in almost a month. I know it's not much, but Mike says I just have to try again, start over from today."

Kate suddenly realized how wrong she had been about Mike. "That's where you were going on the ferry the other day."

"To an AA meeting." Caroline nodded.

"I still don't understand how you came to tell Mike."

"Remember when I told you I ran my car into a ditch on Hawkins Road because a dog ran out in front of me? There was no dog. I was drunk. Mike found me. He told me if I didn't get my act together, I would kill myself. But he didn't have to tell me that, Kate, because I already knew. That accident scared the hell out of me. I didn't realize how out of control everything had gotten. I could have hurt someone else, too."

"The bruises on your arm, were they from the accident?"

Caroline smiled at that. "No, that was just me tripping down the stairs and banging my arm into the door, just like I told you." Her smile faded. "Maybe Dad is right. Maybe I am a klutz."

Kate barely registered the explanation. She was still reeling with the reality of Caroline's drinking. Caroline had almost killed herself driving drunk into a tree. It was awful, beyond awful. She should have realized. She was the big sister. She was supposed to take care of things.

"Don't blame yourself," Caroline said. "I can see it in your eyes. You're feeling guilty."

"How can I not?"

"Because it's not your fault. It's mine. I'm the one who started drinking. I'm the one who has to stop. I let Dad get to me last night. He insisted on putting a beer in front of me, and, once I drank that, it was easy to keep going. I went over to Jake's later and downed a few more shots of tequila. Mike found me there and took me back to his boat. I was in no condition to go any farther. He didn't take advantage of me. He really has been a friend. But I feel like shit today with a god-awful hangover. It must be the result of a few weeks of clean living, because I haven't felt this bad in years."

"I'm glad you had someone to take care of you. I just wish you would have confided in me." Kate stood up and paced restlessly around the room. "I thought we were moving on, getting by, forgetting," she muttered, a thousand thoughts running through her mind so quickly they collided with one another. "But you were drinking, Dad was drinking, and Ashley was taking anxiety medication for panic attacks. I did this to us."

"No, you didn't."

"It was me. It was all me. Every last bit of it. I'm not keeping us together the way I promised Mom. I'm killing us off slowly but surely."

"Why is my drinking your fault?"

"Because it is."

"Doesn't that sound a little egotistical?"

Kate heard the words, but she ignored them. It didn't matter what Caroline said, whether or not she tried to take the blame. Maybe Kate hadn't forced Caroline to take a drink, but she'd given Caroline, Ashley, and even her father the need to find a way to escape.

And hadn't she done the same in her own way, turning a simple bookstore into fantasyland? Turning her back on the water, and all that had happened out there? Forcing everyone to keep the promise they'd made no matter what the personal cost?

"Stop it, Kate. Stop making this about you," Caroline said with irritation as she sat up on the bed. "It's about me. It's my problem. And I'll have to solve it myself."

"When is your next AA meeting? I'll go with you."

"Oh, sure, that's just what I want—strong, invincible Kate by my side, making me feel even more inadequate."

"I wouldn't do that," Kate said, feeling hurt.

Caroline made a face. "Dammit, Kate, there you go again, making me feel guilty. I know it's not you. You can't help it that you're so good, so perfect. You can't help it that you're Daddy's favorite. Or even that you were Mom's favorite. After all, you're the one she asked to make a promise. Not me. Not Ashley."

"You were too young. So was Ashley," Kate said in astonishment, then she started to get mad, too. "Don't you realize how much responsi-bility comes with all this favoritism that you see? Don't you think I ever get tired of worrying about all of you? Because I do, Caroline. I'm only four years older than you, but sometimes I feel like I'm a hundred years older."

"I'm sorry," Caroline said.

"You should be." She paused. "We should call Ashley. She'll want to help."

Caroline rolled her eyes.

"What does that mean?" Kate asked.

"I think Ashley has her hands full at the moment. I saw her last night on the back of Sean's motorcycle."

Kate sank back down on the bed and met her sister's knowing eyes. "Oh, dear."

"I'm sure she won't say anything after all this time," Caroline offered halfheartedly.

Kate hoped Caroline was right, because she wasn't sure of anything anymore.

"Hello, Ashley. Can I come in?" Tyler asked, as Ashley opened her apartment door. Dressed in slim-fitting denim shorts and a sleeveless top, her long hair pulled back in a ponytail, Ashley looked young and pretty, full of life. In fact, there was a light in her eyes that Tyler didn't remember seeing before.

"What do you want?" she asked warily.

"A few minutes of your time."

She hesitated, then stepped aside. "All right."

He was surprised at the chaos in her small apartment. She had obvi-ously not gotten the same neat and tidy gene that Kate had. There were magazines, photos, and books spread out in the living room as well as a few items of clothing.

"I wasn't expecting anyone," Ashley said apologetically, moving some clutter from the couch. "Do you want to sit down?"

He paused by the coffee table and picked up some photos. They were pictures of boats and racing crews. "For the Castleton?" he asked.

"Yes, I photographed each and every entry."

"They're good. Nice light, excellent color, good angle."

"You sound like you know something about photographs."

"I've worked with a few photographers in my time."

"Photos to go with your articles?"

"Exactly," he said. "That's why I'm here. I was wondering if you might have any photos I can use."

She looked taken aback by the idea. "I—I don't know what you mean."

He wondered if Kate had told Ashley he was dropping the article on them. It didn't appear that way, because Ashley suddenly seemed very nervous. She was fidgeting with a chain around her neck and looked like she wished him anywhere but here. "Do you have any photos of your race, shots you took on the Moon Dancer of you, your sisters and your father?" he asked, figuring her answer would tell him just how much she knew.

"I had some, but I don't know where they are."

"It seems funny, you being a photographer and all, that you wouldn't have them displayed." He looked around her apartment. There were lots of photographs but none of the family. He couldn't quite believe that Ashley had spent nine months on a boat with a pregnant sister and hadn't taken one photo revealing that fact, unless she'd been the one who was pregnant.

"I change my pictures frequently. That race was a long time ago. And I put a lot of stuff in storage when we got back."

Tyler sat down on the couch, deciding to switch tactics. "I met your friend Sean the other day. He told me you two were high school sweethearts."

"That's true." She perched on the edge of an armchair.

"It must have been difficult for you to go to sea and leave him behind."

"I didn't have a choice."

"Of course." He smiled to ease the tension he could see tightening the muscles in her face. He sensed he would have to go easy with her or he'd get nowhere. "I bet the boys were all over you and your sisters at the various ports of call. Three good-looking, adventurous blondes. It doesn't get much better than that. You must have been beating them off with a stick."

"Sometimes. But racing men are different. They're so focused on their boats, the other competitors, the weather, the course that every-thing else is unimportant. Besides, we were pretty young."

"Jailbait," he agreed. "Everyone but Kate." He paused. "What happened with you and Sean when you got back?"

"Nothing. I mean, we broke up."

"Why?'

"Because," she said with a helpless shrug. "It just wasn't going to work anymore. It's hard to come back and start over with someone you haven't seen in a few years."

"True. He still seems very fond of you, though."

She flushed. "I care about him, too."

More than a little, he suspected. "Maybe you'll get back together someday."

"I don't know." She paused, looking decidedly uncomfortable. "Is there something else you wanted? I have some things I need to take care of."

"Well, I know you said you don't have photographs of your race, but I wondered if you have anything of some local sailors or past Castleton races that might be a good accompaniment to my article. I would be happy to pay you for their use, of course."

"I have lots of photos from last year's race week. Let me get my file."

"Sure, take your time," Tyler said as she walked into her bedroom. He didn't really want any photos, but he needed a moment to think about how he could win her trust, and maybe look around a little. Surely this investigator who was communicating so avidly with Mark's attorney would be copying one of the McKenna sisters on what was happening.

The coffee table didn't boast anything personal, so Tyler got up and walked over to the desk where Ashley's computer was located. His gaze caught on an envelope on top of a stack of bills with the return address Castleton Family Health. The envelope was open, so he pulled out the bill. It was dated a month ago, an office visit, patient Ashley McKenna, physician Dr. Myra Hanover. That didn't tell him much. He turned to the accompanying letter, which was much more interesting. In the letter, Dr. Hanover referred Ashley to two different psychiatrists specializing in anxiety and depression, both located in Seattle. That confirmed his earlier suspicion that she had mental health problems. He slipped the bill into his pocket, doubting she'd miss it, since she'd obviously already paid it, and he might just need it.

Hearing Ashley, he turned away from the desk and returned to the middle of the room.

She handed him a thick manila envelope. "You can have these from last year. I have to warn you, though, that they're not action shots. There's another guy in town, Nate Raffin, who takes shots out on the water. He might have better photographs. In fact, he's doing this year's races, so you might want to talk to him."

"Thanks, I will." He took the envelope out of her hand. "How come you don't take the action shots? An experienced sailor like yourself, I can't imagine that anyone else could do a better job."

She paled at his question. "I just don't."

"Oh, that's right. You don't like to go out on the water anymore, do you?"

He could see that she remembered their first meeting at Kate's house when she'd confided her inability to get on the boat and take a picture.

"What happened to make you feel that way?" he asked, pressing deeper. He was running out of time, with Mark's threat to take Amelia and run hanging over his head.

"I... It's a long story."

"Was it the storm? Were you traumatized? Or was it something else? Someone you left behind, perhaps?"

Her face turned completely white. "What do you know?" she whispered.

His heart sped up. Maybe it was Ashley. Maybe she was Amelia's mother and she was traumatized because she'd left her baby behind.

He started as the phone rang. Ashley hesitated. "Aren't you going to get that?" he asked.

"I'm sure the machine..." Her voice trailed away as they listened to the message: Ashley, it's Kate. I'm at Caroline's. You need to call me or come here as soon as possible.

Tyler frowned at the concern in Kate's voice.

Ashley grabbed the phone. "Kate, are you there? What's wrong? Is Caroline okay?" She paused then said, "Why can't you just tell me now? Fine. I'll be there in a few minutes."

She hung up the phone and turned to Tyler. "I have to go."

"Is everything all right?"

"I doubt it. Things haven't been all right in a long time."

She picked up her purse and keys and headed toward the door. Tyler had no choice but to follow.

"I'll bring these back later," he said. "Maybe we can finish our conversation then."

"I won't be here later. Just leave them by the door. No one will take them." She hurried down the hall before he could say anything more. Short of running after her, there was nothing more he could do. Damn. He'd been so close to getting somewhere. Now he would have to wait.

Unless he went over to Caroline's apartment. All three girls would be there. But they would undoubtedly form a united front, he realized. He would have more success when they were apart. He would simply have to divide and conquer, one sister at a time.

Kate had tidied up Caroline's apartment, put on some hot water for tea, and checked on her sister for the third time in a half hour when there was a knock on the door. Ashley, she thought with relief. Maybe it wasn't right to burden Ashley with this problem; she had enough to worry about. But Kate needed to share it with someone who would understand. Maybe someone who could tell her that it wasn't that obvious, that she had also been fooled by Caroline's behavior.

Kate opened the door and let Ashley in. "Thanks for coming so fast."

"What is it? What's wrong now?"

"Caroline is..." How could she say it?

"She's what? Is she sick?"

"Not exactly." Kate closed the door behind Ashley.

"Why are you being so mysterious?"

"Because she's trying to find a nice way to say it, but there isn't any," Caroline said from the doorway of the bedroom.

Caroline looked like she was feeling better. She'd changed into a pair of leggings and a T-shirt, and there was color in her cheeks now. But as she sat down on the sofa, Kate could see how thin her baby sister had gotten. Too much booze, not enough food—another sign she'd missed.

"Does someone want to tell me what's going on?" Ashley asked.

"I'll say it. I think I can do it." Caroline took a deep breath. "I'm an alcoholic, Ashley. There I did it again. It's getting easier."

"You—you're what?" Ashley stumbled over her words.

"An alcoholic. A drunk. A boozer. Whatever you want to call it."

Ashley stared at Caroline for a long moment. "I don't understand."

"Do you want me to spell it out for you?"

"I understand what you're saying; I just don't understand how it happened." Ashley looked at Kate. "Did you know?"

"Not until an hour ago. Although maybe I did notice but I just didn't want to see it."

"Well." Ashley sat down in the chair across from Caroline. "What do you want me to do?"

"Nothing. Kate was the one to call you, not me."

"We need to support one another," Kate said, sitting down on the couch. "We're still a family." A family that had given Caroline that first drink, Kate realized. How old had her sister been then? Fourteen, fifteen? "It was that champagne we opened the first day we set sail," she murmured. "Dad wanted to toast our trip. That was the first time you ever drank, wasn't it?"

"Probably."

"You liked it a lot," Ashley commented. "I remember you sneaked back into the galley and finished it off later that night."

"Busted," Caroline said. "I guess you two are to blame for my bad habit."

"Yes," Kate agreed.

"I'm just kidding," Caroline said. "No one held my head and forced me to taste that champagne, and it's not like either of you turned into drunks because of it."

No, but that had opened a door they'd never closed. It had been easy to get alcohol on their trip. When they'd hung out with their father, there had always been glasses left unattended and sailors eager to give you a taste of this or that. Caroline had loved to sit by their father's side and listen to him tell stories. She'd always been the closest to the booze, and to the boozers, for that matter.

"You can't blame yourselves. This is my problem, and I'll fix it." Caroline stood up. "First I'm going to take a shower, then I'm going to work for a few hours and hope they won't kill me for blowing off this morning's appointments."

"You're going in to work?" Kate asked in confusion. "I thought we could spend time together."

"I need to work. So do you. Don't you have a bookstore to run?"

"Theresa is there," Kate replied, but in truth she did need to get to work.

"Look, I'll be okay. Maybe not today or tomorrow, but eventually. Mike said it will take awhile. In the meantime, I have to live as normally as I can. If you want to have dinner or something tonight, I guess we could do that, but oh, damn, I almost forgot, the charity picnic auction is tonight. I promised I'd put in a basket this year, and I don't have a thing in the refrigerator."

"I promised as well." Kate added that to the rapidly growing list of things she had to do. The annual picnic auction was a big fund-raiser for the local library. All of the eligible women on the island made up big baskets of food that were auctioned off to participating bachelors. The couples would then share a picnic supper together. Kate had always enjoyed the event, although some of her bachelors had been better than others. A shiver ran down her spine as she thought about Tyler. Would he come? Would he bid? Would their self-control be tested once again?

"Kate?" Ashley asked.

"What?" She suddenly realized she'd been daydreaming.

"I said that I made extra chocolate cookies if you and Caroline want to put them in your baskets."

"That sounds great." Kate looked at Caroline. "Do you think it's a good idea for you to go? It's usually traditional to include a bottle of wine in the basket."

"I can't avoid every situation where there's alcohol, or I'll never go anywhere. I'll just clue Mike in and ask him to bid on my basket. That way I won't have to pretend with anyone else."

Kate frowned, still not comfortable with the idea of her baby sister and this much older man. "Are you sure—"

"He's really nice," Caroline said, cutting her off. "He has changed since he stopped drinking. He told me so. And he's been nothing but a gentleman. Really. I know how a guy acts when he wants sex from you. I'm not naive."

Kate realized Caroline was probably less naive than she was where men were concerned, so she supposed she'd have to let her do what she wanted. She probably couldn't stop her, anyway.

"Speaking of men who want things..." Caroline cast Ashley a curious look. "I saw you and Sean last night riding on his motorcycle. I couldn't believe it. When did you decide to take a walk on the wild side?"

"It was just a ride."

"And?"

"It was nice," Ashley admitted with a guilty smile. "We went down Sorenson's Hill at about a hundred miles an hour. Okay, maybe not that fast, but it felt like we were flying. I can't remember the last time I did anything that thrilling or risky. I felt so alive."

Now Kate had something else to worry about. "Are you sure it's wise to get involved with Sean again?"

"I didn't tell him anything," Ashley said. "But—"

"No buts," Kate replied sharply. "Not now, not ever. If you think you can be with him and keep the past locked away, then fine, but if you can't, you shouldn't start something you can't finish."

"I really like him," Ashley said quietly. "And I've missed him. I've missed who I am when I'm with him. I'm not sure I can say good-bye to him again." She sighed. "But it may not be my choice. He's still planning to race in the Castleton and on to Hawaii."

"That might be the best thing," Caroline chimed in. "It will be easier for you if he's not here."

"That's what I thought when he left eight years ago. But I was wrong. I think this might be my last chance with him, and I'm really tempted to take it." Ashley turned to Kate. "By the way, Tyler stopped by my apartment. In fact, he was there when you called."

Kate tensed. "What did he want?"

"Some photos of us from the race. I told him they were all in storage."

"But he told me that he dropped the article idea about us. He's working on a new angle for a story."

"Are you sure? He asked me some rather probing questions about my fear of the water and what might have happened to cause it. I didn't get the feeling he'd given up on the story at all."

Kate's heart sank. Tyler had lied to her. Why? Why was it so important for him to do a story on them?

"I gave him some photos from last year's Castleton Invitational," Ashley continued. "Maybe he'll find something interesting in there to build a story around. In fact, maybe we should think of a new angle for him, since he seems to be having trouble coming up with one of his own."

"That's a good idea," Caroline said. "Why don't you introduce Tyler to Ronnie Burns? He can tell Tyler about that shipwreck he discovered off the coast of Oregon last year."

Kate nodded, knowing it was a good idea, but her mind was still wrestling with the fact that Tyler had gone to Ashley behind her back.

"Maybe I misunderstood Tyler," Ashley said. "Maybe he was just making conversation. You should ask him about it."

"Believe me, I intend to." And this time she would force herself to listen with her head instead of her heart.

CHAPTER NINETEEN

HOKEY, silly, stupid, corny, old-fashioned. Tyler could think of a hundred adjectives to describe the auction taking place in Castleton's town square. But none of those adjectives would adequately describe the excitement of the crowd. There were more than thirty picnic baskets up for auction and at least a hundred people milling about, preparing to make their bids.

"Mr. Jamison, are you bidding on a basket tonight?" a woman named Margaret asked him. Margaret was in her mid-fifties and worked the front desk of the hotel where he was staying.

"I'm not sure yet. They look good, though. I'm starting to get hungry."

"Mine has a big pink bow," she said with a wink. "If you like crab sandwiches, check it out."

Tyler smiled as she disappeared into the crowd. Crab sandwiches didn't sound bad, but he was more interested in finding a McKenna sister, one in particular, to share a picnic supper with. He hadn't seen Kate all day, and he very much wanted to.

His cell phone rang, and he dug it out of his pocket with irritation. Mark was probably calling him for another update, another reminder that time was running out, that if he didn't get an answer soon, he would disappear with Amelia. He did not want Amelia to live the life he had led. There had to be another solution. He would simply have to find it.

He was relieved to see a different number on his screen, that of one of the editors he frequently worked for, Kenny Weinman.

"Hi, Kenny," he said. "What's up?"

"Where the hell are you, Ty?" Kenny asked. "I've been calling your apartment for days and get nothing but your damn machine. Finally dug up your cell phone number from that cute blonde in the lifestyle section that you dated last year."

"Jenny?"

"Julie," Kenny said with a laugh. "Jesus, you haven't changed. Love 'em and leave 'em Jamison."

"Why are you calling me, exactly?" Tyler asked, somewhat annoyed with the analysis.

"I've got an article that only you can write," Kenny said. "But you have to get to Paris by Friday."

"I can't do it," Tyler said automatically.

"I haven't even told you what it is yet."

"I'm taking some time off. Family business."

"You have a family?" Kenny asked in surprise. "I didn't know that."

"Yes, I have a family," Tyler snapped. "And I'm taking care of them at the moment. I'll be in touch when I'm free."

"I'll pay you triple your usual fee. This is Paris, Ty. You'll love it."

"Send someone else."

"I can't believe I'm hearing this. You never turn down jobs."

"I'm turning this one down," Tyler said and hung up the phone. He could hardly believe he'd actually done it. Maybe Kenny was right. Maybe he had changed. When had that happened? When Mark had gotten hurt? Or when he'd met a woman he wanted to get to know a lot better? Shit! That was a frightening thought.

The microphone on the stage crackled as the auctioneer made the last call for baskets. Tyler looked around, hoping to see Kate. Sure enough, there she was, setting a dark brown basket on the table. He noted the silver ribbon hanging from the handle. Reaching into his pocket for his wallet this time, he checked his cash. He might have to hit an ATM machine before the auction started. There was no way anyone would outbid him for Kate's basket.

"Tyler is over there," Caroline said to Kate as they put their baskets down.

"Where?" Kate couldn't help asking as she took a quick look around.

"At the back of the crowd. Oh, he's gone now."

"He'll be back," Kate said with certainty. "He's like a bad penny; he keeps showing up."

"And you like him," Caroline said with a knowing smile.

"It's not like that."

"It's exactly like that. And it's not a crime, you know. He's a hot guy. And you're a normal red-blooded female with—"

"Please, don't say urges."

"Feelings and desires. It's been a long time since you've looked at a man the way you look at Tyler. It's long overdue."

"It's crazy. And I'm going to ignore those feelings and especially those desires from here on out."

"Good luck," Caroline said with a laugh. "Tyler seems to be a man who gets what he wants."

Kate decided to change the subject. "Before I forget, I meant to tell you that I had a chat with both Dad and K.C. earlier. Dad bet our portrait against the Moon Dancer."

Caroline raised an eyebrow in surprise. "No way. He wouldn't do that. He knows you love it."

"He would, and he did," she said flatly. "So much for me being the favorite child. Although I have to admit, it made me think twice about racing with him, not to help him, but to protect that portrait from K.C."

Caroline stared at her. "Would you do it, Kate? Could you race again?"

"I'm not sure. But I realize now that there was more between Dad and K.C. than we ever knew."

"Like what?"

"It's a long story. The auction is starting. I'll tell you later."

The auction began and grew more lively with each competitive bid.

"Look, there's Ashley's basket," Caroline said a few minutes later. They watched in amazement as the bidding flew around the crowd fast and furiously, until only one bidder was left.

"Sean," Kate murmured, not really surprised. "I think I liked it better when Ashley was afraid of her own shadow."

"I didn't. I missed the old Ashley," Caroline said. "The one who would jump into the water with fearless abandon."

Kate nodded, remembering all the times they'd sunbathed on the boat then jumped into the water to cool off. Ashley had always loved to swim and snorkel. She'd even taken a deep-sea diving class the year before they'd started racing. "You're right," she said slowly. "I've missed her, too. And I think she might be back." For there was Ashley, greeting Sean with an exuberant hug and an ear-to-ear grin. They walked off, arms linked, as if they were daring anyone to part them ever again. "I hope she doesn't tell him anything she shouldn't."

"If she doesn't, I don't think it will be to protect our secret, but to protect her heart," Caroline said wisely. "Ashley knows deep down that telling Sean will be the end of it all. She won't risk it. She loves him too much."

"Love makes you do crazy things."

"That's true," Caroline said with a laugh. "Your basket is next, Kate."

Kate couldn't help stiffening as her basket was handed to the auctioneer. She hadn't seen Tyler all day, nor had she even hinted to him the night before that she'd be participating in the auction. There was no way in this crowd, even if he was here, that he would know which basket to bid on. She should be happy about that. No long evening of avoiding tense questions. No heart-stopping, spine-tingling moments that would make her consider acting in a reckless manner. Thank heavens.

The bidding began slowly, gathering steam as new parties entered into the auction. She had almost relaxed when she heard Tyler's voice. She couldn't see him, but she knew it was him. Her heart stopped and her spine tingled, just as she'd anticipated. How had he known? Did he know? Maybe it was a coincidence.

But when the bidding stopped and she walked forward to meet her date, she knew without a doubt that, like everything else in their relationship, this was no coincidence.

"We were supposed to have a picnic on the beach or in the park," Kate said as she led Tyler into her house.

"We already did that. And, since I paid for this date, I get to choose the location."

She turned on the hall light and set her purse down on the table. She felt tense and nervous and couldn't quite believe she'd agreed to bring him home. It would have been much safer to picnic someplace where the crowds would have prevented them from talking seriously or acting foolishly.

"You lied to me," she said abruptly, wanting to let him know from the start that she was on to him. "You told me you were dropping the story, but then you went to Ashley and asked her for pictures."

His smile faded and his expression turned somber. "Yes, I did do that."

"Why?" She silently pleaded with him to tell her the truth.

"I went to Ashley to get some photos of the Castleton from last year, but when I got there I started thinking about your family again, and Ashley didn't seem to realize that I'd dropped the story, so I asked some questions."

"To see what she would tell you."

"Something happened to you during that race, Kate. Something that you and your sisters can't tell anyone. I have an instinct for a story, and I know there's one you could tell me if only you would. I can see in your eyes that I'm right."

"What you see is anger that you're invading my privacy."

"That's not what I see at all." He took a step closer, and she took a step back.

"Don't," she said, putting up a hand.

He didn't say anything for a moment. "Why don't we just have our picnic and save this discussion until later?"

"I won't change my mind."

"Then you won't," he said simply.

She hesitated. "All right, fine. We'll eat. Then you'll go." She started to head toward the kitchen, but he caught her by the arm.

"Let's eat in the living room."

"There's only a coffee table in there."

"We'll eat on the floor. You'll spread out a blanket, and we'll pretend this is a grassy park."

She rolled her eyes. "Is this part of your seduction strategy? I just told you—"

"I heard you, believe me. But I paid for a picnic supper, and you owe me one."

"You're a very annoying man."

"So I've been told."

She led him into the living room, and he set the basket down on the coffee table. "I'll get the blanket," she said, but he followed her down the hall. "This isn't exactly a two-person job, you know."

"I want to check out your house."

She opened the linen closet and waved her hand toward the neatly stacked piles of towels and bedding. "This is where I keep the sheets. Excited?"

"Actually, sometimes sheets do get me excited."

She reluctantly smiled. He was a hard man to dislike. "That's a very bad line. And you, a writer, should be ashamed." She tossed him a blanket. "Everything else we need is in the basket."

"Are you sure there isn't anything in your bedroom that we need?" he asked, stopping to peer through a half-open door.

Kate grabbed his arm and pulled him along. "Bedroom tours are not part of the picnic auction."

"They should be, for the price I paid."

She ignored that, returning to the living room where Tyler spread the blanket out on the floor.

"How about a fire?" he asked.

"It's not that cold."

"I heard there might be a storm coming in this weekend. The racers will not be happy."

"Actually, most sailors love a good storm. It's the calm that makes them crazy."

"So they'll race even if it's raining."

"If there's a good brisk wind, you bet. The boats will run even faster." She paused. "Are you still going out with my father tomorrow?"

"That's what he said."

"I hope it's before he gets drunk."

"So do I," he said.

"Tell me again why you're sailing with him?"

"To get some firsthand experience on a boat. It will make my story more realistic."

"Yeah, whatever story that is—if there even is a story." She paused. Had Tyler just flinched? Maybe there wasn't a story. But he was a reporter. She'd already checked that out.

"Of course there's a story," he said quickly. "There's always a story."

"You can probably find one anywhere, can't you?"

"Yes. It's just a matter of simple curiosity and a sharp eye."

"What about your story, Tyler? What if I said I was going to write an article and tell the world about your father stealing you away from your mother? Would you want that revealed to the world? Or would you be protective of your family, maybe even of your father, who you probably have a lot of mixed feelings about?"

Tyler met her questioning gaze with a small smile. "You're very good, Kate. Very perceptive. Smart. Beautiful. Sexy. A deadly combination."

Beautiful? Sexy? Smart? Did he really think she was all those things? Kate shook her head and cleared her throat, realizing he'd successfully sidetracked her once again with his unending charm. She sat down on the blanket. "Let's eat. You can serve me. I did all the cooking."

"Is that part of the date? I thought you would serve me. In fact, I thought you would feed me."

"Not likely." She slid across the blanket, resting her back against the coffee table. Tyler made the same move a second later, his shoulder touching hers, their legs stretched out in front of them.

"I'm not that hungry yet, are you?" he asked.

"Not really," she admitted. Although, if they didn't eat, they'd probably have to talk or, worse yet, they'd find something even better to do.

For a moment they just sat. Then Tyler said, "Is everything okay, Kate? With your sisters?"

"Why would you ask that?" She turned her head so she could look at him.

"You seem preoccupied. A little down, not your normally cheery self."

"Is that the way you see me? An overly perky woman?"

"I think you try to be cheerful, even when you don't feel like it. You're big on putting up a front. A don't-let-anyone-see-you-sweat kind of girl."

"You're the same. You hide what you're thinking behind those unreadable eyes."

"You mean you can't read my mind right now?" His eyes had darkened, and his gaze focused on her mouth. Her lips tingled. She felt as if he were kissing her, yet he hadn't even touched her.

Tyler put his arm around her shoulders and pulled her close until her head was resting against his chest. She should have pulled away, but it felt too good.

"This is better," he said

"I can hear your heart beating."

"Thank God for that."

Kate slipped her hand inside the neck of his polo shirt. "It's beating faster new."

"Want to see how fast it can go?"

"Tyler—"

"Shh." He pressed her head back against his chest. "Did I tell you what I did today?"

She relaxed a bit at the casual question. Maybe they could just sit and talk. "Besides grill my sister? No."

"I stopped at the drug store."

Her body tensed again. So much for just talking. She knew what was coming. What she didn't know was what she would do about it.

"Like a good boy scout, I'm prepared," he added lightly.

"That will be nice for whatever girl scout you run into."

"I don't want a girl scout, I want you."

"I thought we just agreed..."

"I think the only thing we agree on is that we both want each other."

She lifted her head and gazed into his eyes. "That's true, but—"

"No buts." He paused, his eyes very serious. "I know there are a hundred reasons why we shouldn't do this, but I can't stop thinking about you. This kind of feeling doesn't happen every day of the week, you know. I can't make any promises. I can't offer you my heart and my soul, because, in truth, I don't know what's left of my heart. It took a big hit a long time ago when my father ripped my family apart. I don't really know how to love."

She was touched by the admission. "You knew how to love once," she reminded him.

"It almost killed me."

"I understand."

"I know you do. That's why we keep coming back to this place."

Their eyes met in a moment of deep connection.

"I can't stop thinking about you, either, Tyler, but I've never been one to leap without looking. And I'm afraid to look where you're concerned."

"I think there was a time when you could leap. Then you got hurt, and you grew wary, and safe seemed better than sorry."

"It still does," she admitted.

"We're a lot alike."

"In some ways."

"Whatever happens between us tonight is separate from everything else," he said. "There's no past, no future, just tonight. I want to make love to you, Kate. You and me, nothing between us, no clothes, no secrets, no questions, no lies, no memories, no ghosts. Just the two of us."

She drew in a breath and slowly let it out. She was tempted, but it was madness. They couldn't escape the reality of the morning, could they? And how would she feel then?

His hand stroked the side of her face, a gentle, tender caress that made her heart skip a beat. What was coming was inevitable; she'd known that when she'd brought him home.

She leaned forward and touched her mouth to his with a deep sense of relief. Closing her eyes, she let him take over and allowed him to deepen the kiss, sweeping her away from all conscious thought. Her brain shut down and her senses took over as she tasted his mouth, ran her hands through his hair, around his neck, down his shoulders.

No matter what happened, she wouldn't regret this night. There were plenty of things in her life she could feel sorry about, but this wouldn't be one of them.

She broke the kiss and put her finger against his lips when he started to protest. "Is that boy scout kit of yours handy?"

"As close as my pocket."

"Good, because I'm going to show you how a girl scout makes a fire without any matches." She ran her tongue along the edge of his ear and heard his swift intake of breath. "I think I just got a spark."

"I'll show you a spark," he growled, tumbling her over so she was flat on her back.

She waited for his kiss, but he didn't move for a long second; he just stared at her, stripping her bare with his eyes, looking right into her soul. Could he see everything that she was hiding? It was both terrifying and thrilling.

"Touch me," she said softly, putting her hand on the back of his neck and pulling him down to her. She closed her eyes as his mouth trailed along the side of her face, her neck, down to her collarbone. "Don't stop."

"I won't," he promised, and then kissed her on the mouth.

She ran her hands up under his shirt, loving the play of the taut muscles in his back. He was a strong man, a solid man, but he was complicated; he had hidden motives and secret agendas. In some ways he reminded her of the ocean—deep, mysterious, dangerous. It was part of his appeal, and she couldn't resist. She wanted him, wanted to see his control snap, wanted to feel the power in his body, wanted to get closer to him than anyone ever had and fill that emptiness in his heart.

She helped him off with his shirt, then slipped her sweater over her head as he removed his pants and helped her slide out of her jeans. It was a blessed relief when his naked body covered hers. There was nothing left between them. They were breast to breast, hip to hip, toe to toe, mouth to mouth.

Tyler shifted slightly, taking his weight to one side as his hand cupped one full breast, his fingers caressing, pulling, tugging. His mouth followed suit in the most delicious, wicked manner until her nerves were screaming and her breath was coming in rapid gasps of pleasure. His hands and his mouth were relentless, marking every inch of her body with passion and purpose until she was begging him to finish it.

He was in her head, in her heart, under her skin, but it wasn't enough. She pulled him on top of her body and welcomed him inside. She was finally home. And, Tyler might not know it yet, but so was he.

CHAPTER TWENTY

SHE'D TOLD him she wouldn't ask him for anything, wouldn't beg him to stay the night or make promises he couldn't keep. But Kate was still disappointed to find Tyler gone when she woke up Thursday morning. A quick glance at the pillow next to her showed nothing but a single strand of dark hair, no note, no rose, no silly sentimental anything. She smiled at her own foolishness. It was just sex, not love, not romance. But she picked up the pillow, took a deep breath and sighed. She could still smell the musky scent of his body. And, if she closed her eyes, she could see him in her mind, could feel his hands on her body, those wonderful, magic hands.

A wave of heat ran through her. She had been a fool to think one night would be enough. At least not for her. Tyler, on the other hand, had taken off at first light. Maybe it had been enough for him. With that disturbing thought, she stretched her arms over her head and forced herself to get out of bed. Her body felt deliciously sore. Muscles she'd forgotten she had were aching, but it was a good ache, a satisfied ache. It was pointless to look for a note from Tyler, but, after putting on her bathrobe and slippers, she managed to check every table between her bedroom and the kitchen. There was nothing.

Coffee, she decided; maybe some breakfast, then off to work like it was any other day, like all the days that would come next. She didn't miss him. And she wouldn't miss him. Not today, not tomorrow... Well, maybe for just a few days. Then she'd move on.

They had no future together. Tyler didn't belong here. And she couldn't be anywhere else.

Kate shivered. The house seemed colder this morning. Was this the way it would feel from now on, as if someone or something was missing, some heat, some magic? She should never have brought Tyler home. It wasn't smart to have a casual affair at home. She should have kept it separate, gone to a neutral location, a place she wouldn't have to visit every day. She was sure those rules were in a book somewhere, a book on how to have a love affair without breaking your heart.

Like Tyler, she'd thought she didn't have a heart left to break, but there was a distinct ache in her chest. Had her heart somehow reawakened when she wasn't looking? Maybe when Tyler had arrived in town? Tyler, who had all the things she wanted in a man: strength, humor, compassion, and a body to die for. She smiled at that thought— a silly little smile that she would make sure never crossed her face when anyone was looking. She'd keep her feelings for Tyler a secret, just like she kept all the other secrets.

That thought immediately sent her smile packing. No matter what she felt for Tyler, there were still secrets between them. They'd both acknowledged that fact, made no pretense of believing that they were being totally honest with each other, but it had felt honest last night. It had felt like love. But how could there be love without trust?

She was doing exactly what she'd promised herself she wouldn't do: rethinking and regretting. It had to stop right now. Whatever happened from here on out, she'd have last night. She'd know that somewhere out in the world was a man who could touch her heart even if she couldn't touch his.

The phone rang and Kate reached for it, feeling a surge of ridiculous hope.

"Katie?"

The line crackled with static, but she could still make out her father's voice. "Where are you?" she asked. "I can barely hear you."

"I'm at the pay phone on the dock. I'm about to take that reporter friend of yours out for a sail. I need to know if you've changed your mind about racing on Saturday. Rick is pressuring me. If you don't race, then I can't race."

"I already told you—"

"K.C. is spreading rumors, talking trash about us, smearing our name."

Rumors or memories? Kate hoped it was the former.

"Your mother is probably turning over in her grave," Duncan continued. "You have to change your mind. We need to pull together as a family. I need you, Katie. Don't let me down. Say yes."

Kate closed her eyes as her hand gripped the phone. How many times had he said those words to her? How many times had she gone along with him? She'd always supported him, always run interference if she could, always been his backup, but he was asking for too much.

"I can't," she said finally. "I can't race with you." There was nothing but static now, his silence as potent as any argument.

"Good-bye, Katie," he said with a finality that alarmed her.

"Wait, Dad." Her only answer was a dial tone. She stared at the phone for a moment, then dialed the number of the hotel where Tyler was staying. Maybe he'd stopped there to change before going down to the docks. She wanted to tell him...

What did she want to tell him? Don't go. Don't talk to my father. Or, take care of my dad. He's depressed. He's not getting what he wants, and he's dangerous when that happens.

There was no answer in Tyler's room. He must already be with Duncan. Damn. He'd probably been standing right next to her father. Kate hung up the phone feeling angry and worried. Even if she threw on her clothes and raced down to the docks, her dad would probably be gone by the time she got there. At least he'd sounded sober. Mad, but sober. Hopefully that would last.

They would probably be fine. Her father would just have to deal with her decision, live with the disappointment. It wasn't as if she hadn't had to do the same.

"Kate?" Ashley called out, slamming the front door. "Are you here?"

Kate met Ashley in the hall. "Is something wrong?"

"Something is right, actually," Ashley said with a smile. "Sean bought my basket last night."

"I saw."

"We had a great time."

"Why don't you come into the kitchen and have some coffee with me? This sounds like a long story."

Ashley followed her into the kitchen, taking a seat at the table while Kate poured her a cup.

"So, speak," Kate said, sitting down across from her.

"We ate in the park and talked until almost midnight. Neither one of us wanted to end the evening."

What did you talk about?"

"Mostly what Sean has been doing for the past few years. He really wants to work for his father, Kate. He loves designing and building boats; that's where his heart is. It's not in racing. And that's the really good news. He decided not to race in the Castleton. He's going to stay here on the island and build boats. I think it's what he was always meant to do."

"So do I," Kate said with a sigh. She was happy for Sean, but she knew this only meant more trouble ahead for Ashley.

"You think it's going to be a problem, don't you?" Ashley asked.

"Don't you?"

"Well, it doesn't matter. Sean shouldn't have to stay away from his family. If anyone should leave, it should be me."

"But you won't, will you?"

Ashley thought about that. "I love this island, Kate, probably as much as you do. But I want Sean to be happy. And I want him to be safe. If that means he stays here, then I want that, too. If it gets too hard, I'll figure out what to do then."

"You seem so strong all of a sudden."

"He gave it back to me, Kate. I don't know how he did it, but I feel so much better since Sean came back. I'm starting to believe my old self might still be in there somewhere."

"I hope so. I like that girl."

"Me, too." Ashley got up. "I've got work to do."

"I'll walk you out."

Kate followed her sister down the hall, realizing a second too late that she should have steered her past the living room.

"Oh, my!" Ashley exclaimed. "You had quite the picnic last night, didn't you?"

Kate was almost afraid to look into the room. She wasn't sure what state it was in, but it had to be bad. She forced herself to peek around the corner. The sofa pillows were on the floor, along with the blanket, which was completely twisted and tangled among containers of food, some still half full.

"Is that whipped cream?" Ashley asked in amazement. "Just what did you put in your basket?"

"It was for ice cream sundaes. They weren't part of the original basket."

"I bet they weren't." Ashley turned to her with amusement edged with concern. "Are you sure that was smart?"

"I am nowhere near sure. But it happened. And, before you ask, there was no pillow talk, no spilling of secrets. Just a lot of really great..." Kate couldn't quite find the right word.

"Conversation?"

"Exactly," she said with a grin.

"I'll bet. Tell me, big sister, did the whipped cream actually go on the ice cream?"

"Ashley!"

"Hey, you're supposed to be my mentor. If there's something more interesting to be done with whipped cream, I think it's your sisterly duty to tell me about it."

"I think it's time you went to work."

Ashley paused at the front door. "I'm glad you had a good time. You deserve it." She paused. "I kind of wish you would have had this emotional breakthrough with someone else, though."

"That would have been easier," Kate agreed.

"Well, easy has never been the McKenna way."

"I was selfish, though. I could have put us all in a bad position."

"It's not selfish to fall in love."

"I'm not in love."

"Oh, Kate, come on. You don't have sex with guys you don't care about."

"It was just a fling. He's leaving in a few days. It's nothing."

"It may be nothing to him, but it's something to you. You don't give your body or your heart lightly. I don't care what you told Tyler Jamison; I know that for a fact. And if you slept with him, then you're falling for him."

"He's all wrong for me, Ash. I don't want to care for him."

"And I don't want to care for Sean, but we don't choose love. It chooses us. Once it grabs hold, it doesn't let go." She paused, bending over to pick up a piece of paper. "What's this?"

Kate's heart skipped a beat. Had Tyler left her a note after all?

"Kate?" Ashley looked at her with a question in her eyes. "Where did you get this?"

"What is it?"

"It's one of my medical bills."

A flash of disappointment swept through her, followed by confusion. "How did that get there?"

"I have no idea. I didn't even bring my purse in." They stared at each other for a moment, both coming to the same conclusion at the same time.

"Tyler," Ashley muttered. "He was in my apartment yesterday."

"And in my house last night," Kate added. But it didn't make any sense.

"Why would Tyler swipe a copy of my medical bill? What on earth could he hope to find there?" Ashley asked, echoing her thoughts.

"He must be on the wrong track."

Ashley looked at her through troubled eyes. "Or maybe we are."

Tyler sat back in the boat as Duncan steered them out of the marina and past the buoys that marked the beginning of the day's races. There were lots of boats sailing in the area of the start, which would take place in approximately thirty minutes, but Duncan apparently had a different course in mind. He headed them away from the racing area toward the north end of the island.

"Are you eager to be out there racing?" Tyler asked.

Duncan nodded. "I can't wait. There's nothing like a fast start to get your blood pumping."

"It must be different when the race is longer. You have to stay ahead for weeks, months at a time. Must require a great deal of endurance, not just a fast start."

"Long-distance ocean sailing is like running a marathon. You have to pace yourself and take into account changes in weather, temperature, sails, every little detail that could alter the outcome of the race."

"And you don't stop for anything, do you?" Tyler asked. "Not even if someone is sick or injured. You just keep going."

Duncan shot him a thoughtful look. "We didn't have to worry about that."

"The girls were healthy the whole time?"

"They were as fit as any of the crews out there."

Except one of them had been pregnant. Why hadn't anyone realized that fact? Tyler frowned, knowing that this tack was no better than the last. Duncan was too smart to give him an easy answer.

Looking out at the water, Tyler tried to drum up some enthusiasm for his quest. But he had to admit that after spending an incredible night with Kate, he felt even less inclined to hunt down the truth. She was an amazing woman, everything he'd ever wanted—not just beautiful but sexy, warm, funny, smart, the kind of woman a man could be friends with, not just have sex with. Although the sex had been good, very good.

But he hadn't deserved to have her. He was lying to her.

The fact that she also was probably lying to him didn't make it better. He didn't want walls between them. Then again, maybe he should be happy the walls were there. It would make it easier to do what he had to do and walk away.

And he would walk away. There was no question about that. His life and his job were miles away from this island in the Pacific Northwest. And why would Kate be willing to give her heart to a man who had come to town to destroy her or one of her sisters? She wouldn't be able to forgive someone who hurt her family. Her loyalty ran deep. It was one of the things he loved about her. Not love, he told himself fiercely. Just like. He just really liked her.

"Look, there," Duncan said, pointing to the right.

Tyler got to his feet, stunned to see two incredibly large gray whales just a few feet away. They sliced through the water with power and grace. "Amazing," he murmured. "I didn't realize we could get that close."

"They're used to the boats. They don't pay us much attention."

He saw the joy in Duncan's face. "You love this world, don't you?"

"Every last bit of it. But I won't be back this way for a while. It's time to move on."

"You're going to race down to San Francisco next week?"

"And then on to Hawaii. Maybe," he added, surprising Tyler.

"Maybe? I thought it was a done deal."

"Rick wants the girls onboard. I thought Kate would change her mind. She always came through before." Duncan's voice grew weary. "I guess she's finally given up on me. Hold the tiller, would you?"

"What?"

"Just steer toward those trees. I want to adjust the sails."

Tyler felt awkward with the tiller in his hands. Unlike Duncan, he did not feel comfortable on the water, especially when their progress seemed to be contingent on a couple of pieces of canvas and the stick in his hands. Not exactly high technology. But then this boat had obviously seen better days, much like its owner. They were relics from a past era. They'd never be what they'd once been, but they both had stories to tell. He'd bet his life on that.

"I'll be right back. You're doing fine," Duncan said as he disappeared into the cabin.

Doing fine? What the hell was he doing? He was just holding on to the tiller and hoping he didn't run into anything, but they were away from most of the other boats now, and the islands were getting smaller, too. He'd never realized the Sound was so large, so empty.

A shiver ran down his arms as the wind picked up and the boat suddenly seemed to take off. But the wind disappeared as quickly as it had come. Tyler relaxed as the boat's speed decreased. He liked adrenaline as much as the next guy, but he would have liked it more if he knew what he was doing.

Tyler wondered what the old man was up to. He hoped Duncan didn't have a stash of vodka in a cabinet somewhere. He suspected that was a foolish hope. Duncan didn't seem to keep much distance between himself and a bottle of booze.

Tyler reached into the jacket of his windbreaker for his cell phone. He had Kate's numbers, both the bookstore and house, programmed into the phone. He'd try the bookstore first.

"Fantasia. Can I help you?"

The sound of her voice stirred him in a way he'd never imagined. Instantly he was taken back to the night before, to the soft, breathless words she'd spoken in passion. His body hardened; his muscles tightened. He didn't want to be out on this damn boat. He wanted to be with Kate, making love to her.

"Is anyone there?" she asked.

"It's me, Tyler," he said quickly, realizing she was about to hang up.

"What? Tyler? I can't hear you."

"I wanted to make sure you were all right," he said loudly. "I wanted to say good-bye to you this morning, but I didn't want to wake you."

"I can't hear you, Tyler. Is everything okay?"

"It's fine."

"Tyler? Are you there?"

He sighed, knowing she couldn't hear him. They were too far out, and getting farther away by the minute. He'd thought this would just be a nice little sail around the island, but Duncan seemed to have other plans. "I'll call you later. I miss you, Kate. I wish you could hear that." Maybe it was better that she couldn't.

Tyler closed the phone and slipped it back into his pocket. That's when he realized that Duncan was standing at the top of the stairs, watching him.

"Was that Kate?" Duncan asked.

"Yes. She couldn't hear me, though. Bad connection."

Duncan lifted the silver flask in his hand to his lips and took a long drink. "Katie won't leave Castleton. She's dug her heels in. And you're not a man to stay in one place." He paused. "So why are you messing with my daughter?"

"I'm not messing with her. I like her."

"And she likes you?"

"I think she does."

"I thought she had more sense than that. But then, she is her mother's daughter. Nora was a sucker for a smooth line and a charming smile."

"K.C.," Tyler guessed.

"It took her awhile to realize he wasn't who he said he was. Even then she was too softhearted to push him away. Just like Katie should be pushing you away."

"She's been trying."

"Not hard enough. You're still in town." Duncan walked forward. "Move aside."

"Gladly," Tyler said, giving the tiller back to Duncan. "Are we turning back?"

"We're just getting started."

"Where are we going?"

"Wherever the wind takes us."

"That's it? We're at the mercy of the wind?"

"You like to be in charge, do you?"

"Yes, I do," Tyler admitted.

"Then why are you working for K.C.?"

Tyler was once again surprised by the question. "Why would you ask me that?"

"It's just a coincidence that you two turn up in town the same week? I don't think so. You're part of K.C.'s plan to destroy me. He remembers, doesn't he?"

"Remembers what?" Tyler asked, sensing that Duncan was taking off on a tangent that might finally lead to the truth.

"What happened that night," Duncan said impatiently. "Don't play the fool with me. You can romance Katie, intimidate Ashley, or sucker Caroline into talking, but none of them knows what I know."

"What do you know, Duncan?"

"What's it worth to you?"

"I don't understand."

"We can make a deal. Something I want for something you want."

"You don't have anything I want," Tyler said.

"I have Katie." Duncan looked him straight in the eye. "You want her, don't you?"

CHAPTER TWENTY-ONE

KATE WAS STILL WAITING for Tyler to call back several hours later, but the phone remained silent. His voice had cut in and out, making his words incomprehensible. Had he said he missed her? Or had she just imagined that part?

And why did she care? The man she'd made love to the night before had some explaining to do, like why on earth he would have taken a medical bill from Ashley's apartment. Her mind was still wrestling with that question. Unless the bill had been in Ashley's pocket and fallen out and she'd just forgotten it was in there...

No, come to think of it, Ashley had been wearing short shorts and a tank top, no big pockets. It had to have been Tyler who'd dropped it there. Why would he care about Ashley's health? Or was it something else? Was there some type of number on the bill? A social security number? Kate didn't think so, but she supposed it was possible. Maybe that number would lead Tyler to something else, or maybe he thought it would.

Kate sighed as one of her favorite customers approached the counter with a couple books.

"Tough day?" Wanda Harper asked as she reached into her purse for her wallet. "Or do you have race fever like everyone else in this town? All those boats out there make it hard to concentrate on work and chores and all that."

"I know what you mean. I've been restless all day." Kate cast a glance toward the window and was surprised to see some clouds blowing in.

Wanda followed her gaze. "The weather is changing. They're predicting rain for tonight."

"I thought that was tomorrow."

Wanda shrugged. "You know what summer storms are like; they pop up when you least expect them. Thanks," she added, taking her books and walking out of the store.

Yes, Kate knew what summer storms could be like. Intense and powerful. She walked around the counter and stood by the window. In a way, Tyler was like a summer storm, blowing into her life without any notice and drowning her in completely overwhelming emotions. And just like a summer storm, gone by the morning.

The door to the bookstore opened, and Caroline walked in. Dressed in low-rise jeans and a hot pink sweater, she had a smile on her face and energy in her step. Her baby sister was back in form.

"Hi, Kate."

"You look good."

"I feel good. I'm working, so I only have a second. I wanted to give you this." She handed Kate a white paper bag.

"What is it?" She laughed when she pulled out the carton of choco-late-chip cookie-dough ice cream. "You used to give me this when you were in trouble or when you wanted something. Which is it this time?"

"It's a *thank you* for not criticizing, not judging, just being my sister."

"I'll always be your sister, and I'll always love you, no matter what you do."

"Don't say that, because the down side of being sober is that I feel like crying every other second." Caroline took a deep breath. "Anyway, I stopped by the docks to see Dad, but his boat was gone."

"He took Tyler out sailing."

"Are you serious?"

Kate shrugged. "Tyler said he wanted a sailing experience so he could write more intelligently on the subject."

"And he picked Dad to give him that experience?"

"I'm sure he had another reason."

Caroline's eyes narrowed. "You look worried, but you shouldn't be. Dad won't say anything. Sometimes I don't think Dad even remembers what happened, or maybe he's just rewritten the race in his mind so that it actually happened the way we told people it happened."

"You could be right about that. I'll feel better when they get back, though." She checked her watch, startled to see it was almost four o'clock. "They should have been home by now. They left at nine o'clock this morning."

"It's not that late."

Kate walked Caroline to the door. She was surprised at the blast of cold air that greeted them. "The wind is really picking up."

"The racers should be having a hell of a ride about now."

"Hopefully they'll have the sense to come in if it gets worse."

"Since when did sailboat racers have any sense?"

Kate smiled somewhat weakly as Caroline took off down the block. She pulled the door shut behind her and walked across the street. She could see a few boats heading for the marina. She hoped her father was on one of them.

There was no reason to worry. Her father was a good sailor. As long as he wasn't drinking. As long as he had the good sense to check the weather reports.

As long as he didn't try to do something stupid and daring. As long as he didn't let the memory of another storm creep back into his head.

Okay, so she would worry. She couldn't help it, especially since he had Tyler with him. Tyler wouldn't be much assistance to her father.

The wind lifted her hair off the back of her neck, sending chills through her. This day reminded her so much of that other day, the one that had started out so bright and full of promise.

She'd been standing on the deck when the clouds began to gather. The afternoon sun had vanished. The moon had not yet risen. It was dark. Then it got darker. The swells grew into full-sized waves that rose like dragons from the deep. The wind whipped those waves into white-capped frenzies.

But today wasn't that other day,, she told herself firmly. This storm wasn't as bad or as dangerous. Everyone would be all right. No one was going to die.

Tyler hung on to the rail of the boat, feeling his stomach take another nauseating roll. His first experience at sailing had gone on far too long. The beautiful scenery had long since faded away as thick mists descended upon them, socking them into what felt like their own personal cloud. The colors had faded to grays, blues, and blacks. It was hard to tell where the water ended and the sky began. He had no idea if they were a mile from shore or ten miles.

"We've got to get back," he said,

"We will," Duncan shouted. "Don't worry. I've got everything under control. I love it when it gets like this."

Tyler believed that. Duncan was the happiest he'd ever seen him, also the most dangerous. Gone was the weak, tired old drunk. In his place was a man on fire, obsessed, determined to beat back Mother Nature. Determined to win at all costs. For a split second, Duncan McKenna reminded Tyler of his own father, the man who had stolen him from his mother, taken him away from everyone he loved, because it was what he wanted, what he needed.

Selfish obsession—some thought it led to greatness. It took that drive, that impossible ambition, that foolish courage to tackle insurmountable odds. But, ultimately, Tyler thought it led to defeat. His father had died a broken man. Duncan was battling to continue a career that in reality had ended eight years earlier.

"Give it up," he said out loud.

Duncan shook his head. "Never. Never give up. Go into the wind. It's the only way to win."

"Or go back, reevaluate, live to fight another day."

"That's the safe way."

"That's the smart way."

"I've been sailing longer than you've been alive. I know what I'm doing."

"How far are we from shore?"

"Not far. I thought you had more guts than this—a hotshot reporter like yourself."

Tyler was knocked sideways as the boat surfed up one side of a big swell and down the other. He had a life jacket on, but no safety harness, and he didn't think it would take much to go overboard. Still, he felt better on the deck than in the cabin below. "Shouldn't you put on a life jacket?" he asked Duncan.

"Only got the one."

"What? You mean you don't have a vest?"

"I won't need it. You worry too much," Duncan added. "Just like Katie. She was always looking over my shoulder, second-guessing my decisions, wanting to take charge." Duncan pulled out his flask and took another swig.

"Are you sure you should be drinking right now?"

"Just a little something to warm my bones."

"It could slow your reaction time."

"I'm fine, Jeremy, just fine."

Tyler stared at Duncan, wondering if the old man realized he'd just called him Jeremy. But Duncan was fiddling with the sails again and not looking at him at all. Why would he call him Jeremy?

Because he was getting drunk and confused. And Tyler had been an idiot to get himself into this mess. He wondered if Kate had ever felt this helpless with Duncan, this vulnerable. But her situation had been different. She'd known how to sail the boat. She could have taken over if she had to. Tyler had no idea what to do. He had seen a radio down below. Maybe he should call for help. Duncan would probably kill him for casting aspersions on his ability to make it back to shore. Then again, at this rate, Duncan might just kill him anyway.

"Whoo-hoo!" Duncan screamed with delight as the boat went straight up a wave and down the other side.

"Holy shit!" Tyler swore, managing to hang on as water crashed over them. "What the hell are you doing?"

"Living," Duncan yelled. "Isn't it grand? I'd forgotten what it's like. I'm never going back to that life."

"But we are going back to shore, right? You can race again on Saturday. You can sail all the way to Hawaii and wherever else you want to go, but right now we're going home."

"It hasn't been home since Nora died."

"Your daughters are there."

"They hate me."

"That's not true. Kate loves you."

Duncan shook his head. "She blames me. They all do."

"For what?"

"I didn't mean to hurt him."

"Hurt who?"

Duncan took another drink. "Jeremy."

Tyler saw a flash of pain in Duncan's eyes. "How did you hurt Jeremy?"

"He pissed me off, telling me I was cheating, threatening to turn me in. He didn't know what was at stake."

Tyler was having a hard time following the conversation. "Cheating at what?"

"The race. K.C. had sent him to spy on me. That's why Jeremy was looking through my things. I didn't want to hurt him," Duncan repeated. "I just shoved him. I didn't even know he went off the damn boat until I heard Kate scream. Then she was gone. I had to save her." Duncan's eyes turned wild as he grabbed Tyler's shoulders and shook him. "You understand, don't you? I had to save my daughter."

"I understand," Tyler said, which was only partially true. What he really understood was that Duncan was getting more drunk and more agitated by the minute, his mood turning as dark as the storm surrounding them. "We've got to get back to shore. We can talk about this later." He stepped out from under Duncan's grip and grabbed the tiller as the boat began to spin. "Help me here. I don't know what I'm doing."

"K.C. knows," Duncan said, ignoring him. "Everyone says he doesn't remember, but somewhere in his brain, he knows. And someday he'll tell. I hate the waiting. But it's part of the plan. I still think you're a part of it, too. Admit it."

"I don't have anything to do with K.C."

"You're a liar. I can see it in your eyes."

He was lying, but not about that. Before he could say so, it suddenly occurred to him that his feet were wet. He looked down and realized he was standing in three inches of water.

"Duncan. What's happening?"

"I don't know anymore. I don't know which way to turn. I'm tired, Tyler, tired of living with this awful guilt."

"I'm talking about all this water," Tyler said sharply.

Duncan's gaze finally focused long enough to understand what Tyler was saying. "Sweet Jesus," he said. "The pump must be broken."

"What does that mean?"

"It means if we don't get this water out of here fast, we're going to sink to the bottom of the Sound."

———

Caroline stared at the empty boat slip. Why wasn't her father back? It was almost six o'clock, and the wind was growing wilder. The distant thunder and lightning over the water was getting closer by the minute. Something bad was coming; something bad was already out on the water—the water where her father was. The storm had come in much more quickly than anyone had anticipated.

Just like the last time—eight years ago.

The weather reports coming in over the radio that awful day had gotten worse as the morning turned into afternoon. There had been some concern from race officials and the other boats that perhaps they should turn back or change course. Her father had refused to listen. It was a beautiful day for racing, and he wanted to race. They were on a roll. He didn't want to lose their momentum. Kate had voiced some concern, but that was typical. Kate was always more conservative than

Duncan. Caroline had taken pleasure in siding with their father and gained approval from him at the same time. Ashley had gone back and forth as she always did. In the end they'd continued on with the race.

The other boats had also agreed to continue. If the McKenna "girls," as they were called, were willing to stay the course, so were they.

Five men had lost their lives that night. Five men.

Caroline shuddered at the memory. She still held herself somewhat responsible for those five men, especially for one man. If she hadn't supported her father, if she'd sided with Kate, maybe together they could have convinced him to wait or at least postpone the start. But aside from wanting to see approval in her father's eyes, she had also wanted to get it all done and over with. It had gone on far too long, and she was yearning for home, desperate to get there, in fact.

"Caroline?" At the sound of her name, she turned to see Kate approaching, a worried look on her face. "Dad's not back yet?"

Caroline shook her head. "I'm sure he's fine. It's not even raining yet."

"It is out on the Sound. And, even if it weren't, where the hell are they? This was supposed to be a little cruise around the island, not an all-day trip."

Caroline heard panic in Kate's voice, and her own tension increased. Kate was always the calm one. She was reasonable, rational, and in control. But not this time. "We can try him on his radio."

"I just did that. I stopped by the harbor master's office on the way over here. There's no answer. And I don't even know if his radio works. He rarely takes his boat out past the first buoy. I don't know why he did today."

"Probably trying to act macho in front of Tyler."

"Tyler has never been on a sailboat before. He doesn't know a thing about them. If Dad got into trouble, he wouldn't be able to help. He wouldn't be able to make his way back here."

Caroline didn't like the chill creeping up her spine. Her father was a seasoned sailor, a veteran of blue-water sailing. He could handle a storm like this. Couldn't he? Or was she still thinking of him as a hero instead of just a man, an older man, a man who was no longer fit and drank far too much. "What should we do?" she asked.

"I don't know. I talked to the coast guard. They've had two distress calls, but neither boat fit the description I gave them of Dad's boat. They said it was getting bad out there and some of the training runs had gone farther out to stay away from the racing and hadn't come back in yet."

"That's probably why Dad went farther out," Caroline said.

Kate put a hand to her stomach. "I feel sick inside. I know something is wrong. I just know it. The last time I felt like this was eight years ago."

Their eyes met, and Caroline knew that Kate had no more forgotten that night than she had. "We can pretend all we want that it's long behind us, but it isn't really," Caroline murmured. "It's always there, waiting, ready to burst out as soon as we open the door."

"I don't want to open that door."

"I think you already have."

Kate shook her head, but they both knew it was true.

"I was just thinking about the morning of the storm," Caroline continued. "We were all so confident in our racing ability, our weather forecasting, and our gut instincts. We thought we were invincible, every single one of us. Even Ashley. She wasn't afraid at the beginning. It wasn't until later, until we realized that it wasn't going to be just a storm. It was going to be a monster, and we would have to fight it to survive."

Kate looked out at the dark water. "At least we knew how to fight. Tyler doesn't have a clue. I don't want to lose him, Caroline. I'd rather have him walk away from me than have something terrible happen to him. I don't think I could stand it."

Caroline put her arm around Kate. "You won't lose him. Tyler may not know how to fight, but Dad does."

"I wish I could have as much confidence in Dad as you do."

"McKennas don't quit," Caroline said, repeating Duncan's favorite refrain. "Dad may be a lot of things, but he isn't a quitter."

"And neither am I," Kate said. "I'm going back to the harbor master's office. If they haven't heard anything more, I'll find someone with a boat to take me out there."

"What?" Caroline asked in amazement. Was Kate really considering going out on the water?

"You heard me. I can't sit here and do nothing. And I can't just hope that the coast guard will find them. We both know there isn't always time to rescue everyone."

"You'll be hard-pressed to find anyone to take you out in this weather."

"Then I'll go myself."

Kate turned away and started down the dock. "Wait," Caroline called after her, making a quick decision. "I'll come with you."

Kate hesitated. "Maybe you should stay here, find Ashley. If anything should happen, she'll need you."

"Nothing will happen," Caroline said forcefully. "This is not going to be like the last time."

Ashley walked down the street, telling herself not to get worked up over the fact that the weather was changing again, the wind getting stronger with every breath she took, the thunder and lightning moving closer. She would not let the fear take her. She wouldn't go back to being the scared, neurotic woman of the last eight years. She couldn't. She didn't want to live like that anymore.

She stopped and took a deep breath, looking at the building in front of her. The Amberson and Sons Boat Works was housed in a large, barn-like building at the far end of the marina, the back door of the building leading to a ramp where they could launch their boats directly onto the water.

Ashley couldn't remember the last time she'd come here. It had to be years. But Sean was here. He was going to tell his father that he wouldn't be sailing away on Saturday or any other day. He would finally be taking on the role of son in Amberson and Sons. It was a role that had been empty for too long. She knew the Ambersons would be happy to have Sean at home. He was the only son they had left, and he belonged here. She'd known that all along.

In some ways, Sean's absence had only added to her guilt. He shouldn't have had to leave home. Their breakup had never been about him or even their love; it had been about all the things she couldn't tell him, things that involved Jeremy and Kate, Caroline and her father, things they had promised to take to their graves. The only way she had been able to keep the promise was to distance herself from Sean. In doing so, she'd hurt him and herself. Hurting herself had been a just punishment. Sean, however, had never deserved that pain.

She wanted to tell him that. She wanted to say she was sorry, to let him know that if it became too difficult again, she would be the one to leave, she would be the one to sacrifice. And she was prepared to do it. It wouldn't be an empty promise. If one of them had to leave, it would be her. She still didn't know if it would be possible to be with him, to see him day in and day out, without ever talking about the past.

Squaring her shoulders, she opened the door and walked inside. The building was quiet. She walked down the hallway past the business offices and into the main building. There were two boats under construction, one barely begun and one almost finished, a sleek twenty-five-foot sailboat. It was beautiful. The wood was smooth, rich, expensive. She couldn't help running her hand along the side.

The touch brought back feelings of another lifetime—the rail on the Moon Dancer warmed by the noonday sun, hot beneath her fingers. To cool her hand, she'd put it over the side, trailing her fingers in the chilly water of the deep blue sea. So many days of the sun, the wind, the moon, the stars. Endless hours of watching the different shades of water play out in front of their eyes. The sudden squawk of a seabird sometimes the only thing to break the endless quiet.

But it wasn't always peaceful out there. Sometimes the wind sounded like a freight train roaring down the tracks. Sometimes the night was so dark, the mist so thick, that she'd felt like she was sitting in a cloud, suffocating.

Just the thought shook her up. She turned her head, instinctively seeking air, escape. Sean was standing there, watching her.

"Hi," she said somewhat nervously.

"Hi, yourself."

He looked at her as if he wanted to kiss her again, and she couldn't help licking her lips, bringing his gaze to her mouth. Maybe this was a bad idea.

"Did you talk to your dad?" she asked, breaking into speech, anything to cut the tension between them.

"This morning. He was thrilled. I finally did something to make the old man happy."

"I bet your mom is happy, too."

"Over the moon. She's making my favorite dinner, fried chicken, mashed potatoes, and pecan pie. You're invited, by the way. She's sure you had something to do with my change of mind."

"It wasn't me," she said with a self-deprecating shrug.

"Of course it was you. It's always been you, Ash."

She swallowed hard. "I wanted to tell you something." She hesitated, not sure how to say it.

Sean held up a hand. "I don't like the expression on your face. Things are good between us right now. Let's just leave it that way, at least for today. What do you say?"

"I just wanted to tell you that I don't want you to ever go away again because of me. If anyone needs to leave, I'll be the one."

"No one needs to leave. We're grown up now. Can't we just put the past behind us?"

She wanted to do exactly that. "Do you think that's possible?"

"I know it is." He paused. "When you first came back from the race, I badgered you constantly about Jeremy and the storm and what had happened out there. It wasn't fair. You were traumatized, and I didn't see that I was making it worse. I just wanted answers. I wanted something to ease the pain, you know?"

"I know," she whispered.

"But I drove you away, and I regret that."

"You don't have anything to apologize for, believe me."

"Well, it won't happen again. A few days ago I told you I wanted to race, to follow in Jeremy's wake, to experience what he did, but the truth is I don't want any of that. I never did. I never wanted to be him, I just wanted him to be here."

She was confused. "Then why did you say you were going to race?"

"Maybe I was looking for another way to get to you. It kind of worked," he said and gave her a crooked grin. "It got you talking to me again."

"Your mother did that."

"I'll have to give her a big present on Mother's Day. So, do you want to go for a sail?"

She stiffened. "Uh, no, not in this weather."

"Relax. I was talking about this boat." He tipped his head toward the boat next to her. "It's as ready as you are for a dry-dock test run." He pushed the box steps over to the boat. "Want a closer look?"

"All right."

Sean climbed into the boat and held out his hand to her. After a moment's hesitation, she climbed aboard.

Sean sat down on the bench seat and patted the spot next to him. "Sit here with me."

She did as he asked, feeling an odd sense of comfort as she sat down, as if she'd come home.

"Remember when we had a picnic in Mr. Garcia's motorboat?" he asked her.

She smiled at the memory. "Your father was furious at us for getting jam on the seats. I don't think we were more than twelve."

"The good old days."

"The good old days," she echoed.

"What do you think of this boat?" Sean asked.

"It's beautiful."

"It's my design. I sent it to my father a couple years ago. He finally found a customer who wanted it."

She looked at him in surprise. "You did this? That's incredible."

"A little better than all those bad drawings I used to show you, huh?"

Ashley nodded, remembering how Sean had always been busy

scribbling on pieces of paper. "As I recall, most of those boats looked like supersonic jets. You had a fascination with speed."

"I'm learning to slow down," he said, putting an arm around her shoulders.

"I don't think that's slowing down," she replied, not quite sure she was ready for what was coming, but she wanted it all the same.

The kiss started out slow but took off fast as Sean groaned and swept the inside of her mouth with his tongue, taking all she had to give, and asking for more.

A door slammed shut, breaking them apart. "What was that?" she asked breathlessly.

"Just the wind," Sean said. "No one else is here. They've gone home for the night."

"I hate the wind. It makes me crazy. I feel so out of control."

"I like you out of control." He swooped down and stole another kiss.

She put a hand against his chest. "Maybe we should stop."

"Is that what you really want?"

She stared into his beautiful gold-flecked brown eyes and knew it was the last thing she wanted. But was she ready for Sean? She could feel the energy, the tension he barely had under control. This wouldn't be a gentle love affair; it would be wild and turbulent and unpredictable, exactly the way she didn't like things.

"1 can't," she said slowly. "It's too much, too soon."

"Then I'll wait. I'm used to it," he said, an annoyed edge to his voice. He pushed her away and stood up. "Let's get out of here."

"And go where?"

"Wherever there are people, crowds, noise, action. Someplace where I won't be thinking every second about making love to you."

She followed him off the boat, not particularly liking his mood or trusting it. "Maybe we should just take a break from each other," she said as they reached the hallway.

"No. No more breaks. We've had too many already. Let's go to my house. We'll be fine with my parents as chaperones."

Ashley liked that idea even less. "I'm not sure I'm ready for a family dinner."

He put his hands on his hips. "What the hell are you ready for, then?"

She glared at him. "Sean, you are being a jerk. You've been back in town less than a week. Don't rush me."

"Maybe I'm afraid you'll change your mind, that this is some bout of temporary insanity, and you'll suddenly wake up and shut me out the way you have the last eight years. Perhaps that's why I'm rushing you a little."

She saw the insecurity in his eyes and could understand where it came from. "You have a right to feel that way, but we can't go from nothing to everything in five minutes. That won't work, either. We need to get to know each other again. Why don't we go down to the marina and get a soda? Then you can meet your parents for dinner, and we'll set up something for tomorrow."

He seemed to relax at the promise of tomorrow. "Okay, I guess I can do that." He grabbed his jacket off a hook and opened the front door. A blast of wind hit them right in the face.

"Oh, my God," Ashley murmured, her already tense body stiffening. "The sky is black." Her heart sped up. A shiver ran down her spine, and her breath came faster as thunder rocked the night, taking her right back to the very place she didn't want to go. She shook her head, trying to get the memories out of her head, but all she could see were the clouds, swirling, swooping, then the waves doing the same, all mixing together, bearing down on her. "I can't do this," she murmured. "Close the door."

Sean shut the door. "It's just a storm, Ashley. It won't hurt you. We'll be fine."

His voice sounded just like Jeremy's voice. She closed her eyes and saw Jeremy in her mind, his brave face lined with worry, but his eyes alight with the magnificence of it all. He hadn't been scared.

He'd been positive they would come out of the storm all right.

She opened her eyes, seeing Sean, seeing Jeremy, their similar features blurring in her mind, just as the past was blurring with the present.

"That's what Jeremy said, but he was wrong," she murmured.

"What? What are you talking about?" Sean grabbed her by the shoulders, gazing deep into her eyes, into her soul. "Did you talk to Jeremy the night of the storm? Did you hear his voice on the radio?"

The truth pressed against her lips. She couldn't let it come out. She couldn't.

CHAPTER TWENTY-TWO

"ANSWER ME," Sean said, giving her a little shake. "If you heard Jeremy's voice on the radio, those might have been the last words he ever spoke. I can't believe you never told me this before."

Ashley winced as his grip tightened on her arms, but she deserved the pain. A flash of light illuminated the room, spotlighting the torment in Sean's eyes. The loud clap of thunder that followed seemed like a sign from the heavens that it was time to come clean, time to tell the truth.

Before she could speak, the door to the building burst open, and Caroline and Kate ran in.

"Thank God, you're both here," Kate said, her eyes lit up with worry and fear.

"What's wrong?" Ashley asked, her uneasiness escalating.

"It's Dad," Kate said shortly. "He took Tyler out on his boat today. They haven't come back yet, and the radio is dead."

"What are you saying?" Ashley asked.

"He's missing, Ashley. He's caught in the storm, and we need to find him." Kate looked at Sean. "I need a boat. I've asked everyone else, Sean, but there are three other boats missing and everyone willing to search is already out on the water. Do you think you could take me out on your dad's boat? If you don't want to do it, will you let me take the boat myself?"

Ashley couldn't believe what her sister was asking of Sean. Nor could she believe what Kate was contemplating. "Kate, you can't be serious."

"I am serious," Kate said, determination in her eyes. "It's not just Dad. Tyler is with him. They're in trouble. I know it. I'm desperate, Sean. I know I shouldn't ask, but I don't have another choice."

"I'll take you out," Sean said abruptly. He looked over at Ashley. "But when I get back, you and I are going to have a long talk."

"Meet us at Kate's house," Caroline told her as the three of them walked toward the door. "Bring some of your cookies, Ashley. Make some tea. We'll probably need it when we get back."

That's what she had been reduced to—tea and cookies. She'd once been as good a sailor as both of them. But they didn't trust her now. She'd lost their respect along with everything else. Wasn't it about time she tried to get it back?

The three people she loved most in the world were on their way out the door when she finally found the courage to speak. "Wait, I'm coming with you."

Kate couldn't believe Ashley would actually get on Sean's boat, but she didn't want to waste time arguing. When Ashley balked, they'd simply leave her behind and deal with that problem when they came back. Right now she had to concentrate on finding her father and Tyler as quickly as possible.

"We won't be able to stop and bring you back," Kate told Ashley as they ran down the dock. "Maybe you should just wait here."

"She's right, Ash. You don't have anything to prove," Caroline said.

"I'm part of the family. I have to go. One for all, all for one, remember?"

Ashley's words of bravado were accented by sheer terror as she grabbed Kate's arm to steady herself on the dock, which was moving up and down with the water. "Just help me get on the boat. I'll be fine from there."

"It's okay, Ashley," Kate replied. "You don't have to do this. We love you. Dad loves you. He'll understand why you didn't come."

"He won't understand. He never understood. It was my fear that caused our problems before. Dad told me to grow up, to stop crying, or someone would get hurt." Ashley looked at Kate with anguish in her eyes. "I just didn't know it would be Jeremy."

Kate caught her breath at the sharp blast from the past. "Stop it. That was a long time ago and a completely different situation." Besides that, Ashley was wrong, completely wrong. If anyone was to blame, it was herself.

"Let's go," Caroline said impatiently from aboard the boat.

"It's now or never," Kate said, glancing at Ashley's white face.

"Now." Ashley reached out her hand to Caroline, who helped her onboard. Kate untied the rope and jumped onto the boat behind her sisters. They huddled on deck as Sean started the engine of his father's thirty-two-foot cabin cruiser and steered them out of the harbor, right into the heart of the storm.

The rain was coming down steadily. Tyler wiped his eyes, wishing he could see better, but the clouds had obliterated all light. "We should try the radio again," he said to Duncan, who continued to bail water out of the boat, which was looking to be a hopeless task.

"It's dead," Duncan said, pausing in his task. He straightened and pulled out his flask once again. "Maybe this was meant to be."

"What was meant to be?"

"That it would end like this."

"Hey, nothing is going to end tonight. That's for damn sure."

Duncan smiled with defeat. "You and Jeremy, so much alike— strong, energetic, determined, convinced you can overcome. I used to be like that."

"You still are like that, Duncan. You're going to race on Saturday, remember? You're winning back the Moon Dancer. Come on, man, don't give up on me."

"I won't be able to race. Rick won't let me sail without the girls. And they won't come with me."

"I'll help you change their minds." Tyler knew that he had to get Duncan out of this depression so they could fight the storm.

"It's over. I have to accept it. The girls have finally given up on me. It was only a matter of time. And this is the time."

"It's not the time. It's not the time at all. Kate will never give up on you. And Caroline is crazy about you. I don't know as much about Ashley, but I do know this: you're their father. You mean something to them."

"Ashley is a sweet girl, so quiet, so sensitive. I never know what is going on in her head. She's a mystery, has been from the day she was born." Duncan took another drink. "The only thing I know for sure is that she doesn't like me much. Sometimes I think she hates me."

Tyler stared at Duncan, realizing the old man had just given him a big clue. "Why would Ashley hate you?" He wondered if he'd finally hear the words—because I gave up her baby.

"They all hate me for taking them to sea, making them race, not letting them go home when they wanted to go," Duncan said instead. "They didn't know how much was at stake. I couldn't just quit. I'd bet everything: the life insurance money, the mutual funds set up for the girls, Nora's jewelry, her wedding ring. It would all be gone if we didn't win that race. I'd made side bets they didn't know about, and I'd used some of the money to help ensure our victory. It wasn't really cheating, even though Jeremy wanted to blow the whistle on me. He just didn't understand how things were done."

"Jeremy wanted to turn you in?" Tyler asked, trying to make sense of what he was hearing.

Duncan didn't answer him. His eyes were glazed, his face and clothes soaked from the steady rain pouring down on them. Tyler wondered if he even realized where they were.

"I thought he loved Kate," Duncan said. "But he loved the truth even more. Or maybe he just wanted to prove that he was better than me. I should have kicked him off the Moon Dancer when I had the chance."

"How did Jeremy get on the boat?" Tyler asked, still not sure he was following what Duncan was saying. The old man was rambling in a dozen directions at the same time, and it was hard to keep up.

"Kate snuck him aboard," Duncan said, "at the last minute, as we were leaving for Hawaii. She was clever about it. No one knew. We were underway before I realized he was there. I would have lost time kicking him off."

"So you let him stay. And then there was an argument. You fought with him about something to do with cheating."

"I just shoved him away. He was in my face. I didn't mean for him to fall. I didn't know he hit his head. I never saw that." Duncan's voice filled with anguish. "It was an accident, I swear it. I heard Kate scream, and when I turned around she was in the water. My daughter had jumped into that angry sea. My precious girl. I had to save her." His eyes begged Tyler to understand. "You understand, don't you? A man has to save his child."

"What about Jeremy?"

"He disappeared. He was there, and then he was gone. The storm was huge, far worse than this. No one could survive more than a minute or two. I didn't let him die."

"But they thought you did." Suddenly it was all so clear. "That's it, isn't it? The girls think you killed Jeremy. That's the big secret." Tyler suddenly realized why Kate had been stonewalling him all this time. It had nothing to do with a baby and everything to do with Jeremy's death.

Or maybe Jeremy had had something to do with the baby? Had he come on board to help take care of Kate because she was nearing the end of her pregnancy? Hadn't Duncan said that Kate wanted Jeremy with her? What other reason could there have been? They were in the middle of a race. And they would have been together forever only a few weeks later when it was all over.

"Why would Kate jeopardize everything by taking Jeremy onboard on the second-to-last leg? Wasn't that against the rules?" he asked.

"Wouldn't you have been disqualified as soon as you got to the next port?"

Duncan shook his head. "You could have a crew of up to six. It didn't matter who they were." Duncan paused, looking at Tyler. "I didn't kill Jeremy. I just couldn't save him."

"But he was going to blow the whistle on you. That's a good motive for letting him drown." Tyler knew it was stupid to speak so frankly at this moment. Lord knew he wasn't in a position to piss Duncan off, but he couldn't stop the words from coming.

"I couldn't find him. I tried. He must have been unconscious. Otherwise he would have been swimming."

"Why was his name listed on the other boat's manifest?" Tyler asked. "Why didn't anyone know he was with you?"

"The only people that knew were on the Betsy Marie. And I'm not even sure they knew Jeremy was with us. They might have thought he'd bailed at the last port. When the Betsy Marie went down, everyone but K.C. went down with it."

"And K.C. didn't remember." It all made sense now in a terrible way. Kate's boyfriend had died off their boat, and no one had said a word. The girls had circled the wagons around their father. Loyal to the end, they'd protected him.

"I'm sorry," Duncan said, the alcohol slurring his words. "If we don't make it, I'm sorry. Tell the girls I loved them."

"No good-bye speeches. We're both going to make it. Tell me what to do, Duncan."

Duncan's eyes began to drift shut. His hand let go of the tiller, and the boat went into a spin. The boom came flying across. Tyler tried to get out of the way, but it caught him on his back and sent him sprawling onto the floor of the boat. Dazed, his only real thought was that he was going to drown, and he didn't even like to sail.

Kate and her sisters stood in the weather-protected cockpit next to Sean, watching as he steered the motorboat through the rough swells.

They could see a search plane off to the right, its lights blazing across the water. There were Mayday calls on the radio, but none from her father's boat. She told herself it would be all right. Just because his radio was out didn't mean they were in severe trouble. She had to keep the faith. She couldn't let the fear overtake her, but it was there in every breath she took. This was too much like the last time. Maybe not the size of the storm, but certainly the stakes.

"Where to?" Sean asked briskly.

"Captain's Cove. He loved that spot. He might have tried to get a break from the wind over there," she said.

"No, he'd sail straight into the wind," Caroline countered. "The way he did before. Remember? He wouldn't listen to us. He was convinced that the only way out was straight ahead."

Sean looked from one to the other, then over at Ashley, who was huddled in the small space with them, her face white, her eyes huge, her grip on a nearby rail as tight as she could get it. "You okay, Ash?" he asked her.

"No." She shook her head.

"It's going to be fine. I won't let anything happen to you."

Kate felt her breath catch in her throat. Sean looked so much like Jeremy right now, confident, strong, sure of himself. He had no idea...

"Captain's Cove or straight ahead?" Sean asked Kate.

"Straight ahead. Caroline always understood the way Dad thought better than I did."

"Jeremy didn't want Dad to sail into the wind," Ashley murmured. "He thought we should go east, don't you remember? But Dad said we'd lose even more time, and it was just a summer storm. It wouldn't get that bad."

Kate stiffened. If she was closer, she would have given Ashley a good swift kick, but she couldn't reach her.

"What are you talking about, Ash?" Sean asked.

"She's confused," Caroline said quickly. "Look at her, she's terrified."

"They were arguing so loudly," Ashley continued as if neither Sean nor Caroline had spoken. She looked at Kate. "I'm sorry."

"Was Jeremy talking to your dad over the radio? I thought there wasn't any contact during the storm," Sean said, also turning his gaze to Kate.

She didn't know what to say, how to answer. Ashley was at the breaking point. The current storm was bringing it all back into her head. Anyone could see that.

"Jeremy was on our boat," Ashley burst out. "I'm sorry, Kate. I can't keep it in anymore. I'm so tired of lying."

"What did you just say?" Sean demanded, looking from Ashley to Kate. "Jeremy was on the Betsy Marie. He went down with that boat. That's the truth."

Kate took in a deep breath, knowing it was over. If she didn't tell him, Ashley would. "I brought Jeremy onboard the Moon Dancer just before that leg of the race. I wanted him to sail with us, Sean." Her stomach twisted into a knot as she thought back to those awful days. "I needed him with me. No one knew, not even my father, until it was too late to turn back."

The boat bounced and Sean stiffened, taking a minute to get the boat back under control before gazing back at her. "I don't understand. If Jeremy was on your boat, then what happened to him? You all survived. Why didn't he make it, too?"

"So many things happened all at once," Kate murmured. "I'm not even sure I know the sequence of events."

"It started with me," Ashley said. "I was down in the main cabin, and I was crying. I wasn't feeling well, and I was scared. The storm was just starting then. It wasn't that bad yet. Jeremy told me it would be all right. Just like you did a minute ago, Sean." She paused. "That's when he put his arm around me, and I kissed him. I wanted to distract myself from the storm. I wanted to forget where I was. Then Kate walked in." Ashley looked at her sister. "You had the most awful look in your eyes when you saw us, like I'd just stabbed you in the heart."

"I couldn't believe it," Kate said painfully. "I misunderstood the situation. I went a little berserk, and I said things I shouldn't have." Her eyes watered as guilt swamped her. She'd never had a chance to tell Jeremy she was sorry.

"But he knew you didn't mean it, Kate. And he knew Ashley was just scared," Caroline interrupted. "Because I talked to Jeremy right after that. He understood that tensions were running high. We were all on edge. We had been for months, but when Jeremy came onboard, it tipped the scales. Dad was furious. That's why he started drinking. He'd been so good the rest of the time. But, that night, it all came to a head."

"Yes, it did." Kate wished the memories weren't flooding back, but they were, and she couldn't stop them. "Dad and Jeremy were fighting about something. I don't even know what really. I was too mad at Jeremy to talk to him about it, and then I was too busy trying to keep the boat afloat to worry about it."

"Jeremy accused Dad of cheating," Caroline said. "I was down in our cabin, and I heard them talking. Jeremy said Dad had been cheating all along, bribing some of the crew members of the Betsy Marie to slow K.C. down, stuff like that. Then Dad accused Jeremy of coming onboard for K.C. and not for Kate." Caroline stopped, an odd look in her eyes. "I just remembered that. He thought Jeremy was K.C.'s spy."

"You never said that before," Kate said.

"I didn't remember until now."

"Get back to how my brother ended up in the ocean," Sean said harshly, drawing all three women's eyes back to him.

"It was later that day," Ashley said. "Kate was at the wheel. Caroline and I were down in the cabin. I don't know which one of us was crying more." She exchanged a poignant look with Caroline. "Jeremy came down to check on us. I guess that's when he took off his safety harness."

"And when he came back up, Dad started shouting at him," Kate continued. "I told them both to stop fighting and come help me with the sails. They started toward me, and then they collided." Kate saw the scene unfolding in front of her eyes. Jeremy rushing toward her, then Duncan getting in his way, the shove, hands, fists, arms, legs flying, Jeremy landing on his back with a crack. She had turned in horror, and as she'd done so, the boat was hit by a huge wave, and suddenly Jeremy was sliding away, right over the side of the boat and into that awful, monstrous sea. "Jeremy fell. And then he was gone, over the side," she muttered.

"Oh, my God!" Sean said, horror in his eyes.

"I remember unhooking my safety harness. I ran to the side, and I saw him in the water," Kate continued.

"And then you jumped in after him," Ashley said. "I couldn't believe it. Dad and I went running for the lines so we could rescue you both."

"I had Jeremy's hand in mine." Kate looked at the brother of the man she had loved so fiercely. "I tried to save him, Sean. I swear I did." Her voice broke. "But I couldn't hold on. His hand was too slippery, and he wasn't conscious. His eyes were closed. I screamed at him to look at me, to talk to me, but he wouldn't. And then he was gone." Kate saw the awful pain in Sean's eyes, but it was nothing to the pain she'd felt when Jeremy had disappeared. A tear ran down her face as she took in a breath and let it out. "The next time I came up, I saw the Moon Dancer in front of me, and I managed to get to the life preserver Dad had thrown out to me. He and Ashley pulled me onboard."

"We looked for Jeremy, but we couldn't find him," Ashley said. She put a tentative hand on Sean's arm, but he threw it off in anger, glaring at each of them.

"How hard did you look?"

Kate flinched. "We looked, Sean. Don't you think I would have saved Jeremy if I could have? I loved him. He was everything to me."

"But your father hated him. Maybe he made a choice that night. Maybe it was easier to let Jeremy's accusations drown."

"That's not true," Caroline said. "Dad wouldn't have done that. He might be a drunk, but he's not cruel."

"Why didn't you say something?" Sean asked in bewilderment. "All these years, you let me and my parents believe that Jeremy went down with the Betsy Marie. How could you do that?" Sean stared at them as if he'd never seen them before. And he hadn't. He was seeing them for the first time the way they really were. Kate felt naked and ugly and totally ashamed.

"We didn't set out to lie," she said. "But when we got back to shore, everyone was talking about the guys who went down on the Betsy Marie. They were comforting me, knowing that I was involved with Jeremy. Dad asked us not to correct them. When it became clear that no one knew Jeremy had been with us, it was too late to come clean."

"Because you were afraid that your father might have been held accountable," Sean said roughly. "He killed my brother. He shoved him, knocked him out, and then didn't try to rescue him."

"That's not what we just said," Kate said.

"Isn't it? That's what I heard. And then the three of you covered it up."

"Because Jeremy was dead, and nothing we said would change that," Caroline explained.

But her explanation didn't satisfy Sean. Kate could see it in his eyes, eyes that were so much like Jeremy's. Only Jeremy's eyes had never condemned her, never wished her to hell as Sean's eyes were doing now. She couldn't blame him for the hate. It was the same hate she'd felt for herself every day for the last eight years.

"I loved Jeremy," she said. "If I could have died in his place, I would have."

"But your father saved you, so you saved him in return." Sean shook his head. "What the hell am I doing out here with the three of you? How could you even ask me to do this?"

"I asked you because I was desperate," Kate said. "That's why. Because it's not just my father who is missing. Tyler is with him, a man I care very much about. A man I don't want to lose the same way I lost Jeremy. You can hate me, Sean. You can hate all of us. We probably deserve it. But there's an innocent man out on the water who has no idea about any of this. And he doesn't deserve to die because of something that happened eight years ago, something we can't take back no matter how much we want to."

Sean stared at her for a long moment, then turned his attention to the water in front of him. "We probably won't be able to find them, anyway. They could be anywhere."

"But you won't turn back, will you?" Kate asked, holding her breath for his answer.

"Not yet," he said finally.

For a few moments no one spoke. The only sounds were those of the increasingly furious storm. Kate, Ashley, and Caroline huddled together, arms linked, drawing strength from one another as they stood behind Sean, their father's fate resting in his angry hands.

They peered through the darkness. The spotlight running from the top of the boat illuminated patches of water, but it was difficult to see much of anything. The radio continued to relay distress and rescue calls, but none that fit the description of their dad's boat.

It couldn't end like this. Not like this, Kate prayed. There were too many things she wanted to tell Tyler. And even her father. Too many questions left unanswered. Too many feelings left unspoken.

"There they are!" Ashley shouted, drawing her attention back to the water. "Look, there's Dad's boat."

Sean seemed to hesitate. For a split second Kate wondered if he would turn back, leave her father to save himself.

"Sean?" Kate questioned.

"I don't leave anyone in the water," he said abruptly, turning in the direction of Duncan's boat.

When they drew closer, Kate could see Tyler, waving and shouting something, but the wind took away his words. Not that it mattered. Kate could see they were in trouble. The boat was sitting precariously low in the water and going lower by the second. Each swell seemed to push it even farther down.

Sean steered them as close as he could, but the waves pushed them apart.

"I need someone to take the wheel," Sean said urgently.

"I'll do it," Caroline offered.

Sean hurried out onto the deck, and Kate followed quickly behind him.

"We'll throw them a line and try to tow them closer to us," Sean yelled to her.

The rain seemed to pick up as their efforts intensified, creating a thick curtain between the two boats. Kate barely felt the water or the wind. She was too focused on Tyler and her father. She didn't understand why Duncan was just sitting there doing nothing. Why wasn't he helping? Why wasn't he trying to grab the line?

The first few attempts fell short. Finally the line made it into Tyler's hands. Kate let out a gasp of relief as Tyler tried to tie the line to the boat. But he couldn't do it. The boat was sinking, she realized in horror. Her father and Tyler were going underwater. And her father didn't have on a life jacket. Why not? Had her father gone completely crazy? Unless he only had the one, and he'd given it to Tyler.

As she watched, Tyler began to shrug out of his life jacket, clearly intending to put it on her father. She clapped a hand to her mouth, realizing that he would be completely vulnerable if the boat went down. "The life preserver," Kate shouted to Sean.

Sean was already tossing a life preserver to Tyler. Tyler caught it and tried to get it over Duncan's head.

What was wrong with her father? He seemed completely out of it. Was he drunk? The horrifying thought made her sick to her stomach. Was that why they hadn't come back? Had her father taken Tyler along on some drunken joyride? Damn him!

"Dad must be hurt," Ashley said as she came on deck. "Or sick."

"Or drunk," Kate said bitterly.

"What are we going to do?" Ashley asked as they watched Tyler try to wrestle their father into the life preserver.

"I'm going in," Kate said decisively. "I'll swim over there and help Tyler."

"You can't," Ashley said. "Not again."

The last thing Kate wanted to do was jump into that black, swirling water, but she couldn't stand by and do nothing, not when another man she loved was in danger of drowning.

"I have to," she said.

"I'll go." Sean put his hand on Kate's shoulder. "You went after my brother. I'll go after your father."

"No, Sean!" Ashley screamed, rushing to the side as Sean went into the water. "No, don't go," she cried, sobbing as they waited for Sean to come up.

"He'll be okay," Kate said, putting her arm around her sister and holding her close. She was relieved to see Sean's head pop out of the water and the beginning of a strong freestyle. But it seemed to take forever for Sean to reach the boat. He was swimming in a life jacket, his movements hampered by the bulky vest, and he had his arm hooked around another life preserver. Despite the fact that he was a good swimmer, the waves kept pushing him back toward their boat.

"This is just like before," Ashley said. "I was watching you struggle in the water. Dad was trying to save you, and I didn't think I would ever see you again."

"But you did." Kate pulled Ashley into a tight hug as they both started crying. "And Sean is just as stubborn as I am, probably more so. He'll make it, and he'll save Dad and Tyler."

Kate looked toward the other boat. Sean was almost there. So close. And then Tyler was leaning over. He grabbed Sean's hand and pulled him onboard. Together, they put the preserver around Duncan's body. But he seemed to be wrestling with them, arguing, shouting something.

Please, Dad, Kate prayed. Please, just let them save you.

A huge swell came up, crashing over all three of them. One minute they were on the boat, the next they were in the water, and the boat was gone.

Kate heard screams. She didn't know if they were hers or her sisters', but they echoed the screams of the past. The storm had returned. The day of reckoning had come.

"I don't see them," Ashley cried. "Oh, my God, Kate! I don't see any of them."

CHAPTER TWENTY-THREE

IT WAS JUST LIKE BEFORE. One minute he was there, the next he was gone, Kate thought. She shook her head, wiping the rain and tears from her eyes so she could see better.

"They can't be gone," Ashley sobbed. "I love Sean. I never told him."

She'd never told Tyler she loved him, either, Kate realized. She'd let the opportunity pass by, afraid to put her heart on the line, afraid to even admit to herself that she'd fallen for him. Now it might be too late. And what of her father? Had she protected him all these years, only to lose him now?

Then the clouds suddenly parted. The moon peeked through, lighting up the water next to them like a spotlight on center stage.

"There they are!" Kate shouted. The bodies drew closer, but she couldn't tell how many. Were there two or were there three?

Finally they reached the boat, and she could see Tyler and Sean, each with a hand on the life preserver holding her father afloat. She threw the rope ladder over the side and Tyler pulled himself halfway out of the water. Then, with what looked like a superhuman effort on his part, he managed to get Duncan to the ladder.

Kate and Ashley both reached out for their father. Duncan's movements were awkward and slow. His eyes were open, but he seemed barely conscious or aware of his surroundings, and his body was like a deadweight. With Sean and Tyler pushing him up, they managed to pull Duncan over the side and onto the deck of the boat. Caroline ran up the stairs from the cabin below, her arms full of blankets. While she wrapped a blanket around her father's shaking shoulders, Kate reached out to Tyler.

He grabbed her hand and she held on tight. She would not let this man go. He would not slip from her fingers. As he climbed up the ladder, their eyes met, and she almost burst into tears, knowing that she could have easily lost him forever. Then he was over the side of the boat and holding her in his arms, his cold lips touching hers in a passionate kiss that warmed them both from the inside out.

"Are you okay? Are you hurt anywhere?" she asked, pulling away from him long enough to take a good look.

"I'm fine." He turned toward Sean, who was wrapped up in Ashley's arms. "Thanks to your friend here."

Sean drew back from Ashley and stared at all of them, his gaze finally settling on Duncan, who was half lying, half sitting on the deck, his breath still coming in ragged gasps.

"You should have let me drown," Duncan said, looking at Sean. "It's what I deserved."

"Probably," Sean agreed. "But, unlike you, I don't let people die." He stomped into the cockpit, ignoring the blanket in Caroline's hand, and a moment later the engines roared to life.

Kate squatted down next to her father. "He knows everything. We told him on the way out here."

"And he still jumped into the water?" Duncan asked in bemusement.

"He's a good man."

"Just like his brother," Duncan muttered. "I never wanted Jeremy to die, Katie. It was an accident. I didn't like him, but I didn't mean to hurt him."

She'd heard it all before. But the words of forgiveness wouldn't come. "What about Tyler? Did you mean to hurt him when you brought him all the way out here? What the hell were you thinking? Why didn't you turn back when the weather changed?"

"Katie, I—"

"You were drinking, too. Drinking and sailing without a working radio, without two life jackets! It's madness, and you know it. You taught us the rules years ago, but you keep breaking them. Over and over and over again. How many times do you think I can rescue you? How many times can I keep doing this, Dad?"

He looked at her with intense pain in his eyes. "I'm sorry. I'm sorry for everything, for Jeremy, for the cheating, and for the lies I asked you and your sisters to tell." He looked over at Ashley and Caroline. "You girls were the best thing that ever happened to me after marrying your mother. I know I didn't raise you right, taking you out of school and sailing around the world. I made a lot of mistakes. I'm still making them. But I love you, girls. If you don't believe anything else, I hope you'll believe that. And I hope you'll forgive me." His sentence ended with a fit of coughing that turned his face red.

Caroline came over with a bottle of water. Kneeling down beside him, she took off the cap and lifted it to his lips. "Here you go, Daddy," she said. "Don't talk anymore. You need to rest."

More tears came to Kate's eyes at the emotional scene. Caroline loved Duncan so much, in spite of everything.

"I don't know if I can ever forgive him," Ashley said quietly to Kate. "Apologies are fine and good, but what happens tomorrow when he picks up another drink?"

Kate couldn't give her an answer, because she didn't know. But she did know one thing: Life wouldn't be the same after this night. Sean knew the truth, and, turning her head, she could see that Tyler knew it, too.

Two hours later, Kate and her sisters tucked their father into Kate's bed, then returned to the living room where they collapsed on the nearest available sofa or chair. No one said anything for a long time. There had been too many words spoken already.

Sean had taken off as soon as they docked. Tyler had headed to the hotel in search of dry clothes. And the McKenna sisters had come home. As Ashley and Caroline looked at Kate, she knew it was her job now to say something wise and reassuring, but for the life of her she couldn't come up with a single thing. Who knew what would happen now that the awful truth was out in the open, and in front of a reporter, no less. The story could be all over the newspapers, sailing magazines, and online sailing chat rooms in twenty-four hours. Everyone would know that the McKennas had covered up the death of Jeremy Amberson. And if someone probed further, they might find other discrepancies, incidents of cheating that her father had tried to cover up. She hadn't been aware of that part of it until Jeremy had come onboard and mentioned to her that he thought Duncan was paying off crew members on the Betsy Marie to slow things down. She still didn't know if that was the truth or not; her father had been unwilling to ever admit to that, and no one had ever come forward. Perhaps K.C. still had something up his sleeve, something else they would have to face before this week was over.

Kate sighed wearily at the thought of more drama. She looked at the portrait hanging over the fireplace and saw her mother's smiling face. Nora McKenna looked beautiful, innocent, happy. What would she have thought of all this?

Her mother might not have been surprised. She'd lived with Duncan for almost seventeen years; she'd known her husband wasn't all good or all bad. But he'd been different with her, Kate thought. He'd changed after her mother's death, crossed lines that before he'd never crossed. Without Nora, without his anchor, he'd gone adrift.

What now? Would he change? Would this brush with death finally make him stop drinking? Would he see that it was time to stop racing, that he had to give up the glory days of the past, that he couldn't recapture them? He had to find some other way to be happy, but how? And would he even have the opportunity if the consequences of this night resulted in criminal or civil charges?

"What do you think will happen now?" Caroline asked, obviously reading Kate's mind.

"I have no idea."

"I didn't mean to blurt it all out," Ashley said, a guilty expression on her face. "It just came out. I couldn't stop it."

"You wanted to tell Sean. You've wanted to tell him for a long time," Caroline said with her usual bluntness. "I knew you couldn't keep it in forever."

"I tried. And for eight years I succeeded. But tonight with the wind and the rain, all the memories, it just came out."

"I'm not blaming you," Caroline said "I'm kind of glad, in a way. It's almost a relief. Hopefully the consequences won't be too horrible."

"I suppose the race victory could be overturned, although it wasn't illegal for Jeremy to be onboard, but we did cover up his death," Kate said. "And I guess his death might be investigated as something other than an accident. If the other allegations of cheating and bribery come to light, then that will make what happened look more sinister."

"You don't think Dad could go to jail?" Caroline asked in alarm. "It was an accident. We know it was."

"Sean's family may not be so certain," Kate replied. She offered Ashley a sympathetic glance. "It won't be easy for him, Ash. Jeremy and Sean were very close. The whole family was. They're going to be furious with us, and rightly so."

Ashley nodded, her face tight, her mouth set in a grim line. "I know. We need to talk to Mr. and Mrs. Amberson as well as to Sean."

"Tomorrow," Kate said. "We'll do it tomorrow. Well do it together, the way we should have done before."

"I don't want Dad to go to jail," Caroline said again. "The rest of it I can handle. If we have to give back the trophy, who the hell cares? If we have to find a way to repay the money we won, we'll find a way to do it. But I don't want Daddy to go to jail."

"We'll do everything we can to make sure that doesn't happen." Kate pressed her fingers together, hoping it wouldn't go that far. Her father would never be able to survive such an experience. And in truth, he didn't deserve a jail sentence. He was a lot of things, but he wasn't a killer. Jeremy's death had been an accident. If she had ever believed anything else, she would have made sure her father had paid for it a long time ago. "One thing that surprised me tonight," she said, "was that the two of you blamed yourselves for what happened to Jeremy. Why didn't you ever tell me that before?"

"You never wanted to talk about any of it," Ashley said quietly. "And who could blame you? You were going to marry him. You had so many plans. Remember all those bridal magazines we bought at every port? Every time you took a break, you were poring over wedding dresses, flowers and cakes."

Kate remembered. After two years at sea, she and Jeremy had found each other again, just before the start of the Winston. For three weeks they'd been in the same port, and they'd discovered that the love they'd kept alive by phone calls during the past two years was just as strong as ever. Those three glorious weeks had been spent in love and laughter, and, just before the start of the Winston, Jeremy had asked her to marry him. They'd set the date for a month after the race. Their families and friends had been thrilled.

Actually, that wasn't true. Her father had not been happy at all. He liked Jeremy, but he had visions of the McKenna family racing into the history books. Kate had thrown him a bone by telling him that Jeremy would race with them after they were married; he would be a useful addition to the family and to the crew.

"You're thinking about Jeremy, aren't you?" Ashley asked quietly.

"Yes, I guess I am."

"I'm sorry I hurt you by kissing Jeremy that night."

Kate waved her hand dismissively. "I knew it was nothing, even then. Maybe momentarily I saw red, but I knew you and I knew him. The stress of the situation was getting to all of us." Kate turned to Caroline. "And just because Jeremy took off his safety harness to check on you, Caroline, doesn't mean you were responsible for him not putting it back on when he came on deck. Besides that, neither of you had anything to do with the argument between Jeremy and Dad. I'm the one who created the situation. If I hadn't asked Jeremy to come onboard, none of it would have happened."

"But he might have died that night, anyway, on the Betsy Marie," Caroline said. "Who knows what would have happened? If he would have survived along with K.C., or if he would have drowned with the others."

"I know what you're saying. I've thought of that a thousand times, but—"

"But it always has to be about you." Caroline gave Kate a smile that took the edge off her words. "Some things are just fate, accidents, circumstance. Some things you can't control, no matter how hard you try."

Kate let out a sigh. "Lord, what a long day it's been." She checked her watch and realized it was almost eleven o'clock. It was quieter now, too. Glancing out the window, she could see moonlight. The storm had passed as quickly as it had come.

"I could really use a drink right now," Caroline said. Then she added quickly, "Relax, Kate, I was thinking along the lines of some tea or hot chocolate with marshmallows."

"I agree." Ashley stood up. "I'll make the hot chocolate."

"I think there are marshmallows in the cabinet," Kate said as her sisters headed toward the kitchen. "And cookies, too, if you're hungry."

Kate sat back in the chair as her sisters left the room. She needed to think about all that had happened. And she probably needed to start thinking about what to do next, how to deal with the consequences of their confession.

The doorbell rang, putting an end to her ruminations. She got to her feet, knowing it was Tyler even before she opened the door. She just didn't know what on earth they would say to each other now.

Tyler had changed into dry jeans and a gray sweater. His hair was still damp, his face red from a long day in the wind.

"Hi," she said softly, not sure how to greet him this time. "I didn't think you'd be back this soon."

"But you knew I'd be back," he said without smiling.

"I figured. Do you want to come in?"

"Where's your dad? Your sisters?" he asked as he stepped inside.

"My dad is asleep in my bed, and my sisters are foraging for food and drinks in the kitchen." She led him into the living room and took a seat on the sofa. She could hardly believe she'd made love to this man in this very room only twenty-four hours earlier. She'd lain naked in his arms, been as intimate with him as anyone in her life, but now he seemed almost a stranger. The day's events had put a distance between them that she wasn't sure how to cross. "I guess you finally got your story."

"I guess I did." He sat down on the chair by the coffee table and stared at her for a long moment. "Duncan told me about Jeremy. He even called me Jeremy at one point. He said we were a lot alike." He offered her a grim smile. "Of course, that didn't make me feel any better when I realized he'd shoved Jeremy overboard in the middle of a storm."

"It wasn't like that. It was an argument that got out of control."

Tyler leaned forward, resting his elbows on his knees. "Okay, let's say I buy that. Duncan gave Jeremy a shove, and he ended up in the water. In the confusion, Duncan was only able to save you, his daughter, and not Jeremy. A terrible choice for any father."

"Don't you think I've kicked myself a hundred times for jumping in that water? If I hadn't, if I'd kept my cool, maybe I could have gotten the line to Jeremy, or my Dad and I together could have found a way to save him."

"Not if he was unconscious, which he apparently was. He wouldn't have been able to grab a line. Your only hope was to jump in after him. You didn't have time to think about all that, but instinctively you knew it was the right thing to do. And very brave, too," he added quietly. "I can't even imagine having a woman love me enough to jump into a raging sea to save me. Jeremy must have been a hell of a guy."

"He was, but I would have gone in after you tonight, Tyler, if Sean hadn't done it. I let him because I thought he was stronger, and I didn't want to make the same mistake as the last time. I didn't want to cause a bigger problem, with Sean having to rescue me instead of you and Dad."

"I know you would have jumped in, Kate. Your bravery has never been in question." He paused. "Only your judgment. Why did you cover it up? Because your father cheated during the race? Because Jeremy had something on him? What? What was the reason?"

She could have told him that it hadn't started out as a cover-up, that they'd just let people believe what they already believed, that Jeremy had died going down on the Betsy Marie, but was that really the truth? Or just the truth she'd told to herself? Hadn't a part of her always known that things hadn't been done quite right, that if there was an investigation, her father might be in serious trouble?

"It was family loyalty," she replied finally. "I was afraid my father might go to jail."

"Because if the cheating came out, what was an accident could have looked like murder. So you chose to protect your father."

"Yes, I did," she said fiercely. "Ashley and Caroline, too. I was the oldest. I had to watch out for all of us. And he was our father, the only parent we had left."

"How could you look Jeremy's parents in the eye? How could you look Sean in the eye, knowing what you knew?"

"Weeks passed before that happened. His parents were notified by the race officials long before we ever got home. In fact, they held Jeremy's funeral and placed his headstone before we sailed back into the harbor. They had come to terms with what happened, believing that he'd gone down with the Betsy Marie, that he'd died heroically trying to save others on the boat. The Mayday calls painted those sailors as heroes. It was easier to let it be, to leave it alone. It was too late to tell the truth. Jeremy was dead, whether he'd died off of our boat or not."

Tyler frowned. "Do you really believe that, Kate? Do you really believe you were right?"

She met his gaze and saw the sharp, ruthless pursuit of the truth in his eyes. "Not completely," she admitted. "But I wasn't thinking clearly at the time. I did love Jeremy. I was emotionally distraught when he drowned. I couldn't believe it at first. I thought it was a horrible nightmare. But I couldn't wake up, and every time I closed my eyes I saw Jeremy's head going under the water. I felt his hand slipping out of mine." She took a breath, emotion threatening to overwhelm her. "I've seen two people die, two people that I loved very much. I guess I didn't want to lose anyone else."

"Like your father?"

"Like my father," she agreed. "I can say I'm sorry, but it won't change the facts. I lied, whether it was by omission or not. I am sorry, though. I didn't realize how one lie could spiral so far out of control, how our lives would be forever influenced by that one hasty decision."

"You must have been worried that K.C. would recover his memory. He knew Jeremy hadn't been onboard his boat. That must have given you some sleepless nights. He could have recovered his memory at any time and blown the whistle on you all. In fact, your father thinks he does remember, that's why he's come back now."

"Then why hasn't he said anything?"

"I have no idea. Perhaps he's waiting for the right moment." Tyler paused. "Your father wanted to die out there tonight. He gave up. He knew you weren't going to race with him on Saturday, that he wouldn't ever get the Moon Dancer back. He was going to let us drown."

His words horrified her. "Oh, my God, Tyler! I had no idea. I just thought the storm came up too fast or he drank too much and couldn't get the sails going right. I didn't know he quit on you. That's a first. McKennas don't quit," she said with a bitter sadness. "You don't know how many times I've heard those words spoken."

"But you don't quit, do you?" Tyler sent her a hard look that she didn't understand.

"What do you mean?" she asked hesitantly, sensing his anger had just gone up a notch and not sure what had triggered it.

"I just want to know one thing, Kate. Why, after screwing up your own family, did you go looking to screw up someone else's family?"

Who are you talking about? Jeremy's family, the Ambersons?"

"No."

"Then who?" Kate asked in confusion. "I don't understand."

"I want to know why you went looking for the child you gave up eight years ago."

Kate's breath fled from her chest as the last secret came to the surface. "You know about the baby? My father told you that, too?"

"He didn't have to. That baby is my niece. Her name is Amelia. She was adopted by my brother Mark in Hawaii eight years ago. She has a locket with Nora McKenna's name on it."

Kate put a hand to her heart. She'd never expected this. "Amelia? Her name is Amelia?"

"That's right. And she's happy, healthy, and she loves her father."

"What about her... her adoptive mother?"

"You mean her real mother? The one who took care of her, stayed up with her at night, that woman?" His voice was unforgiving. "What does it matter, Kate? You gave your baby up. You can't have her back." He shook his head. "I still can't believe you did it. But Jeremy was dead, so it all makes sense now. He came onboard to be with you when you had the baby. After he died, you couldn't bear the thought of keeping his child. So you gave it away. You pretended it had never happened, just like everything else you denied."

"You must think I'm a terrible person," Kate murmured, seeing the hardness in his eyes.

"I think you've had second thoughts and decided to hire a shark attorney to get your daughter back, but you can't have her. I have enough on all of you to thwart any efforts to take back Amelia. So don't even try."

"You have enough..." Her voice trailed away as her brain finally caught up. "You came here to find your niece's birth mother, not to do a story about us winning the Winston, didn't you?"

"That's right, Kate. I couldn't care less about the damn race. I only care about what happens to Amelia. I won't let you take her away without a fight."

Kate snapped her fingers. "That's why you took that medical bill from Ashley's apartment. And you mentioned that you thought Caroline had a drinking problem. You were collecting evidence. What about me? What did you find out about me when you made love to me last night?" A terrible pain stabbed at her heart as she realized the depth of his deceit.

For the first time, Tyler looked guilty. "Last night wasn't about

Amelia. It was about us, but we both knew there were secrets between us."

"Yes, we both knew," she said wearily. Her heart was as heavy as a stone.

His eyes softened just for a minute. "Why couldn't you tell me, Kate?"

"I didn't even know that was your question. I thought you were probing into what happened during the race. I had to protect my family."

"And I have to protect mine. I'm sorry if it hurts, but you made the decision to give your baby up. Now let her be."

"It wasn't Kate's decision, it was mine."

Kate drew in a shaky breath as Tyler turned to the woman standing in the doorway.

"What did you say?" he asked.

"Kate isn't the mother. I am."

CHAPTER TWENTY-FOUR

TYLER WAS STUNNED to hear the words coming from Caroline's mouth. Caroline? No. That wasn't right. Kate was the mother. It had to be Kate. Kate and Jeremy. Was this just another ploy to confuse him? The McKenna sisters sticking together, no matter what?

"That's right, Tyler," Caroline repeated with a forcefulness he couldn't ignore. "I'm the one who got pregnant and gave up a child." Caroline walked into the room, her head up, her step purposeful.

"You? But I don't understand," Tyler said. "You were only—"

"Sixteen years old." Caroline held up a hand as Kate started to interrupt. "It's okay, Kate. I want to tell him, to be done with the secrets. It's true. I had a baby, and I gave her away."

"Willingly?" Tyler asked. "Or did your father make the decision for you?"

"It was a combination of both," Caroline said tightly.

Not exactly what he wanted to hear, but close enough. "Then you had no business hiring an attorney to go after my brother. Do you know what kind of pain and turmoil you've caused by threatening to take away his child? Do you have any idea what it's like to spend eight years loving and raising a daughter only to find out that the birth mother suddenly wants a second chance?"

Caroline appeared shocked by his comments. Her eyes had grown wider with each word. Was it all an act? Or had she just not considered the consequences of her actions?

"I didn't," she said finally. "I didn't threaten to take her away."

"Your hotshot attorney did."

"Steve? He must have done that on his own."

"You hired an attorney?" Kate asked. "When did you decide to do that? Why didn't you tell me?"

So Kate didn't know about the attorney. For some reason, that made Tyler feel better. Maybe if Kate had known, she would have advised Caroline not to do it. Maybe there was still some hope that he and Kate might wind up on the same side.

"What's going on?" Ashley asked, returning to the room with a tray of hot drinks. "Don't tell me something else is wrong."

"Tyler came here to find out which one of us gave up a baby," Kate answered her sister. "I can't believe that possibility never even crossed my mind."

"You were too busy covering up the Jeremy story," Tyler told her. "Ironic, isn't it?"

"Sorry, I'm a little too tired to appreciate the irony." Kate glanced back at Ashley. "Tyler's brother adopted the baby."

"I think I'd better sit down." Ashley put the tray down on the coffee table and took a seat on the couch next to Kate. Caroline sat down on the other side of her big sister. They were a united front, but Tyler wasn't intimidated.

"I'd really like to know how you became pregnant with Amelia," he said.

"Amelia? Is that her name?" An eager light blossomed in Caroline's eyes.

"Answer the question."

"Don't interrogate her," Kate said sharply. "She's not on trial here."

"It's okay," Caroline said. "I want to tell. In fact, I've been dying to talk about the baby, but I knew I couldn't talk about it with Kate or Ashley."

"Why not?" Kate and Ashley asked at the same time.

Caroline looked at both of them and shook her head. "Because we never talk about the past, especially that night."

"We didn't want to cause you more pain," Kate said. "We figured if you wanted to talk about it, you would."

"To answer your question," Caroline said, turning her attention back to Tyler, "I was a little wild back then. I started drinking on the boat, swiping some of my dad's stuff, and it was easy enough to drink onshore, too. I just sat by my dad at the bar, and people were always willing to give me sips of this and that. Kate and Ashley tried to keep the reins on me, but I was a rebellious teenager, and we were living like gypsies. One night I got into trouble. I wound up going further than I wanted to. It wasn't like rape or anything," she added quickly. "I let things get out of control. I didn't try to stop until it was too late. The worst thing is that I didn't even know his name or who he was."

"I'm sorry," Tyler said sincerely. Despite Caroline's brave words, he had a feeling the night had been more traumatic than she was saying. "But how could you keep it a secret? That's what I don't understand. Didn't anyone see you?"

"We wore heavy weather gear a lot of the time," Caroline explained. "And once I was showing, I didn't really go off the boat much. Besides that, I was a teenager in great shape. I wasn't eating that much. We were racing. We were working hard. I didn't even know I was pregnant until I was five months along."

"That doesn't seem possible," he said.

"It was, believe me. My periods weren't that regular. I never threw up. And if I felt queasy, I just chalked it up to being on a bouncing boat. But my growing stomach finally got my attention, and I had to tell Kate and Ashley that I thought I might be pregnant."

"It must have been some conversation," Tyler commented, looking over at Kate.

"It was pretty scary," she replied. "Caroline was so young, and I wasn't that much older. I had no idea what we were going to do."

"Kate bought me a pregnancy test at the next stop, and we found out for sure," Caroline continued. "Kate thought we should drop out of the race."

"Of course you should have dropped out of the race," Tyler said sharply. "What did your father say when you told him?"

"He said no," Kate replied, answering for Caroline. "Caroline wasn't due to deliver until after we got back, and at the moment we were in second place. We were very close to everything he'd dreamed about. Later, I discovered that there was some money involved in the race, some creative financing that my father had done."

"With your mutual funds and your mother's jewelry," Tyler said with a nod. "He told me about that."

"You had quite a chat out there, didn't you?"

"It's amazing what a man will say when he thinks he won't see tomorrow. But, let's get back to a pregnant teenage girl on a world-class racing boat with only her father and sisters to take care of her. You were miles from land at times, days from help. What if something had gone wrong? What would you have done?"

"I don't know," Kate answered. "It's easy to look back now and say we were crazy, but you don't realize how powerless we all felt. My father was in charge. Caroline was underage. I couldn't take her and run away, even if I wanted to. I didn't have any money. We'd been living on a boat for more than two and a half years. I had to listen to Dad. I didn't have another choice. None of us did."

"Why keep it a secret? Would it have disqualified you?"

"No, but Dad didn't want Caroline to be the focus of a lot of unwanted attention. He was protecting her."

"Bullshit!" Tyler leaned forward. "He didn't tell anyone because he didn't want to lose the spotlight. He didn't want the press to be side-tracked by a pregnant teenage girl hard-luck story. Isn't that the truth?"

"Yes, that's the truth," Ashley said, speaking for the first time. "Dad was obsessed with that race. He was a different person during those eleven months. He wouldn't let anything get in the way of winning. I don't remember having one conversation with him that didn't include some worry about the course, the sails, the boat speed, or the weather. He was on one track and one track only. When we told him about Caroline, he barely blinked. His response was 'All right, we'll deal with that later, when we get home. Right now we have a race to win.'"

"Dad didn't want to deal with the fact that Caroline was pregnant," Kate added. "He knew he was responsible for what happened, for not keeping a better eye on her, and I think he felt guilty about that, even though he didn't say so. I believe that deep in his heart he felt he'd let Caroline down."

"Really? Do you think so?" Caroline asked. "Do you think he felt bad? Because he always seemed angry. Then he got distant and pulled away from me until we barely spoke. I figured he was just so disappointed he could barely stand to look at me."

Tyler couldn't believe what he was hearing. Actually, he could believe it. Having spent the day with Duncan, he now had a better understanding of just how difficult and complicated a man he could be. He was extremely likable at times, and a real bastard at others. "So, your father wouldn't let you tell anyone. He made Caroline hide away on the boat and swore you all to secrecy."

"He did buy me a stack of baby magazines and baby books," Caroline said.

"Bully for him." Tyler shook his head in disgust. "He didn't treat you right, Caroline. He should have made sure you had proper medical care. He should have tracked down the boy who got you pregnant. There were a hundred things he should have done that he didn't do, and you all know it. But you're still protecting him, even now."

"You don't know him as well as we do," Caroline said with a soft plea in her eyes. "He could be a great dad at times. He could be the best time you ever had."

"But mostly he was a terrible dad and the worst time we ever had," Ashley said. "Don't you agree, Kate?"

Tyler waited for Kate to speak. He had a feeling her viewpoint fell somewhere in the middle of theirs.

"He's our father, Tyler. And you're judging our actions eight years after the fact. In retrospect, things always look a lot more clear than they did at the time," Kate said.

"I'll give you that," he conceded. "Tell me about the birth. It must have happened right after the storm. Was it after you got to port?" The three sisters exchanged looks that made him even more curious. "Well?" he prodded.

"I went into labor during the storm," Caroline said. "I don't know if it was the stress or the fear or whatever, but there it was. I started having contractions about ten minutes into the storm. That's why I stayed down in the cabin. I was in a lot of pain. Jeremy kept coming back and forth to check on me."

"Jeremy," Tyler echoed, realizing this was another piece of the puzzle. He turned to Kate. "You wanted him on board to help you with Caroline and the baby in case it came earlier."

"That was part of it," Kate admitted. "I was scared. Caroline had been having some smaller contractions, and while it didn't seem possible she would deliver that early, I was worried something might happen. Our father wasn't seeing very clearly back then. I couldn't even talk to him about it."

"When did the baby come and who delivered her?"

"She was born at dawn, and it was a group effort," Kate replied. "Ashley did the most. She'd read all the books. Frankly, I was still in shock from losing Jeremy to be much of a help. Dad was around, too. Jeremy's death had sobered him up quickly. But it was mostly Ashley who talked Caroline through it."

"I can't even imagine that night. First you're fighting for your life, then you lose your fiancé, then your sister goes into labor." He looked at Kate and shook his head in amazement.

Kate gave him a grim smile. "It all happened so fast. In twenty-four hours we saw someone go out of the world and someone come in. It was almost surreal. That morning was eerily quiet. The sun seemed to mock everything we'd gone through, as if we'd imagined that awful storm, as if it had all been a bad dream. But Jeremy's things were on his bunk, and he wasn't coming back to get them. And Caroline was holding her baby in her arms as we limped into port, ravaged, exhausted, overwhelmed." Kate's voice petered out, and Tyler saw Ashley put a hand on her sister's knee. Then she looked at Tyler and continued the story.

"When we got to Hawaii, there were lots of reporters waiting,"

Ashley said. "We were one of the first boats to arrive. But already news had spread like wildfire that the Betsy Marie had gone down. That's all anyone was talking about. Dad went out first and gave interviews. Then he sent Kate and me out to run interference. As long as the news people could talk to the 'girls,' as they liked to call us, they were satisfied. I kept waiting for someone to ask us about the storm, about Jeremy, but no one did. In fact, people came up to Kate, trying to comfort her. A lot of the other crews knew that they had gotten engaged just before the start of the race. It quickly became clear that no one knew Jeremy had switched boats at the last minute."

"And you didn't tell them?"

"No, we didn't."

"Dad took me to the hospital to get me checked out," Caroline said. "Actually, it wasn't a hospital. It was a clinic, I think. I don't remember, exactly. I do remember the doctor telling Dad that he knew someone who would love to take the baby." She drew in a deep, emotional breath at the memory. "I gave her one last hug and said good-bye, and I put the locket around her neck. I wanted her to have something of mine, and that locket was given to me by my mother." Caroline paused. "I cried for three days straight."

"We all did," Kate added. "I wanted to help Caroline raise the baby. I didn't want to let her go, but my father convinced Caroline that it wouldn't work. Maybe if Jeremy hadn't just died, maybe if the race had been over and we'd been home, I would have been able to make him see that we couldn't give Caroline's baby away. She was part of our family. But that wasn't how it was, and when Caroline came back to the hotel room alone, we didn't know where the baby had gone or who had adopted her. The decision had been made, and we would have to live with it."

"Exactly. So what happened three weeks ago, Caroline?" Tyler demanded. "What made you decide to try and take your baby back now?"

"I didn't decide to take her back. I just wanted to know if she was all right. That's all. I swear."

"Your attorney said differently."

"My attorney is a friend of a friend. I don't know what he told you or what he did, but all I asked him to do was to see if he could find out if my baby was okay. A few weeks ago, I came to terms with the fact that I have a drinking problem. I went to AA and listened to all the talk about taking responsibility for your actions and saying you're sorry and all that. That's when I decided that I needed to know that the baby was all right." Caroline looked at Tyler with her heart in her eyes. "Is she all right, Tyler?"

Tyler hesitated, knowing he was about to take a step his brother would not want him to take, but he was leaning toward believing Caroline's story. She had no reason to lie to him now. She could just have easily told him that she thought her baby had been taken illegally, and she wanted to get her back. But Caroline seemed genuine in her concern and remorse. "Yes," he said finally. "Amelia is fine. She's a happy and healthy little girl. But she did suffer a huge tragedy a month ago when her mother was killed in a car accident."

Caroline put a hand to her mouth in horror. "Oh, no."

"My brother Mark was badly injured, but Amelia was fine. A few scratches, that's it. I'm only telling you this because I believe you when you say you don't want to hurt Amelia. She doesn't know she's adopted. She doesn't know anything about you. She loves her father, and she misses her mother, and the last thing she needs is to find out that she's adopted. Not right now, anyway. Not while her world is so shaky."

"I understand," Caroline said. "What is she like? Is she pretty?"

Tyler smiled. "Yeah, she's pretty." He reached into his pocket and pulled out his wallet. "Would you like to see a picture?"

"Would I ever."

Tyler took a photograph from the wallet and handed it to Caroline. "That's last year's school picture."

"Oh, my God!" Caroline whispered. "Is that really her?"

"She's you, Caroline," Kate murmured.

"Only the best parts of me, I hope." Caroline traced Amelia's sweet face with her finger. "She's real, isn't she? Sometimes I lie in bed at night and think I imagined the whole thing. But then I remember how it used to feel when she'd kick me, first a little flutter, then I could actually feel her toes or her fist. She was my greatest achievement and yet my worst failure."

"No," Tyler said. "You didn't fail. She already means so much to a lot of people. She's bright, loving, kind, smart. You would be very proud of her."

"Because of your brother," Caroline said. "I wish I could thank him."

"Why didn't your brother come himself?" Kate asked.

"He's still rehabilitating from the accident," Tyler answered. "And he didn't want to leave Amelia at home or bring her here."

Kate nodded, a gleam of understanding in her eyes. "In case one of us recognized her. Just out of curiosity, why was your brother so worried? I mean, he adopted her legally and all."

Damn Kate for being so smart, so perceptive. "It was legal, wasn't it?" she continued.

"Close enough."

"I don't think so, or you wouldn't have come here," she said. "I'm not surprised things were done in an underhanded way. After all, my father was involved."

"Look, Mark might have played loose with the rules, but, like you said, so did your father. You can be assured that Mark and his wife Susan desperately wanted a baby. And they loved Amelia from the first second they saw her. They devoted themselves to her. Amelia has had a very good life. Mark only became worried because of his wife's death and his injuries. He didn't think any of that would help if your sister came calling. He was afraid that whoever was looking for the child would use the accident to try to overturn the adoption. I didn't think that could happen, but I wasn't sure, and Mark wasn't willing to take the chance."

"So your whole reason for being here was to find out which one of us was Amelia's mother. There was never any story, was there?" Ashley asked.

"No, that was just my way of getting to meet you. All we knew was that one of the McKenna sisters was the mother. We didn't know which one. And frankly, Caroline, this jerk of an attorney that you hired made it absolutely clear that you wanted your baby back. I couldn't just come out and ask which one of you had a baby. I was afraid it would lead you straight to Mark, and I needed to find out who you were and what you wanted before that happened."

"I understand," Caroline said. "I didn't mean to cause such turmoil. I know it's too late for me to be Amelia's mother. I won't try to take her away. I won't even try to see her. I just want to know about her, if that's okay."

Before he could reply, he was interrupted by Kate, who now had a very purposeful look in her eyes. "You lied," Kate said. "Or omitted the truth. Amazing how easy that can be, isn't it, when you're trying to protect someone you love?"

"It's not the same. We're not the same." He got to his feet, feeling suddenly restless and edgy. He'd known it would come back to him and Kate. The race, the baby, all of that had been explained, but not what had happened between them.

"Aren't we?" Kate asked as she stood up to face him. "Wouldn't we both do just about anything for our families?"

"I didn't cover up a murder."

"It wasn't a murder. It was an accident. And you were willing to cover up an illegal adoption."

"It wasn't illegal. It was just not done quite as properly as it should have been done."

"You're making excuses."

"So are you."

"Why did you sleep with me?" she demanded.

"Why did you sleep with me?" he returned.

Their heated exchange sent sparks flying between them. Kate couldn't look away. Tyler couldn't, either.

"I don't think you need us anymore," Caroline said.

Tyler was dimly aware of Ashley and Caroline leaving the room. His entire focus was on Kate.

"Answer the question," he said.

"I asked you first."

He drew in a deep breath. "I made love to you for one reason, Kate, and one reason only. I wanted you more than I've ever wanted a woman in my life. You got under my skin, into my head. I couldn't stop thinking about you. I told myself not to get distracted, but every time I saw you that thought flew right out the window." He paused. One thing he'd learned out there on the water tonight was that he didn't want to die without telling her how he felt about her. "I love you, Kate. I fell in love with you probably the first time I saw you. I didn't know it then. I didn't know it last night, if you want to know the truth. But I knew it today, when I thought the world might end. I finally saw what meant the most to me, and it was you." She blinked rapidly, moisture pooling in her beautiful blue eyes. "Believe me, Kate. Please."

"I want to," she whispered. "But how can I believe anything you say when you've lied to me the whole time you've been here?"

"Not the whole time. Not the times I kissed you, not last night when we made love. That was the real me, Kate."

"But you came here to discredit me. Maybe this is still part of the plan, to make the oldest sister believe you love her so she won't put up a fight."

He shook his head. "No, Kate. The desire to do you wrong left a long time ago. You have to understand that when I came here, you were just a name in a news article, a picture on a magazine cover. I didn't know you. But I did know my brother and Amelia. I knew how much they had suffered, how much they loved each other. I couldn't let anyone hurt them. Especially Mark. He had just lost his wife, the woman he loved more than anyone in the world. You know how that feels, don't you? You, more than anyone, know how that feels."

"Yes, I know," she admitted.

"Mark threatened to leave. He said he'd take Amelia and disappear before he'd give her up. I didn't want that life for her, the kind of life I had led, always on the run, always hiding from someone."

"So you set out to ruin each one of us. And we made it so easy."

"You didn't. I had nothing on you. You were smart and caring, kind and compassionate, beautiful, nurturing, loyal to a fault." He reached out, unable to hold himself back from touching her. Her soft hair drifted through his fingers, and he rested his hands on her shoulders. "I couldn't think of one reason why you wouldn't be a terrific mother. You're an incredible woman. Don't you know that?"

"Keep talking."

He smiled, sensing the battle was half won. "All I could think about on the water today was getting back to you, asking you to forgive me."

"I don't think I've actually heard the words."

"Will you forgive me, Kate?"

She made him wait a long, tense moment, then her lips, her beautiful, generous lips curved into a tender smile. "Yes, I'll forgive you. I love you, too, Tyler. That's why I made love to you last night, even though there was more to be discovered between us. Deep down inside, I knew you were a good man. Maybe you weren't being completely honest, but then I hardly hold the title for honesty myself."

"What else did you know?" he asked, teasing her cheek with a soft kiss. He liked the way she caught her breath, and he did it again, just to hear that small sound.

"I knew… You're distracting me, Tyler."

His tongue swept the curve of her ear. "I'm listening, Kate."

"I knew you could make me feel like this, crazy, reckless, not that those are necessarily good things but they sure feel good," she said with a sigh. "You make me laugh, and you make me think about the future, and I've never let myself think about the future. Not in a long time. I'm not proposing or anything," she added with a nervous laugh. "It's too soon for that."

She kissed him again, and he wrapped his arms around her, pulling her up against him until he could feel every inch of her. Only it wasn't enough, it would never be enough. "Did you say your father was in your bed?" he grumbled.

She grinned. "Yes, and my sisters are in the kitchen. This house is way too crowded."

"I know where there's a hotel room with lots of privacy."

"Will you show me?"

"Oh, I'll show you lots of things." He grabbed her by the hand and pulled her toward the door.

"Tyler, wait, I need my purse, my coat, my—" He cut her off with a deep, passionate kiss.

"Hey, where are you two going?" Ashley asked as she and Caroline came out of the kitchen.

Tyler put his arm around Kate. "She'll see you tomorrow," he told them. "We have a few things to discuss in private."

"You're leaving us with Dad?" Caroline asked in shock. "You can't leave us with Dad."

Kate laughed. "As a matter of fact, I can. Good night."

Tyler kicked the door shut behind them and looked down into Kate's smiling face. "You're okay with this, right?"

"I'm more than okay. I'm madly in love, and tonight is ours. Tomorrow I'll worry about tomorrow."

"Well, what do you think of that?" Caroline asked in dismay. "Kate just runs off with the sexy reporter when we've got a huge mess on our hands."

"Sounds like something you would do," Ashley replied.

Caroline didn't appreciate the smug look in Ashley's eyes. "Very funny. Do you think it's serious between them?"

"I hope so. I haven't seen Kate look so happy in a long time."

"It would be great if they got together, because then I'd have a chance to know Amelia, not as her mother but as her aunt. Wouldn't that be cool? Not that I don't want Kate just to be happy, but this could work out well for everyone."

"Certainly for you," Ashley said, but she smiled to take the sting out of her words. "I hope you do get to know Amelia."

"Amelia is beautiful, didn't you think? Like Mom."

"Like you."

"Thanks. That's nice to hear." Caroline's eyes narrowed when she saw Ashley glance at her watch, then the door, then her watch again. "Where are you thinking of going?"

"I want to talk to Sean."

"Maybe you should let him cool off."

"That would probably be smart, but I feel like time has never been on our side, and waiting would be more of a mistake." Ashley opened the hall closet and took out one of Kate's coats. "I'm going to borrow this. I'll see you tomorrow."

"Tomorrow?" Caroline echoed in alarm. "Hey, you can't leave me here with Dad."

"You always wanted to be his favorite," Ashley told her. "Now is your chance."

Before Caroline could reply that both of her sisters were being totally unfair, Ashley was gone. The house was suddenly quiet, too quiet. Caroline was alone. Well, not exactly alone. Her gaze turned down the hall toward Kate's bedroom. Maybe she should check on her dad, make sure he was all right.

She walked down the hall and pushed open the door to see her father asleep in Kate's bed. His face was red, his hair still damp, but he appeared to be sleeping, breathing normally. It suddenly occurred to her that everything her father owned was gone. Even his favorite cap had sunk into the Sound. All he had were the few items of clothing he'd left at Kate's house over the years. The rest of it had disappeared into the sea.

She walked farther into the room and sat down on the rocking chair next to the bed. She wondered if he was dreaming or reliving the experiences of the day. His breathing seemed to have quickened, and his chest was moving up and down more rapidly. Whatever he was thinking about was disturbing him in some way. She was tempted to put her hand on his shoulder and tell him to relax, that everything would be all right.

Weren't those the very same words he'd told her when the pain of labor had grown too much to bear? When she hadn't thought she could go on? He'd held her hand the morning Amelia had been born. He'd cut the umbilical cord and held his grandchild in his arms. There had been something in his eyes that morning, something that looked like love, but still he'd taken them both to the hospital and given away her child. She'd hated him for it. But she'd loved him, too, because he'd taken care of her after that, and he'd told her how proud he was of her, how strong she had been. For the first time in a long time, she'd felt worthy of his love.

She didn't really know how they had sailed that last leg. She had been weak and hurting. Kate had been grieving. Ashley had been traumatized. But somehow they had pulled through for this man—this man who wouldn't let them quit, who aroused so many mixed emotions in their hearts.

Her father's breathing caught, changed, and then he turned over on his back. His eyes opened as he awoke. "Where? Where am I?" he asked in a thick, slow voice.

"You're at Kate's house." Caroline pulled her chair closer to the bed. "I'm here if you need anything."

"Where's Kate?"

Caroline should have figured that would be his first question. "Kate is sleeping with Tyler at his hotel, I imagine. Any other questions?" She supposed she could have sugarcoated it, but why bother? They'd told too many lies already.

Duncan sighed wearily. "She's angry with me, isn't she?"

"For almost killing her second love? Yeah, I'd say she's angry. By the way, Ashley and I aren't too happy about what happened, either. Not that you care."

He turned his head to look at her, and for a long moment he didn't say anything. The silence almost undid her. It made her want to jump into speech, offer an apology for whatever needed to be apologized for so he wouldn't be angry. But she forced herself not to speak, not to give in. She wasn't in the wrong. He was.

"I didn't set out to hurt anyone," he said.

"You never do, but somehow people always seem to get hurt."

"You most of all."

"Yes," she agreed. "The worst time was when you took my baby out of my arms and gave her away to that doctor. You ripped my heart in two that day. I wasn't sure I'd ever feel whole again."

"Hardest thing I ever did. I should have let you keep her. Nora must have turned over in her grave when she saw me give our grandchild away." He shook his head. "But I was barely keeping us afloat. I didn't think we could manage a baby, too. And you were just a kid yourself."

"It wasn't about that. It was about the race. You didn't want to stop, and if I'd kept the baby, we would have had to stop. It took me a long time to realize that was the real reason I had to give her up." She paused. "It's over. Tyler knows everything, and Sean, too. By morning the rest of the world will be talking."

"You all should have let me drown out there tonight."

"That would have been too easy," she said sharply.

His gaze flew to hers. "Now, you listen, young lady—"

"No, you're going to listen to me for a change. You made some huge mistakes in your life, and it looks like you'll have to pay for some of them, just like I've had to pay for giving up my child, and Kate for losing Jeremy, and Ashley for having to lie to Sean. You don't get to drink yourself into oblivion anymore. You have to face the consequences of what happened. Maybe that means we give back the trophy and pay back the money. Hopefully, that's all it means. But we need to move on, and we can't be worrying about you every second, especially Kate. She's in love with Tyler, and she deserves a chance to start over. So you're going to have to pull yourself together and fast." She looked him straight in the eye. "We need a father, and you're it. Starting tomorrow, you're going to start acting like a father."

"I don't know if I can."

"You can and you will. But tonight you get to sleep."

Caroline smiled as her father's eyes drifted shut. He probably wouldn't remember their conversation, but she would. She'd meant every word—words she should have said a long time ago. Now the dam had burst. Little did her sisters and father know that from here on out, she probably wouldn't shut up.

No more going along with the family. She was standing up for herself. She would stop drinking, keep working, and find a way to be proud of herself and hope that someday her daughter Amelia might be proud of her, too.

Ashley walked down the damp, dark streets of Castleton wondering if this would be the last time she spoke to Sean or if she would even have the chance to speak to him. Would he send her away without a word? Would there be only anger and hatred in his eyes? She deserved nothing more than that. She just wanted a chance to say she was sorry.

Doubting that he would have gone home to his parents' house just yet, she went back to the marina, hoping he'd be on the boat. He would need time to think about how to tell his parents what had really happened to Jeremy. Besides that, it was past midnight; his mom and dad were probably asleep.

As she walked down the dock, she thought how odd it was that everything was quiet now. No more wind, no more rain. The storm had passed. Just like that.

Ashley climbed onto the Ambersons' motorboat without a second thought for the water below. That fear had been well and truly vanquished. She realized now that it was never really the water she'd been afraid of, but all the things buried beneath it, like Jeremy's death and Caroline's baby, her father's lies, their cover-up. She'd been terrified all the secrets would come up and hurt them all, so she'd stayed away from the water. Now the secrets were out, and the water was just water.

She walked down the stairs to the cabin and found Sean sitting on the couch, a bottle of beer in one hand. He'd changed into an old sweatshirt and a pair of jeans. But it was his face that had changed the most. There were new lines in his forehead, new shadows under his eyes, and a new hardness in his gaze.

"Can I come in?" she asked.

"Looks like you're already in." He took a swig of his beer.

She sat down on the edge of the couch, careful to keep some space between them. "I wanted to tell you I was sorry."

"Yeah, well, it's a little late, isn't it?"

"Yes. But I still mean it." She paused, not sure what to say now that she had a chance to say it. "Jeremy—"

"I don't want to hear any more lies about Jeremy," he said sharply.

"What about some truths?" she challenged. When he didn't reply, she continued, "Jeremy spent the last day of his life doing what he'd always done, taking care of Kate and her family."

"He shouldn't have been with you."

"I know, but he was. He was with the woman he loved, Sean. Those days before the storm hit were good ones for both of them. They were finally together. They'd wanted to be together for so long. I'm glad they had that time. And I think Jeremy was, too."

"He shouldn't have died."

"You're right. He shouldn't have died. He didn't deserve to die that night. But it was an accident."

"Your father pushed him."

"Not overboard. They were arguing, yes. And my father shoved Jeremy, but Jeremy hit his head, and the storm did the rest. The water crashing over the boat is what swept Jeremy over the side." She paused, taking a breath as she forced herself to relive that night. "I saw Kate jump into the water after your brother. And I helped my father try to rescue them both. I wish I could have done more. You don't know how much I wish that. I've blamed myself for not trying to get Jeremy while Dad was getting Kate, or not being able to spot Jeremy in the water. If only I'd done something differently, maybe the result wouldn't have been the same. Kate feels the same way, and I suspect my father does, too."

"Your father hated Jeremy."

"My father and Jeremy were a lot alike. They lived for the sea. They butted heads because they both cared deeply about what they were doing. Sailing and racing were as much a part of Jeremy as they were a part of my father."

"He still shouldn't have died," Sean repeated, with a hitch in his voice. He rubbed a hand across his eyes. "He was so young. He had his whole life ahead of him. And he lost it for what? A stupid sailboat race."

"He didn't think it was stupid. He thought it was the most exciting thing he'd ever done in his life and the most exciting thing he might ever do. We spent a lot of time together at the various ports along the way. Jeremy loved what he was doing. If you don't believe anything else, I hope you'll believe that. He also loved you very much. He talked about you all the time to me. He knew I was missing you." She stumbled over the words as emotions swamped her. "I loved you so much, Sean. The only reason I broke up with you was because I couldn't stand to lie to you. I knew eventually we would come to this point, when you would look at me and know the truth, and you would hate me. It was inevitable."

She paused, wishing he'd say something, but he was staring at his bottle of beer. "Anyway, I just wanted to say I was sorry. I still love you, Sean, but I'm going to leave the island. I'm going away so you don't have to look at me every day or, worse yet, try to avoid me. I want you to be happy. I really want that." She got to her feet, but he reached out and caught her hand in his. She looked into his eyes and saw what looked like forgiveness and so much more.

"Don't go," he said, pulling her back down onto the couch. "Don't ever go." And his mouth covered hers before she could tell him that the last thing she wanted to do was leave...

Kate rolled onto her side and ran her hand down the center of Tyler's chest. His eyes were closed, but she knew he wasn't sleeping. He'd already tensed with the slightest brush of her fingers against his skin. They'd made love twice already, but it wasn't enough. She wanted to feel him inside her again, filling all the empty spaces in her heart and her soul.

"You're living dangerously, Kate," he murmured.

"You may not know this about me, but there was a time when I liked to live dangerously, and I'm beginning to want to do it again." She lifted her head and smiled as he opened first one eye, then the other.

"How dangerous are we talking?"

"Really dangerous." She hesitated, not sure he was as ready as she was to talk about the future. "But we can discuss that later."

"Why wait?" he asked. "I'm right here. I'm not going anywhere."

"Maybe not today," she said slowly, "but I suspect soon." She put her head on his chest and closed her eyes, listening to his heart beat steadily beneath her ear. She wished she hadn't said anything. She could feel the tension in his body now, tension she'd created by wanting to talk about the future.

He gently stroked her hair. "Kate?"

"What?"

"I don't know the best way to work things out between us. But I do know that I want to make it work, more than anything."

She lifted her head and turned over on her stomach so she could look him straight in the eye. "I want that, too. I love you."

"I love you back," he said with a gaze so tender, so full of promise, she felt tears in her eyes.

"Wherever you want to live," she said, "I'll go with you. I want you to know that."

"You'd give up this island, your garden, your little house in the hills? You'd give that up for me?"

She didn't answer right away, because she wanted him to know that she was taking this question seriously, that her answer mattered and meant something. She saw his eyes darken with uncertainty. "Yes, I would," she said finally. "I'd give up everything for you. I would have jumped into the water for you tonight, if I'd needed to. I don't want to lose you. If my grip gets too tight, you'll have to let me know."

"I'll be holding on to you just as tightly, Kate." He put his hand behind her head and pulled her close for a kiss. "You're the best thing that ever happened to me. I'm not going to ask you to give up anything for me. We'll find a way to work it out." He kissed her again, then set her aside.

"Hey, that wasn't enough," she complained.

He smiled as he reached for his cell phone on the bedside table. "There's one call I need to make."

"To your brother?"

"Yes. I need to let him know that Caroline is no threat to Amelia. He'll be very relieved."

Kate frowned. "How do you think he'll feel about you being

involved with the sister of Amelia's birth mother? That could be complicated."

"He'll deal with it, just as Caroline will. I think Amelia is a lucky little girl to have so many people love her. And hopefully one day she can know the true circumstances of her birth. I think it's important, and I hope Mark will realize it, too. Amelia should know her biological family."

"Even my father?"

Tyler groaned. "Well... maybe not my first choice, but he is your father. However, I will never sail with that man again. In fact, I may never sail again."

"Fine by me." Kate sat up in bed, wrapping the sheet around her bare body. "Before you make that call, there's something else I wanted to talk to you about."

"What's that?"

"I've been thinking, and this will sound crazy, but I want to race in the Castleton on Saturday and try to win back the Moon Dancer." Her words came out in a rush, and she waited for him to say she was a fool, it was a ridiculous idea. But he didn't say anything, he just smiled at her.

"I think that sounds like a terrific idea."

"Really?"

"It's the last bit of unfinished business, isn't it?"

"As long as K.C. has our boat, he'll always be in our lives. I want him out. I want all of the past to be over with." She sighed. "Now I just have to convince Caroline and Ashley to sail with me."

CHAPTER TWENTY-FIVE

"ALL FOR ONE, ONE FOR ALL." Caroline held out her hands to Kate and Ashley as they stood on the dock in front of the Summer Seas, the boat they would race against the Moon Dancer in just a few minutes. Rick Beardsley had agreed to let them participate in the race around the island with a few of his crew, who would then take the boat on to San Francisco and eventually to Hawaii.

Kate had persuaded her father to sit the race out. Yesterday she'd notified the race officials from the Winston Around-the-World Challenge of the true events of eight years ago. There would be an investigation and probably some type of recompense to be made in terms of the prize money they'd already spent. Kate had no idea where they'd get the money to pay it back or whether her father would suffer any further penalties, but it didn't matter. It was a relief to have it all out in the open.

They'd also faced the Amberson family and had come clean on every detail of the last few days of Jeremy's life. The Ambersons had been understandably furious and hurt, the pain once again as fresh as it had been eight years ago. But hopefully in time they would understand that Jeremy had still died a hero.

He'd come onboard the Moon Dancer to help and support the

McKenna girls, and he'd done exactly that right up until the last minute.

It didn't take long for the news to race around the island, and gossip and speculation were running rampant. The McKennas had been the talk at every bar and on every boat on the island. But today was a new day. A new race. And, like all good sailors, they weren't looking behind them. Their eyes were fixed on the horizon.

"I can't believe I'm doing this again," Ashley murmured.

"Me, either," Caroline said with a dimpled smile. "But it feels good. I feel good."

"So do I," Kate said.

"That's because you're in love," Caroline teased.

Kate was in love—lust, infatuation, she had it all. She still didn't know what the future would hold. Loving a man like Tyler would no doubt offer its own set of challenges. He was a roamer at heart, and, even though he claimed he wanted roots, she wasn't sure how the reality of island living would fit him. Something else she'd deal with as she went along. She could live anywhere. She knew that now. She no longer needed a place to hide, but a place to live.

"Hello, girls," a familiar voice said.

They turned to see K.C. and David bearing down on them.

"Hello," they said in unison.

"It's been quite a week, hasn't it?" K.C. said, looking at Kate.

"Yes, it has."

"I didn't remember, you know. I almost wish I had. I almost wish my plan had been as devious as you no doubt thought it was," K.C. said. "I realize now that Duncan thought I came back here to torture him with the possibility of revealing the truth. But I just came back to rub his face in the sight of me sailing his boat."

"Not for long," Kate said. "We're going to win it back. The bet still stands, right? Whether my father races or not?"

"Why would you want the Moon Dancer? You girls don't want to race or even sail."

"Because it's ours. It's our home, our legacy. My mother would want us to have it."

K.C. met her gaze with a long, serious look of his own. "I wish you luck, then," he said, tipping his head.

"We won't need luck. We're McKennas," Kate called after him, repeating her father's favorite phrase.

"I'm not so sure we don't need luck," Ashley said somewhat darkly. "We haven't raced in eight years. We're a little out of practice."

"That's true, but we're still strong and fit, and, frankly, I think it's ingrained in us, don't you? There was a time when we could do this in our sleep. I'm hoping it comes back. But, if it doesn't, at least we will have tried our best." Kate paused, giving her sister a curious look. "By the way, how is Sean?" Ashley blushed and Kate had her answer. "That good, huh?"

"We're working things out."

"I'm so glad."

"I left him a message that we were racing today, but I'm not sure he wants to be a part of it." Ashley looked around. "I thought Dad might come down to see us off. Although he's probably angry with us for finally speaking the truth."

"He is, but he brought a lot of it on himself. He told Tyler quite a bit of it when they were on the boat together. I think in a way he was almost as relieved as we were to speak the truth... At any rate, I told him I didn't want him here today unless he was sober. We have to make some changes in our lives, starting now," Kate added, but since her father was nowhere in sight, she had a feeling he hadn't been able to do as she requested.

"That's a lot to ask."

"It's past time to be asking," Kate said. "It's bad enough, all the risks he took with us by his side, but I can't forgive him for endangering Tyler's life the way he did. We're not going to lie to one another anymore. We're not going to pretend things are right when they're wrong."

"He may not be capable of changing," Ashley said.

"I know. But I am capable of changing how I deal with him."

"Let's go, girls," Caroline said, waiting for them on deck with two other crew members whom Kate had met the day before. "It's time to get this show on the road."

Kate and Ashley climbed onto the boat, and within minutes they were in the familiar groove of race day preparations.

The starting line was crowded with boats. Kate felt a rush of excitement as the boats jockeyed for position. Then they were off. It was a tight race to the first buoy marker. The boats were neck and neck. There were barely inches between them at times.

The next two hours were exhilarating, exhausting, and renewing. Turn after turn, tack after tack, into the wind with speed and grace. Their lives had come full circle. As they turned and headed for home, the Moon Dancer falling behind them, Kate knew that the victory was theirs.

"Look, Ashley," she said with a wave of her hand. Standing on the bluff were the two most important men in their lives, Tyler and Sean. "They're waiting for us."

"I can't believe it," Ashley said, tears coming to her eyes.

"Me, either." Kate wished there was someone waiting for Caroline, too. But her sister wasn't looking at the bluff; she was concentrating on the finish line. For Caroline, it wasn't about love—it was about the future. She also felt a bittersweet sadness that Duncan wasn't there, but perhaps he couldn't bear to see them race without him. Maybe it was better this way.

They'd finally cut the ties between father and daughters. They were on their own, for better or for worse.

"Stay focused," Caroline said. "We haven't crossed the finish line yet," she added as the Summer Seas and the Moon Dancer battled back and forth for position.

Kate adjusted the sails and ran the boat boldly and bravely into the wind, remembering who they'd once been and who they would be again.

EPILOGUE

S<small>HIP'S LOG</small>, Moon Dancer, July 14

Wind: 840 knots
Sea Conditions: calm, peaceful
Weather Forecast: clear skies

Kate McKenna picked up her pen with a smile. It had been eight years since she'd written in this log—this weather-beaten, storm-battered log that had been stored in her attic until today. She was supposed to write down only the facts, but she couldn't help herself, not this time. She turned to the last empty page in the book.

I never thought I would write in this book again, but today the Moon Dancer will sail around Castleton Island, a proud victory sail for my sisters, my father, and myself. We have taken back our boat. We have taken back our lives. That terrible storm of eight years ago destroyed much, but it did not destroy us. We are stronger now. We have learned to let go, to forget and to forgive, but, most importantly, we have learned how to love again.

Kate set down the pen and closed the book. She took it up on the deck where her sisters were waiting, along with her father, Tyler, and Sean.

"What do you have there?" Tyler asked, a curious glint in his eyes.

"The ship's log. The history of our trip around the world. And the forecast for today's sail."

"Did you embellish?" her father asked with a slightly grumpy smile.

He'd been sober for almost twenty-four hours, so he was bound to be a bit out of sorts. Kate didn't know how long it would last, but they would take it one day at a time.

"Just a bit." She handed him the book. "This belongs to you, Dad. So does the Moon Dancer. Caroline, Ashley, and I agree that you should live on it here in the harbor. But we'd prefer that you don't take it out unless you invite one of us along for the ride."

"Would you go?" he asked, sounding slightly astonished by the idea.

"I would," Caroline said quickly.

"I would, too," Ashley replied a bit more slowly. Kate simply nodded.

"Well, then..." Duncan shook his head in bemusement. "You girls always come through for me, don't you? I'm not sure I deserve it. Actually, I'm sure I don't deserve it. But I'm going to try harder." Duncan looked over at Sean and Tyler. "I guess you two will be hanging around, huh?"

"I certainly will," Sean said firmly, putting his arm around Ashley.

"What about you, Mr. Hotshot Reporter? What's your story?" Duncan asked.

"My story is just beginning," Tyler replied, sending Kate a tender smile. "Or should I say *our* story?"

"Our story," Kate agreed.

"And my brother has promised to think about bringing Amelia for a visit as soon as he's back on his feet," Tyler added, his gaze turning to Caroline.

"I promise I'll never reveal who I am unless your brother wants Amelia to know."

"I've told Mark that. It's difficult for him to trust, but he's trying."
He paused. "I should thank you for sending that attorney after us.
Otherwise, I never would have met Kate." He smiled at her. "Funny
how things work."

"Funny," she echoed. "And wonderful."

"So, are we ready to set sail?" Caroline asked.

Duncan held up a hand. "First," he said, walking over to the side of
the boat, "we need to get rid of this log."

Kate gasped as Duncan tossed the ship's log into the harbor. She
rushed to the side in time to see it sink beneath the surface of the water.

"What did you do that for?" Caroline asked.

"It's over," Duncan said simply, directing his words to Kate. "Isn't
that what you've been trying to tell me?"

Kate blinked back a happy tear. "Yes, Dad. It's finally over. Today,
we begin again."

# # #

I hope you enjoyed Summer Secrets. Next up is Golden Lies. Keep
reading!

GOLDEN LIES

PROLOGUE

San Francisco-1952

The fire started easily, a small spark, a whisper of breath, and the tiny flame leaped and crackled. It slid quickly down the length of rope, growing in size and beauty with each inch it consumed. It wasn't too late to stop it, to have second thoughts. A fire extinguisher was nearby. It would take just a second to grab it and douse the small flames. But the fire was so beautiful, mesmerizing—gold, red, orange, black—the colors of the dragons that had promised so much: prosperity, love, good health, a second chance, a new start.

The fire began to pop, the small sounds lost in the constant boom of firecrackers going off in the streets of San Francisco in celebration of the Chinese New Year. No one would notice another noise, another spark of light, until it was too late. In the confusion of the smoke and the crowds, the dragons and the box they guarded would disappear. No one would ever know what had really happened.

The flame reached the end of the gasoline-soaked rope and suddenly burst forth in a flash of intense, deadly heat. More explosions followed as the fire caught the cardboard boxes holding precious inventory and jumped toward the basement ceiling. A questioning cry came from somewhere, followed by the sound of footsteps running down the halls of the building that had once been their sanctuary, their dream for the future, where the treasures of the past were turned into cold, hard cash.

The cost of betrayal would be high. They would be brothers no more. But then, their ties had never been of blood, only of friendship— a friendship that some would think had died this night of fire, but in truth had died much earlier.

There was only one thing left to do, grab the dragons and their box of secrets. The back door offered an escape route. The wall of fire would prevent anyone from seeing the truth. No one would ever know who was responsible.

The crate where the dragons were stored beckoned like the welcoming wave of an old friend. It took but a moment to pry off the lid. Eye-watering smoke and intense heat made it difficult to see what was inside, but it was impossible not to realize that something was missing.

Only one dragon was inside! The other dragon was gone, as was the box. How could it be? Where were they? The three pieces were never to be separated. They all knew the importance of keeping them together.

There was no time to search further. A door on the opposite side of the basement was flung open. A man holding a red fire extinguisher shot a small, helpless stream of chemicals at what was now a raging inferno.

The fire could not be stopped, nor the future. It was done. For better or worse, the dragons would never dance together again.

CHAPTER ONE

"They say that dragons bring good luck to their owners," Nan Delaney said.

Riley McAllister studied the dark bronze statue in his grandmother's hands. Ten inches tall, it appeared to be a dragon, although the figure looked more like a monster with its serpent body and dirty scales. Its brilliant green eyes blazed like real stones, but those eyes couldn't possibly be jade. Nor could the golden stripe that ran around its neck really be gold. As for luck, Riley had never believed in it before, and he didn't intend to start now. "If that dragon were lucky, we'd be at the front of this line," he grumbled.

He cast a frustrated look at the people around them, at least a hundred he estimated. When he'd agreed to help his grandmother clear out her attic, he'd never imagined he'd be standing in the parking lot at the Cow Palace Arena in San Francisco early Monday morning with a bunch of people who wanted to have their trash appraised by a traveling antiques show.

"Patience, Riley." Nan's voice still held a touch of her native Irish brogue even though she'd lived in California for sixty years.

He frowned at his grandmother's perky smile, wondering where she got her energy. She was seventy-three years old, for God's sake. But then, she'd always been a pint-sized dynamo. Pretty, too, with her stark white hair that had been the same shade for as long as he could remember, and her pale blue eyes that always seemed to see straight into his soul.

"Good things come to those who wait," she reminded him.

Not in his experience. Good things came to those who sweated blood, pulled out all the stops, sacrificed everything, and never let sentiment cloud reason. "Why don't you let me sell this stuff on the Internet?" he suggested for the twentieth time.

"And let someone take advantage of me? I don't think so."

"What makes you think these people won't take advantage of you?"

"Because *Antiques on the Road* is on television," she said with simple logic. "They can't lie in front of millions of people. Besides, this will be fun, a new experience. And you're a peach to come with me. The perfect grandson."

"Yeah, I'm a peach, and you can stop the buttering up, because I'm already here."

His grandmother smiled and set the dragon gently on top of the other treasures in the red Radio Flyer wagon she'd also found in the attic. She was convinced that somewhere in her pile of pottery, dolls, baseball cards and old books was a rare find. He thought she'd be lucky to get five dollars for everything in the wagon.

A loud clattering noise drew his head around. "What the hell is that?" he asked in amazement as a tall man dressed in full armor lumbered toward the front of the line.

"He looks like a knight in shining armor."

"More like the tin man in need of a brain."

"He probably thinks he has a better chance of getting on the show if he wears the armor. I wonder if we have anything interesting we could wear." She squatted next to the wagon and began digging through the pile.

"Forget about it. I'm not wearing anything but what I have on." Riley pulled up the zipper on his black leather jacket, feeling like the only sane person in the middle of a freak show.

"What about this?" she asked, handing him a baseball cap.

"Why did you bring that? It's not an antique."

"It was signed by Willie Mays. It says so right there."

Riley checked out the signature scrawled across the bill of the cap. He hadn't seen the cap in a very long time, but he distinctly remembered writing on it. "Uh, Grandma, I hate to tell you this, but I'm Willie Mays. I was planning to sell that hat to Jimmy O'Hurley, but somebody tipped him off."

She frowned. "You were a very bad boy, Riley."

"I tried."

The busty redhead standing in front of them turned her head at his comment, giving him a long, sexy look. "I like bad boys," she said with a purr that matched her cat's eyes.

The old man standing next to her tapped his cane impatiently on the ground. "What did you say, Lucy?" he asked, adjusting his hearing aid.

The redhead cast Riley a wistful look, then turned back to the stooped, old buzzard who had probably put the two-carat ring on her third finger. "I said, I love you, honey."

"That's just sick," Nan whispered to Riley. "She's young enough to be his granddaughter. It goes to show that men can always get younger women."

"If they have enough money," Riley agreed.

"I hate that you're so cynical."

"Realistic, Grandma. And I don't think you'd be happy if I was walking around San Francisco in armor, pretending to be a knight. So be glad I have a job. The line is moving," he added with relief, as the crowd began to shift toward the front doors of the arena.

The Cow Palace, once known for its livestock shows, had been divided into several sections, the first an initial screening area where experts scoured the items brought in. When it was their turn, the first screener riffled quickly through Nan's stash, pausing when she came to the statue. She told them to continue to the next screening area with the dragon only. The second screener had the same reaction and called over another appraiser to confer.

"I think we might get on the show," his grandmother whispered. "Now I wish I'd had my hair done." Nan patted her head self-consciously. "How do I look?"

"Perfect."

"And you're lying, but I love you for it." Nan stiffened as the two experts broke apart. "Here they come."

"This is a very interesting piece," one of the men said. "We'd like to put it on the show."

"You mean it's worth something?" Nan asked.

"Definitely," the man replied with a gleam in his eyes. "Our Asian art expert will be able to tell you much more, but we feel this piece may date back to an ancient dynasty."

"A dynasty?" Nan murmured in wonder. "Imagine that. Riley, did you hear him? Our dragon came from a dynasty."

"Yeah, I heard him, but I don't believe it. Where did you get that statue, anyway?"

"I have no idea. Your grandpa must have picked it up somewhere," she said as they made their way across the arena. "This is exciting. I'm so glad you came with me."

"Just don't get your heart broken," he cautioned in the face of her growing enthusiasm. "It could still be worth nothing."

"Or maybe it's worth a million dollars. Maybe they'll want to put it in a museum."

"Well, it is ugly enough for a museum."

"We're ready for you, Mrs. Delaney," a smiling young woman said as she ushered them onto the set, which was cluttered with lights and cameras.

An older man of Asian descent greeted them. After inspecting the dragon, he told them the statue had probably been crafted during the Zhou dynasty. "A rare find," he added, launching into a detailed explanation of the materials used, including the jade that made up the eyes, and the twenty-four karat gold strip that encircled the dragon's neck.

Riley wondered if he could possibly be hearing the man correctly. It appeared that this very odd-looking dragon had some important place in Chinese history and quite possibly had belonged in the private collection of an emperor. The expert estimated that the dragon might be worth thousands of dollars, maybe hundreds of thousands.

When their segment ended and they were escorted off the set, they were immediately swamped by appraisers and other experts, who handed them business cards and shook their hands. Riley kept a tight grip on the dragon as well as his grandmother's arm. The dragon was like a prime steak tossed into a pack of hungry wolves. He'd never seen such covetous looks, such outright greed and hunger.

His grandmother wanted to stop and chat, but he forcibly propelled her through the crowd, not relaxing until they were in his car with the doors locked. He let out a breath. "That was insane. Those people are crazy."

"Just excited, I think," Nan said, looking at the statue in his hands. "Can you believe this thing is thousands of years old?"

For a brief second he almost could. There seemed to be an intense heat radiating from the dragon, burning his hands. Oh, hell, it was probably just his imagination. Whether it was a year old or several thousand years old, it was still just a piece of bronze, nothing to get worked up over. He set the statue on the console between them, more relieved than he cared to admit to have it out of his hands.

"And it was in our attic," Nan continued, a dreamy note in her voice. "Imagine that. It's like a fairy tale."

"Or a nightmare."

Nan ignored him as she flipped through the pile of business cards she'd received. "Oh, my goodness. The House of Hathaway. Look." She held up the simple, engraved card naming San Francisco's most famous and elegant store. "They want me to call as soon as possible. I have a very good feeling about this."

"Do you? Because I have a very bad feeling."

"You worry too much. Don't think about the problems—think about the possibilities. This could be the beginning of something amazing."

"Is it possible that this dragon was actually crafted during the Zhou dynasty?" Paige Hathaway asked her father, David, as she froze the frame on the videotape one of their scouts had sent over from *Antiques on the Road*. If anyone could date the piece, it was her father, the head buyer for the House of Hathaway and their resident expert on Chinese art.

"It's possible," he said, a note of excitement in his voice and a glitter of anticipation in his eyes as he moved closer to the screen. "I wish I could see it better. That man keeps getting in my way. They really should make the object clearly visible to the camera."

The man her father was referring to was a tall, ruggedly built guy in a black leather jacket, who had started out looking uncomfortable in front of the camera and now appeared completely amazed and very, very skeptical. He was a striking contrast to the sweet, sparkling old lady he called Grandma, who seemed more than a little thrilled at the thought of her good fortune. And it might be incredibly good fortune if her father was right about the age of the object.

"Why hasn't she called us?" her father asked in irritation. "Are you sure you told her it was imperative we speak with her today?"

"On both messages that I left," Paige reassured him. "I'm sure she'll call back." Although, as Paige checked her watch, she realized it was almost six o'clock. "Maybe not until tomorrow."

"This can't wait until tomorrow. I must have that dragon."

David paced restlessly around Paige's fifth-floor office. The room was decorated with simple, beautiful Chinese furnishings that were meant to relax and inspire. The calming atmosphere was obviously having no such effect on her father.

"Do you realize what a find this could be?" he continued. "The Zhou dynasty is estimated to have begun around the year 1050 B.C. This could be a very early bronze. That dragon must have an incredible story to tell."

"I can't wait to hear you tell it," she murmured. She liked her father the most at moments like these, when there was passion in his eyes, in his voice, in his heart.

"I can't tell the story until I see that dragon, until I hold it in my hand, measure its weight, listen to its voice, feel its magic." David walked over to the window that overlooked Union Square. Paige doubted he was looking at the city lights. He was caught up in the pursuit of a new acquisition. When that happened, nothing else mattered to him. He was completely focused on his goal.

And, for the first time, he'd included her. Usually, acquisitions went through preliminary calls made by his assistant buyers, depending on the type of piece and area of expertise. If they deemed the object of interest, they would call in her father. But this time, he'd come straight to her, asking her to call Mrs. Delaney. She couldn't help wondering why, but she wasn't inclined to ask. If he wanted her involved, then she'd be involved.

She smiled as he ran a restless hand through his wavy brown hair, messing it up. It drove her mother, Victoria, crazy that her husband often looked as creased as the dollar bills he stuffed into his pockets, instead of in the expensive wallet she'd given him for his fifty-fifth birthday several months earlier. But that was David Hathaway, a little bit rumpled, often impulsive, and always interesting. Sometimes Paige wished she was more like him. But, despite having inherited her father's dark brown eyes, she was more her mother's daughter. Maybe if he'd spent more time at home, if he'd taught her the things he knew instead of leaving her education up to her mother, if he'd loved her as much as he'd loved China...

No, she wouldn't go there. She wouldn't be jealous of an entire country. That was ridiculous, and Hathaways were never ridiculous or anything else that was less than perfect.

Her grandfather and her mother had instructed her every day of her life to sit up straight, be responsible, never show emotion, never lose control. The lessons of a lifetime still ran through her head like an irritating song, one she couldn't ignore. Her impeccably neat office reflected those lessons, replicating the atmosphere in which she had grown up, one of sophistication, money, culture, and coldness. Even now, she felt a chill run down her arms that had nothing to do with the cool February weather and everything to do with her family.

Maybe if her sister, Elizabeth, had lived, things would have been different. She wouldn't have had to bear the burden of expectations, especially those of her mother and her grandfather, who looked to her as the only Hathaway heir upon whom all responsibilities would one day fall. Paige felt guilty at the thought, because there were a million reasons why her older sister should be alive and none of them had anything to do with making Paige's life easier.

"She found it in her attic," David said abruptly, turning back to her. "That's what the old woman said, right?"

"Yes, that's what she said on the show." Paige forced herself to focus on the present.

"You need to call her again, Paige, right now."

The strange gleam in his eyes increased her uneasiness. "Why is this so important, Dad?"

"That's a good question." The voice came from the doorway.

Paige turned to see her mother, Victoria, enter the room. A tall, rail-thin blonde, Victoria was a picture of sophistication, the ultimate feminine executive. There was intelligence in her sharp blue eyes, impatience in her voice, and a hint of ruthlessness in her face. Dressed in a black power suit; Victoria was too intimidating to be truly beautiful, but no one who met her ever forgot her.

"I asked you a question, David," Victoria repeated. "Why are you stirring up the staff, asking Martin and Paige and God knows who else to find this Delaney woman? Is the dragon worth that much?"

"It could be priceless."

She uttered a short, cynical laugh. "Everything has a price, darling."

"Not everything."

"Have you seen something like this dragon before in one of your books? Or perhaps you've heard a story, a fairy tale? We know how much you love fairy tales, especially ones coming from China. You know everything there is to know about that country and its people." Victoria spit out the word people as if it had left a bad taste in her mouth. "Don't you?"

"Why do you care, Vicky?" he asked, deliberately using the nick-name she hated. "It's not as if actual art holds any interest for you."

"Its value certainly does."

Paige sighed as her parents exchanged a glance of mutual dislike. Her father was right, though. Her mother rarely even looked at the inventory in the store. She was the financial wizard, the company spokesperson. David was the passionate art expert, the one for whom each piece told a special story. And Paige, well, no one had figured out her place at Hathaway's yet, least of all herself.

"Oh, I almost forgot." David reached into his pocket and pulled out a velvet pouch. "I bought this for Elizabeth's birthday, to add to her collection."

Paige watched as he slipped out a small, exquisitely carved jade dragon that had probably been designed to fit on the top of a sword. "It's perfect. It will go nicely with the others," she said as her mother turned away. Victoria had never been comfortable talking about Eliza-beth or acknowledging the tokens that David continued to buy each year in honor of his oldest daughter's love of dragons. "Do you want to leave that with me now?" she asked.

Her father returned the dragon to its pouch. "No, I'll keep it until we go to the cemetery next week."

"Really, David, these ridiculous birthday parties of yours. They're so distasteful," Victoria said with a frustrated shake of her head. "It's been twenty-two years. Don't you think—"

"No, I don't think," David said, cutting her off. "If you don't want to go to the cemetery, then Paige and I will go on our own. Right, Paige?"

Paige looked from one to the other, feeling very much like a wish-bone. But she couldn't say no to her father. Elizabeth's annual birthday party was one of the few occasions they always spent together. "Of course."

The phone on her desk rang. Paige pushed the button for the inter-com, grateful for the distraction.

"Mrs. Delaney is on line one," her secretary said.

"Thanks, Monica." She put the phone on speaker. "Hello, Mrs. Delaney. I'm glad you called. We'd love to talk to you about your dragon."

"I'm so excited," Nan said. "It's been such an incredible day. I can't tell you."

Paige smiled at the enthusiasm in the older woman's voice. "I'm sure it has been. We're hoping we might persuade you to bring the dragon down to the store tomorrow so we can take a look at it. Maybe first thing in the morning?"

"The morning is out, I'm afraid. Riley can't drive me until tomorrow afternoon."

"That will be fine. In fact, we have a wonderful tea. I don't know if you've heard of it, but—"

"Oh, yes, yes, I have heard of it," Nan said. "I've heard it's fantastic."

"Good, because we'd like to treat you and a friend or a family member to tea and a private appraisal. What do you say?"

"That sounds terrific," Nan replied.

"Good, why don't we—"

"Just a second," Nan said. There was a rustling, then a male voice came over the speaker.

"Miss Hathaway, I'm Riley McAllister, Mrs. Delaney's grandson. We'll be entertaining offers from numerous dealers, you understand," he said in a brusque voice.

"Of course, but I hope you'll give us a chance to make you an offer after we verify the authenticity of your piece."

"Since your store has had people calling my grandmother all day long, I'm fairly certain we have the real thing. But we will not be making any decisions without doing considerable research into the company making the offer. The House of Hathaway isn't the only game in town. And I will not allow my grandmother to be taken advantage of."

Paige frowned, not caring for the implication. The House of Hathaway had an impeccable reputation, certainly not one of taking advantage of little old ladies.

"My grandmother will bring the dragon in tomorrow," Mr. McAllister continued. "She'll be coming with a friend and myself. We'll be there at three o'clock."

"That sounds—" The dial tone cut off her reply. "Well, that was rude," she said, pressing the button to disconnect the call.

"Why did you suggest the tea?" her father asked, irritated. "That's not until the afternoon."

"She said she couldn't do it in the morning."

"I just hope that doesn't mean she's taking the dragon somewhere else. I want that dragon, whatever it costs," he said.

"Don't be absurd, David," Victoria replied. "We don't have an unlimited budget. Need I remind you of that?"

"Need I remind you that I make the buying decisions?" David looked Victoria straight in the eye. "Don't get in my way, Vicky, not on this." And with that, he turned on his heel and exited the room, leaving Paige alone with her mother.

"Always so dramatic," Victoria murmured.

"Why do you think this dragon is so important to Dad?" Paige asked.

"I have no idea. What's important to your father has been a mystery to me for some time." She paused. "Keep me informed about the dragon, won't you?"

"Why?"

"Because I run the company."

"I've never known you to care about an old statue."

"I care about everything that concerns this store, especially things that make your father believe he has a blank check."

Paige frowned as her mother left the office, shutting the door behind her. It had been a long time since both her parents had been interested in the same thing. That couldn't possibly be good.

CHAPTER TWO

RILEY COULD FEEL the hairs on the back of his neck standing up. They matched the goose bumps that ran down his arms as his every instinct told him that someone was watching them. He'd had the feeling the night before when he'd stayed at his grandmother's house because he hadn't wanted to leave her alone with a potentially valuable art object that had just been seen on national television. And he had the feeling now as he pulled his car into the underground garage at Union Square. Although it was the middle of the afternoon, and the garage was fairly well lit, his uneasiness grew as he debated his options.

"Aren't we getting out?" Nan asked, a curious note in her voice as he flipped the automatic car locks back down.

"In a minute." He scanned the area with a practiced eye. Running his grandfather's security business for the past four years had made him appreciate details. He looked for something out of place. Someone sitting in a car. A broken light. A shadow that didn't belong. Everything appeared normal.

"What are you looking for?" Millie Crenshaw asked, sitting forward in the backseat.

His grandmother's best friend and next-door neighbor had come along for the tea and, like Nan, seemed more interested in what type of food might be served than whether they should actually consider selling the dragon to the House of Hathaway. Riley would have preferred more time to research the company as well as some of the other companies that had contacted them. But his grandmother had refused to talk to anyone else until after she'd had the tea that everyone in San Francisco raved about.

"He's looking for bad guys," Nan whispered to Millie. "He thinks someone might try to steal the dragon from me."

"I just think you should be careful," Riley said. "Despite the fact that the thing is ugly as sin, quite a few people seem to want it."

"Isn't it amazing that it was sitting in your attic all these years?" Millie said. "I went down to the basement yesterday and looked through all our things. I'm going to make Howard take me to the show the next time it comes to town. You just never know what you have."

"That's true." Nan cradled the dragon in her lap like it was a precious baby. "I don't think I ever saw this until a few days ago. The attic was Ned's place. He was always puttering around up there." She looked at her watch. "We're going to be late, Riley. I think we should go."

"I'll carry the dragon, just in case."

"Just in case what, honey?"

"Whatever," he said cryptically, not wanting to worry his grandmother. Despite the fact that everything looked okay, his instincts told him something was off. He hoped he wasn't making a huge mistake by not following those instincts. He got out and walked around the car so he could open the door for his grandmother. As the women exited, Riley perused the garage, acutely aware of every sound.

A car came around the corner, its tires squealing on the cement. He immediately threw himself in front of Nan, blocking her with his body. As the car sped by, he saw two teenagers in the front seat; they barely gave him a glance.

"Good heavens, Riley," Nan said, straightening her dress. "You're strung so tight you'll snap if you're not careful. Maybe I should hold the dragon," she added, as he slipped it into a heavy canvas bag.

"I'll take it. Let's go." He'd feel better when they were out on the sidewalk.

Nan and Millie hurried along in front of him. They were both breathless when they reached the elevator that whisked them up to Union Square and the blessed sunshine.

"Everything okay now?" Nan asked as they paused to get their bearings.

"I wish you'd let me handle this on my own." He continued to look around as they made their way across the square.

"And miss the tea? Not a chance." Nan smiled at him and stopped walking. "Now, tell me, how do I look? Any lipstick on my teeth?" She flashed him a perfect set of white teeth.

"Beautiful," he replied. Nan was dressed in what she called her Sunday best, a navy- blue dress, nylons, and low heels. Millie was a taller, more colorful version of his grandmother, dressed in hot pink pants and matching top, her bright red hair flaming in the afternoon sunshine. "You could both pass for at least sixty."

"Oh, you're such a charmer," Millie said with a wave of her heavily ringed hand. "I don't know why you're still single."

"Neither do I," Nan said. "I keep telling him I want to see some great-grandchildren, but he always pretends to be hard of hearing at crucial times. Isn't that right, Riley?"

"What did you say?"

"See," Nan said, exchanging a laugh with Millie.

"Let's go." Riley led them around the corner, past Saks, Neiman Marcus, and the St. Francis Hotel with its glass elevators that ran up the outside of the building. They walked past the cable car stop, where a group of tourists was snapping photographs of one another. The House of Hathaway stood proudly on the east corner of the square. At six stories, it was nowhere near the most imposing building in a city of tightly knit skyscrapers, but its Roman columns and ornate gold carvings over the front doors were impressive.

Riley held open one of the large glass doors, then followed Millie and his grandmother inside.

Nan paused, putting a hand to her heart. "Oh, my, isn't this grand? I haven't been here in years. I'd forgotten."

Riley wasn't a shopper, but he had to admit the store was amazing. It was cool, quiet, and well lit, with paintings on the walls, wide aisles between glass display cases filled with art objects, a thick carpet beneath his feet, and a magnificent central ceiling that reached up six stories and was capped by a stained-glass skylight. He felt as if he'd stepped into another world, one of money and culture, one in which he didn't feel particularly comfortable.

"Look at this dollhouse," Millie said, moving toward a nearby display case. "It has miniature people and everything. And it costs..." Her eyes widened. "Three thousand dollars. Can you imagine? I think we sold my daughter's dollhouse in a garage sale for two dollars."

"It's amazing what some people will pay for junk," Riley commented.

"Hush, now," Nan said. "One person's trash is another person's treasure."

"I guess that's why we're here." Riley was beginning to wonder just what his grandmother's dragon was worth.

"Mrs. Delaney?"

Riley turned and caught his breath as a beautiful young woman approached them. Her hair was long and blond, held back with an ornate clip at the base of her neck, her eyes a dark chocolate brown. She was dressed in a silk turquoise dress that clung to her breasts and hit just above her knees, showing off a nice pair of legs. He'd thought he'd lost the ability to feel sucker punched by an attractive woman, but apparently not. His breath seemed to be trapped in his chest, and he had the terrible feeling that his jaw had dropped low enough to hit the floor. He cleared his throat and forced in some air as his grandmother shook hands with the woman.

"And you must be Mr. McAllister." She offered him a much cooler smile than she'd given his grandmother. "I'm Paige Hathaway."

He should have figured that by the expensive jewelry and the hint of perfume that probably cost more than a month's rent on his apartment. Well, he'd always wanted what he couldn't have. Why should this be any different? "Miss Hathaway," he said curtly.

"Will you follow me? My father is waiting for us in the lab." She led them to a bank of elevators nearby. "We're so glad you could come," she said as they waited. "Have you been in the store before?"

"Not for some time," Nan replied. "It's a bit beyond my means, you know. But it looks lovely."

"I'd be happy to show you around before you leave. We offer a variety of items in our emporium on the third floor that are quite reasonably priced."

"That would be wonderful. I've heard so much about the tea. It's the talk of San Francisco, you know," Nan added as they stepped on to the elevator.

Riley was bothered by his grandmother's eagerness. She was soaking up Miss Hathaway's charm like a dry sponge desperate for water. He supposed it was understandable; his grandmother's life had been difficult in recent years. He couldn't remember the last time he'd taken her out shopping or when they'd shared a meal that hadn't been at her house or at the cafeteria in the hospital his grandfather had been in and out of so frequently. He'd neglected her. He hadn't meant to, but he'd done it all the same. He'd have to do better in the future.

The elevator opened on the fifth floor. A set of glass doors labeled Executive Offices faced them, but Paige turned toward the right, leading them down a long hallway. Riley couldn't help noticing the discreet cameras in the hallways. There had been one in the elevator as well. Security seemed to be in good shape at the House of Hathaway. Paige punched in a code on the pad next to the door, then turned the knob. They stepped into an office with a desk and several chairs. The far wall was glass and looked into a lab area where two men were scrutinizing a vase. Riley noted a more sophisticated electronic keypad on this door.

Paige tapped on the window, and one of the men turned. He had Paige's brown eyes—or maybe she had his. Riley didn't need an introduction to know this man was a relative and more than likely her father. A moment later, the door buzzed, and the dark-haired man walked out.

"This is my father, David Hathaway," Paige said, offering introductions.

Handshakes were exchanged as David greeted them with a charming smile. But there was a distance in his eyes when he looked at Riley that showed his distraction, or perhaps his focus, which was on the canvas bag in Riley's hand.

"May I see the dragon?" he asked.

Riley began to reach into the bag, but David stopped him

"I'm sure you've handled it a great deal, but from here on out, I'd like to limit the number of hands that touch the piece."

Riley watched as David pulled a pair of thin latex gloves from his pocket and slipped them over his hands.

"We will be examining your dragon in what we call a clean room, an environment that we keep as sterile as possible to protect the art pieces," David said. "Our initial appraisal will run about one hour. Paige will take you to tea while you're waiting, and we'll meet after that."

"I think I'll stay and watch." Riley felt slightly annoyed by the look of relief that flashed in Paige's eyes. She would obviously be happy to get rid of him.

David didn't look nearly as pleased. "There's really nothing to see. We can't allow you in the clean room, and most of our work will not be visible from the window."

"Why can't I go inside?"

"Insurance, liability, you understand," he said with a vague wave of his hand. "Please enjoy the tea. It will be an experience you will not forget."

"Oh, come with us, Riley," Nan said. "I want to share this with you."

His grandmother slipped her hand through his arm, taking any idea of further argument out of his head. Before he knew it, the lovely Miss Hathaway was leading them back into the elevator and up to the top floor, where the tearoom was located.

When they stepped inside, Riley felt as if they'd just crossed the Pacific Ocean and landed in Beijing. The tearoom was filled with expensive mahogany tables, glass display cases showing ornate teacups and pots, paintings on the wall depicting scenes from the Far East. This dining room was a far cry from the restaurants where he got take-out potstickers and Mongolian beef.

A woman in an Oriental silk dress ushered them to a table in a corner surrounded on three sides by ornate screens painted with flowers, fruit, and birds. She disappeared as quietly as she had arrived, leaving them to seat themselves at the marble and carved wood table.

"Mr. Lo will be with us shortly," Paige said "He's a Chinese tea master, and he'll conduct a tea ceremony for you."

"There's such a thing as a tea master?" Riley asked.

"Absolutely. Although the Japanese tea ceremony called chanoyu is better known, the Chinese also have their own ceremony. Since your dragon is believed to have come from China, we thought you might enjoy the Chinese version."

Riley leaned forward. "We've already dropped the dragon off with your father; you don't have to give us the dog and pony show."

Paige bit down on her lip. Judging by the slightly chapped look of those beautiful pink lips, he suspected he'd just noticed another important detail. Paige Hathaway didn't always find it easy to say the right thing at the right time.

"According to legend," Paige said, turning her attention to Nan and Millie. "In the year 2737 B.C., an emperor named Shen Nung was boiling some hot water while he rested under a wild tea tree. Some tea leaves dropped into his pot, and when he drank the hot water, he found to his surprise that he felt rejuvenated. He believed the leaves were responsible for this feeling of well-being, which then triggered further experimentation. This was the beginning of tea drinking in China. Today there are more than fifteen hundred types of tea to choose from. While more than twenty-five countries cultivate tea, China is still the main producer."

"Really?" Nan said. "I never knew that. Did you know that, Riley?"

"I had no idea. Sounds like quite a coincidence, those tea leaves dropping into the pot."

"There are other stories to explain the origin of tea drinking, but

that's the most popular one," Paige added. "What's important to understand is that tea still plays an important role in Chinese culture. It's part
of daily life. Tea is believed to have benefits that affect the physical,
mental, and emotional well-being of those who drink it."

"I better switch from coffee," Millie said with a laugh.

"What kind of tea are we going to have?" Nan asked. "I've heard of
green tea, but I know there must be lots of others."

"Lots," Paige agreed with a smile, "but I'll let Mr. Lo explain them
to you." She looked up as a stooped, old man with thick black glasses
and only a single tuft of gray hair on his balding head sat down at the
table with them. "Mr. Lo. May I present Nan Delaney, her grandson,
Riley McAllister, and her friend, Millie Crenshaw."

"Welcome. I am Yuan Lo." He set down a tray upon which there
were several items—a shallow lacquered box, four small cups shaped
like spools of thread, and four additional drinking cups. A moment
later a waitress entered with a pot of tea that she set on a decorative hot
plate. More small cups were also placed on the table.

Everything was so miniature that Riley felt as if he'd entered a
child's tea party. He squirmed uncomfortably on the narrow chair,
which was also too small. He tugged at the tie that his grandmother had
insisted he wear and wished he was anywhere but here. He should have
stayed in the lab. At least then he could have been bored in more manly
surroundings. And he could have kept an eye on the dragon, maybe
gotten some insight on how much it was really worth. Instead he was
about to partake in some ceremonious, sanctimonious, hyped-up tea
party.

"Relax, Riley," his grandmother said softly, as if she'd read
his mind

"This has no purpose," he muttered.

"Of course it doesn't. Not everything in life has to have a purpose.
Sometimes it's just about a little fun!"

Riley McAllister didn't like their tea, Paige decided. He'd stopped
listening completely about the time Mr. Lo had begun discussing the
differences among black tea, green tea, and oolong. While he obedi-
ently sniffed the scent of the tea leaves, and tasted at appropriate times,

he didn't appear to be at all affected by the sensuous experience. She, on the other hand, was feeling warm, and a little dizzy. From the hot tea, she told herself, not from sitting next to Riley.

She had to admit he was an attractive man, with his raven black hair that was curly and thick and a little longer than it should be. His blue eyes blazed against his tanned cheeks, and there was a hint of a dark beard along the jawline. He wasn't the sophisticated executive she was used to seeing, but the rugged, extremely physical, very masculine sort of man that she almost never encountered. The kind of man who didn't tend to frequent high-scale gift and antique emporiums or museums, two places where she spent most of her time. Which was probably why she felt a little rattled around Mr. McAllister.

It was annoyance, irritation with his impatience, that made her feel hot and bothered, nothing more, certainly not attraction. Even if she were attracted, he obviously was not. He hadn't spared her more than a few disgusted glances in the last twenty minutes. It was clear that he wanted this over and done with, so he could get on with his life. She felt exactly the same way. She didn't need his condescension, his disinterest. She'd gone out of her way to entertain his grandmother, and she was sure her father would be making a more than generous offer to Riley and his grandmother in very short order. She didn't have a damn thing to apologize for, and she would not let him make her feel uncomfortable.

She straightened in her chair as the waitress brought over plates of food for them to sample. This was a lovely tea, and she was going to ignore Riley and enjoy it. At least Nan and Millie were fun. They chattered on, never seeming to notice the tension between Riley and Paige, which grew with each passing moment. She almost wished he'd talk. His silence, his unreadable expression bothered her. She was used to men who spoke about themselves, about their work, about everything they were interested in. She knew how to handle such men. Actually, you just had to listen, and she'd always been a good listener. If she hadn't been, she never would have gotten her father's attention. He was a great storyteller, and everyone knew that a great storyteller needed a great audience. That's what she'd been—her father's audience.

What was she now? The annoying question entered her mind again. Each day it seemed to come back louder than before, more insistent, more demanding of an answer. And it wasn't just about her father, but about her mother and her grandfather and her role in the company. She was restless, itching to do something more important at Hathaway's than plan parties and museum events. But with her grandfather at the helm of the company, her father as head buyer, her mother in charge of operations, and long-time family friend Martin Bennett overseeing the retail division, there was nowhere for Paige to go. The company ran smoothly without her. No one really needed her—except they did, because the irony was that she was the heir, the only heir. The company could never belong to Victoria, because she wasn't a blood Hathaway. David didn't want to do anything but buy art objects, and Martin wasn't a blood relative. Which meant it would all one day belong to Paige.

But what was she supposed to do in the meantime? Just wait for her turn? That's what they all seemed to want. A sigh escaped her lips as her thoughts led her down a familiar, wearying maze from which there was no way out. She was relieved when Riley cleared his throat and made a point of checking his watch. At least his irritation distracted her from her thoughts.

"This is all very fascinating, but how much longer do you think your father will be?" he asked. "It's been over an hour."

"I'm sure he'll be here soon."

Mr. Lo stood up and bowed to them. "Thank you very much for your attention."

"Thank you for the delightful presentation. I learned a great deal," Nan said.

"I am glad you were pleased."

"Thank you, Mr. Lo," Paige said as he left the table.

"Now then, Miss Hathaway," Riley said. "Let's talk about my grandmother's dragon."

"Before we do that, I need to use the ladies' room," Nan interrupted, getting to her feet.

"Out that door to the right," Paige told her.

"I'll go with you," Millie said. "I drank so much tea I'm about to float away."

As soon as they left, Paige wished she'd gone with them. Riley had the sharpest, bluest eyes she'd ever seen, and right now his gaze was fixed on her. She shifted in her chair, not used to such a close, deliberate appraisal. She wondered what he saw, and she practically had to sit on her hands to prevent herself from reaching up to make sure her hair was still in place.

"You look nervous," Riley commented. "Why is that? Is there something about this ugly dragon I should know?"

At least he thought the dragon was making her nervous and not him. That was a relief. "I'm just distracted. I have a lot of work to do."

"So do I. Yet here we are, having tea."

"What kind of work do you do, Mr. McAllister?"

"I run a security company."

"What does that entail? Bodyguards? Computer security? Burglar alarms?"

"All of the above, whatever the customer needs. Who does the security for this store? Do you know?"

"Of course I know. It's Wellington Systems."

He nodded. "I thought I recognized some of their work, but they're not the best anymore. Bret Wellington spends more time on the golf course than he does on keeping up with the latest security systems."

"Mr. Wellington is a good friend of my grandfather."

"That explains it, then."

"I suppose you think your company is better."

"I suppose I do," he replied, a small smile on his lips.

She played with the napkin in her lap, wishing the ladies would come back because Riley made her nervous.

"So, why is my grandmother's dragon so popular?" Riley asked. "Frankly, when I first saw it, I thought we should toss it in the trash."

"It's good you didn't. If it's truly a bronze from the Zhou period, then it's quite old. Besides its age, dragons are revered in Chinese culture. They are believed to be divine mythical creatures that bring with them prosperity and good fortune. The Chinese dragons are the angels of the Orient. They are loved and worshipped for their power and excellence, boldness, and heroism. I don't know what story your dragon has to tell, but I suspect it will be fascinating."

"You think that dragon is going to talk to you?"

"No, but I think my father will be able to tell us something interesting about it."

"Speaking of your father, maybe we should go find him."

"It takes time to do an accurate appraisal. I'm sure you want him to be accurate."

Riley rested his elbows on the table and leaned forward. "There are quite a few places interested in the dragon—Sotheby's, Butterfields, Christie's, not to mention an incredible number of smaller dealers. That makes me wonder if it might be better if we worked with one of the auction houses. If everyone wants the dragon, they can bid on it."

"While that certainly is an option for you, I believe we can make you an excellent offer. The House of Hathaway is secondary to no one, Mr. McAllister." It was a phrase her grandfather, Wallace Hathaway, had said on a thousand occasions. She was surprised at how easily the words crossed her lips, and somewhat annoyed, too. Her grandfather usually sounded like a pompous ass when he said those words, and she had a feeling she'd just presented herself in exactly the same way.

"We'll see about that," Riley replied.

"See about what?" Nan asked as she and Millie returned to the table.

"We were just discussing the dragon's value," Riley told her.

"I can't wait to find out what your father thinks," Nan said. "And I want to thank you again for tea. It was fabulous."

"It was my pleasure. I enjoyed myself, too."

As Paige finished speaking, her father entered the tearoom, his hands noticeably empty.

Riley stood up abruptly. "Where's the dragon?"

"In safekeeping, I assure you," David said smoothly. He then directed his attention to Nan. "I'd like to keep the dragon overnight, if I may. I know an appraiser who won't be available until tomorrow, but I'd very much like him to look at it. While the piece appears to be very promising, there are many fakes in today's market. And I want to be absolutely sure the piece is truly an antiquity. We'll need to run numerous tests."

"That sounds fine," Nan replied.

"Wait a second. Why don't we bring the dragon back in the morning?" Riley suggested.

"I'd like to study it further this evening," David replied. "We have excellent security, Mr. McAllister, if that's what you're concerned about. Your piece will be very safe in our hands, I promise you, and it will be insured as is every other piece in the store. I've taken the liberty of writing up a receipt." He handed a piece of paper to Nan.

"I'm not worried at all," Nan stated.

"Grandmother—"

"Riley, this is the House of Hathaway. They have an impeccable reputation. I trust them completely." She turned back to David. "I'd be happy to leave the dragon here until tomorrow."

"Thank you. If you'll give Paige a call tomorrow afternoon, we'll set up a meeting." He extended his hand to Nan. "On behalf of the House of Hathaway, I want you to know how very much we appreciate the opportunity to evaluate your dragon, Mrs. Delaney."

"Oh, it's my pleasure," Nan said, stuttering somewhat under David's charming smile.

David departed, leaving Paige to say the good-byes. She walked the ladies to the door and was not surprised when Riley lagged behind.

"Is this really necessary?" he asked her.

"My father thinks it is." She didn't know the appraiser her father was referring to but he was the expert, and if he felt they needed a third party's judgment, then that's what they needed. "You can trust us, Mr. McAllister."

He gave her a cynical smile. "Nothing personal, Miss Hathaway, but I don't trust anyone. If anything happens to that dragon, I'll hold you responsible."

"Nothing will happen, I assure you."

"Then neither one of us has anything to worry about."

CHAPTER THREE

WEDNESDAY AFTERNOON HAD COME TOO QUICKLY, David Hathaway thought as he walked purposefully across town, the strap of the heavy canvas bag clenched tightly in one hand. There was still much to do, but the hour was growing late. The air had cooled, the traffic had grown noisy with the early evening commute, and the sun was falling lower in the sky, sometimes completely blocked by the tall skyscrapers of San Francisco. It was almost four o'clock. Mrs. Delaney and her grandson would be arriving at the House of Hathaway in one short hour. They would expect to receive the dragon or an offer of purchase. While he might be able to stall Mrs. Delaney, her grandson was another story.

David paused on the corner, wondering if he shouldn't have put off this visit until after they'd purchased the dragon. But he had to show Jasmine—to be sure. He would have liked to come earlier, but Jasmine had been out all day. When he had finally reached her, she had told him not to come, but she always said that. And this was too important.

Crossing the street, he walked under the concrete foo dogs guarding Chinatown's main gate and past a red-faced deity protecting a local herbal shop from atop a rosewood shrine. He was only a few blocks from San Francisco's financial district, but the atmosphere, the neighborhood, had completely changed. Leaving Grant Avenue, the main thoroughfare through Chinatown, David headed down a narrow side street, past Salt Fish Alley, where the odors of fish and shrimp being cured in large vats of salt was overwhelming, past Ross Alley, once notorious for gambling, and past the Golden Gate Fortune Cookie Factory, where women still filled hot cookies with Chinese fortunes.

This wasn't his Chinatown, this tourist-attraction that played to the interests of tourists and locals who wanted to experience a little of the Orient in their hometown. His Chinatown was a continent away, in the streets of Shanghai. Veering away from the commercial avenues, he entered a residential neighborhood where apartment buildings were crowded together, one after another, hugging each other as tightly as the large, close-knit families that lived inside the small rooms. Jasmine's building was at the end of a lane. He used the back stairs leading up from the garden to her apartment. Three short knocks, and he waited.

For a moment he thought she wouldn't answer. His uncertainty was uncomfortable, unthinkable, an emotion he didn't know how to handle. Jasmine would come. She would let him in; she always had before. She had loved him like no one else. She had said she always would.

He hadn't treated her well. He knew that deep in his soul, in a place he never chose to visit. There were too many painful emotions there, feelings he kept hidden away. Sometimes he wished he could change, but as Jasmine once told him, it was easier to move a mountain than to change a person's character. For better or worse, he was who he was. It was too late for regrets. In his hand was something special. A thrill of excitement ran through him as he considered the possibilities.

The door slowly opened. Jasmine stood in the doorway, looking far older than her forty-eight years. She wore a black dress that was but a variation of her usual black pants. He remembered a time when she had dressed in colors as bright as those she used in her paintings, when her face had lit up with joy and wonder. Now there was nothing but dark-ness—in her eyes, her face, her voice, her apartment. The heavy incense she burned made it difficult to breathe. He sometimes wondered what she was mourning, but he had a feeling he already knew. So he didn't ask questions, and she didn't offer explanations.

"You shouldn't have come. I asked you not to," she said in a somewhat hoarse voice. He wondered how often she spoke to anyone. Had her voice grown raspy from disuse? A twinge of guilt stabbed his soul. Had he done this to her? If they had never met, would she have ended up here?

"I had to come," he said slowly, forcing himself to focus on the subject at hand.

"It is always this way in the week before Elizabeth's birthday. That is when you seek me out. But I can no longer comfort you. It isn't fair of you to ask."

Her words put a knife through his already bleeding heart. "This isn't about Elizabeth."

"It has always been about her. You must leave now."

He ignored the anger in her eyes. "I have a dragon that looks very much like the one in your painting, Jasmine."

Her eyes widened. "What did you say?"

"You heard me."

"It doesn't exist. You know that. It was something I saw in a dream."

"I think it does exist. Let me come in. Let me show you."

Jasmine hesitated. "If this is an excuse—"

"It's not." He glanced over his shoulder, not seeing anyone but feeling as if they were being watched. There were many eyes behind the thick curtains that covered the nearby windows. "Let me in before someone sees me."

"Just for a moment," she said, allowing him to step inside. "Then you must go before Alyssa comes."

"I will go," he promised, "after you look at this." He pulled the dragon out of the canvas bag and watched her reaction.

Her gasp of disbelief told him everything he needed to know.

Riley McAllister pedaled harder, the street in front of him rising at an impossibly steep angle. Even the cars were parked horizontally to protect from accidental runaways. Most people were content to ride their bikes along the bay or through Golden Gate Park, but Riley loved the challenge of the hills that made up San Francisco.

He could feel the muscles in his legs burning as he pumped harder, the incline working against him. He switched speeds on his mountain bike, but it didn't help. This wasn't about the bike; it was about him, what he was capable of doing. It didn't matter that he'd conquered this hill a week ago. He had to do it again. He had to prove it wasn't a fluke.

His chest tightened as his breath came faster. He was halfway up the hill. He raised his body on the bike, practically standing as he forced the pedals down one after the other, over and over again. It was slow going. He felt as if he was barely moving. A car passed him, and a teenage boy stuck his head out the window and yelled, "Hey, dude, get a car."

Riley would have yelled back, but he couldn't afford to waste a precious breath. Nor could he afford to stop pedaling. Otherwise, he'd go flying backward down the hill a lot faster than he'd come up. He pressed on, telling himself this was what it was all about, pushing the limits, forcing the issue, achieving the impossible. He was only a few feet away from the top of the hill now.

Damn, he was tired. He felt light-headed, almost dizzy. But he wouldn't quit. He'd faced bigger challenges than this. He couldn't give in. Quitting was what his mother would have wanted him to do, what she'd told him to do many times. *If you can't do it, just quit, Riley. You're just not that good at things. You're not smart. You're not artistic. You're not very musical, but you can't help it. You take after your father.* Whoever the hell he was. Aside from his name, Paul McAllister, Riley knew absolutely nothing about his father.

The funny thing was the more his mother told him he couldn't do something, the more he wanted to prove her wrong. That feeling had driven him through boot camp and a stint in the marines, and it was still driving him today. Maybe he was as big a fool as his grandmother, believing that his mother might actually care that he'd ridden up the steepest hill in San Francisco today.

Forget about her. He heard his grandfather's stern, booming voice in his head now. This isn't about your mother; it's about you. No one else can fight your battles for you. In the end we all stand alone. So when it comes your time to stand front and center, raise your chin high, look everyone straight in the eye, and know in your heart that you're up to the challenge.

The words sent him over the top of the hill.

Pumping a fist in the air, he coasted across the intersection. In front of him was one of the best views in the world, the San Francisco Bay and the Golden Gate Bridge. He could see sailboats bouncing along the bumpy water. Alcatraz was in the distance, a ferry boat pulling up to the famous old island prison. Angel Island lay beyond, Marin County, the rest of Northern California. The world was literally at his feet. At least his small part of the world. And it felt good. Damn good.

He flew down the next hill, loving the wind in his face. His cheeks began to cool, his heart slowed to a more comfortable beat, and his breathing came much easier. This was supposed to be the best part. But in truth, the best part had been those last few seconds before he hit the top, the moments when he wasn't sure he could do it. Now he knew. But he also knew that the good feeling would only last until tomorrow. Then he'd have to find some other hill to climb.

He let out a sigh and began to pedal as he reached a flat area. A quick glance at his watch told him he needed to get back to the office, wrap up a few loose ends, then pick up his grandmother and meet the Hathaways. He had to admit he was curious about the value of his grandmother's dragon. Finding a treasure in a pile of junk seemed too good to be true. But if it wasn't valuable, he doubted the Hathaways and all the other dealers in the country would be so hot to get their hands on it. In this case, his grandmother's dragon might just put a dent in his comfortably cynical approach to life.

Forty minutes later, Riley strode through the front door of his office and greeted the lobby receptionist with a warm smile, then headed down the hall. His secretary, Carey Miller, sat at a desk in a cubicle next to his office. The distinct smell of nail polish wiped the smile off his face, which was followed by a frown when he saw her bare feet propped up on her desk, little foam pads stuck between her toes.

"I hope I'm not interrupting you," he said sarcastically.

She shrugged. "You're not. How was the bike ride? You must have stopped off at home and taken a shower. You don't smell as bad as you normally do."

"Speaking of smells, do you have to put the paint on here?"

"If you paid me more, I could afford to get a pedicure."

"If you worked harder, you might actually earn more money."

He strode into his office, knowing she'd follow. It took her a few extra minutes, as she walked through the door on her heels, carefully keeping her toes from hitting the carpet. "So, did you accomplish anything besides the perfect shade of red?" he asked her.

"Did you accomplish anything besides a near heart attack?"

"Exercise is good for you. You should try it sometime."

"Please. If I'm going to work out, I prefer to do it in the bedroom." She gave him a mischievous grin. "Don't you remember?"

"I remember throwing out my back."

"That's because you did it wrong. You were on position seven when I was on six. The book said you needed to do it in order."

"Why I ever agreed to try anything in that book, I'll never know." He sat down in the leather chair behind his desk that had served his grandfather so well for so many years.

Carey flopped down in the armchair in front of his desk. "I've got another book now. You'd be surprised at some of the things in there. You should read it."

"I'll wait for the movie." With a pleased smile he surveyed the stack of papers on his desk, the half-filled coffee cup, the afternoon's sports page. His grandfather's office was beginning to feel more like his own, a place where everything was under his control. He picked up a small plastic basketball on his desk and sent it swishing through the hoop mounted on the opposite wall. "Any messages?"

"Nothing I couldn't handle." Carey popped a chunk of gum in her mouth.

"Do you have to do that?"

"It beats smoking. You know I'm trying to quit." Carey hooked her jean-clad leg over one arm of the chair. An ex-stripper, ex-smoker, ex-drinker, and ex-girlfriend, she was now his right-hand man, make that *woman*. While she hadn't been a particularly good stripper, smoker, drinker, or girlfriend, she was a good assistant, even with the painted toenails.

"What else has been going on around here?" he asked.

"As you requested, I got the goods on Paige Hathaway." She tapped the file folder in her hand.

His heart skipped a beat. "What did you learn?"

"Well, it's all incredibly..." She tilted her head to one side. "What's the word I'm looking for? Oh, I know. Boring. It's incredibly boring."

"Excuse me?"

"Boring, dull, put-you-to-sleep kind of reading. I can give it to you in a nutshell. Paige Hathaway grew up in a fancy mansion in Pacific Heights with her parents, Victoria and David Hathaway, and her grandfather Wallace Hathaway. Apparently, the grandmother died before she was born. There was a whole slew of housekeepers, maids, gardeners, and chauffeurs over the years, but apparently they were paid well, because no one has had anything negative to say." Carey popped her gum. "Paige moved out a few years ago. She lives in an apartment in one of those high-rise buildings with a view of the bay. David Hathaway spends most of his time in China. And Victoria Hathaway and the old man, Wallace Hathaway, spend most of their time at the store."

Riley opened the folder she handed him and read through the facts Carey had just recited. "What else?" he asked, looking back at her.

"The family is a pillar of society. They support many nonprofit organizations, especially those connected to the arts, the ballet, the symphony, the opera. They're hosting an exhibit on Chinese art at the Asian Art

Museum in a few weeks. They're on the A-list for parties. Oh, and get this—Paige Hathaway was actually a debutante. Can you believe they still have debutantes? Not that she isn't pretty. There's a photo in the file." Carey sent him a knowing look. "But you already knew that, didn't you?"

"She's not my type."

"She sure isn't," Carey agreed.

He felt annoyed by her assessment. "Why? Am I too blue-collar?"

"Yes, as a matter of fact. Because Paige Hathaway is not blue-collar. She is blue blood. If San Francisco had a royal family, Paige would be the princess."

"What did you learn about the rest of the family?"

"Victoria Hathaway is the queen. She's the CFO of the company. Wallace Hathaway, the old man, retains the CEO title despite the fact that he's eighty-something. He apparently still comes into the store every morning to review the profit and loss reports or perform surprise inspections in unsuspecting departments. David Hathaway is the main buyer for the store, and quite the jet-setter. He spends more time in China than he does here. Paige seems to be drifting through the company right now. She plans a lot of parties. I'm not sure what else she does. Those are the main family players. Although..." She paused. "I'm not sure if you want to know this or not, but there was a small tidbit in one of the gossip columns that Paige is engaged to Martin Bennett. He's a vice president at Hathaway's and another blue blood. A match made in Tiffany's no doubt."

"No doubt."

So Paige was engaged, huh? As he recalled, she didn't have a ring on her finger. He wondered why not. Probably couldn't find a stone big enough. He tossed the folder onto the desk. He'd read the rest of it later —if he bothered to read it at all. If the Hathaways made his grand-mother a respectable offer, he'd encourage her to take it and be done with the whole thing. "Did you call my grandmother and tell her I'll pick her up?"

"She said she couldn't leave. You should go on your own, and she trusts you to make the best deal for her."

"What?" he asked in surprise. "Why doesn't she want to go? Is she sick?"

"You're not going to like it."

"Just tell me."

"She said the phone rang and there was no one there, just the sound of breathing, but then she heard someone clear their throat, and she thought it might be a woman." Carey paused. "She thought it might be your mother."

"Goddammit. She can't keep doing this every time someone calls the wrong number. It's been fifteen years since my mother walked out the door. She's probably dead." He jumped out of his chair, pacing restlessly in front of the window.

Carey stood up. "What do you want me to do?"

"Call my grandmother and tell her that she's coming with me. She's the legal owner of the dragon, and she's the one who needs to sell it."

"What about –"

"Tell her I'll be there in twenty minutes, and she better be ready." He was relieved to hear the door shut as Carey left. His chest was tight again, but this time it had nothing to do with exercise but with the past.

It had not been his mother on the phone—he knew that. There was no reason to think otherwise. None at all. But despite the ruthless affirmations, deep down inside there was a part of himself that still wondered where she was, and if she was ever coming back.

An hour later, Riley was less concerned about his mother's whereabouts and more interested in when David Hathaway would show up with his grandmother's dragon. They'd been cooling their heels in the executive offices of Hathaway's for fifteen minutes and there was no sign of David or his daughter, Paige.

"This is ridiculous," he said with irritation. He'd never been good at waiting, but he especially didn't like waiting for what belonged to him.

Nan worked her knitting needles with quiet, competent hands. He had no doubt that by his April birthday he'd have another sweater to put in his closet.

"Relax, Riley," she said. "I'm sure they'll be with us at any moment."

"It's after five. We should take our dragon and leave. There are plenty of other potential buyers out there. We don't need Hathaway's."

"Why don't we wait and see what they have to say? They gave us that lovely tea yesterday, and Paige is such a sweetheart. Pretty, too, don't you think?"

He frowned as he stretched out his long legs. "I didn't notice."

"Blind now, too, as well as hard of hearing," she teased.

Riley ignored that and jumped to his feet when the receptionist said, "Miss Hathaway will see you now."

Paige met them at the door to her office. She wore a blue suit with a lacy white see-through blouse that offered just enough cleavage to distract him. But he wouldn't be distracted, not today, not by someone he had no intention of ever seeing again.

"I'm sorry to have kept you waiting—" she began.

He cut her off. "Where's the dragon?"

"Why don't you come in?"

Riley followed her into her office, his grandmother close behind. He'd hoped to see David Hathaway, or at the very least, the ugly dragon statue, but neither was there. Paige looked decidedly nervous as she stood behind her desk, motioning for them to sit down in the chairs in front of her desk. Nan did as suggested. Riley decided he preferred to stand.

"Well?" he asked.

"My father has been delayed."

"Where's the statue?"

"He'll be here very soon, I'm sure." She offered him a tentative smile. "Can I get you some of that strong coffee you like so much?"

"No."

"Mrs. Delaney?"

"I'm fine, dear." Nan pulled out her knitting and sat back in her chair, content to wait. During the past year, Nan had spent a lot of time waiting for doctors to come back and tell her what was happening with her husband. She didn't deserve to have to wait for this, too.

"Miss Hathaway," he began again.

"I know. I'm very sorry. My father probably lost track of time. He does that sometimes. He doesn't mean to make anyone feel as if they're unimportant. He just gets caught up in the moment."

"I used to know someone like that," Nan said, a sad note in her voice. She glanced over at Riley, but he looked away.

She was talking about his mother, and he didn't want to go down that road. "This is ridiculous." He waved an impatient hand as he glared at Paige. "You're running a business here, aren't you?"

"Yes, but I can assure you that everything will be fine. This is just a small delay. If you'd rather come back tomorrow—"

"Absolutely not. I don't know what kind of scam you're running, but I'm not putting up with it."

She stiffened, her conciliatory smile turning angry. "I'm not running a scam. My father is simply late."

Riley's instincts told him that something was wrong, the same instincts that had been raising goose bumps along his arms since they'd discovered the damn dragon might be worth something. He leaned forward, rapping his knuckles on the top of Paige's mahogany desk. "I don't give a damn about whether or not your father is late for our meeting. I want the dragon."

"I can't conjure it up out of thin air."

"Why don't you have someone bring it up here? Isn't it in one of the vaults or a clean room of some sort?" He didn't like the way she avoided his gaze. "Isn't it?"

"The dragon doesn't appear to be in the lab. My father must have already retrieved it."

"And where is he?"

"I'm not exactly sure."

"Are you saying your father took the dragon out of the store? I don't believe we gave him permission to do that."

"I don't believe I said that he left the store. I just haven't been able to track him down."

"What the hell are you up to?"

"Look. I appreciate the fact that you're angry, but there's nothing going on here. I can assure you of that. Hathaway's has never lost a piece of art, and we're not starting with yours. I'm truly sorry for the inconvenience."

"Inconvenience, my ass!"

"Riley, I don't like it when you swear," Nan chided. "Now stop yelling at Miss Hathaway. There's nothing she can do about the delay. I'm sure Mr. Hathaway will have a reasonable explanation when he returns."

"I'm sure he will," Paige said.

The door behind them opened. Riley turned, expecting to see David, not another nervous young woman.

"I'm sorry for interrupting you, Miss Hathaway," she said.

"It's all right, Monica. Did you find my father?"

"That's the thing. He doesn't seem to be in the store." She paused, darting a worried look at Riley. "And the dragon isn't here, either."

CHAPTER FOUR

VICTORIA HATHAWAY SAT down in front of the mirror on her dressing room table and began to brush her hair. It was a pre-bedtime ritual that she'd followed every night since she was a little girl, living in a small two-bedroom apartment with her drunk of a mother and her two older sisters. Her mother had used one bedroom, her sisters the other. She'd had the couch, the bumpy, lumpy, bright red couch that her mother thought was so pretty.

Her surroundings now were quite different. Her elegant four-poster bed could be seen through the gold-edged mirror that David had bought her for their fifth wedding anniversary. As she pulled the brush through her smooth blond hair, she remembered a time when David had actually brushed her hair. She could almost see his reflection now in the glass, his dark hair rumpled, his brown eyes warm and caring.

It was foolish to turn her head, to see nothing but blank air. She knew he wasn't there. She couldn't remember the last time he'd been in her bedroom. David had moved out a few years earlier, because he was a night owl and she was an early bird, because he liked to read in bed, and she liked to get up early and do her hundred sit-ups in the privacy of her own room. God forbid anyone should know how hard she worked to keep her size-six figure. But those were only the reasons he said out loud, not the real reasons, not the ones that had isolated them in their own very private and personal hells for too many years to count.

She glanced back at the mirror and sighed. She could keep her body lean and trim, but not even the most expensive creams in the world or BOTOX treatments were managing to keep the wrinkles at bay. Already she could see the tiny lines around her eyes and lips. She could cover them in the daytime, but with her makeup removed, they were clearly visible. Perhaps some women would have turned away, but she forced herself to look, to examine, to be critical. It was the only way she knew to be.

When she was a young girl, she had made herself look at her life, her family, the way they lived and the manner in which they behaved. She remembered cutting out pictures from magazines of big houses and fancy restaurants. She'd made a list of how to get what she wanted, and she had followed that list to the letter. She'd gotten an education when many of her friends had dropped out, taken ugly, messy jobs in order to make enough money to go to college, always keeping her eye on the prize. Putting herself in a position to meet David at a party, marrying him, making her way into the Hathaway business had all been steps in the plan. She was no longer Vicky Siminski; she was Victoria Hathaway, and no one could ever take that away from her. She would not allow her life to be tarnished in any way.

Which brought David again to her mind. He'd postponed a trip to China when that old woman had discovered the dragon statue in her attic. David never postponed trips to China, which meant the dragon was special. She didn't know why it was different from any other arti-fact that had come to light, but something about it had filled him with barely restrained energy. He knew something about that dragon, some-thing he had not seen fit to share with her and she didn't like it. Nor did she like the fact that he'd been out of the office all day.

A knock at her bedroom door cut into her thoughts. For a moment, the quiet tap reminded her of other times when the loneliness had grown too keen, and David had come to the door. A shiver ran down her straight, stiff spine. What would she say if he'd come to her tonight?

The knock came again, followed by a voice. "Mother? Are you awake?"

Paige. The disappointment was not as annoying as the anger Victoria felt at herself. She didn't need David. She had everything she wanted in life.

"Come in," she said. "What are you doing here so late on a Wednesday night?" she added as Paige came into the room wearing running shoes, tight-fitting navy blue leggings, and a short matching warm-up jacket. "What on earth do you have on?"

"I came from my gym," Paige replied. "I'm sorry it's so late, but I need to speak to you."

"Why? What's wrong? And you know you can work out here in the house. The gym downstairs is state of the art and completely private."

"I like to be around other people when I exercise. It's inspiring."

"It's unsanitary. All that sweat on the machines after people use them. Heaven only knows what you might catch."

"I wipe the machines down with a towel, but that's not what I came to talk to you about." Paige sat down on the chaise next to the bed. "Have you seen Dad today or tonight?"

"No." Victoria picked up her brush and ran it through her hair, watching Paige through the glass. Her daughter was biting her nails, a nasty little habit Victoria had never been able to break her of. She remembered when she'd painted Paige's hands with a bad-tasting black polish just to make her aware of how many times she put her fingers in her mouth. It had worked for a while, but apparently the fix had not been permanent. Why was she surprised? Paige had a lot of her father in her.

"Dad didn't show up for an important meeting this afternoon," Paige said. "He's also not answering his cell phone, and no one seems to know where he is, not even Georgia."

Victoria's lips tightened. She hated the fact that David's secretary was more up-to-date on his whereabouts than she was, but she didn't particularly want to waste her time keeping track of him, so she'd allowed that to slide.

"I can't imagine where he is," Paige muttered.

Victoria heard the worried note in Paige's voice and tried not to let it concern her. Paige was a natural-born worrier. David's unexplained absence meant nothing, absolutely nothing. He was always missing. She'd spent too many hours to count waiting for David to show his face, to be where he'd promised to be, to support her when times got tough. All that had gotten her were more lines on her face. "He'll turn up. He always does—sooner or later."

"This isn't just about Dad. The dragon is missing, too."

Victoria's hand paused in mid stroke. "The dragon he was so eager to acquire?"

"Yes, but he never made an evaluation or an offer. He must have taken it somewhere for some reason. Mrs. Delaney is being incredibly patient. Her grandson is another matter. If Dad doesn't bring that dragon back to the store tomorrow, Mr. McAllister will be a huge problem."

That would be bad publicity for the store. Damn David. He never thought before he acted.

"Do you have any idea where he might be?" Paige asked.

Victoria had a terrible idea, one she didn't care to contemplate, one she couldn't possibly speak to her daughter about. "I'll see if I can find him." She set down the brush and got to her feet. "Why don't you go home and let me worry about your father?"

Paige rose, hesitating. "Do you think I should speak to Grandfather?"

"Good heavens, no. Why on earth would you want to do that?"

"Maybe he and Dad—"

"No, absolutely not. Your father doesn't confide in your grandfather. You know that. And let's not borrow trouble. Your father will turn up, he always does. There's no reason to upset Wallace." Her father-in-law was hard enough to please as it was, always looking for reasons to keep her in her place, to remind her that she could never run the store as well as he could.

"I guess you're right," Paige said slowly.

"Is there something else?"

"I just wonder—"

"Don't wonder, Paige. It's pointless where your father is concerned."

"Don't you ever worry about him?"

"Does he ever worry about us?" She knew her words hurt Paige, and she wished she could take them back. Hurting her daughter was never her intention, but sometimes it seemed inevitable. Paige had been disappointed by her father time and time again, yet she never seemed to see him for who he really was.

"You're right," Paige said.

"Well, he does worry about you," Victoria amended. "You're very important to him. And to me. Since you're here, there's something else I wanted to talk to you about."

Paige's expression turned wary. "What's that?"

"Martin. His mother tells me he's falling madly in love with you."

"Martin doesn't do anything madly. And we've known each other for years."

"But things have changed between you in recent months, isn't that true?"

"We've gone out together a few times," she said with a shrug. "The six-year age gap between us doesn't seem so big anymore, but that doesn't mean—"

"Six years is nothing. And I shouldn't have to remind you that you're not getting any younger. All your friends are married or about to be. Cynthia McAuley's wedding is in two weeks. Isn't that the fifth or sixth wedding you've been a bridesmaid in?"

"Tenth, but who's counting?"

"Don't be flippant, Paige. This is not a joking matter. The fact that Cynthia McAuley, who has the IQ of a lamp shade, is getting married before you is just ridiculous."

"She's a sweet girl. I'm happy for her."

"Of course you are. We all are. But we're not talking about her—we're talking about you. Martin is an excellent candidate for a husband. He's very successful and extremely smart."

"You make it sound like he's running for office."

"You should make a pro and con list, Paige. You'll see that Martin is right for you. It's important for you to marry someone who can work in the business with us. After all, the store will be your responsibility someday, and a husband who can help you shoulder that burden would be very good."

"Because you don't think I can handle it?"

"I didn't say that. You're so sensitive, Paige." She felt a twinge of remorse, but she forced it aside. "This isn't personal. It's business."

"I'm your daughter. That's personal. Getting married is even more personal. I have to go. Tell Dad to call me." Paige shut the door behind her.

Victoria let out a frustrated sigh and a muttered curse as she stared at herself in the mirror. Why couldn't the people she loved do what she wanted them to do? If she told Paige to walk, her daughter would run. If she told David to go out, he would stay home. It was as if they took perverse joy in making her life difficult. Paige needed to get married. And David—well, the list of what David needed to do was very long. Right now she'd settle for him coming home and bringing that damn dragon with him. He better have a good reason for taking a valuable artifact out of the store without the customer's permission. He knew better than that. A surge of uneasiness swept through her body. Had something happened to him? Or was this just another one of his famous disappearing acts?

Victoria walked across the room and looked out the window. A bright moon illuminated San Francisco Bay just a few miles from her home in Pacific Heights. All was quiet and peaceful in this part of town. Too quiet and peaceful for David. She knew where he'd gone, where he always went when he was on the mainland, as he called it. He'd gone to Chinatown. And she had a terrible feeling she knew exactly who he had gone to see.

She should have known better than to visit her mother. She'd accomplished nothing. Paige tried to slam the front door behind her, but it was so damn heavy and expensively made that it merely swung shut with a quiet thud. So much for venting her anger. She stopped at the bottom of the steps and drew in a deep breath. She tried counting to ten, but she was still feeling angry when she got to twenty.

Something was wrong. She knew it. She could feel it. But she had no facts, nothing to go on but instinct. She crossed the graveled drive, got into her Mercedes, and buckled her seat belt. There was nothing more to accomplish here. She might as well go home. Halfway down the street, she realized she didn't want to go home, didn't want to sit in her quiet, empty, lonely apartment—whoa, where had that *lonely* come from? She wasn't lonely. She liked living on her own. She didn't need a man in her life, even one that was as good a candidate for marriage as Martin was.

Her mouth turned down at the thought of her mother's suggestion to make a pro and con list. Marriage was supposed to be about love, lust, breathlessness, recklessness, falling head over heels; it wasn't supposed to be about IQ, credit rating, college degrees, family connections, business mergers—was it? How would she know anyway? Her mother and father were hardly a shining example of passionate love. Still, they'd been married for thirty-one years. Maybe they'd had all that earlier on, and she just hadn't been old enough to see it.

She hit the brake as the traffic light in front of her changed to red. She should turn right. It was the fastest route home. But she didn't want to go home. She wanted to talk to someone who would understand.

Unfortunately, as her mother had pointed out, all of her friends were married or about to be. Besides that, it was almost nine o'clock on a Wednesday night. She couldn't just drop in on anyone, especially not her married friends. Something happened once a woman walked down a rose-strewn aisle toward the man she loved; she changed, became one of a pair, half of a couple, someone you didn't stop by to see without a reason.

And, to be completely honest, most of her friends hadn't been all that close to her before marriage; they'd been girls she'd gone to private school with, college friends, or fellow debutantes. They were women she had lunch with, not women she confided in, at least not confidences that were more serious than the chocolate she'd sneaked after a Pilates workout. She wasn't in the habit of sharing personal information with anyone. The Hathaways had always been targets of gossip-mongers. No matter how close the friendships were supposed to be, confidences always seemed to leak out.

Making a quick decision, she turned left at the green light and drove across town to the neighborhood known as the Avenues. She found a parking spot just down the street from a popular neighborhood bar. It wasn't the kind of bar a Hathaway was supposed to be caught dead in but she wasn't dead yet, she thought with a smile as she got out of the car and walked down the street.

Fast Willy's was a cozy sports bar with photographs of athletes in every available space, some signed to the owner, Willy Bartholomew, a third-generation Willy from what she understood and a former minor league baseball player. There were four television sets, one placed at each corner of the room, with small tables crowded together on what was sometimes used as an impromptu dance floor. On the weekends, the bar overflowed with customers, but tonight there was a quiet after-work crowd, content to talk and listen to the jukebox.

She avoided the tables and headed to an empty stool at the long bar.

"What's an uptown babe like you doing in a joint like this?" the red-haired bartender asked her as he set down a napkin.

"Looking for a friend," she replied.

"Aren't we all? Just how good a friend are you looking for?" he asked with a wicked grin. "Because I can be pretty damn good, you know what I mean?"

"A monkey would know what you mean. Does that line work on intelligent women?"

"Did I say intelligence was a requirement?" He gave her an exaggerated wink.

"My mistake," she said with a laugh.

"What do you want, the usual chardonnay in a pretty glass?"

"I'd like a vodka gimlet."

"You don't drink vodka."

"I do tonight. In fact, forget the gimlet part and just get me the vodka."

"Oh, my God!" He clapped a dramatic hand to his forehead. "You went to see your mother. Why on earth would you do that?"

"It was a last resort, believe me."

"Paige, Paige, when will you learn?"

"Shut up, Jerry. I didn't come here for a lecture. I came here to get drunk."

"You don't get drunk." Jerry Scanlon pulled out a bottle of mineral water, poured it into an ice-filled glass, and handed it to her. "Try this."

"There better be some vodka in there."

"Then I'd have to hold your hair while you threw up. I'm not going to do that again."

She tried to frown, but ended up smiling instead. Jerry was the closest thing she had to a brother. The son of one of their housekeepers, Ruth Scanlon, Jerry and his mother had moved into the apartment over the garage when Paige was eleven years old. At thirteen, Jerry had been a tormenting pest, an irritating big brother, and a best friend. He'd saved her from lonely isolation, and their friendship had nourished for five years, until his mother had gotten fired during one of Victoria Hathaway's annual servant purgings.

Paige could still remember the sixteen-year-old angst she'd felt when Jerry and his mom had moved away to San Diego. Seven years later, Jerry had come back to San Francisco, and they'd found each other again. They'd kept in touch over the years, an odd but close friendship between a red-haired, freckle-faced pro athlete wannabe turned bartender and a sophisticated, blond debutante. She hated to think of herself in those terms, but she knew most of Jerry's friends thought of her in exactly that way. Not that they mingled with friends much. They moved in different circles except when they were together, which wasn't as often as she would have liked. Paige felt guilty about that, but Jerry understood how often she was torn between what she was supposed to do and what she wanted to do.

"My mother wants me to marry Martin," Paige said, reminded of what she was supposed to do now. "If I make a pro and con list, I will see that he's perfect for me."

"Martin Bennett? You can do better." Jerry wiped down the bar with a damp towel. "Is that all that's bugging you?"

She shook her head. "My father is nowhere to be found."

"What else is new?"

"It's different this time. He took a valuable artifact from the store. The owners are very upset. I managed to stall them until tomorrow, but I haven't been able to find my dad. He doesn't answer his cell phone. He's not at the store. He's not at home. I'm worried."

"He'll show up. He always does. You know what you need?"

"I have a feeling you're going to tell me."

"A game of pool. Or, as you Hathaways call it—billiards," he said in a mocking British accent.

"I don't think so," she replied with a shake of her head.

"Come on. When was the last time you played?"

"Probably the last time you talked me into it."

"I've got a break coming up." He set his towel down on the bar. "Let's rack 'em up."

"Why do I let you talk me into these things?"

Jerry grinned. "Because you love me."

Paige Hathaway got off the bar stool and followed the bartender through a door leading into a back room. Riley frowned, wondering what the hell she was up to. He hadn't been surprised when she'd gone to the gym or even to her mother's house, but this latest stop didn't make sense at all. This wasn't the kind of upscale bar she would frequent. These people weren't her crowd. And who was the bartender she'd been talking to for the past few minutes? Their conversation had looked more than friendly. Riley could hardly believe that Paige Hathaway, the princess of San Francisco's royal family, would be friends with a bartender.

Maybe this stop had something to do with the dragon, a back room deal. It was a reach, he knew it. She certainly didn't have the dragon with her, but it was possible she knew more about its whereabouts than she'd let on earlier. His grandmother might be content to wait until morning to get her dragon back, but he wasn't. In fact, his impatience had been growing since he'd left Hathaway's a few hours earlier. Something was wrong. He could feel it in his gut. David Hathaway had taken the dragon out of the store and missed their meeting. Paige had been concerned despite her best efforts to appear calm. That's why he'd decided to follow her.

Deciding to risk his cover, he walked into the bar. He needed to know what Paige was doing in the back room.

Five minutes later he couldn't quite believe what he was seeing.

Pool! She was playing pool. Paige's sweet ass was all he could see as she bent over the table, her attention focused on the cue stick between her fingers and the ball she was about to hit. It was a good shot, better than good, and she cleared the last two balls from the table. A murmur of appreciation from three old guys watching the action echoed his own thoughts. But he suspected they'd been watching her more than the game.

Paige exchanged a bouncing high five with the bartender. "Who's the best?" she demanded.

"That was a lucky shot," the guy replied.

"Luck had nothing to do with it. So tell me who's the best. Come on, you can say it."

"You're the best," he grumbled. "And not a pretty winner, by the way. Do you want to play again?"

"Do you feel like another butt-kicking?"

"Cocky, aren't you?"

"I could take you with my eyes closed."

"What about me?" Riley interrupted. "Could you take me with your eyes closed?"

Paige whirled around in surprise, her jaw dropping when she saw him. "What are you doing here? Oh, my God, did you follow me?"

Ignoring her questions, he said, "How about a game?"

"I don't think so." As she spoke, she stiffened, and there was no sign left of the unrestrained, laughing young woman he'd watched from the doorway. Her face went to stone. Her lips tightened. Her chin lifted in the air. Despite her casual clothes, she now looked exactly like the elegant, reserved businesswoman he'd met hours earlier—untouchable, unreadable, and unlikely to spend more than five minutes in conversation with him. He didn't care for the transformation.

"I have to go," she added.

"So, you're afraid you can't beat me," he drawled. "I can understand that."

"I am not afraid of losing. Tell him I'm not afraid, Jerry."

The bartender laughed. "Why don't you show him, Paige? You like a challenge."

"I'm tired."

"Scared." Riley smiled as a spark of anger flickered in her eyes. He had the urge to provoke her, to do anything to bring down the wall she'd put up when he entered the room.

"Fine. You want a game, I'll give you a game."

"I want a game, Miss Hathaway."

"I should have my head examined," she muttered as she moved to collect the balls.

"What did you say?"

"She said she should have her head examined," Jerry said helpfully, a big grin on his face. "I take it you two know each other."

"Yes," Riley replied.

"Barely," Paige corrected. "Don't be nice to him, Jerry. I think he followed me here."

"You're stalking her?" Jerry asked, his smile vanishing. "Maybe you should get the hell out of my bar, then."

"No, no," Paige said quickly. "It's not that way. It's not personal."

"She's right. It's not at all personal. It's business."

"Mr. McAllister's grandmother is selling a statue to us," Paige added.

"*Maybe* selling a statue, if it ever shows up again." He gave her a pointed look.

"It will."

"I hope so."

Jerry moved toward the door. "All right then. I'm not getting in the middle of this. But I'm warning you, dude. You mess with her, you mess with me. Let me know if you need anything," Jerry added to Paige.

"Good friend of yours?" Riley asked as Jerry left.

"Yes, he is, as a matter of fact."

"I'm surprised. I didn't figure you for a Fast Willy's kind of girl."

"I don't think you know me well enough to make any assumptions about me. Not that that will stop you. Stereotyping is hardly confined to the rich, is it?"

"At least you admit you're rich."

"It's hardly a secret that my family is wealthy, but believe it or not, I'm nowhere near as rich as they are."

"Maybe not now, but I'll bet there are some hefty inheritances in your future."

"Not that it's any of your business."

"Until you return my grandmother's missing dragon, everything about you is my business."

"It's not exactly missing. It's just unaccounted for at the moment."

"Splitting hairs, don't you think? Why did your father take the dragon out of the store, anyway? I thought you had state-of-the-art testing equipment on the premises. Isn't that what your brochure says?"

"You've read our brochure?"

"I've read a great deal about your company in the past twenty-four hours."

"Then you shouldn't be worried."

"Maybe I wouldn't be—if you weren't worried. But you are, aren't you, Miss Hathaway? This isn't standard operating procedure. This isn't the way things normally go down." She glanced away from him, guiltily he thought. "I can't help wondering what's coming next."

"Nothing is coming next. You just need to be patient."

"I'm not a patient man."

"I can see that." She paused. "Do you actually want to play pool?" She waved her hand toward the table.

"Do you really know how to play, or did the red-haired guy give you a break?"

"Jerry give me a break? Not in this lifetime. And, yes, I do know how to play pool. Although at our house we refer to the game as billiards." An impulsive smile broke across her face as she said the word. "Or, as Jerry calls it, billiards." She added a British accent and a laugh that broke the tension between them. "My grandfather always refers to it as that."

God, she was beautiful all loosened up again, her long blond hair falling out of its ponytail, her slender body encased in tight-fitting sweats, a pair of running shoes on her feet. Looking like this, he could almost forget she was the princess of San Francisco and way out of his league. He could almost forget that this was business.

She cleared her throat. "You're staring." She tucked a strand of hair behind her ear. "I look a mess. My mother would have a fit if she knew I was out in public looking like this."

"I like it."

"You do?" she asked, amazement in her voice. "It's not at all appropriate."

"Who cares about appropriate?"

"I always have to be careful what I wear, because with my luck some photographer desperate for a photo to fill tomorrow's empty slot will snap me in my sweats and suggest that maybe Hathaway's is losing money, and the incident will be blown completely out of proportion."

"Gone a few rounds with the press, have you?"

"More than a few."

"Well, there's no paparazzi here. And I don't have a camera. Although I wish I did, because you don't look anything like the woman

I saw earlier today. In fact, since you've been in this room, you've undergone several transformations. You remind me of a lizard I used to have as a kid."

"A lizard? I remind you of a lizard? That's quite a compliment."

He laughed at her look of outrage. "A chameleon. The kind of lizard that changes colors to fit its environment. That's what you do. And it was a compliment. I don't know many women who can be comfortable in the back room of Fast Willy's and the next day go to work in the executive offices of Hathaway's."

She frowned at him. "I still think you could do better than lizard if you're looking to give a compliment. It's no wonder why you had nothing better to do tonight than follow me around. That's what you've been doing, isn't it? I should call the cops."

"I don't think you want to call the police, not with my grandmother's dragon missing."

"I told you before—"

"I know what you told me before. But my instincts tell me something else is going on. Have you spoken to your father since we met earlier?"

"Since you've been following me, you know that I haven't."

"I thought he might have called you."

"He didn't."

"Is that unusual? Not hearing from your father when he has a valuable artifact out of your store?"

"Potentially valuable," she corrected.

"Oh, come on. If it was a fake, it would have been returned to us hours ago."

"There's nothing to worry about, Mr. McAllister."

"Riley," he corrected. "And I am worried, because as I said before —you're nervous."

"Maybe I'm nervous because you've been following me around." She paused as her cell phone rang. She hesitated, then pulled out of her purse to answer. "Hello."

"Hello?"

Riley watched the color drain from her face.

"What did you say?" she stuttered. "Where? When? Yes, I'll come right away."

"What's wrong?" he asked as she ended the call.

"My father," she said, her eyes dazed, frightened.

"Where is he?"

"He's in the hospital. He was attacked in an alley in Chinatown. He's in critical condition."

CHAPTER FIVE

PAIGE FOUND her mother in the waiting room on the fourth floor of St. Mary's Hospital. Next to Victoria was her closest friend, Joanne Bennett, another well-to-do socialite in her fifties, and Joanne's son, Martin, the object of their earlier discussion. A tall, lean man in his mid-thirties with perfectly styled dark blond hair, Martin was still wearing the charcoal gray Armani suit he'd had on at work earlier that day. While sometimes his never-a-hair-out-of-place demeanor annoyed Paige, right now she found it reassuring. Things couldn't be that bad if Martin looked so calm

Martin got up to greet her, putting his arms around her in a comforting hug. "It will be all right, Paige."

She wanted to linger. It felt good to let someone take care of her, but she knew she couldn't hide in Martin's arms. She had to see her mother's face, look into her eyes, and then she would know the truth. She pulled away and said, "Mother?"

Victoria's face was white. There were tight lines around her eyes and mouth. She'd come out of the house without touching up her lipstick, without wearing hose, for God's sake. In fact, she had on a blue skirt and a yellow sweater that didn't match, all the little details her mother took such pride in. It was bad. It had to be bad.

"How is Daddy?" she forced herself to ask.

"They don't know yet. He's unconscious. He has a bad gash in his head, maybe a skull fracture." Victoria cleared her throat as the words came out choked and emotional.

"But he's going to be all right? He'll recover?"

"I'm sure he will," Victoria replied, but there was no strength in her voice, no confidence, just fear. "The doctor said it may be awhile before we know anything."

"I don't understand what happened. Was he robbed? What was he doing in Chinatown?" The questions tumbled out of her mouth. "Did they find the person who did this to him?"

"Paige, slow down," Joanne chided gently. "There's time to know everything."

"Is there time? Are you sure there's time?" Paige asked, meeting her mother's gaze.

"I hope so," Victoria muttered.

"This is a private conversation. Do you mind?" Martin said.

Paige turned to see Martin bearing down on Riley, who had stopped a discreet distance away. She'd forgotten he was there, forgotten he'd given her a ride to the hospital.

"Are you with the press?" Martin demanded.

"He brought me here," Paige answered. "Riley McAllister, Martin Bennett." She turned to her mother, leaving the two men to shake hands or not. "Have you spoken to the police?"

"Just for a few moments. They don't know anything. Or at least they're not saying what they know. Someone found your father lying in an alley in Chinatown." Victoria put her head on her hand. "God. An alley, of all places."

Her mother's words created a vivid picture in Paige's mind, one of her father defenseless and in pain, maybe crying out for help, for family. Paige felt nauseous at the thought. "I don't understand how this could happen—"

"Paige, I know you're terrified, and you want answers," Joanne cut in with a compassionate smile, "but your mother is also upset, and she doesn't know anything more than she's already told you."

"Except that he was in Chinatown," Victoria said a bitter note creeping into her voice as she exchanged a pointed look with her friend. "Probably with that damn woman."

"Dad was with another woman?" It was too much to take in. Paige started to sway.

Riley was suddenly behind her. He caught her by the arm, and she sank back against his solid chest. His arm came around her waist. "Hang on," he said, leading her to a nearby chair. She sat down, and he pushed her head down between her knees. "Breathe."

"I'm okay." She sat back up. "I'm okay," she repeated, looking into Riley's skeptical eyes. "I just felt dizzy for a second."

"What can I do to help?" Martin asked, drawing her attention back to him.

She didn't know how to reply to that. What could anyone do to help except make her father be all right again? But Martin wanted to do something. "Maybe some water."

"I'll get it right away."

Riley took one of her hands in his and gave it a squeeze. "The hardest part is the waiting."

"You sound like you know something about it."

"I've done this a few times."

His compassionate gaze completely undid her. Was this the same man who had stormed into her office yesterday? Who had followed her all over San Francisco tonight and practically accused her and her family of lying and stealing? Because he wasn't acting like that man right now. He was acting more like a friend. And they weren't friends. She couldn't start thinking they were. He'd given her a ride because she'd been too frantic to get her keys in the lock of her car door, and he'd insisted she go with him. Why had he insisted? Probably to find out whether the dragon had come in with her father.

"You don't have to stay. I can get a ride home," she said. "This is a family matter." Paige dropped her voice down a notch. "As soon as my mother gets her bearings, she'll be horrified that you've witnessed such a private moment. And she doesn't need that right now. I'll find out about the dragon as soon as I can. I know that's your main concern."

"I do hope your father is all right."

Her eyes misted. "So do I. He's not the best dad," she whispered, "but he's the only one I've got."

Riley squeezed her hand once again. "Keep the faith."

His words brought back memories from the last time someone had said that to her, the night before Elizabeth died. She had been only six years old, but those words were forever burned in her memory.

Keeping the faith then hadn't stopped the worst from happening. And now it was happening again. Why? Was it a random attack? A mugging gone bad? Or something else?

He'd been in Chinatown—maybe with another woman. An affair? God, she didn't want to go there.

"Here's your water." Martin handed her a bottled water.

"Thank you."

"Are you a friend of Paige's?" Martin asked Riley as he got to his feet.

"His grandmother is the owner of the dragon we're interested in acquiring," Paige explained, as the two men sized each other up. They were night and day, she thought. Riley was midnight with his black hair, olive skin, and light blue eyes. Martin was sunlight—blond, clean, a golden boy. They were both good-looking men, but they didn't seem to care for each other at all. Their matching frowns showed wariness and distrust, maybe a bit of rivalry. Which was completely idiotic, because Riley was a customer and Martin was—well, she didn't know exactly what he was, but this little display of showmanship was the last thing she needed. "Riley was just leaving," she added, breaking the tension.

"I'll talk to you tomorrow." Riley tipped his head in her direction, then strode off down the hall.

"What were you doing with him, Paige? It's after ten o'clock." Martin sat down in the chair next to her, looking decidedly put out.

"It's a long story."

"I think we have time."

She sighed. Sometimes Martin was like a dog with a bone. "I

wasn't out on a date, if that's what you're thinking. Mr. McAllister's dragon has gone missing. I think my father took it from the store."

Martin looked surprised. "That doesn't make sense at all."

"No, it doesn't. But right now it's the least of my worries. Where's Grandfather?" she asked abruptly. "Does he know what happened?"

"Yes, of course. He's upstairs with the chief of staff, Dr. Havenhurst. They're making sure the best doctors are on the case. He'll be down shortly."

She tapped her fingers against her legs. "What's taking so long? Damn, I hate this. And where are the police? Why aren't they here telling us what happened?"

"A detective checked in with your mother when we first got here. He'll report back as soon as he has any more information. They're investigating the crime scene now."

"What was my father doing in Chinatown?" She didn't like the way Martin avoided her gaze. "If you know, you have to tell me. My mother said something about a woman?" She lowered her voice, not wanting her mother to hear her, but Victoria and Joanne were engaged in a low conversation of their own. "Do you know who that would be?"

Martin shifted in his seat and tugged at his tie. She'd never seen him appear so uncomfortable. "What matters right now is your father's health." He took her hand in his.

His fingers were colder than Riley's had been. His reassuring squeeze chilled rather than comforted. Maybe because she knew he was keeping something from her, and she didn't like it. That was one of the problems with their relationship; she didn't think Martin respected her, or perhaps it was just that his loyalties always seemed to lie more with her parents or her grandfather than with her.

"I'm sorry, Paige," he said quietly, concern in his eyes. "I wish I could make this go away for you."

Now she was sorry for being so annoyed with him. He was a good man. And he'd come running to the hospital as soon as he'd heard the news. "I'm just on edge." She pulled her hand from his and stood up. "I can't sit here. I'm going to take a little walk, see if I can find someone who knows something. I'll be back in a few minutes. Watch out for my mother, all right?"

"Always," he said reassuringly. "And you, too, if you'll let me."

That was a question she'd save for another day.

Riley ran into the police detective getting off the elevator. A short, squat, muscular man with thick brown hair and cynical black eyes, Tony Paletti was a third-generation San Francisco Italian and a fifteen-year veteran with the SFPD. Riley knew Tony from some of the events on which they'd coordinated security.

"Hey," Riley said with a nod. "Are you working the Hathaway mugging?"

"You know something about it?" Tony stepped off to one side to avoid an orderly pushing a wheelchair down the hall.

"I was with Paige Hathaway when she found out about her father. Was he robbed?"

"Looks like it. Wallet, money, credit cards are missing. Hathaway was in the wrong place at the wrong time."

"Was anything else found at the scene?"

"Like what?"

Riley hesitated, debating the wisdom of saying anything, but then again secrecy would help the Hathaways more than his grandmother. "A statue that looked like a dragon?"

Tony's eyes narrowed. "No, but do you want to tell me why you're asking?"

"My grandmother found an antique statue in her attic. Hathaway's was appraising it."

"And you think he had it with him?"

"Possibly."

"Is this thing worth much?"

"Could be worth a lot, but we don't know yet."

Tony took out a small spiral notebook and jotted down some notes. "I'll speak to Mrs. Hathaway. See if she knows what her husband was doing in Chinatown, who he might have gone to see. I need to drum up some witnesses fast. I already got a call from the mayor. The Hathaway family is very important to the city. They want his assailant behind bars ten minutes ago, if you know what I mean."

Riley nodded, knowing the pressure the cops would be under to solve this case as soon as possible. By morning the press would be all over it, too.

Paige came around the corner, startling him with her sudden appearance. She looked just as surprised to see him standing with the police officer.

"Are you the officer investigating my father's attack?" she asked Tony.

"And you are?"

"Paige Hathaway. I'm his daughter."

"I'm sorry about your father, Ms. Hathaway."

"Thank you. Can you tell me any more about what happened?"

"Not yet, I'm afraid. We're still investigating the scene. Do you know what business your father had in Chinatown?"

"I have no idea."

"Did he have friends there? Business associates?"

"Probably both. My father specializes in purchasing Asian art. He has many contacts in the Chinese community."

"Sounds like we'll need a big net. I'll need you to sit down with someone and give us a list of names. But right now I'd like to speak to your mother. Is she available?"

"She's in the waiting room."

Before Tony could move down the hall, the elevator doors opened and a uniformed officer stepped out. Tony walked over to greet him, and they began to converse in hushed tones.

"What do you think that's about?" Paige asked Riley.

"Probably your father's case."

"I hope they caught the bastard."

"If they didn't, they will," he reassured her.

"They better. It's cold in here, don't you think?" She shivered, clasping her arms more tightly about her waist.

Riley shouldn't have put his arms around her. He knew it as soon as her breasts brushed his chest. But it was too late then. Her cheek was pressed against his heart, her hair tickled his chin, and her arms crept around his body, holding on to him with a tight desperation that he suspected had a lot to do with fear. He wished he had as good an excuse for hugging her back.

"I'm sorry," Paige said, pulling away far too soon. "I don't know what came over me. I don't usually throw myself into people's arms like that."

"Miss Hathaway?" Tony walked back to join them. "Do you recognize this bracelet?" He extended his hand, a gold bangle in his palm.

She shook her head. "I've never seen it before. Where did you find it?"

"It was found near your father. It might not have anything to do with him, but there's an inscription. It says '*Jasmine, my love*'. Do you know anyone named Jasmine?"

"Jasmine," Paige echoed, looking confused. "I—I don't think so."

Despite her denial, Riley had the feeling something in the name had registered with Paige.

"I'll ask your mother." Tony closed his fingers over the bracelet.

"Wait," Paige said. "Do you need to ask her now? She's upset."

"If this bracelet can help us find who assaulted your father..."

"You're right," Paige agreed. "Go ahead."

"From what I've seen, your mother is a very strong woman," Riley said quietly as they watched the detective stride away.

Paige looked at him with indecision in her eyes. "Yes, she is."

"You've heard the name Jasmine before, haven't you?"

She hesitated. "There's a painter named Jasmine Chen. We've bought some of her work for the store. But that doesn't mean that she and my father... He wouldn't do that. He's not a bad man. At least, I don't think he is." She pressed a hand to her temple, looking paler than she had before. "The truth is I don't know what kind of man he is, and I'm terrified that I won't have the chance to find out. What if he doesn't make it? God, I shouldn't have said that."

"Give yourself a break. You're human."

"No, I'm a Hathaway. The press will be all over this before morning. And if there's speculation about another woman..." she let out a
sigh. "I should get back to my mother. She might need me." She
paused, then let out an odd laugh that sounded incredibly sad. "Who
am I kidding? She doesn't need me. I didn't even think she needed my
father until a few minutes ago." Paige seemed to be talking to herself
more than to him. She suddenly started. "Was I talking out loud?"

"I didn't hear a thing," he lied.

She stared at him for a long moment. "I can't quite figure you out."

"Likewise," he replied.

"Thanks for the ride."

Riley watched her walk away, the stiffness of her spine no doubt
worthy of the very best Hathaway. She had her game face back on, and
she would do anything to protect her family.

But right now he had his own family to worry about—his grandmother's possibly priceless dragon. And the only clue he had was
Jasmine Chen, a local painter. She shouldn't be that difficult to find.

Jasmine turned over in bed, her legs twisting in the hot sheets. She
wanted to escape from the dream that raced through her head once
again, but it had her in its grip, the jade green light burning from two
bright eyes, the makeshift altar with the candles, the fireworks bursting
outside. Then there was nothing but darkness, the swish of fabric
against her face, the terror of no way out, the screaming, the terrible,
terrible screaming of a woman, the harsh grip on her arm, the
wrenching pain...

She woke up abruptly, sweat dripping down her face. The dream
always began and ended the same way. But tonight was worse, because
today the dream had become a reality.

The dragon from her nightmares existed. It wasn't a figment of her
imagination, as her mother had assured her over the years. It was real.
David had shown it to her. It matched the vision in her head, the one
she had painted so many times, trying to understand what her dreams

might mean. For there had to be a meaning, a reason why her mind kept taking her back to that place. What was she was supposed to learn? And why couldn't she learn it, understand it?

Untangling herself from the sheets, she walked over to the window and threw it open. The cold air washed over her, cooling the fever in her body, in her head, but she still felt frustrated. She was close to something. She could feel it in her heart, a heart that sang to the past more than to the present. It was a love she shared with David, a love of history, of China, of people and places that seemed both magical and yet very real, as if she had lived there once. But she hadn't lived there. Her parents had been born in China, but she had been born here in Chinatown, just a few blocks away in an apartment that she'd shared with her three brothers and one younger sister. How could she know of things that had happened a continent away and several lifetimes ago? Was it just her imagination, or did she have an old soul, as a fortune-teller had once told her?

Shivering, she stayed by the window, refusing to give in to the cold or to the reality of her life. She tried not to look down, not to see what was right before her, because so much of her present was not what she wanted it to be. Instead, she looked up at the moon and the stars, to her dreams, her desires. She was a fool, she knew that, too. Foolish to believe in miracles. Her life had been hard since the day she was born missing the index finger on her left hand, a sign of just how inadequate she was and would be. She had disappointed so many people in her life. So why was she here on this earth? What was she supposed to accomplish with her life?

The answers had something to do with the dragon. She knew it with a certainty that she couldn't explain. David knew it, too. He was as much a dreamer as she was. And her persistent dreams had always intrigued him. Over the years, they had looked through centuries of stories about dragons to find some similarity to the one in her dreams. Only one tale had come close, but that tale involved two dragons connected together. She never dreamed about two, only one. Unless they were a perfect match, unless they blended together as one in her dreams. She remembered seeing a rough sketch of those dragons in a book of Chinese fairytales, and there had been a small similarity, but neither had really matched the dragon in her dreams. Another dead end, she had thought. But today... when her fingers had traced the joint opening where two dragons could become one, she had known the truth.

And if there were two dragons...

Where was the other one?

CHAPTER SIX

PAIGE WALKED through the front doors of the hospital and blinked against the brightness of the early Thursday morning sun. She couldn't believe the night had finally ended. For a while she had thought it might go on forever.

Her father was in a coma, the doctors said. There was severe swelling in his brain. They didn't know the extent of the damage, if it was permanent or temporary. In fact, they didn't know much of anything. Only time would tell. So they waited and they waited. When the sun came up, Paige had ventured down to the lobby, grabbing a cup of coffee from the cafeteria, finally making her way out here, to the front of the hospital where a horseshoe driveway allowed for pickups and drop-offs.

She sat down on a cold bench and let out a long, frustrated, anxious breath—the breath she'd been holding most of the night. But she couldn't relax, not yet. The immediate danger wasn't over. And she had to be ready for everything that would follow, the press, the police, Riley McAllister. She knew he'd be back. And she'd have to deal with the question of the missing dragon.

Maybe it was somewhere in the store. She would have her secretary search every floor. She'd ask Martin, too, and whomever else she could enlist to both help and keep the search confidential. The last thing she wanted was for the public to catch wind of not only her father's attack but also the fact that a piece of art that Hathaway's had not yet acquired had disappeared from their care.

"Paige, there you are." Martin came through the hospital doors, looking as crisp as he had appeared the night before. She couldn't imagine how he did it. "I'm glad you waited," he said. "I'll drive you home."

"I'm not going home yet."

"You've been here all night. You need some sleep."

"I can't sleep now, not until I know for sure my dad is all right."

"Paige, it could be hours."

"My mother should be back shortly," she said, taking a quick look at her watch. "I'll leave when she gets here."

"Do you want me to wait with you?"

She shook her head. "No, but thank you for the offer. You've gone above and beyond the call of duty."

"It's not duty. I care about you."

She looked away, not liking the gleam in his eyes.

"Paige, I know this isn't the time, but—"

"You're right, it's not the time. I have a lot on my mind."

He frowned. "I'm sorry. Is there anything I can do for you before I go?"

She thought about that for a moment. "There's something you can do when you get to the store. You can find out if that dragon statue is anywhere on the premises. I think my father had it with him, but I have to know for sure. I don't want to think there's a connection between the dragon and my father's attack, but it's possible."

"Does your mother know about this?"

"I mentioned it to her last night before Dad got hurt. I don't think it's at the top of her list right now. And I really don't want Grandfather to know, although I suspect he already does. He seems to have an uncanny ability to know every single thing that goes on at the store."

Martin smiled. "The sign of a good executive. Don't worry, Paige.

I'll do everything I can to help." He leaned over and kissed her on the cheek. "Maybe someday you'll realize I'm a good guy to have around."

She was saved from answering by the appearance of her grandfather's car pulling up in front of the hospital. She stiffened at the sight. Wallace Hathaway was the most intimidating individual she had ever known. He demanded perfection, and he made no allowances for family. If anything, he expected more from those who shared his blood. She stood up as her grandfather got out of the backseat of his black BMW, which was driven by his longtime chauffeur.

Eighty-two years of living might have turned his hair a pepper gray and drawn thick lines across his forehead and around his dark eyes, but time had not lessened his stature. At six foot four, her grandfather still seemed like a giant.

"Grandfather," she murmured, walking over to him. "I didn't expect you back so soon."

"What are you doing out here? Why aren't you upstairs with your father?" he demanded.

"I was just—"

"How is David?" he interrupted.

"The same," she said.

Her grandfather's lips tightened with anger, or maybe it was fear. He was a difficult man to read. She wanted to tell him she was scared and worried and have him respond that it would be all right, that her dad would pull through. But to do that would mean admitting personal weakness, something her grandfather never wanted to see.

"I've hired a private nurse," Wallace said abruptly. "I want someone with him at all times."

Paige immediately felt guilty for having abandoned her post for even a few moments.

"I'll walk up with you, Mr. Hathaway," Martin said. "Paige needs a little air."

She sent Martin a silent thank you, knowing he'd made the offer to give her some space. She sat back down on the bench, retrieving her rapidly cooling cup of coffee.

Martin and her grandfather got along well, she thought, taking a sip of the tepid liquid. Another item to put in the pro column. And he'd just saved her a few minutes of awkward tension. But deep in her heart she knew there was still something missing in their relationship. Despite all of Martin's good qualities, she couldn't seem to feel more for him than fondness and appreciation. Her mother would say those emotions were enough to base a marriage on. But she wanted more. She wanted that reckless, breathless, falling-in-love kind of feeling. She wanted her stomach to do flip-flops when Martin was close by. She wanted to be acutely aware every time his hand touched her shoulder or the small of her back. She wanted to be swept off her feet. But Martin didn't make her feel any of those things.

He was a good date. Generous, concerned, able to pick fine wines, good restaurants, appropriate movies. He read extensively, traveled when he had the chance, worked out, kept fit, handled money well, had a good job. Damn. She was doing just what her mother had suggested, making a pro and con list in her head. Only the pros were all logical, and the cons were all emotional. Big surprise there. She'd spent most of her life torn between reason and desire. And she always chose reason. She always did the right thing in the long run. That was who she was; even when she wanted to stray, she couldn't. She should probably conserve her energy and just agree to marry Martin now, save herself all the stress and turmoil of a decision that would probably end up there anyway.

With a sigh, she leaned back, resting against the building. This wasn't the time to be thinking about marriage. Not with her father's life on the line. A rush of worry hit her once again. She didn't want to lose him. It couldn't end like this, without warning, without a chance to say good-bye.

She closed her eyes for a moment, seeking a peaceful image, but she was taken back to an even more painful place—her sister's bedroom. She'd had more than one chance to say good-bye to her sister, but she hadn't been able to make herself go into the room, so she'd stood in the doorway as her parents sat by Elizabeth's bed. She could see them now, the sunlight streaming in through the window, lighting up Elizabeth's face as if she was already an angel, already gone to heaven. Her mother had asked Paige to come in, to say good-bye to her sister. But she hadn't been able to enter that room. Not with Elizabeth lying so still, her eyes closed, her small hands folded on her chest. It was the way she would look a few days later when they put her in the casket, like she was sleeping, only she wasn't.

God, how Paige wished she hadn't had to see that. But her mother had insisted that she face it, that she understand that death was a part of life. *You must be strong, Paige. You must not cry. You must go on with your life.* She hadn't been strong, and she hadn't understood. She'd been six years old and terrified that whatever was happening to her sister would happen to her, too. She hadn't been able to sleep on her back for years. In fact, she still hated that position, still refused to put her hands together on her chest, as if she were inviting the same result.

Her eyes flew open so she wouldn't see the images in her head. She knew that the reason she was sitting out here was so she wouldn't have to look at her father in the same position. She was twenty-eight years old now, but seeing her father lying so still in bed, looking so old, so fragile, made her feel as if she were six years old again. She wanted it all to go away. She wanted everything to be the way it was yesterday.

Rolling her head around on her shoulders, Paige felt the aches of the long, stressful night. The sudden ringing of her cell phone made her jump. She answered the call with a wary hello.

"Paige? This is Riley. We need to meet."

"What? How did you get this number?"

"It wasn't difficult. How's your father?"

"No change."

"It sounds like he's holding his own."

"For the moment, yes."

"We need to talk, Paige. I think you should meet me in Chinatown."

"Why?" she asked, shocked by the suggestion. She never went to Chinatown. Her mother insisted it was a tourist trap, a neighborhood where Hathaways didn't belong. Even on the few occasions when a girlfriend had dragged her there for dim sum, it had always been to visit a certain restaurant, not to go anywhere else, not to walk down the streets, or stop in the shops, or talk to the people.

"Paige? Are you still there?"

"I can't go to Chinatown. Why would you ask me to? The police are investigating the area. There's nothing I can do. There's nothing you can do, either."

"I've already done something."

"What?" Her heart beat in triple time. "What have you done?"

"I found Jasmine Chen. She lives two blocks from where your father was attacked. I want to talk to her. Don't you?"

Her mind whirled with the information. Did she want to talk to Jasmine? Did she want to face the woman who might be her father's lover? Oh, God. She couldn't do this, not on no sleep, not with her brain in a fog. "I can't leave right now," she said hastily.

"All right. I'll go on my own."

"No. This is family business. I want you to stay out of it."

"Until I get my grandmother's dragon back, your family's business is my business. I'm going to see Jasmine Chen with or without you. If your father went there yesterday, he might have had the dragon with him. She might be the last person who spoke to him. I'm sure the police won't be far behind me, but I figure she might rather talk to me than a uniform, especially if her relationship with your father—"

"Stop." She couldn't let Riley, then the police, then God knows who talk to Jasmine without her there. What if Jasmine said something to compromise her father, his reputation, his name? "I'll go with you. I don't want you to talk to her without me there."

"Do you need a ride?"

"I'll take a cab." She made a mental note of the address he gave her, then closed her phone and stood up. Her grandfather and Martin were with her dad, and her mother would be back soon. She might as well take care of this now. She hoped Jasmine Chen had nothing to do with her father, that all they'd had was a business relationship. Just because the woman lived in Chinatown near the scene of her father's assault didn't mean anything. Her bracelet could have fallen off at any time. It didn't have to be connected to her father. It didn't have to be from him.

The rationalizations made her feel better. With any luck, this whole misunderstanding would be cleared up within the hour, and they'd never have to talk about Jasmine Chen again.

Riley walked down one of the many alleys that ran behind the main streets of Chinatown. David Hathaway had been attacked some thirty yards into the alley, and apparently no one had seen or heard anything, not an unusual occurrence in a neighborhood where it was better for your health not to be too observant. Even now, a young man sweeping the brick in front of his store hurried quickly inside and shut the door, obviously not wanting to engage in conversation.

Riley stopped at the spot where remnants of yellow tape lay on the ground and wondered again what the hell a rich man like David Hathaway had been doing down here. A glance around the alley showed nothing out of the ordinary. The bottom floors of the buildings housed various businesses, a trading company, a photography studio, an accounting office, certainly nothing that would appear to have anything to do with a dragon statue. There were, however, several unmarked doors opening off the alley that could have led anywhere, to anyone.

He looked up, noting the apartments on the second, third, and fourth floors. There were clothes drying off fire escapes, open windows with tattered curtains blowing in and out in the breeze, and a halfhearted attempt at a window garden in the dark alley. Everything he saw spoke of people struggling to survive in a densely populated city. He imagined that the apartments above were cramped, the plumbing and electrical antiquated, too many people living in too small a space. Was it any surprise that David Hathaway had been robbed in a place like this? He should have had more sense than to come here alone at night.

Bringing his gaze back down to the ground, Riley checked to see if anything else had been missed by the police, but found nothing. A few feet away was a doorway set back from the street, an overhang offering shelter, perhaps a hiding spot as well. He walked over to the door and saw women and sewing machines through the metal grille that protected the shop from burglary. He rang the bell. A moment later, a short young Chinese woman approached the door. She looked through the upper glass portion of the door, then tentatively opened it, leaving the metal grille between them.

"Hello," he said, offering her a friendly smile. "I wonder if I could talk to you for a minute."

She said something to him in Cantonese and started to shut the door.

"Wait, I wanted to ask you about a man who was attacked here last night."

"No English," she said in a heavy accent. Another woman came up behind her and grabbed her by the arm, forcing her away from the door.

"Police?" the other woman asked him.

"No. I'm a friend of the man who was assaulted in the alley last night. Were you here when it happened?"

She shook her head, then shut the door firmly in his face. He had no idea if they were protecting someone else, or just themselves.

Checking his watch, he realized he had only a few minutes to meet Paige. He walked down the alley toward the main street, passing a temple on the corner. Gold dragons were wrapped around two columns in front of the doorway that boasted a sign with Chinese writing. Below, in English, those seeking blessings were invited to enter. He wondered if David Hathaway had stopped at this temple, seeking a blessing on the dragon. Apparently, dragons were quite a symbol in Chinatown. He saw them virtually everywhere, promising protection, long life, and good fortune. But he hadn't experienced any good fortune since his grandmother discovered the dragon, and David Hathaway certainly hadn't, either.

Leaving the alley, Riley traversed two short blocks, leading him away from the commercial area to a neighborhood of apartment buildings that shared common walls. He wondered again if he shouldn't have gone ahead and talked to Jasmine on his own. While he wanted to believe Paige knew nothing about the dragon's disappearance, another part of him, the part that reminded him that women could lie and cheat with smiles on their faces, told him to be wary and not to take anything at face value. Paige Hathaway had grown up in a different world with different rules.

David Hathaway had already broken one rule by taking the dragon from the store. Who knew what else he'd had in mind? Riley needed to do more research on the art world, find out what scams were running. He was concerned that someone might try to copy the dragon, return the counterfeit version to his grandmother, insisting it was a fake, and sell the real thing on the black market. He would not allow that to happen to his grandmother.

A taxi pulled up alongside the curb, and Paige stepped out, still dressed in the navy blue leggings she'd worn the night before. She'd brushed her hair, put on some pink lipstick, but her eyes were tired, her face drawn. She was scared. He could see it in every tiny, tense line.

"You look like hell," he told her. "Why don't you go home and let me handle this? I can call you and tell you what I find out."

"You'll tell me what you want me to know," she said tersely. "Which one is her apartment building?"

"It's at the far corner."

"She probably doesn't have anything to do with my father," Paige said as they began to walk in that direction. "It's just a coincidence that her bracelet was found in the alley. It didn't have my father's name on it. Any man could have given it to her. Or it could have been there for days. Maybe she goes through that alley all the time."

The explanations tumbled out of her mouth one after the other. Paige was already deep in denial. That meant she had doubts about her father's fidelity, suspicions that had probably been hidden away with the family jewels all these years. "Relax," he said, halting in front of the building. "Let's take it one step at a time. No one is accusing your father of anything."

"You are. You've been accusing him of all kinds of things. And me, too."

"I'm simply opening my mind to the possibilities. The truth will come out in the end."

"And then you'll owe me an and my family an apology."

"We'll see." He tipped his head toward the back stairs. "Second floor, 2C."

She paused. "Let me do the talking."

"I don't think so."

"It's my father who's lying in a hospital bed in critical condition. I have the most at stake here. Don't forget that."

She had a point. He waved her forward. "After you."

Paige took a deep breath. Now that she had the control, she wasn't quite sure what to do with it. Despite her best efforts to take charge, she was trembling. She kept thinking about the fact that her father might have taken this same route the day before, climbed these stairs, raised his hand to knock on this door. But why?

"Aren't you going to knock?" Riley asked when her hesitation lengthened.

"Just give me a second."

"To do what? It's a door. Knock."

She flung him an irritated glare, then rapped her knuckles against the wood. For a split second she thought no one might be home. Then she heard footsteps, a rustling, the jangle of a chain. The door opened slightly, the chain still in place. An Asian woman peered out suspiciously, her eyes as black as her hair.

"Yes?"

"Are you Jasmine Chen?" Paige asked.

"I don't have any money to give."

"Wait," Paige said, but the door shut in her face. She looked at Riley.

He simply reached over and rapped again. "Ms. Chen," he said loudly. "We need to speak to you, please. We're not leaving until we do."

The door cracked open again. "What do you want?"

"Tell her, Paige. Tell her who you are," Riley instructed.

She hesitated, knowing this might be her last chance to forget the whole thing.

"Paige?" the woman questioned, her gaze narrowing. "Paige Hathaway?"

Her stomach turned over. This woman knew her. Okay, don't panic, she told herself. Jasmine did business with the House of Hathaway. She'd probably seen her in the store. There was nothing mysterious about that. "Yes. I'm Paige Hathaway. I think you might know my father, David." She drew in a deep breath. "He was hurt last night. He was mugged in an alley not far from here."

The woman put a hand to her heart, her eyes widening in shock. "No, not David."

"We need to talk to you."

Jasmine unhooked the chain and opened the door to allow them to enter. The living room was small and sparsely furnished, with a simple black couch and matching chair, a coffee table with candles on it, a sewing machine on an old desk, piles of fabrics stacked on the floor, and a few photographs of a young woman on a side table. But while the room was simple, the walls were cluttered. Paintings filled every available space, conveying a frenzy of emotions that were not reflected in Jasmine's now unreadable expression as she stood in the center of the room waiting for them to speak.

Now that they were here—now that the questions could be asked— Paige couldn't bring herself to speak. How could she ask a woman, a stranger, if she was sleeping with her father? She'd told Riley she wanted to take charge of this meeting, but now she looked to him for help.

"Did David Hathaway come to see you yesterday?" Riley asked Jasmine.

Paige let out a small breath of relief at the fairly innocuous question. It was certainly an improvement on the question she'd been considering.

"Yes," Jasmine said.

"Why?" Riley asked.

"He came to speak about a painting."

Maybe that was all it was, a simple business meeting, Paige thought desperately. Then she saw Jasmine's gaze stray toward the wall, toward one of the paintings, and she saw something she didn't want to see, something that appeared very familiar.

"Oh, my God," she whispered, as she walked over to the wall to take a closer look. "Riley, look. It's your dragon."

CHAPTER SEVEN

RILEY MET Paige's gaze in shocked awareness. He turned to Jasmine. "How did you come to paint that dragon?"

"I have seen it many times in my dreams."

"In your dreams? What does that mean?" he asked.

"What I said."

"Why don't we get more specific, Ms. Chen," Riley continued. "Did you see a dragon yesterday that looked like the one in your painting? Did David Hathaway show you just such a dragon?"

Jasmine hesitated again, then nodded. "Yes. David came by yesterday with a dragon statue that looked like that one."

Why?" Riley asked sharply.

"He thought I might like to see it."

"Because you'd seen it before?"

"In my dreams, as I told you. I didn't know it actually existed until yesterday."

Riley paced back and forth in front of the painting, his gaze darting around the rest of the room as if he were memorizing all the details. Paige thought she should probably get into the conversation, but for the life of her she couldn't think of a thing to say. Why had her father brought the dragon to Jasmine? How had Jasmine known to paint something that looked so similar? And what the heck did she mean by saying she saw it in a dream?

"What time was Mr. Hathaway here?" Riley asked.

"I think it was around five o'clock."

"Is that when he left or when he arrived?"

"When he left."

"Did he leave with the dragon?" Riley asked.

"Yes."

Jasmine was nothing if not brief. "Ms. Chen," Paige said slowly, "When my father was found last night, he didn't have the dragon with him. Do you know where he was going when he left you yesterday?"

"I didn't ask."

"Do you think he was taking it to an appraiser, someone here in Chinatown that I might not be aware of?"

"I don't know. You must go now. I have an appointment." Jasmine walked across the room and opened the door.

Short of being rude, Paige didn't see any alternative but to leave the apartment. Riley followed her out to the landing.

"Your father," Jasmine said, her expression softening, "Will he be all right?"

"They don't know. He's unconscious."

There was a tiny flicker of what looked like pain in Jasmine's eyes. "I will burn some incense for him, ask for blessings."

"Thank you. I'm sure he would appreciate that."

"What hospital is he in?" Jasmine asked.

"St. Mary's."

"And your mother—she is with him?"

Paige stared into Jasmine's dark eyes. "Yes, my mother is with him."

Jasmine nodded, then gently shut the door in her face, leaving Paige feeling sick to her stomach. There was something between this woman and her father; she knew it. Jasmine hadn't called him Mr. Hathaway as most of their customers did. She'd called him David. And there had been more than a little familiarity in her voice.

"You could have asked her," Riley said, reading her mind.

Yes, she could have asked, but Paige couldn't bear the thought of an answer that would destroy her family. "It's not the issue. It's not important right now." She looked into Riley's eyes and saw understanding, compassion, pity. She stiffened. She didn't want this man feeling sorry for her. She was a Hathaway. No one should feel sorry for a Hathaway. "It's all speculation, anyway. You heard Ms. Chen. She and my father met to discuss a painting. End of story."

"That's not the end, and you know it. He brought the dragon to show her."

"You think my father was attacked because of the dragon, don't you?"

"I believe the dragon is involved in some way. He had it with him when he left this apartment yesterday. Now it's gone."

"But hours passed between the time he was here and when he was found in the alley."

"Exactly. Where did he go in between? What did he do with the dragon? Did he leave it somewhere else? That's what we need to find out."

She hated his even, cool tone. "Yes, that's what we need to find out. Because this isn't just about your dragon. My father could die, and I will not let whoever did this to him get away with it."

"Then we're both extremely motivated," he said, meeting her gaze.

"But you don't trust me."

"No, I don't."

She stopped at the bottom of the stairs. "My father almost died last night. How can you possibly think I'm involved in something underhanded?"

"Sometimes events get out of control. Things happen that aren't meant to happen. People considered friends, family, associates turn out to be enemies. And money, greed, desire can turn a man's head; or a woman's for that matter."

His eyes hardened down to cold, blue steel. She sensed he spoke from experience, that there was pain behind the harsh words, but she doubted he would admit that. A less vulnerable man she had yet to meet. But at the moment his vulnerability was the least of her worries.

His stubborn pursuit of the truth might take her to a place she didn't want to go. Not that her father was guilty of anything. He must have had a good reason for taking the statue to Jasmine. He just needed to wake up so he could tell her that reason.

"I have to get back to the hospital," she said abruptly.

"Do you want a ride?"

She hesitated, part of her wanting to get as far away from Riley as possible, but it would certainly be more convenient to accept his offer. "Yes, thank you. Actually, if you could take me back to Fast Willy's, so I could get my car, I'd appreciate that. I'd like to go home and change my clothes before returning to the hospital."

"No problem. I'm parked in the Portsmouth Square garage just down the street."

She had to walk quickly to keep up with his long-legged strides. When they reached the square, she moved closer to him. The area was crowded with Chinese men, mostly older men, she realized as they headed toward the elevator leading to the parking garage under the square. Their voices were pitched high and loud, the unknown words of their language producing an odd kind of music. She felt suddenly and self-consciously blond, aware of the looks she and Riley were generating. This was not her world. She didn't belong here.

"Relax. At this time of day, we're fine," he said.

"I'm not worried."

"Sure you are."

"Well, it makes good sense to be cautious." She stepped into the elevator, the walls of which were covered with Chinese graffiti. It was probably a good thing she couldn't read the characters.

"Too bad your father didn't think the same way."

"My father gets wrapped up in what he's doing. He loses track of everything and everyone around him."

"Which would make him an easy target."

"Yes," she agreed, as they stepped off the elevator and entered the garage. It was dark and quiet down here, and her uneasiness increased. She was grateful to see Riley's black Jeep Cherokee parked in a nearby spot. The car was sporty, rugged, and unpretentious, very much like its owner. She got in, fastened her seat belt, and pushed down the automatic door lock.

Riley smiled at the action. "I won't let anything happen to you, Paige."

"Yeah, right. You and I are such good friends."

"You're very important to me right now."

"A means to an end. I figured that out awhile ago. Just get us out of here. I hate underground parking garages."

"Better?" he asked a moment later when they pulled out onto the street.

"Yes," she said, letting out a sigh. "It's been a long night."

"You should go home and get some sleep."

"I need to see my dad, to be there when he wakes up. I shouldn't have even come here, but I didn't want you to talk to Jasmine alone." Paige looked out the window, feeling calmer as Riley drove away from Chinatown, heading toward the Financial District. "It's amazing how quickly the neighborhood changes."

"And how little the neighbors mingle. You live only a few miles from here, yet you never come here."

"How do you know where I live?"

"I have my ways."

"I don't like my privacy being invaded."

"Well, I don't like the fact that my grandmother's dragon is missing. So we're even."

He had her there. "What about you? Where do you live? It seems only fair that I should know as much about you as you know about me."

"I have a condo south of Market," he told her.

"The new 'in' neighborhood according to *San Francisco Magazine*."

"It's convenient to my work. I don't care much about trends."

"What about your grandmother? Does she live with you?"

"God, no." He uttered a laugh. "She has a house in the Sunset. It's too big for her now that my grandfather is in a rest home, so she's thinking about moving. That's why we cleaned out her attic last week."

"I am sorry about all this," she said, feeling even more guilty now that she knew his grandfather was in a rest home. When I promised you that the dragon would be safe in our care, I was sincere."

He sent her a thoughtful look. "I'd like to believe that."

"You can. I'm a very honest person. I don't lie about anything."

"Everyone lies about something."

She shot him a curious look. "You're really a glass half-empty kind of guy, aren't you?"

He smiled at that. "When it's half empty, it *is* half empty."

"Or half full, depending on your point of view, and yours seems to be extremely cynical."

"And yours is extremely optimistic. You remind me of my grandmother. She still believes in Santa Claus."

"I liked your grandmother. She's really nice. Nothing like you."

"She'd be the first to agree with you."

"You're close, aren't you?"

"We're all we have left since my grandfather got sick. I try to watch out for her as much as I can. I don't let anyone take advantage of her. Although I may have screwed up in this case."

"You didn't. We'll get the dragon back."

"You can't make that promise. You don't even know where it is."

"Then we'll compensate your grandmother in some other way," Paige said, knowing her mother would probably have a heart attack at the thought of paying for a dragon statue she couldn't sell. But then again, Hathaway's had lost the statue, and Paige doubted the insurance would cover the item since it had been taken out of the store.

Riley concentrated on the traffic, maneuvering across three lanes. His profile was strong and masculine, his hands firm on the wheel, his shoulders broad. He was a beautifully made man, attractive, virile. Good heavens, where had that word come from? A knot in her stomach squeezed tight as she was overwhelmed by an unfamiliar feeling of lust. She had the sudden urge to reach out and trace his jawline, maybe run her fingers through the thick strands of dark hair.

What was she thinking? Her father was fighting for his life. Her family business was going to be under intense scrutiny when the press got wind of the disappearance of the dragon. Her mother would be beside herself. That's what she needed to be thinking about, not how good-looking Riley McAllister was, or how much she wanted to touch him.

She rolled down the window, letting in some fresh, cooling air.

"I can turn on the air conditioner," Riley said.

"This is fine."

He turned the corner and slowed down as Fast Willy's came into view. He pulled over behind her car, leaving the engine running.

Paige put her hand on the door handle, then paused. "What are you going to do now?"

"Follow the trail."

"There isn't a trail. The only evidence the police have is that bracelet. I can't believe we didn't even ask Jasmine about the bracelet," she added, realizing the subject had never come up.

"The bracelet doesn't matter. It led us to her. That's all we needed to get out of it."

"But she didn't tell us anything. I don't see any trail, Riley."

"The trail of the dragon. It came from somewhere. It seems to have some value. Maybe if we know more about it, we can figure out who would want it badly enough to steal it. Surely someone in your family or someone at Hathaway's might have more information about such a piece and its history."

"That someone would be my father. But I think you're overlooking something."

"What?"

"Your family. Where did your grandmother get the dragon?"

"She doesn't know."

"Maybe someone in your family knows," she said, repeating his earlier statement and liking the fact that the Hathaways weren't the only ones under the microscope.

"There's no one else in my family to ask. My grandfather has Alzheimer's. He can't even remember his name."

"No other relatives?"

"Nope. Dead or gone pretty much accounts for all of them."

She thought about that blunt statement. "What about your parents?"

"Dead or gone," he repeated.

She didn't know what to say to that. Riley certainly didn't know how to make polite conversation. "I'm sorry," she said awkwardly.

"It's not your fault. But you're right. We can't overlook anything, in my family or in yours. I'll do some digging. Hell, I'll even pay my grandfather a visit. Maybe he'll have a lucid moment."

"Does that happen often?"

"Almost never."

"That must be difficult for your grandmother."

"She was crazy about him. Still is, even when he doesn't recognize her, which is most days. The hardest times are when he's struggling to remember something, when he has enough awareness to realize it's gone. That's when it gets to me—when I see that look of panic in his eyes, and I can't do anything to stop it." He shook his head. "I hate feeling helpless."

She knew exactly what he meant. She'd felt that way when her sister died, and she'd felt that way all last night. "Thanks for the ride. I guess I'll see you later."

"You can count on that."

By seven o'clock that night, everyone in San Francisco knew that David Hathaway had been assaulted in Chinatown, that he was fighting for his life, and that a potentially valuable Chinese dragon might have been the motivation for the attack. Riley hit the mute button on the television, irritated with himself for mentioning the dragon to the police detective the night before. Obviously, Tony had not kept that fact to himself. With the press watching the Hathaways every second, it was no wonder the news had leaked out. At least his grandmother's name had not been mentioned. He didn't care if the Hathaway reputation took a hit, but he'd prefer not to have his grandmother in the spotlight.

His phone rang, and he leaned over to pick up the extension, seeing his grandmother's number. "Hello, Grandma."

"Riley, I just saw the news. I feel terrible about what happened to poor Mr. Hathaway. And that my dragon might be the cause of it all is so upsetting."

"We don't know that for sure."

"The reporter who talked to me seemed to think it was the reason."

His gut tightened. "What reporter?"

"Someone from the *Herald* called. He was very nice. He asked me all kinds of questions about the dragon. Of course I could only tell him what they told us, and I didn't even remember all of that."

"I wish you weren't mixed up in this," he grumbled. "Don't talk to anyone else, Grandma. Just let the answering machine pick up the phone. Maybe I should come over there."

"And do what? Babysit me? I'm too old for that, honey. Besides, Patty and Lila are coming over to play cards in a few minutes. I won't be alone."

"What about later tonight?"

"I'm a big girl. I'll lock the doors and windows, and I'll make sure I turn on that security system your grandpa put in a few years ago."

"All right, but be careful."

"Of course I'll be careful, but I don't understand why you sound so concerned."

"I'm concerned because someone may have been willing to kill David Hathaway for your dragon." He heard Nan's small gasp of breath and cursed himself for being so blunt. He should have chosen his words more carefully.

"Well," she said, "I didn't quite see it like that, but I don't think I have to worry. After all, I don't have the dragon anymore."

She had a point, but he still couldn't shake the feeling that he was missing something.

"I'm beginning to think I wasn't meant to have that dragon, Riley," she added.

"Why would you say that?"

"I've been racking my brain trying to figure out where it came from. It had to have been brought into the house by one of two people, your grandfather or your mother. Now, I usually knew what Ned was up to. He didn't have many secrets. But Mary was full of surprises. I wonder if she didn't pick up that dragon on one of her trips. Maybe..." Her voice drifted away. "But I don't want to think that."

"That she stole it." The thought had already crossed his mind.

"Your mother isn't a thief."

"My mother doesn't know right from wrong, up from down, red from blue. Her vision of the world was skewed most of the time, even when she wasn't on drugs. You know that."

"If she took the dragon from somewhere, she didn't think it was stealing."

"It doesn't matter," he said, trying not to show his exasperation with Nan's loyalty. After all, she'd extended that same loyalty to him.

"It might matter. Maybe your mother saw us on TV the other day. I've gotten a couple of strange hang-up calls recently."

"Why would she call and hang up?" Riley asked, trying to be logical and practical instead of emotional. "Why wouldn't she just say hello?"

"She might be working up her courage. We had words that last day before she left, and I told her that she couldn't come back unless she said she was sorry. I had no idea I was asking something that was just impossible for her to give."

Riley knew his grandmother still wanted to hear those words, still wanted to believe that her daughter would one day realize how much she'd hurt them all and apologize. Riley had hoped for the same thing for a long, long time. But not now, not after fifteen years.

"She must think about you, Riley. I'm only her mother, but you're her son, her child. I know she thinks about you. I know she wants to see you."

"You don't know anything of the kind," Riley said somewhat harshly. "I'm sorry, Grandma, but the truth is we don't even know if she's alive. And the odds of her calling and hanging up are really long. It's more likely a wrong number, or maybe even Grandpa dialing the phone and forgetting who he's calling. You should have caller ID on your phone; I don't know why you don't. I'll get that added tomorrow."

"Oh, Riley, more security measures? I don't want to feel like I'm living in a prison. You're probably right. It's probably your grandpa. He does have that phone by his bed."

Riley paused as the buzzer for his apartment rang. "Someone is at the door. Call me if you have any problems." He hung up the phone and walked over to the intercom. "Yes?"

"It's Paige. I need to speak to you right away."

He buzzed her in, having a pretty good idea of what she wanted to see him about.

She made it to the second floor in less than a minute and, judging by the flushed red of her cheeks, she'd taken the stairs. He waved her into his apartment.

"Before you—" he began.

"What the hell were you thinking, talking to the press about this?"

"I didn't."

"You must have. They have the whole story. My phone has been ringing off the hook all day. They want to know about the dragon. And our other customers want to know if their priceless artifacts are in danger of disappearing. My mother is livid. This is the last thing we needed, with my father fighting for his life." She finally took a breath.

Riley jumped in. "I didn't call the media, Paige. I mentioned the dragon to the police detective last night. I asked him if they'd found anything in the alley."

"The police told the press?" she asked with a disbelieving frown.

"I'm sure someone has a source in the department. And you said yourself that the Hathaways are always news, aren't they?"

"Yes." She let out a sigh. "I need to sit down."

Riley swept a pile of newspapers off a nearby chair so she could take a seat. "How did you find me, by the way?"

"Your secretary was very helpful."

"I'll fire her in the morning."

Paige smiled weakly. "I guess I should apologize. I shouldn't have come here. I just had to yell at someone."

"How's your father?"

"No change. It's hard to see him lying so still. My mother is there now, along with a private nurse. My grandfather is planning to stop by tonight. He'll probably just order my father to wake up."

"Does he have that much power?"

"He thinks he does, but my dad tuned out my grandfather years ago. The two of them have never gotten along. I think that's why Dad started traveling so much. It was his escape."

"Do you need an escape, too?" he asked curiously.

"I already made my escape. I moved out of the family house a few years ago. I couldn't breathe there. My grandfather has portraits of all the Hathaway ancestors lining the hallway. Every time I'd walk down that hall, I'd feel like they were looking at me, wondering why I should be the only Hathaway left to carry on the family bloodline. I can't even carry on the name officially, since I'm a girl, which has caused endless turmoil. I think my mother would consider adopting my husband just to give him the Hathaway name."

Riley smiled. "That would be extreme. And I can't see many men willing to give up their name."

"The woman gives up hers. Why shouldn't the man do the same?"

"Because it's very..."

"Very what?"

"Wrong. Trust me, Paige, if the man you marry is willing to give up his name to take yours, you should run away as fast as possible." He sat down on the sofa across from her, resting his arms on his legs. "Speaking of which, you're engaged, aren't you?"

"Who told you that?"

"My assistant, Carey."

"Then you should fire her."

He grinned. "Are you saying it's not true?"

"You don't see a ring, do you?"

"No, but I thought I saw a jealous boyfriend last night at the hospital."

She shrugged, avoiding his direct gaze. "Martin was just being protective. He wasn't jealous of you. Why would he be? It's not like you and I are together. You don't even like me."

"Did I say that?"

"Didn't you?" she countered, her gaze seeking his.

"I don't think so."

"You said you didn't trust me."

"That's not the same thing."

She tilted her head, giving him a considering look. "It's not just me you don't trust, though, is it? What made you so cynical—or should I say who?"

"I was just born this way."

"No one is born distrusting. That's not how it happens."

"Why don't you tell me about it over pizza?" He got to his feet and moved toward the phone. "What kind do you like?"

She looked at him in surprise. "I'm not staying for pizza."

"Why not? Aren't you hungry?"

"Well, yes, but—"

"You can help me with some research while we're waiting for the food," he added, tipping his head toward the laptop computer on the table. "I've found some interesting dragon tales, but nothing that looks like my grandmother's dragon. Maybe you know of some better sites."

"I suppose I could try," she said slowly.

"What do you want on your pizza?"

"Surprise me."

He raised an eyebrow. "Are you sure? I don't want to hear any complaints later on."

She gave him a serene smile. "Hathaways never complain."

Forty-five minutes later, Riley knew that Paige liked black olives, mushrooms, pepperoni, and onions but picked off the bell peppers when no one was looking. Only, he was always looking; she just hadn't caught him at it yet. She'd been too busy surfing through various art sites on the computer.

He liked the way she worked, the way her eyes focused on the screen, sometimes squinting over tiny print. He liked the way she frowned with impatience when the computer worked too slowly or a lead turned into a dead end. But it didn't make her quit. She just worked harder. And she was right; she didn't complain, not about the fact that the only drink he had to offer was beer, or that he had run out of napkins and paper towels and had only toilet paper to offer for dripping cheese and tomato sauce.

She'd probably also noticed the fact that his apartment was decorated in leftovers, as he liked to call the furniture he'd collected from his bachelor friends every time they moved in with a woman or got married. It seemed that along with commitment came interior design. Sooner or later, his friends' furniture showed up at his place while the women filled their joint living space with new stuff.

Well, not for him. He was happy with his big-screen TV, his oversized reclining armchair, his leather couch and his football memorabilia, including a signed jersey from the San Francisco 49ers. No woman was worth losing that for.

"Hello..."

Paige's voice brought his attention back to her. "What?"

"I've been talking to you for five minutes."

"Sorry. What did you find?" He moved around the table so he could see the monitor better. Unfortunately, the close contact with Paige distracted him once again. Her hair smelled good, like a field of wildflowers that he wanted to roll around in for a few hours.

Paige tapped the screen with her fingernail. "A legend about a dragon that looks a lot like yours."

Riley forced himself to focus. The unsophisticated sketch could be his dragon, he supposed.

"The period referenced is the Zhou dynasty," Paige continued, "Which is the period my father thought your dragon might be from. What's interesting about this story is that it actually speaks of two dragons that connect together and open a special box."

"That doesn't sound like what we have at all."

"Maybe not. But..." Her voice trailed away.

"But what?" he asked impatiently.

"It's a fascinating story. Do you want to hear it?" She turned her face toward him, and he saw the eager light in her brown eyes. Whatever she'd found had caught her imagination.

"Go ahead."

"It's about a little girl, the daughter of an emperor. The emperor suffered severe, violent headaches, and the kingdom was in despair over how to ease his pain. It was said that he went on rages during these episodes. People were killed. Things were destroyed. One day the daughter was in the woods, and she found a long piece of bamboo that made music when she blew through it. She took the bamboo flute back to the palace, and that night, when her father was suffering from another headache, she played it for him. The music was magical. It instantly soothed his pain. He pronounced the flute to be a gift from the gods, and this child, this daughter, had succeeded in comforting him when no one else could—"

"What does this have to do with a dragon?" Riley interrupted, sensing Paige could go on like this for a while. She was obviously captivated by the tale.

"I'm getting to that. The emperor decided that the flute must be protected above all else. He had a box created to hold the flute. Then he had two special dragons fashioned out of bronze to guard the box. The dragons had to be connected together in a special way in order to open the box. If either dragon was damaged or lost, the box could not be opened. And the little girl, the first daughter of his second wife, was treated like a princess."

"Yeah, yeah. So?"

Paige gave him an irritated look. "So, these three pieces were very valuable. Others in the kingdom were jealous of the little girl's new status. You can imagine what happened next."

"Someone stole the flute."

"The whole thing, the dragons, the box, and the flute. What was worse, the emperor had his daughter killed, because he was so angry. He then had a ton of bamboo brought to the palace, but no one else could make any of the pieces sing like the original flute. There was no longer any healing magic. Nothing could be heard but the sound of weeping throughout the kingdom."

"Where's the happy ending?"

"There isn't one. The emperor swore a curse of revenge on all first daughters. He said that until the box and the flute were put back in their rightful place, all first daughters of whoever came in contact with any piece of the set, the box, the dragons, or the flute would suffer terrible misfortune."

"So what happened?"

"I don't know."

"What do you mean you don't know?" He reached over and pushed the scroll key only to find that they had come to the end of the passage. "That's it? That's the whole story?"

"There's a moral."

"Right. I got that. Stealing is a bad thing. What I want to know is who took the box and the flute and the dragons, and what the hell happened to them?"

Paige smiled. "That sounds like a security expert talking. You have to solve the crime, otherwise the world is off balance. One plus one always equals two. Missing things must be found. Every beginning has to have an ending."

"That's the natural order of things. I still don't see what that story has to do with my grandmother's dragon."

"Maybe nothing, but it might be worth looking into. Did you happen to notice a connecting joint on the dragon, a piece that looked like it might fit into another piece?"

Riley shook his head. "I didn't look at it that closely. I'll bet your father did, though. What about that other guy who was working in the lab that day?"

"Raymond Li?" Her eyes widened. "My God. I just remembered. I never spoke to Mr. Li. He called in sick yesterday. I know that, because I was looking for my father, and I went down there thinking they'd be together, but Mr. Li's assistant told me that he was out."

Riley felt his heart begin to pump faster. He checked his watch. It was almost nine o'clock. "Do you have his home number?"

"I'm sure it's in the personnel file, but I don't have that."

"You can get it, can't you?"

"Tomorrow when the store opens."

"What about tonight?"

"I don't have access to those files on my computer."

"Don't worry about that. You get me into the store. I'll get you into those files."

CHAPTER EIGHT

"THIS FEELS WRONG," Paige said as she let Riley into her dark office just before nine thirty. The store closed by six o'clock on weekdays, five o'clock on the weekends. The Hathaways had never felt compelled to offer longer hours. Her grandfather always said if the people wanted to buy their goods, they could damn well find a way to come during the day.

She flipped on the lights, but it still didn't ease the tension in her body. She'd been at the store after hours before, but never for the purpose of looking into files that weren't any of her business.

"You own the store, Paige," Riley reminded her. "You have the right to access any information having to do with it."

"My mother would not agree with you." Paige walked around her desk to turn on her computer. "She's the boss."

"More so than your father? Isn't it his family's business?"

"Yes, but my mother doesn't think of it that way. She's probably more of a Hathaway than my father is. Once she married my dad, she got rid of her own family. I've never even met my maternal grand-mother or my mother's sisters."

"Really?" he asked with a note of surprise in his voice. "So, your mother has some skeletons in her closet. That's interesting."

"My mother grew up poor and angry about it. Now, she's rich and angry about other things, like the fact that my grandfather won't name her CEO. She's not a blood Hathaway, and therefore she can't have the title. My father can't have it, either, because he doesn't spend enough time at the store. But that's not an issue, because he doesn't want the title."

"Which leaves you."

"Exactly. If I prove myself worthy, someday all of this will be mine, but it certainly won't be anytime soon."

"Sounds like your grandfather still runs the show," Riley commented.

"He's a very strong-willed person, strong in body, in mind, and in opinions." She punched a button on her computer, then stepped aside so Riley could sit down. She perched on the edge of the desk, watching as he quickly riffled through the programs.

"Passwords?" he asked.

She gave him the ones she had and watched his fingers fly across the keyboard as if this were very familiar territory. She couldn't help wondering about his background. "Where did you learn to do this?" she asked, noting how quickly he got into the personnel files.

"Self-taught," he said, his attention still focused on the screen.

"You majored in computers in college?"

"I didn't go to college."

"Really? Why not?" Everyone she'd ever known had gone to college. Even Jerry had managed to make it through a state school.

"No money. What's the name of the guy we're looking for?"

"Raymond Li. They have scholarships, financial aid to help you get through school."

"Yeah, what would you know about that?"

"Enough to know that you were smart enough to go if you wanted to go."

"I went into the service instead. Here it is, Raymond Li." He jotted down the address on a piece of paper.

Riley had been in the service? Although given his commanding air, that wasn't all that surprising. "Which branch of the military?"

"Marines."

"You seem to be more comfortable giving orders than taking them."

"One reason I'm an ex-marine," he said with a brief smile.

She frowned as her gaze drifted to the screen and she realized that Riley wasn't looking at the personnel files anymore. "What are you doing?"

"Just checking a few things out."

"Our inventory?"

"Wouldn't someone have recorded the dragon as part of the inventory on the day we brought it in? Your father gave us a receipt for it. But I don't see it."

"It would have been temporary, most likely under possible acquisitions or something like that." She paused, knowing she should probably stop him, but reviewing their inventory list was hardly worth shouting about, and at the moment she was interested in learning more about him. "What was it like being a marine? Did you see any combat?"

"Some. Nothing I want to talk about," he added, flinging her a pointed look before turning back to the computer.

"What's that expression the marines always say? Semper something."

"Semper Fi. Always faithful."

"And are you?"

"To my country—absolutely."

She picked up a pen from her desk and played with it. "What about with a woman?"

"I've never been married."

"But you've been in relationships."

"What makes you so certain?"

"Because you're—you're not bad to look at."

He smiled. "You think so?"

She felt a wave of heat cross her cheeks. "I was speaking from a purely observational point of view."

"Is that what they call it these days?" He suddenly swung the chair around and stood up. He put his hands on either side of the desk, trapping her in what could have been an embrace, only he wasn't touching her, just crowding her, making her very, very aware of every inch of his long, muscular, masculine body.

"What—what are you doing?" she asked quickly, her heart speeding up at the look in his eyes.

"Getting a better look at you—from a purely observational point of view."

She licked her lips, then wished she hadn't as his gaze settled on her mouth. "We should get back to..." What were they supposed to be doing, anyway? She couldn't seem to remember. He was too close. He was stealing her breath, making it hard to think, to concentrate. And then he moved closer still, his mouth covering hers in a kiss that he hadn't asked for, a kiss he simply took, a kiss she couldn't help giving back. He tasted good, his mouth warm, demanding, impatient as his tongue swept inside, deepening the kiss, making her want to melt right into him. His hands were hot and firm on her waist as he pulled her against the solid wall of his chest.

She stroked his back, loving the feel of the hard muscles beneath her fingers. Their legs tangled up as they each searched for a better position. It wasn't until her back touched the top of her desk that she realized how quickly things were moving along. Was that Riley's hand on her leg, on her hip, sliding up under her shirt?

Good God! Another minute and she'd be having sex on top of her desk.

Paige hastily sat up, pushing him away with a breathless "Stop."

Riley stared at her with dark, intensely blue eyes that were filled with desire for her. She almost wished she hadn't asked him to stop. But this wasn't right. She wasn't the kind of woman to have sex with a man she didn't know. And she didn't know Riley, not enough, anyway. The fact that he was the sexiest, most attractive man she'd met in a long, long time, and that he made her want to do reckless, impulsive things wasn't a good enough reason—was it? Suddenly logic didn't seem important. Nor did common sense or rational thinking.

Riley had made her feel good, like a woman, like a sexy feminine creature. But she wasn't just a woman. She was a Hathaway. Hathaways didn't have sex on the office furniture.

Paige drew a deep breath and ran her hand over her hair, still acutely conscious that Riley hadn't taken his eyes off her. "Why did you do that?" she asked, stumbling over the question.

He thought for a moment, then said, "I wanted to."

"Well, you can't just do what you want like that—without asking."

"Do men always ask before they kiss you?"

"As a matter of fact, yes, they do."

"And what do you usually answer?"

"That depends on the situation and the man and everything else." She waved her hand in the air, not liking the grin spreading across his face. "It's not funny."

"Yes, it is."

"Well, don't do it again. Don't kiss me without any warning."

"So you didn't like it? I must have imagined your fingernails burrowing into my back, the little gasp you made when my tongue—"

"Would you stop?" she interrupted, feeling awkward and embarrassed. "It's bad enough that we kissed. We don't have to talk about it."

He laughed again. "God, you're funny. You're not a virgin, are you?"

She bristled in defense. "What I am or am not is none of your business."

"Maybe I'm making it my business."

"Why would you want to?"

"Because I want you, Miss Hathaway. What do you think about that?"

She caught her breath at his blunt words. She wasn't a virgin, but her experience wasn't all that extensive. In fact, she could count her lovers on the fingers of one hand, and she suspected Riley would need more than a few hands to total his conquests. He was cocky and confident, a man who knew he was attractive to women. That arrogance should have turned her off, but for some reason she found it oddly appealing, almost irresistible, in fact.

"You're just trying to get to me," she said finally. "And we're done here."

Sliding off the edge of the desk, she pushed him aside to look at the computer. Her eyes widened as she took in the details of the screen. Riley had somehow hacked his way into the accounting program—not just the company's financial records, but what looked to be her father's personal money program. "What is this?"

"Your father's electronic checkbook. Apparently, he does all his transactions online. He's very efficient that way. Probably because he's out of the country so much."

"You should not be looking at that. It's private."

He leaned over her shoulder and hit the scroll key, showing the check transactions for the past few years. "See anything interesting, Paige?"

"No. I don't want to see anything at all. This is none of our business." She moved to close the window on the computer, but Riley stopped her.

"Wait a second. There's something I noticed before you distracted me."

"I didn't distract you. I was merely asking a few questions."

"Whatever. Check this out—payments to Jasmine Chen, once a month like clockwork."

She saw the look in his eyes and knew what he was thinking. It was what she was thinking, too. "That probably confirms they were having some sort of an affair," she said slowly, a sinking feeling in the pit of her stomach.

"An expensive sort. We're talking several thousand a month. The number varies a bit." He scrolled through a few more screens, taking them back to the previous year and the year before that. "There are also several payments to UC Berkeley. Is that where you went?"

"I went to Stanford."

"Did you take classes at Berkeley?"

"No." She frowned, wondering why her father would have made payments to the university. "Maybe it was some sort of Hathaway grant, although that wouldn't have come out of my father's checkbook."

She moved aside as Riley sat back down in the chair, his fingers flying once again. She should stop him. This was going beyond the investigation of the dragon. Riley was delving into her father's business, his personal life, a life she was beginning to realize she knew very little about. She'd never given much thought to the possibility that there were other people who meant something to him, people besides her mother or her grandfather or herself. Friends never seemed to be that important to him. In fact, most of the couples her parents spent time with seemed to be her mother's friends, not her father's.

"Who is Alyssa Chen?" Riley asked, interrupting her thoughts.

"I don't know. Why?"

"She's the one who was going to Berkeley. Your father referenced her name on several transactions."

Alyssa Chen? A relative to Jasmine? A daughter?

Paige suddenly felt a knot in her stomach, a knot that grew tighter and twisted painfully with each passing second. "Turn it off."

Riley shot her a quick look. "Turning it off won't make it go away."

"Yes, it will. I don't want to know."

"Then don't look. But my gut tells me Jasmine Chen has something to do with the dragon. And maybe this Alyssa does, too."

Paige walked away from him, staring out the window behind her desk, which overlooked Union Square. She wasn't seeing the stores or the park; she was seeing Jasmine Chen's face, her apartment, the painting of the dragon on the wall, the photographs of a young woman on the table. Alyssa?

Well, so what if her father gave Jasmine money?

It also didn't matter if Jasmine had a daughter, and her father had generously given that daughter money for college. He was a generous man. He gave to lots of charities. Jasmine probably couldn't afford to send her child to college; she was a painter, an artist, and her father would have wanted to support an artist. He was all about art, about making it possible for people to create freely, to express themselves without worrying about how to make a living.

"Hmm, this is interesting," Riley murmured behind her.

She didn't like the sound of that. She was almost afraid to ask. But she had to. Turning, she asked, "What are you looking at now?"

"Vital statistics."

"Whose?"

"Alyssa Chen. She's twenty-two years old. Mother: Jasmine Chen. Father: Unknown."

Paige's heart skipped a beat. "Why is that important? Lots of women have children without knowing who the father is."

He cast her a speculative look. "True. But how many receive money from a complete stranger for that daughter every month for the past four years at least?"

"Okay, maybe my father has been involved with Jasmine, but that has nothing to do with your dragon, so turn it off."

"She has a picture of my dragon on her wall. I don't think that's a coincidence. And your father took the dragon to her. Another connection."

"He just showed it to her. He didn't leave it there."

"So she said."

"Their relationship is not relevant to you. An affair is only important to me, to my family."

He didn't say anything right away, but his silence was damning. She didn't need his words to put the equation together.

"Paige—"

"Don't say it."

"Fine. I won't say it."

She stared at him for a long moment. "You think Alyssa Chen is my father's..."

"Daughter." Riley met her gaze head-on. "And you think so, too."

It was easy to get his room number. Jasmine's neighbor's daughter worked in pediatrics. So Jasmine bypassed the information desk and took the elevator to the fourth floor. Visiting hours were almost over and the hallways were quiet. Now that she was here, she wasn't sure she could go through with it. She had spent most of the day worrying about David. What if he died? She didn't want to face that possibility, but it was there all the same.

David Hathaway had been so many things to her. She had liked him, loved him, hated him, then loved him again. Every time she had tried to cut him out of her life, he had come back in some unexpected way. He had brought with him nothing but trouble, nothing but pain. He had shamed her, and in turn she had shamed her family. She had spent the past twenty-two years being shunned by the people who had once loved her. And all because of David. So why had she come here now?

Because she still cared. God help her.

She found herself in front of his room. The door was closed. Was he alone? What would she say if he was not? They would wonder who she was, why she was here. Or maybe they knew. She thought back to Paige's visit. There had been a question in Paige's eyes that had nothing to do with the dragon or her father's accident. Paige suspected something; she just hadn't had the courage to ask, and for that Jasmine was grateful.

She tapped quietly on the door. No one answered. She slowly opened it. The room was small but private. There was a man in the bed, lying perfectly still. There were machines surrounding him but no one else. Where were they—this family that he adored, that he could never leave, that he had chosen over her? Why weren't they here by his bedside, praying for his recovery, holding his hand, talking to him, pleading for him to wake up?

Once in the room, she stopped by the bed, her heart breaking yet again as she looked at his face. There was a huge, ugly bruise just beneath the bandage around his head. Her eyes blurred with tears. It couldn't end like this. The charming, outgoing David Hathaway, who spoke so passionately about art and history and life, could not go so quietly out of this world.

She picked up his hand. It had been a long time since she had held his hand. His skin was cool, as if the blood couldn't quite reach his fingers, as if his heart was slowing, his body shutting down. But the machine was still bleeping. She could see jagged lines of what must be his heartbeat. His chest moved in and out. He wasn't gone yet.

"Don't leave me," she murmured. "Not like this, not without a good-bye."

"What on earth is going on?" A woman's sharp voice broke through the silence.

Jasmine turned, knowing whom she would find behind her.

Victoria Hathaway stood in the doorway, her face shocked, her eyes angry. She drew herself up, throwing back her shoulders, lifting her chin. She was so beautiful, with her blond hair, her blue eyes, her perfectly made-up face, not a wrinkle, not a shadow anywhere, nothing to show she was worried about her husband. Dressed in a white suit with sheer stockings and high heels, she looked as if she'd come from work, as if her life hadn't changed at all since her husband's assault.

Jasmine felt short and heavy, uncomfortable with her old, unstylish clothes and her heavy, thick black hair that hadn't seen a hairdresser in several years. Not for the first time she wondered how David could have left Victoria to come to her. But she hadn't always looked this way. There had been a time when men thought she was pretty, when she had laughed and enjoyed life. Meeting David had changed all that.

"Who are you?" Victoria demanded, walking farther into the room.

"Jasmine Chen," she replied.

Victoria's face paled. Did she recognize the name? Had David actually spoken of her? Jasmine's heart lightened just a bit.

"You have no right to be here." Victoria's harsh words sliced through Jasmine like a knife. "How did you get in here? Where is the nurse?"

Jasmine didn't reply right away, not sure what she wanted to say. Although she had feared it was not her place to be, now that she had come, she wanted to stay. She had lost so much because of this man. Didn't she deserve to at least stand by his bedside at this moment? Everyone would say no. She was not the wife. She was not family.

"How is he?" she asked, ignoring Victoria's request that she leave.

"That is none of your business. Please go."

"Why haven't you asked me who I am, how I know David?" Jasmine saw the truth in Victoria's eyes. "You know, don't you?"

"I know that you don't belong here in my husband's room."

"I love him, too." Jasmine was shocked by the words that had come from her mouth. She hadn't said them in twenty years, not to anyone, not even out loud to herself.

Victoria stuttered over a reply, as if she couldn't believe what Jasmine had said.

But it was done. It couldn't be taken back. Jasmine looked at David, wondering if he would be angry when he woke up. He had asked her for secrecy, and she had always given it to him. Until now. She had betrayed him to his own wife. Would he be able to forgive her? She told herself she should not care. But she did. And she was sorry. Would she have a chance to tell him how sorry she was?

"Get out of this room now," Victoria hissed. "You have no right to be here. I don't care who you love. For that matter, I don't care who he loves. He's my husband. I'm his wife. And that's the way it will stay."

"I didn't come here to cause you trouble. I simply wanted to see him." Jasmine cast David one last lingering look, wondering if this truly would be the last time she saw his face. She wished she could commit it to memory forever, so that she would never lose him. Not that she had ever really had him. She had been his lover, not his wife. That title belonged to the woman on the other side of the bed. "I'm sorry," she added belatedly.

"I don't want your apology."

"I shouldn't have told you, but I—"

"I already knew," Victoria said harshly. "Did you think I was stupid?"

A look of truth passed between them, and Jasmine realized that she had not betrayed David's secret at all. It had never been a secret, or perhaps only for a short time. His wife was not the fool; Jasmine was. In some strange way, the secrecy of their affair had made the love between them seem deeper, more important. Theirs had been a passion forbidden by society. In her heart she had always believed that only great passions dared to cross the bounds of propriety.

"Did you think you were the only one?" Victoria added, taking delight in sending another shaft through Jasmine's heart. "Ah, I see. You did believe that. What a pity."

Victoria was wrong. David had told her many times that he had only come to her and no one else. *Was he the liar? Or was it his wife?*

She turned away from the bed, then stopped, startled by the presence of another woman in the doorway—Paige. Behind her was the man who had come to the apartment with her earlier. She wondered how long they had been standing there, how much they had heard.

"Mother?" Paige asked. "Is everything all right?"

"Everything is fine," Victoria said with ice in her voice. "Ms. Chen was just leaving. And she won't be back."

No, she wouldn't be back. This was not her place. This was not her role. She didn't come to David; he always came to her, and having met the cold-hearted woman who called herself his wife, Jasmine understood much more clearly just why he had come to her in the first place and why he couldn't seem to stop himself from coming back. A spiteful part of her wanted to tell Victoria exactly that. But when Paige moved to stand next to her mother, the spitefulness faded. Paige was David's daughter, and unlike her mother, she seemed terribly worried about her father. Even now she had her hand on his arm, as if she would protect him from the tension in the room. Paige didn't deserve to be caught in the middle.

"I am leaving," Jasmine said. "I wish your father well."

"Ms. Chen, wait," Paige said unexpectedly.

Jasmine felt a shiver run down her vine at the question in Paige's eyes, the nervousness in her stance as she looked from her mother to her father, to Jasmine.

"Don't get involved in this," Victoria warned her daughter. "It does not concern you."

"I think it might. I think she's Dad's—"

"I know what she is." Victoria cut her off abruptly.

"You do?"

"Yes, I've known about her for years."

"Have you also known about Alyssa?"

Jasmine's heart stopped. How did Paige know about Alyssa? That was one secret she was sure David had kept. Victoria, too, looked taken aback, her face as white as her suit.

"Stop, Paige, please just stop. Don't say whatever it is you're thinking," Victoria said.

"I can't. I have to know. Do Alyssa and I share the same father?"

CHAPTER NINE

ALYSSA CHECKED her watch as she got off the bus early Friday morning and headed toward her mother's apartment in Chinatown. She hated going into the neighborhood, with its crowded buildings, the smells of fish and livestock in the butcher shops, her mother's small apartment with its dark rooms, its heavy cloud of incense, the memories of so many nights when she had gone to sleep hearing her mother cry—because of him. The *him* who remained a mystery even today. The man who had fathered her, who had left her and her mother, who had caused them to live in shame, who had made her half white, half Chinese, half of nothing.

Her friends told her that her unusual looks—her brown eyes, long black hair, pert, pointed, very un-Asian nose—made her more beautiful, more exotic, but she knew the truth. Different wasn't beautiful; it was just different. And her looks made her feel... wrong. There was no other way to describe it. Her own family didn't accept her, especially her grandparents, who treated her illegitimate birth like a mark of shame upon the family. Every New Year, they prayed at the family altar that her mother's sins would be forgiven and that the rest of the family would not suffer for those sins. They also prayed that she would not travel the same road, that she would not dishonor the family as her mother had done.

She had no intention of dishonoring anyone. She just wanted to live her own life. She had a college degree now and a career in banking. Maybe it was just an entry-level job as a loan officer in a downtown bank, but she thought of it as a stepping stone to a future in high finance. She would not live hand-to-mouth as her mother had done. She would not have to sew late into the night to make enough money to eat, or sell precious pieces of her soul, as her mother had sold her paintings, to keep a roof over their heads. Someday she would have plenty of money and she would buy her mother a big house, and it wouldn't be anywhere near Chinatown.

The familiar smells were already turning her stomach. She usually made her mother meet her downtown in a café where they could eat with a fork, drink Diet Pepsi, and munch on potato chips, instead of sipping tea and using chopsticks to scoop up endless piles of rice. It wasn't that she didn't like Chinese food. She did. She'd grown up on it. But she had a love-hate relationship with everything Chinese.

Sometimes she wondered what kind of ethnic background her father had. Was he Italian? Irish? German? English? Was he a mix of something like she was? The only thing she knew for sure was that he wasn't Chinese.

Crossing the street, she quickened her pace. She didn't know why her mother had asked her to come so early, but the tension in her voice had persuaded her not to argue. Still, she didn't want to be late to work. She took her job seriously. She supposed she took everything seriously, but she didn't know how else to be. It had become clear early in her life that she had not brought joy and lightness into the world with her birth. She had to work hard to make that better. To be worthy of being born.

She took the steps to her mother's apartment two at a time, grateful for the tennis shoes she wore to work. They might look silly with her business dress, but they were comfortable. At work, she would put on her heels and add three inches to her five-foot-two inch frame. Then she would be ready to deal with the world. But that world would have to wait, at least for a few minutes. She had this world to deal with.

Her mother opened the door before she could use her key.

"What's wrong?" Alyssa asked quickly, sure now that something was up. It wasn't that her mother was crying or looking stressed, but rather that there was an unusual light in her eyes, an energy in her stance, maybe even a bit of anger in the tilt of her chin. Anger? That wasn't Jasmine Chen. Her paintings could be angry, but she was always quiet, complacent, accepting of her fate, her penance, her punishments. Sometimes Alyssa wanted to shake her mother, tell her to get mad, to tell her family to go to hell—that she didn't deserve to be treated like some lesser human being just because she'd had a child outside of marriage.

"Come in." Jasmine took her hand and pulled her into the apartment. "We must talk."

"You're not sick, are you?"

Jasmine shook her head. "No. It's not that. I wasn't going to say anything, but somehow they know. I don't know how they know, but they do. They'll come to see you. I couldn't allow that to happen, not without talking to you first."

Alyssa couldn't make sense of what her mother was saying. "Okay, start over and slow down. Who knows what?"

"Your father."

"My father?" Alyssa asked in wonder. She'd asked her mother many times to tell her about her father, to describe him, identify him, but Jasmine had always refused.

"He is hurt. Hurt badly."

"You know where he is? I thought you didn't know where he was."

Her mother's expression was usually unreadable, but not today. Today the truth was written all over her face. Her mother knew where her father was. She had probably known for a long time. Every time Alyssa had asked, she had been told that he had disappeared and that her mother could not bear to speak of him.

Jasmine wrung her hands. "I didn't want to tell you. I still don't. But I am afraid they will."

"Who? Who will tell me?"

"Paige."

The name didn't ring a bell.

"She is his daughter, too," Jasmine added, drawing in a breath. "Paige Hathaway."

"Hathaway? As in the Hathaways? My father is a Hathaway?" Alyssa asked in shock.

"David Hathaway. He was attacked in Salmon Alley two days ago."

"That's only two blocks away."

"He came to see me."

"He came to see you after all these years?" Alyssa's mind was spinning. "Why? Why now?"

"He has come before. I am sorry, Alyssa. I only wanted to protect you. But his family knows of your existence now, and they may want to talk to you."

Alyssa couldn't believe what she was hearing. "They want to talk to me? Why?"

"Because it's possible that your father may not survive."

She didn't know how she was supposed to take that information. Was she supposed to feel sad about a man she didn't know? Angry—because now it might be too late to know him? But why would she want to know him? Had he known about her? Had he ignored her all these years? She took a breath. "You said he came to see you. Why?"

"That's not important."

"Of course it's important. Does he know about me? Does he know I'm his daughter?"

"Yes," Jasmine said quietly, painfully. "He knows."

"For how long?" Her mother's dark eyes pleaded with her for understanding, but Alyssa wasn't sure she could give it. "How long?"

"Since you were born."

Her mother's words were shocking. "How can that be? How can he have known and not come to see me? He doesn't live that far away. My God! David Hathaway is an incredibly rich man. He lives in a mansion in Pacific Heights. I know, because there's a picture of the house on the wall of the bank I work in." Her anger grew with each word, each new realization. "And he let us live here, in this small apartment? You had to work two jobs when I was small. We barely had enough to eat."

"I wouldn't take his money in the beginning. But when you got older, when you needed things, I asked him to help. He paid for your college. He bought my paintings to help us out."

"To ease his guilt, you mean. He should have supported us, or at least me. I don't care what you told him."

"He did give me some money. That's the only way I could afford for us to live here alone. But I hated every penny that I took from him. If I couldn't have him, I didn't want his money, but pride wouldn't pay the rent, so I took a little when I had to."

Alyssa sat down on the couch, not sure she would have the energy to get back up again. She'd never felt so overwhelmed in her life. She had hated not knowing who her father was, but now that she did, she almost wished for that innocence again. It was bad enough to know that her father hadn't loved them enough to stay—but even worse to know he was a rich, powerful man who lived only a few miles away but had never wanted to see her.

Jasmine sat down in the chair across from her. She tapped the teapot on the table with her finger. "Would you like some tea?"

Alyssa shook her head. How could they have tea? How could they pretend that nothing had changed between them?

For long minutes there was nothing but silence in the room. It wasn't unusual that they were quiet. Her mother had never been a talker, but now the air was filled with tension and distrust. Alyssa couldn't help it. She loved her mother, but she couldn't understand how she had kept such a secret all these years.

"You don't have to see him," Jasmine said haltingly.

"Of course I don't have to see him. I don't want to see him. He didn't care enough to see me." Alyssa paused, her mind catching up with everything that had been said. "You said he was attacked in the alley?"

"Yes. He was struck in the head. He has been unconscious since then." Jasmine's voice caught, and she lowered her gaze to the floor.

Alyssa felt as if she were seeing her mother for the first time. She had known that her mother had loved a man, and obviously slept with him since she'd been born as a result, but Jasmine hadn't dated anyone since then. She'd always been alone, content she said with her daughter and her painting. Now Alyssa couldn't help wondering what her mother felt for David Hathaway. Was it possible she still cared about him? It seemed unthinkable. He had left her to fend for herself alone, with a child. But Jasmine had never said one angry word against him. She'd never complained about her life, just accepted her fate.

It wasn't fair. David Hathaway had so much, and they had so little.

"You must not blame him," Jasmine said, breaking the silence.

She met her mother's gaze. "How can I not?"

"There are things you don't understand. I feel responsible for what happened to him."

"Why would you be responsible?"

"He came to show me something. If he hadn't come, he wouldn't be hurt."

"What did he show you?"

Jasmine hesitated. "The dragon, Alyssa. He found the dragon."

Alyssa's gaze flew to the wall, to the serpent-like creature her mother had painted so many times Alyssa could have drawn it herself simply from memory. "You said it didn't exist."

"I know now that it does. I held it in my hands."

Alyssa's body tightened. That dragon had been a part of her life for as long as she could remember. On many nights her mother had awakened from sweat-drenched nightmares, mumbling about the dragon. Sometimes it saved her. Sometimes it threatened her. Sometimes she couldn't find it.

"So he..." She couldn't bring herself to call him her father yet. "He has the dragon?"

"I think it was stolen from him in the alley."

"Why? Who would steal it? Is it valuable?"

"It must be."

Before Alyssa could ask her to elaborate, a knock came at the door, surprising them both. "I'll get it," she said, rising to her feet. She didn't know whom she was expecting when she threw open the door, but it certainly wasn't two uniformed police officers.

"Jasmine Chen?" one of the officers asked.

"I am Jasmine Chen," her mother said from behind her.

"We'd like to talk to you about a robbery that occurred down the street and a man you may know—David Hathaway."

Paige walked into her apartment and shut the door with a weary sigh. She'd spent the night at the hospital, catching a few hours sleep on a couch in the waiting room. She could have gone home. Her grandfather had hired private nurses to stay with her father twenty-four hours a day, but after Jasmine's surprise appearance in her father's room, Paige had felt compelled to remain close by. Even though neither Jasmine nor her mother had answered the question about Alyssa's parentage, Paige knew the answer. She'd seen it in Jasmine's eyes. And she'd seen it in her mother's eyes before they'd both left the room, leaving Paige alone with her father. She'd stared down at him for a long time, wishing he would wake up so she could ask him the questions burning her tongue, but he had slept, and he was still sleeping now. At least, that's what she liked to call it. Sleeping sounded so much better than coma.

Setting her purse on the table, she considered her options. She could nap, go to work, take a shower... she usually had a dozen things on her to-do list and today shouldn't have been any different, but it was. Since her father's attack, her priorities had shifted. She picked up her favorite family photograph from the table. Her father looked so young, vibrant and healthy. How she wished she could have that man back. Her mother looked good, too, happy as they posed in the front yard on the occasion of her grandfather's birthday. Her grandfather stood in the back, his tall, sturdy body like a solid tree, his arms around his son on one side and his daughter-in-law on the other. Paige and her sister, Elizabeth, sat on a bench in front of them, dressed in beautiful, fluffy white dresses.

Looking at her sister's sweet face, a face that had never grown old, never worn makeup, never kissed a boy, made her incredibly sad. Maybe it was the reminder that it was almost Elizabeth's birthday that brought tears to her eyes. Her father had to wake up soon. He hadn't ever missed Elizabeth's birthday. He had a present for her, a present only he could give.

Maybe it was a sick tradition, as her mother thought. But at the moment Paige clung to it, because continuing the ritual meant everything was going on the way it was supposed to go on. Paige set the photo down. The happy family portrait was really nothing more than an illusion. Her father had had an affair. He'd slept with another woman. Jasmine Chen was hardly the prettiest, sexiest woman Paige had seen. Maybe she had been in her day. Obviously their affair went back twenty-something years.

Alyssa was twenty-two years old, and Elizabeth had been dead almost twenty-three years. That meant that her father had had this affair almost immediately after Elizabeth's death. Paige's pulse quickened as she calculated the possibilities. Was that why it had happened? Had her father been so lost in grief, despair, and unhappiness that he'd reached out to another woman?

Or was she just trying to excuse his behavior the way she always did?

The doorbell rang, and she started, glancing down at her watch. It was ten o'clock in the morning. Who would be calling on her now? She went to the intercom and said, "Hello?"

"It's Riley. Can I come up?"

Riley? Her heart skipped a beat. Did she want him to come up? It seemed as if they were living in each other's pocket these days. And yet, at the same time, it felt as if it had been too long since she'd last seen him. The bell rang again, more insistently. Patience was not his strong suit. She buzzed him in.

She made a quick dash to the mirror. Her hair was falling out of its ponytail. There was not a speck of makeup left on her face, nothing to hide the shadows under her eyes. And her clothes were wrinkled. She was basically a mess, and she hated to face Riley looking like this. But he was already knocking at the door; she had no choice but to open it.

She wished she could say he looked as bad as she did, but it was just the opposite. His hair was damp from a recent shower, his skin scrubbed and glowing. He smelled good. He looked even better in a pair of black trousers and a long-sleeve, gray knit shirt.

"You look awful," he said. "Did you sleep in those clothes?"

"As a matter of fact, I did."

"Any change in your father's condition?"

"None. I don't know why it's taking so long for him to wake up. But he will wake up. I just have to be patient."

Riley walked into her apartment. "This is nice."

The apartment wasn't really her. While she'd expressed her independence by getting her own place, she'd followed true Hathaway form by allowing her mother to decorate it with antiques, paintings, and expensive furniture. A cleaning lady came once a week to keep everything sparkling clean, and since Paige never made a mess, the apartment was always spotless, but not particularly warm and inviting.

"I feel like I just stepped into the page of a magazine," Riley continued. "Where's the clutter? The shoes you kicked off when you got home, the newspaper you just read, the keys you tossed on the table when you came in?"

"My shoes are still on my feet. The newspaper is in the recycle bin, and the keys are in my purse where they belong."

He raised an eyebrow. "Obsessive-compulsive?"

"Just neat. Do you have a reason for being here?"

"I have some information for you. I called Raymond Li at home. His daughter told me he's on vacation, and she doesn't know when he'll be back." He paused. "Raymond Li wasn't scheduled for a vacation, was he?"

"I don't know. I don't keep track of the vacation time of every employee."

"She said it was a sudden trip, destination unknown."

"You make it sound mysterious."

"As far as we know, Mr. Li is the only other person at Hathaway's who had a chance to examine the dragon. He might also be the only other person who knows why your father went to Chinatown. I'd say that makes him a key player. The fact that he's now nowhere to be found is too big of a coincidence for me."

"Do you think that Raymond Li had something to do with the assault on my father? I can't believe that. He's worked at the store for twenty years. He's had plenty of opportunities to steal, if that's what you're implying."

"I'm not implying anything. Just saying his sudden vacation is suspicious. Let's say that he knew your father took the dragon out of the store. He might have even known where David was going. Or he could have followed him. I don't think someone just happened by that alley, found your father, and took advantage of his presence by robbing him. Someone followed him to Chinatown or knew where he was going and set the whole thing up. We know your father saw Jasmine a little before five o'clock and that the police found your father around nine o'clock. It certainly didn't take him four hours to walk those short blocks from Jasmine's apartment. And it doesn't appear that he was lying there for four hours, either. I'm figuring he went somewhere else and was coming back, maybe to tell Jasmine what he learned. Or else he had business in that area and was leaving that location."

Paige hated the way Riley was dissecting everything so clinically, so dispassionately. This was her father they were talking about. Just thinking about his attack made her feel sick.

"I've asked my assistant to see if she can locate Mr. Li," Riley added. "For now, I think we should concentrate on the Chen family."

She turned away from the sharp look in his eyes. She knew what was coming next, and she didn't want to hear it. Instead she walked back over to the table and picked up the family photograph. She handed it to him. "This is my family."

"Nice picture. Who's the other girl?"

"My sister, Elizabeth. She died when I was six, and she was seven. That picture was taken just a few months before she got sick."

"You had a sister who died?" He looked surprised. "I never heard about that."

"It's not a secret, but it happened a long time ago."

"How did she die?"

"She had leukemia. It was awful." A word that didn't begin to describe the horrible disease that had stolen Elizabeth's life. "Nothing was the same after she died." Paige stared at the photograph in his hand. "It happened almost twenty-three years ago. If that girl, Jasmine's daughter, is really my half sister, then she was born in the year after Elizabeth died. Maybe that's why the affair happened. Or maybe that's what I want to believe. Either way, I'm not sure I can accept this other girl as my sister. Elizabeth is my sister. It would be wrong to put anyone else in her place. It would be as if she hadn't existed."

"Alyssa Chen isn't going to make you forget or love your real sister any less."

"I'm not so sure." She debated telling him what she was feeling, but her emotions and words seemed to run amok when Riley was nearby. "Sometimes I forget what Elizabeth looked like, sounded like, smelled like," she confessed. "I see the pictures and I remember her, but I'm not sure I remember her from my memories or from the pictures. Does that make sense?"

"It makes a lot of sense. It's been a long time, Paige. Memories fade. And you were a little girl. How much do you remember from when you were six years old?"

"Probably not as much as I should." She took the picture from his hand and set it back on the table. "Every year on Elizabeth's birthday, my father and I go to the cemetery, and he gives her a birthday present. It's always a dragon. She loved dragons. My father started her collection, and he still contributes to it every year. In fact, we're going to display the collection in the new Hathaway exhibit at the Asian Art Museum."

"A dragon like the one my grandmother had?" Riley asked sharply.

"Any kind of dragon. The gifts have all been different. But, yes, he was interested in your grandmother's dragon for that reason, as well as a dozen others, I'm sure. Elizabeth's birthday is next Wednesday. He has to wake up before then."

"I hope he does, but everything you've told me, Paige, only makes me believe that your father knew something about that dragon that we don't. We have to find out more about it."

"You're right. Now I wish I'd majored in art history instead of business economics."

"You majored in business economics?" he asked with a raised eyebrow.

"After my mother. She said it was more important to be able to run the business than to appreciate the goods that we sell. Unfortunately, right now that's not helping us at all."

Riley's cell phone rang, interrupting their conversation. "I better take this," he said, checking the number. "Hello? Grandma?"

Paige watched Riley's demeanor change. His face tightened. His eyes grew hard. He looked as if he wanted to hit something or someone.

"Stay at Millie's," he said. "Don't go back to the house. I'll be there as soon as I can."

"What happened?" Paige asked as he ended the call.

"My grandmother's house was broken into."

"Is she all right?"

"She's fine. She wasn't home when it happened. I have to go."

"I'm coming, too." Paige grabbed her purse as she followed him to the door. "What do you think they were looking for? Your grandmother doesn't have the dragon anymore."

"Maybe someone thinks she has the other one." He sent her a pointed look. "Didn't that story say there might be two?"

CHAPTER TEN

THE DRIVE across town seemed to take forever as the Friday morning traffic was heavy in the downtown area. Riley hit the brakes hard as yet another red light stopped him in his tracks.

"You couldn't have predicted this," Paige said quietly.

"I certainly should have. Dammit." He hit the steering wheel with his fist. "As soon as you told me that story about the two dragons, I should have connected the dots. And those hang-up calls—"

"What hang-up calls?"

"My grandmother said someone kept calling and hanging up. She thought it was my mother, which I immediately dismissed as ridiculous."

"Why would your mother be calling and hanging up? That seems odd."

He uttered a short, bitter laugh. "That's my mother, odd."

"What do you mean?"

"Never mind." He turned the corner sharply and pulled up in front of his grandmother's house before she could press him further.

Riley jumped out of the car and ran up the driveway to where Millie and Nan were standing. Paige followed, feeling a strange tightness in her throat as she watched him hug his grandmother with a fierce tenderness.

"Good heavens, Riley. You're squeezing the breath out of me," Nan told him. She smiled and stroked his face with her fingers. "I'm fine. But the house is a mess. They went through everything, dumping out my drawers and undoing all the beds. I don't know what kind of fortune they thought I was hiding in there, but I don't think they got much for their trouble. I couldn't have had more than twenty dollars in cash lying around. And my jewelry isn't worth much."

"I'm going to check it out. You wait here. Paige will keep you company."

"Oh, dear. I didn't even see you, Miss Hathaway." Nan looked from Riley to Paige, then back to Riley. "Did I interrupt something when I called?"

"Nothing that can't wait. I'll be back in a few minutes. Just stay put. You, too," he told Paige.

As Riley sprinted across the yard, Paige found herself being perused by two pairs of very curious eyes. "It's nice to see you both again. I'm sorry the circumstances are so distressing."

"Let's go to my house and have some coffee," Millie suggested, leading them next door.

Paige followed them into the kitchen, where Millie filled several mugs with coffee and placed a chocolate cake on the table in case anyone was hungry. Then she excused herself to answer the phone, leaving Nan and Paige alone.

"I was so sorry to hear about your father," Nan said, patting Paige's hand where it rested on the table. "How is he doing?"

"He's still unconscious." Paige paused. "I'm sorry your dragon has gone missing in the midst of all this. I feel terrible. The House of Hathaway has never lost an art object before."

"Someone wanted that dragon very badly. What I don't understand is why anyone would break into my house. I don't have it anymore."

Paige wasn't sure if she should tell Nan about the possibility that there might be two dragons. It was only a theory, and not much of one at that.

"I'm a little afraid it might be Mary behind this break-in," Nan said, surprising her with the comment.

"Who is Mary?" Paige asked.

Nan looked a little guilty at the question, as if she wished she hadn't brought it up. "She's my daughter, Riley's mother."

"Why would your daughter break into your house?"

"Well, she wouldn't." Nan shook her head. "I'm sure none of this has anything to do with her. She left Riley with us a long time ago, when he was a teenager. Even before that she was barely around. She wasn't much of a mother to him, that's for sure."

"That's too bad. Riley said something about hang-up calls?" she queried.

"Sometimes I think Mary is calling me and hanging up because she just doesn't have the nerve to speak." She sent Paige a thoughtful look. "I'm surprised Riley mentioned his mother to you. He must like you."

"Barely mentioned, and he doesn't like me at all. He thinks my family is trying to cheat you."

Nan brushed that away with a wave of her hand. "Riley always believes people are out to con him. He doesn't trust anyone. That's the legacy my daughter left him with, I'm afraid. I wish I could have stepped in sooner to take care of Riley, but she took him away from us early on, and there were years when we didn't know where they were."

Paige saw regret and sadness in Nan's eyes. It must hurt her deeply to speak ill of her daughter. Nan seemed like such a nice lady. Paige couldn't help wondering how her daughter had turned out so badly.

"She got involved with drugs at a young age," Nan said, answering Paige's unspoken question. "Barely fourteen when she started. Mary had the kind of personality that needed a lot of attention. She was never happy with what she had. I thought it was teenage years," Nan said reflectively. "I blame myself for not seeing that she needed real help. I did so many things wrong."

This time Paige reached across the table and covered Nan's hand with her own. "Sometimes people are just born with a personality that takes them into trouble."

Nan smiled. "You're a sweet girl, and very kind not to blame me.

Riley doesn't blame me, either, and he should. He's the one who had to pay."

"Riley seems to have turned out okay."

"I know it looks that way, but I still worry about him. Sometimes I wonder if I did the right thing asking him to come home and run his grandfather's business."

"The security business belonged to your husband?"

"Yes, but when Ned started getting sick about four years ago, I asked Riley if he could come back and help us out. He was debating whether or not to re-up with the Marine Corps at the time. He was doing so well in the service. He was always cagey about what he was doing or where he was going though. I knew it was dangerous, and he was probably being reckless, because Riley has always believed he has nothing to lose." She shook her head, with regret in her eyes. "At any rate, he came home to help out and has been here ever since. Now he runs the business better than my husband did, and he's settling down, a little bit, anyway. I wouldn't mind seeing a woman in his life," she added hopefully. "He is a good man. A little pushy sometimes."

"That's an understatement," Paige said with a wry smile. "How on earth did he ever learn to take orders?"

"It took awhile. But the marines straightened him out. He got into some trouble when he was young. Ned, that's my husband, thought the service would put Riley on the right track, and he was right. Riley is very smart, caring, and he's loyal to a fault. A woman could do worse."

Paige smiled. "Well, that may be true, but just so you know—I have a boyfriend." It felt strange to call Martin her boyfriend, but she needed something to dampen Nan's growing enthusiasm for a possibility that would never happen. As soon as they found Nan's dragon, Riley would be out of her life, and she would be out of his.

"Of course you do. I keep telling Riley that if he doesn't hurry up and get serious, all the good ones will be gone."

"I don't think he'll have any trouble finding someone."

Paige looked up as Riley entered the kitchen, a grim expression on his face. "The house is a mess. It will take some time to clean it up. I think you should stay here for a while, Grandma. And I definitely don't want you in the house tonight."

"Surely they've taken what they wanted," Nan replied.

"They may have been interrupted when you came home."

"What do I have that anyone would want so badly?"

"There may be another dragon. Paige and I have been doing some research, and we've found information about two dragons that connect together, and they both look like the one you had. Someone might think you have the other dragon, too."

"I'm sure I don't. We cleaned out the attic last week, Riley. You know that."

"But no one else does. Why didn't you turn on the security system when you left the house?"

"I only went to the store. I thought I'd be gone for just a few minutes. And it's broad daylight. I thought burglars usually came at night."

"You should turn it on every time you leave, no matter what."

"I'll do better, Riley, I promise."

"And you'll stay here with me today and tonight," Millie said, returning to the room.

"I don't want to impose on you and Howard," Nan protested.

"You could never do that. We'll go shopping. You've been wanting to walk down Union Street. And tonight we'll have dinner and then you'll keep me company while Howard plays on that computer of his. I'll be glad to have the company."

"Then it's settled," Riley said.

"I'll still need to get some clothes. I don't have anything with me."

"I'll go with you to the house. We'll get whatever you need."

"Riley, the police are still there, aren't they?" Nan asked.

"Yes, but—"

"Then I'll be fine. I'll go over and talk to them. I won't stay there alone. Once they leave, I'll come back here. You and Paige can go on and do whatever you were doing."

He frowned. "I hate for you to see your house that way, Grandma."

"I've already seen it, honey. It was a shock, I'll admit, but it is what it is, and not looking at it won't make it go away."

"I'll come back later and clean it up for you."

"Don't worry about that. It's nothing that can't wait. Maybe after we go to Union Street, Millie and I will drive out and see your grandfather. I want to ask him if he's been calling the house." Nan paused. "Thank you, Paige, for keeping me company. I'll pray for your father."

"I'd appreciate that," Paige said, getting to her feet.

"You take care of yourself, and don't let Riley boss you around too much."

"Don't worry. I'm used to bossy people," Paige said with a smile. She followed Riley out to the street. It bothered her to see the police car in front of Nan's house. She was a nice lady. She didn't deserve to have trouble like this.

Riley opened the door for her, closed it, then walked around the car to slide in behind the wheel. "Thanks for staying with my grandmother."

"It was no problem. Her house was in bad shape?"

"Ripped apart. Even her china was broken."

"It seems so pointless."

A lot of life is exactly that—pointless. Just crazy people doing crazy things."

She wondered if he was talking about someone in particular. "Is it possible your mother is involved in this?"

He sent her a sharp look. "What did my grandmother tell you?"

"A little about your past. Doesn't it bother you—not knowing if your mother is even alive?"

His eyes turned a cold, dark blue. "None of it bothers me anymore. I turned that page a long time ago. And I'm not turning it back."

"But the emotions aren't gone—the disappointment, the bitterness, the hate, maybe even the love—they're still there, aren't they?"

"Save the psychobabble for your own shrink, princess. I don't need my head examined by a rich girl who has no idea of the way I've lived."

"And you have no idea of the way I've lived," she retorted.

"I have a pretty good idea. I've seen the family mansion. It must have been rough growing up with your own bedroom, your own housekeeper. Hell, you probably had one of those butlers, didn't you?"

"Stop baiting me, Riley. I'm not getting into a competition with you on who had it the hardest."

"Because you can't compete. You can't even get in the starting block. You grew up in a rose garden."

"I grew up in a cold, lonely house." She gazed out the window and drew in a breath. "My parents barely spoke, and my grandfather's anger and bitterness chilled every room."

"And he had so much to be bitter about, all that money weighing him down."

She turned her head to look at him, but he was staring at the traffic, his profile hard. He seemed almost unreachable. She told herself not to try, but the words wanted to come out. "My grandfather lost his wife and daughter in a car crash when my father was nine years old," she said quietly. "He never recovered from their deaths. He hired housekeepers and nannies to raise my father because he couldn't do it himself. He was too full of hate at the universe for what had happened to him. When my father got married and started a family of his own, my grandfather felt renewed hope that the house would once again be filled with laughter and happiness. When I was really small he used to smile more, he used to laugh. Then Elizabeth got sick and died, and that ended. The last bit of life went out of our house for everyone. The rooms were so quiet I could hear my own heart beating, my own breath going in and out of my chest. It was that still."

She stopped herself from going on, wishing she hadn't told him so much already. She was opening herself up to get hurt. And he could hurt her. She didn't know why his opinion mattered, but it did. Maybe it was because she was used to people liking her, trusting her, and Riley's attitude was difficult to understand. Maybe she really was a spoiled little rich girl who didn't know how good she had it. Riley wasn't going to feel sorry for her; he'd grown up with a mother who was a drug addict, a woman who'd abandoned him.

"Say something," she muttered, wanting to get it over with. "Tell me how not sorry you are for me."

"I'm not sorry for you, Paige," he said, but when he turned to look at her there was a softness in his eyes that took the sting out of his words. "But maybe I understand you a little better. I shouldn't have judged you. I'm just in a bad mood. I don't like it when people I care about are in danger." He pulled the car up in front of her apartment building and shut off the engine. "How about a truce? We need to work together."

"You just want to keep an eye on me."

"That, too. Look, Paige, it's not just you. I don't trust anyone."

"Except your grandmother."

He tipped his head. "Except her. She's special."

"One day you might manage to feel that way about another woman."

"I'm not looking for a wife. I don't know what my grandmother told you; I'm happy with my life."

"I'm happy, too, and I'm not looking to make any changes," she said pointedly.

"You may not be looking, but your life is changing. You now have a half-sister."

She sighed. "I've been trying to forget about that."

"You have to deal with her, sooner or later."

"Let's make it later. I want to change my clothes and get back to the hospital."

"I'll wait for you and give you a ride."

"You don't have to do that. I can get myself there."

"We're keeping an eye on each other, remember?"

"What do you think I'm going to do, make some shady deal with an art buyer while I'm in the shower?"

He gave her a sexy smile. "If you think I need to follow you into the shower, just say so."

She saw the gleam in his eyes and gave a bemused shake of her head. "I can't figure you out. First you're nice, then you're sarcastic and cold, now you're flirting. Who is the real Riley?"

He grinned. "You like me, don't you?"

"I said you were complicated; I didn't say I liked you."

"Same thing."

"It's not at all the same thing." But as she got out of the car and slammed the door on his mocking smile, she was afraid he was right.

Alyssa couldn't concentrate on the loan application she was reviewing. Usually she loved her job as a loan officer for the First National Bank in San Francisco, but today her mind was back in her mother's apartment, hearing the words *your father is David Hathaway*. She still couldn't believe it.

For so many years she had wanted to know her father's name, but now that she did, she didn't know what to do with the information. How was she supposed to feel? Her emotions were all over the place. She was angry, hurt, jealous, but at the same time she was curious about the man who had fathered her. She'd seen David Hathaway in the newspaper. She'd known that the House of Hathaway had bought her mother's paintings. She'd been in the store—that beautiful, rich store. Her father owned that store.

Her father. She'd been without one for so long.

But she didn't really have one now. David Hathaway, was lying in a hospital bed, fighting for his life. Even if he weren't, would he suddenly recognize her as his daughter? If his other daughter, Paige, hadn't found out, would he have kept the secret forever? Would her mother have done the same? She suspected the answer was yes, but it didn't matter. The secret was out. Now she had to deal with it. She could wait for them to come to her, or she could go to them.

She got up and walked over to the desk where her manager, Jenny Conroy, was ending a phone call. "I'm not feeling well," she said. "I need to go home."

"Oh, all right." Jenny appeared surprised. No wonder: In the year that she had worked at the bank, Alyssa had never missed a day of work or been late. She was too focused on her goal to get ahead to allow her private life to interfere. Until today.

"I've finished a couple of loan applications and put them through," she added. "I'll leave the information with Mark in case anyone calls while I'm out."

"You do look flushed," Jenny commented. "I hope you're not catching that flu."

"Me, too." Alyssa returned to her desk, grabbed her purse, and left the bank, relieved to be out in the fresh air. Maybe the crisp breeze blowing between the tall buildings would clear her mind. It wasn't just her father she was thinking about; her mother was also on her mind.

The police had shown them a bracelet found near the scene of David Hathaway's assault—a bracelet with the name Jasmine on it. Alyssa had recognized it immediately. She'd seen the bracelet in her mother's jewelry box, but she'd never known it was from her father. Another secret.

Her mother claimed she cut through the alley every day and that she didn't know when she'd lost the bracelet. The police had continued to ask her questions about her whereabouts on Wednesday night, about when she'd last seen David Hathaway and why he'd come to visit her. Her mother had given out little information. She was a pro at saying nothing.

How strange that, after all these years, the dragon from her mother's dreams should appear as an actual piece of art that someone had crafted, someone had owned someone had stolen. Alyssa sensed her mother knew more than she was saying. But the dragon was not her concern. She had a father at last. Now she just had to figure out what to do with him.

———

Paige walked into her father's hospital room and smiled at the private duty nurse who sat by his bedside. "Why don't you take a break? I'm going to be here for a while."

Paige moved closer to the bed as the nurse left the room. She reached out and touched her father's arm. He didn't move. His breathing didn't change. His eyelids didn't flicker. He'd never been a heavy sleeper, but today he was lost in some other world.

"Daddy," she whispered. "I'm here. It's Paige." What could she say to bring him back? "It's almost Elizabeth's birthday. We have to go to the cemetery. It's tradition. We can't miss it. You know that." She wouldn't remind him that he'd missed her own birthday a dozen times, not to mention other important events in her life. This wasn't the time for accusations.

His skin was so cool. She pulled the covers up over his body, tucking in the blanket next to his side. "I need you, Daddy. Mother needs you, too, even though she'd never admit it." She paused. "Your secrets are spilling out. Jasmine Chen came to see you last night. She said she loved you. I wonder how you feel about her. I wonder how you feel about her daughter, Alyssa. I wonder if you have any idea how wrong all this is."

"I wonder that, too," a woman said from behind her.

Paige whirled around. The woman in the doorway looked very familiar, a little like Jasmine, and a little like... her father. "Who are you?" she asked with a shaky voice, even though she already knew.

"I'm Alyssa Chen." The woman gave her a hard, angry look. "I think I might be your sister."

CHAPTER ELEVEN

SISTER? No.

Elizabeth was her sister, her only sister. Not this petite Asian woman, who was beautiful, exotic, and furious. There was no mistaking the anger in her brown eyes when she looked at David. Paige instinctively moved closer to the bed, feeling as if she had to protect him.

"He doesn't look like me." Alyssa walked around the other side of the bed and stared down at David Hathaway. "Not really. Maybe a little in the nose."

And in the shape of her face, and the freckle at the side of her nose, the Hathaway freckle. Elizabeth had had one. Paige did not. It bothered her that Alyssa did.

"I can't believe he's my father." Alyssa looked over at Paige. "How long have you known about me?"

"Since last night. I found out my father paid your college tuition. When I saw your mother, she didn't deny it or corroborate it. She said nothing."

"My mother is very good at saying nothing."

Paige heard the bitterness in Alyssa's voice and saw something else in her face: fear. "When did you find out he was your father?" Paige asked.

"This morning. My mother always refused to talk about my father. But she was afraid you were going to tell me the truth, so she told me first." Alyssa stared down at the man in the bed. "He never came by to see me, never wrote to me, never gave me anything that I knew about, although I guess he gave my mother some money."

"Quite a bit of money, actually."

"It couldn't have been all that much. We didn't live well."

Paige felt guilty, as if that was her fault, as if she should apologize for being the daughter he had raised and supported. But it wasn't her fault. And, to be fair, it wasn't Alyssa's fault, either. The man between them was the only one to blame.

Alyssa didn't say anything for a moment, then murmured, "I should go."

Paige wanted her to go, wanted to be able to pretend that she'd never come at all, but as Alyssa turned toward the door, she knew she had to stop her. "Wait. We need to talk."

"About what?" Alyssa asked warily.

Paige wasn't sure. Where could they begin? There were so many questions to ask. "About everything. About your mother and my father. About us."

"Look, just because we found out we're half sisters doesn't mean we have to have a relationship. I doubt we have anything in common."

"We have *our father* in common."

"You had everything. I had nothing. I don't want to like you. I'm not even sure I want to know you," Alyssa said.

Her blunt words hurt, but in a way they mirrored exactly what Paige was thinking. Wouldn't getting to know Alyssa only cause trouble? Her mother certainly wouldn't like it. Her grandfather would be furious. And her father... Her gaze drifted over to her father. What would he want? Had he ever thought about introducing them? Of course not. That would have meant admitting he'd cheated, confessing to his infidelity. He couldn't do that. He couldn't jeopardize his marriage. And what did that mean? That he had never loved Jasmine, that she had never been worth giving up what he already had? It seemed the most likely answer. An affair was an affair. A marriage was forever, or was supposed to be, anyway.

"I'm not sure I want to know you, either," Paige said finally. "I'm also not sure we have a choice. Something is going on between your mother and our father—even now. He went to see her only hours before he was attacked."

"The police already spoke to my mother. She told them what she knew."

"Did she tell you about the dragon?"

"I know my mother is obsessed with a dragon that looks like the one your father supposedly showed her. I don't know anything more than that."

"Maybe if we put our heads together, we can figure out why that dragon is so important to our parents. It seems strange that your mother could have painted it without seeing it before."

"My mother paints from her imagination. She's a very good artist and an extraordinary person. She didn't deserve... *him*," Alyssa added, casting another angry glance at her father.

"Neither one of us knows much about their relationship, but what I do know is that your mother was quite possibly the last person to see him alive. And that makes her very important."

"What are you saying? That you think she assaulted him?"

"No. But she's going to be a part of the investigation. My family is very important to the city. The mayor, the police chief—they want the assailant caught. The press is covering the story every day. As soon as they find out about your mother, they'll be all over her. She'll be under the microscope. She'll be asked tougher questions than the ones I'm asking. The press will delve into her background, where she came from, how she met my father. They might even find out about you."

"Is that some sort of threat?"

"I'm just pointing out the reality of the situation. I need your help. My father got hurt in Chinatown. I bet people there would be willing to talk to you before they would talk to me. You may hate him, but I'm sure you love your mother. We both want to protect our family."

Alyssa considered her words. "I'll think about it."

Paige took out her business card and scribbled her home and cell phone numbers. "Please call me. Don't wait too long."

Alyssa took the card. She paused on her way out the door. "Are you going to tell the press about me?"

"Are you?" Paige countered.

"Why would I?" Alyssa asked with surprise.

"Money. Someone would pay you well for the story."

Alyssa nodded, her mouth set in a bitter line. "I'll keep that in mind."

"Dammit," Paige swore under her breath as Alyssa left the room. She hadn't handled that particularly well. The door opened, and she wondered if Alyssa had come back with more to say, but it was the nurse and Riley.

"I found this man listening at the door," the nurse said with a frown. "Do you want me to report that to your grandfather?"

"No, he's a friend of mine." Paige moved into the hall to speak to Riley while the nurse moved to the bed to check on her father. "What did you hear?"

"Some of your conversation with Alyssa," he admitted. "I don't think I would have given her the idea of selling her story to the tabloids."

"She would have thought of it eventually. She's very angry. She didn't know about my father until today."

"Then she has a right to be angry. Let's go."

"Go where?" she asked in surprise.

"To follow Alyssa, of course," he said, taking off down the hall.

Paige jogged after him, barely keeping up with his long strides. As they exited through the front doors of the hospital, they saw Alyssa heading toward the bus stop.

"I'll get the car," Riley told her. "You keep an eye on her. If she gets on a bus, make a note of the number."

"Okay. But why are we following her?"

Riley just gave her a quick smile. "So we can find out where she goes."

Paige didn't particularly care for his sarcastic answer, and she couldn't see what following Alyssa would accomplish, but at least they were taking action. Anything was better than sitting in that hospital room wondering if her father would ever wake up.

Alyssa got off the bus and walked up the steps toward the top level of Portsmouth Square, a popular gathering spot in Chinatown. Her discomfort grew with each step, especially when she passed the children's playground where old Chinese grandmothers watched the babies for their young mothers who worked during the day. Chinatown never really changed. While new immigrants moved in and out of the neighborhood, there were many who lived their whole lives here, like her grandparents, who had gotten married just after the Second World War ended.

They'd spent several years living in a small, cramped apartment with two other families they referred to as uncles, aunties, and cousins. In truth there was no blood between them, just a friendship borne of being strangers in a strange land. Eventually, her grandparents had managed to get their own apartment, where they'd raised five American-born Chinese children. But while those children, her mother Jasmine included, grew up American, her grandparents still held tight to their traditions and superstitions.

Her grandmother, An-Mei, was a strong-willed woman who had worked hard to help support the family, shelling shrimp, sewing in sweatshops, and making fortune cookies for tourists. She had done it all while her husband, Lee, cooked herbs in the kitchen and eventually opened an herb shop on a narrow street in Chinatown, which they still ran together.

Alyssa had heard the many stories of their struggles to survive in America, and she admired the strength and courage it must have taken for her grandparents to start over in a new country. But she didn't admire the way they treated her mother and herself as outcasts who had dishonored the family name. Her mother was the true culprit, but by virtue of her illegitimate birth, Alyssa was considered a mark of shame as well, at least by her grandmother, who had told her many times that she would have to work hard to overcome her birth, that she would have to prove to the gods that she was worthy. Worthy of what, Alyssa wasn't quite sure, but she hadn't dared to ask.

Questions were never welcome in her family, not with her mother, not with her grandparents, not with anyone. So why had she come back to the old neighborhood with even more questions? Who did she think would answer them?

Part of her wanted to turn and run back across town to the small apartment she shared with three of her college friends, who didn't worry about old secrets, who were only concerned about getting ahead, meeting nice guys to marry, living their lives the way they wanted to live them. But she still had to worry about her mother. It was for her mother's sake that she had come here. Perhaps her grandparents would speak to her more freely than they would to Jasmine.

A cluster of men sat on the stairs, playing cards. She hurried past them, past the chess tables where more old guys turned to stare at her. The top level of Portsmouth Square was a male bastion of gambling and other vices she didn't want to consider. She remembered once walking alone through the square late at night and having men come up to her asking if she wanted a date. She'd been so frightened by those groping hands, those leering voices that she'd avoided the square for years. Even now she felt uneasy.

But it was daytime and no one bothered her. She paused, seeing a familiar stooped figure bending over a bench where several men were playing Mahjong. It was her grandfather, Lee Chen. She hesitated, then approached the group, careful not to disturb anyone during the play. Her grandfather must have sensed her presence, for finally he turned and looked at her. He broke away from the group and walked over to join her. He was a short, square man; at one time, he had been a gymnast, but that had been a very long time ago. Now he was thin and frail and occasionally seemed confused by his very existence. Since he had turned seventy-nine years old on his last birthday, she supposed some confusion was understandable. She smiled as he put a hand to his head to pat down the few loose-flying strands of hair he had left. His face was square, plain, his eyes somewhat hidden by the old-fashioned black-rimmed eyeglasses he wore. But he had a smile on that face, a cautious smile, as if he wasn't sure he should give her one.

"Alyssa, what are you doing down here?" he asked.

"I'm on my way to the shop. I need some herbs."

"You are too thin. Must eat more. You come for New Year's. An-Mei fatten you up."

"You know Grandmother won't let us come for New Year's. It's a sacred holiday. We have too many sins, we taint the New Year with our presence." Alyssa heard the bitterness in her voice, but she couldn't do anything about it. While their presence was tolerated at other family parties, the traditional New Year's Eve dinner had always been held just out of reach.

"You come anyway. I invite you," Lee said firmly. "She do what I say. She's my wife."

"I can't come without my mother."

"Jasmine lay in the bed of her making. Not you. You come."

"I'll think about it." She paused. "Do you remember Ma telling you of her dreams about a dragon?"

He frowned. "She dream too much. She must stop."

"Ma thinks she saw a dragon just like the one in her dreams."

"She always see dragons. She imagine it."

"A man," she said, deliberately not calling David Hathaway her father, "brought her a dragon statue the other day. She said it looked exactly like the one in her dreams. But that man was robbed, and the dragon was stolen." Alyssa watched her grandfather's face for a reaction but saw nothing in his eyes. He might be the friendliest of her relatives, but he had the same unreadable expression as the rest of the Chens. "Did you hear of a robbery in Salmon Alley on Wednesday night?" she added.

"I hear many things, some lies, some truths. Who knows which is which?" he said with a shrug.

"The man who was robbed was David Hathaway. I don't suppose you know who he is?"

"I must go. It is my turn to play. You be a good girl, Alyssa, go home, go to work. Make good life for yourself. Forget about dragons."

Her grandfather was gone before she could say another word. He knew who David Hathaway was; that much she was sure. Although that wasn't completely surprising. The Hathaways were a famous San Francisco family. Did her grandfather know that David Hathaway was also her father?

With a sigh, she walked out of the square. She was tempted to end her quest and go home, but Paige's reminder that her mother might be connected to their father's attack worried her. She couldn't let her mother get into any more trouble than she was already in. The Hathaways had a lot of money. They could make things happen. She hadn't needed Paige to tell her that. It was strange to think she had a sister now—a half-sister, but still a sibling. She'd been an only child forever.

Paige was beautiful—blond, sophisticated, smart. She'd never had to struggle, never worried about her family name or lack thereof, never wondered where she came from, who her parents were. It wasn't fair, and Alyssa was jealous. Not really of the money, although it would have been nice to grow up rich. No, what she really hated was that Paige had grown up with two parents who loved her, two parents who could probably trace their family tree back to the Mayflower. Paige had never had to be half of anything.

Not that it was Paige's fault. She wasn't responsible for the situation any more than Alyssa was. In a way, Alyssa was surprised that Paige had been friendly. She wondered if she would have felt the same way if the situation was reversed. Well, she'd have to deal with Paige later. Right now she had to speak to her grandmother, and that would require all of her attention, strength, and courage.

Squaring her shoulders, she headed down the street and opened the door to the family herb shop. The smells of ginseng root and honeysuckle made her want to breathe deeply, to inhale the peace and calm that filled the shop. Despite her often anti-Chinese stance, she secretly loved the herb shop: the floor-to-ceiling mahogany cabinets filled with hundreds of long, narrow drawers where the various herbs were stored; the soft flute music that played in the background; the rows of books on Oriental medicine, self-healing, meditation; the candles that burned brightly along the counter no matter what the time of day.

Her cousin Ona, who at thirty-five was the oldest of the cousins and a favorite of their grandmother's, was helping a customer complete a purchase. She smiled at Alyssa and said she'd be just a moment.

"Is Grandmother here?" Alyssa asked deliberately using the word grandmother. While the other grandchildren affectionately called their grandmother Nai Nai, Alyssa refused to do so. Her grandmother had made it clear that, because of her mixed blood, she wasn't a true member of the family.

"No." Ona bagged the customer's order and wished her a good day. "Can I help you with something? Maybe some ginkgo biloba or some licorice. You look anxious, tense. What have you been eating? Are you drinking too much coffee again? You know you have to keep a balance in your life."

"Yes, yes, I know." Unfortunately balance was the last thing she had right now. She was so weighted down it was hard to stand upright, but she didn't want to tell Ona the reason for her anxiety. As the oldest, Ona was also the nosiest, believing she had some inalienable right to butt into everyone's business.

"You're a big-time banker now," Ona continued. "You should take care of your health."

"I take ginseng every day."

"What about ginger? It disburses the cold, adjusts nutritive and protective qi."

"Fine, I'll take some ginger. But I think you're just trying to show a profit so our grandparents will leave the shop to you and not to cousin Lian."

Ona smiled. "You are a smart girl, little cousin."

"Don't let the family hear you say that or you'll be disowned for good."

"It's the twenty-first century. Our grandparents need to get over the facts of your birth," Ona said firmly.

"They never will. I don't expect it anymore. And I don't really care."

"Don't you?" Ona asked softly, compassion in her dark eyes. "It's not right the way you've been treated. I wish you would come to New Year's. I miss you every year."

"That's sweet of you to say, but I won't come without my mother, and she's not welcome." Alyssa took the bag of herbs off the counter. "By the way, I heard there was a robbery in Salmon Alley two nights ago. Do you know who did it?"

"I have no idea. Why do you ask?"

"Just curious. I read about it in the newspaper. You always seem to know what's going on in the neighborhood. I heard the victim was a Hathaway and that he might have had a priceless statue with him."

"I heard the same thing. Assaulting rich white men is very bad for business. If the tourists are afraid to come here, we'll all suffer."

That was Ona, a homeopathic herbalist but also an unemotional pragmatist. Of course, Ona didn't realize that the rich white man was Alyssa's father.

"Our grandparents were very upset about it," Ona added. "I heard them talking in the back room. They don't like it when crime gets too close. It makes them remember the old days when they had to pay for protection from the gangs running through the streets."

"They had to pay for protection?"

"Of course. It was a way of life for many years, but thankfully not now."

"Do you think a gang was responsible for the attack?"

"No one is boasting about it, but who can say? Ancient art pieces can be sold on the black market for a lot of money. I'm surprised Mr. Hathaway didn't have more security with him. Actually, I'm surprised he was here at all. I bet he was going to see Lonnie Yao. He's an expert on Chinese bronzes. He has a reputation for being able to spot a fake from three feet away."

"You'd think a rich man like Mr. Hathaway would have his own expert right in the store."

Ona shrugged. "Is something wrong? You seem awfully interested in this robbery."

"Nothing is wrong. So, where is our grandmother?" Alyssa asked,

deciding she better change the subject before Ona became more curious. "Is she upstairs cleaning the apartment for the New Year's celebration?"

Ona groaned. "Every day she cleans—up there, down here, in the
garden. And every night she buys fresh oranges and tangerines and
tells me to take them home so I can have more babies. She doesn't
think my two are enough."

Alyssa laughed. Ona's two energetic boys were more than enough.
"Maybe she wants you to have a girl."

"I don't think so. She says three boys would be lucky."

"I think I'll go upstairs and see her."

"She isn't upstairs. She went out, and she didn't say where. She was
in a bad mood, so I let her go without asking why."

"Why was she in a bad mood?"

"She's seventy-eight years old. Does she need a reason? Besides,
she's always in a bad mood around the New Years'. I guess counting up
all her sins for the year depresses her." Ona rested her arms on the
counter as she leaned forward. "So, how are you, Alyssa? Any new
men in your life?"

"I'm too busy for men."

"Ben was asking about you the other day. He always asks about
you when he comes into the shop."

"I'm sure he was just being polite."

"You know, he might get tired of waiting for you."

"He's not waiting for me, and I'm not interested."

"Because he's Chinese."

"Because we're too different."

"You should talk to him, Alyssa, give him a chance. He might
surprise you."

"I doubt it. He wants a traditional Chinese wife, and I could never
be that."

"Do you want me to tell Nai Nai you came by?"

"No, I'll catch up to her later. Thanks."

Alyssa stepped onto the sidewalk and paused, debating her options.
Maybe she should talk to Ben. Not about her love life, but about the

dragon and the robbery. Ben was a reporter for the Chinese Daily News. He covered everything that happened in Chinatown.

Still, she hesitated. She hadn't seen Ben in several years. They'd been friends throughout childhood and had started dating in high school, but when she'd moved away to college, she'd ended their romance the same way she'd cut the ties to the old neighborhood. There was no future for her in Chinatown. And that's where Ben wanted to be.

He probably didn't care about her anymore, she told herself. He just asked about her out of politeness and friendship. He probably had a girlfriend. There was no reason not to see him. She needed answers, and he was in the position to give them. They'd have a simple conversation, and that would be it. Thankful she had a plan, she walked briskly down the street.

"She's leaving," Paige said, watching Alyssa from Riley's car. "Are we going to follow her again? I don't really see how this is accomplishing anything. We've seen her talk to an old man and go into an herb shop. What have we learned? Nothing."

Riley ended the call he'd been making on his cell phone to his assistant. "The herb shop is owned by Alyssa's grandparents, An-Mei and Lee Chen. They've owned it for the past thirty-five years."

"Your assistant got that information in the last five minutes?"

"It's all a matter of public record."

"I have a feeling everything is public where you're concerned."

Riley laughed. "True. I believe the old man she was talking to in the square was her grandfather, Lee Chen."

"So what now?"

"I think you're looking a little stressed, Paige."

"Thanks for pointing that out." She pulled down the sun visor and checked her face in the mirror. "I don't look that bad."

"You look perfect, but maybe the herbalist won't notice, especially if you tell him or her how tired you are all the time, and how you need a pick-me-up."

"And why can't you be the tired and pale person in need of an energizer?" she asked, realizing his intention.

"Me? I'm the picture of health."

Riley was the picture of a gorgeous male in the prime of life and didn't she know it. "Fine. But I draw the line at actually taking anything. You don't know what's in those Chinese herbs. They could be dangerous."

"Or they could save your life. Chinese medicine has accomplished some amazing things. In fact, many of our modern medicines are based on herbs that first appeared almost two million years ago."

Paige raised an eyebrow. "Who are you?"

He laughed. "Sorry. I have one of those minds for trivia. Things come into my brain, and they don't leave."

"And it doesn't get crowded in there?"

"The human brain is quite a large organ—"

"Please. I do not want to hear about the size of your organs," she said with a mischievous smile. She hadn't seen Riley in this light-hearted mood before. Everything had been so intense, so fast-paced, so filled with drama that they hadn't had much time to laugh, and she was enjoying it—probably more than she should be.

He smiled back at her. "It doesn't have to be just talk."

She shook her head. "Let's stay focused on the task at hand." She opened the car door and stepped out onto the sidewalk.

"Okay, all kidding aside," Riley said, as they paused in front of the door. "You distract the clerk. Do whatever you have to do while I look around. My assistant told me the grandparents live upstairs over the shop. If I can get up there or in the back office, I will."

"What are you looking for?"

"I'll know when I find it."

"This doesn't seem very efficient."

"And Hathaways are always efficient?"

"Always," she said with a nod. "If you don't find anything, you're buying me lunch."

"Or you're buying me lunch. I have a craving for a lobster and steak combo at the fanciest restaurant in town."

"What? Do you think I'm made of money?"

"You said it; I didn't." He opened the door to the herb shop. "After you."

CHAPTER TWELVE

PAIGE HAD no idea that *do whatever you have to do* would mean participating in an acupuncture demonstration. But when Riley had asked for a restroom, and the clerk had sent him toward the back room, she'd known she had to do something to keep the clerk busy until he returned.

"Have you done this before?" she asked nervously, watching the woman, who had introduced herself as Ona, twirl a long needle between her fingers.

"Lots of times. Now, tell me where the pain is."

Paige had made up a headache on the spur of the moment, which was what had led to the acupuncture demonstration, but now the prophecy was actually coming true. Anxiety had brought a throbbing to her left temple. She pressed the point of pain with the tips of her fingers.

Ona nodded. "That is an easy spot to fix. You'll feel better within a few moments."

"You're not going to stick that thing in my head, are you?"

"No. There are pressure points throughout the body that can relieve pain."

Paige lost track of what Ona was saying as her mother's voice entered her head. Are you out of your mind, Paige? That needle could be unsanitary. You could be sticking yourself with a fatal disease. You don't let some woman in an herb shop in Chinatown stick a needle into you.

"Um, maybe I don't want to do this," Paige said anxiously.

"The needle is sterile. You saw me take it out of the package. And I've worn latex gloves the entire time, yes?"

"Yes, but—"

"It's perfectly safe. I promise you. Now give me your hand."

Damn that Riley. Where the hell was he? Paige extended her hand, watching as Ona slowly inserted the needle into the back of her hand, the fleshy part between the thumb and first finger. There was a little pinch, but no real pain. Ona turned the needle back and forth, concentrating on her task. Paige was so tense she felt as if every muscle in her body was on red alert, ready to flee at any second.

"Relax," Ona said softly.

"I don't think—"

"Close your eyes. Let your mind drift. Find a picture that pleases you."

She closed her eyes and Riley's image came to her mind, unbidden and unwanted. His image did please her, but it did not make her feel relaxed. On the contrary, she felt her heart speed up and her palms dampen with sweat. Not that she was sweating because of him. Her nerves had more to do with the needle in her hand. Didn't they?

She saw his laughing face in her mind, his sexy smile, the lazy grin, and she wanted to smile back at him, run away into the sunset, find a deserted sandy beach and a big soft blanket, and fall into Riley's arms.

"Paige?"

His voice was so clear. She could hear him calling out to her, see him raising his hand to beckon her forward.

"Paige?"

She started, realizing his voice was much too clear to be part of her dream. Her eyes flew open, and she looked into his astonished face.

"What are you doing?" he asked.

"I—uh, I had a headache."

"And how is it now?" Ona asked, as she removed the needle from Paige's hand.

"Oh, my goodness, it's gone." She wrinkled her brow, surprised that the tension had eased. Had the acupuncture done the trick, or was it due to the fact that Ona had removed the needle from her hand? Or maybe it was because Riley had returned, and she no longer had to cover for him. Whatever the reason, she felt a lot better.

"I told you," Ona said. "Now what else can I do for you?"

Paige looked at the array of herbs she'd already agreed to buy. "I think we have everything."

"You bought out the store, honey." Riley put his arm around her. "I hope you have something to take away those headaches every night," he said suggestively. "Or maybe a little aphrodisiac that won't make you feel so tired around bedtime."

Paige elbowed him in the gut, but Ona laughed. "Oh, we can take care of that, no problem. In fact, I have something for you, too," she said to Riley.

"That's good," Paige said, "because you know your stamina isn't what it used to be, sweetie."

Riley's jaw dropped. "My stamina is just fine."

Paige exchanged a commiserating look with Ona but said out loud, "Of course it is."

"Don't worry, we'll fix you right up," Ona said, reaching for some other herbs.

"I don't need fixing. Thanks, anyway," Riley said quickly.

"Now, dear, you know we agreed we'd keep an open mind," Paige reminded him. "Just give us whatever you think, we need," she said to Ona. "Honey, why don't you give her your credit card, so we can pay up?"

"You'll be paying up later," Riley said in hushed annoyance as he handed Ona his credit card.

Paige simply smiled. Hey, she'd had a needle stuck into her hand. The least he could do was pay for the herbs. She wondered if he'd found anything on his search through the back room.

"Thank you. Come again." Ona handed Riley his purchase, then said to Paige, "If your headache comes back, you can always massage and put pressure on the point in your hand where we did the acupuncture. Sometimes that works, too."

Paige nodded and followed Riley out onto the sidewalk. "Well?" she asked impatiently.

"In the car," he muttered.

She got into the car and shut the door. "Did you find anything? Or did I just get myself stuck for no good reason?"

He reached into his pocket and pulled out a piece of paper. It was a newspaper article written in Chinese characters. She had no idea what the article said, but she recognized the picture of the dragon that accompanied the piece. "That's our dragon," she breathed.

"The photograph could have been taken from the antiques show," Riley said. "I know there were photographers there as well as the television cameras. Or it might have come from somewhere else."

"How do we find out?"

"I think we should pay a visit to the *Chinese Daily News*." He pointed to the byline. "Benjamin Fong should be able to tell us where this photograph came from and what else he knows about this dragon." He started the car engine. "By the way, you owe me lunch."

Alyssa could see Ben through the plate-glass window that separated the small lobby of the *Chinese Daily News* from the ten or so cubicles that made up the newsroom. Ben had a computer at his elbow but was writing on a yellow pad of paper, his fingers painstakingly precise, his attention focused on the task at hand. It reminded her of when they'd both taken calligraphy lessons from his uncle Guy. Ben had loved calligraphy, putting ink to paper, detailing the Chinese characters with absolute perfection.

She had been too impatient to take such time. But not Ben; he loved tradition and history. He was a twenty-four-year-old dinosaur in the twenty-first century. Which was why she was here. If anyone could tell her where to start her search for an ancient dragon, it was probably him.

"Can I help you?" the receptionist asked as she entered the lobby from a back room.

"I'd like to speak to Benjamin Fong."

"May I tell him your name?"

"Alyssa Chen."

Alyssa watched Ben through the glass as the receptionist made the call. He looked up as soon as he heard her name, his gaze meeting hers. He was surprised she had come. Why wouldn't he be? She'd cut the ties to their friendship a long time ago. "

"You can go on back," the receptionist said.

Ben waved to her, but now that she had the okay, she was hesitant to take it. What on earth would she say to him? She saw him get to his feet and realized she hadn't moved an inch. The last thing she wanted was to have this conversation in front of the receptionist, who was already giving her a curious look. Forcing herself to put one foot in front of the other, she walked down the hall, meeting Ben halfway.

"Hi," she said, offering him a tight smile. She'd never been a warm, affectionate person, and she didn't think she could start now.

"Alyssa. It's good to see you." Ben's eyes were truly welcoming, and she relaxed a bit.

"How have you been?"

"Great. Busy. What are you doing here?"

"I need some help, and I thought you might be the right person to ask. It's not personal," she said hurriedly, then wished she hadn't added the disclaimer as his smile dimmed.

"Business, of course. Come on back." He walked toward his cubicle and waved her toward a chair by the desk. "Have a seat."

"Thanks." She sat down, holding her purse on her lap.

"What's up?"

"My mother saw a statue that she thinks might be really old, maybe valuable, and I thought you might be able to tell me about it. You always seemed to know so much about Chinese art"

He shrugged somewhat modestly. "I know a little. What does the statue look like?"

"It's a dragon with a serpent-like body, about ten to twelve inches tall. The eyes are jade. There's a gold strip around the neck. It probably sounds like a million other statues."

Ben's eyes darted to the newspaper on his desk. He reached for it and handed it to her. "Does it look like this?"

"Oh, my God! That's it exactly." The dragon in the photograph resembled the painting on her mother's wall, which her mother said was a perfect match to the statue David Hathaway had brought to show her. "Why do you have this picture in the paper?"

"That statue was discovered on the television show *Antiques on the Road*. It's believed to date back to the Zhou dynasty. You can read the article, unless you've forgotten how to read Chinese characters."

She frowned at his reminder that she had not always embraced her culture. "Does it say anything more than what you just told me?"

"Not much."

"Do you know more about the history of the dragon?"

"There are several theories. Unfortunately, no one has gotten a good look at it. The owner took it to the House of Hathaway to have it appraised. Since David Hathaway was assaulted a few days ago, no one has been able to get any information on the statue."

Alyssa nodded, her body tensing at the mention of her father's name. She had no intention of sharing that information with Ben. As long as she and her mother didn't speak of it, no one else would know. She doubted anyone in the Hathaway family would rush to tell the press about a long-lost illegitimate daughter. Unless, of course, as Paige had suggested, the disappearance of the dragon drew a connecting line between David and Jasmine. That's what she had to prevent from happening.

"Does anyone have any idea who might be responsible for assaulting Mr. Hathaway?" she asked.

"Not the usual suspects, from what I've heard."

"What does that mean?"

"That someone with experience and knowledge of ancient art was behind the theft. That it was more than likely David Hathaway was mugged because he had the statue with him and not just because he was in the wrong place at the wrong time."

"You said there are several theories about the dragon," she continued.

"There are, but I have a meeting in a few minutes. Perhaps we could do dinner."

She didn't like the wicked sparkle in his eyes and knew getting involved with him again was probably a bad idea, but she needed his help. "Where do you want to go?"

"I'll cook for you."

"You'll cook for me?" she echoed in astonishment.

"Yes. And trust me, you won't starve. I'm a very good cook." He jotted down an address.

She saw the street names and realized he hadn't gone far. "China-town, Ben?"

"Is that a problem?"

"No, of course not."

"Good." He got up and walked her out to the lobby area. "Is seven o'clock good for you?"

Before she could answer, the outer office door opened. To Alyssa's surprise, Paige and Riley walked into the lobby. They stopped abruptly when they saw her.

"Alyssa?" Paige questioned, her gaze narrowing suspiciously. "What are you doing here?"

"I could ask you the same thing," she retorted.

"We'd like to speak to Benjamin Fong," Paige said, giving Ben a questioning look.

"That would be me," Ben replied. "You're Paige Hathaway, aren't you?"

"Yes, and this is Riley McAllister. We'd like to speak to you about the article you wrote regarding the dragon belonging to Mr. McAllister."

"It seems that many people are interested in that story. Do you all know each other?" Ben asked, his gaze moving back to Alyssa.

"We've met," Alyssa said shortly. "They spoke to my mother earlier. You know she has sold several of her paintings to the House of Hathaway."

"What do you want to know?" Ben asked.

"Paige and I have read about a legend involving two dragons, a box, and a flute," Riley said. "Have you heard of such a thing?"

Alyssa started. This was the first she'd heard that there might be two dragons. Or a box. Or a flute for that matter. She glanced over at Ben and saw a spark of excitement flash in his black eyes.

"I know the story," Ben replied. "It is believed that an emperor had the box and dragons made out of bronze to protect a flute that his daughter, the first daughter of his second wife, found in the woods. When the daughter played the flute for her father, his violent headaches would ease. He was so happy that he treated the daughter like a princess and her mother like a queen. The first wife, however, did not like the change in status. She had a son who was meant to be emperor, but now there was talk of this girl becoming an empress. In a fit of rage, she stole the dragons and the box. With the flute gone, the father's headaches returned. In a violent frenzy, he had his daughter killed for losing the flute and swore a curse on all first daughters of anyone who should touch the dragons or the box or the precious flute."

"That's very similar to the story we read," Paige said. "Do you know if the pieces ever resurfaced since the origin of the legend and the curse?"

"I believe there have been several sightings of the pieces, whether as a unit or individually I'm not sure. However, the age of the bronze alone would make it of great value today. Of course, if all three pieces of the unit were together, it would be even more valuable. Where did your grandmother get her dragon, Mr. McAllister?"

"She has no idea, unfortunately. She found it in the attic."

"Too bad. It would be easier to trace." Ben paused. "If there was a curse on the dragon, it might have affected your grandmother."

"I don't believe in curses," Riley said sharply.

"You might want to rethink that," Ben said. "To not understand the power of the past is to be a fool."

"Is that a Chinese saying?" Riley asked.

"No, it's good advice." Ben checked his watch. "I'm afraid I have a meeting."

"Thank you for your time," Paige said. "If you think of anything else, please call me." She took out a business card and handed it to Ben.

Alyssa lingered behind as Paige and Riley left.

"I guess I don't need dinner after all," she said. "Interesting story. You could have shared that with me when I asked."

He smiled. "I needed a bargaining chip so you'd come to dinner. We haven't seen each other in a long time. I'd like a chance to get reacquainted." He paused. "If you give me a few hours, I'm sure I can find out something else about the dragon."

"That sounds like bribery."

"Whatever it takes."

She hesitated, then said, "All right. I'll come to dinner."

"Good. I'm sure we'll have plenty to talk about—including how you know Paige Hathaway and why you're both interested in a dragon statue from thousands of years ago."

"I can't believe Alyssa came here, too," Paige said to Riley as they waited in the hall for Alyssa to emerge from the newspaper office. "She obviously knows Benjamin Fong."

"Yes, she does," Riley mused. "There are a lot of players getting in this game."

"It's not a game."

"I think it might be," he said.

"You think everyone is conspiring against you. That's called paranoia."

"That's called being smart," he said, tapping his temple with his finger.

"Too smart to believe in legends or curses, right?"

"My grandmother had that dragon in her attic for God knows how long. Nothing happened to anybody."

"Are you sure?" She saw his eyes darken and had second thoughts about bringing it up, but it was too late. "The curse is about first daughters. Wasn't your mother a first daughter?"

"Don't be ridiculous. I'm not going to blame a statue for my mother's problems. She created most of them herself. It's just a story, Paige. It doesn't mean anything. It isn't real."

She'd been working around antiques too long not to believe in the power of the past, but she didn't know enough about Riley's mother to pursue an argument.

The door opened and Alyssa stepped out.

"I figured you'd be waiting," she said with a sigh. "How is your— our... I don't even know what to call him."

"He's the same," Paige said quickly, not eager to get into labels either. "Is Mr. Fong a friend of yours?"

"Since childhood."

"You came to ask him about the dragon, didn't you?"

"He didn't tell me anything he didn't tell you."

"But he might," Paige said. "We need to work together."

"I'll think about it, but right now I have other things to do."

"Alyssa..." Paige didn't know what she wanted to say, but she felt as if she had to say something. "I'd like to know more about you. I think we should talk or something."

Alyssa sent her a wary look. "Why? Just because we share a few genes doesn't mean we have to know each other."

"It doesn't mean we can't, either. Wouldn't it be easier if we tried to get along?"

"Easier for who—you? You've always had it easy. I'm used to it being hard, really hard." And with that she walked away.

"That went well," Paige said. "Alyssa has a chip on her shoulder that's almost as big as yours."

"You can't just expect her to open up her heart to you. She's protected it for too long."

"I think she has the Great Wall of China built around it. I can understand her distrust of my father, but why doesn't she want to know me? What have I done to her?"

"You haven't done a thing. But you had everything she didn't, especially a father. It would be natural for her to resent you."

"That wasn't my fault. And I do feel bad about the fact that my father ignored her. He shouldn't have done that, and when he's better, I'm going to tell him so." Riley didn't look as if he believed her, so she added, "I won't sweep this into the closet like a dirty little secret."

"I doubt your mother will let you make anything public. It is a dirty little secret, Paige. And if it gets out, your high-society friends will have a field day gossiping about it."

He was right. Victoria would fight any kind of public disclosure. But this wasn't about the public acknowledging Alyssa; it was about her father doing the right thing.

"Come on, Paige, it's time for a break," Riley said. "You owe me lunch."

"Fine, I'll buy you lunch. Just remember when you're ordering that I don't come into my trust fund until I'm thirty."

"How old are you now?"

"Twenty-eight."

"Looks like we're going to have a very long lunch."

CHAPTER THIRTEEN

"I TOLD you I wasn't cursed," Riley said as he pulled into a parking spot directly in front of a restaurant called the Mad Hatter on Union Street. Because it was a popular shopping street just a few blocks from the marina, Riley had indeed scored a coup.

"I didn't say you were cursed. I said your mother might have been," Paige reminded him. "The curse has nothing to do with sons."

"That's because men don't believe in curses."

"Need I remind you that it was a male emperor who put down the curse?"

He smiled at her. "You can remind me over lunch. I'm starving. Let's go."

Paige followed him into a small sidewalk café. A hostess wearing a top hat with sequins and feathers asked them if they'd prefer to sit inside or out. Out of habit, Paige chose an inside table, but almost immediately regretted her choice when they were seated at a cozy table in a dark corner of the room. It was difficult to keep their relationship in perspective when they were alone.

"This is nice, private," Riley said with a wink. "I like it."

"I should have figured you'd feel comfortable in dark corners." She paused. "I feel a little guilty that I'm having lunch instead of going back to the hospital to see my dad."

"Your father is not alone, and we're working hard to figure out who hurt him. That's worth something."

She sighed. "Fine, you've convinced me. You're very persuasive and good at coming up with excuses. I'll be sure to call you when I want to get out of a root canal or something."

"I can't be of any help to you there. I love going to the dentist."

"No one loves the dentist."

He smiled. "The chairs are cool. When I was a kid I felt like I was in a spaceship."

"What about the drill and the shots of Novocain?"

He shrugged. "A little pain is good for the soul. It builds character."

"Who told you that—the dentist?"

"As a matter of fact, yes," he said with a laugh. "My first crush was on a female hygienist. I was thirteen. I loved the way she smelled, the way her hair drifted against my face, her breasts—they were so perfect—"

"I get the picture," Paige said, holding up a hand. "You're a fan of big breasts."

"I'm a fan of any female breasts."

"Of course." She picked up her menu, deliberately placing it in front of her not overly endowed chest.

"Hiding?" Riley asked.

"Just trying to order."

He pushed the menu down so that it lay flat on the table. "I think you have beautiful breasts, Paige."

She cleared her throat, hating the way her breasts responded to his words, her nipples drawing into tight, hard peaks that she prayed weren't evident through her silk blouse. "This isn't exactly lunch conversation."

"We can talk about them over dinner if you prefer."

"We're not talking about them at all, unless you want to talk about a few of your own private parts."

"Whatever you want."

What she wanted was to slap that lazy, knowing grin right off his face. Actually, she didn't want to slap it off; she wanted to kiss it off. "There must be something terribly wrong with me," she muttered.

"Why? Because you're turned on? It's a natural response. It happens all the time."

"I'm so happy to know that you turn on all of your lunch companions. But thanks for reminding me, because you just turned me off."

"No, I didn't."

"Oh, shut up," she said in exasperation. "Can we just order some food and talk about something else?"

"Sure. Have you ever been here before?"

"No. Is the food good? Or are the hats supposed to distract you from what you're eating?"

"The food is excellent, especially the hot roast beef sandwich."

"That sounds perfect. I'll have that."

He raised an eyebrow. "It's a good size and it comes with fries—do you know how many calories are in that?"

"I don't want to know. But since I've missed most of my meals the last few days, I think I have room for a few extra calories. Do you watch your weight?"

"Do I look like I should?"

He looked like a man in perfect condition, muscled, toned, trim, but she didn't want to make his ego any bigger. "How old are you?" she asked instead.

"Thirty-one. Does that make a difference?"

"Of course it does. Once you pass thirty, it's all downhill."

"I thought that was forty."

"That's what all thirty-one-year-olds think," she said with a smile.

"Well, you don't have to worry since you haven't hit the magic number yet."

"That's right. I can even order dessert."

"You're paying," he reminded her.

She looked down at the menu in front of her. "It could have been a lot worse. Where's the steak and lobster combination? Did you decide to go easy on me?"

"Since you don't have your trust fund yet, I had no choice."

The waiter came over to take their order and for a few minutes they were busy answering questions about drinks and food and whether or not they'd like to purchase one of the hats on display. When the waiter left, a silence fell between them, a tense silence, Paige thought, the teasing laughter of a few minutes ago no longer in evidence. She glanced over at Riley and caught him staring. A little shiver ran down her spine. "What are you looking at?"

"You."

"I know that, but you look like you have something on your mind."

"I do. You," he added with a slow smile that took her breath away.

"I'm sure you have a lot more interesting things to think about."

"I can't remember one." He paused, his gaze still intent on her face. "Are you really going to marry that stiff shirt who was at the hospital the other night?"

"Martin? I told you I'm not engaged to him."

"Does he know that?"

"He should," she replied. But she had a feeling she'd let things drag on too long where Martin was concerned. "It's a tricky situation. Our families are friends. Martin works at the store. He's a vice president now. Somewhere along the way someone got the idea that we would make a good match. So we started going out, but—"

"But you don't want him," Riley finished.

"He's a good man. I could do worse."

"You could do better."

"You don't even know him. And why should I care what you think?"

"No reason," Riley agreed. "It's none of my business. A week ago I probably would have thought you were a good match, too."

"Not now?"

He didn't answer right away, just continued to study her with a thoughtful expression on his face. Then he said, "You're not exactly what I thought. You're more complicated. The person most people see isn't the person you really are, is it? Somewhere in there lies the problem with Martin."

How could he know her so well after a few days when people she had known her whole life didn't have a clue?

"I think on the outside you're cool and collected but inside you're teeming with frustration and maybe a little anger," he continued.

"That's enough," she said, shaken by his assessment.

"Am I wrong?" he challenged.

"You're oversimplifying things. And even if you're not, you're no different. You play the tough guy, but that's not who you are."

"That *is* who I am."

"And more. Caring and loyal... Your grandmother said you gave up your career in the marines to come back and take care of the family business when your grandfather got sick."

He shrugged. "It wasn't a big deal. I was ready to come home."

"And your family was important."

"My grandparents are important to me, just those two people. I wouldn't use the general term *family*. Are you done with the analysis, Princess, or is there more?"

"You always call me princess when we get too friendly. I wonder why."

"It's a reminder that we don't travel in the same circles."

"Today we do."

"Tomorrow we won't."

He was probably right, and she should be happy about that. He'd been a thorn in her side since the day they'd met. But he'd also been other things, including the first man in a long time she felt she could really talk to, say the things she wanted to say, not the things she was supposed to say.

"Riley?" a feminine voice called out with a delighted squeal.

Paige looked up to see a gorgeous, statuesque redhead heading straight toward them. Riley jumped to his feet just in time to be swept into a tight hug against a pair of very large breasts. He must be in heaven, Paige thought, sitting back in her seat.

"Riley, you devil, I've missed you," the woman said with a sparkling laugh. Then she planted a long, smacking kiss on his lips that he didn't make any move to avoid.

As their kiss went on, Paige cleared her throat. Riley still didn't look over at her. "Riley," she said more loudly as the two broke apart. "Who's your friend?"

He finally turned toward her. "This is Brenda Sampson—Paige Hathaway."

"Paige Hathaway?" Brenda raised an eyebrow as she cast Riley a speculative look. "Moving up in the world, are you?"

"Right now I'm having lunch."

"Did you order the hot roast beef sandwich?"

"It's the best," he said.

"I put it on the menu just for you. I'll go have a word with the chef, make sure you get extra meat and fries. It was nice to meet you, Miss Hathaway. I hope you enjoy your lunch. And, Riley, you better call me soon. It's been too long."

"I will," he promised. He returned to his seat as Brenda moved on to greet another table of customers.

"You have lipstick all over your face," Paige told him.

Riley picked up his napkin and wiped off his mouth.

"It's on your cheek. You didn't get it," she said.

"Maybe you could help."

"Fine." She dipped her napkin into her water glass and leaned across the table to wipe the lipstick off his face. Unfortunately, the move put her into closer contact with his body. Her leg brushed his under the table. Her shoulder collided with his arm, and she became acutely aware of how near his mouth was to hers. It wouldn't take much to lean in just a little bit farther...

She heard a catch in his breath, and her eyes met his in shocking awareness.

"Do it, Paige," he said huskily. "You know you want to."

"I—I don't know what you're talking about," she lied. She rubbed at his face with brisk ruthlessness, then sat back in her seat. "It's gone now."

"So is half my skin." He put a hand to his cheek. "What the hell is wrong with you?"

"Nothing is wrong with me."

A gleam entered his eyes. "You're jealous."

"I am not. I've never been jealous in my life."

"You didn't like Brenda."

"She's a pushy redhead, and the two of you made a scene."

He sent her a knowing grin that irritated her more. "You didn't like that she kissed me."

"I couldn't have cared less. You know, I'm not hungry. I think I'll catch a cab and go to the hospital."

"Running away, Paige? I thought Hathaways had more guts than that."

He knew just which buttons to push. She tapped her fingers on the table, considering her options. Why was she acting so crazy? Was she jealous? Was that possible? She certainly wouldn't admit that to him, nor was she going to admit that she had actually wanted to kiss him a moment ago. She needed to calm down, pull herself together, and—as he'd reminded her—act like a Hathaway.

"Fine, I'll stay."

"Good." He paused as the waiter set down his beer and her diet Coke. He raised his glass. "To your father's speedy recovery and to finding the dragon."

She hesitated, but how could she resist that toast? She clinked her glass against his. "Thanks for putting my father first. I know you believe he created this situation."

"I think he had a lot to do with it, yes."

"Guilty until proven innocent."

"Most people are guilty."

"I'm not. And we're on the same side, Riley."

"Maybe for the moment." He leaned forward, resting his arms on the table as he gave her his full attention. "We don't know yet how this will play out. We don't know what your father's intentions were. But we do know that you are a loyal Hathaway. And at some point you may have to choose between doing what's right and supporting your family."

"That won't happen. My family is as trustworthy and honest as I am."

"I hope that's the case, Paige, I really do. Because if it comes down to your family or mine, who do you think I'm going to pick?"

Paige was reminded of Riley's words an hour later when she approached the front doors of the hospital. Off to the side of the main entrance were at least two television crews lying in wait. Unfortunately, they spotted her just a second after she spotted them. There was no time to escape.

"Miss Hathaway, how is your father?" a young woman asked as she stuck a microphone in Paige's face, nearly knocking out her teeth.

Paige jumped back, only to trip over a man coming up on the other side of her.

"Is it true that your father was robbed of a valuable piece of art that didn't belong to Hathaway's?" he asked.

"What is Hathaway's doing to recover the piece?"

"Do the police have any leads on your father's assailant?"

"Do you think this was a personal attack? Does your father have any known enemies?"

Paige blinked at the rifle-shot questions. She could barely keep up with them all, and each time she turned her head, there seemed to be another reporter in her face as well as more microphones and cameras. She certainly hoped this wasn't a live shot, because she had the distinct feeling she was coming across as an idiot.

Think, Paige told herself. You're a Hathaway. You can do this.

"My father," she began, drawing immediate silence with the mere sound of her voice. The sense of power gave her confidence. "My father is in stable condition, and we expect a full and complete recovery."

"What was your father doing in Chinatown?"

"The police are continuing their investigation," she replied. This wasn't so bad. A lifetime of watching her parents handle reporters had prepared her for this moment. She hadn't realized just how well prepared she was until now. "Thank you for your concern. As soon as we know more, we'll be sure to inform you."

"Is it true that your father went to see a woman in Chinatown?"

The question pierced Paige's confidence like a pin to a balloon. Jasmine? They knew about Jasmine? Oh, God. What about Alyssa? Did they know about her, too? She had to say something to head them off.

"No further comment," Martin Bennett said, appearing at her side. "The Hathaways will be holding a press conference later today."

Paige felt Martin's strong grip on her arm as he pulled her through the crowd of reporters and into the hospital lobby. They didn't stop walking until they were on the elevator, and even then he put a finger to his lips, motioning for her to be silent until they were alone. They got off at the fourth floor, and she yanked her arm out of his grip.

"Why on earth did you do that?" she demanded.

"Do what? I saved you from saying the wrong thing. You know you're not supposed to talk to reporters. What were you thinking?"

"That I could handle the situation," she snapped. "Which I was."

"No, you weren't. They were leading you for a fall, and you were going right along. You should have done what I did, told them there will be a press conference forthcoming and any further questions should be directed to me as the spokesperson for Hathaway's in this time of crisis. That's the way we do things. You know that."

She stared at him in amazement. He was talking to her like a child. "I'm a Hathaway, Martin. I know how to handle myself and the press. And if I want to speak on behalf of the store or my family, I will. I don't care if you're the designated spokesperson or not."

"Your mother won't feel the same way."

"My mother isn't here."

"No, she's with your father, talking to him instead of the media, which is where you should be."

"And where I was going." She saw the anger in his eyes but didn't understand it. "What are you mad about, anyway? I'm the one who has the right to be annoyed. You came in and swooped me away like an eagle snatching an unsuspecting bird."

"You are an unsuspecting bird," he said as he ran his hand through his hair in obvious frustration. "Where do you think those questions were going, Paige? Someone has obviously been following the police investigation. They know by now that the police went to see Jasmine Chen. Curiosity as to how a simple Chinese woman could be connected to David Hathaway was sure to follow."

"And we should have an answer ready. *'No comment'* will only fuel the curiosity."

"The answer is coming from your mother. We've already planned a press conference for early this evening. That's why the media are outside right now."

"No one told me that."

"I tried calling you earlier, but your message machine was on at home, and you didn't pick up your cell phone. Where have you been?"

She felt a slight surge of guilt at the memory of her delicious lunch. "I've been doing some research of my own about the dragon."

"With Riley McAllister? What are you doing with him, Paige? He's not on our side. He's using you."

"And I'm using him. We both want to get the dragon back. We both want to know who is responsible for the attack on my father and who might have the dragon now. Riley is a security expert. He has connections. He can get information I can't."

"Like what?"

"Like he's the one who figured out Jasmine's daughter, Alyssa, is my sister," she said.

Martin's jaw tensed. He cast a quick look around them to make sure they were alone. "What the hell are you talking about?"

"My father's illegitimate daughter."

"Damn," Martin frowned, then shook his head. "Now McAllister has ammunition to blackmail you."

She was shocked by the suggestion. Riley wouldn't do that. He was an honorable man. Wasn't he? A niggle of doubt crept into her mind. Was she being naive? He'd laughingly told her she shouldn't have suggested to Alyssa the possibility of selling her story to the tabloids, but couldn't Riley do exactly that? If they couldn't find his grandmother's statue, maybe Riley would have to find another way of getting his grandmother the money he thought she deserved.

"I need to see my father," she said abruptly, hating the way Martin had derailed her.

"Look, Paige, I'm sorry if you think I came down too hard on you. I just want to protect you from more pain. And I don't think hanging around with this McAllister guy is a good idea."

"You don't need to protect me. I can take care of myself. Understood?"

"As long as you understand that there's a good possibility your father was up to something by taking that dragon into Chinatown in the first place."

"Up to what? We know he took it to show Jasmine. Big deal."

"She might not be the only one he showed it to. Maybe he took it to someone who could make him a fake."

His suggestion left her speechless. "My father doesn't deal in fakes. How can you say that, Martin?"

"Because he didn't have a good reason to take it out of the store. It went against company policy, our insurance guidelines, our security measures, everything."

She couldn't refute that. She didn't know why her father had taken the dragon from the store, but Martin's doubts gave her even more motivation to find out. "When he wakes up, he'll tell us why he went to Chinatown. And his reason won't have anything to do with the commissioning of a fake statue. He cares too much about art to even consider such a thing. You'll see I'm right. When my father wakes up, he'll tell us what really happened. And then there won't be any more doubts or questions."

"I'm looking forward to that moment," Martin replied. "Until then, don't talk to any more reporters, Paige. You'll only add fuel to the fire."

The fire eating away at her family's reputation. She had to find some way to put it out.

CHAPTER FOURTEEN

AFTER DISCUSSING her husband's case with the private duty nurse, Victoria dismissed the woman so she could be alone with her husband. As she stood now by his bed, she couldn't remember the last time she'd watched David sleep. He looked old, she thought, panic filling her chest. And he was two years younger than she was. This shouldn't be happening now. They weren't the right age to be facing this crisis. They had so much left to do.

But she wasn't dying, she reminded herself quickly. She was okay. And David would be all right, too. She had to believe that. He was the foundation of her life. Maybe not him exactly, but who he was. She hadn't married just him; she'd married his family, his heritage. She knew more about his ancestors than he did. She was the one who made sure the distant relatives got Christmas cards and birthday presents. She was the true Hathaway, and she wouldn't lose that.

She certainly wouldn't lose it to divorce. She still couldn't believe the nerve of that woman coming here to her husband's bedside. Well, it wouldn't happen again. The nurses had strict instructions not to let Jasmine Chen anywhere near David.

How could he have picked a woman so unattractive, so unappealing, so unstylish, so lower-class? He had a wife who was beautiful, smart, sophisticated. Why had he needed someone else?

Angry tears blurred her vision, and she drew in a sharp breath, hating the fact that she still cared about him at all. Look at how he had treated her, cheating on her with another woman, and God knows how many others. And now the daughter had surfaced. She had known of Alyssa's existence, of course. Her private investigator had researched every aspect of Jasmine Chen's life, including the birth of her daughter, Alyssa, nine months after she'd slept with David. If Jasmine had gone after David then, Victoria would have stopped it. But it appeared that the woman actually cared about David, maybe even loved him—too much to go after his money. What a fool Jasmine Chen was.

But she was a fool, too. She should have made sure that the connection between Alyssa Chen and David could never be made. She'd slipped up. Now Paige knew about the whole sordid mess. It was embarrassing and awkward, and Victoria dreaded the conversation she knew was coming. Paige would want to talk about the affair, the last thing Victoria cared to discuss with her daughter. Her marriage was personal and private and none of Paige's business.

"Damn you, David," she said aloud. "The least you could do is have the guts to wake up and face this mess you've created."

"Do you really think yelling at him is the best approach?" Paige asked as she entered the room.

"I've run out of other ideas," Victoria retorted, glad to see Paige was alone. She suspected that Riley McAllister was behind her daughter's newfound knowledge, and she resented his intrusion into their lives. "What's wrong?" she asked, noting a flush on her daughter's cheeks.

"I ran into some reporters downstairs."

"You didn't tell them anything, did you?"

"Not really. Martin cut them off at the knees." Victoria nodded approvingly. "He's a very smart businessman. Where is he?"

"He said he'd be by later. How is Dad?"

"I don't know. The same, I guess."

They both glanced down at David, who seemed to be barely breathing. "He sleeps so deeply," Paige murmured. "You're worried, aren't you?"

"I'd feel better if he was awake." Victoria felt Paige's gaze on her face, but she didn't want to look into her daughter's eyes and see the questions there. "Now isn't the time," she muttered.

"I wasn't going to ask."

"Thank you for that."

"But you knew, didn't you?"

"I thought you weren't going to ask."

"I'm sorry. It's just so confusing. I believed our family was so solid, so secure."

"Our family is fine. A few bumps in the road along the way, but nothing more than that." Victoria looked at her daughter's worried face. "We are Hathaways, Paige. And we're survivors. Don't ever forget that."

"I hope Dad hasn't forgotten. What would we do without him?"

"Hopefully, we won't have to find out."

"You still love him a little, don't you?"

"Good heavens, why would you ask that?" "That's not an answer, Mother. Do you still love him?"

"We've been married for thirty-one years. Love isn't that easy to define at my age."

"I don't think it should be that difficult, either."

Some latent motherly instinct made her want to reassure Paige. "Your father and I are not going to split up. We'll never get a divorce, if that's what you're worried about."

"Because you love him, or because you want to be a Hathaway?"

"I am a Hathaway. I'm more a Hathaway than he is. I've worked hard to be one. I won't give it up. I don't care how many women and daughters come out of the woodwork."

"I guess I have my answer."

"No, you don't have your answer." Victoria took a deep breath. "I love him, and I hate him. I can't help it. I'm sure he feels much the same way. We've shared some of the best days of our lives and some of the worst. We understand each other, and yet we don't. We make each other laugh, and we make each other cry."

"I guess that's better than feeling nothing."

"Sometimes I'd rather feel nothing." Victoria stared down at the familiar lines of her husband's face and realized that what she felt was fear. She didn't want to lose David. She didn't want him to die.

"Damn you, David, wake up. Wake up and answer your daughter's questions." She smiled at Paige, and for the first time in a long while there was a connection between them. "I shouldn't be the only one on the hot seat. He has a lot more to answer for than I do."

"That's for sure." Paige put her hand on her father's arm. "Come on, Daddy. Open your eyes. We need you."

"Oh, my God," Victoria whispered as David's eyelids began to flicker. "I think he's trying to wake up." She leaned over in excitement. "David? Can you hear me?"

His eyelids moved. Another blink and she was staring into his brown eyes.

"Jasmine," he said, and then his eyes shut again.

"You bastard," Victoria hissed. "You lying, cheating bastard."

"He didn't know what he was saying," Paige said quickly, trying to defuse the situation.

"The hell he didn't."

"Mother, please." Paige pressed her lips against her father's cool cheek. "Daddy, try to wake up again."

"Bright," he murmured in a raspy voice.

"I'll turn off the light," Paige said, hurrying over to the light switch.

"Vicky? Is that you?" he asked, squinting as he tried to focus.

"Who did you think it was?"

"Mother," Paige warned. "He's coming out of a coma. Try to remember that."

Victoria drew in a long breath and slowly let it out as she gazed into his dazed eyes. "How do you feel, David? Do you have any pain?"

"Head hurts. Where am I?"

"You're in the hospital." She leaned over and pushed the button for the nurse while Paige took her father's hand.

"It's going to be okay, Dad. Just relax and don't try to do too much too soon."

A few moments later the nurse entered and proceeded to check David's vital signs.

"Welcome back, Mr. Hathaway," she said.

"What happened?" David murmured, continuing to blink in confusion.

"You were attacked," Victoria answered. "Don't you remember?"

David slowly shook his head, then winced at the pain the movement generated.

The doctor entered a moment later and conducted a brief examination. "You're doing well, Mr. Hathaway. I'd like to run some tests, but it looks like you're on the road to recovery. It's about time, too."

"What—what day is it?" David turned to Paige with desperation in his eyes. "Elizabeth's birthday. When is her birthday? I didn't miss it, did I?"

Page shook her head, tears filling her eyes. "Today is Friday. Her birthday is next Wednesday. You have plenty of time."

"Thank God."

"I'll be back," Victoria said, following the doctor out of the room and leaving Paige alone with her father.

"You had us worried, Daddy."

"What happened to me?"

"You were mugged in Chinatown."

"What? Why was I in Chinatown? God, I'm tired."

"Dad, before you go back to sleep, I have to ask you. Do you know what happened to the dragon?" He looked at her in confusion. "What dragon?"

"The dragon that belongs to Mrs. Delaney, the one you took out of the store when you went to Chinatown."

"Did I go to Chinatown to meet Mr. Yee for dim sum?"

"Mr. Yee? No, that was last month. I'm talking about this week."

His eyes drifted shut, and Paige realized he had fallen asleep. Why didn't he remember? Was there something wrong with his memory? She walked quickly from the room, finding her mother and the doctor in the hall. "He doesn't remember the dragon or going to Chinatown or anything that happened recently," she blurted out. "Something is wrong with his mind."

"Short-term memory loss is common in cases of trauma like this. It usually comes back," the doctor reassured her. "He just needs time. I'll check him in the morning, but I think you can both relax. He'll probably sleep for a while. His body is still recovering. But the worst is over."

"So you think his memory will return?" Paige asked.

"I'm fairly certain it will. Maybe not the actual event of the assault, but probably most of what occurred before that time."

"Thank you, Dr. Crawley," Victoria said.

"No problem. Now, both of you go home and get some rest. That's an order." He smiled and tipped his head as he walked away.

"Well, it looks like your father will make it," Victoria said with relief.

"Yes, it appears that way."

"What's wrong now, Paige?"

"I wish he could have told me what happened to him."

"He will. He needs time. You heard the doctor. Why don't you go home? The nurse will stay with your father through the night. If he wakes, she'll make sure he has whatever he needs."

"I'm wondering if we shouldn't have more than a nurse."

"What are you talking about?"

"I'm talking about a security guard. What if whoever tried to hurt Dad finds out he's awake? He might be afraid that Dad can identify him. He might come back."

Victoria's gaze narrowed suspiciously. "What else aren't you telling me?"

Paige hesitated. "There may not be any connection, but Mrs. Delaney's house was broken into this morning."

"Mrs. Delaney, the owner of the dragon?"

"Yes, and I've been doing some research. It's possible that her dragon is part of a set. It's Riley's theory that—"

"Riley McAllister? The grandson?"

"Yes, he's a security expert, and he thinks that someone might have broken into his grandmother's house to see if she had another dragon."

Victoria let out a long, weary sigh. "Fine. I'll call our security company and have them send someone over here right away. Will that ease your mind?"

"Yes, thank you." Paige paused, watching her mother's gaze drift back to her dad's hospital room. "Are you going to stay?"

"For a while."

"What Dad said when he first woke up—"

"I didn't hear a thing."

"I didn't, either," she lied.

"Go home, Paige, and for God's sake, run a comb through your hair. It looks like a bird made a nest in it. And put on some lipstick. There could be press snapping your picture on your way out of the hospital. You have to think about these things, you know. Appearance and image are very important, especially when we're under such close scrutiny. Speaking of which, I think you should distance yourself from Mr. McAllister. We need to keep our business private."

"Our family business went public when Dad lost Riley's grandmother's dragon. Riley is determined to find out what happened, and I can't blame him. I feel bad for his grandmother. One minute she's sitting on a possible fortune, and the next minute it's gone."

"There's no room for sentiment in business, Paige," her mother replied. "Mr. McAllister is a customer, not a friend. Try to remember that."

She would try, but her mother had no idea how difficult that would be, because Paige wasn't thinking of Riley as a potential friend but as a lover.

"So you decided to actually come to work," Carey said, dumping a pile of pink message slips on Riley's desk late Friday afternoon. "Where have you been all day?"

"I've been trying to track down my grandmother's dragon," he replied. "I knew I could count on you to keep things going."

"You can—for most things," she said somewhat ominously.

Riley sat back in his chair. "What does that mean?"

"The three musketeers want another assignment."

"Bud, Charlie, and Gilbert?" he asked, referring to the three older men who'd been with the company since his grandfather had started it forty years ago. They were now in their early to mid-seventies and insisted on continuing to work. His grandfather had made him promise when he first came back to help out that he would not terminate their contracts for any reason except gross negligence, certainly not for age or any other discriminatory reason. "Actually, I have a job for them," he said. "I want them to take turns monitoring my grandmother's house. I'm not expecting any trouble, but another pair of eyes wouldn't hurt."

"I'll let them know. They'll be thrilled."

Riley smiled. "Maybe we should look into getting them into some computer classes. If they're going to work for me, I need to find something worthwhile for them to do."

"And you're too soft to fire them."

"Hey, they're cheap, loyal labor. I'm looking out for my own interests."

"Yeah, yeah, tell it to someone who doesn't know you."

"What else is going on?"

"Tom picked up a new Internet client. Richie called in and said the film company shooting in Marin needs security guards for three more days. That's about it. Oh, and Josh called and said he got an A on his chemistry test, so can he please come back to work?"

Riley smiled at that. "Good for him."

"Good for you for making him care about his grades. You're pretty smart when it comes to teenagers and old guys. Women—now that's another story. And speaking of women, or woman in particular, are you going to be tagging along with Paige Hathaway all night, too? Just so I know where to reach you in case of emergency."

He ignored her amused smile. "You can always reach me on my cell phone. You don't have to know where I am."

"That's no fun. Seriously, Riley. Is this thing with Paige Hathaway business or funny business?"

"It's none of *your* business," he said pointedly.

"Just be careful," Carey warned. "Don't fall in love. Girls like Paige can break your heart."

"That's never going to happen."

Carey walked out of his office with a disbelieving laugh. But she was wrong. He had no intention of falling in love. Long-term commitments were not for him, and not even a beautiful, brown-eyed blonde was going to change that. Besides, he had more important things on his mind right now. He had a dragon to find.

When Jasmine opened her door, she was shocked to see her mother, An-Mei, on the doorstep. She couldn't remember the last time her mother had come to visit. They lived only a few blocks from each other, but the distance between them was as big as a continent.

"Ma," she stuttered. "Is everything all right?"

"No, all wrong," An-Mei said shortly, brushing past her into the apartment.

Jasmine closed the door and waited for An-Mei to state the purpose of her visit. A flicker of nervousness ran down her spine as she watched her mother critically peruse the contents of her apartment. Her mother would find some fault with the way the furniture was arranged or the color of the painted walls. There would be something to criticize. She waited quietly, patiently, feeling as if she deserved whatever criticism was coming. Because she was bad; she'd always been bad. Her mother had told her so over and over again.

Sometimes she wondered if anyone else saw the temper in the tiny, barely five-foot-tall woman in front of her with the long black braid down her back and the baggy clothes that covered her from head to toe. Jasmine couldn't remember the last time she'd seen her mother's bare legs or arms. Modesty was a virtue, An-Mei believed, along with many other virtues that Jasmine had never been able to live up to, even before the biggest sin of them all.

She'd always been a disappointment. When she'd been born missing a finger, her mother had screamed in fury, according to her auntie Lin. Ever since then, Jasmine had been treated as an outcast. Her mother had once told her that the missing finger was the mark of shame she would grow into. And Jasmine hadn't disappointed her.

By sleeping with a married man, she'd committed a terrible sin, and having an illegitimate baby made it even worse. Her mother probably wouldn't have spoken to her again if it hadn't been for her father's influence. His heart attack a few years earlier also had softened her mother's stance, perhaps made her realize that too many years had passed with this anger between them.

Jasmine wouldn't have taken the scraps of affection if it hadn't been for Alyssa. She'd buried her pride and forged a tenuous relationship with her parents so that Alyssa would become part of the family. But that hadn't really happened despite her efforts. The sins of the mother were forever visited on the daughter.

An-Mei walked over to the painting of the dragon that hung on the wall. She stared at it with piercing black eyes, then turned those same eyes on Jasmine. "You take down. Hide away. Never speak of dragon again." Her heavily accented voice was sharp, pointed, definite. Despite the fact she'd lived in San Francisco for fifty-some years, An-Mei still spoke as if she'd only recently gotten off the boat. Her heart had never really left China.

"I saw it," Jasmine said somewhat defiantly. "I saw the dragon. It's real."

"You are a liar. You make up stories."

"I'm not lying. I saw the dragon." She watched her mother closely, seeing something in her eyes that looked like fear.

"You see nothing. You are a bad girl."

"I'm not a girl. I'm a middle-aged woman with a grown child of my own. When are you going to realize that?"

"You send Alyssa to see your father. She make him worry about dragon. She tell him you in trouble. Mixed up in Hathaway robbery."

"I'm not in trouble. But David Hathaway did show me a dragon statue that was taken from him later that evening. Someone else must have wanted it very badly." Jasmine paused, seeing the pulse beating rapidly in her mother's neck. An-Mei knew something about the dragon. But what? "I read a story about my dragon. I think there are two, and together they open a box," she continued.

An-Mei didn't blink, her gaze unwavering.

"I wonder if whoever took Mr. Hathaway's dragon has the other one."

"If you know of such a set, you know there is a curse. Your dreams come from the curse reaching out to touch you. You must not let it touch you. And you must not touch the dragon."

"I held it in my hands," Jasmine said with a shiver of uneasiness as she remembered the coolness of the bronze beneath her fingers.

"Where is Alyssa?"

"Alyssa? I don't know."

"You must find her. You must make sure she is safe."

"Why wouldn't she be safe?"

"The curse is on first daughters."

The words stabbed deep into her heart. So it was true, the story she and David had found. And something else was suddenly clear. "I'm a first daughter."

"Yes," An-Mei said, meeting her gaze. "And your dreams have cursed you, too."

"My dreams?" Jasmine echoed. "Or the dragon?"

"No more!" An-Mei shouted, her eyes blazing.

Jasmine took a step back, feeling suddenly afraid. But why did she fear her own mother? This small woman had cut her many times with unkind words, but she had never actually struck her. At least, she didn't think that had happened. Sometimes her childhood seemed like a vague, dull memory that never came into focus.

"The gods are watching," An-Mei said, her voice quieter now but still sharp.

Jasmine crossed her arms over her chest, fighting the impulse to look around and see if someone was watching. "Why can't you just tell me the truth? Did I see the dragon somewhere?"

An-Mei stared at her for a long moment. "Yes. You see the dragon at the museum in Taiwan when we went there on a trip. I tell you don't touch, but you do. Bells go off. Guards come running. Lee almost go to jail. You touched it, and you were cursed."

Jasmine stared at her mother in confusion. The story sounded convincing, but it was so innocent, so bland. Why hadn't they told her before where she'd seen the dragon? Why pretend it didn't exist, that it was only in her dreams? Was her mother lying?

It seemed an impossible thought. An-Mei had punished each of her children for every small lie she had caught them in. She believed that lies told eventually came back and stabbed you in the heart. In fact, she thought heart attacks were caused by too many lies. When her husband had had his attack, An-Mei had prayed for forgiveness every minute of every hour until his heart was beating strongly again. Which made Jasmine wonder something else. What were the lies her father had told?

"Please," An-Mei said. "No more, Jasmine. No more talk of dragons. Stop now, before it is too late."

Jasmine had the terrible feeling it was already too late for her. But maybe not for Alyssa. She had to find her daughter. She had to make sure Alyssa stayed away from the dragon before she, too, was forever cursed.

CHAPTER FIFTEEN

"ALYSSA, COME IN," Ben said, as he opened the door to his apartment. "You're right on time. Can I take your coat?"

Alyssa was tempted to hang on to her coat so she wouldn't get too comfortable, wouldn't let down her guard, but it was warm in the apartment, so she took off her suede jacket and handed it to Ben. Underneath she wore a red knit sweater and a pair of black pants.

"Nice sweater," he said approvingly. "At least you haven't shunned red."

"Why would I? The Chinese don't have a monopoly on the color."

He smiled at her. "It's still considered lucky, you know."

"I look good in red. Don't read anything more into it than that."

"You do look good." He hung up her coat in the closet. "Joey is out for the evening, so make yourself comfortable."

"You still live with your brothers?"

"Henry lives in Seattle, but Joey lives here. He has a night class. So it's just you and me."

"Great," she murmured warily. A few minutes with Ben had reminded her of why she had avoided him all these years. He was too attractive, too likeable. And he had a way of seeing into her head that made her feel uncomfortable. Besides that, he reminded her of the past and a lifestyle she'd rather forget. Even now, looking around his apartment, she saw all the signs of a traditional Chinese family getting ready for the upcoming New Year's celebrations. There were fresh flowers everywhere as well as a platter of oranges and tangerines and a candy tray that she was sure was filled with eight varieties of dried sweet fruit.

"My mother," Ben said quickly, following her gaze. "She brings flowers and fruit every day. I tell her we have more than enough, but she won't stop. She wants to make sure we have good fortune in the New Year. Would you like a drink?"

"Absolutely," she said with a fervor that made him laugh.

"I take it that means alcoholic."

"If you have anything like that—wine, beer?"

"I'll get you some wine."

"Thanks." While he was getting her a drink, she looked around his apartment. The furniture was mostly old and comfortable. Nothing really matched, and it was clear that it was a male-dominated room, no traces of female sentiment anywhere in sight. Three tall bookcases overflowed with books, and she moved closer to take a look at the titles. "Have you read all of these?" she asked, taking the glass of wine from Ben's hand when he returned to the room.

"Most of them."

She pulled one out of the stack. "The History of Porcelain. That looks fascinating."

"It is, if you like porcelain." He tipped his head toward the couch. "Sit down. Tell me what you've been doing with your life since you moved away from Chinatown."

"Getting a college degree, a job, an apartment. I live in Noe Valley with three girls I went to school with," she said, taking a seat.

"Sounds good. I heard you graduated from Berkeley with a four-point GPA."

"Who told you that?"

"Someone in the neighborhood."

"I can't imagine how they'd know." She didn't keep in touch with any of the kids she'd grown up with, just a few of her cousins, and that was because they insisted on keeping up with her.

"How's your mother? I haven't seen her in a while." He sat down in a chair facing her.

"She's all right, I guess." Alyssa set her glass of wine on the coffee table between them. She had the sudden urge to tell Ben everything that had happened, which was unusual. She always kept her thoughts private. It was easy to keep quiet with her other friends, none of whom were Asian, because they wouldn't understand the way her family operated. But Ben wouldn't need long explanations. He'd seen firsthand how she and her mother had been treated by the rest of the Chen family.

"Alyssa?" His gentle voice called her back to the present.

"Sorry. I was just thinking."

"Want to talk about it?"

She looked into his kind eyes and knew she could trust him. "My mother might be in some trouble. David Hathaway brought that dragon statue to my mother's apartment the day he was assaulted. The police came to visit her. They asked all kinds of questions about where she was, and why he was there, and where he was going when he left. But she couldn't tell them anything, because she didn't know."

"Why would David Hathaway visit your mother?" Ben asked curiously.

"He purchased several of her paintings in the past."

"Right. I forgot about that. Is that how you know Paige?"

She hesitated, tempted to share it all, but in the end her guard came back up. "Yes."

"Now, tell me again why he took the dragon to your mother. Surely that didn't have anything to do with her painting?"

Damn, he was too smart. She should have remembered how quick his mind was. She cleared her throat, stalling. "Actually, my mother painted a dragon that looks exactly like the one he found. That's why he wanted to show it to her. And that's why I'm interested in finding out more about it. You said you'd research it for me. Did you find out anything?"

"Are you going to run out the door as soon as I give you my answer? I've worked very hard on dinner."

"Of course I won't run out the door. That would be rude."

"I did make Chinese food. Still sure you'll stay?"

"Yes," she said, seeing the challenge in his eyes. "I know you think I'm wrong to feel the way I do, but I wasn't raised to be proud of who I am. I was raised to be ashamed of my mixed blood."

"You can't run away from who you are, Alyssa."

"My God, Ben, you think I don't know that? I've spent half my life wishing I could wake up in a different body and be someone else."

"You shouldn't feel that way. I hate that your family made you think you were unworthy. It was wrong."

"Well, I don't think they'll agree with you. But it doesn't matter anymore. I have a good life away from here. And I'm never coming back."

"I know," he said softly, meeting her gaze. "I figured out a long time ago that you probably hated Chinatown more than me, but it was easier to get rid of us both."

His words reminded her of how much there was between them. "Maybe this wasn't a good idea," she said.

"I want you to stay for dinner."

"I don't want to discuss the past, Ben. There's no point. We broke up a long time ago."

"You broke up with me."

"You would have done it eventually, if I hadn't. We want different things out of life."

"We used to want each other," he reminded her. "I don't think that desire is gone. I felt it the moment you walked into my office this afternoon."

She swallowed hard at the look in his eyes. "Ben, I only came here to discuss the dragon. If that's not going to happen, I should leave."

"It will happen. I made you a promise, and I'll keep it. As for the rest, we'll see how it goes. Now stay here, drink your wine, and let me show you what a good cook I am. I've got some appetizers you will love."

And if she stayed too long, she'd fall in love with more than his appetizers. He was right. The desire was still there, maybe even stronger than before. When had he become so good-looking, so grown-up, so manly? Why was she feeling such a strong attraction to him? They should have felt comfortable around each other, like two old shoes, not tense and nervous and on edge. She picked up her glass of wine and took a long sip, willing herself to relax. This was just Ben. This was just dinner. Nothing was going to happen.

"So, what have you been doing with your life?" Alyssa asked a while later as they finished the incredible dinner Ben had prepared. She was feeling calmer now that she had a full stomach. She rested her arms on the dining room table and smiled at him. "Are you happy writing only for the Chinese audience? Is that enough for you?"

"Probably not," he said, surprising her.

"Really?"

"You're not the only one with ambition, Alyssa. I'd like to work for one of the bigger metropolitan newspapers, or maybe an arts magazine "

"That might mean moving away from Chinatown."

"It's not a ball and chain around my leg. I could leave—if I had a good reason." He paused. "I like your hair. I'm glad you left it long."

"It's too thin and too straight."

"It's perfect. You're perfect."

"I'm not," she said with a shake of her head.

"I wish you could see yourself the way I see you."

Alyssa got to her feet, suddenly restless under his intense gaze. She walked over to a desk that held a computer and more books. "What's all this?"

"Research on your dragon." He came up behind her. "I found out that the set I told you about was discovered in an archaeological dig in southern China in the early 1900s. The pieces were sent to China's National Palace Museum, but at some point they were lost."

"From a museum? That sounds odd."

"There was a lot of turmoil and war in China. Many artifacts were lost."

"My mother only saw one dragon. She didn't see a box or another dragon."

"It's not surprising that the pieces have been separated. It would probably be more shocking if they were still together."

"True." She picked up a pile of newspaper clippings. "What are these?"

"I'm doing a story on the Chinese New Year celebrations in San Francisco, a composite look at the traditions. My cousin Fae is going to be Miss Chinatown this year."

"That's great. She must be excited."

"She is, because she's the third generation." He flipped through the photos on the desk. "Here's the one of her mother getting crowned, and here's the one of her grandmother."

Alyssa looked at the photos. The Miss Chinatown Pageant was a very big deal. When she was a young girl, she'd even had thoughts of trying out for it herself. Until she was reminded that only a pure Chinese girl could win.

"See anyone familiar in this picture?" Ben asked her, pointing to the one of Fae's grandmother. It had been taken at the party after the pageant, and there were a number of people in the picture, but none really jumped out at her. Although...

"Is that my grandfather?" she asked in astonishment, recognizing the familiar profile.

"Yes, and he's talking to Wallace Hathaway. David Hathaway's father."

And her grandfather.

A shiver ran down her spine at the connection.

"Hathaway was probably the Master of Ceremonies for the pageant," Ben continued. "They usually had someone from the city council or chamber of commerce announce the winner."

"I had no idea they'd ever met," she murmured. These two men, who had shaken hands some fifty years ago, were her grandfathers.

"It's a small world," Ben commented.

"Yes," she agreed. And it was getting smaller by the moment.

Riley set his grandfather's armchair back into its upright position and adjusted the cushions. He looked around at the living room his grand-mother had always kept so neat and wondered if it would ever look that way again. Whoever had ransacked her house had been hastily and ruthlessly brutal in their search. Obviously time had been a factor. There was also a sense of purpose. This hadn't been a random burglary. It didn't appear that anything had been taken.

He moved over to the end table, staring down at the piles and piles of photographs that had been dumped out of the box his grandmother kept them in. It had been a family joke for years that Nan was not a photo-album kind of person. She'd been talking about organizing the photos of her life for as long as he'd been alive, but here they were, a mass of black and white and color photographs from a lifetime of living.

He sighed. He wished he could just hire a cleaning service to come in and tackle this mess, but his grandmother had already told him that she didn't want any more strangers in the house. She'd do it herself tomorrow, and that would be fine, but he couldn't let her face this.

His cell phone rang, and he answered. "Yes?"

"There's a beautiful blonde casing the house," Gilbert, one of his security guards, told him. "She's been standing on the sidewalk for almost five minutes. You want me to talk to her?"

"No, I think I know who it is," he said, feeling an unexpected jolt at the information.

"She's walking up to the door now."

"I've got it, thanks."

Riley slipped his phone back in his pocket and went to open the front door. Paige was in the process of reaching for the doorbell. "Looking for me?" he asked, surprised and pleased to see her. He'd spent most of the day with her, but he'd missed her the past few hours. Damn, not a feeling he wanted to examine too closely.

"How did you know I was out here?" Paige asked.

"I have a sixth sense."

Her gaze narrowed speculatively. "You have an undercover guy sitting in a car at the corner."

He grinned at her. "Very good, Miss Hathaway. He said you were stalling. Why?"

"I was having second and third thoughts. Can I come in?"

Riley held the door open for her. "It's a mess, I warn you."

Paige walked into the room, her eyes widening as she took in the destruction. "My goodness. When most people say their house is a mess, it's usually spotlessly clean. But this really is a mess."

"They did quite a job. Take a look." He led her around the downstairs, showing her the living room, dining room, and kitchen, where they had to step over pots and pans to get to the back stairs. The upstairs was just as bad. The bedding had been tossed off all the beds, the drawers upended, items pulled off the shelves.

"Oh, Riley." Paige shook her head at the sight of his grandmother's bedroom. "Whoever did this was very serious."

"I know. You live in a secure building but you should be careful, Paige. Until your father can tell us what happened, we need to be cautious."

Paige's face lightened at his words. "That's what I came to tell you. My father is awake."

"That's great. How is he?"

"He's okay, I think. But he doesn't remember what happened this week at all. He only spoke for a few minutes, and he seems to have lost a few weeks. I asked him about the dragon, but he didn't know what I was talking about. The doctor said it's not unusual for there to be short-term memory loss."

"Probably not, but it's damned inconvenient," Riley grumbled. He couldn't help wondering if David really couldn't remember or if this was just another trick, but in light of Paige's happiness at her father being awake, he decided to keep that thought to himself.

"Everything seems so much better now," she said. "I know we don't have the dragon back yet, but I feel as if we're getting closer. As soon as my dad can tell us why he went to Chinatown, we'll have an idea of who is behind all this."

Her smile took his breath away. He liked the optimism in her voice. She reminded him of his grandmother in that way, always wanting to see the best, the potential, the possibilities. Meanwhile his brain was spinning with the complications. "Your father may not be safe," he began.

"My mother is hiring a security guard."

"That's good. We don't want anyone to take another shot at your father."

"My mother will make sure that doesn't happen. She knows how to protect what's hers." She paused. "Anyway, why don't I help you clean up? That's what you came here to do, right?"

"Surely Hathaways don't clean."

Her brown eyes sparkled. "Not usually, no. But I think I can stumble my way through the process. Besides, I've seen your apartment, and I don't think you're exactly an expert."

"You don't have anything better to do with your Friday night? No hot date with Marty?"

"Martin."

"Whatever. How come you're not out with him?"

"He didn't ask."

"Are you one of those girls who must be called by Wednesday for a Friday date?"

"Monday or Tuesday at the latest. What about you? Are you one of those guys who calls at four o'clock on Friday and says, " 'Hey, babe, want to hang out tonight?' "

"What's wrong with that?"

"No finesse. No style." She walked into Nan's room and picked up one of the drawers from the floor. She set it on the bed and began folding his grandmother's shirts and shorts.

Riley watched her from the doorway. Once again, her behavior was surprising him. She should have been out celebrating her father's awakening with her fancy friends in a fancy restaurant. Instead she'd come here—to him. That thought was more than a little disturbing. What was she doing here? What did she want?

"Are you going to help?" She cast him a curious look. "Or are you going to stand there and stare at me?"

"I haven't decided yet."

Paige finished with one drawer and returned it to the dresser. "You probably don't want to go through your grandmother's underwear, do you? I can understand that women's lingerie would make you a little uncomfortable."

"My grandmother's underwear definitely makes me uncomfortable," he said with a smile. "Women's lingerie is another story entirely."

"I'll bet. Red teddies and black garter belts, right?"

"I keep an open mind. And I don't discriminate."

She rolled her eyes. "I'm sure you don't. Do you have a woman in your life right now?"

"Yeah, an irritating, nosy blonde who asks a lot of questions."

Paige finished with another drawer. "Help me get the bed together," she said, ignoring his comment. "Maybe we should wash the sheets. I bet your grandmother would feel better if everything was cleaned."

"She is a big believer in clean sheets. I had to strip my bed every Saturday morning like clockwork. For the first fourteen years of my life, I was lucky to sleep on any kind of sheets. Sleeping bags and old blankets were more the norm." He was sorry he'd mentioned it when he saw the pity come into her eyes. "It was like camping. It was fun," he added, not wanting her to feel bad for him

"It was wrong. Every child deserves at least the basics—food, shelter, clothes, security."

"That requires money. I don't expect you to understand."

Paige tossed the bedding in a pile on the floor, leaving the mattress bare. "You always bring up money. You always point out how different we are. It's as if you want to make sure I know there's a line between us that we can't cross."

She was right. He was drawing a line between them, because right now, alone in a bedroom with a bed only a few feet away, it would be easy to forget there was anything to keep them apart. Her flowery scent was tantalizing, her brown eyes beckoning with the fire of challenge in them. And her body. Hell, he'd have to be a saint not to notice the curve of her breasts through her silk blouse or the shapely ass encased in a pair of black pants. She was quite a package, and he was dying to unwrap her.

"Well? Nothing to say?" she asked.

"You seem to be talking enough for both of us."

"Show me your room, Riley."

"I haven't lived here in a long time."

"Show me where you slept when you did live here."

It was another dare; he could see it in her eyes. She wanted to get to know him better, to get inside his head. And he wanted to get inside her body. Two distinctly opposing goals. Although they didn't have to be, if he gave her what she wanted...

He turned and walked down the hall to his old bedroom. It had been his mother's room when she was a girl, but there was no sign now that any female had ever lived here. Now the room housed a full-sized bed with a blue bedspread, a simple oak dresser and matching desk where he'd once done his homework. There were a few items from childhood in the room, the model airplanes he'd made when he'd dreamed of being a pilot and flying away from it all, the posters of football players that had never quite come down. Now he was almost embarrassed to see them.

"Did you make these?" Paige asked, pointing to one of the airplanes.

"Yeah." He picked up the globe and the stand that his grandfather had given him. It had been knocked over during the burglary.

"You like to fly."

"I do. I like looking down on the world. How about you?"

"I love flying, especially takeoff, when you're speeding down the runway and the plane is shaking and suddenly you're up and away. It's a wonderful feeling."

He frowned, hating the way she'd echoed his own feelings. He didn't want to have anything in common with her. "I'm sure it's a better experience in first class than in coach."

She groaned. "Oh, my God, Riley, would you knock it off? You may have grown up poor, but you're not poor anymore."

"How do you know?"

"Because I know. There's nothing wrong with this house, either. It's nice, comfortable, a lot warmer than the one I grew up in."

She sat down on the bed, which was disheveled but intact. Apparently, their uninvited guest had done only a cursory run through this room. Probably because there wasn't much in it. Riley swallowed hard as Paige did a little bounce on the bed. His bed. His teenage bed. The bed he'd dreamed of sharing with a beautiful, sexy blonde like Paige.

"This is much softer than mine was," she told him. "My mother believes a firm mattress keeps the posture straight and the body supported. It's also extremely uncomfortable. I used to pile extra blankets on the mattress and sleep on top of them. Now, of course, I have a nice soft mattress, like this." She laid back on the bed, her legs dangling off the end. "Look, you have the universe on your ceiling. That is so cool."

He glanced up at the ceiling, which his grandfather had painted like a nighttime sky, a dark blue with twinkling gold stars. "My grandpa got tired of me climbing up on the roof. When my mom would leave, I'd go up there to watch for her. Then I started stargazing."

"What's that one?" She pointed to the ceiling.

"Orion. Get up, Paige."

"What's the problem?" She sat up halfway, resting on her elbows.

"I want you out of my bed." He could have bit his tongue at the way that came out, but he was fighting an overwhelming feeling of lust at the moment, and it was that or jump on top of her and show her just how much the bed could bounce.

"Sorry," Paige said hastily as she scrambled off with a hurt look on her face.

He caught her by the arm. "That's not what I meant."

"You were pretty clear."

He gazed into her face and knew he couldn't look away, couldn't walk away, couldn't make her go away.

"Riley," she whispered, "let me go."

"I can't." He leaned over and covered her mouth with his. She tasted sweet, sinful, sexy, sophisticated. It was a heady combination and completely irresistible, especially when she moved into his body, when her breasts came into contact with his chest, when her hands crept around his waist. She should have been resisting, pushing him away, not kissing him back like she didn't want to stop. And when he slipped his tongue into her mouth, she absolutely should not have met him halfway. Nor should she have made that lusty little gasp of desire that he wanted to hear again and again.

"Riley, I need to breathe," she murmured against his mouth.

He played his lips across her face, her neck, the curve of her shoulder. He moved behind her and used his hands to memorize her body, from her slim waist to her soft breasts. He rolled his palm over one breast, feeling the nipple tighten beneath his fingers. It was too much of an invitation to resist. He slipped his hand inside the V neck of her blouse, into her lacy bra so he could touch her bare skin, feel the heat rising between them. He used his other hand to bring her bottom flush against his groin, where he was hard as a rock.

There was that little gasp of desire again. It made him crazy.

His name rolled off her lips like a plea for more. And he intended to give her more, much more. He turned her to face him again, backed her up against the bed until the backs of her knees hit the mattress, and they both went down. He landed on top of her, exactly where he wanted to be, and found her mouth again. He wrestled with the buttons on her blouse, one, two, three. Finally, he had them undone, and as he pulled open her shirt, he broke away from her mouth to gaze down at her. Her beautiful breasts were rising up and down, her nipples peaking through the sheer lacy cups. God, he was in heaven.

He leaned over and pushed her bra aside, putting his mouth to her breast, rolling his tongue around her nipple until she groaned. But she didn't push him away; she put her hand around the back of his neck and pressed him closer.

"Don't stop," she whispered. "Don't stop."

"I won't," he promised. But the words had barely left his mouth when the sound of a door slamming penetrated his foggy brain.

A voice came from down below. "Riley? Riley, are you here?"

Paige shoved him off, panic in her eyes. "Is that your grandmother?"

"Riley?" Nan called out again.

"Oh, my God. She can't see us like this," Paige said.

Riley sat back in a daze, watching as Paige fumbled with the buttons of her shirt. She looked incredible, with her blond hair tangled from his fingers, her lips red from his kisses, her breasts moist from his tongue. He knew he needed to move, get up, go to the door, tell his grandmother he'd be right down, but all he could do was look at Paige and wish to hell they could go back to doing what they had been doing.

"Riley, help me," Paige begged as they heard footsteps on the stairs.

He finally got his brain to function. "I'll head her off." He got off the bed and took a deep breath, willing the rest of his body to cooperate. His grandmother might be in her seventies, but her eyesight was still perfect.

"I'll be right there, Grandma," he yelled. He gave Paige a rueful smile. "She always did have bad timing. I'll get rid of her."

"How are you going to do that?"

"I don't know."

"Don't tell her I'm here."

"I wasn't planning on it." He walked out of his bedroom and took care to close the door behind him. He found Nan in her room, staring at the mess.

"It's worse than I remembered." She walked over to the dresser and set up the photo of herself and Ned at their fortieth anniversary party. "That's better."

Riley's heart began to slow down as he realized his grandmother's distraction was definitely to his benefit. "What are you doing here? I thought you were staying at Millie's."

"I needed my robe. I forgot to get it earlier. I saw your car so I figured it would be all right to come in. Plus, I saw Gilbert sitting in his car at the corner, so I know I'm safe. You hired those old boys to watch over me, didn't you?"

"Yes," he admitted, still feeling a bit uncomfortable when she turned her gaze on him.

She stared at him for a long minute, and he wondered what she was seeing. Did he have lipstick on his face? Was his hair as messy as Paige's? He distinctly remembered feeling her fingers run through his hair.

"What's wrong?" she asked him.

"Nothing."

"You look—funny."

"It must be all the dust I've been stirring up."

"Must be."

"There's your robe." He grabbed it off the chair in front of her dressing table. "This is your favorite one, isn't it?"

"Yes, it keeps me warm." She gave him another long look. "I guess I'll go back to Millie's, unless you want me to stay and help."

"No. You take the night off. There will be plenty to do tomorrow."

"Are you going to sleep here tonight, honey?"

Sleep was the last thing he had on his mind. "I don't know yet. I'll see how late it gets."

"If you are, you should change the sheets on your bed. I have extras in the hall closet. Why don't I help you do that before I go?"

"No," he said abruptly. "I mean, I already did it. So you can just go back to Millie's."

"You already did it? I must have taught you something after all." She smiled at that. "Well, don't work too hard."

He followed her down the stairs, praying she wouldn't suddenly stop and decide she needed to get something else. But they made it to the front door without a hitch.

"I'll watch you walk next door," he said.

"You always take good care of me, Riley."

"That's my job."

She stood on her tiptoes and gave him a kiss on the cheek. "Good night, honey." She walked down the steps, then paused. "By the way, tell Paige I said hello." Her knowing grin made him feel fourteen years old again. "I hope you didn't make her hide in the closet like you did Jenny Markson."

"Paige is definitely not in the closet," he replied. Her laughter lasted all the way next door. When be shut the door, Paige was right behind him.

"I am totally embarrassed," Paige said. "She knew I was here the whole time."

"I never could get away with anything." He took a step toward her. "Now, where were we?"

She put a hand on the middle of his chest, holding him at arm's length. "Who is Jenny Markson?"

"She's not competition, if that's what you're worried about. I think she has a couple of kids by now, and at least one husband."

"Was she your girlfriend?"

"For about two weeks in the tenth grade."

"Did you make out in your bedroom?"

"We tried, but my grandmother came home early."

"So I wasn't the first." Paige crossed her arms in front of her chest, a sexy little pout on her face.

He grinned. "You were definitely not the first."

"Did you have sex with her?"

"Unfortunately, that bedroom has never been lucky for me in the sex department. I'm hoping tonight we can change my luck."

She dodged his oncoming embrace. "Are you kidding me? Your grandmother knows I'm here. I can't possibly have sex with you in that bedroom tonight."

"The idea wasn't bothering you a few minutes ago."

"I went a little crazy," she admitted.

"I like you a little crazy." This time when he put his hands on her waist, she didn't move away. "Want to know what else I like?"

"I don't think so," she said breathlessly. "I should go home."

"I could come with you. Your bedroom would certainly be more private."

She hesitated, and he saw the answer in her eyes even before she said it. She'd had time to think—too much time, apparently.

"You have a lot to do here," she said.

"It's not going anywhere."

"Riley—"

"The moment is over. I get it."

"It's not that I don't want to." She looked at him with her heart in her eyes, and he felt a rush of emotion as well as panic. What was he thinking? What was casual for him would probably not be casual for Paige. She wasn't a one-night-stand or a three-day-fling kind of girl. She was marriage and children and happily ever after, and he'd given up on that a long time ago.

"Fine. Whatever," he said.

"It's just more difficult to make the choice than to simply let it happen, you know? I guess that makes me a coward."

"Or smart."

"I don't feel smart. I feel... frustrated."

"That makes two of us. You should go."

"I want to help you with the cleaning."

"Why?"

"Because I do, and because, dammit, I don't want to go home yet. Is that the deal, if I don't sleep with you, I have to leave?"

He smiled at her obvious annoyance. "That's usually how it works."

"That's not the way it works with me. But to be on the safe side, we'll clean down here." She entered the living room. "Has this room been lucky for you?"

"Nope."

"Good."

He laughed. "Not so good for me."

She knelt down next to the pile of photographs on the floor. "This is quite a mess. Your grandmother sure has a lot of pictures."

"My grandmother has been talking about putting those in photo albums since I was a kid. She just never gets around to it."

"Is this you?" She held up a baby picture.

He squatted down beside her, his chest tightening. "No, that's my mother."

"Oh, I'm sorry. I should have guessed." She picked up more

pictures of his mother at various stages of her life. Riley didn't want to look. He tried not to remember his mother at all. He certainly didn't want a visual reminder. But as Paige went through them, he found himself looking over her shoulder. His stomach clenched at the one in her hand. His mother was holding him in her lap at what was probably his third Christmas. She was trying to hand him a doll, but he was pushing it away.

"Now, I know this is you." Paige looked at him with tenderness in her eyes. "I recognize the scowl."

"I wanted a fire truck. Not that stupid rag doll."

"Oh, this is you, too." She pulled out a photo his grandmother had taken at his junior high school graduation. "There's that scowl again. Do you ever smile for the camera?"

"I didn't see any point in recording those moments in my life." He paused, remembering that day. He'd only been at his grandmother's house since that Christmas. He'd transferred into yet another school to finish up the eighth grade. His mother was supposed to be at the graduation, but she'd gone off on a weekend retreat that had lasted six months. That's when his grandparents had told him he would be living with them from now on.

"Aren't there any of those naked baby pictures in here? I'd like to see your bare ass on a blanket," Paige said, lightening his mood.

"I'd be happy to show it to you. It's much more impressive now than it was then."

Her brown eyes sparkled at him. "So you say." She picked up another photograph. "This must be your grandparents at their wedding."

"You're really going back in time now As I said, my grandmother never organized any of these. She always said she was too busy living life to look at it."

"That sounds nice." Paige let out a sigh. "There are six photo albums of my life to date, every minor or major event captured on film for generations to see."

"Who was the photographer? Your mother or your father?"

"They usually hired photographers."

"Of course. My mistake."

"They were at my kindergarten graduation and all the other school graduations to follow, birthday parties, Christmas, holiday events, and of course the off-the-shoulder drape portrait for my debutante ball."

"Poor little rich girl. My heart is bleeding."

She tossed the pictures at him. "Then you can clean these up."

"Fine with me." He swept them into a pile, then stopped. The photograph in front of him was an old black-and-white taken in San Francisco. It was the sign in the background that made him pause. "Look at this."

Paige peered over his shoulder. "That's my store," she said in wonder. "That must have been taken years ago. Look at the car."

"I was looking at the men in front of the store." Riley pointed to a man wearing a security uniform. "That's my grandfather. Do you happen to know who he's shaking hands with?"

"Oh, my God. I certainly do. That's my grandfather, Wallace Hathaway."

Their eyes met as they both came to the same conclusion.

"My grandfather must have worked for Hathaway's," Riley said.

"It sure looks that way. And he obviously knew my grandfather. It's quite a coincidence, isn't it?"

"I've never believed in coincidences." Riley felt sick to his stomach. He glanced over at Paige. "Have you spoken to your grandfather about the dragon?"

She shook her head. "No."

"I think it's time you did."

CHAPTER SIXTEEN

THE STORE CLERKS chatting behind a counter stopped the instant they saw him. Good, but not good enough, Wallace thought. They shouldn't have been wasting time in the first place. Their business was to serve the public, not to entertain each other. He stopped in front of the counter, eyeing the name tag on the younger woman, Megan.

"May I help you, Mr. Hathaway?" she asked nervously, sending a pleading look to her cohort, a man who quickly busied himself with the countertop display.

"What time do you begin work?" he asked. "Ten o'clock."

"What time is it now?"

"Ten thirty."

"Exactly. I assume your duties do not include pointless conversation with other store clerks?"

"No, sir. But there aren't any customers right now."

"Whether there are customers present or not does not mean you should shirk your duties. Am I clear?"

"Yes. It won't happen again."

"See that it doesn't." He strode briskly away. Now that his presence had been noted in the store, everyone got busy. He walked down the aisles, surveying the displays, making mental notes that he would later dictate to his secretary. He made the same inspection on each subsequent floor, stopping at times to speak to the department managers. Some had been at the store for decades, but he didn't allow any friendliness to creep into his voice. There was a line between them. He liked it that way. He trusted no one, not even those who reported to him on a daily basis. They served a purpose, but that was the extent of the relationship.

As he headed toward the executive offices, he couldn't help but worry about what would happen to Hathaway's when he was gone. Paige needed to step up to the plate. Maybe she didn't have it in her. He hated the thought of his store going into anyone else's hands, including Victoria's, but he had to admit that so far his granddaughter was a dismal failure as an only heir.

"Is my grandfather coming in today?" Paige asked, when her grandfather's secretary answered the phone. Although it was Saturday, she expected him to make an appearance. Saturday seemed to be his favorite day for checking up on employees, especially her mother. Victoria acted as if she didn't care and made a point of not coming to work on the weekends, but Paige suspected her mother made sure there was nothing out of order for Wallace to find.

"I expect him any minute," replied Georgia Markham, her grandfather's longtime secretary who always worked on Saturday. "Would you like an appointment?"

"Yes. I mean no. Well, maybe."

"Which is it, dear?"

"I'll check back with you in a few minutes. I'm not sure about my schedule yet." Paige hung up the phone, feeling like a big fat chicken. The man was her grandfather, for heaven's sake. There was no reason to be intimidated by him. Unfortunately, logic did little to dispel the nervous butterflies in her stomach.

Well, it could wait a few more minutes. While she was stalling, she decided to tie up some of the final arrangements for the grand opening party of the Hathaway exhibit at the Asian Art Museum, now only two short weeks away. She updated the response list, reviewed the catering, floral, and photography arrangements, and took another look at the budget. Everything was as it should be. In fact, her assistant had done most of the work, reminding Paige that she wasn't all that vital to the success of the company.

Paige looked up as a knock sounded at the door. "Come in," she called.

Martin walked into the office, dressed in his usual Armani business suit. "Hello, Paige. It's good to see you back at work and things returning to normal. I just came from the hospital. Your father looks well."

"Yes, he does. I stopped in early this morning and caught him having his first real meal in a while. Of course, he complained about the eggs and the toast and the fact that there was no bacon. But he seemed in good spirits."

She got to her feet as Martin walked around the desk to offer her a hug and a kiss on the cheek. His touch did absolutely nothing to raise her blood pressure, and she couldn't help thinking about the night before when she'd had a meltdown in Riley's arms. At least one truth had come out of this past week. She didn't feel enough passion for Martin to even consider marrying him. It wouldn't be fair to either one of them.

"How are you doing?" he asked.

"I'm fine. Catching up."

"I'm happy to see you concentrating on work instead of pursuing that dragon."

"It needs to be pursued. We still don't know what happened to it. My father's short-term memory is apparently absent at the moment"

"That's what I hear."

She didn't like the doubt in his voice. "You don't believe him?" She paused, tilting her head to one side. "You don't really like my father, do you?"

"Don't be ridiculous. I have a great deal of respect for him."

The words were right, but the lack of emotion in his voice told

Paige that Martin wasn't being completely honest with her. "You already suggested to me that my father might have been looking into commissioning a fake. There's no point in backtracking now."

"That was a mistake on my part. I realize your father would never do such a thing. As for the dragon, our security people are investigating it, Paige. You don't need to do it personally. In fact, your mother and I both agree that it would be better if you stayed out of it. Your father has already been hurt. We certainly don't want you in the line of fire. Your mother tells me that the Delaney woman's house was broken into as well. Another sign that you should leave this to the experts. This is not the job for you."

She couldn't stand his patronizing tone, never mind the fact that he glossed over the words with a smile. "I don't think it's up to you, Martin, to decide what job is right for me."

"I didn't mean to offend."

"But you did."

"Paige, you're misreading me."

"I don't think I am. I realize you have an important job here at the store, that Mother considers you her right-hand man. But I'm the Hathaway heir, not you."

He looked shocked by her words, and she had to admit she had surprised herself by speaking so bluntly. Maybe Riley had rubbed off on her.

"I didn't mean to overstep—" he said.

"You did overstep. It is obvious that as far as you're concerned, I'm pretty much good for planning parties and nothing else, but you're wrong. And so are my mother and my father and my grandfather and whoever else thinks that way. I intend to do more for this store than party planning."

"That's great," he said soothingly. "My point and concern were only for your safety. I wasn't criticizing your judgment."

"I appreciate that. Thank you."

He looked at her for a long moment. She refused to glance away, knowing that they had to get something else straight between them.

"You're not interested, are you?" he asked.

"I like you as a friend and a coworker."

He offered her a wry smile. "Not exactly what I was hoping to hear."

"I'm sorry, Martin. I realize I may have given you the wrong idea in the past, but I don't want to lead you on any further."

"We could be good together. We have so much in common. I feel as if you and I are a perfect match."

"Maybe on paper, but a marriage is real life. Quite frankly, I don't think you have any idea who I really am. I suspect I haven't seen the real you, either."

"I am what you see."

"I doubt that," she said with a softening smile. "You're going to make someone a great husband."

"But not you."

"Not me."

He tilted his head to one side, studying her thoughtfully. "You've been different this past week. Your father's brush with death sparked something in you."

"That was part of it," she conceded, not wanting to mention that the real spark had come from Riley. She liked Martin far too much to throw another man in his face.

"You've come alive." He nodded approvingly. "It looks good on you. And I don't think all you're capable of is party planning. I simply followed your lead, Paige. If you've been unhappy or feeling restricted, you should have said something. After all," he added with a smile, "you are the Hathaway heir, as you just reminded me."

"I guess that sounded a little high-handed, didn't it?"

"Actually, you sounded a lot like your mother."

"God forbid."

Martin laughed, and she realized in that moment that he wasn't at all disappointed that their relationship wasn't going to be more than friendship.

"You aren't upset about this, are you?" she asked.

"Don't get me wrong, Paige. I like you. However, I must admit I was feeling a little heat from our respective mothers. I've been so focused on my career the past few years that I hadn't given much thought to marriage and, well, you are pretty near perfect."

"Not even close."

"Let me know if you want to branch out into some other areas of the company," Martin said, as he opened her office door. "I'd be happy to explore the possibilities with you."

"Thanks. That's very generous of you."

Martin paused, his expression turning serious. "I do think you ought to stay out of this dragon business. Your father was almost killed. I don't want you to get hurt."

"I'll be careful, but I have to see it through. I have to know what happened, not just to Dad, but to the dragon. Mrs. Delaney put her trust in me, and I failed her. I want to make it right."

"To her or to her grandson?"

"To both. My family's reputation is on the line."

"And you are the Hathaway heir. Don't forget to remind your mother of that."

She made a face at him. "I don't think she'll take it as well as you did."

"I don't think she will, either."

"I have to talk to someone else first," she said. "My grandfather."

"Are you sure you want to climb that mountain?"

"I've been putting it off for far too long."

"Your grandfather knows everything that happens around here. He's uncanny that way."

"I suspect he has a few spies helping him out. Maybe even you," she added thoughtfully. "Hmm. I'm right, aren't I?"

"I'm a loyal employee, Paige. That's all I am."

As Martin left, Paige couldn't help wondering if that's really all he was. Her grandfather did seem to know everything that occurred in each nook and cranny of the store, and she knew he had to have help. Why not Martin? He'd risen through the ranks faster than anyone.

Not that it mattered. Whether he had a spy or not, her grandfather was the boss. He had a right know to what was going on in his own business. But she knew it was past time for her to find out exactly what he knew about the dragon. Picking up the phone, she dialed his secretary's extension.

"Hello, Georgia, it's Paige again. I would like to make an appointment to see my grandfather, as soon as possible."

"I'm sorry," Georgia replied, "but your grandfather has already left the store. Can I give him a message for you?"

"No, I'll catch up to him later," she said, hanging up the phone. Maybe it would be better to talk to him at home, anyway. There were too many eyes and ears at the store, and this was one piece of business she'd prefer to keep private.

Ned Delaney lived on the second floor of the Woodlake Assisted Living Center, a three-story building set in a quiet grove of trees on the western edge of San Francisco. Riley and his grandmother had chosen the center after looking at all the available options and had found this one to offer the most in terms of quality surroundings, care, and compassion. But it was still a depressing place, and Riley had to force a smile as he opened the door.

His grandfather sat in a chair by the bed, staring at the television set. There was a basketball game on, but whether he was actually watching it was debatable. Dressed in casual clothes, Ned looked normal, as if nothing was wrong with him. He'd always been a big man, taller than Riley's own six feet by another two inches. But his girth had diminished in the past few years, and now he was dangerously thin, Riley thought. Not like the man who used to chow down three hamburgers or a twenty-ounce steak at one sitting.

In fact, the man in the chair was nothing like the man who had taken him to task, made him clean up his act. His grandfather had once dragged him out of a pool hall where he'd gone to hustle money when he was fifteen. That Ned had been larger than life, an Irishman who talked loudly, gestured with every word, and knew how to tell great stories. Where had that man gone?

His body was still there, debilitated by various illnesses that came with old age, but still relatively stable. It was his mind that was off balance.

Maybe Riley would get lucky. There were times when his grandfather was coherent, when he remembered somebody or something. This could be one of those times. Damn, he was starting to sound like an optimist, a role better left to his grandmother or to Paige.

Ned's head turned as Riley entered the room, a good sign that he was alert.

"Hello, Grandpa." Riley deliberately used the title to help his grandfather remember.

"Who are you?" Ned asked, a somewhat belligerent note in his voice.

"I'm Riley, your grandson."

Ned narrowed his eyes suspiciously. "You're that guy who owes me twenty bucks. Did you come to pay up, or do you have another sob story?"

"I've come to pay up." Riley took his wallet out, removed a twenty-dollar bill, and handed it to Ned.

"What's this for?" Ned asked, already confused.

Riley shook his head and took the bill back. "You okay? You got everything you need?"

"I'm cold. It's damn cold in here. Can't get no heat. They don't turn it on for me. They're cheap."

"How about a blanket?" Riley took a blanket off the edge of the bed and put it over his grandfather's legs. "I remember when you tucked me in that first night I came back to your house. You made sure the covers were real tight."

His grandfather looked at him with bemusement, his dark eyes suddenly clearing as if a cloud had passed. "Riley?"

"It's me." He squatted down next to the chair. "How's your grandmother? I haven't seen her in a long time. Is she still mad at me?"

"She's not mad at you. How could she be? You always make her laugh."

Ned grinned at that. "She was the prettiest thing I ever did see. I remember when I met her the first tune at a dance at the YMCA. She had beautiful legs. I loved those legs."

"Do you remember Wallace Hathaway?" Riley asked, knowing he had to take the shot while he had an opening.

"Is that you, Wally?" Ned's eyes changed once again as he tilted his head and studied Riley's face. "You hate when I call you Wally, don't you? Well, I don't care. I saved your sorry butt more than once, and what did you do? You turned on me, that's what you did."

"I didn't mean to," Riley said, trying to keep the conversation going.

"It wasn't right what you did, Wally. I thought we were brothers."

"I'm sorry about what happened."

"That was a hell of a crash. I can still hear the engines screaming as we went down, the treetops splitting off as we hit 'em. Hell of a ride. We were lucky he found us."

Was he still talking about Wallace Hathaway? Riley couldn't make sense of the rambling sentences.

"Do you remember working at Hathaway's store as a security guard?"

"Damn fire ruined everything. Nan doesn't know. Can't tell her. Want to tell her but can't tell her. She'd get mad." Ned grabbed Riley's sleeve. "You don't tell her, Wally."

"I won't," Riley promised as his grandfather grew more and more agitated.

"Where's Betty?"

"Betty? I don't know a Betty."

"Who are you?" Ned asked, lost again. His gaze drifted back to the television set, and he lapsed into silence.

Riley stared at him for a long moment, feeling incredibly depressed by the sight of his grandfather, once so vital, so strong, so important to him, fading away, adrift in a mind that raced from one subject to the next. At least his grandfather didn't know that he didn't know. That was a cold comfort, but it was all Riley had to hang on to..

"Riley? I didn't know you were coming here." Nan entered the room with a vase of fresh flowers in her hands. "You should have told me. We could have driven over together."

"I didn't know until this morning."

She leaned over and kissed Ned on the cheek. "Hi, honey. I love you."

Ned pulled away from her, his gaze focused on the television. Riley saw the hurt in her eyes and wished he could take the pain away. "He asked about you. Talked about your beautiful legs."

"He did? Really?"

"Yes. He was sort of clear for a couple of minutes."

"Did you come here to ask him about the hang-up calls, about whether he was trying to call the house?" Nan asked.

"I didn't get a chance. I think the hang-up calls were someone casing the house, to see if you were home or not. The next thing we need to do is get you an unlisted number."

"If you do that, I'll start to feel invisible. It's bad enough getting old. I don't want to disappear, too."

"That could never happen."

"Did your grandpa say anything else?" Nan asked.

"I asked him about Wallace Hathaway, Paige's grandfather. When I was going through your photos, I saw a picture of Grandpa in a security uniform posing in front of Hathaway's store with Wallace Hathaway."

"I don't remember a picture like that. But I hardly ever look at those old photos."

"Grandpa must have worked at the store."

"Well, yes, he did, when we were first married. Didn't I tell you that?"

"No, you didn't."

"It was a long time ago. And he worked at so many stores in those early days; I could hardly keep track. I was too busy having a baby and making a home."

"Did you ever meet Wallace Hathaway?"

"Good heavens, no. I would have remembered that, Riley. He's quite famous in San Francisco. But your grandfather was a security guard. He didn't spend time with the Hathaways."

"Grandpa mentioned someone named Wally. Did you ever hear him talk about a Wally?"

She pondered that. "I know your grandfather flew with someone named Wally in the war. I don't think it was Wallace Hathaway, though. He talked about Wally like he was a friend. If Wallace Hathaway was Wally, I think he would have mentioned that to me at some point."

"You're right. Wally is probably somebody completely different. I doubt a Hathaway would ever let himself be called Wally."

She smiled. "How was your evening with Paige'?"

"Too short."

"I'm sorry I interrupted."

"It was probably for the best." He glanced over at his grandfather, whose eyes had drifted shut. "Looks like he's going to sleep for a while."

She nodded. "I'll just leave the flowers and hope they cheer him up."

"I'll walk you to your car."

"Good-bye, Ned," she said quietly and kissed him on the cheek once again.

Riley drew in a sharp breath of air, feeling as if he'd been punched in the stomach. The look in her eyes when she gazed at her husband just about undid him. The only real love he'd ever seen in his life had been between these two people. Even now, it was still there, at least on his grandmother's part.

"He squeezed my hand," she said, her eyes bright, drawing Riley's gaze down to their hands clasped together. "I think he knows it's me."

"I'm sure he does."

"I feel better. I can go now." She squeezed Ned's hand again. "I'll be back soon."

Riley was glad she didn't say anything as they left the room. He didn't know why he felt so choked up. He'd come here before. He'd seen how bad it was. He knew it wasn't going to get better. So why was it still getting to him?

Paige, he thought with annoyance. It was her fault. He'd been living a nice emotion-free existence up until a few days ago. She'd knocked down some of his walls, and he needed to get them back up fast. He didn't want to feel like this, like there was a pain in his heart. He didn't even want to admit he had a heart or that it could break again.

"I'm going back to clean the house," Nan said when they reached her car, parked just a few spots down from his own. "You made a good start on putting things right. I can finish the rest."

"I'll come stay with you tonight."

"No. I'm a big girl, and I have my watchdogs out in front. In fact, I told Bud he could stay on my sofa tonight instead of the car. He'll be more comfortable there, and I'll have someone right in the house."

"Someone who is seventy-four years old. I'm not sure what good he'll do inside. At least out front, he can call 911 if he sees anything."

"I trust Bud. And I'll put on the alarm so you don't have to worry. I'm sure you have better things to do than babysit your grandmother. It's Saturday. Maybe you should make a date—maybe with Paige."

"You have to call Paige by Monday or Tuesday at the latest for a weekend date."

"Somehow I think she might make an exception for you. You've got a devilish charm when you choose to use it."

"Don't go thinking there's some possibility of a longterm relationship with Paige. That won't happen."

"Why not?"

He shrugged. "Because we aren't right for each other and we are definitely not in the same financial bracket."

"So what? Money isn't everything, not if you love each other. But that isn't the real problem, is it? You don't think you know how to love. And you're afraid to trust anyone who says she loves you."

He shifted his feet, uncomfortable with the conversation. "Paige hasn't said she loves me, because she doesn't, and I sure as hell don't love her. I barely know her."

"You knew her well enough to make out with her last night. Or are you going to tell me you were just talking?"

"It's a different world, Grandma."

She laughed at that. "It's the same world, Riley, and I'm not so old I don't remember what desire feels like."

"You know, I have to go." He was not going to discuss desire with his grandmother.

"To see Paige? Give her my love, or better yet—give her yours."

Paige let herself into the mansion in Pacific Heights that had housed four generations of Hathaways. She was met almost immediately by the latest housekeeper, Alma Johnson.

"Let me take your coat, Miss Hathaway," Alma said. "Did you come to see your mother? Because she's at the hospital."

Paige handed over her coat. "Actually, I came to see my grandfather. Is he in?"

"Yes, he is."

"I'll go on up, then. Thanks." Paige made her way to the third floor with heavy feet and a reluctant heart. She told herself that her grandfather wasn't a bad guy; he was just impatient, opinionated, ruthless. Okay, maybe he was a little bit of a bad guy. He certainly didn't suffer fools, and he could definitely hold a grudge. He'd told the story a hundred times of a childhood friend who'd asked out the girl he was interested in. Wallace had never forgiven him. Their ten years of friendship had ended with that one lapse in judgment.

Which was why Paige hesitated in the hall outside his study. Talking to her grandfather about the Delaneys and the dragon or even her role at Hathaway's could be a definite lapse in judgment on her part. She wished Riley were here, but she knew she had to do this by herself. This was her family, after all.

She glanced at the portrait of her grandmother that hung on the wall near the door to her grandfather's study. It had been painted on the eve of her wedding to Wallace. Dolores Cunningham Hathaway had a beautiful smile and a serene expression on her face, as if she knew exactly what she wanted out of life. Paige wondered if her grandmother had been able to soften the sharp edges of her husband, if she had stood up to Wallace, or if he had controlled her the way he did everyone else. Unfortunately, she would never know. Her grandmother had died long before her birth, and Wallace had been single ever since. She supposed there must have been other women in his life at some point, but if there had been, he'd kept them away from the family.

Was that because he'd been so in love with her grandmother he couldn't bear to be with anyone else? Was that the kind of love he'd known? It seemed difficult to believe. He was such a hard, cold man. Maybe he'd been different then. Maybe he'd changed. The death of a wife and child would be enough to change any man.

How odd that both her father and her grandfather had lost their daughters—their first daughters.

An eerie shiver drew goose bumps along her arms. They weren't part of this curse. They didn't have the dragon, which had only just surfaced in Ned Delaney's attic. If anyone had felt the curse, it would have been Ned. But Ned Delaney and her grandfather had known each other. They'd posed for a photograph together. Was that all it had taken? Had just touching Ned Delaney's hand, the hand that had held the dragon, been enough to launch a curse? Or was all this foolishness?

Shaking her head, she pushed the disturbing thoughts to the back of her mind. She needed to concentrate on the present, not the past. Although, she might have to bring up that past in order to get to the present. Damn, she was going in a circle.

She raised her hand and rapped on her grandfather's door. A moment later, she heard his gruff, "Come in."

He stood in front of the fireplace, poised to hit a golf ball into a can of some sort. He raised a hand when she began to speak, and she waited patiently while he sank the putt.

"There," he said with satisfaction, reaching down to take out the ball. He finally looked at Paige. "What's wrong?"

Okay, so it wasn't the warmest greeting. She didn't need warmth;

she needed answers. "Nothing is wrong. I just wanted to talk to you about something."

"Did something happen at yesterday's press conference?"

"I don't know. I haven't heard anything. But that's not what—"

"You weren't there?" he interrupted with annoyance. "Why weren't you there?"

"Mother wanted to handle it, the way she always does."

"Goddammit, Paige, you're the Hathaway, not your mother. When are you going to start acting like one?"

She was taken aback by the question. "I, uh, Mother is the CFO of the company. She outranks me."

"You let her outrank you."

"Excuse me?"

He sat down on the arm of the couch, golf club still in hand. "I haven't stepped down as CEO because you're not ready to step up. Maybe you never will be. Maybe you've got more of your father in you than I thought."

"I don't understand. I can't just take over. I don't even have a title."

"You don't need a title. You're a Hathaway."

"All I've been doing is planning parties."

"And that's all you will do until you stand up for yourself."

She stared at him in bemusement. "I didn't know you wanted me to."

"You're all I've got," he said in a tone that didn't sound exactly loving or appreciative. In fact, it was almost an insult. "If your father had had a son, that would have kept our line alive, but no, he had to have girls," Wallace continued. "He couldn't even do that for me."

His words cut her to the quick. "I'm sorry we were such a disappointment."

"You don't have to be. You've been well educated, well trained. You know what to do, so do it. Prove you're worthy of being a Hathaway."

She didn't know what to say, how to react to the challenge he'd thrown down before her.

"Well, cat got your tongue? Speak up, girl."

"I came here to ask you about something else." She needed more time to think about what he'd just told her. "There's a dragon statue that my father wanted to acquire. We got it in the store on Tuesday afternoon, but it disappeared along with Dad on Wednesday."

"Do you think I'm a fool, Paige? I'm eighty-two years old, for goddamn sake, but I can figure out what's going on in my own company. Your father was an idiot for taking it out of the store. Insurance won't cover the loss." His angry brown eyes held not a hint of concern for the son he'd almost lost.

"That's true, but we can't change what happened. Right now, I'm more interested in trying to find the statue."

"How the hell will you do that? Whoever took it probably sold it the same day."

"Sold it to who? Do you have any ideas?"

"Could be thousands of people. Ask your father. He's the Chinese art expert."

"He doesn't remember what happened or why he even went to Chinatown." She watched her grandfather's face carefully, wondering if he knew about Jasmine and Alyssa, but he didn't give a thing away. "It's possible that this statue," she continued, "might have been part of a set consisting of two dragons and a box. There's a legend, a curse, the whole bit. I've been reading up on the subject."

"There are always legends, always curses. What else have you got?" He stood up and placed the golf ball back on the carpet in preparation for making another putt.

"Ned Delaney. Do you know who he is?"

"I don't think so," he said.

"He was a security guard at Hathaway's. I saw a photograph of the two of you together."

"I've taken a million photos with a million different employees."

"He was also the owner of the dragon in question. His wife, Nan Delaney, is the one who brought it to us. It seems an odd coincidence that he would have worked for us a long time ago."

"A lot of people have worked for us over the years."

"Not people who have priceless artifacts discovered in the attics of their modest homes. This is not a man who collected antiques or

Chinese art. He had nothing except this statue, and no one seems to know where it came from." She paused, debating whether or not to ask a question that had been bothering her for some time now, a question she didn't really want to put into words because it made her feel disloyal to Riley. But that was wrong. Her loyalty was to her family. She had to remember that. "Are you sure that Hathaway's never owned a statue like this a long time ago?" she finally asked.

"You think this Delaney stole the statue from us?"

"It did occur to me, yes."

He focused on his putt, sending the ball into the can. "Interesting theory."

"Unfortunately, the computer records at the store only go back ten years and the files another ten. Judging by the photo I saw, Mr. Delaney must have worked for Hathaway's in the fifties or sixties. And I don't think we still have those records anywhere, do we?"

"No. That's that, then," Wallace replied. "Anything else?"

"You're sure you don't remember the dragon statue?"

"I've bought and sold thousands of statues in my lifetime, Paige. Not many stand out in my mind."

"I guess not." She turned toward the door, but his voice stopped her.

"What happened to this Delaney guy? Is he dead?"

"No, he has Alzheimer's. He's in an assisted living place. Riley says he doesn't remember much."

"Too bad." Wallace picked up the golf ball and set it up again. She watched him measure the distance to the hole. Then he stroked the ball. It missed by a good two inches. Wallace Hathaway was nowhere near as steady as he usually was. Paige wondered why.

CHAPTER SEVENTEEN

AN HOUR LATER, Paige was still thinking about her conversation with her grandfather as she leaned over the pool table, trying to concentrate on the shot in front of her. It was nice to focus on something simple for a change. All she had to do was hit the ball into the corner pocket. She slid the cue between her fingers and took the shot. It was perfect. She stood back, admiring her handiwork.

"Not bad," Jerry said as he stepped into the back room of Fast Willy's in search of empty glasses. "But don't you think it's kind of pathetic that you're here all by yourself on a Saturday afternoon shooting pool?"

"It's not nice of you to point that out."

"How's your father?"

"He's much better, almost ready to go home. I'm incredibly relieved."

"Are you?" Jerry picked up two empty beer bottles and set them on the tray. "Then why are you shooting pool today? You usually only do that when you've got some problem on your mind that you can't figure out how to solve."

"I do not have one problem, I have many problems," she replied.

He gave her a thoughtful smile. "Any involving that guy who followed you here earlier this week?"

"That is none of your business."

"Come on, Paige. Give a little. This is your old pal Jerry you're talking to."

She let out a sigh. "I think I'm falling for him."

"Does he feel the same way?"

"Who can tell? I know he wants me, but the rest, all the emotional stuff, I don't think it's going to happen." She sighed. "But my love life or lack thereof isn't really the problem. It's my family, it's my job, it's what I want to do with the rest of my life."

"That's going to take a lot of games of pool to figure out."

"Tell me about it." She set her cue back in the rack. "What's up with you?"

"Actually, I'm thinking about moving on. I have a job offer, if you can believe it."

"Seriously?"

"Yes. I know that surprises you but I don't want to tend bar forever."

"What kind of job is it?"

"Computer programming. It's in Seattle. And I've always wanted to live in the Pacific Northwest."

She frowned. "Since when?"

"For a while," he said with a shrug.

"It rains all the time in Seattle."

"I like the rain."

She snapped her fingers. "That's not it. There's a girl there."

His freckled face flushed at her statement. "Maybe," he conceded.

"No maybe about it. Is it serious?"

"There's some of the emotional stuff, as you called it, involved."

She threw her arms around him and gave him a big hug. "I'm so happy for you."

"All right, don't get mushy."

She felt mushy. She felt like crying. She was happy for Jerry, but it seemed like everyone was moving on except her. Why was she stuck in one place?

"I need a drink," she said as she let him go.

"I'll get you one."

"Don't bother; I've got it covered," Riley said. He walked into the back room with a beer in one hand, a diet Coke in the other.

Her jaw dropped at the sight of him. "Did you follow me again?"

"Actually, I came on a hunch. Couldn't find you at home, at the hospital, or at work. Process of elimination."

"You went to all those places?" she asked, amazed at his persistence.

"I called around."

"Oh." So he hadn't tried that hard; but he had tried a little. And here he was, looking even better than he had the day before. And she wanted... she wanted a thousand things that all had to do with kissing and touching him and getting really, really close. She was still kicking herself for not making love to him when she'd had the chance. Maybe she should have thrown caution to the wind instead of playing it safe the way she always did.

"I don't think you two need me anymore," Jerry said with a laugh, since Paige seemed unable to do anything but stare at Riley. "And, Paige, I don't think you're going to need to play as much pool as you think."

"What did he mean by that?" Riley asked when they were alone.

"Nothing. What's up?"

"How's your father?" Riley asked.

"Getting better. He's coming home tomorrow. He still has no memory of what happened, though." She paused. "You don't think he's faking, do you?"

"You know him better than I do," he said, his expression carefully neutral.

Did she know her father? She used to think so. Now she wasn't nearly as sure. "I suppose if he was trying to cover up going to Jasmine's apartment, he might claim a memory loss. I'm not sure. I'll ask him about it when he gets stronger. I don't want to put too much pressure on him too soon."

"That's understandable. Why don't we sit down?" he suggested as a group of men came back to play pool. He chose a table by the window. "I think we need to talk."

"Yes," she said, joining him at the table. "I spoke to my grandfather today. I asked him if he'd met your grandfather."

"And his reply?"

"He said the name sounded familiar. Then he pointed out to me that he's eighty-two years old, and he's met a lot of people in his life. He also said that he's sold thousands of statues in his time and none stand out as the one we're looking for."

"That sounds about as productive as my conversation with my grandfather." Riley took a sip of his beer. "Although, he did ramble on about someone named Wally. I wondered if Wally was short for Wallace, but my grandmother said she didn't think so."

"I don't either," she said with a shake of her head. "I can't imagine my grandfather allowing anyone to call him *Wally*."

"My grandmother did mention that Ned worked at Hathaway's when they were first married, which would explain the photograph."

"Yes. And it might also explain where your grandfather got the statue," she said.

His gaze narrowed. "What are you talking about? You think that statue was owned by your family?"

"It's a possibility, isn't it? I mean, think about it. Where would your grandfather have gotten such a piece?"

"Just what are you accusing my grandfather of doing? Stealing from Hathaway's?" he demanded, protective fire in his eyes now.

"I didn't say that."

"Yes, you did. I knew you'd go down that road, Paige. It just came a little sooner than I thought."

"What came sooner?"

"The choice between your family and mine."

"I'm not making a choice; I'm just pointing out some things."

He jumped to his feet, obviously angry.

"Riley, wait. Don't go."

He paused at the door, his blue eyes as cold as steel when he looked at her. "Why not?"

"Because we're not done."

"I think we are. You've already decided—"

"I haven't decided anything." She got to her feet and walked over to him. "I just said what came to my mind. I'm sorry. I thought we were past the point of having to pick and choose our words. I thought we were friends."

"How could we ever be friends?" he asked, as if that would be totally impossible.

"We can be friends if we're honest with each other."

"My grandfather wouldn't have stolen a statue from your store. He wasn't that kind of man. He was honest to a fault. He set the standards of behavior for me. He taught me what was right and what was wrong."

In other words, Riley couldn't bear to believe his grandfather wasn't perfect. She understood that. Too many people had hurt this man with their actions; he couldn't afford another disappointment.

"Okay," she said evenly. "Then there must be another reason why your grandfather had the statue. Don't make me the enemy, Riley, because I'm not. I'm your partner. Now, what do you say to starting this conversation over?"

He hesitated, then let out a long sigh. "Fine."

"You can finish your beer. I'll drink my diet Coke. And we'll both take a deep breath."

Riley sat back down at the table and picked up his beer. "I'm sorry if I jumped on you, but my grandfather was a good man, Paige. He ran into a lot of prejudice when he was young. He used to tell me that when he was a teenager, the Irish in San Francisco were considered second-class citizens, thieves and robbers. It made him very determined to live the kind of life he could be proud of. I won't let his reputation be smeared at this late date."

"I understand. And I was just talking off the top of my head. From here on out, let's try not to point any fingers unless we have hard proof. Deal?"

"Deal." Riley ran his finger around the edge of his glass beer mug.

"What was your grandfather like before he got sick?" she asked curiously.

"Typical Irishman. He liked his drink, his food, his wife, his stories. He wasn't wild, though. He had all these rules for himself."

"Like what?"

"Like no more than two drinks before dinner. No dancing with anyone other than his wife. No stories that made fun of women. No laughing in church." He smiled to himself as if he were lost in a fond memory. "That was a tough one, though. Father O'Brien used to fall asleep during the readings and snored so loud he could have woken the dead. My grandfather and I could barely get through those moments without a laugh." Riley took another drink. "For the most part his rules worked for him. He said they kept him out of trouble."

"He sounds like a good man."

"He is—or he was. He's not the same now. I must admit I've wondered where he got that statue, but if anyone stole it from some-where, it was my mother, not my grandfather."

"Or maybe it wasn't stolen at all," she said soothingly. "We really don't know. It is odd though, isn't it—this connection between us, between our grandfathers."

"So, did your grandfather have anything else of importance to say?"

"Not about the statue. We did talk about my position at Hath-away's. He shocked the hell out of me by telling me that I can take control at any time. I just have to stand up and do it. I'm not quite sure how that's supposed to happen since I have no title, no real power."

"Do you want to take control of the store?"

"I think so," she said slowly. "I've been raised to believe it's my destiny. Everything I've done has been to that end. I've never worked anywhere else. Every summer since I was fifteen, I've been at the store, filling out sales slips, working the floor, tracking inventory. But now all I do is plan events or host tea parties for clients whose art objects we wish to acquire."

"So do what your grandfather said, take charge."

"And what do you think my mother will do, roll over and get out of the way?"

"You need to be as smart and ruthless as she is."

She sent him a doubtful look. "I'm not sure I have it in me."

"And that's the problem," he said with a knowing nod. "You have to believe in yourself before anyone else will."

"I'm trying."

"I have an idea," he said after a moment. "Are you free for a few hours?"

"Why? What do you have in mind?"

"Just answer the question."

"I guess. My father is resting. My mother has hired a private detective to look for the dragon. Alyssa has not returned my calls. And I'm not accomplishing anything here, so sure, I'm free."

"Good. I know just the thing for you. Come with me." He stood up, holding out his hand. She hesitated as anticipation raised the hairs on the back of her neck.

"Where are we going?"

"To my apartment."

His eyes dared her to say no, but she couldn't. There were a lot of things she wanted to do at his apartment, and they all involved saying yes.

"Bike riding?" Paige asked in surprise as they stood in the center of his small garage a few minutes later. "You want me to ride this bike somewhere?" She looked down at the mountain bike he'd pushed over to her.

Riley laughed at her look of dismay. "It's a good bike. There are fifteen speeds."

"I don't ride bikes that actually move."

"Then you've been missing out. This is a great city we live in. You should be out in it."

"I was just out in it—in your warm, comfortable car. Besides, it's cloudy. It might even rain."

"And your point is? Come on, live a little. You might like it."

He walked his own bike out of the garage, pleased when she slowly followed. He handed her his extra helmet. His bike riding passion had grown so much over the years that he was always replacing his equipment with newer and better, which meant he had extras to share.

"Are we planning on crashing?" she asked.

"No, but Hathaways aren't the only ones who are prepared for every possibility. You need to wear the helmet."

"There's so much traffic in the city. Why don't we drive to a park and start there? Golden Gate Park is really nice."

"It's too flat." He adjusted his helmet and watched as she reluctantly put hers on.

"This isn't really my color," she said, referring to the bright orange helmet now covering her blond hair.

"But the cars will be able to see you." He was actually surprised she was such a good sport. Most debutantes probably would have bailed on him by now. He handed her a clip for her pant leg. "Put this on. It will keep your pants out of the chain area."

"You are prepared for everything." She clipped her pant legs and straddled the bike. "You couldn't have had a girl's bike, could you?"

"I think you can handle it."

"Okay, I'm ready, but I haven't ridden an actual bike since I was a kid, and I only did that about three times."

"You'll be fine. Just follow me, and yell if you have a problem." He got on his bike and began to pedal slowly down the street.

"Riley," she yelled.

He stopped immediately, turning his head in anticipation of seeing her sprawled on the ground, but she was still standing where he had left her. "What?" he asked with annoyance.

"Just testing to see if you'd really stop."

"Get on the bike, Paige."

"Okay, okay." She perched gingerly on the seat and began to pedal so slowly the bike was in serious danger of falling over.

"Faster," he encouraged. "It will be easier."

"So you say," she grumbled, increasing her speed until she passed by him.

He headed after her, pleased to see her gaining confidence as they moved down the block. The beginning of their ride was flat. He took her along the Embarcadero, past the magnificent Bay Bridge that connected San Francisco to Oakland, the ferry buildings where the cruise ships docked, and the downtown Financial District that edged North Beach and Fisherman's Wharf, closer to the hills he wanted to tackle today.

He motioned for her to follow as he cut across the Embarcadero toward a residential area. The hills of San Francisco called to him like a beacon in the night. But Paige's voice yanked him back. He stopped his bike and looked over his shoulder at her. "What's the problem now?"

"We're not riding up that hill, are we?" she asked in disbelief.

"Sure we are."

She shook her head. "It's too steep. I'll never make it."

It wasn't nearly as steep as the next one, but he wasn't about to tell her that. "I thought you wanted to find out what you were made of."

"By riding a bicycle up a hill?"

"It's a test of your strength, courage, stamina, stubbornness. You can do it."

"I don't think so."

He saw the uncertainty in her pretty brown eyes and knew that she needed to do this for herself. "You're stronger than you think, Paige."

"This isn't going to prove anything."

"Try it and see."

"I don't like to fail."

He smiled. "So don't fail." He sent her an encouraging look. "It's not a test if it's too easy."

"Who said I wanted to take a test?"

"Fine. I'm going up this hill with or without you. Your choice."

"That's not very gentlemanly."

He laughed. "I thought you'd figured out by now that I am not a gentleman."

"You're not a very good date, either. I can think of a lot of other things that would be more fun than this."

"You haven't even tried it yet. And this isn't a date." He turned his head toward the hill in front of them. He drew in a deep breath and counted to ten. Then he got on his bike and pedaled hard, wanting to get as much speed as possible for the ascent. He heard Paige muttering to herself and saw from the corner of his eye that she was on the bike and riding after him.

So far so good. He just hoped she really could make it up the hill. Maybe she was too pampered, too spoiled, too weak for such a challenge, and maybe he was a fool, wanting to believe she was someone she wasn't.

Paige knew she'd passed the insanity mark when her legs began to burn and her chest tightened with each breath. She was only halfway up the hill; there was no way she would make it. She wasn't in shape for this. She should have trained, prepared, worked up to it. But wasn't that what she'd spent the last thirteen years doing at Hathaway's: training, preparing, but never actually doing? At least here she was being aggressive, taking a chance.

But it hurt.

And damn Riley. He was already at the top, off his bike, watching her, waiting for her. He shouted words of encouragement.

If he believed in her, maybe she needed to believe in herself. So she told herself to focus, keep pedaling, and don't even think about quitting.

"Come on, Paige. A few more feet," Riley yelled.

The last part was very steep. She really didn't think she could do it. Her eyes were glazing over from sweat or terror or exhaustion, she didn't know which. The road was wavy, the bike was wobbling, her hands were beginning to cramp from her grip on the handlebars.

"You're almost there, Paige. Bring it home!"

Her heart pounded against her chest as she forced her feet down again and again and again, until she hit the top and the ground flattened.

"Keep riding, Paige, take a circle around the intersection," Riley said.

She wanted to get off the bike the way he'd done, but she needed to bring her heart rate down to a safer level. She knew that much from her cardio classes at the gym. So she took a wide circle around the quiet intersection, finally returning to his side, her breath still ragged but her heart slowing to a more reasonable beat.

His smile was her reward. It was big and broad and totally amazed. She couldn't help smiling back. And when he tossed his bike on the ground and held out his arms to her, she slid off her bike and ran to him.

She threw her arms around his neck. "I did it," she said with more joy than she could ever remember feeling.

He hugged her tight and hard, as if he didn't want to let her go. They were both hot and sweaty, their helmets clanking as Riley swooped in to kiss her mouth. He tasted so good, better than the last time—better than any time. He tasted like success, freedom, wonder, and all the emotions that seemed so often out of reach for her. But he'd made her feel them.

He pulled back and undid her helmet, taking it off of her head. "You're awesome."

"I'm a mess." She put a hand to her hair, which was loose and tangled, then laughed. "But I don't care."

"Neither do I." He took off his own helmet and tossed them both to the ground. "Now, let's do this right."

She met him more than halfway, as eager for the kiss as he was. She wrapped her arms around his waist, pressed her breasts against his chest, and let her tongue sweep the inside of his mouth with a demanding need she hadn't thought herself capable of. Today was a day for firsts.

A honking horn broke them apart as a car maneuvered around them and headed up the next hill.

Paige knew she should have felt embarrassed, ashamed by her behavior on a public street no less, but there was laughter bubbling up from deep down inside. And she couldn't stop it from bursting out, especially when Riley was already laughing.

"Stop," she said, getting a side ache. She turned away from him. "If I look at you, I'm going to keep laughing."

"It's good for you."

She turned back around. "You're good for me." His laughter stopped. His expression changed like a cloud over the sun. "Paige—"

"Don't say anything." She held up her hand. "This is a great moment. Let's just leave it at that."

"I knew you could make it up that hill."

"You had more faith in me than I did. You've done this before, haven't you?"

"A few times."

"Like every day?"

"Three or four times a week," he admitted. "But not just this hill. There are always higher hills to climb, especially in this city."

She wondered what the hills really stood for. She doubted he would tell her even if she asked. Instead, she looked down the hill from where they had come. "I did pretty good."

"You did. Ready for the next one?"

"No way."

"You said that before."

"Maybe next time."

He studied her thoughtfully, then nodded. "Maybe next time. Ready for the best part?"

"Going down?"

"Absolutely. You earned it. Now enjoy it."

She put her helmet back on and picked up her bike. She had a momentary fear of the steepness of the downhill ride, but she pushed it away. Today was not a day for holding back but for going forward.

She sailed down the hill, the wind in her face bringing tears to her eyes—at least that's what she wanted to blame the emotion on. She knew she was lying to herself. It wasn't the wind making her cry; it was the feeling that she'd finally broken through. And the odd thing was she hadn't even realized she was holding back until now.

"How was that?" Riley asked her as he joined her at the bottom.

"It was good, but it wasn't the best part," she admitted. "The best part were those last few feet at the top of the hill."

His eyes burned bright at her reply, and they exchanged a long look of complete and total understanding.

"Was it that way for you, too?" she asked.

"It usually is," he admitted. "But today the best part was when I was kissing you, and you were kissing me back."

She smiled at him. "I hate to break this to you, Riley, but you could have had that kiss an hour ago when we were standing in your garage."

He laughed. "Now you tell me."

"I'll race you back to your apartment."

"Feeling cocky, are you?"

"Absolutely. And I like it!" She hopped on the bike and began riding back the way they had come. It didn't matter if she beat Riley or not. She'd already won the biggest battle of the day, the one going on inside herself.

CHAPTER EIGHTEEN

ALYSSA JOGGED up the stairs to her mother's apartment Saturday afternoon and knocked on the door. As she waited, she found herself foolishly smiling, which was pretty much what she'd been doing since she'd left Ben's apartment the night before. She'd had a good time with him, better than she'd expected. In fact, he'd reminded her of what she'd liked in him before, his intelligence, his dry sense of humor, his ability to see into her head, to make her take life less seriously.

If only he weren't Chinese, or, at the very least, if only he didn't live in Chinatown and wasn't so closely tied to this neighborhood, maybe then she could consider him as someone she could date. But... she glanced over her shoulder, realizing how close he lived to this building, only three short blocks away. It wasn't nearly far enough.

Her mother finally opened the door and beckoned for her to come in. "Are you all right?" Jasmine asked, her gaze traveling up and down Alyssa's body, as if she were checking for bruises or broken bones.

"I'm fine. Why wouldn't I be?"

"I've been calling you since yesterday. Why didn't you call me back?"

"I didn't get a chance," Alyssa said, knowing that she'd had plenty of chances, but she'd been battling herself over how much she wanted to get involved with the missing dragon, her mother, and her newly discovered father. "What's wrong?" she asked, seeing the deep worry lines stretching across her mother's forehead. "Why are you so upset?"

"You shouldn't have spoken to your grandfather about the dragon."

"Oh. Well, I ran into him in the square. I was going to talk to Grandmother, but I couldn't find her. She wasn't at the shop."

"She came to see me."

"She came here?" Alyssa echoed in amazement. "What did she say? What did she want?"

Instead of answering her, Jasmine walked over to the nearby easel and stared at the still-wet painting. She was stalling, Alyssa thought, wondering why. She also noticed that her mother had once again painted the dragon, and this one was more distinct, the details sharp and clear where before they had always been hazy.

"You can't stop painting it, can you?" she asked.

"I try, but whatever object I start to paint always turns into this."

"What did Grandmother want?"

"She told me that I had seen the dragon at a museum in Taiwan, that I had tried to touch it, and the alarms went off, frightening me. That's why I have such bad dreams about it."

Alyssa considered the explanation. It was so simple, so easy. "Why didn't she tell you that before? When I asked Grandfather, he said you had never seen a dragon like the one you dream about."

Her mother looked as confused as she felt. "I don't know, Alyssa."

"They're not telling us the truth, are they?"

"We should not speak ill of our elders. It is wrong, disrespectful. We must honor them."

Alyssa had heard those words a thousand times, but she had always had a difficult time equating her grandparents' behavior with honor.

"My mother reminded me that the story of the dragons includes a curse on all first daughters," Jasmine continued. "Because I touched the dragon the other day, I may have brought the curse down upon you, Alyssa. I am worried about you."

Her mother's words rocked her back on her heels. She'd never thought about the curse in terms of herself. Did she even believe in curses? Wasn't that just more superstitious foolishness?

"I'm not worried," she said, trying to ignore the unease sweeping through her body.

"You should not taunt fate."

"Ben already told me about the curse, but we don't even know if the dragon you saw is part of that story, that set."

"You went to see Ben?" her mother asked in astonishment. "Why? Why would you do that? You don't care about the dragon or Ben."

"I care about you. I care about the fact that the dragon is missing, and you might have been the last person to see it before Mr. Hathaway was attacked just a few blocks from here." She couldn't quite bring herself to call him her father. It still didn't seem real.

"I didn't hurt David."

"Of course not. But he's a rich man, and his family has connections. If they need someone to blame, who better than you?"

"You don't have to worry about me."

"I'm afraid that's not possible. I love you. You're my mother."

Tears came to Jasmine's eyes. "I brought you into a world of shame."

"You brought me into a world of opportunity. And I thank God that you did. I can be whoever I want to be."

"I know it hasn't been easy for you."

"You were the one who had it the worst," Alyssa said generously, even though she still couldn't quite forgive her mother for withholding the name of her father for so many years.

"What about David?"

"What about him? He obviously didn't want to know me. If he did, he would have asked you about me. He would have wanted to see me."

"It is much more complicated than that," Jasmine replied with a helpless wave of her hand. "He did ask at times. I refused. I had my reasons. I didn't want you to be confused any more than you already were."

"That I don't understand, but it was your choice."

"Yes, perhaps it was wrong. I don't know anymore, but he is awake now."

"He is?" she asked, her body tightening.

"It was on the news last night."

"Well, that's good, I guess. He can clear you if the police come back." Alyssa paused, not sure she was ready to ask the question in her head, but it came out before she could stop it. "How did you two meet? How did a humble Chinese girl from Chinatown meet a rich, handsome man like David Hathaway?"

"It is a long story."

Alyssa sat down on the couch. "Tell me."

Jasmine stood in the center of the room, looking decidedly uncomfortable, but finally she began to speak. "I met him at a party at his home. I was working as a waitress for a caterer, and the Hathaways had ordered a special Chinese feast in honor of David's birthday." She paused. "He was very sad that night. His daughter had died only a few weeks earlier."

"His daughter?" Alyssa asked in shock. "I thought Paige was an only child."

"No, there was an older girl. Her name was Elizabeth. David left the feast as soon as possible. I was on the terrace collecting glasses. He started talking to me. I think for some reason I was the only one in the house that night that he could talk to. He said they were all pretending —his wife, his father, his friends. They were acting as if life was normal, but he didn't think it would ever be normal again." She took a breath, collecting her memories. "I don't know how it happened. One minute we were talking, and the next minute we were kissing. It was wrong. He was married. But there was something between us, a connection. I felt as if we belonged together, as if this was meant to be for some reason."

Her mother made it sound romantic and lovely, but the consequences of that night had been anything but. Her own existence was a testament to that fact.

"I fell in love with him at first sight," Jasmine continued. "I've loved him ever since."

"But he never really loved you, did he?" she asked sharply.

"I suppose not," her mother admitted, her voice edged with pain.

"And he never loved me, either." Alyssa made it a statement, not a question.

"He couldn't. He thought loving you would be a betrayal of his love for his daughter Elizabeth. He had come to me out of grief. When I became pregnant; when I had a daughter, he didn't know how to react. For him to care about you seemed wrong."

"Were you together after I was born?"

Jasmine cleared her throat somewhat awkwardly. "A few times in the early years, usually around Elizabeth's birthday. I thought that's why he had come this past week to see me. Her birthday is on Wednesday. I was surprised when the reason for his visit was the dragon."

Alyssa nodded, her mind reeling with the information she had just received. "So you and my father met by chance at a party. It seems like such a coincidence."

"What do you mean?"

"When I was at Ben's apartment, I saw a photo of my two grandfathers. Wallace Hathaway was shaking Grandfather's hand at a New Year's celebration a long time ago. Don't you think it's odd that they knew each other?"

"It's not odd at all. When my father first came to San Francisco, he worked at the House of Hathaway."

"He did?" Alyssa asked in amazement, wondering when she would stop being surprised.

"Yes, but it was only for a short time. It was a long time ago, before he and your grandmother started the herb shop. I used to wish when I was a little girl that he worked at Hathaway's still, so he could take me inside. At Christmas when we'd walk by the store, I thought it was so beautiful, all the lights, the glass, the fancy people. My mother would never let me go inside. She said it was not the place for a poor girl from Chinatown."

Alyssa heard the wistfulness in her mother's voice and wondered if that was when the love was born. Had her mother coveted something Hathaway from the time she was a little girl? Was that why she had an affair with a married man twenty-something years later? "Do my grandparents know that David Hathaway is my father?" she asked.

"No, they don't," Jasmine said immediately.

"Are you sure about that?"

"Yes, absolutely. I told no one."

"Did my father tell anyone?"

"No, he kept it a secret. He couldn't bear for his family to know what he had done."

She could certainly believe that. "Well, they know now."

"We can't cause them any trouble, Alyssa. I have always promised David that I would not hurt his family."

"I'm his family, too," she reminded her mother. "In fact, I just realized something. I'm a Hathaway. And I should own a piece of that fancy store that a poor girl from Chinatown didn't belong in."

"Alyssa, no. You can't upset things."

She was tempted, very tempted. She could make big trouble for David Hathaway and his family. She could sue him for paternal support, for a stake in Hathaway's and the rest of the family investments. She could win enough money to support her mother in the fashion she deserved for the rest of her life. Even if she didn't win a lawsuit, she could sell their story to the tabloids for a fortune, as Paige had suggested. The Hathaway's deserved everything they got.

Well, maybe not all the Hathaways, maybe not Paige. She seemed nice, friendly. Of course, Paige had also reminded Alyssa that her mother could be in a heap of trouble if the stolen dragon was linked back to her. Maybe Paige had only been looking out for her own interests. Maybe that was the Hathaway gene she had truly inherited, the one that was telling her now to look out for herself and her mother and not to worry about anyone else.

"I love him. I love you," Jasmine said, interrupting her plan of attack. "Alyssa, listen to me—I don't want you to fight with David or his family. I couldn't bear it. I committed the sin. If you must punish him, you must punish me."

"You've already been punished enough," Alyssa said.

"And so have you. I want you to have your life, Alyssa, the life you want, wherever you want to live it. I don't want it to be a life based on pain and anger. You have told me many times that you know what you want, and you know how to get it. So get it. Don't do it by hurting the Hathaways. I already did that, more than you can ever understand."

Paige didn't understand how Riley could change gears so quickly. Since they'd returned to his apartment from their ride an hour earlier, he'd parked himself in front of the computer, pounding the keyboard in search of more information on the dragon. He seemed to have forgotten all about her, about their kiss, about the fact that if they'd wanted to continue that kiss in the privacy of his apartment, they could have done just that. Obviously, he'd had second thoughts. But why?

She felt annoyed, restless, wanting answers to questions she didn't have the courage to ask, so she did what he was doing, turned her attention to the mystery surrounding them.

"Have you found anything?" she asked.

Riley didn't answer her. She wasn't even sure he'd heard the question. That was the thing with him. He gave one hundred percent to every task, whether it be attacking a monster hill on a mountain bike or researching an ancient artifact. She liked that about him. She liked a lot of things about him. More important, she liked the way she was when she was with him.

Sitting down on his couch, she stretched out her legs, feeling a delicious ache of weariness. Defeating that hill had given her a sense of confidence and self-worth that she hadn't felt in a long time. She remembered the feeling from when she was at college and she'd spent two years on the crew team. Rowing had also made her feel as if she was using her body, her muscles, her mind, accomplishing something. She'd been drifting the past few years, going from one mundane task to the next. She'd lost her focus, her purpose. She'd just been waiting, counting minutes, passing time until the magic moment when she would assume her intended role at Hathaway's.

She realized now that taking over Hathaway's would not happen by chance, that she would have to make it happen. She couldn't keep moaning about unimportant duties; she needed to find her own work, her own role at the store. Maybe it wouldn't be as CEO or CFO, since those jobs were already taken, but surely there was something she could do to leave her mark on the company. She just had to find it and then do it—tomorrow or the next day. She didn't have to find herself a job right this second. In fact, she could think of lots of other things she could be doing right now, including finishing that kiss she'd started with Riley in the middle of an intersection in San Francisco.

She was tempted to get him out of his chair and into the messed-up bed she could see through the half-open door to his bedroom. Sheets and blankets were tossed in abandon, making her want to jump into the middle of them and roll around with Riley. A shot of heat swept through her body at the thought. She couldn't do what she was thinking, could she?

She had to get a grip. Sex with Riley would only complicate things. They'd never work out as a couple. *Would they?*

Even if they could get past the differences in the way they'd grown up, what about the way they lived now? She might rail against Hathaway standards, but there was no denying the fact that she liked some of the culture she'd grown up with—the ballet, the symphony, the art museums. And she wanted commitment, a husband, children, the happily-ever-after she'd read about in so many books.

Did Riley want any of that? He loved his grandparents, but he couldn't seem to let himself get close to anyone else. She knew his mother had hurt him deeply. Too deeply for him to be able to trust, to love another woman?

"Paige. Yoo-hoo, Paige."

She started, realizing the object of her thoughts was now staring at her. "What?"

"I've been talking to you for three minutes."

"That's funny. I asked you a question awhile ago, and you didn't even answer."

"I found something," he said, ignoring her comment.

"About the dragon?"

"About my grandfather."

She looked at the screen. "Where are you?"

"Social Security. My grandfather worked at Hathaway's from 1946 to 1952, when the store burned to the ground."

"That makes sense, because the store was closed down while it was rebuilt. I'm sure a lot of employees were let go."

"I'm sure they were." He closed one screen and went to the next. He brought up an old newspaper article. "Did you know that the fire occurred during the Chinese New Year's Parade?"

Another bell went off in her head. "I remember hearing that. They thought it might have been started by some errant fireworks."

"Actually, the article claims there were traces of gasoline in the basement and suspicion of arson."

"Really? I never heard that, but it happened a long time before I was born."

"Do you know who was the first man on the scene?"

"Your grandfather?" she ventured.

"Guess again."

"My grandfather?"

"You've got one more choice."

She frowned. "I don't see what it is."

"Lee Chen."

"Lee Chen?" she echoed, seeing the excited light in Riley's eyes.

"Alyssa's grandfather," he said. "We're connected, Paige, all three of us. It says in the article that Lee Chen, an employee at the store, was the first one on the scene. He tried to put the fire out but it was too hot, and he suffered burns on his hands before he was pulled out of the store."

"What a strange coincidence," she said, still trying to make sense of all the connections.

"Is it a coincidence? What do you bet that Lee Chen was never rehired after the fire?"

"Why wouldn't he have been—if he tried to save the store?"

"Did he try to save it? Or did he start the fire? The first one on the scene could have also been the person who started it."

"That's quite a leap. You got angry at me for making that same jump to your grandfather. We should be careful who we accuse."

"Agreed. But at least we're narrowing down the suspects."

"The suspects to what, Riley? Are we trying to figure out who set fire to the store fifty years ago? Or are we trying to figure out what happened to a dragon that disappeared last week?"

"That depends on whether that dragon ties the two events together."

"Which would take us back to the idea that the dragon might have been owned by the store at one point. You didn't like that scenario, remember?"

He tipped his head. "I still don't think my grandfather stole it. But I'm willing to keep an open mind on where it's been in the last hundred years."

"That's big of you."

"I also think that the fact that these three men knew each other at one point is somehow very important. They all worked at Hathaway's in some capacity."

"I agree," Paige said. "Maybe Alyssa or Jasmine could tell us about Lee."

Paige's cell phone rang as she finished speaking, and Paige had the eerie sensation that someone had been reading her mind. Her suspicion was confirmed when Alyssa's voice came over the phone.

"Alyssa," she said. "Riley and I were just talking about you. We found an odd connection between not just you and me, but Riley, too. Your grandfather's name is Lee Chen, right?" It suddenly occurred to her that Lee Chen was a fairly common name.

"Yes," Alyssa said. "Why do you ask?"

"We discovered that he worked at Hathaway's a long time ago."

"I just learned that as well."

"Riley's grandfather worked there, too. And, of course, my grandfather. They must have all known one another. I don't know what it means. It could be a small world, a really big coincidence, or a great lead. That doesn't narrow it down much, does it?"

"No, but perhaps we can narrow it down further," Alyssa said. "I spoke to Benjamin Fong again. He says his uncle has some information for us about the dragon. I'm meeting them in a half hour—that's why I'm calling."

She was thrilled that Alyssa had thought to let her know. "I'd love to come with you. Riley would, too."

Alyssa hesitated. "I've been thinking about everything. I don't completely trust you, Paige. You might be trying to frame my mother for some sort of theft."

Paige's heart sank. Another distrusting soul. She seemed to be surrounded by them. She looked at Riley and caught him watching her with a thoughtful expression on his face. He didn't completely trust her, either. She would just have to prove herself to both of them. "I don't want to hurt your mother in any way," she said firmly, returning her attention to the phone call. "What's between my father and your mother is separate from all this. I want to know who attacked my father, and you want to protect your mother. We're on the same side. And we want to make sure no one else gets hurt. The only way we can do that is to find out what happened to the dragon, if we can."

"All right. Meet me at 3712 Stockton Street, Jimmy Lee's martial arts studio."

Paige ended the call and explained the situation to Riley. "We can go if we want," she told him.

"Of course we're going."

"You're loving this, aren't you?" She could see the sparkle in his eyes, hear the energy in his voice.

"I've always liked a puzzle, and this one is finally starting to come together." He stretched his arms up over his head, then got to his feet. "So, thirty minutes, huh?"

"Yes." She stiffened as Riley took a predatory step in her direction. "What are you doing?"

"I'm walking over to you."

"I can see that, but why are you—Oh," she gasped as his mouth pressed against hers in a crushing, passionate kiss. "You're never going to ask me first, are you?" she muttered when he let her catch her breath.

"Are you complaining?"

"Yes, I'm complaining. I've been here for almost an hour, and this is the first move you've made."

He laughed. "You never say what I think you're going to say." He swooped in and stole another kiss.

"We only have thirty minutes," she reminded him.

"There are a lot of things we can do in that amount of time, princess," he said, a husky note in his voice.

"Like what?" she asked breathlessly.

"Use your imagination."

David felt himself sliding into sleep. The familiar dream welcomed him home.

He was walking through the long dark alley, hearing footsteps coming closer. There were eyes following him, watching him, or maybe it was the dragon's eyes. They glowed in the night, two jade points of light from thousands of years ago. Jasmine's dragon. He had to get back to her. She was the only one who understood. Why couldn't he get to her? Why didn't the alley end? Was it always this long, this narrow? He heard voices hushed, then growing louder, one especially cold and shrill—Victoria? She stepped in front of him, and something flashed in her hand. A knife? A gun?

"I know what you did, David. You betrayed me. You ruined our name. You hurt your daughter. You must pay."

The gun was pointed straight at his heart. It exploded. He jerked, feeling the shock, the pain, the knowledge that he had really screwed up this time.

"Mr. Hathaway. Mr. Hathaway?"

He blinked as a bright light blinded him. Was this it? The light that would lead him straight to heaven? No, he probably wasn't headed there. Not after the way he'd lived.

"Mr. Hathaway. Wake up. You're dreaming." The hand on his shoulder was firm.

He opened his eyes, looking into the concerned face of the nurse who'd been hired by Victoria to babysit him

"Are you all right?" she asked him. "You screamed bloody murder a minute ago."

"I'm fine." He put a hand on his chest, feeling as if Victoria really had shot him. But there was no bullet hole, no blood, no pain. It was just a nightmare. She didn't know. She couldn't know. He'd never said a word, and Jasmine certainly wouldn't have told her.

Jasmine. She'd been on his mind since he'd woken up. She must have heard the news of his attack. She was probably worried.

"Can I get you anything, Mr. Hathaway?" the nurse asked.

"Yes," he said huskily. "Could you get me a soda from the cafeteria downstairs?"

"There's water right here."

"I'm tired of water. I want a Coke." And he wanted her to leave him alone for a few minutes so he could call Jasmine. Maybe Jasmine could tell him why he'd gone to Chinatown. He didn't know why he couldn't remember anything since Christmas, which according to Paige was a month earlier. Why had his brain cut off the last few weeks? What was his mind hiding?

"All right. I'll get it for you. Shall I have the security guard stand inside the door?"

"No, you shall not," he said grumpily. "I'm fine. Go. And take your time."

She did as he asked, and he was blessedly alone. Thank goodness. He wasn't used to having anyone around twenty-four hours a day, and even though it hadn't been that long, he was already tired of the constant attendance of nurses. He wanted to go home, to his own room, where he could sort things out.

Reaching for the phone, he dialed Jasmine's number, hoping she was home. She always told him not to call or come by, but he needed to talk to her.

The phone rang three times, then her voice came over the line. "Hello?"

"It's me," he said, relieved that she was there.

"David?" she asked in wonder. "Are you all right?"

"They told me I was assaulted in an alley near your apartment, that I was in a coma for a few days."

"You don't remember?"

"I wish I could." Silence followed his words. "Why did I come to see you?"

"You showed me the dragon."

"The dragon I bought for Elizabeth's birthday?"

"No, David, it was the dragon from my dreams. Someone brought it to your store to have it appraised. You showed it to me. I held it in my hands." Her voice wavered. "I believe now that it was part of that set, the one we read about, the one with the curse on first daughters. And I touched it. I released the curse on my own daughter, on our child."

His brain was still too foggy to follow her reasoning. He knew about the dragon, of course. It was important to Jasmine. "Are you sure the dragon was the same one?"

"Exactly the same. You saw it, too, David. I am so afraid of what will happen next. First, you are almost killed. Now I worry about Alyssa, and what the curse will do to her. You must remember, David. You must remember where you went when you left me. You didn't go back to the store. If you had found the dragon, where would you have gone?"

"I don't know," he said slowly. "I wish I did." He strained to remember, but the effect only brought a throbbing pain to his head.

"There is something else. I told Alyssa that you're her father."

"Why? Why would you do that?" he asked, shocked to the core. They had kept the secret for so many years. It was difficult to believe it was out.

"Your daughter found out about Alyssa."

"Paige? That's not possible."

"It's the truth. I don't know how she did, but she did. I couldn't let Alyssa be blindsided. I had to tell her first."

Paige knew about Alyssa and Jasmine? His heart sank to the bottom of his toes. She must hate him. She hadn't said anything yet, probably because he'd been so badly hurt. But when things were back to normal, she would remember that he'd betrayed her and her mother. And she wouldn't understand. He couldn't bear it if Paige turned on him. She was the only daughter he had. Except Alyssa, of course, but he didn't know her. She didn't know him. It was a choice he'd made a long time ago. There was no turning back now. Unless...

"Does Alyssa want to see me?"

"She isn't sure. But you know she will not make trouble for you, and neither will I."

No, the trouble would come from Victoria. No doubt about that.

"I have to go," he said, hearing the nurse outside his room. "I'll call you when I get home." He hung up the phone, almost wishing he could return to the unconscious state he had just left. His daughter and most likely his wife knew about his mistress and his illegitimate child. Maybe he would have been better off dead. The thought sent a shiver down his spine.

Someone had wanted him dead.

Who? Did he know? Was that why he couldn't remember? Maybe he didn't want to remember. Maybe he didn't want to know who had attacked him.

Or worse, maybe the person who had attacked him was someone he knew. He wasn't the only one with secrets.

CHAPTER NINETEEN

"You're awfully quiet," Paige said as Riley drove them across town.

"Just thinking about everything."

"It makes my mind spin. There seem to be so many secrets."

"Yeah," he said. But he wasn't thinking about secrets; he was thinking about Paige, about the kisses they'd shared before she'd reminded him that they had to leave, that they didn't have time to take those kisses into the bedroom, which was the only place at that moment he wanted to go.

He needed to stop kissing her, stop torturing himself with possibilities that could never be. Paige was a long-term girl; he was a short-term guy. He could have women in his life without making a commitment. In fact, he'd probably get more sex if he stayed single; at least that's what most of his married friends told him.

If Paige wanted a fling, he was her man, but anything longer, forget about it. He didn't carry the commitment gene. He knew that without a doubt. Neither his mother nor his father had been able to handle a relationship or a family. Although... his grandparents had had a good marriage.

Sure, they'd fought over the years. He'd heard them yelling at each other and driving each other crazy about not filling up the car with' gas or forgetting to buy toilet paper. But they'd also hugged and kissed and laughed together. They'd been best friends as well as lovers. They'd had a special connection, something rare, something most people didn't have. What was the likelihood of him finding such a connection? A million to one.

And the truth was—he didn't have the stomach for those odds. He didn't want to put his heart on the line, make himself vulnerable. He'd lived his childhood like that. The pain was still with him years later. He'd loved his mother and she'd abandoned him. She'd lied so many times, broken so many promises. He sighed, wondering why the memories were coming back now. It was because of Paige. She was breaching the emotional wall he'd built. He would have to be careful, or she'd sneak in when he least expected it. And he couldn't let that happen.

It would all be over soon. They might not find the dragon, but he was confident they would get closer to the truth. The pieces were falling into place. He just had to concentrate on the task at hand and forget about the woman sitting next to him. If only she didn't smell so good. Did she wash her hair with perfume? The scent of sweet wild-flowers seemed to fill the car. He pushed the automatic button for the window to let the breeze in, anything to break the intimacy growing between them.

Paige shot him a curious look. "Are you all right?"

"Fine," he said gruffly.

"You're not acting fine. You seem tense. You're angry because we didn't get to finish what we started."

"We were finished," he said shortly.

"Really? I wasn't."

"Well, you don't get everything you want, Paige. I know that's probably a foreign concept for you, but it's the truth. Some things, some people you just can't have, and it doesn't matter what your last name is."

She sent him a curious look. "Jeez, what brought that on?"

He shrugged. "It's just the way it is."

"Are you under the impression that I think I can get anything or anyone I want? Because believe me, that's not the case. In fact, very few people in my life ever do what I want them to do. I've often thought I have absolutely no impact on anyone's choices."

"That's not true."

"Oh, it's true. For example, my mother let me get a cat when I was a little girl. She thought it would keep me company after my sister died. It was a small black-and-white kitten and I adored it, but it refused to sleep on my bed. When I tried to pick it up, it hissed at me."

"You should have gotten a dog."

"The point is I couldn't even make my own cat do what I wanted it to do." She shook a finger at him. "And don't you dare call me poor little rich girl again. You'd feel bad if your pet didn't like you."

"I never had a pet, not one that belonged just to me. There were some animals at one of the communes we lived in. It was actually more of a farm with pigs, chickens, dogs, cats."

"You lived in a commune? Like a cult kind of place?"

"More like a transient, don't-feel-like-being-a-responsible-citizen kind of place."

"What a crazy life that must have been."

"It was. Moving into my grandparents' house was culture shock. They ate dinner every night at six o'clock, not six-fifteen or six-thirty, but six. My grandfather always had the same cocktail before dinner, a Manhattan. And my grandmother used to watch game shows on a small television set in the kitchen as she cleaned up after us. They had so many rules I thought I'd gone to prison."

She smiled at him. "You liked it."

"I liked the structure, the predictability," he admitted. "It was sometimes stifling, and I complained a lot, but deep down it felt good to know what was going to happen from day to day."

"And that's what you liked about being a marine, too?"

"Yes. Plus I got to combine that structure with danger and excitement."

"Do you miss it?"

"Sometimes." He thought about her question far more seriously than she'd probably intended, but then again, he'd been considering the subject a lot lately. "But this is where I'm meant to be."

"Do you like the security business? Or are you doing it out of a sense of responsibility to your grandparents?"

"I like it. There are certainly opportunities for improved security these days."

"So it's going to be a long-term commitment?"

"Did I say that?"

She smiled. "You don't like that word—commitment."

"Most things don't last. Not jobs, not relationships."

"You're very cynical. And yet you have grandparents who adore each other. They grew together not apart."

"They're the rare exception."

"Maybe," she admitted, her smile dimming. "My parents certainly aren't a shining example of anything."

"Let's go find your sister," he said, as he pulled the car into a parking space.

"Words I never thought I'd hear again," she muttered. "I'm not sure I want you to call Alyssa my sister. We haven't figured out what we are to each other yet."

"You're sisters by blood."

"But we don't know each other. She doesn't trust me. I'm not sure I trust her."

He smiled. "Sounds like every family I've ever known, Paige. At any rate, she called, and we're here, so let's go meet her. The trust issues can wait."

"The class started a little late," a young Asian woman told Alyssa. "Ben said to tell you to wait for him." She waved her hand toward the gym. "There are chairs along the wall if you want to sit down."

Alyssa walked into the studio and paused just inside the door. Ben and another man faced off in the middle of the room. They were both bare to the waist, dressed in black pants and barefoot. She watched in fascination, every move, every attack, every defense. There was strength, skill, stubbornness, determination, agility, and courage in the way they fought.

Ben had taken martial arts classes for years, but she'd never actually seen him fight, and she hadn't realized he'd become so masterful at the art. She tended to think of him as an intellectual man, not a strong physical being, but it was quite clear now that that impression did not do him justice. She felt her heart speed up at the sight of him.

Today, at this minute, he wasn't a modern-day reporter. He was an ancient warrior, a man of power, a force to be reckoned with, a man who was making her feel really hot and very female. She waved her hand in front of her face and sat down in a nearby chair. The match continued for another five minutes. Ben finally took his opponent down with a spinning kick.

She let out the breath she had been holding as Ben extended his hand to his opponent. He helped him to his feet, then they bowed to each other. The instructor said a few words to both of them, then Ben turned toward her, a soldier returning from battle to the woman left waiting for him. She had to fight back the ridiculous impulse to run into his arms and hold him tight, to make sure he hadn't been hurt.

This wasn't a fantasy. This was reality. Ben was her childhood friend, her pal, not some godlike warrior out of a movie. So why did she feel so anxious and tense around him?

"Hi," he said, his voice deep and husky.

Had he always sounded this sexy? She cleared her throat. "Hi. You said you had some information?"

"Actually, I said we should talk to my uncle."

"Right." She could barely remember what he'd said. "Do you want to put on a shirt or something?"

A small smile played across his lips, and she damned herself for being so obvious.

"Sure, I'll put on a shirt." He walked over to a chair and grabbed a T-shirt, pulling it over his head in one swift gesture. "Better?"

"I don't really care. I thought you might be cold. It's not good to get sweaty and then walk around in the cold air. You'll stiffen up."

"Thanks for the concern."

"There's something else. I called Paige Hathaway and asked her to meet us here. I hope that's all right?"

"That depends on why you called her." His eyes sharpened with curiosity. "I know she's interested in the dragon, but there's more to it than that, isn't there?"

"Yes." She took a step back, drawing him into a private corner so they wouldn't be overheard. "My mother actually had a more personal relationship with David Hathaway than I led you to believe." She drew in a deep breath, not sure she could actually say the words. It would be the first time she'd said them out loud to anyone except her mother. But Ben was her friend. She could trust him. "David Hathaway is my father."

His eyes widened. "You're kidding."

She shook her head. "No, I'm not."

"That's quite a piece of news." His expression changed. "Oh, wait a second, he's hurt, isn't he?"

"He's getting better. He's conscious now."

"Have you spoken to him?"

"Not yet. Which is fine, because I'm not even sure what I want to say to him."

"So Paige Hathaway is your half-sister," he said slowly. "And the two of you are interested in the dragon because... Okay, I've lost the thread."

"Because David Hathaway showed the dragon to my mother the day he was assaulted. She might have been the last person to see it."

"You want to protect your mother."

"And Paige wants to protect her company from a lawsuit since they hadn't purchased the statue when Mr. Hathaway took it from the store."

"Do you think you should be calling him Mr. Hathaway when he's your father?"

"I don't know what to call him," she said with frustration. "The whole thing is strange. I've wanted to know who my father was for so long. I had this dream that I fit in better with him and his family than I did with my own. I used to think about running away to find him."

"Alyssa—"

"Now I know who my father is," she said, cutting him off, "and it doesn't make any more sense. I'm not a Hathaway. I can't fit in with them."

"You don't know that. You don't know who they really are."

"What would we have in common?"

"You won't find out if you don't try. And I suspect you want to try, or else Paige wouldn't be joining us."

"I just don't want her making trouble for my mother." She wouldn't let herself look at any other motives right now. "I think it's better if I know what she's up to than let her do this on her own."

"Whatever your reason, it's a start." He looked up as the front door opened. "There they are now." He waved them over.

"I hope we haven't kept you waiting," Paige said as she and Riley joined them.

"Not at all," Ben replied. "I need just a moment, and then I'll take you upstairs."

"Upstairs?" Riley queried.

"My uncle knows a great deal about Chinese artifacts. I asked him to speak with us about the dragon you're seeking. I'll be right back."

"Thanks for calling," Paige said to Alyssa. She could see that Alyssa had stiffened upon their approach, and she wanted to put her at ease. "We really appreciate your help."

"Whoa, what is this?" Riley murmured in amazement.

Paige turned to see two men sizing each other up in the middle of the studio. In their hands were long, curved, single-edged blades.

"They are using broadswords," Alyssa said.

"I didn't think weapons were involved in the martial arts," Paige replied.

"The swords were used in ancient times, as the hand weapons of military foot soldiers."

"I would have liked one of those," Riley said with macho enthusiasm.

Paige rolled her eyes. "You are such a guy," she muttered. They all sat down together in the corner as the sparring proceeded.

Alyssa leaned in closer to explain what was going on. "The use of the broadsword requires speed and strength and excellent footwork. One wrong move could mean death."

"It looks dangerous," Paige commented.

"It is, but these two are highly skilled. And they will use every resource they have. Wisdom and courage, sharp eyes, fast hands, and the ability to confuse the opponent."

Paige saw exactly what she meant as the two men spun and kicked, thrust and parried, moving like dancers in an odd, brutal, killing ballet. Yet there was something beautiful about the fight, something intriguing. Ever since that dragon had appeared, her days had taken such a strange turn, leading her into a world she'd never seen before. She wouldn't have believed she'd enjoy watching a fight like this, but these men were so warrior like, so elemental in what they were doing. They were pushing themselves to the limit, a mental, physical, emotional, and spiritual battle. They were living the way she should be living.

A few moments later the sparring ended. The two men bowed to each other and moved off the floor amid sporadic clapping from the spectators sitting around the room.

"That was very cool," Riley said with enthusiasm. "I think I might have to take a class."

"Have you studied martial arts?" Alyssa asked.

"A little tai chi, some kickboxing, karate, nothing for any length of time. I think I'll grab a flyer from the front desk."

Paige shook her head, a rueful smile on her lips as she saw him heading fast and furiously into something new and exciting. What kind of woman could ever keep a man like this happy and feeling challenged? It would take a unique person. Someone who lived life to the fullest, who wasn't afraid of new experiences, who loved a good fight. Was that her? Or was she just kidding herself?

"Is there something between you two?" Alyssa asked, her question mirroring Paige's own thoughts.

"Well, uh, Riley's grandmother is the owner of the dragon."

"That's not what I asked. He's very attractive."

"Yes, he is."

"And you like him?"

"Yes, I do," Paige admitted. "Although I'm not sure I want to."

For the first time Alyssa smiled, and they exchanged a female look of commiseration.

"What about you and Ben?" Paige asked.

"He's been a friend to me my whole life, but we've seen little of each other since high school. I'm not sure it's wise to get involved again, but here I am."

"That damn dragon is causing all kinds of trouble."

Alyssa nodded her head in agreement. "I'm not sure we'll be able to find it. But I want to make certain no one thinks my mother had anything to do with its disappearance."

"I don't think that." And Paige realized it was true. Jasmine might be her father's lover, but she didn't seem like someone who would steal an ancient artifact. She was an artist herself. Still, she couldn't help wondering... "I don't quite understand why my father took the dragon to your mother. Why was it so important that she see it?"

"She has dreams."

"She told me that. But it's not clear to me what the dreams mean."

"Or to me. She has always had them. They're nightmares really. They leave her shaking and trembling, as if she is terrified of some-thing. We have both wondered if there was some experience in her early life that was tied to seeing such a dragon. She told me today that her mother now says she saw the dragon on a trip to Taiwan when she was a small girl. That it was in a museum, and she tried to touch it, setting off many alarms."

"Really? That's interesting."

"I don't think it's true. Which makes me wonder why my grand-mother would make up such a story."

"If it isn't true, where did your mother see the dragon?"

"I don't know. Maybe it truly is in her dreams. She's very spiritual. Not at all like me."

"Or me. My father—our father—he's a dreamer, too. Maybe that's what they had in common," Paige added. "I used to be so jealous of his fascination with China. I loved hearing his stories when he came home from his trips, but in a way I hated them, too, because he was so much happier when he was there than when he was home, when he was with me."

"He loved all things Chinese, and yet he couldn't love me," Alyssa said, bitter irony in her voice. "But then, I'm only half Chinese. He made me that way."

Paige didn't know what to say. The hurt in Alyssa's eyes was so deep, so dark, she wondered if it could ever be mended. "I'm sorry," she said with heartfelt sincerity. Even though her father hadn't always been there, at least he'd been around some of the time.

"It doesn't have anything to do with you."

"I know that. What you should know is that I wasn't the favorite daughter, either. I had a sister. Elizabeth died when she was seven and I was six. She was his favorite. He loved her more than anyone or anything. He still goes to her grave every year on her birthday to give her a present. It's on Wednesday, by the way—her birthday. I think he might have woken up just so he could make that trip. God, I sound like a jealous sister, don't I?"

"I don't know. I was an only child."

"Not any more." Paige didn't know when she had decided she wanted Alyssa to be part of her life. An hour ago, she'd been waffling, but it suddenly seemed clear that she had a chance to make this relationship whatever they both wanted it to be. "We've got the power now," she said. "My father didn't tell me about you. Your mother didn't tell you about him. But now it's just about us, what we want to be to each other. That's a good thing."

Alyssa seemed a bit taken aback by her words. "I suppose," she said slowly. "I understand our father is awake now. Has he told you anything more about his visit to Chinatown?"

"No. He can't remember the last week. Hopefully it will come back. Until then, we'll work together to protect our parents." Paige looked up as Riley returned with a flyer in his hand. "Find any classes?"

"A few, not that I have time."

"I have a feeling you'll make time."

"You could take the class with me."

She laughed. "You'd trust me with a long blade in my hand?"

"Only if mine is bigger."

"Spoken like a true man."

Before Riley could reply, Ben rejoined them. "I'm ready now. Please forgive the delay. If you'll follow me, we'll go see my uncle."

Paige smiled at Riley as he sent a look of longing at the sparring about to take place, this time with long, pointed spears. "Come on," she said, grabbing his arm. "You can play later. We have work to do."

CHAPTER TWENTY

"MY UNCLE, Guy Fong, still teaches calligraphy classes every Saturday night," Ben said as they approached the upstairs apartment. "He may be finishing up with his students. If so, we will have to wait patiently and quietly. He does not tolerate interruptions."

Paige nodded as Ben opened the door. As he had said, there were three adolescents sitting at the dining room table, carefully painting Chinese characters with long, ornate brushes.

They moved in closer so they could watch what the children were doing. Paige was surprised by the preciseness of their script, the attention to detail, the concentration of three kids who surely would have wanted to do something else on a Saturday night. Ben's uncle stood at one end of the table, a short man with a square face and thick black hair. His eyes were a piercing black, his expression stern and uncompromising as he watched his young charges. If she'd had to guess at his age, she would have said mid-forties, but she couldn't be sure. Perhaps it was the otherworldliness of what was happening in the room that made him seem older.

Time obviously passed slowly in this apartment where an ancient art was being taught to children who were being raised in an age of video games and fast food, fast everything. It seemed extraordinary that they would be painting characters instead of pounding a keyboard or moving a mouse. But apparently Mr. Fong was a man who believed in traditions. Paige respected that. It was nice to see something being preserved and passed on from one generation to the next. There was too little of that in the world.

She was also beginning to see where her father's passion for China and everything Chinese had come from. He loved old things, traditions that never changed, rituals and ceremonies. He'd been born in the wrong century and the wrong place. Maybe it was people like her father and Mr. Fong who were meant to show others the value of such time-honored customs.

A few moments later, the children set down their brushes and the tension in the room eased as Mr. Fong nodded approvingly at each paper passed to him. He said some words in Cantonese that Paige didn't understand. The children's faces broke into smiles that were matched now by the one on their teacher's face. He reached into the cabinet and pulled out three bright oranges and handed one to each.

"For prosperity and good luck," Alyssa said, answering Paige's unspoken question. "A long and fruitful life."

"Uncle," Ben said as the children left the apartment. "These are the friends I spoke to you about. You remember Alyssa Chen."

"Alyssa." Guy bowed to her. "How is your family? Your grandparents are well?"

"Yes, thank you."

Ben continued the introductions and Mr. Fong greeted each of them with a welcome and a bow. After refusing his offer of refreshments, they sat down together in the living room.

"As I told you on the phone," Ben said, "my friends are seeking information about three pieces of art, two dragons that join together to open a box that we believe once held a flute."

"Yes." Mr. Fong picked up a folder from the table. "I made a copy of the article I found."

At Ben's nod, he handed it to Paige. She opened the folder, sensing that she was about to see something very important. Her instincts were right on the money. The photograph in front of her showed two dragons, one facing to the right, one to the left, interlocking together in front of a long, rectangular box. "This is it," she murmured. Riley and Alyssa crowded in next to her as she read the caption under the photograph. "*An ancient Chinese bronze excavated from a burial site in 1903, now on display at the National Palace Museum.*" She looked at Mr. Fong. "Where did you get this?"

"From a very old book I have on Chinese art. Is this the piece you are seeking?"

She glanced at Riley. He was staring at the picture with an intense frown. "What do you think?"

"I think that's my grandmother's dragon on the left, with the head going to the right, don't you?"

"I don't really remember."

"It looks a lot like the dragon in my mother's painting," Alyssa commented.

"If it was in the museum, what happened to it?" Paige asked.

"The National Palace Museum was taken apart piece by piece during World War Two," Mr. Fong replied. "Almost thirty thousand crates filled with artifacts were sent all over China for protection against the invading enemies. After the war it took sixteen years to put the museum back together. Some items were lost during that time, the dragon set among them."

"Do you know what happened next?" Riley asked. "Is there any record of these pieces reappearing at auctions or in private collections?"

"Some believe the box and the dragons came to the United States along with other pieces of art that were sold discreetly and privately."

"But there are no records, no proof that these pieces, this set, still exists?" Paige asked.

"Not until Mr. McAllister's grandmother found a dragon in her attic," Mr. Fong replied. "Ben told me what happened. I wonder how it got there—in your grandmother's attic."

"I wonder the same thing," Riley said, his expression grim. "Do you mind if I keep this photo?"

"Please do."

"Thank you for your time," Paige said as they all stood up and walked toward the door. "Just out of curiosity, Mr. Fong—if someone were looking for that dragon or its match here in San Francisco's Chinatown, where do you think they would go?"

"They would follow the pattern. The dragons and box connect. I suspect the owners do as well. If Mr. McAllister's grandfather had one dragon, then who do you think would have the other?"

Wallace Hathaway or Lee Chen. Those were the connections, Paige realized. But both of those men denied having knowledge of the dragons. Someone was lying.

Victoria raised her hand to knock on the door of David's bedroom late Sunday afternoon, knowing she'd put off this visit as long as she could. She'd managed to avoid her husband since she'd brought him home in a limousine just before lunchtime. She'd rationalized that she was letting him rest, but in truth she was avoiding him. His near brush with death had scared her more than she wanted to admit. Although she and David had grown apart in recent years, she didn't want him to die. In fact, faced with that possibility, she'd been shocked at how much she wanted him to live. She'd prayed for another chance, but now that she had it, she didn't know what to do with it.

They could no longer pretend that Jasmine and Alyssa did not exist. Jasmine might be willing to stay hidden, and Paige might be willing to let Jasmine stay that way, but not Alyssa. Paige wouldn't take kindly to sweeping Alyssa under the carpet. Victoria would have to deal with Alyssa herself, make it clear to her that she wasn't going to be a part of anything Hathaway. Victoria couldn't bear the thought of her husband's lover's daughter getting anything that she, Victoria, had worked so hard to achieve for herself and her own child.

One of the maids walked down the hallway. Unwilling to be caught waffling in front of her husband's door, she knocked and entered without waiting for a reply. David was still dressed in the casual clothes he'd worn home from the hospital. He was lying on the middle of his bed surrounded by art and antique books.

"What are you doing? You're supposed to be resting."

He looked at her with bemusement in his eyes, as if he wasn't quite sure why she was there. "I'm reading."

She picked up one of the books and saw a photo of a dragon. She sighed. "Dragons and more dragons. Is this the same one?"

"No."

"I thought you didn't remember the dragon statue."

"I asked Martin to send over a copy of the videotape from the antique show so that I could see the statue that sent me to Chinatown."

She wasn't quite sure she believed him—he'd lied about so many other things—but his words had a ring of truth to them. "Maybe you just went to Chinatown to see that woman. It wouldn't have been the first time. We both know that."

David took off the reading glasses that had slipped to the bridge of his nose and put them on the bed. "Must we deal with this now?"

"Paige knows about your illegitimate child. That damn security expert she made friends with has dug into our personal life."

"But you already knew about Alyssa, didn't you?" he said, through shrewd, tired eyes.

"I know everything, David." She could have sat down on the chaise lounge next to the bed, but she preferred to stand, to be taller, bigger, more in control than he was.

"Why didn't you say anything?"

"It wasn't important as long as she stayed away."

"What do you want to do now?"

"Pay her off, of course."

"Of course," he echoed wearily. "It doesn't matter that she's my daughter."

"You haven't acted like her father, have you? I didn't think so," she added when she saw him flinch. She knew this man too well, maybe better than he knew himself. She knew what made him strong and what made him weak. She knew his fears and the limits to his courage, and once upon a time he'd known something about her. But he'd forgotten or she'd changed—maybe it was a little of both.

"Alyssa is a young woman. She can't hurt us," David said.

"I won't be made a target of gossip."

"Don't worry, Vicky, you can play the martyred wife and become even more popular."

She ignored his cutting comment. "The least you could have done was use birth control. Where was your mind anyway? Forget it, I don't want to know. What I do want to know is if there are any other children about to come out of the woodwork."

"No," he said shortly.

"Thank God for that." She walked over to the window, gazing down at their beautifully manicured backyard lawn, next to the swimming pool and the gazebo. The sight of her surroundings immediately calmed her.

"You're so cold, Victoria. So sure of yourself, so self-righteous. I almost died this week, but all you can think about is your image, your reputation."

"You almost died this week because you went to see her," she said fiercely, turning to face him. "How do you think I felt knowing you were almost killed two blocks from her apartment? What do you think the press has been asking me all week? *Where was your husband going? What was he doing in Chinatown?* I'm lucky I managed to cover up your connection with that woman. Thankfully our good friend the police chief made sure that piece of information was put to rest by suggesting that the police visit to Jasmine's apartment had no connection to your attack."

"You mean your good friend, don't you? I'm not the only one with friendships in unlikely places, but while you can take the girl out of the slum, you can never quite take the slum out of the girl."

"How dare you!"

"How dare you?" he echoed. "You haven't said a kind, warm word to me since we buried Elizabeth, since you decided to blame me for her dying. It was my fault she got cancer. It was my fault the doctors couldn't save her. It was all my fault."

"Yes, it was," she hissed. "It was your fault. It was your fault I had to hear the diagnosis by myself because you were out of town. It was your fault that Elizabeth didn't go to see that specialist in Europe because you let her pleas that she just wanted to stay home sway your judgment. Maybe he could have saved her."

"And maybe he would have caused her more pain. She was dying, Victoria. You knew it, and I knew it, and neither one of us could stop it, not even you, the superwoman, and certainly not me, because I've never been good enough to do anything in your eyes. Except marry you. I got that right, didn't I? It wasn't me you wanted. It was my name, my house, my business, my parents. But was it ever me? Tell me the truth for once in your life."

Staring into his demanding eyes, she wondered—had it ever been him? She'd set her sights on him and made sure she got an introduction. She'd learned everything she could about him, his likes, dislikes, ambitions, fears, and she'd made herself into the perfect wife-to-be. She wouldn't apologize for it. She'd been a good wife. She'd given him children, managed his house, taken over his company, made his life simple and easy. "You've had it good, David. You have nothing to complain about. You had what you needed."

"I didn't have love."

She shook her head, remembering those same words coming out of her poor, drunken mother's mouth. "What is love, anyway? It doesn't pay the bills. It doesn't get you through life. It doesn't make trouble go away. You have to fight for things. You have to take care of yourself." She walked back to the side of his bed. "Haven't you figured that out yet?"

"I figured out I couldn't depend on you, except for the basics of our life together. What about friendship? Companionship? Caring? Kindness?"

"Is that what *she* gives you?"

"She did at one time."

His gaze was clear and direct. She found herself feeling uncomfortable, but she wasn't the one who was wrong; he was. So why was she feeling as if she had to explain or justify her own actions? "Don't turn this around on me."

"Was I doing that?"

"I never walked out on you. I never cheated on you."

"You never wanted anyone more than you wanted the store. That's why you didn't cheat. It wasn't out of faithfulness to me; it was out of your desperate need to keep your position. That's what you love. That's the only thing you love."

"That's not true," she said, her voice shakier than she wanted it. "I love Paige. And I loved Elizabeth. And at one time I even loved you, dammit. Is that what you want to hear? Well, there it is. When we first got married, I thought I was the luckiest girl in the world, because you didn't just have everything I wanted; you *were* everything I wanted— funny and passionate and charming. But when things got tough, I couldn't count on you. And you're right, I want more for my life than someone who drops in and out of it every few weeks, whose heart is on another continent. If I'm cold, it's because it got damn chilly in our bed."

"You locked your door against me. The day Elizabeth died, you turned away. Every night that week you went into your room alone, and every morning when you came out, there was another piece of you that you'd hidden away from me. It was the same with my father. When my mother and sister died in that car crash, he turned away. He couldn't love me, because I had survived. Just like you couldn't love me, because Elizabeth was gone and I was still there."

His words shocked her to the core with a truth she couldn't refute. She put a hand to her heart, feeling weak. A moment later she was sitting on the edge of his bed, looking into the eyes of a man she had never really seen. "You never said that before."

"I was hoping you'd figure it out for yourself. You were so damn smart about everything else."

"I—I never wished you dead in her place."

"It doesn't matter anymore, does it, Vicky? We're done. We've been done for a long time. What are we trying to hang on to, anyway? What do we have left? Why don't you just give me a divorce and call it quits? You can have the store. You can have whatever you want."

"And what will you have?" she asked. "Will you have her?"

"I hurt Jasmine more than I ever hurt you," David said with brutal honesty. "I used her for comfort and friendship and kindness. When she got pregnant, I gave her money to get an abortion, money she threw back in my face. When she had Alyssa, I offered to send support, but she turned me down. For years I didn't give Jasmine or our daughter one penny of my money. Finally, Jasmine broke down. She needed help. Her family had turned against her because she'd had a baby out of marriage and out of her own race. So I sent her a few dollars when she asked, never one cent more than she requested, and I never saw Alyssa, never even spied on her in the playground. Jasmine didn't want me to confuse Alyssa, and I couldn't betray..." He rubbed a rough hand across his eyes, eyes that were suspiciously wet.

Victoria was still reeling from his suggestion that they get a divorce; she could barely keep up with what he was saying, the words pouring from his heart. The dam had burst and twenty years' worth of feelings were rushing out in a wild torrent of emotion. She was feeling it, too, more than she wanted. All those old feelings of young love were coming back. She'd told herself for so many years that she hated David, but she'd never really told herself why. Now she wasn't sure she could remember why. She just knew how badly he had hurt her, and she supposed she had hurt him, too. She'd known that he didn't get along with his father, but she hadn't realized that it stemmed from the accident in which David had survived and his sister and mother had perished. Why hadn't she put those facts together?

Everything made so much more sense—even to some extent the affair that he had had. Deep down in the honest part of herself, she knew she had turned away from him. She'd been overcome with sadness, depression and pain; she just hadn't wanted to feel anything else.

"I don't expect you to forgive me," David said wearily. "I'm too old to start over, to change, to make things better. I'm too damn old."

Now here was one good reason why she had grown to dislike him so. "You're such a quitter, David. Why don't you ever fight for the things you want? Why didn't you fight for your father's attention, for my attention? Why didn't you fight Jasmine, so you could see your own daughter? Why do you always give up, take the easy way out?"

"Because I never win, even when I try."

"I don't think you try. You blame yourself the way you expect others to blame you. I think you're the one who feels bad for surviving all the tragedies."

"You've been in therapy too long, Vicky."

"I *have* been in therapy too long," she agreed. "I realize now I wasn't the one who needed it. It was you, always you." She got up from the bed. "Here's the bottom line, David. If you want a divorce, you're going to have to fight like hell to get it. Maybe it's time you found out what you're made of. Maybe it's time you gave me a chance to see if you're worthy of my affection."

He uttered a short, bitter-edged laugh. "Goddamn, Vicky. Do you know how crazy you are? You're saying the only way you'll love me again is if I can beat you, if I can make you divorce me."

"I need an equal, not a doormat. It's your call. Frankly, I don't think you have it in you to do anything more than run back to China and lick your wounds in private. I fully expect things to go on exactly the way they've gone for the last twenty years at least."

"We'll see about that."

"Yes, we will."

CHAPTER TWENTY-ONE

"I CANNOT BELIEVE you want to sneak into my parents' house and search the cupboards and closets for a dragon statue," Paige said. "This is your worst idea yet."

"You didn't have a better one," Riley replied as he settled himself more comfortably in the driver's seat of his car. "Mr. Fong told us to look for the connections, and we both agree that your grandfather is one of those links."

That was true, she silently conceded. She'd been thinking about their grandfathers' connections ever since she'd left Mr. Fong's apartment, but she hadn't had time to do anything about it, having spent most of the day helping her mother get her father settled back home. "Did you talk to your grandmother again?" she asked.

"No. Not yet," Riley said.

She stared down the dark shadowy street. Riley had parked several mansions down from the one she'd grown up in, and she couldn't shake the uneasy feeling that they were heading into trouble. But they weren't really breaking in anywhere. They were just going to take a look through the family home while her mother and grandfather were out. She checked her watch. It was nearly six. "They should be heading out any minute now."

"If they're as punctual as you say they are."

"They are, trust me. I inherited the on-time gene. But don't forget my father will still be in the house, not to mention his private nurse and a couple of servants. We won't be alone."

"Too bad." He smiled. "So, what was it like to grow up with servants. What did they do for you?"

"They kept the house, cooked, that kind of stuff."

"If you dropped a candy wrapper on the ground, someone was there to rush over and pick it up for you?"

"I wasn't allowed to eat candy. It's bad for you."

"Some bad things are really good," he said with a wicked smile.

And suddenly the quiet in the car grew more intimate. She'd been trying to keep her attraction to Riley at bay, to remind herself that Riley didn't want the things she wanted, like commitment, marriage, family. Maybe she didn't want all that tomorrow or the next day, but eventually she would. What was the point in wasting time in a relationship that wouldn't lead in that direction? She wasn't twenty-one anymore. She was almost thirty.

So why couldn't she listen to her head instead of her heart? When he'd stopped by her apartment an hour earlier, she'd jumped at the chance to join him on this latest escapade, not even asking him what he had in mind until they were in the car. She was crazy. *Crazy in love.*

She'd just have to get over it. Treat it like a bad cold or a case of the flu. She could recover. She'd just have to work at it.

Of course, working at it probably didn't include spending more time with him. Well, she'd start working on it tomorrow. Her weary sigh drew his attention.

"Something wrong?" he asked.

"Just thinking."

"You do that too much." He shifted, putting his right hand along the back of her seat.

"What are you doing?"

"Passing the time."

She scooted to the edge of her seat. "We can't do that here."

"I think we can."

"This car is way too small," she protested, just before his hand crept around the back of her neck and pulled her toward him.

"It's perfect. You're perfect," he muttered.

He sealed the words with a lingering, tender, playful kiss that wasn't really meant to start anything. Just the same she felt her body responding with passion and intensity that went far beyond his intention. He seemed able to light her up without even trying.

Riley must have read her mood, because the kisses suddenly changed, deepened, intensified. Or maybe he was just feeling what she was feeling.

When they broke apart, there were no smiles, no teasing jokes, nothing to ease the tension between them.

"Dammit, Paige."

"What?"

"I shouldn't have done that."

"And you're blaming me."

"Yes, because you're irresistible. Every time I kiss you it's better than the last time. I keep telling myself that can't possibly be true, but it is."

His look of bemusement made her like him even more. "I feel the same way," she confessed. "I keep thinking it will burn itself out."

"We might have to make that happen."

"You mean, get each other out of our systems?"

"It's an idea."

She couldn't help smiling as she shook her head. "Another bad one. You're full of them tonight."

Before he could reply, their attention was drawn to the street where her grandfather's car pulled out of the drive. They could see two people in the back, the driver in the front.

"Looks like it's show time," Riley murmured. "Ready?"

"Yes." Because right now she had a feeling her grandfather's rooms were far less dangerous than this car.

Alyssa spotted her grandfather through the blinds of the Plum Rose Café. He was seated at the second booth, the newspaper in front of him. it was probably the racing form, she thought. When he wasn't playing mah jong or pai gow he went to the track at Golden Gate Fields and watched the horse races from around the country. She knew this was her best opportunity to speak to him alone. Tomorrow was New Year's Eve and the entire family would gather together for a huge feast of Chinese specialties that her grandmother and a half dozen cousins were working on even now. Of course she hadn't been invited to help prepare the food. Just another slight to make her remember that she didn't quite belong.

She shook the thought from her head. She had more important things to worry about right now than fitting into the family. Since Mr. Fong had suggested the possibility that the connection between the dragons and the box might mimic a connection between the various owners of those three pieces, she couldn't stop thinking about the connection between the three grandfathers. If Riley's grandfather had a dragon, then it made sense that one of the other two men might also have one. But probably not her grandfather. He'd simply worked in the stockroom at Hathaway's. He hadn't been in a position of power.

Still... there was something about the dragon that bothered her grandparents, and she had to find out what that something was.

"Alyssa?"

She turned her head to see Ben crossing the street. "What are you doing here?" she asked in surprise, feeling her heart skip a beat at the sight of him.

He smiled at her. "Trying to catch up to you. I saw you as I was leaving my friend's apartment." He pointed to a building down the street. "I couldn't believe you were actually making another trip to Chinatown."

"I want to talk to my grandfather. He's in the café."

"I can see that. He's eating alone. Hiding out from the family?"

"Avoiding the New Year's Eve preparations, I'm sure."

"You're going to ask him about the dragon?"

"I thought I might ask him about Wallace Hathaway instead, see if I can find another way into the conversation."

"Want some company?"

"I don't think so. Although he did always like you."

"What's not to like?" Ben asked teasingly. "Wait, forget I asked. You probably have a list somewhere."

"I left it at home."

Ben glanced toward the window of the café. "He's having pie. Looks like dinner is almost over. If you're planning to go, you better do it now."

"All right. Would you wait for me out here? Unless you have other plans or something. You probably do have other plans. I don't know what I'm thinking. Forget I asked."

"You are one crazy woman," Ben told her. "You argue both sides before anyone has a chance to say anything."

"I know. I should have been a lawyer. But I wanted to make money now, not in three years. I couldn't wait any longer to be independent. And I want to get this issue with the dragon resolved so I can go back to my own life." Her words erased the smile from his face, the light from his eyes.

"I'm sure you must be eager to get away from here," he said. "I actually have something to do. I'll see you around."

"Ben, wait."

"What?"

"I didn't mean it the way it sounded. I'm grateful for all the help you've given me, and especially for your friendship, which I don't deserve."

He walked back to her with deliberate, purposeful steps that made her want to step back, but she couldn't move. Because this was Ben, and she suddenly wanted very much to hear what he had to say.

"You deserve everything you want, Alyssa. And I hope you get it all."

"I wish you wouldn't be so nice."

"That's my problem. I'm the nice guy, the one who doesn't get the girl."

"It's not you, it's me," she whispered. "Until I figure out who I am, I don't feel as if I have anything to offer."

"I already know who you are. I've known for a long time. When you figure it out, give me a call." He put his hand under her chin, tipping up her face so he could look into her eyes. "Just don't wait too long."

Before she could reply, he brushed her lips with his, a brief, teasing kiss that made her want more. He was halfway down the street before she got her breath back. Turning toward the café, she forced herself to move, up the steps, through the door, and into the seat across from her grandfather.

"Alyssa," he said with surprise.

"I saw you through the window," she said. "Did you play the races today?" She tipped her head toward the racing form that was marked up with numbers and circles.

"I won a few dollars. I don't bet much, you know that. Your grandmother counts every penny. Do you want something to eat?"

"No, thanks. I actually wanted to talk to you about something."

He grimaced. "Not the dragon, please."

"About your work at Hathaway's."

His gaze dropped to his empty plate. "I worked in the stockroom. Nothing more."

"Did you get to know Wallace Hathaway?"

"He was a big man. I was a small man."

She waited for him to elaborate, but he didn't say more. Instead, he picked up his empty coffee cup and waved the waitress over. He remained quiet while his cup was refilled. Even after the waitress left, he still didn't speak.

"Can you tell me anything more about him?" Alyssa prodded. "Or about the fire? I know you stopped working there after the fire."

"I can still see those flames in my mind, jumping up the walls like angry snapping snakes." He shook his head as if to dislodge the memory. "It was the end of everything."

"The end of what?" she asked.

His gaze sharpened. "The end of my job."

She had a feeling that wasn't what he'd been thinking at all.

"Why do you ask these questions—because of the dragon that your mother can't forget?"

"Partly. But also because I want to know more about the Hathaway family."

His lips formed a tight line. "Do not speak of it, Alyssa."

And just like that she knew that he knew—about David and her mother and herself. She had been brought up not to ask questions, especially of her grandparents, and she had always respected that policy... until now. There was a need to know burning inside of her.

"Just tell me one thing—did my mother's affair with David Hathaway have anything to do with your relationship, whatever it was, with Wallace Hathaway?" she asked. "I know why my mother wanted David, but I don't know why he wanted her. And I can't help thinking, that maybe getting my mother was some sort of revenge or payback or a way of getting in someone's face, maybe even yours."

Her grandfather's face tightened. "You talk crazy. He pulled out his wallet and tossed some money on the table.

"I'm sorry if I upset you," she said as he got to his feet.

"You go home, work hard, forget about this. It was over a long time ago."

That was the problem. It wasn't over, not by a long shot.

"What do you think are the odds that we're actually going to find something in here?" Paige asked as she and Riley entered her grandfather's study. She turned on the small lamp over his desk. "I've been here before. In fact, I was here yesterday. And I didn't see a dragon or anything else suspicious."

"He wouldn't have it sitting out on his desk," Riley replied, glancing around the room. "This is nice. A man's room." He nodded approvingly at the dark wood, the heavy furniture. "Is this where your grandfather spends his time?"

"Yes. He considers these rooms his private sanctuary. Which is why we shouldn't be doing this. We have no right to be in here."

"Paige, get a grip. We're not stealing anything. We're just looking. You know your grandfather is hiding something. Asking him straight out didn't get you anywhere."

"That's true," she conceded.

"Don't forget, this missing dragon almost sent your father to the morgue."

Riley had a way of cutting to the chase that was really effective. "All right. You've convinced me. But be careful. I don't want him to know anyone was here." She glanced around the neat room. "Where do we start?"

"You check out the desk. I'll look through the filing cabinet."

Paige did as he asked, and for a few moments there was nothing but quiet rustling in the room. The desk revealed common business items, stationery, paper clips, pens. Everything was organized, nothing out of place. She closed the desk and waited for Riley to finish with the filing cabinet.

"Nothing," he said. "Where would your grandfather hide something incriminating?"

"I don't think he has anything incriminating." She couldn't stop the automatic defense. It was second nature to protect the family name.

"Let's go into his bedroom," he said, ignoring that comment. He walked through an adjoining door. She hastily followed. If there was anything to find, she wanted to be with him when he found it. She stood in the middle of the room as Riley went through the drawers of the bureau with a quiet efficiency that scared her. He looked very at home in this role of burglar. It reminded her of how different they were, where they'd come from, the lives that they'd led up until this point.

Maybe Riley was right. Maybe they were too different to belong together. Her head told her he might have a point. Her heart told her the differences didn't matter. And weren't those differences in the past? They were together in this. She might be hesitating, but if she were really honest with herself, she'd have to admit that he hadn't dragged her into it. She wanted to find the answers as much as he did. She was just letting him be the one to do it.

Wasn't that cowardly? As if not helping in the search made her actual participation seem less. But it wasn't less. They were a team, a partnership. And she'd come into this room with her eyes open. She couldn't pretend Riley was making her do it. He wasn't.

She turned and deliberately opened the door to her grandfather's walk-in closet. It was lined with suits on one side, shirts and pants on another, everything from formal to casual wear, dozens of shoes on racks, ties, hats, sweaters. It was the closet of a very rich man. She looked to the shelves that ran around the top of the closet. Her gaze caught on a square plastic container in which there appeared to be several books. She looked around for a step stool but couldn't find one.

"Anything in here?" Riley asked, moving into the closet.

"I don't know yet. But that plastic container looks interesting."

Riley reached up and pulled it off the shelf, setting it on the ground between them. She squatted down, putting her hand on the lid, but she stopped when Riley covered her hand with his. She met his eyes. "What?"

"You don't have to do this. At least, you don't have to do this with me here."

"Why wouldn't I?"

"If I find anything to incriminate your grandfather, I'll use it," he said with his usual brutal honesty.

She drew in a tight, worried breath. Maybe she should be doing this alone. But she didn't want to do it alone. She wanted to do it with him. Gazing into his passionate blue eyes, she knew she could no more send him out of the room than she could send herself. They'd already crossed that line, and there was no turning back.

"We're in this together," she murmured. "And if I find anything incriminating against your grandfather, I'll use it, too."

"Then we know where we stand."

"Not really. But let's at least open this box and find out if it's anything at all."

She pulled off the lid and realized the box was indeed something.

There were three photo albums inside and a manila envelope. She grabbed one album. Riley took another. Her album showed her grandfather's childhood, black-and-white photographs of her grandfather and his parents. She flipped through it, wishing she had more time to really think about where her grandfather had come from, what kind of life he had lived as a young man.

"What did you get?" she asked Riley.

"Your grandparents' wedding pictures. Your grandmother was a beautiful woman. Looks a little like you in the eyes."

"Yes," she murmured, gazing at the page he had turned. "I wish I could have met her. Anything else?"

"Doesn't look like it."

Paige reached for the third album, wondering where this book would take them. The first page of photographs sent goose bumps down her arm. "Hathaway's," she muttered. "Look, this is the store way back when."

"In the 1920s?" Riley guessed, coming around so he could sit next to her on the floor.

"It looks that way. My great-great-grandfather started the store in the late 1800s. The Hathaways were part of the gold rush, only we weren't digging for gold; we were outfitting the miners and selling dry goods."

"When did the focus turn to antiques and art?"

"After World War Two when my grandfather took over," she said, wondering if there was any significance to that. "I remember him saying that his own father never had much vision, but after he'd seen the world, he realized that bringing the rest of the world to San Francisco would be a gold mine."

"It certainly was," Riley agreed.

Paige flipped through several more pages, noting the mix of photographs and yellowed newspaper clippings. There were a few pages devoted solely to the 1906 earthquake that had flattened the city and the fires that followed. Hathaway's had moved to Union Square with the rebuilding of the square after the quake. The clippings from the next few decades showed the Hathaways gaining importance as city leaders.

"This is amazing," she murmured, seeing her family history unfold before her. "I wonder why this has been hidden away. I would have loved to see it."

"Your family was really something. It looks like they built half the city."

She turned another page and stopped, the headline turning her blood cold: *Wallace Hathaway Missing In Action.* "Oh, my God. What's this?" She skimmed through the article, knowing Riley was keeping pace along with her. "My grandfather's plane was shot down over mainland China," she exclaimed.

Riley met her gaze with an excited gleam in his eyes. "We just hit pay dirt. Turn the page."

She was almost afraid to do that. Her grandfather had never mentioned being shot down over China during the war. In fact, she only vaguely knew that he'd been in the war, but that was it. No one had ever spoken about that time in his life.

Riley grew impatient and turned the page for her. "Damn," he said. "Would you look at that."

It was a newspaper photograph of two men dressed in ragged uniforms, their arms around each other: *Hometown Heroes Found Alive*

"Our grandfathers," Paige said in amazement, recognizing both men.

"Two of San Francisco's finest, shot down over China almost three months ago, were found alive," Riley read. "They credit their survival to a young Chinese man named Lee Chen, who gave them food and shelter and kept them hidden from the enemy."

"Lee Chen?" Paige could hardly believe it. "The same Lee Chen who is Alyssa's grandfather?"

"The third connection," Riley said, meeting her gaze. "This is amazing, Paige. It's all coming together. Our grandfathers flew together in the war. Wallace must have been the Wally my grandfather talked about."

"And Alyssa's grandfather was the one who saved their lives in China."

"When they returned from the war, they all went to work at Hathaway's with a new focus, Asian art. Imagine that," Riley continued.

"The three of them worked together until a fire destroyed the store," she continued. "They went their separate ways, nothing connecting them to each other until now."

"Until a dragon statue in my grandfather's possession came to light."

"The dragon set that was lost in China during the war."

They both came to the same conclusion at the same time.

"You think they brought it back from China?" she asked.

"It sure looks that way to me."

"But that would mean they stole it. Not just my grandfather, Riley, but yours, too. Is that what you're saying?"

He ran a frustrated hand through his hair. "Someone stole it. I'm just not sure who."

"You can't still be trying to pin this all on my grandfather?"

"He did end up with the most money."

"He had the most money to start with."

"Okay. Let's back up a little."

"Good idea, because I don't think it would be that easy to smuggle national art treasures out of a foreign country. In fact, I wonder how Lee Chen got out of China so quickly."

"Probably courtesy of your grandfather, Paige. He came from a powerful family. He had political connections, didn't he?"

"I'm sure my great-grandfather did."

"There you go. Your grandfather was grateful for the rescue, and in return he got Lee Chen to the States."

"I suppose it could have happened that way. But that still doesn't explain the dragon."

"It was wartime. I have a feeling a lot of things were smuggled out of China."

"You can't just steal ancient artifacts and sell them without anyone noticing," she argued.

"The black market has been around forever. Who says you can't do exactly that?"

"I don't know, but we still don't have real proof of any of this. It's all speculation. The only person we know who had a dragon was your grandfather. I'm not accusing him of anything," she said hastily as the storm clouds gathered in his eyes. "Like you said, he could have gotten it anywhere. He could have come across it at a flea market. The possibilities are endless."

"The possibilities are not that endless, Paige, not when we now know that the three of them were in China together during the war, the same time these art pieces were being shipped around the country." He paused. "Let's go over it again. When they came back to the States, Wallace returned to work in the family business. My grandfather was hired as a security guard, and Lee Chen went to work in some capacity in the storeroom."

"Then there was a fire," Paige continued.

"Discovered by Lee Chen."

"After the fire, neither your grandfather nor Lee Chen returned to the store."

"There was speculation that the fire was arson, but no conclusions. The Hathaways didn't press for an investigation."

"How do you know that?" she asked.

"Simple. If they had pressed for an investigation, it would have happened. They had too much clout to be ignored. Which leads me to believe that Wallace, for whatever reason, didn't want to pursue the arsonist. Hell, maybe it was him."

"He wouldn't have burned down his own store."

"Maybe for the insurance money? Things couldn't have been that good after the war."

"They weren't that bad, either," she replied. "It's just as likely that Lee Chen or your grandfather was responsible. And if you're going to accuse my grandfather, then you can take some heat yourself. Because everything you're implying, including getting national treasures out of China, involves all three of them."

Riley thought about that for a moment, and she could see he wasn't too pleased by the idea. Which was tough. Because she didn't want to believe her grandfather would have done any of the things they were talking about, either.

"Is there anything else in the album?" Riley asked. She checked the next page, but it was empty.

"Nothing," she said, closing the book.

"What's in the envelope?" he asked.

She pulled a stack of letters from the manila envelope. "They're all addressed to my grandfather." She opened the first one and began to read aloud.

"Dear Wallace, I miss you so much already. I hate this war. I hate that we can't be together. And most of all I hate that we didn't get married before you left. I think about you every day. You have my heart, Wallace. Keep it safe until you return. Love always, Dolores."

Paige felt a wave of emotion as she folded the paper and returned it to the envelope. "A love letter from my grandmother. Who would have thought anyone could love that cranky old man?"

"He probably wasn't always so cranky."

She opened the next one and read softly, "Dear Wallace, I'm so afraid. We haven't heard from you in a long time. You've been declared missing in action. I was with your parents when they were told. Your mother fainted. Your father said it wasn't true, that you couldn't be gone. I don't believe you're gone, either. In my heart I know that you're alive and that you're coming home to me. We're going to have a future together, children, grandchildren. We'll grow old together. I miss you so much, Wallace. I'd do anything to get you back, and I know you'd do anything to get back to me. You're so strong, determined, stubborn. You'll get through this. We both will..." Paige's voice trailed away as she glanced at Riley. "She must have been so scared."

"She didn't give up on him."

"No, she didn't. And he came back to her just like she said he would."

"He did whatever he had to do to get back."

"Maybe," she said, wondering what bargains her grandfather had made to get himself out of China. "Anyway, I'm sure these letters are

more of the same. I don't feel right reading them. They're so personal."
She placed the envelope and the photo albums into the box and stood
up. Riley put the box back in its place on the top shelf. "I think we're
done in here."

"Yeah." Riley took one last look around the bedroom before they
turned out the light and walked into the hall. "There's one more place I
want to see before we go."

"We can't do the downstairs," she said quickly. "The housekeeper is
here, maybe one of the maids. And my father is resting in his
bedroom."

"I'm not interested in the downstairs or your father's bedroom. It's
time for payback."

"What does that mean?"

"I showed you mine. Now you show me yours."

"Just what exactly are we talking about me showing you?"

"Your bedroom. I want to see where the princess slept for most of
her life."

CHAPTER TWENTY-TWO

AGAINST PAIGE'S BETTER JUDGMENT, she snuck Riley down the stairs and into her old bedroom, which was thankfully at the far end of the hall on the second floor, separated from both of her parents' bedrooms by several guestrooms and two bathrooms. She'd moved down the hall just after her thirteenth birthday in a moment of pure teenage rebellion. Her mother had pouted for a week, but it was one of the few times in her life that her father had actually stuck by her and stood up for her decision, saying she needed more space and privacy.

"This isn't nearly as nice as I thought it would be," Riley said with some disappointment. "Where's the canopy bed and the pink rug?"

"I hate pink," she retorted.

"You must hate every color."

She saw her room through his eyes, cream-colored walls, cream-colored carpet, cream-colored bedspread on the double bed with just a hint of a flower pattern. At least her bed frame, desk, and dresser were a dark wood.

"Where are the teenage rock star posters, the sports trophies, the antique porcelain doll collection?" he asked.

"How did you know I have one of those?"

"Lucky guess." He sat down on the bed, stretching out against her fluffy pillows, and he had the nerve to actually put his feet, shoes included, on the comforter. "You really were raised to be a princess, weren't you?"

"Do you mind getting your feet off the bed?"

"Afraid of a little dirt?"

"Not afraid of it. I just don't feel like cleaning it."

"Don't you have housekeepers for that?"

She crossed her arms and studied him thoughtfully. "This is another test, isn't it? I'm starting to recognize them. I constantly seem to be auditioning for you, but I'm not quite sure what part I'm trying out for."

His eyes darkened. "What part would you like?"

"How about the part where I get to be myself and you stop judging me by all the stereotypical rich girls you've met in your life?"

"I haven't met any rich girls before you."

"Now, that I find hard to believe."

"Why?" he challenged. "Do you think they lived in my neighborhood? That they were in the marines with me? Or maybe you think they work for my security company?"

"If you aren't comparing me to anyone in particular, then why do you have so many critical judgments about me?" He didn't answer, but she could see she'd struck a nerve by the way his jaw tightened. "I know why. It's because you're still trying to convince yourself that this attraction we're both feeling will take you someplace you don't want to go."

"At least you admit you're attracted to me."

"You know I am. And I think we could be good together."

"What makes you think that?"

Sensing he genuinely wanted to know, she decided to tell him, even though she felt as if she'd run into another test. "You need someone like me in your life to make you see the other side of things, to make you believe in the good stuff again."

"And what about you? Do you want someone to drag you down, to mire you in the bad stuff the way I would?"

"Maybe I need someone to hold my feet to the fire, the way you do." She moved closer to the bed and sat down next to him, putting her hand on his very solid chest. "I need someone to challenge me, and you do that."

"Paige," he warned, "don't start something you can't finish."

"Who said I can't finish it?"

"We're in your bedroom at your parents' house. There is no way it's going to happen here."

She almost laughed at the desperation in his voice. "You don't think so, huh? I seem to have a thing for childhood bedrooms where you're concerned."

"I don't think you want your mother to see my bare ass on your bed."

"That would shake her up," she said with a little laugh. "But I actually like the sound of that." She dropped her hand to the snap on his jeans and heard the sharp intake of his breath. She didn't have to look down to know that his body was not fighting her nearly as hard as his mind was. Since she was a curious woman by nature, she let herself look anyway and was more than a little pleased by what she saw. When she glanced back at Riley, she couldn't hide the smug satisfaction she was feeling.

"I'm a man," he told her. "It doesn't take much."

"That's what you'd like me to believe, but I know it's me making you crazy."

"Feeling awfully sure of yourself all of a sudden."

"At one time, in my youth, I was an inexperienced virgin sleeping in this bed, but that was a long time ago, Riley. I want you to understand something important, all joking aside."

"Okay, tell me."

"I'm not a princess. I'm a woman, a complicated woman with good sides and bad sides. This room is part of who I am. I won't try to defend my family or my background or the privileges I grew up with, and I don't expect you to defend yours. What's important is not where we come from or how we were raised, but who we are today, what we want out of life."

"It's hard to forget where you come from."

"Maybe I can help you forget." She put her hands on his shoulders and leaned forward, whispering in his ear. "I want to make love to you."

"God, Paige, you can't just say it like that."

"I can say it any way I want."

"If you want to go back to my apartment—"

"I don't. And I don't want to go back to my apartment. I want to make love to you here."

"Why here?"

She gazed into his dark blue eyes and knew she had to tell him why. "Because this is where I first dreamed about you."

"Not me. I'm not some prince. You must have me mistaken for some other guy."

"I know who you are, Riley. And I have a pretty good idea of who you're not. I don't mean I dreamed of you exactly. I just dreamed of feeling this way, a little bit wild, reckless, like I'm about to jump off a cliff and I'm not sure where I'm going to land."

"Maybe you should back away from the edge."

"You're the one who makes me want to go higher and see what's on the other side." She touched his lips with hers, tentative at first, then with more confidence when he didn't reject her. "I'm going to make you forget who you are and where you are. The only thing in your head and your heart will be me," she whispered against his mouth, feeling his warm hands run up her back as she pressed her breasts against his chest and ran her tongue along the line of his lips.

Riley groaned deep in his throat. "You're killing me, Paige. I'm going to stop saying no if you're not careful."

"Good, because I don't intend to be careful." She covered his mouth with hers, diving into the kiss with her heart and her soul, giving him everything she'd dreamed of giving a man. No holding back. No second thoughts. It was all about this one moment, this one incredible kiss.

She threaded her hands through his hair, drawing him as close as she could, and when his arm slid around her body and hauled her up tight against his chest, she knew there was no turning back. She let reality go, stroking his tongue and feeling the rest of her body respond with a sense of desperation she'd never experienced before. She wanted him more than she wanted to breathe. She'd never felt so needy, so starving.

A moment later, the breath was completely knocked out of her when Riley moved suddenly, tossing her on her back, his hard body pushing her into the soft pillows.

"You didn't think I was going to let you call all the shots, did you?" he asked.

A shiver of anticipation ran down her spine at the intense male look in his eyes. He cupped her head with his hands, imprisoning her face for his very thorough kiss. Then his mouth left hers to dance along the side of her cheek, down the column of her neck across her collarbone as if he were following a path straight to her heart. But it wasn't just her heart calling him. Her breasts were tight and aching, eager for the touch of his fingers, his mouth. Her legs were moving restlessly between his, her body yearning to complete the connection between them.

"Damn." Riley pulled back with a breathless curse. "What's wrong?"

"I don't have anything. Protection. Safe sex. You know." He ran a frustrated hand through his hair.

"Oh. Don't you have anything in your wallet?"

"I don't have my wallet."

"You don't have your wallet? But you drove us here. Did you drive us here without your driver's license?"

He stared at her in amazement. "Is that really the most important thing on your mind right now?"

"Sorry."

"What about your purse? Don't you keep anything handy in your purse?"

"I own a dozen purses, Riley. And today I used the sneak-into-my-mother's-house purse, which does not come with condoms."

"Then that's that."

No, this couldn't be happening, not now when she wanted sex more than she'd ever wanted it in her life. Think, she told herself. "Wait. Oh, my God. I think I can save us."

"I sure as hell hope so."

"You'll have to let me up."

He sat back, and she slid off the bed, walking over to her bookcase. She ran her fingers along the spines of novels she'd read during her high school years. There it was, The Odyssey, a thousand pages that her mother would never dream of reading. She flipped through the pages until two foil-wrapped condoms dropped out. She picked them up and held them out triumphantly to Riley. "They're still here."

"From what decade, Paige?"

She pursed her lips. "They're not that old. I didn't buy them until after I graduated from college. I was trying to be a grown-up."

"So, you bought condoms and hid them in a book," he said with a laugh.

"I didn't want the housekeeper to find them and report them to my mother, because then I'd get the lecture on strange men and strange diseases."

"You are crazy."

"You want me anyway." She walked toward him, dropping the condoms on the comforter.

"I do," he agreed, taking her hand and pulling her back down on the bed.

"Good."

He pushed her back against the pillows. "Now, where were we? I know." His hand went to the buttons on her shirt, his fingers playing with those buttons for long minutes, while he leisurely kissed her as if they had all the time in the world. She wanted him to pick up the pace. She wanted that hand on her breast, and it seemed to be taking forever for him to undo the buttons.

"You're torturing me," she muttered.

His grin told her just how much he was enjoying the process. "I know."

"Riley."

"Paige," he echoed.

"Touch me."

"Oh, I intend to. I intend to do a lot of touching." His hand slid inside her shirt, his fingers slipping under the lace edge of her bra, circling one nipple and then the other as they tightened and peaked under his caress.

His mouth touched hers again as he explored her breast with his hand and his leg insinuated itself between hers. She moved her hand up under his shirt, caressing the taut muscles of his back. He was a strong, powerful man, and she loved the solid feel of his body, the way they moved together so perfectly. She had always believed that when it was really right, she would know it. And she knew it now. Knew it with all her heart.

Riley sat back, pulling his shirt over his head. She followed his lead, removing each item of clothing with a deliberate seriousness, her gaze never leaving his, answering all the questions in his eyes. She'd never stripped herself so bare before, lights blazing overhead, bodies completely exposed. That's the way she had wanted it. And she faced him bravely, offering herself to him in a way that she'd never offered any other man.

"I don't think I deserve this," he muttered. "Yes, you do. Let me show you why."

They met each other halfway, the slow teasing of the past few minutes replaced by breathless passion as they kissed, touched, stroked, caressed, made love to each other with their mouths, their bodies, their hearts, and their minds. Her dreams had never been this good.

Paige woke up disoriented. The bed didn't feel quite right, and there was something weighing her down. Blinking, she realized there was a strong male arm, flung heavily over her stomach. As she stirred, Riley's hold on her grew tighter, as if he didn't want to let her go, even in sleep. The events of the past few hours came flooding back into her mind. Making love to Riley had been better than she had imagined. He was a generous lover, inventive, adventurous, demanding, making her stretch, reach, be more than she thought she could be. And she'd tried to give him back what she suspected he needed, genuine caring, unconditional love.

Love. The word took her breath away. They hadn't used the word, but she didn't have to say it to know she felt it. She'd been falling in love with him since that first awkward tea party at the store. And she'd tumbled further and further each day. When would it end? When would she stop falling? When would it feel like every other relationship?

The cynical man in her bed would probably predict that possibility happening today or tomorrow or the next day. But she knew deep down it wasn't going to happen. She hadn't gone into this with blinders on. She knew what kind of man Riley was. He was terrified of commitment. He could risk his life on a battlefield but not his heart on a woman. But she also knew that he could love with loyalty and devotion; she'd seen that with his grandparents.

She wouldn't try to change him; she would just wait him out. Eventually he would realize what she already knew, that feelings like this didn't come around more than once in a lifetime. For the first time in her life that she'd made love to a man without all the trappings of romance, dinner, dancing, music, candlelight, flowers, candy. They hadn't needed any of those things, only each other. She put her hand on his arm and smiled to herself. Even if she didn't have tomorrow, she would not regret tonight.

A wave of light flashed through the window and she heard the sound of a car pulling into the garage. "Oh, my God, my mother is home," she said, shooting up in alarm.

"Paige?" Riley muttered in a sleepy voice.

"They're home. My mother and grandfather are home."

"Huh?"

"Jeez, you don't wake up very fast, do you?" She put her hands on his face. "Focus. My mother and grandfather are home. We have to get out of here without anyone seeing us."

His gaze sharpened. "Got it. You don't want Mom to see me."

"See us," she corrected. "Especially not naked here in my old bedroom."

"Right."

Paige scrambled out of bed, tossing clothes at Riley as she tried to find her own. "What time is it?"

Riley looked at his watch. "Ten forty-five."

"I can't believe we slept so long."

"Well, you wore me out." He smiled. "You're not going to turn into a pumpkin, are you?"

"Ha-ha." She walked over to the door and turned off the light, not wanting her mother to see the light when she came down the hall. "She must still be downstairs. What do you think we should do?"

"We could have sex again until she goes to sleep."

She rolled her eyes. "We already used up my stash."

"Are you sure you didn't hide anything in another book, maybe *The Little Princess* or how about *The Scarlet Letter*?"

"You're quite the funny man tonight, aren't you?"

He offered her an unrepentant grin. "I like you flustered."

"You just like me."

"Maybe a little."

"More than a little." She saw him stiffen and added, "Don't worry, this isn't the *tell me you love me and want to be with me forever* moment."

"It's not?" he asked, unable to hide the note of relief in his voice.

She laughed. "You scare so easily." She stopped abruptly at the sound of footsteps on the stairs. They slowed down by her door, and Paige had the sudden thought that maybe her door was usually left open, not closed. Holding her breath, she hoped her mother wouldn't take this moment to notice the anomaly, although her mother was certainly one to notice just such things. The footsteps moved on, and she let out her breath.

She wondered if her mother would check on her father or go straight to bed. Thinking about her father made her feel a little guilty that she hadn't bothered to check on him herself. Not hearing anything more, she opened her door a crack and peeked out. The hallway was empty. "I think it's safe," she whispered. "But be quiet. My mother has excellent hearing."

She took Riley's hand as they crept down the stairs. They managed to make it down the stairs without any doors opening behind them or voices calling out. They were almost to the front door when she realized someone was in the living room. She grabbed Riley and pulled him across the hall into the dining room. There was no way they could open and close the front door without whoever was in the living room hearing them.

"Is that my mother?" she whispered.

Riley peered around the corner then looked back at her. "It's your grandfather. He's opening a safe."

"There's no safe in the living room."

Riley took another look. "Behind the portrait by the window."

"That's not possible." She pushed him aside to take a look herself, and what she saw was shocking. She'd thought she'd known where all the family safes were. There was one in the study, one in her mother's bedroom, another in the linen closet, although why there was one there she'd never been able to explain. But no one had told her about the one in the living room. She was so annoyed by the oversight that she stepped into the hall.

"What are you doing, Paige?" Riley asked. "Do you want him to see you?"

"I think I do," she said decisively.

"You're going to take a step you may not be able to take back," he warned her.

"It seems to be the night for that. Are you coming with me?"

"After you, princess."

She drew in a deep breath, walked across the hall, and entered the living room just as her grandfather turned away from the safe with a very familiar object in his hands.

Her body stiffened in amazement. "Oh, my God! That's the other dragon."

CHAPTER TWENTY-THREE

HER GRANDFATHER DREW himself up to his full height, his eyes blazing with anger. Paige couldn't help but take a step back. Actually, she was tempted to run out of the room, but Riley's solid body blocked her exit.

"What the hell are you doing here, Paige?" her grandfather demanded.

She couldn't speak. The dragon in his hands was the last thing she had expected to see. "I—I came to...." She couldn't think. Her grandfather had the other dragon. How? When? Why? The questions raced around her mind, but she couldn't get any of them out.

"Who are you?" her grandfather asked, his gaze now fixed on Riley.

"Riley McAllister. Ned Delaney's grandson."

Wallace was not surprised. That small fact registered with Paige before anything else. He knew who Riley was. In fact, it was obvious now he knew a lot more than he was telling.

"Where did you get that dragon?" she asked, finally putting a voice to her thoughts. "You told me you'd never seen a dragon like the one that was stolen last week, but this is an exact duplicate. You lied to me. Why?"

"It's none of your business. This is my property. I don't owe you any explanations."

"But you owe me." The voice came from the doorway. David Hathaway entered the room wearing a silk robe over his pajamas. He looked tired and pale, but his eyes were filled with excitement. "Where did you get that dragon?"

"You should be in bed. You look like death," Wallace replied, ignoring the question.

"I got up to get some water. I heard voices." David stared at the dragon in Wallace's hands. "I remember now. I saw the dragon on the television show, and you—" His gaze swung to Riley. "You and your grandmother brought it in to the store."

"That's right," Riley said tersely. "And you took it without telling anyone. The next thing we knew, the dragon was gone, and you were in the hospital."

"I took it to show Jasmine. Then I went to show it to someone, a man who can spot a fake bronze from a mile away. I had to be sure my excitement wasn't misleading me."

"Why didn't that man tell the police he had seen you that day? You were on the news every other hour," Paige said.

David hesitated. "He's very private."

"He works the black market," Riley interjected.

"Let him talk," Paige said. "What happened next, Dad?"

"I remember thinking that I needed to get home. I cut through the alley. And then—"

He stopped. "There were footsteps behind me. Someone was running. I was struck by a terrible force. I felt myself falling." He shook his head. "That's all I remember."

"You hit your head on the pavement," Paige said.

David drew in a breath, then let it out as he nodded.

"Why did you think you needed to get home and not back to the store where my grandmother and I were waiting?" Riley asked.

David glanced at Riley, then back at his father. "I wanted to speak to you," he said to Wallace. "A long time ago I saw a box that you had, and I thought it could be the one that goes with the dragons. I didn't realize you also had the other dragon—"

"What? He has the box?" Riley interrupted.

David didn't answer. Neither did her grandfather. The two men were staring at each other, a look passing between them that spoke of unfinished business. Paige couldn't help wondering just what her father knew and what else her grandfather was hiding.

"The box you saw was from the Ming dynasty," Wallace replied. "It has no connection to the dragon."

"I find that difficult to believe. It looked exactly the same."

"I don't care what you believe."

"Where did you get the dragon, then?" David asked.

"From a private collector. I thought I might one day find the other dragon and the box. Until then, I would keep the dragon safe." Wallace turned abruptly, putting the dragon back into the safe before anyone could move. He slammed the door shut and flicked the combination lock. Paige was startled by the movement. Her father, too, seemed taken aback. But Riley... She could feel the angry energy emanating from his body. She glanced over at him and saw a determination in his eyes that told her he wasn't about to let her grandfather end the conversation so quickly.

"I'd like to see that dragon," Riley said.

"I would, too," David added.

Wallace shrugged. "It's no one's business but mine."

"My grandfather had one just like it," Riley said. "And he worked for you. You were friends."

"We were friends until Ned betrayed me," Wallace replied. "I gave him a job. I treated him like a brother. And he paid me back by stealing the dragon and setting fire to the store to cover up his crime."

"That's a damn lie," Riley said.

"It's the goddamn truth," Wallace said, his eyes blazing. "And you gave me the proof when you and your grandmother showed up on television with the dragon he'd been hiding in his attic all these years."

"I don't believe you. My grandfather is an honest man."

"Then how did he get the dragon?"

"I don't know. But then, we don't know how you got yours either, do we?"

"I told you, a private collector—"

"You also told us only a minute ago that you only had one," Riley reminded him. "Now you're saying you had two, and my grandfather stole one."

For the first time, Wallace looked confused. "Yes, well, I had both originally."

"But not the box?" David asked, rejoining the conversation. "Are you sure the box I saw didn't go with the dragons? If you had both dragons, where was the box?"

"That box wasn't part of the set."

"Open the safe," David said. "I want to see the dragon again."

"No."

"Dad almost died because of that dragon," Paige interjected. "Don't you think he has a right to see the matching one?"

There was a strange glitter in Wallace's eyes as he looked at David. "I'm sorry you were hurt. That shouldn't have happened."

"Why are you sorry? You didn't have anything to do with it." David's eyes narrowed, the expression on his face changing several times. "Did you have something to do with the robbery?" he asked in shock.

"I'm eighty-two years old. You think I go around knocking people off in alleys?"

"Maybe not just anyone," David said slowly, his mouth set in a grim line. "But I'm not just anyone, am I?"

Paige had a sick feeling in the pit of her stomach. "Dad, you can't believe—"

"Can't I?" David interrupted, his gaze still fixed on his father.

The two men exchanged a long look that Paige couldn't begin to decipher.

"Your grandfather certainly could have hired someone to do whatever he needed to have done," Riley said to Paige.

"No!" Paige turned on him in fury. "Don't accuse my grandfather of hurting his own son. Are you crazy? He wouldn't do that."

"Wouldn't he?" Riley looked her straight in the eye. "Look at the facts, Paige."

"There aren't any facts, just speculation. We need to calm down, talk this through."

"Playing the peacemaker again, princess?"

"Someone has to."

"You just want to give your grandfather and your father time to cover up. A Hathaway to the bitter end."

She was stung by the cold fury in his voice and felt her own temper rise. "Maybe you should go."

"So you can hide the dragon?"

"I'm not hiding anything. But you're not helping."

"She's right. Get out," Wallace said shortly. "Or I'll have you thrown out."

"And who's going to do that?" Riley challenged. "Are you going to call the police, Wally? Because I think I'd like them to come. I'd like you to tell them why you have a dragon in your safe that looks exactly like the one that was stolen from me."

"We know there are two," Paige said desperately. "They're identical. This could be the other one."

"Take off the rose-colored glasses, Paige. This isn't the other one. This is the same one."

"Please, just go." She had to think. She needed time to sort things out, to make sense of it all.

He looked as if she'd just stabbed him in the heart. "You really are choosing them, aren't you?" he asked.

"It's not a choice. It's too much too fast. I can't keep up with it all."

"Sure you can; you just don't want to. But this isn't over. I'll find out the truth, and when I do, someone will pay."

"That someone will be your grandfather," Wallace said.

"We'll see about that." Riley strode from the room without another glance in Paige's direction. His exit was punctuated by the slamming of the front door.

For a moment there was only silence in the room. Paige was afraid to look at her father or her grandfather, afraid of what she would see in their eyes. She had a terrible feeling that Riley might just be right about everything.

"I want to see the dragon again," David said. "Open the safe, Father."

"It's late. I'm going to bed."

She looked up as David moved in front of Wallace, blocking his way. There they stood face-to-face, shoulder-to-shoulder, father and son. Paige had always believed her grandfather was the stronger of the two, but right now her father was holding his own.

"The dragon in the safe is the same dragon I held in my hands," David said slowly. "Mr. McAllister was right. That's what you don't want me to see, isn't it? You didn't have two dragons. You had none. Until you stole the one from me in the alley."

"No," Paige breathed, but neither one of them was paying any attention to her.

"Did you mean to kill me, too?" David asked in a voice that sounded almost dispassionate. "Was that part of the plan?"

Wallace didn't say anything for a moment, then said, "I didn't want you to get hurt. They were supposed to take the dragon and bring it back to me. No one was supposed to get hurt."

Paige sank down on a nearby chair as her legs gave out from under her. Her grandfather had had his own son robbed? And she'd just stood up for her family? Taken their side over Riley's? She'd made a terrible, terrible mistake.

"Why didn't you tell me you wanted the dragon?" David asked. "Why steal it?"

"I didn't want to pay for it. It was mine. Ned stole it from me. I wanted it back. It was simpler just to take it"

"Simpler?" Paige echoed in disbelief, drawing their attention back to her. "Dad was almost killed. You call that simple?"

Wallace's face tightened at her criticism. "I told you that was an accident."

"And you expect him to forgive you for it? I don't understand you at all."

"You don't have to understand. I was settling an old debt. And your father will be fine." He paused. "No one will ever know. It's done now. Tomorrow this dragon, too, will disappear."

"It's not done," Paige countered. "Riley won't let it go. He's probably on his way to tell the police right now. He'll get a search warrant. They'll come to get the dragon."

"It won't be here, and surely you don't think Mr. McAllister is any match for a Hathaway?" Wallace's cool, ruthless smile made Paige shiver. "The police chief is a friend of ours. He will not be obtaining any search warrants. Your Mr. McAllister will run into one brick wall after another until he gives up."

"He doesn't give up easily."

"He'll have no other choice, not if he wants to run his business in this city."

"You're really flexing your muscles, aren't you?"

"I'm showing you what it means to be a Hathaway. Maybe it's time you decided whether or not you're up to the challenge."

And with that Wallace left the room, leaving chaos and confusion in his wake.

David sat down on the couch, resting his head in his hands, looking exhausted, overwhelmed, and defeated. "He always wins, Paige. He always wins."

She went to him, kneeling down in front of him, putting her hands on his knees, forcing her father to look at her. "Not this time," she said. "We can't let him win this time. This isn't about honor. It's about cheating. That's not what Hathaways are about."

"Isn't it? I cheated on your mother."

"That's not the same thing."

"Your mother cuts corners at the store every chance she gets."

"That's just good business sense."

"And your grandfather—well, where do you think he got the dragon in the first place, Paige? You're the only one who still has some goodness left. You should get out of this family while you have the chance."

"I don't think I can." Paige sat down on the couch next to him, her mind reeling with information. They'd never spoken this frankly in their lives. It was difficult to take it all in.

"I've made so many mistakes," David said.

Which reminded her... "You have. You should have told me about Jasmine and Alyssa, especially Alyssa. She's my sister. I should have known about her," Paige said. "Why didn't you support her? See her, even if it was only in secret?"

"Her mother wanted it that way. And your mother would have wanted it that way, too. I'm a very weak man, Paige. I couldn't stand up to either one of them. The last thing I ever wanted was for you to know the truth about me. But now you do. And I'm sorry."

A part of her wanted to put her arms around him and give him a hug, tell him that it didn't matter, that he would always be her father. But that was the old Paige. Sometime in the past week—or maybe in the past few minutes—she'd grown up. "I don't think sorry is enough. Maybe for me, but not for Alyssa. You owe her, Dad. You owe her support, love, and acceptance. She's your daughter. She deserves that as much as I do or Elizabeth did."

"I was missing Elizabeth," he said quietly. "That's how it started. Jasmine was there. She was kind. She listened. It's not an excuse, just a reason. We met at a party. She was a waitress working for the caterer. She was beautiful then, warm, kind. She reminded me that there was still some life in me. But I destroyed her life just as she gave me mine back."

"Did you know that Jasmine's father, Lee Chen, was the man who rescued Grandfather during the war?"

"What?" David looked surprised. "How can that be?"

"The three of them knew each other, Ned Delaney, Lee Chen, and Grandfather. I think they found at least one of the dragons and maybe even the box in China and brought them back here to San Francisco. After that, I'm not sure what happened. But it's strange that you and Jasmine should end up together. And that she should dream of dragons. It all seems so unexplainable."

"The mysteries of the universe. Perhaps I've spent too much time in the Far East, but I believe that there are patterns and connections everywhere. Destiny plays a bigger role than we imagine. Maybe those dragons want to come back together. That's why they're pulling all of us toward each other."

It was an eerie, mystical explanation for what was happening, but there seemed to be some truth in it. The dragons were bringing them together, this third generation. Maybe they were the ones who were meant to put the pieces of the set back together, too. "Do you still think Grandfather has the box?"

"Yes," David said without hesitation. "I'm sure of it."

"Then that leaves one dragon missing. If Ned had a dragon and Grandfather had the box, then it stands to reason that Lee Chen had the other dragon. I think it's time you and Jasmine had a talk. And Alyssa, too," she added. "We'll need everyone to get to the bottom of this."

Riley didn't sleep all night, considering the options available to him. After leaving the Hathaway house, he'd gone to the police station but hadn't gotten beyond leaving messages for the officers investigating the robbery. He'd gone home, tried to sleep, but gave up as the sun rose.

Getting out of bed, he went on a grueling bike ride around the city, watching San Francisco come to life. It was the day before the Chinese New Year he realized as he passed by traffic control officers putting up signs and roadblocks for the parade that would begin at five o'clock in the afternoon. Tonight all of Chinatown would celebrate the dawning of a new year.

He wished he could feel a sense of hope and wonder, that he could look forward to a new year filled with good fortune, but he couldn't feel any of those things. He'd left them behind in the Hathaway mansion. He still couldn't believe Paige had stood up for her grandfather. The old bastard was a liar. That was obvious to anyone. But no, not Paige. She still couldn't see past her last name. Well, why should he have expected it to be any different? He knew who she was. He'd known all along. He'd just forgotten for a while.

Lost in her arms, in her kiss, in her body, he'd forgotten pretty much everything. Even now his body was hardening at the thought of her, which was damn uncomfortable considering he was riding a mountain bike. But the pain in his body was nothing compared to the pain in his heart. He'd let her in. And she'd hurt him. When was he ever going to learn to stop believing in fairy tales and happily ever afters? They didn't happen to guys like him. They never had, and they never would.

He pedaled harder, keeping his head down, his heart racing, his mind occupied so he wouldn't have to think. Somehow, he ended up at his grandmother's house. He got off the bike and walked up to the front door. It was almost eight now, and he suspected his grandmother was already up and making coffee for whichever one of the three muske-teers had spent the night on her couch. He could probably call them off now. He suspected Wallace Hathaway had been behind the burglary. He'd probably been looking for the other dragon, the one still missing.

Bud opened the door for him. "Riley. Saw you coming. Anything wrong?"

"No," he lied. "How's my grandmother?"

"I'm fine, honey," Nan said as she came down the hall from the kitchen. "And while I've enjoyed having the company of Bud, Charlie, and Gilbert, I think their wives would be happy if you ended this assignment."

"I was just thinking the same thing. You can go on home, Bud. Thanks for your work."

"Are you sure it's safe now? I don't want to leave Nan in any danger."

"I think she'll be all right, and I'll keep an eye on her."

"I'll be fine," Nan said with a firm tone.

Bud grabbed his jacket and headed out the door without any more encouragement. Riley followed his grandmother into the kitchen. "Is that bacon I smell?"

"Yes, it is. Take a seat. Do you want eggs, too?"

Riley sat down at the kitchen table as his grandmother put a plate of bacon in front of him. "This is plenty."

"You look like you sweated off enough calories this morning to eat whatever you want. Don't tell me you rode that bike of yours all the way over here?"

"Okay, I won't tell you."

Nan sat down across from him. "'What's wrong?"

"Everything," he said heavily.

"It's Paige, isn't it? I knew you liked her."

"Yeah, well, it doesn't much matter."

"Why not?"

"It's a long story, but let's just say that Paige will protect her family's reputation no matter who else gets hurt in the process."

Nan's eyes sharpened. "Who else is going to get hurt?"

"Maybe Grandpa."

"Oh, honey, I don't think your Grandpa could get hurt right now."

"Wallace Hathaway claims that Grandpa stole that dragon from him and tried to burn down the store fifty years ago. It's crazy, I know. Grandpa would not do any of that. And I know they don't have any proof, or they would have done something before now. But I don't want your name being dragged through the mud."

Nan's expression grew troubled. "Oh, dear. That doesn't sound good."

"You don't sound as shocked as I thought you would be." An uneasy feeling ran through him.

"I don't know anything about what you just said, honey, but I know Ned had a bit of a temper when he was younger. And he could be a show-off, a braggart. He liked to impress people. I thought it was rather charming. I kind of liked his bad boy image to tell you the truth."

Riley's eyes widened. " 'His bad boy image'?"

"He drank quite a bit when I first met him. He was always hanging out at the Irish pubs, telling stories. He was a little wild back then. All the girls loved him, but he didn't always treat them right. Until he met me, of course. Then he changed. Not all the way, though—there was always a toughness about him " She paused. "Life wasn't that easy for Ned. He grew up poor, got drafted when he was eighteen, went to war, almost got killed from what I understand. Then when he came back, he had to find work in a city that didn't think much of Irishmen. He always struggled. But he always found a way to survive."

"Do you think he could have stolen something from Hathaway's?"

"No," she said quickly. "He wasn't a thief."

"I didn't think so," Riley said, much relieved.

"But there could have been a misunderstanding," she continued.

And just like that his relief fled. "What kind of misunderstanding?"

"I couldn't say. But now that we're talking about all this, I do remember that Ned was very upset after the fire at Hathaway's. I thought it was because he would be out of a job for a few months. Maybe there was more to it. I don't know. We didn't talk about his work much. I do know this. Your grandfather wasn't perfect. He made mistakes. He was human. I know you love and respect him, Riley, but don't put him up on a pedestal or under a microscope. Not many of us could withstand such scrutiny."

"It might not be my choice."

"Paige won't hurt you. She likes you too much. I saw it in her eyes." She smiled at him. "And I am never wrong."

"You might be this time."

"We'll see. I have faith in that girl. She'll come through. She'll do the right thing."

He had a feeling that Paige's idea of the "right thing" would be vastly different from his own.

CHAPTER TWENTY-FOUR

"WE NEED TO DO THIS," Alyssa told her mother as Jasmine prepared breakfast for them in her apartment.

"We are not invited to the New Year's Eve celebration."

"It's a family party, and we're family. I say we go."

"Why?"

"Because this is the most important holiday of the year. It's a time when families are supposed to be together, and I feel a strange and intense need to be with my family this year."

"You do?" Jasmine asked with surprise.

"Yes. I want you to come with me. I don't care what Grandmother has to say about it, or anyone else for that matter. Just this once, Ma. Please say you'll come with me."

"You're up to something," Jasmine said. "What is it? What are you planning?"

"Nothing," Alyssa lied. Actually, her plan was only half formed at the moment. She knew one thing for certain, though. She needed to stop running away from who she was and face up to it. Ben was right about that. Tonight would change that. Tonight would be a step forward for all of them. "Will you come?" she asked again. "I won't take no for an answer."

"I will bring dishonor to the occasion."

"No, you will bring pride and strength and love." Alyssa got to her feet and kissed her mother on the cheek. "It's about time the rest of the family sees what I have always known."

"You have such faith in me. I don't deserve it."

"Yes, you do. And you deserve a lot more. This past week has made me realize so many things."

"You are not still angry with me about your father?"

"Well, I wouldn't go that far," she said with a gentle smile. "Which brings me to my next request. I want you to ask him to come over here before we go to Grandmother's tonight. I want to meet him face-to-face."

"Oh, Alyssa, I don't know if that is wise. And he may not be strong enough. He just got out of the hospital."

"Ask him and see."

"I don't call him. I never call him."

"If you don't, I will. And I'll leave a message with his wife, if I have to."

Jasmine frowned. "I think I like it better when you stay away from Chinatown, when you want nothing to do with family."

"You're never happy. I'll see you after work. We have a new year to welcome in."

"Are you sure you won't change your mind?"

"I'm sure. Call my father. Tell him it's about time he saw his daughter."

Paige had plenty of time to change her mind on her way to Riley's apartment. In fact, she drove around the block twice before pulling into a parking spot and shutting off the engine. It was after nine on a Monday morning. He might not be home. But she'd already checked the office, and his secretary had said he hadn't come in yet. He could be on a bike ride. She'd have to check the highest hills in San Francisco next. But maybe she'd get lucky and find him at home.

As she walked down the street toward his building, she realized his garage door was open. Bypassing the front door, she slipped into the garage and saw that both bikes were there. Since she doubted he'd leave his garage open if he wasn't there, she went through the door leading up the stairs into his laundry room.

"Riley?" she called. There was no answer. Venturing farther into his apartment, she heard water running. He was in the shower.

Damn. She wanted to get this over with, wanted to apologize to him, beg his forgiveness, claim a moment of temporary insanity, and hope he was willing to meet her halfway. She had hurt him, and she regretted everything she had said. She knew the truth about her family now. And she knew that the man in the shower was the most honorable man she had ever met. The father she had adored was weak. The grandfather she had admired was a ruthless liar. But Riley—a man who came from nothing, who had struggled to survive a neglected childhood, who had served his country, who had come back to support his grandmother—was a strong, courageous man, an incredible human being. He was the man she really loved. And she hoped to God she hadn't lost him forever.

She walked into the bedroom and saw the open bathroom door, wisps of steam coming from the shower like tantalizing fingers beckoning her forward. She couldn't do that, could she? A knot of desire grabbed hold of her as she thought about stripping off all of her clothes and joining him. He'd be shocked. She'd be shocked. It was not Hathaway behavior at all. But then, Hathaway behavior wasn't what it used to be.

She unzipped her high-heeled boots and slipped them off. Her jeans and shirt followed. Standing in his bedroom in nothing but a bra and panties, she had more second thoughts. He'd been so angry with her last night. He was probably still furious. Maybe he wouldn't want her. Or maybe he would. Maybe they could connect in a physical way even if they couldn't connect on any other level. It was worth a shot. She was desperate.

She unhooked her bra and slid off her panties. She heard the shower being turned off. The shower door opened.

Damn, she was too late. She wanted to grab something to cover herself, but she'd made the dramatic point of tossing her clothes across the room.

Riley walked into the bedroom with a towel in his hand and nothing else on his body. He stopped in surprise when he saw her. "Paige'?"

"You weren't supposed to get out of the shower yet."

"I was done."

"I guess I'm too late then."

"That depends on what you want. I'm all out of hot water."

She took a deep breath. "I wasn't really looking for hot water. I was looking for you." "Why?"

"You're not going to make this easy, are you?"

"No way."

"I'm sorry, Riley. I was wrong. My family is basically pretty sick. I shouldn't have defended them. I shouldn't have asked you to leave. I was afraid." She drew in a deep breath. "I hope that maybe you can forgive me."

"Why? Because Paige Hathaway always gets what she wants?"

"No, because Paige Hathaway has finally found a man worth loving, and she really doesn't want to lose him because she was stupid."

His mouth tightened, and she could see a battle going on in his eyes. She didn't know if he was fighting himself or her. "You should have left well enough alone," he said harshly. "I told you before this wasn't going anywhere."

"I can't accept that," she said simply. "I love you, Riley. You don't have to say it back. You don't even have to feel it. I'm feeling enough for both of us right now. Just give me a chance to show you what kind of person I really am." She crossed her arms in front of her breasts. "Did you happen to notice that I'm naked?"

"I noticed."

"What do you think about that?"

"I think you're pulling out all the stops."

"That's right. Whatever it takes, I'm willing to do it."

"Anything I want, huh?"

She swallowed back a knot of nervousness. "Anything. I'm just hoping that anything includes making love to you."

"Oh, it definitely includes that."

"Good." She saw a teasing light blossom in his eyes and felt the ugly tension between them dissolve. "Now, let's see how willing you are." She walked over and grabbed the towel he was holding in front of himself. "Not bad. I know you're a guy, and it doesn't take much."

"Just you," he said on a husky note.

She tossed the towel on the floor with her clothes, liking the way it fell on top of her bra and panties. That's where she wanted Riley to be —on top of her, inside of her, all around her. Their eyes locked in a moment of complete and utter intimacy.

His arms came around her body. His mouth claimed hers in a hard, passionate kiss. His hands cupped her bottom, puffing her into the heat she was craving. She was on fire, one burning need fueling every action. She wanted to get closer, but instead of letting her pull him into her very willing body, Riley took a step back, his breath ragged.

"We gotta slow down."

"No." She reached for him again, but he sidestepped.

"Patience, princess." He reached into the drawer by his bed and pulled out a foil-wrapped square packet. "Why don't you open this for me?"

She'd never done that before. What an odd realization that was. She smiled at Riley, then ripped open the foil packet with her teeth. She laughed at the astonished expression on his face, then moved forward until her body was only inches from his. She cupped him, hearing a deep groan of appreciation as she slid the condom on. "Is there anything else I can do for you?" she whispered.

"Hell, yes." He backed her up against the wall, gripped her bottom with his hands, and raised her until she could slide right down on top of him, taking him deep inside.

He filled her completely—and not just her body but her heart and her soul. She closed her eyes as they began to move in absolutely perfect unison.

Paige was sleeping on him, her head on his chest, her arm flung across his waist, her leg over his, as if she wasn't planning to let him go any time soon. And that certainly wasn't a problem, since he didn't want to let her go, either. He couldn't believe she'd come into his apartment, stripped down, and offered herself to him. He'd spent most of the previous night trying to convince himself she was all wrong, and here they were—back where they'd been yesterday. Because she was a beautiful, generous person, he realized. Because he cared about her more than he had ever thought possible.

"I can hear you thinking," Paige whispered. "Your heart started beating a little faster. What are you thinking about?"

"You," he muttered.

She raised her head and looked into his eyes. "Really?"

"You had a hell of a lot of nerve coming here like you did. How did you get in, anyway?"

"For a security expert, you don't keep your apartment very secure. I came in through the garage. It was wide open."

"Damn. That's right. The phone was ringing when I got back from my bike ride, and I must have forgotten to close the door. I bet half my stuff is gone by now."

"Do you want to go look?"

"Are you kidding? I'm in bed with a beautiful blonde. What's a bike or two?"

She laughed, her eyes sparkling with pleasure. God, she was pretty. Every time he saw her he thought she looked more appealing than the last time. Maybe it was because he wasn't just seeing her physical beauty now. He was seeing her, all the complicated feelings and emotions and actions that made her Paige.

Paige Hathaway, a little voice inside reminded him. A woman who'd only the night before chosen her family over him. Sure she'd apologized, but how could he be sure it wouldn't happen again?

"Now you're stiff, and I don't mean stiff in a good way," Paige said, frowning. "What's wrong?"

"Nothing."

"Liar. You're thinking about last night again. I was hoping we'd gotten past that."

"We will," he said, stroking her silky hair with his hand, "but we still have some things to resolve."

"I know—the dragon for one. My father and I talked last night. We agree that the dragon in the safe is the one you brought in. We think my grandfather has the box, which means there's one dragon missing, and there's only one other person I can think of who might have it."

"Lee Chen," Riley said. "I think so, too."

"My father said something else that was interesting. He thinks the dragons are calling us together. They want to be reunited. They're making it happen."

"They're doing a damn good job of it," he said with a grin.

"Yes, they are. Now it's up to us, Riley, the third generation, to put those pieces back together and return them to China where they belong. What do you think about making another trip to Chinatown tonight?"

"It's a good idea."

"I'm going to call Alyssa. We'll go to her grandparents' house together."

"It's the Chinese New Year's Eve," he reminded her. "The anniversary of the fire."

"And the perfect time to figure out just what happened that night."

"What are we going to do until then?" He was getting hard again, already wanting her, already feeling as if it had been too long since he'd last made love to her although it had only been an hour or so.

"I can think of a few things," she said with a smile.

"So can I."

"Good. But this time you can open your own damn condom." She gave him a wicked smile. "I have a few other things I'd like to do with my mouth."

He groaned and knew he wasn't just lost; he was hopelessly lost.

"He's late. He's not coming," Alyssa told her mother as she paced restlessly back and forth across the living room. "It's almost five o'clock."

Jasmine sat on the couch, her hands folded calmly in her lap. "Sit down, Alyssa. You're wearing a hole in the carpet."

"This is a mistake. I shouldn't have asked you to call him. He doesn't want to see me. He doesn't want to know me."

"He will come. You will see."

"Fine. He'll come. I'll see. And then we'll go to my grandparents' house and ask them where the dragon is."

Jasmine's lips tightened. "I don't think it's a good idea. It's New Year's Eve. It is a special occasion. We cannot do it tonight."

"We have to do it tonight. I already spoke to Paige and Riley. We're going. And I hope you'll come, too."

"I will think about it."

A knock came at the door just as her mother finished speaking. Alyssa sent her a desperate look. "Maybe you should open it."

"You are my brave daughter," Jasmine said with a rare smile. "The one who always tells me I must not be so afraid. Now it is your turn."

Alyssa took a deep breath, squared her shoulders and answered the door.

"Alyssa." David Hathaway stood in the doorway, a handsome man with dark hair and dark eyes, eyes that looked like hers. Those eyes were pleading now, pleading for understanding. "I'm—I'm your father," he said.

God. She felt like crying. Why did she feel like crying? He hadn't wanted her. He hadn't taken any time to see her before, and only now because he'd had a near-death experience. That had to be the only reason he'd agreed to come.

"Can I come in?" he asked tentatively.

She nodded, her throat still too tight for words. She took a step back as he entered the apartment, dimly aware of him greeting her mother.

"Alyssa, shut the door," Jasmine instructed.

She hesitated. This might be her last chance to run. But she forced herself to shut the door, to look at the man who had fathered her. He was tall, almost six feet. He still had a bandage on his forehead, but it was obvious he was almost back to normal.

"You look like your mother," he said. "As beautiful as she is."

"I'm afraid I look more like you," she said, speaking for the first time. "Ma has always said I have your nose."

"And the Hathaway freckle," he said idly. "Paige is the only one who doesn't have it." He paused. "You met Paige, I heard."

"Yes. She's nicer than I expected."

"She chastised me for abandoning you."

"Is that why you've come now?"

"No. She only said what I have known for a long time. I want to apologize. I can't make up for what happened. But I want you to know that I do care about you, Alyssa."

"Why should I believe you?"

"I guess there's no reason," he said wearily.

"Why didn't you want to see me before?"

He sent Jasmine a desperate look, as if hoping she'd throw him a lifeline. Her mother remained stonily silent, letting him answer the question for himself.

"Ma already gave me the reasons she could think of," Alyssa told him. "I'd like to hear yours."

"It was never you I didn't want to see, it was myself. Looking at you would have been like looking at a mirror that showed all my flaws, all the bad things I've done in my life—cheating on my wife and hurting your mother. And it was also because of Elizabeth, my oldest daughter. She was my heart. I loved her so much. I wanted to die when she died. It was the end of everything good. For those few years in my life that I had Elizabeth, I was happy." He took a deep breath. "I had lost a mother and a sister when I was a child. For the next twenty years I was searching for something good. Elizabeth gave me back the joyous feeling. And then that was gone, too." He took a breath and continued. "When your mother and I got together, I knew it was wrong, but I did it, anyway. When she became pregnant with you, I felt as if my sin was being held up for the world to see. Everyone would think I was trying to replace Elizabeth with you. It felt like betrayal. I couldn't bear it."

It hurt to hear how much he had loved her half-sister. And she couldn't help noticing that Paige's name hadn't been mentioned throughout any of it. Hadn't Paige told her that their father had always loved Elizabeth the most? She wondered how Paige had felt growing up in a house with a favorite daughter, and how she'd felt afterward when she was the only one left, but not the child he really wanted.

"I can't change the past," he added. "I hope you'll give me a chance in the future to get to know you."

"Do you really want to? Or is this gesture just because you've been found out?"

"I want to," he said with surprise in his voice.

"Does your wife feel the same way?"

"No. In fact, she wants me to offer you a financial settlement to stay out of our lives."

Another stinging rejection. Alyssa didn't know why she hadn't expected it. The Hathaways weren't going to want her in their family any more than her own family did. "No, thank you," she said. "I don't need anything from you. In fact, I'm going to start repaying the money I owe you for my college education. It might take a while, but I can do it," she said proudly.

"I don't want your money, Alyssa. And I'm not offering you a payoff. I'm done with hiding. I almost lost my life cutting through a dark alley." He smiled at Jasmine. "And I hope someday you'll forgive me, too, for not supporting you when you needed it the most."

"I always knew what I was getting," Jasmine said. "You never lied to me, David. Maybe to everyone else, but not to me."

Alyssa followed the look that passed between them and saw something that resembled love. Maybe she hadn't been the product of a sordid affair. Maybe her parents really did have feelings for each other. The thought made her feel better. "Why did you bring the dragon to show my mother?" she asked, the question still bothering her.

"I knew how much the dragon meant to her." He smiled again at Jasmine. "When I saw it, I wanted to give it to you, to free you from the dreams that kept you awake night after night. I probably should have left it with you. It would have been safer here. Or perhaps not. It might have brought you even more trouble."

"It is cursed, David. I believe that now even more."

"Yes." He paused. "I do need to ask you both a favor."

Alyssa's newfound serenity quickly fled. "What do you want?"

"Paige told me you are all going to your grandparents' house tonight. I want to go with you."

"Oh, David," Jasmine said. "They would not like it."

"Who cares if they like it or not?" Alyssa asked. "We know they've been lying to you about the dragon. We have to confront them, and you must come with us."

"I am afraid," Jasmine replied. "I don't have a good feeling about this."

David took Jasmine's hand in his "I will be there for you. It's about time I gave you back some of the strength you once gave me."

CHAPTER TWENTY-FIVE

THE COLORS WERE AMAZING, lighting up the twilight sky with mystery and excitement, Paige thought as she and Riley stopped to look at the parade that was currently blocking their way into Chinatown. There were children in costumes, some playing instruments, some dancing, others just walking and waving amid the colorful floats weaving their way down the street.

"This is incredible. I've never seen this before," she said loudly as Riley bent down to hear her.

"Me, either, except on the news."

He wrapped his arm around her waist and pulled her close, reminding her of just how close they'd spent most of the day. They'd made love several times, each time more passionate and demanding than the last, as if they both were testing the limits of their feelings. Her body felt sore and achy, but wonderfully satisfied, she thought with a smile. Whatever happened tonight, she would never regret this day.

"Look at that," Riley said, pointing to several enormous lions that were now dancing through the streets. Each lion was operated by two men. The head was carried by one dancer who would rear up, then crouch down, while the other man carried the body, carefully copying his moves. The lion danced to the accompaniment of gongs and drums. As they watched, more characters, including monkeys and clowns, entertained the crowd with acrobatics.

"Amazing," Paige said. "I never knew until this past week how really isolated I've been. I live in a city of intensely different cultures, and I've hardly experienced any of them."

"Hard to do that from a mansion on the hill."

"I'll be spending more time on the street from now on. I like all the excitement, the music, the laughter, the life. Don't laugh at me," she said, seeing amusement on his face. "I can't help how I was raised. It's what I do with the rest of my life that counts, isn't it?"

"Absolutely. And I can't wait to see what you do with it."

"Neither can I."

"We better go."

"Wait, there it is, the dragon." But she wasn't talking about the dragon statue, she was talking about the enormous paper dragon coming down the street toward them. A man paraded in front of the dragon, carrying a lantern. The dragon's head was held up by a pole carried by another man. The tail of the dragon followed, as far back as she could see, with thirty, forty, maybe fifty people carrying the tail as it danced down the street.

Once the dragon had passed by them, Riley took her hand and pulled her down the street, looking for an opportunity to cross to the other side. Most of the crowd was following the dragon, so the streets were thinning out quickly. A few minutes later they were passing in front of the herb shop, which was currently closed. There was a door next to the shop leading into the building itself.

"I wonder where Alyssa is," she said, checking her watch.

"Right there," Riley replied.

She turned to see Alyssa coming down the street, flanked on both sides by her parents, Jasmine and David. Paige supposed she might have felt angry or upset to see her father with another woman, another daughter, but in truth she felt pleased that he'd done the right thing. When he'd told her his intention to accompany Alyssa to the Chens' tonight, she hadn't been sure he'd go through with it. Maybe there was hope for him yet.

"I'm glad you all came," she said, reassuring them with a warm smile. "There is strength in numbers."

Riley opened the door to the building. "Shall we go in?"

Paige stood back, allowing Alyssa and Jasmine to go first. It was their family, after all.

At the top of the stairs, Alyssa knocked on the door. "They might not be home," she said. "They're probably still at the parade. But everyone will come back here for dinner."

"Do you have a key?" Riley asked.

"I do," Jasmine said, holding up a long, silver key. "I haven't used it twenty-two years."

"Then it's time," Alyssa said.

They all waited as Jasmine inserted the key into the lock and turned the handle.

The Chens' apartment was small, crowded with mismatched furniture and knickknacks. The delicious smell of many Chinese dishes wafted from the kitchen. The dining room table was set for a feast. Paige had a terrible feeling they were about to ruin what was supposed to be the happiest day of the year.

A loud sound from the next room set them all back on their heels.

"Someone is here," Jasmine whispered in a panic. "We must go."

But it was too late to leave. A tiny Asian woman came through the door in a rush. Her eyes widened at the sight of them. "What are you doing here?" she demanded. "You go. You all go. Too early for dinner." She tried to shoo them away, but no one was moving.

"We want to talk to you," Alyssa said. "Before the others come back."

"No, you come back later."

The front door opened behind them to reveal a short, elderly man. Lee Chen, Paige realized, the man who had rescued her and Riley's grandfathers so long ago. He appeared taken aback by their presence, and as his gaze went from one to the other, he seemed to grow more alarmed.

"Jasmine, explain," he said. "Who are these people?"

Jasmine couldn't seem to get her mouth open. Paige almost felt sorry for her. She looked completely overwhelmed. Her father went to Jasmine's side and took her hand in his. Paige was stunned at how oddly dispassionate she felt. Her father was holding the hand of another woman, a woman not her mother. And while she would never have put Jasmine and her father together before, they seemed almost right for each other.

Jasmine needed him. And that was something his own wife had never felt—need. Jasmine looked up to him as if he were important, and her mother had always looked down. It suddenly became so clear to Paige what had drawn these two rather eccentric people together. Alyssa was watching them, too. Alyssa, her sister, watching her own parents together for the first time. A rush of emotion threatened to overwhelm her. Paige sought out the hand of the man standing next to her, and his strength filled her with resolve.

"I'm Paige Hathaway," she said, taking charge. "This is my father, David. And my friend, Riley McAllister, who is the grandson of a man you might remember, Ned Delaney."

Lee Chen's face paled at her words. "Why did you come here? Why did you bring him?" he said to Jasmine in anger. "You dishonor us, dishonor the family. You should go."

"You're a fine one to talk of dishonor," a man said from the doorway.

Paige was shocked to see her grandfather, Wallace Hathaway, walk into the room like a king visiting the local peasants. He was dressed in an expensive suit, and he looked every inch the successful business-man, a direct contrast to the old, baggy clothes worn by Lee Chen. The room went still at his appearance. She had the distinct impression that this was the first time in many years that these two old men had laid eyes on each other. But they were looking now, staring at each other with an intensity that spoke of a troubled past.

"What are you doing here, Grandfather?" she asked.

"I came to get my dragon back. Where is it?"

"I don't have your dragon. You steal it and keep it for yourself,"

Lee Chen said.

"You and Ned conspired against me. If he had one, you must have the other," Wallace replied.

"I do not," Lee said firmly, waving his hand in the air. "Get out of my house. You are not welcome here."

"Don't tell me where I'm not welcome. I'm the one who got you to this country, and how did you repay me? By stealing and burning down my store—"

"I thought you said my grandfather did that," Riley interrupted. "So you really don't know who did it, do you? Maybe you did it yourself. Maybe you wanted to cover something up, take the insurance money, start over."

"The person who burned down my store is the person who took the dragons out of the basement that night. That would be Ned or Lee," Wallace said. "I've known that all along."

"Why did you wait until now to come looking?" Riley asked, echoing the question in Paige's mind.

"Because I thought that the dragons had been destroyed in the fire. The store was a twenty-feet high pile of junk after that blaze. The cleanup wasn't as efficient as it would be today. I lost everything. When I saw your grandfather's dragon, I realized it had escaped the fire, and I suspected the other one had, too."

"And you knew my grandfather didn't have the other dragon because you had his house searched," Riley said. "You probably had my grandmother watched, too, didn't you? I knew someone was tailing us that very first day we went to the store."

Paige's eyes widened as Riley put together another piece of the puzzle that hadn't yet occurred to her. Wallace didn't confirm or deny the accusation, but Paige could see the truth in her grandfather's eyes. When he hadn't been able to get the dragon away from Riley and his grandmother, he'd had someone follow David until there was an opportunity to snatch the dragon back.

"Why did you wait until now to come here?" Riley asked.

"I don't have to explain anything to you. Where is the other dragon?" Wallace said turning his attention back to Lee. "I want it."

"I don't have it," Lee Chen stubbornly repeated. "I never had it. And I didn't set the fire."

"You were just the first one on the scene, is that it?"

"Yes. I was there. I tried to put the fire out. I tried to save the store. I never saw the dragons. I don't know where they are."

"You must know where one is," Jasmine said quietly. "It's here, somewhere in this apartment, isn't it?" Lee's face turned pale at his daughter's words. He started to shake his head, but Jasmine interrupted. "I saw it one night. A night like this."

Jasmine had barely finished speaking when a loud crack rocked the room. Fireworks! The parade must be over, for there was an explosion of noise, flashes of light coming through the windows. Jasmine jumped, putting a hand to her mouth. "It was just like this," she said. "I remember now."

"You remember nothing," An-Mei said fiercely. Suddenly the battle was between the two women and not the two men.

"I was frightened. I ran into your bedroom?" Jasmine's gaze darted to the door behind her mother, and she gasped.

Paige followed her gaze and saw the reason for the sudden horror on her face. Smoke was coming from under the door behind Mrs. Chen.

"Fire!" Alyssa cried.

An-Mei threw open the door to her bedroom, and they saw the curtains going up in flames. She ran into the room with a scream. Riley followed behind her, trying to pull her away from the fire. Paige rushed toward them both, while David, Jasmine, and Alyssa ran to the kitchen to get water to throw onto the fire.

"Get her out of here," Riley said. "Call 911." He tried to push An-Mei out of the room, but she was surprisingly strong for a small woman of her age. Paige tried to take her arm as well but she shrugged it off. Jasmine came into the room and begged her mother to leave it alone, to get out. An-Mei wouldn't move. She looked at Jasmine with a gleam of madness in her eyes. "The curse. It has finally come true. We all die here tonight."

"We're not dying," Riley said as he ripped the curtains off the rod and stomped on them until there was nothing left but smoke.

An-Mei looked at Wallace with hatred in her eyes. "It is your fault. You make it all happen. You promise much gold and prosperity. But you curse us all."

"I made us a fortune. I brought your husband to this country. He was nothing without me. Then he betrayed me."

Wallace's eyes suddenly lit up, and as Paige followed his gaze, she saw the dragon on a table that was set up like an altar, the statue surrounded by dripping candles, one of which had fallen on its side, lighting the bedroom curtains that were now water-soaked and black-ened. The dragon stared at them mockingly, as if wondering why it had taken them so long to come. Its jade eyes flashed through the lingering smoke, throwing colors across the ancient bronze.

"Oh, my God," Paige said.

"You had it all along," Jasmine said in a daze. "I saw it here before. You were praying at the altar. I came up to you and asked you about it. You threw me in the closet. You locked the door. It was dark. I could hear the fireworks. I was terrified." She looked at her mother. "And when you pulled me out, you almost broke my arm. You spanked me many times and told me I was bad, I must forget. I must never tell." Jasmine turned to her father, who stood in the doorway of the bedroom. "Did you know what she did to me? Did you?"

Lee Chen didn't answer right away. He stared at his wife, who was holding her arms around her waist and rocking back and forth. "An-Mei," he said softly. "It's all right."

"It's not all right," Jasmine said. "Don't you understand that?"

Lee wasn't looking at his daughter. He was looking at his wife.

"The dragons were not meant to belong to any of us," An-Mei said. "They should have been returned years ago."

Wallace turned to Lee. "After all we had been through together, you betrayed me. You stole this dragon. But you couldn't do anything without the other dragon and the box. So you kept this one hidden away all these years. Did you know Ned had the other dragon?"

"I wasn't sure," Lee said, coughing as he finished speaking.

"We should get out of this smoke," Paige said.

"She's right," Riley echoed.

No one moved. No one wanted to leave the dragon on the altar. But no one seemed to have the nerve to touch it.

Riley took a step forward. Paige called him back. "Don't," she said. "Don't touch it. It might really be cursed."

He hesitated, then moved ahead in typical Riley fashion. He picked up the dragon statue and walked out of the room. There was a scramble to follow him, people bumping into one another as they made their way into the living room. Paige was the last one out, closing the bedroom door behind her.

"Time for some straight talk." Riley set the dragon on the coffee table. "Where did the dragons come from?"

"Tell him, Wallace," An-Mei ordered. "Tell him you steal dragons from China."

"I didn't do it alone," Wallace retorted.

"Then, how did you do it?" David asked his father.

"It was Lee," Wallace said. "He found the crate in the woods. It must have fallen off a truck. It was just waiting there, a treasure to be discovered. I knew right away we should keep it. We might need to trade it for freedom. It was wartime. The enemy was getting closer every day. Lee agreed with me. So, did your grandfather," he added, looking at Riley. "We were good friends then, brothers. We smuggled the crate out of China and brought it back here to San Francisco. Inside, there were many artifacts from the museum."

"More than just the dragons and the box?" Paige asked.

"Yes," Wallace said shortly. "We knew we were sitting on a potential gold mine. We made a pact to sell the objects one at a time, discreetly of course, so no one would know. Ned and Lee worked at the store with me. We shared the profits from those sales equally. Until she..." He tipped his head at An-Mei. "She started worrying about the damn curse. She got Lee and even Ned all worked up about it. Stupid woman." He turned to Lee. "But you—I couldn't understand why you would steal the dragons and burn down the store. We were friends."

For the first time, Paige saw a chink in her grandfather's armor, a sign that he wasn't as emotionless and cold as he pretended to be. He'd been betrayed by his friends. No wonder he'd never trusted anyone again.

Lee didn't seem able to speak. His eyes were watering. His shoulders shaking.

Paige wanted to tell her grandfather to stop, but she couldn't interrupt. This was between the two of them, and it was time they settled it.

Lee put a hand to his heart. Jasmine ran to his side. "Papa," she said with concern.

He waved her off. "I'm okay." He drew in a breath, then said, "When I set the fire, I thought I could take everything, but only one dragon was there. The other two pieces were missing. I set the fire to cover the theft. It was my fault."

"No!" An-Mei cried. "Not you. *Me*."

The tiny Chinese woman walked to the middle of the room and slowly but defiantly pushed back her sleeves. Paige saw the crisscross of scars that ran from her wrists to her elbows, and suddenly the truth was clear.

"I start fire," An-Mei said. "I want to send dragons and box back to China. Break curse forever. I have no choice." She shook her head. "But only one dragon there. The fire jumped. Too late to stop." She looked at her husband. "I hide it away. You don't see. You don't know."

"I knew," Lee said heavily, meeting her gaze. "I saw it a long time ago, but I didn't want to speak of it."

"And I saw it, too," Jasmine reminded her once again.

"I tell you to forget. You never forget. You cursed."

"I think it was the moment I realized how much you hated me," Jasmine said. "That's why I couldn't forget. I knew I was a disappointment, but I didn't know why—a disappointment long before David came along."

"You first daughter, Jasmine. You born with no finger. The curse struck you because of him," she said, shooting another dark, stabbing look at Wallace. "He say they too valuable to send back."

"They were too valuable, and it was too late to turn back," Wallace replied. "We would have had to reveal where we got the dragons in the first place. And we couldn't do that. The scandal wouldn't have just done us in; it would have hurt the entire country. The United States and China were not exactly friends." He looked at the statue on the coffee table. "And neither were we—after the fire."

"I can't imagine that my grandfather ever went along with this theft, this plan," Riley said.

Paige heard the pain in Riley's voice; it matched the pain in her own heart. It was hard to believe that the men they loved and respected had made a very bad decision a long time ago.

"He went along with it," Wallace said. "You don't have to understand. It was a different time. We'd seen our friends die in front of us. We'd faced our own mortality, and when we got back to the States, times were hard. Those art pieces gave us a leg up. Lee and Ned were able to start their own businesses with the money they made, and I put Hathaway's back into the black. No one got hurt."

"How can you say that?" Paige asked. "It looks to me like a lot of people got hurt, our families most of all."

"I don't understand," Jasmine interrupted, looking at her mother. "If the dragon was cursed, why did you keep it all this time?"

"I couldn't do anything else with it," An-Mei said. "The pieces were separated. I thought they were destroyed in the fire. So every New Year I pray to the Dragon God for forgiveness and a chance to make it right. When the other dragon came to light I thought—but then it was gone again."

"How did my grandfather get the other dragon?" Riley asked.

"I think Ned must have taken it to show some friends at the bar, to impress them," Lee replied. "He was always doing that. I didn't realize he hadn't returned it to the store before the fire."

"But then the store burned down, and my grandfather probably thought he'd be blamed if Wallace knew he had one of the dragons," Riley said. "It makes sense."

"You still have the box, don't you, Father?" David asked. "I saw it a long time ago. It wasn't in the basement when Mrs. Chen started the fire, was it?"

Wallace hesitated for a long moment. "We kept the records of our transactions in the box. I had removed it to my house for safekeeping."

BARBARA FREETHY

"So, you have my grandfather's dragon and the box." Riley picked up the other dragon from the coffee table. "I think it's time we put the pieces back together again."

An hour later they were gathered together in the dining room of the Hathaway mansion with one more member of the family in attendance, Victoria. Paige's mother was furious at all that had transpired outside of her presence and had made that quite clear to Paige when the motley group, as Victoria referred to them, had descended on the mansion. But no one was paying much attention to Victoria. There were now three pieces on the mahogany table, the two matching dragons and a long narrow box with an ornate lock.

"We should do it together," Paige said, motioning for Alyssa and Riley to come forward. "I believe we three were meant to put the pieces back together."

"I agree," Riley said, handing Alyssa the dragon that had been kept in her grandparents' apartment for so many years. Then he picked up the one belonging to his grandfather.

Paige picked up the box and held it out to them. She felt a shiver of excitement run down her spine as the box seemed to grow warmer in her hands. She could almost hear voices from the past, or was it music? For somewhere in her mind she could hear the distinct sound of a distant flute.

Riley and Alyssa moved forward, joining their dragons together. With Paige's help, they inserted the back joint of each dragon into the box. Their eyes met at the same moment the lock turned, and the lid snapped open.

Paige reached for the pieces of paper that were inside the box, but Wallace grabbed the papers from her hand. Before anyone could move, he had pulled a lighter from his pocket and set the papers to flame, the evidence burning quickly.

"Damn, you're good," Riley said, not making it sound like a compliment. "No one will ever know the extent of your thievery."

"Or your grandfather's involvement," Wallace said. "We did this together."

"He is right," Lee said. "We made our choice a long time ago. It was wrong. We were cursed because of it, but now it is over."

"Not quite," Riley said. "These pieces are going back to China, to be restored to the National Palace Museum." He paused. "You agree with that, don't you, Paige?"

She looked at her family standing across from her, waiting, watching. She couldn't remember when she'd had their attention before. And it was time to stand up, to take control as her grandfather had told her to do.

"Yes," she said. "The pieces will be returned to the museum as soon as possible. My father will make sure of that, won't you, Dad?"

"It would be my honor," David replied.

"But—" Wallace sputtered.

"Don't try to stop us, Grandfather," Paige said. "It's the right thing to do, and we're going to do it."

"And just how do you think you're going to do it?" Wallace asked David. "Where are you going to say you got the set?"

"He's going to say," Victoria interrupted, "that the House of Hathaway in association with their friends, the Chen family and the Delaney family, discovered a rare and previously lost piece of Chinese art that is now being returned to its rightful place."

Her mother was so smart, reading the situation quickly and coming up with a solution that would turn the three men from thieves into heroes. Everyone in the room seemed dumbstruck by her suggestion. But who could argue? Each family wanted to protect their own.

"Shouldn't they have to pay for what they did?" Alyssa asked finally.

"Everyone has paid in his own way," David replied. "My father lost his wife, his daughter, and his granddaughter. Your grandfather suffered the shame of knowing that his wife had burned down the store. Your grandmother suffered horrible burns on her arms. Your mother lived a life of shame and dishonor, from which you suffered as well."

"And my grandfather lost his daughter to drugs," Riley continued. "He also lost his mind and can't even remember his name, much less what he did fifty years ago. Mr. Hathaway is right. Everyone has paid a price for what was done." He paused. "Now, knowing that we've all agreed on what has to happen, I want to ensure it actually does happen. I think we should have the pieces put into a secure vault until they can be transported back to China."

"I'll make sure of that," Victoria said. "But first we'll put them on display in the upcoming Hathaway exhibit at the Asian Art Museum." Her eyes lit up at the thought. "You'll all be given due credit, of course. I'm a genius with a press release. Just ask anyone. I'd better make some calls."

"She's really something, your mother," Riley said to Paige as the group began to disperse.

"Yes, she is. I guess it's finally over." She couldn't help wondering where they would go from here now that they no longer had a dragon to chase.

"Not quite. I need to fill in my grandmother."

"Give her my love," Paige said. She watched him walk out the door with a heavy heart. Would she ever see him again?

"My family and I are leaving now," Alyssa said, coming up to Paige. "It's almost the new year. I think it's going to be a good one."

"I do, too. By the way, how do you feel about a new job?"

"What do you mean?"

"The House of Hathaway could certainly use another Hathaway."

"But I'm not a Hathaway."

"Aren't you?"

"Really? Can you do that? Hire me on without asking anyone?"

Paige smiled. "As a matter of fact, I can. You see, I'm the Hathaway heir. Only, I just recently discovered that I'm not the only one. And if I have to run that damn store one day, so do you. Of course, we'll have to get my mother out of it first."

"She's not going to want me there."

"No," Paige agreed. "But it's about time she realized that she's not the only woman in this family who gets what she wants. I want you in the store, and in my life. You're my sister. And I can't wait to get to know you."

Alyssa threw her arms around Paige and gave her a hug that Paige gladly returned. Out of this entire mess had come a new, wonderful relationship with a woman she could call a sister.

"I have to go," Alyssa said. "I have a man to meet."

"Ben?"

"I'd like to ring in the new year with him." She paused. "Maybe you and Riley should do the same thing."

"He's already gone."

"So go find him. You want him, too, don't you?"

She did. But this time he would have to come to her.

Paige entered her apartment just before midnight, exhausted from the night's events. All she wanted was a hot bath, a glass of wine, and bed. Two out of three were waiting for her in her bedroom. She smiled in pure delight. Riley had come to her. Granted, he was asleep, but it was the thought that counted.

She sat down on the side of the bed and put her hand on his chest. He stirred ever so slightly as she leaned over and put her mouth to his. She knew the moment he awoke, the moment he gave his heart to hers in one long, tender, passionate kiss.

He cupped her face when she tried to pull away and kissed her again as if he wanted to make sure she'd gotten the message the first time.

"Beautiful Paige," he murmured as he released her. "What took you so long?"

"I didn't know you would be waiting. How did you get in here?"

"I know a little bit about locks. And you need a better security system. In fact, I can think of a lot of things you need."

"Anything in particular—or should I say anyone?"

"Me," he replied with a grin.

"What about you? What do you need?"

"You, Paige."

"I want a long-term commitment."

"How long term?" he asked warily.

"Marriage, children, pets, a house of my own, furniture I choose, a garden."

"Whoa. Time out."

"What's the matter? Scared?"

"Terrified," he admitted.

"Okay, then, we'll start out slow. How about a real date involving dinner, maybe a little dancing, some champagne, rose petals on satin sheets?"

"Now you're talking. When can we go?"

"Any time you want."

"Paige," he said more seriously, "I don't know if I have it in me to be the kind of man you want and deserve. I don't want to disappoint you."

"You couldn't do that, Riley. And while I do hope for everything I said before, what I really want is you, on whatever terms you can give me. The truth is I'd rather have a few days with you than a lifetime with someone else. You've set me free, brought out a side of me I didn't know I had. I'll never be the same again."

"You've done the same thing for me." He pulled her hand to his heart. "I thought this had broken a long time ago. But you brought it back to life."

"I'm glad. We ended up on the same side after all," she said.

"Yes. Both our grandfathers were thieves. And Alyssa's, too. So much for protecting our families' names."

"Let's just hope our generation can turn things around."

"We will." He paused. "Are we going to have to wait for our romantic date to... you know?"

"I think so. You should have to work for it this time."

"Paige," he groaned, "you're going to kill me."

"You better believe it. Starting now," she said with a wicked smile.

"I thought you just said—"

"It's a woman's prerogative to change her mind. Besides, we

haven't made love in this bed yet." She leaned over to kiss him, but he put a finger against her lips.

"Uh, Paige."

"What now?"

"I just remembered. I don't have my wallet."

"You have to start driving with your driver's license, Riley."

"I don't suppose you have another copy of the Odyssey laying around?" he asked hopefully.

"Unfortunately, no, and I hate to admit it, but this bed has seen about as much action as the one in my parents' house. I haven't brought a guy here in a long time. I don't think I have anything."

"That's all right. We have the rest of our lives to make love to each other."

"I like the sound of that."

"So do I," he admitted.

"Do you trust me, Riley, really trust me?"

"Yes, I do. Let me show you how much." He tossed her back on the pillows, his hands slipping under her sweater.

"This feels more like lust," she teased.

"Now it's your turn to trust me. There are a lot of things we can do without a condom."

"Show me."

"I intend to." He gazed into her eyes. "You're an amazing woman."

"And you're an amazing man. By the way, when we get married—and I know we will," she added with a smile of her own, "I'm taking your name. I think I'm going to be a better McAllister than a Hathaway."

"I just want you, Paige. I don't care what your name is."

"I love you, Riley."

"I love you, too." He sealed his words with a lingering kiss.

# # #

Next up is Don't Say A Word...

DON'T SAY A WORD

PROLOGUE

She took her bow with the other dancers, tears pressing against her lids, but she couldn't let those tears slip down her cheeks. No one could know that this night was different from any other. Too many people were watching her.

As the curtain came down one last time, she ran off the stage into the arms of her husband, her lover, the man with whom she would take the greatest risk of her life.

He met the question in her eyes with a reassuring smile.

She wanted to ask if it was all arranged, if the plan was in motion, but she knew it would be unwise to speak. She would end this evening as she had ended all those before it. She went into her dressing room and changed out of her costume. When she was dressed, she said good night to some of the other dancers as she walked toward the exit, careful to keep her voice casual, as if she had not a care in the world. When she and her husband got into their automobile, they remained silent, knowing that the car might be bugged.

It was a short drive to their home. She would miss her house, the garden in the back, the bedroom where she'd made love to her husband, and the nursery, where she'd rocked...

No. She couldn't think of that. It was too painful. She had to concentrate on the future when they could finally be free. Her house, her life, everything that she possessed came with strings that were tightening around her neck like a noose, suffocating her with each passing day. It wasn't herself she feared for the most, but her family, her husband, who even now was being forced to do unconscionable things. They could no longer live a life of secrets.

Her husband took her hand as they walked up to the front door. He slipped his key into the lock and the door swung open. She heard a small click, and horror registered in her mind. She saw the shocked recognition in her husband's eyes, but it was too late. They were about to die, and they both knew it. Someone had betrayed them.

She prayed for the safety of those she had left behind as an explosion of fire lit up the night, consuming all their dreams with one powerful roar.

CHAPTER ONE

PRESENT DAY...

Julia DeMarco felt a shiver run down her spine as she stood high on a bluff overlooking the Golden Gate Bridge. It was a beautiful, sunny day in early September, and with the Pacific Ocean on one side of the bridge and the San Francisco Bay on the other, the view was breathtaking. She felt like she was on the verge of something exciting and wonderful, just the way every bride should feel. But as she took a deep breath of the fresh, somewhat salty air, her eyes began to water. She told herself the tears had more to do with the afternoon wind than the sadness she'd been wrestling with since her mother had passed away six months ago. This was supposed to be a happy time, a day for looking ahead, not behind. She just wished she felt confident instead of... uncertain.

A pair of arms came around her waist, and she leaned back against the solid chest of her fiancé, Michael Graffino. It seemed as if she'd done nothing but lean on Michael the past year. Most men wouldn't have stuck around, but he had. Now it was time to give him what he wanted, a wedding date. She didn't know why she was hesitating, except that so many things were changing in her life. Since Michael had proposed to her a year ago, her mother had died, her stepfather had put the family home up for sale, and her younger sister had moved in with her. A part of her just wanted to stop, take a few breaths, and think for a while instead of rushing headlong into another life-changing event. But Michael was pushing for a date, and she was grateful to him for sticking by her, so how could she say no? And why would she want to?

Michael was a good man. Her mother had adored him. Julia could still remember the night she'd told her mom about the engagement. Sarah DeMarco hadn't been out of bed in days, and she hadn't smiled in many weeks, but that night she'd beamed from ear to ear. The knowledge that her oldest daughter was settling down with the son of one of her best friends had made her last days so much easier.

"We should go, Julia. It's time to meet the event coordinator."

She turned to face him, thinking again what a nice-looking man he was with his light brown hair, brown eyes, and a warm, ready smile. The olive skin of his Italian heritage and the fact that he spent most of his days out on the water, running a charter boat service off Fisherman's Wharf, kept his skin a dark, sunburned red.

"What's wrong?" he asked, a curious glint in his eye. "You're staring at me."

"Was I? I'm sorry."

"Don't be." He paused, then said, "It's been a while since you've really looked at me."

"I don't think that's true. I look at you all the time. So do half the women in San Francisco," she added.

"Yeah, right," he muttered. "Let's go."

Julia cast one last look at the view, then followed Michael to the museum. The Palace of the Legion of Honor had been built as a replica of the Palais de la Legion d'Honneur in Paris. In the front courtyard, known as the Court of Honor, was one of Rodin's most famous sculptures, *The Thinker*. Julia would have liked to stop and ponder the statue as well as the rest of her life, but Michael was a man on a mission, and he urged her toward the front doors.

As they entered the museum, her step faltered. In a few moments, they would sit down with Monica Harvey, the museum's event coordinator, and Julia would have to pick her wedding date. She shouldn't be nervous. It wasn't as if she were a young girl; she was twenty-eight years old. It was time to get married, have a family.

"Liz was right. This place is cool," Michael said.

Julia nodded in agreement. Her younger sister Liz had been the one to suggest the museum. It was a pricey location, but Julia had inherited some money from her mother that would pay for most of the wedding.

"The offices are downstairs," Michael added. "Let's go."

Julia drew in a deep breath as the moment of truth came rushing toward her. "I need to stop in the restroom. Why don't you go ahead? I'll be right there."

When Michael left, Julia walked over to get a drink of water from a nearby fountain. She was sweating and her heart was practically jumping out of her chest. What on earth was the matter with her? She'd never felt so panicky in her life.

It was all the changes, she told herself again. Her emotions were too close to the surface. But she could do this. They were only picking a date. She wasn't going to say "I do" this afternoon. That would be months from now, when she was ready, really ready.

Feeling better, she headed downstairs, passing by several intriguing exhibits along the way. Maybe they could stop and take a look on the way out.

"Mrs. Harvey is finishing up another appointment," Michael told her as she joined him. "She'll be about ten minutes. I need to make a call. Can you hold down the fort?"

"Sure." Julia sat down on the couch, wishing Michael hadn't left. She really needed a distraction from her nerves. As the minutes passed, she became aware of the faint sound of music coming from down the hall. The melody was lovely but sad, filled with unanswered dreams, regrets. It reminded her of a piece played on the balalaika in one of her music classes in college, and it called to her in a way she couldn't resist. Music had always been her passion. Just a quick peek, she told herself, as she got to her feet and moved into the corridor.

The sounds of the strings grew louder as she entered the room at the end of the hall. It was a tape, she realized, playing in the background, intended no doubt to complement the equally haunting historic photographs on display. Within seconds she was caught up in a journey through time. She couldn't look away. And she didn't want to look away—especially when she came to the picture of the little girl.

Captioned *The Coldest War of All,* the black-and-white photograph showed a girl of no more than three or four years old, standing behind the gate of an orphanage in Moscow. The photo had been taken by someone named Charles Manning, the same man who appeared to have taken many of the pictures in the exhibit.

Julia studied the picture in detail. She wasn't as interested in the Russian scene as she was in the girl. The child wore a heavy dark coat, pale thick stockings, and a black woolen cap over her curly blond hair. The expression in her eyes begged for someone—whoever was taking the picture, perhaps—to let her out, to set her free, to help her.

An uneasy feeling crept down Julia's spine. The girl's features, the oval shape of her face, the tiny freckle at the corner of her eyebrow, the slope of her small, upturned nose, seemed familiar. She noticed how the child's pudgy fingers clung to the bars of the gate. It was odd, but she could almost feel that cold steel beneath her own fingers. Her breath quickened. She'd seen this picture before, but where? A vague memory danced just out of reach.

Her gaze moved to the silver chain hanging around the girl's neck and the small charm dangling from it. It looked like a swan, a white swan, just like the one her mother had given to her when she was a little girl. Her heart thudded in her chest, and the panicky feeling she'd experienced earlier returned.

"Julia?"

She jumped at the sound of Michael's booming voice. She'd forgotten about him.

"Mrs. Harvey is waiting for us," he said as he crossed the room. "What are you doing in here?"

"Looking at the photos."

"We don't have time for that. Come on."

"Just a second." She pointed at the photograph. "Does this girl seem familiar to you?"

Michael gave the photo a quick glance. "I don't think so. Why?"

"I have a necklace just like the one that little girl is wearing," she added. "Isn't that odd?"

"Why would it be odd? It doesn't look unusual to me."

Of course it didn't. There were probably a million girls who had that same necklace. "You're right. Let's go." But as she turned to follow Michael out of the room, she couldn't help taking one last look at the picture. The girl's eyes called out to her—eyes that looked so much like her own. But that little girl in the photograph didn't have anything to do with her—did she?

"It cost me a fortune to get you out of jail," Joe Carmichael said.

Alex Manning leaned back in his chair and kicked his booted feet up onto the edge of Joe's desk. Joe, a balding man in his late thirties, was one of his best friends, not to mention the West Coast editor of *World News Magazine,* a publication that bought eighty percent of Alex's photographs. They'd been working together for over ten years now. Some days Alex couldn't believe it had been more than a decade since he'd begun his work as a photojournalist right after graduating from Northwestern University. Other days—like today—it felt more like a hundred years.

"You told me to get those pictures at any cost, and I did," Alex replied.

"I didn't tell you to upset the local police while you were doing it. You look like shit, by the way. Who beat you up?"

"They didn't give me their business cards. And it comes with the territory. You know that."

"What I know is that the magazine wants me to rein you in."

"If you don't want my photographs, I'll sell them somewhere else."

Joe hastily put up his hands. "I didn't say that. But you're taking too many chances, Alex. You're going to end up dead or in some prison I can't get you out of."

"You worry too much."

"And you don't worry enough—which is what makes you good. It also makes you dangerous and expensive. Although I have to admit that this is some of your best work," Joe added somewhat reluctantly as he studied the pile of photographs on his desk.

"Damn right it is."

"Then it's a good time for a vacation. Why don't you take a break? You've been on the road the past six months. Slow down."

Slowing down was not part of Alex's nature. Venturing into unknown territory, taking the photograph no one else could get, that was what he lived for. But Alex had to admit he was bone tired, exhausted from shooting photographs across South America for the past six weeks, and his little stint in jail had left him with a cracked rib and a black eye. It probably wouldn't hurt to take a few days off.

"You know what your weakness is?" Joe continued.

"I'm sure you're going to tell me."

"You're reckless. You forget that a good photographer stays on the right side of the lens." Joe reached behind his desk and grabbed a newspaper. "This was on the front page of the *Examiner* last week."

Alex winced at the picture of himself being hustled into a police car in Colombia. "Damn that Cameron. He's the one who took that photo. I thought I saw that slimy weasel slinking in the shadows."

"He might be a weasel, but he was smart enough to stay out of jail. Seriously, what are you thinking these days? It's as if you're tempting fate."

"I'm just doing my job. A job that sells a lot of your magazines."

"Take a vacation, Alex; have some beer, watch a football game, get yourself a woman—think about something besides getting the next shot. By the way, the magazine is sponsoring a photography exhibit at the Legion of Honor. Your mother gave us permission to use the photographs taken by your father. You might want to stop by, take a look."

Alex wasn't surprised to hear his mother had given permission.

Despite the fact that she'd hated everything about his father's job while they were married, she had no problem living off his reputation now. In fact, she seemed to enjoy being the widow of the famous photojournalist who had died far too young. Alex was only surprised she hadn't pressed him to attend. That might have something to do with the fact that he hadn't returned any of her calls in the past month.

"Why don't you check out the exhibit tonight?" Joe suggested. "The magazine is hosting a party with all the movers and shakers. I'm sure your mother will be there."

"I'll pass," Alex said, getting to his feet. He needed to pick up his mail, air out his apartment, which was probably covered in six inches of dust, and take a long, hot shower. The last person he wanted to talk to tonight was his mother. He turned toward the door, then paused. "Is the photo of the Russian orphan girl part of the exhibit?"

"It was one of your father's most famous shots. Of course it's there." Joe gave him a curious look. "Why?"

Alex didn't answer. His father's words rang through Alex's head after twenty-five years of silence: *Don't ever talk to anyone about that picture. It's important. Promise me.*

A day later Charles Manning was dead.

It didn't take Julia long to find the necklace tucked away in her jewelry box. As she held it in her hand, the white enamel swan sparkled in the sunlight coming through her bedroom window. The chain was short, made for a child. It would no longer fit around her neck. As she thought about how quickly time had passed, another wave of sadness ran through her, not just because of the fact that she'd grown up and couldn't wear the necklace, but because her mother, the one who had given it to her, was gone.

"Julia?"

She looked up at the sound of her younger sister's voice. Liz appeared in the doorway of the bedroom a moment later, the smell of fish clinging to her low-rise blue jeans and bright red tank top. A short, attractive brunette with dark hair and dark eyes, Liz spent most of her days working at the family restaurant, DeMarco's, a seafood cafe on Fisherman's Wharf. She'd dropped out of college a year ago to help take care of their mother and had yet to go back. She seemed content to waitress in the cafe and flirt with the good-looking male customers. Julia couldn't really blame Liz for her lack of ambition. The past year had been tough on both of them, and Liz found comfort working at the cafe, which was owned and run by numerous DeMarcos, including their father. Besides that, she was only twenty-two years old. She had plenty of time to figure out the rest of her life.

"Did you set the date?" Liz asked, an eager light in her eyes.

"Yes. They had a cancellation for December twenty-first."

"Of this year? That's only a little over three months from now."

Julia's stomach clenched at the reminder. "I know. It's really fast, but it was this December or a year from next March. Michael wanted December." And she hadn't been able to talk him out of it. Not that she'd tried. In fact, she'd been so distracted by the photograph she'd barely heard a word the wedding coordinator said.

"A holiday wedding sounds romantic." Liz moved a pile of CDs so she could sit down on the bed. "More music, Julia? Your CD collection is taking on mammoth proportions."

"I need them for work. I have to stay on top of the world music market. That's my job."

"And your vice," Liz said with a knowing grin. "You can't walk by a music store without stopping in. You should have bought some wedding music. Have you thought about what song you want to use for your first dance?"

"Not yet."

"Well, start thinking. You have a lot to do in the next few months." She paused. "What's that in your hand?"

Julia glanced down at the necklace. "I found this in my jewelry box. Mom gave it to me when I was a little girl."

Liz got up from the bed to take a closer look. "I haven't seen this in years. What made you pull it out now?"

Julia considered the question for a moment, wondering if she should confide in her sister.

Before she could speak, Liz said, "You could wear that for your wedding—something old. Which reminds me..."

"What?" Julia asked.

"Wait here." Liz ran from the room, then returned a second later with three thick magazines in her hands. "I bought up all the bridal magazines. As soon as we get back from Aunt Lucia's birthday party, we can go through them. Doesn't that sound like fun?"

It sounded like a nightmare, especially with Liz overseeing the procedure. Unlike Julia, Liz was a big believer in organization. She loved making files, labeling things, buying storage containers and baskets to keep their lives neat as a pin. Since taking up residence on the living room futon after their parents' house had sold, Liz had been driving Julia crazy. She always wanted to clean, decorate, paint, and pick out new curtains. What Liz really needed was a place of her own, but Julia hadn't had the heart to tell Liz to move out. Besides, it would be only a few more months; then Julia would be living with Michael.

"Unless you want to start now," Liz said, as she checked her watch. "We don't have to leave for about an hour. Is Michael coming to the party?"

"He'll be a little late. He had a sunset charter to run."

"I bet he's excited that you finally set the date," Liz said with a smile. "He's been dying to do that for months." Liz tossed two of the magazines on the desk, then began to leaf through the one in her hand. "Oh, look at this dress, the satin, the lace. It's heavenly."

Julia couldn't bear to look. She didn't want to plan her wedding right this second. Wasn't it enough that she'd booked the date? Couldn't she have twenty-four hours to think about it? Julia didn't suppose that sounded very bridal-like, but it was the way she felt, and she needed to get away from Liz before her sister noticed she was not as enthusiastic as she should be. "I have to run an errand before the party," she said, giving in to a reckless impulse.

"When will you be back?"

"I'm not sure how long it will take. I'll meet you at the restaurant."

"All right. I'll pick out the perfect dress for you while you're gone."

"Great." When Liz left the room, Julia walked over to her bed and picked up the catalogue from the photography exhibit. On page thirty-two was the photograph of the orphan girl. She'd already looked at it a half-dozen times since she'd come home, unable to shake the idea that the photo, the child, the necklace were important to her in some way.

She wanted to talk to someone about the picture, and it occurred to her that maybe she should try to find the photographer. After researching Charles Manning on the Internet earlier that day, she'd discovered that he was deceased, but his son, Alex Manning, was also a photojournalist and had a San Francisco number and address listed in the phone book. She'd tried the number but gotten a message machine. There was really nothing more to do at the moment, unless...

Tapping her fingers against the top of her desk, she debated for another thirty seconds. She should be planning her wedding, not searching out the origin of an old photo, but as she straightened, she caught a glimpse of herself in the mirror. Instead of seeing her own reflection, she saw the face of that little girl begging her to help.

Julia picked up her purse and headed out the door. Maybe Alex Manning could tell her what she needed to know about the girl in the photograph. Then Julia could forget about her.

Twenty minutes later, Julia pulled up in front of a three-story apartment building in the Haight, a neighborhood that had been the centerpiece of San Francisco's infamous "Summer of Love" in the sixties. The area was now an interesting mix of funky shops, clothing boutiques, tattoo parlors, restaurants, and coffeehouses. The streets were busy. It was Friday night, and everyone wanted to get started on the weekend. Julia hoped Alex Manning would be home, although since he hadn't answered his phone, it was probably a long shot. But she had to do something.

She climbed the stairs to his apartment, took a deep breath, and rang the bell, all the while wondering what on earth she would say to him if he were home. A moment later, the door opened to a string of curses. A tall, dark-haired man appeared in the doorway, bare chested and wearing a pair of faded blue jeans that rode low on his hips. His dark brown hair was a mess, his cheeks unshaven. His right eye was swollen, the skin around it purple and black. There were bruises all over his muscled chest and a long, thin scar not far from his heart. She instinctively took a step back, feeling as if she'd just woken the beast.

"Who are you and what are you selling?" he asked harshly.

"I'm not selling anything. I'm looking for Alex Manning. Are you him?"

"That depends on what you want."

"No, that depends on who you are," she stated, holding her ground.

"Is this conversation going to end if I tell you I'm not Alex Manning?"

"Not if you're lying."

He stared at her, squinting through his one good eye. His expression changed. His green eyes sharpened, as if he were trying to place her face. "Who are you?"

"My name is Julia DeMarco. And if you're Alex Manning, I want to ask you about a photograph I saw at the Legion of Honor today. It was taken by your father—a little girl standing behind the gates of an orphanage. Do you know the one I'm talking about?"

He didn't reply, but she saw the pulse jump in his throat and a light flicker in his eyes.

"I want to know who the little girl is—her name—what happened to her," she continued.

"Why?" he bit out sharply.

It was a simple question. She wished she had a simple answer. How could she tell him that she couldn't stop thinking about that girl, that she felt compelled to learn more about her? She settled for, "The child in the picture is wearing a necklace just like this one." She pulled the chain out of her purse and showed it to him. "I thought it was odd that I had the same one."

He stared at the swan, then gazed back into her eyes. "No," he muttered with a confused shake of his head. "It's not possible."

"What's not possible?"

"You. You can't be her."

"I didn't say I was her." Julia's heart began to race. "I just said I have the same necklace."

"This is a dream, isn't it? I'm so tired I'm hallucinating. If I close the door, you'll go away."

Julia opened her mouth to tell him she wasn't going anywhere, but the door slammed in her face. "I'm not her," she said loudly. "I was born and raised in San Francisco. I've never been out of the country. I'm not her," she repeated, feeling suddenly desperate. "Am I?"

CHAPTER TWO

ALEX COULD HEAR the woman talking on the other side of the door, which didn't bode well for his theory that he was dreaming. That blond hair, those blue eyes, the upturned nose—he'd seen her features a million times in his mind. And now she was here, and she wanted to know about the girl in the photo. What the hell was he supposed to say to her?

Don't ever talk to anyone about the photo or the girl.

His father's words returned to his head—words that were twenty-five years old. What would it matter now if he broke his promise? Who would care? For that matter, why would anyone have cared?

He'd never understood the frantic fear in his father's eyes the day the photo had been published in the magazine. All Alex knew for sure was that he'd made a promise in the last conversation he'd had with his father, and up until this moment he'd never considered breaking it.

His doorbell rang again. She was definitely persistent.

Alex opened the door just as she was about to knock. Her hand dropped to her side.

"Why did you say I was her?" she demanded.

"Take a look in the mirror."

"She's a little girl. I'm an adult. I don't think we look at all alike."

He studied her for a moment, his photographer's eye seeing the details, the slight widow's peak on her forehead, the tiny freckle by one eyebrow, the oval shape of her face, the thick, blond hair that curled around her shoulders. She was a beautiful woman, and dressed in a short tan linen skirt that showed off her long, slender legs, and a sleeveless cream-colored top, she looked like a typical California girl. He felt a restless surge of attraction that he immediately tried to squash. Blondes had always been his downfall, especially blue-eyed blondes.

"Did your father know the little girl's name or anything about her?" she persisted.

"He never said," Alex replied. "Can I see that necklace again?"

She opened her hand. He stared down at the white swan. It was exactly the same as the one in the photograph. Still, what did it mean? It wasn't a rare diamond, just a simple charm. Although the fact that this woman looked like the orphan girl and had the necklace in her possession seemed like a strong coincidence. "What did you say your name was?"

"Julia DeMarco."

"DeMarco? A blond Italian, huh?"

"I'm not Italian. I was adopted by my stepfather. My mother said my biological father was Irish. And she is—was—Irish as well. She died a few months ago." Julia slipped the necklace back into her large brown handbag.

Adopted. The word stuck in his head after all the rest. "You didn't know your biological father?"

"He left before I was born."

"And where were you born?"

"In Berkeley." Her lips tightened. "I've never been out of the coun-try. I don't even have a passport. So that girl in the photo is not me."

"Just out of curiosity, how old were you when you were adopted?"

"I was four," she replied.

And the girl in the photograph couldn't have been more than three.

He gazed into her eyes and knew she was thinking the same thing.

"I was adopted by my stepfather when he married my mom," she explained. "And she wasn't Russian. She never traveled. She was a stay-at-home PTA mom. She did snacks for soccer games. Very all-American. There is no way I'm that girl. I know exactly who I am."

She seemed to be trying damn hard to convince herself of that fact. But the more she talked, the more Alex wondered.

"You know, this isn't your problem," she said with a wave of her hand. "And I obviously woke you up." Her cheeks flushed as she cleared her throat and looked away from him.

Alex crossed his arms in front of his bare chest, not bothering to find himself a shirt. "I just got off a plane from South America." ·

"Were you taking photographs down there?"

"Yes."

"How did you get hurt? Not that it's any of my business."

"You're right. It's none of your business."

She stiffened at his harsh tone. "Well, you don't have to be rude about it."

Maybe he did, because he didn't like the way his body was reacting to her. The sooner she left, the better. He was smart enough to avoid women who wanted more than sex, and this woman had "more than sex" written all over her.

"Are you sure there's nothing else you can tell me about the photo?" she asked.

He sighed. Obviously, he hadn't been rude enough. "Look, you're not the first person to wonder who that girl was. There was quite a hunt for her when the photograph was first published. Everyone wanted to adopt her."

"Really? What happened?"

"She couldn't be found. Our governments weren't cooperating at that time. International adoptions were not happening. It was the Cold War. In fact, no one was willing to admit there even were orphans in Moscow." It wasn't the whole story, but as much as he was willing to tell her. "Besides the fact that you have blond hair and blue eyes, and you have the same necklace, what makes you wonder about that photo? Don't you have family you can ask about where you were born? Don't you have pictures of yourself in Berkeley when you were two or three years old? What makes you doubt who you are?" Once the questions started, they kept coming.

"I don't have family I can ask," Julia replied. "My mother was estranged from her parents. They washed their hands of her when she got pregnant with me. And there aren't any photos, not of her or of me, until she married my stepfather. She said they got lost in the move from Berkeley to San Francisco."

"That's not much of a move. Just over the Bay Bridge."

Her lips tightened. "I never had any reason to believe otherwise."

"Until now," he pointed out.

She frowned. "Damn. I can't believe I'm doubting my own mother just because of a photograph in a museum. I must be losing my mind."

If she was, then he was losing his mind right along with her, because everything she said raised his suspicions another notch. A familiar jolt of adrenaline rushed through his bloodstream. Was it possible this woman was that girl? And if she was, what did that mean? How had she gotten from Moscow to the U.S.? And why didn't she know who she was? Was she the reason his father had told him to never speak about that photo? Was she part of something bigger, something secret? Had his father found himself in the middle of a conspiracy all those years ago? Alex knew better than anyone that photographers could get into places no one else could.

"I wish I could talk to my mother about this," Julia continued. "Now that she's gone, I have no one to ask."

"What about your stepfather?"

"I suppose," she murmured, "but he's had a rough year. My mom was sick for a long time, and he doesn't like to talk about her."

"There must be someone."

"Obviously there isn't, or I wouldn't have come looking for you," she snapped.

"What was your mother's name before she became a DeMarco?"

"It was Sarah Gregory. Why?"

"Just wondered." He filed that fact away for future use.

She suddenly started, glancing at the clock on the wall. "I have to go. I have a family birthday party at DeMarco's."

"DeMarco's on the Wharf?" he asked, putting her name together with the seafood cafe on Fisherman's Wharf.

"That's the one. Gino DeMarco is my stepfather. It's my aunt Lucia's birthday. Everyone in the immediate family, all thirty-seven of us, will be there."

"Big family," he commented.

"It's a lot of fun."

"Then why go looking for trouble?"

Her jaw dropped at his question. "I'm not doing that," she said defensively.

"Aren't you? You think you're the girl in the picture."

"You're the one who thinks that. I just want more information about her."

"Same thing."

"It's not the same thing. It's completely different. And I'm done with it. Forget I was ever here."

Julia left with a toss of her head. Alex smiled to himself. She wasn't the first blonde to walk out on him, but she was probably one of the few he wouldn't forget. She might be done with the matter, but he was just getting started. Unlike Julia, he did have someone else he could talk to—his mother. Maybe it was time to return her calls.

Kate Manning loved parties, and she especially enjoyed being the center of attention as she was tonight. Actually, the party was in honor of her late husband, Charles Manning, whose photographs were on display, but that was beside the point. She was here, and he wasn't. She'd had twenty-five years to come to terms with that fact, and there was nothing to do but keep moving on. Maybe that seemed cold to some, but she was a practical woman, and as far as she was concerned, the love she'd had for her husband had been buried right along with him.

She was now sixty-two years old, and after two failed marriages in the last twenty years, she'd resumed using the Manning name. This exhibit in honor of Charles's work had put her back on the society A-list, and she was determined to stay there. She'd been dropped from most invitation lists three years ago when her then husband, a popular city councilman, had slept with an underage girl, causing a huge scandal. He'd been booted out of office, and she had been shunned by her supposed friends. But now she was back, and if she had to play the tragic widow of a brilliant photographer, then that's exactly what she would do.

It had also occurred to her in recent weeks that she might be able to augment her income by selling Charles's photographs to a book publisher. While she wasn't poor by any standards, she was acutely aware that her lifestyle required a steady income, and if there was still interest in Charles's work, then who was she to deny the public the opportunity to buy a book of his photographs? She just needed to convince Alex to go along with it. But he was a lot like his father—stubborn, secretive, and always leaving to go somewhere. It was no wonder he wasn't married. He couldn't commit, couldn't settle, couldn't put a woman before his work—just like Charles.

"Kate, there you are."

She put the bitter thoughts out of her mind as Stan Harding came up to her. Stan had been one of Charles's closest friends and the best man at their wedding. He was also one of the many photo editors Charles had worked with over the years. Stan was semiretired from *World News Magazine* as of last year, working only on special projects, like putting together the photographs for this exhibit.

A handsome man, just a few years older than herself with stark white hair, a long, lean frame, and a strong, square jaw, Stan was one of the most intelligent and interesting men she'd ever known. He'd been married briefly years ago, but his wife had died of cancer the year she and Charles had split up. For a brief moment back then, she'd toyed with the idea of getting together with Stan. But his loyalty to Charles, even after Charles had passed away, had always been too high a hurdle to clear. She'd had to settle for his friendship.

"Hello," she said, accepting his kiss on the cheek with a pleased smile.

"Are you having a good time, Kate?"

"Better now that you're here."

"You always say the right thing," he said with a smile.

She certainly tried. "We've gotten a wonderful response to the exhibit. I can't believe how many people have come tonight." The room was literally overflowing with men in formal suits and women in beautiful cocktail dresses. Waiters moved through the crowd offering champagne and gourmet appetizers prepared by one of San Francisco's best chefs. She felt a little thrill run through her as she complimented herself on her efforts. She hadn't thrown the party by herself, but she'd done a lion's share of the work, and it was turning out perfectly.

"You did a fine job," Stan said, as he gazed around the room. "Charles would be proud."

She wasn't so sure about that. Charles had hated her need to socialize and host parties, and he'd never been one to brag about his work or take the credit he deserved. He'd even asked the magazine to print his pictures without a byline on occasion. She'd never understood his reasoning.

"I thought Alex might be here," Stan continued. "Joe said he got back into town today."

And he hadn't called her. She didn't know why she felt hurt. It wasn't as if they were close, even though he was her only child. The rift had started years ago. Alex had blamed her for the breakup of his family. Then Charles had died, and Alex had hated her ever since. He didn't act that way on the surface, and they certainly never spoke about anything as personal as Alex's feelings, but she knew the truth.

"The photos Alex took in South America were amazing," Stan added. "You must be very proud of your boy."

"I am, of course." She grabbed a glass of champagne from a passing waiter and took a sip. "I spoke to Joe earlier about doing an article on Alex and Charles, a side-by-side look at the father and son," she added. "It would sell a lot of magazines."

Stan nodded, a twinkle in his eye. "I'm sure it would. I understand Alex is quite popular with the ladies."

Kate didn't doubt that. Alex had his father's roguish good looks, thick, dark brown hair, light green eyes, and strong, muscular build, with not an ounce of fat on him, probably because he kept too busy to eat. He was always on the run, always looking for the next great shot. She sometimes wondered if he bothered to sleep. She certainly couldn't see herself in him anywhere—he was the spitting image of his father. She suddenly realized that spitting image was walking straight toward her. She threw back her shoulders, feeling a sudden pang of nervousness.

"Mother," he said with a cool smile.

"Alex. What on earth are you wearing?" She couldn't believe he'd come to the party in blue jeans and a black leather jacket. He frowned at her question, and she mentally chided herself for getting his back up so fast. But, dammit, couldn't he think about propriety once in a while?

"It's nice to see you, too, Mother." His smile warmed as he nodded to Stan. "What's up?"

"Not much. Glad to see you made it safely back," Stan said. He stepped forward and gave Alex a brief hug, much as a father would a son. Over the years Stan had tried to fill the gaps in Alex's life by showing up at his ball games or school graduations. It made Kate feel a bit sad and a little angry to realize that Alex could hug Stan but not give her even a light pat on the shoulder.

"You should have called me, Alex," she said abruptly. "I was worried sick after I saw that photograph in the newspaper of you being dragged off to jail." She pursed her lips as she studied the purple swelling around his eye, and some latent maternal instinct made her say, "That must hurt. Did you see a doctor?"

"I'll live. Don't worry about it."

"You have to stop taking so many chances. You're not superhuman. I don't understand why you're willing to risk your life on perfect strangers."

"I'm just doing my job. But I didn't come here to talk about my job."

"Why did you come?" she asked sharply. She didn't like the intense look in her son's eyes. When he wanted something, he tended to go after it with all that he had. Maybe that was the one trait he got from her.

Alex motioned them toward a quiet corner. "It's about one of Dad's photographs—the orphan girl at the gates. Did Dad ever talk to either one of you about that picture or the girl?"

"He didn't talk to me about any of his photos," Kate replied, still feeling the pain of Charles's distance even after all these years. "Especially the ones he took on that last trip to Moscow. Now if you'll excuse me, I have some people to greet. Stop by the house tomorrow, Alex, and we can talk more." By tomorrow, she'd have her wits about her. She'd be ready to deal with Alex's questions then. Tonight she just wanted to enjoy the party.

Alex watched his mother walk away, not surprised that she'd given him such a sharp answer. After twenty-five years she was still pissed off at his father. That would probably never change. She looked good, though. Her hair was a dark copper red, and she had the face and the figure of a woman at least ten years younger. He knew she cared about her appearance. He didn't know what else she cared about. He never had.

Alex glanced over at Stan, seeing a thoughtful look on the older man's face. "What about you?" he asked.

"What do you really want to know? Cut to the chase, Alex."

Alex hesitated, then said, "I want to know if there's a chance that the Russian orphan girl is alive and well and living in the United States."

Stan's eyes narrowed. "Why would you ask that question?"

"Because I think she came to my apartment today." Alex was a pro at reading people's expressions; he'd had plenty of practice behind his camera. Even though Stan tried to cover his reaction with a bland smile, Alex could tell that he was surprised, maybe even shocked. His face paled and his eyes glittered with an odd light. Stan knew something, but what?

"That's impossible," Stan replied.

"Why is it impossible? Do you know what happened to that girl?"

"What I know is that the photo was not supposed to be published. I can't tell you any more."

"Can't or won't? My father has been dead for twenty-five years. Surely there are no secrets left to protect."

Stan stared at him for a long moment, then drew him farther into the corner of the room so that there was no chance they could be overheard. "Like you, your father sometimes got involved in things he should have left alone."

"What does that mean?"

"It means butt out, Alex. Do what your father asked. Don't talk about any of it. If the woman comes back, tell her she's crazy. Tell her that girl in the photograph died a few weeks after that picture was taken. End of story."

"But she's not dead, is she?"

"In all the ways that matter, she is. Forget about her, Alex. Trust me. You do not want to reopen the past."

Alex suddenly wanted nothing more.

DeMarco family birthday parties were always big, loud affairs. Tonight the cafe was filled to the brim with Italians of all ages, shapes, and sizes. The small tables were dressed in red-checkered tablecloths, candles gleaming in each floral centerpiece. The food was plentiful, the wine flowed, and laughter filled the room like music. This was her family, Julia reminded herself. It didn't matter that she was the only blonde in a sea of brunettes. It didn't matter that she wasn't a DeMarco by blood. They loved her. They treated her as if she were one of their own. She just wished she had more in common with her family, that she didn't feel so out of step with her father and her sister. Not that they ever tried to make her feel that way. She just did.

"Julia, you're not eating." Her aunt Lucia, a short, plump woman with pepper gray hair, paused by the table, her face disapproving. She pointed to Julia's untouched lobster ravioli. "Is it too spicy? Shall I get you another plate?"

"It's perfect. I'm just full."

"How could you be full? You ate nothing."

"Hey, she has to fit into a wedding dress in a couple of months. Don't fatten her up yet," Liz interrupted, joining Julia at the table. "But since I hate to see food go to waste..." She pulled Julia's plate across the table and picked up her fork. She took a bite and nodded approvingly. "Excellent."

Lucia beamed her approval. "You, I don't worry about. But Julia..." She gazed at Julia again. "Since your sweet mother died, you just don't seem yourself."

"I'm all right," Julia said. "I'm just not hungry."

Lucia sighed, but held her tongue as Michael joined them at the table.

Michael kissed her aunt on the cheek, then smiled at Julia. "Have you told them?"

"Liz did. She got here before me. You know what a big mouth she has."

"I couldn't keep it to myself," Liz said with a laugh. "I'm so excited. It seems like I've been waiting forever for this wedding."

"I feel the same way," Michael said with a laugh.

"We're very happy for you," Lucia said. "Now, you must be starving. I'll fix you a plate of food."

"That would be great."

"And I'll get you a beer," Liz added, following Lucia over to the bar.

Michael sat down at the table. "Big party."

"Like always," Julia replied. "How did your charter go?"

"Fine. Sorry I'm late. I got hung up talking to my father about our advertising. I want to make changes. He doesn't. Same old argument. What did you do this afternoon?" he asked, reaching across the table to take her hand in his, his thumb playing with the engagement ring on her finger. "Did you go shopping for a wedding dress?"

She shook her head. "No. I'm sure Liz wants to do that with me."

"Just make sure you get something sexy and low cut."

She smiled as she knew she was meant to, but it must have looked halfhearted to Michael, because the light disappeared from his eyes. "What's wrong, Julia? You've been acting strange since we left the museum."

"You'll think I'm crazy if I tell you."

"I could never think that. If something is bothering you, I want you to share it with me. I'm going to be your husband."

She gazed down at their intertwined hands and knew she had to be honest with him. "I'm feeling rushed."

"Because of the December wedding date?"

She glanced back up at him and nodded. "It's fast, Michael. Only a little over three months."

"We've been engaged for a year."

"But not a normal year. Not a year of just being together without my mom being sick and endless trips to the hospital."

"I understand that you're still sad, Julia, but it will get better. And it will get better faster if we're together. I can't wait to get on with the rest of our lives. I have so many plans for us. I promise to do everything I can to make you happy. And I honestly believe that once you get into the wedding planning, you'll feel more confident that this marriage is absolutely right. She thought about his words. He might be right. Maybe she just needed to be settled. But how could she settle down when there were so many questions running through her mind? "There's more," she said slowly. "I've been thinking about my past, about my real father and who my mother was before she married Gino."

Michael looked at her in confusion. "Why would you be thinking about all that now?"

"That girl in the photograph at the museum. She looked just like me, and she was wearing the same necklace that my mother gave me when I was a little girl."

"I don't understand. You're saying you're... Russian?"

She winced at the incredulous note in his voice. It did sound ridiculous coming from his mouth. "I'm saying I don't know who I am," she amended. "I don't have anything from before my mom married Gino.

Nothing—no pictures of anything or anyone. It's like I didn't exist before I became a DeMarco."

"Didn't you ever ask your mother about your real father?"

"Of course I did, hundreds of times. She wouldn't talk about him. She said he left us and what did it matter?"

"It doesn't matter, Julia," he said, squeezing her hand. "You don't need him. You don't need anyone but me, and I don't care about your bloodline."

But she did need something besides him—she needed the truth. "I have to find out who I am, where I come from. It's important to me."

"Before the wedding?"

She nodded, seeing a flicker of annoyance cross his face. "Yes."

"And this is all because of some photograph?"

"That was the trigger, but to be honest, if it wasn't that, it would have been something else."

His eyes narrowed at that comment. "Because you want to postpone the wedding? Is that what you're trying to tell me?"

She wasn't quite sure how to answer that question. "It's just so fast."

"Yeah, that's what you said." He sat back, releasing her hand. "Look, Julia, just let things ride for a few days, see if you feel the same way in a week or two, before we change the date. If we don't take December, we'll have to wait another year. I know how much you love history, and I think the museum would be the perfect setting for you."

"I know." God, she felt so guilty. Michael had been so happy earlier. Now his face was pinched and tight, his eyes filled with disappointment.

"Here's your beer." Liz set the bottle down on the table, glancing from Michael to Julia, then back at Michael again. "Who just died?"

"Julia wants to postpone the wedding," Michael said glumly.

Julia sighed, wishing Michael had not shared that piece of information just yet.

"Are you out of your mind?" Liz asked in astonishment. "Why would you want to wait? You have the best place in the world to get married and the perfect guy. What's wrong with you, Julia?"

"Good question," Michael said, standing up. "Maybe you can talk some sense into your sister, Lizzie. I'm going to find some food."

Liz quickly took his seat. "Tell me what the problem is," she said as Michael left.

"I just need more time. I don't want to rush into marriage."

"Rush? If you go any slower, you'll be moving backwards."

Julia looked away from her sister's determined face, wondering if she could make a quick exit through the front door. But a tall, dark-haired man with light green eyes blocked that door. Her breath caught in her chest. Alex Manning? He'd cleaned up, shaved, showered, and put on more clothes, but it was definitely him. What did he want? Did he know something? Did she want to know what he knew?

Oh, God! She suddenly felt terrified that she was about to go down a path from which there would be no turning back.

"Who's that?" Liz asked, following her gaze.

Julia looked at her sister. "What?"

"Is that man the reason you want to postpone your wedding?"

"Maybe."

"Julia! How could you?"

"It's not what you think, but I do have to talk to him." She jumped to her feet and crossed the room, intercepting Alex before one of her aunts could shower him in cheek kisses, plates of ravioli, and cake. "What are you doing here?" she asked.

"I wanted to see your face again."

Julia fidgeted under his sharp, piercing gaze. "And?"

"I talked to someone about the photograph."

Julia pulled him out the front door of the cafe and onto the deserted pier, where darkness and shadows surrounded them. "What did you find out?"

"I was told to tell you that the girl died a few weeks after the photograph was taken. I was also told to butt out and mind my own business. That's not my style."

She wasn't sure how to read the gleam in his eyes. "What is your style?"

"To find the truth. Are you up for it?" he challenged.

Goose bumps raced down her arms. She should be focusing on her relationship with Michael and her wedding—she had a million things to worry about, things that were far more important than that old photograph. But something inside of her wouldn't let it go. All the questions about herself that she'd never had answered suddenly demanded attention. Maybe once she knew those answers, she'd feel more confident about moving on with the rest of her life.

"Yes," she said. "I want to find out who that girl is."

"Whatever it takes? Because there's no turning back once we get started."

She bristled at his controlling tone. "Look, I'll turn back whenever I want. So—"

"Then I won't help you."

He started to leave. He was actually going to walk away from her? In fact, he was six feet away before she said, "Wait. Why are you acting like this?"

He hesitated for so long she wasn't sure he would answer. Then he said, "The only reason I'm here is because you bear a striking resemblance to that girl. The necklace and the fact that you have no concrete evidence of where you lived before the age of four are also intriguing. But I promised not to talk to anyone about that photo. I won't break that promise with you unless I know you're committed to finding out the truth about that child."

"Who would have asked you to promise such a thing?"

"Are you in or are you out? Because I tell you nothing unless we have a deal."

She could see the resolve in his eyes. If she said she was out, she'd never see him again, and she'd never know if that picture had anything to do with her. She could research it on her own, but she wouldn't know where to start. Alex would have more contacts, more information. Oh, what the hell. It wasn't like she was selling her soul. She drew in a breath, praying she wouldn't regret her decision. "I'm in. Tell me what you know."

He met her gaze head-on. "My father didn't take that picture. I did."

CHAPTER THREE

"WHAT DO YOU MEAN, you took that photograph?" Julia asked, shocked by his statement.

"Just what I said. I was with my father on that trip to Moscow."

"But you're young. You must have been a little boy then."

"I was nine."

"I don't understand." Julia sat down on one of the wooden benches outside the cafe. She could hear the laughter and the music from inside the restaurant, but they sounded like a million miles away.

Alex sat down next to her. "I went to Moscow with my father," he explained. "It was the first and only time he took me with him on one of his assignments. My father was photographing a cultural exchange —an American theater group performing in Moscow. It was 1980. The Cold War was beginning to thaw, and both sides were eager to show that East and West could come together. My father got me a small part in the play so that I could go with him. It's a long story, but bottom line —my parents had separated that year, and this was the only opportunity my dad and I had to spend together. A few days after we arrived, he had a meeting one afternoon in Red Square. I got bored, and I picked up his camera. I wandered away, pretended I was shooting pictures the way I'd seen my father do. That's when I saw the girl at the gates." He paused, his eyes distant, as if he were recalling that moment. "She looked like she was in prison. I moved closer and said something to her, but she answered too softly for me to hear. She was... terrified. So I took her picture."

"I can't believe it. You were actually there? You saw her? You talked to her?" Julia searched his face, wondering if there was any possible way she'd ever seen him before. But she had no memories of her early childhood. She never had. Other people said they could remember events when they were two or three. Why couldn't she?

"After I took her picture," Alex continued, "I heard my father call my name and I ran back to him. I never told him I took the shot. My dad sent his film back to the magazine to be published. It wasn't until the magazine came out a few weeks later with that photo in print that he realized what I'd done. I'd never seen him so furious."

"Why? What did it matter? It turned out to be a famous shot."

Alex's lips tightened and a hard light came into his eyes. "I don't know why he was so upset about it. He wouldn't say, but he made me promise never to tell anyone I took the photo or that I saw the girl. He told me to forget she ever existed. There was fear in his eyes. I don't know if I realized that at the time, but in retrospect I believe he knew something I didn't."

"Like what?" she asked with a bewildered shake of her head. "How could a photo make someone afraid? I don't understand."

"All I can think is that the girl or the background of the picture revealed something that no one was supposed to see."

Julia thought about that for a moment. "Didn't you say there was a public reaction after the publication, that people were searching for that girl, but no one could find her?"

Alex nodded. "Yes. I have to admit I wasn't paying much attention at the time. My father died the day after that picture was published. That conversation we had about it was the last one we ever had, which is why it stuck in my mind."

"What?" Julia stared at him in shock. His voice was matter-of-fact, but his words were horrifying. "Your father died the day after the photo was published in the magazine? What happened to him?"

"Car accident," Alex said shortly, as if he couldn't bear to go into more detail. "My dad managed to travel all over the world without a scratch, but he lost his life a few miles from here on the Pacific Coast Highway." He looked off into the darkness, his profile hard and unforgiving.

Julia wanted to ask more questions, but there was so much pain in his voice, she couldn't bring herself to break the silence.

Finally, Alex turned back to her. "At any rate," he said, "I want to take another look at the photo. I think there's a good possibility the negative might still be in my mother's possession. The magazine gave her all of my father's work after he died. In the meantime, you should try to find some concrete evidence of your life before the age of four, especially when you lived in Berkeley. Your mother must have had friends, neighbors, someone who would remember seeing you as a baby. If you find them, your questions will be answered."

"But yours won't be." She realized his interest had more to do with the promise he'd made to his father than with her. She had just been the catalyst. Her quest had suddenly become his quest. He was taking over, and she didn't like it. What if he found out something about the photo that reflected poorly on his father? Would he share it with her? What if she was that girl and his father had covered something up about her? "I want to look at the photo with you," she said. "Especially if you have the original negative."

"I'll let you know what I find," he said as he stood up.

"That's not good enough. I told you I was in for the long haul. Commitment works both ways. Together means together, Alex."

"You don't sound like you trust me, Julia," he said with a little smile that made her trust him even less.

"I don't. I'm sorry if that hurts your feelings."

He laughed at that. "Don't worry about it. I don't have feelings to hurt. By the way, there's some guy staring out the window at us, and he looks pissed off. Do you know him?"

Julia turned her head to see Michael standing by the cafe window. "Yes, I know him," she said with a sigh. "He's my fiancé."

"You're engaged?"

She nodded, wondering how she would explain Alex to Michael.

"He's going to be a problem, isn't he?" Alex asked.

"I think he might be."

"Why don't you just go out there?" Liz asked, wishing Julia would return to the cafe sooner rather than later. Michael had been staring out the window for a good five minutes, and while Liz would have liked to take a look herself, she'd managed to refrain. She thought if she sat at a nearby table, sipping her red wine and acting unconcerned, Michael would feel the same way, too. So far it wasn't working.

"Who is he?" Michael bit out. "I've never seen him before."

"I'm sure he's no one important."

"Then why is she talking to him out there?" Michael asked, turning to face her. "Why not invite him inside? Why all the secrecy?"

Liz shrugged. "It's quieter outside. Why don't you sit down and have a drink with me?"

"Julia has been acting funny all day—at the museum and here tonight. I don't know what's going on with her. I thought we were finally moving on. I thought I'd given her enough time. I know I can make her happy if she'll give me a chance. Don't you think so?"

"Of course, Michael."

He let out a heavy breath and turned back toward the window. Julia *was* acting oddly, Liz thought, booking a wedding date today, and then telling Michael tonight that she wanted to postpone the ceremony. It didn't make sense. Michael was such a great guy. He had his own business. He was successful, good-looking, kind, and a family man. He'd been supportive during their mom's illness and the funeral. She didn't think they could have made it through their mother's death without him. She couldn't understand why Julia was hesitating for even a second.

If she had been the one Michael wanted, she'd have married him the day after he asked. Not that he'd ever noticed her in that way. She was just the kid sister, the short brunette, the flaky one, who served up shrimp cocktails and clam chowder in bread bowls all day long. Julia was prettier and far more interesting with her passion for music and her job at the radio station. There was no way Liz could compete with her. Although she did have bigger breasts. It was a small distinction, but one she was happy to make.

A loud clatter made her turn her head just in time to see her father, a tall, normally nimble man, stumble into a table and chairs. Her aunt Rita pushed him down into the chair and told him she'd bring him some coffee. Liz frowned. He was drinking so much lately. He'd always loved his red wine, but now it was vodka and scotch and lots of it.

Gino rested his head in his hands. He'd developed prominent streaks of gray in his black hair in the past year. His cheeks were pale and he was far too thin. Liz got up and walked over to him. "Daddy, are you okay?"

"I'm fine," he said, lifting his head. He offered her a dazed, drunken smile. "You're a good girl, Lizzie."

"You should eat something. Have you had any food?"

"I'm not hungry. I think we need another toast. To my daughter and her fiancé." He looked around. "Where's Julia?"

"She's outside talking to a friend. You can toast her later."

"Lucia, we must have champagne," Gino yelled across the room. "We must drink to Michael and Julia."

"Dad, please. Just have some coffee." Liz sent Aunt Rita a grateful look when she brought over a mug of hot coffee. "Here you go."

He waved a hand in disgust. "I don't want coffee. I want champagne. This is a party."

"You're embarrassing your daughter," Rita said sharply. "Drink the coffee, Gino."

He pushed it away, got to his feet, and staggered across the room to the bar. Liz knew she should probably go after him, but dammit, she was tired of chasing him. It was Julia's turn. She glanced across the room and saw that Michael was still staring out the window.

Maybe she couldn't set her father straight, but she could do something about Michael and Julia. She walked over to him and said, "If you're not going to get her, I will."

Michael grabbed her arm as she moved toward the door. "Stay out of it, Lizzie."

"Excuse me?"

"I want her to come in on her own."

"I don't care how she comes in. My dad is drinking himself to death over at the bar, and she needs to help me get him out of here."

"Your uncle is taking care of Gino," Michael said, tipping his head toward the far side of the room. Gino was now sitting down in a booth with her uncle and a pot of coffee.

She felt marginally better seeing them together. "He's really got me worried," she confessed. "He's like a lost soul right now, completely adrift. My mom took care of him. She did everything— the cooking, the cleaning, the housework. She paid the bills. She even did the books here at the restaurant. I don't know how he gets through the days without her. Actually, he's barely getting through the days." She shook her head, feeling helpless.

"You worry too much about your family," Michael said, putting a reassuring hand on her shoulder. "But I understand. I'm the same way."

Liz nodded. It was nice to have someone who understood. "Let's sit down. Yesterday you said you had something to tell me, and I still haven't heard what that something is."

"That's right," Michael muttered, as he pulled out a chair, joining her at the table. "Now I think I may have jumped the gun."

"About what?" she asked.

He hesitated for a long moment, then offered her a sheepish smile. "I bought a house."

"You did what?" She couldn't have heard him right. He hadn't just said he'd bought a house, had he?

"I bought a house. It's down the street from Carol's home," he added, referring to his younger sister. "She knew the seller. I was able to make an offer before the owner put it on the market. It's small and needs a lot of work, but it's perfect. It's near the Marina, on Waterside.

It has a small garden in the yard, and it's close to the rec center where I play basketball."

"Has Julia seen it?"

"No, I want to surprise her. What do you think?"

What did she think? She thought he was crazy. But it was certainly a romantic gesture. She had to give him that.

"Say something, Lizzie. You're making me nervous."

"It's just that a house is such a big thing to do on your own, Michael." Liz had a feeling Julia would not be happy to have been left out of the decision making. "Why didn't you show it to Julia before you bought it?"

"Because she would have put me off, told me to wait until we got married, and this was too good a deal to pass up. I want us to have our own home, Liz. No more apartment living. I want to own something, put down roots, start a family. I want to give Julia back some of what she lost when your mother died." He gave her an earnest smile. "It's a two-bedroom, so we'll have plenty of room for a baby. With my sister down the street, we'll have family nearby. I was so afraid we wouldn't be able to afford a place in the city that I knew I had to grab this one."

"That makes sense," she said slowly. "When are you going to tell Julia?"

"I want to fix it up first. It needs a lot of paint, some landscaping. I'm going to start work on it tomorrow. The escrow doesn't close for another two weeks, but the owner has already moved out and said I could do whatever I wanted."

"Wow." She didn't know what else to say.

"You can't tell Julia about it until I'm ready. Promise me, Lizzie."

"I promise. This is your secret to tell."

"I will make her happy," he said with determination. "I just want her to give me a chance to do it. I thought I'd pinned her down today; then tonight she got the jitters again." He paused. "Did she tell you about a photograph she saw at the museum that she thinks is her?"

"No. What are you talking about?"

"She saw some picture of a little girl standing in front of an orphanage in Russia twenty-something years ago, and for some bizarre reason, she thinks it could be her."

"What?" Liz's jaw dropped in amazement. "That's crazy. She's not Russian, and she was never an orphan."

"Yeah, well, she suddenly doesn't know who she is."

"She's a DeMarco. She's my big sister, that's who she is," Liz said, with a burst of anger. It was one thing for Julia to question getting married, but why on earth would she start thinking she was someone she wasn't?

"You should remind her of that."

As Michael finished speaking, the door opened, and Julia entered the restaurant alone. She sat down next to Liz, her cheeks flushed, a guilty look in her eyes. Liz felt a shiver of uncertainty race down her spine. What was Julia feeling guilty about? That man? Or was it something else? Something that would throw their lives into chaos again? The past year had been horrible. They were finally getting back to an almost normal state where she didn't feel like crying every day. She didn't want to deal with any more problems. Which meant she didn't want to ask Julia what she'd been up to outside the restaurant.

Apparently Michael didn't feel the same way. "Who was that?" he asked, an edge to his voice.

Julia hesitated for a moment, then said, "A photographer."

Liz felt a wave of relief. "Of course, a wedding photographer. I told you it was nothing," she said to Michael.

The tension on his face eased as well. "You were talking to a wedding photographer? I thought you weren't sure about planning the wedding yet?"

"I'm not, but—"

Before Julia could finish, they were interrupted by Lucia, who held a digital camera in her hand. "Come, come," Lucia said. "We're going to take a family picture for my birthday present. Now, before your father falls down."

"Dad is drinking again?" Julia asked Liz.

"I don't think he's stopped in the past six months," Liz replied, wondering why Julia hadn't noticed. "We're going to have to do something."

"He'll be all right," Lucia interrupted with a wave of her hand. "He's grieving. It's understandable. Now, it's picture time. And smiles all around. You, too," she said to Michael. "You're practically family."

"Am I?" Michael asked, looking at Julia. "Am I practically family?"

"Of course you are," Liz said when her sister couldn't seem to get the words out. She grabbed both their hands and pulled them to their feet. A moment later they were swept up in the DeMarco crowd, and Liz breathed a sigh of relief. Maybe if they could just survive this night, Julia would get over whatever was bothering her and return to being her reliable older sister who was about to marry the man of her dreams. But as Liz took her place in the group portrait, she couldn't help glancing toward the door, wondering if the man in the black leather jacket and blue jeans had really been a wedding photographer. He'd had a doozy of a black eye. She hadn't met many wedding photographers who looked like they'd just gotten out of a bar fight. But if he wasn't a wedding photographer, who was he?

––––––––

Julia spent most of Saturday morning going through the storage unit that was filled with the remnants of her mother's life. After the funeral, her father had made a sudden decision to sell their home, saying he couldn't bear to live in it without his beloved wife.

Julia had suggested he wait, but he would have none of it, and within three months the house was gone. Gino now lived in a two-bedroom apartment a few blocks from the wharf, Liz had moved in with Julia, and what they hadn't had time to go through had been put in this storage locker.

Looking through her mother's things was unbelievably depressing. Julia wished she didn't have to do it alone, but she couldn't ask Liz to help. She couldn't talk to anyone about the picture—except Alex Manning. In the cold light of day she'd had to question why she'd agreed to work with a man who'd been beaten up, thrown in jail, and kicked out of Colombia. And that was just last week. She'd found that information in a recent article in the Examiner. Further research on the Internet had unveiled the fact that his reputation for being a brilliant photographer was only surpassed by his reputation for getting into trouble. The last thing she needed was more trouble.

But she'd made her deal with him and she'd stick to it—at least as long as it made sense. Or until she had proof that she was not that girl.

So far she had no proof of anything. As her mother had told her, there were absolutely no photos of either of them before the wedding pictures taken when her mother had married Gino. It was as if they'd come into existence at that moment. But her mother had had a life before Gino, thirty-three years of life. She'd had parents and grandparents, and she'd grown up somewhere. But where?

Her mother had told her she was from Buffalo, New York. That was the only information she'd ever shared. She said if her parents didn't want her, she didn't want them. Julia had often wondered about her grandparents, but loyalty to her mother had kept her from asking questions or requesting to see anyone. After all, they hadn't wanted her, either. Now she had a feeling she would have to find them if only to prove the truth about her birth.

Sitting back on her heels, she considered again how best to do that. How did one find a needle in a haystack? For that matter, she couldn't even find the haystack. She had nothing to trace, not one little clue.

"Julia?"

She looked up as her sister appeared in the doorway. Liz was dressed in running shorts and a tank top, her brown hair swept up in a ponytail. She looked like she'd just come from a jog. Liz was one of those people who liked to run and work out. Julia's favorite form of exercise was a long walk to Starbucks followed by a latte. "What are you doing here?" she asked.

"Looking for you. I stopped by Dad's place. He told me he gave you the key. What are you looking for?"

"I'm not sure."

"Michael told me that you think there's some mystery about who you are," she said with a quizzical look in her eyes.

"I have some questions," Julia admitted.

"How can you have questions now?" Liz demanded, her expression filled with hurt. "Our mother just died. Our father is drinking himself into oblivion every night, in case you haven't noticed. And your fiancé is upset that you want to postpone your wedding. Don't you have enough on your plate? Do you really need to find your birth father now? After all these years?"

Liz made some good points. The timing wasn't right. Then again, it had never been right. Which was how Julia had reached the age of twenty-eight without knowing who her biological father was. But he wasn't really the issue. "I'm not trying to find my father," she said. "I just want to know who I am, where I was born. I saw a picture at the museum. It was the spitting image of me. And the little girl had on a necklace just like mine."

"The one with the swan? That's why you were looking at it?"

"Yes."

"Michael said the girl in the picture lived in Russia. How can you think it's you? You were never in Russia."

It sounded worse coming from Liz's mouth. "I know it seems crazy. But that photo started me thinking about how I don't have any pictures of me or Mom before she married Gino. Isn't that odd? I thought if I came here, I might be able to find something that would prove I was living in the United States when I was three years old."

Liz stared at her like she was out of her mind. "Are you having some sort of breakdown, Julia? You're acting like a mad person."

"No, I'm acting like a person who doesn't know where she came from. It's different for you, Lizzie. You know who both your parents are. I only know about my mother. I don't know about my real father or my grandparents on my mother's side. And I can't remember anything from when I was little, which is also driving me crazy. Why don't I have any memories from that time in my life?"

"A lot of people don't remember when they're really young. I don't remember much."

"You don't have to remember, because I can tell you everything," Julia replied. "I was there from the minute you were born. No one that I know besides my mother was there from the minute I was born. And she's gone."

"All right, fine." Liz perched on the edge of an old trunk. "Did you ask Dad about it?"

"Not yet. He had a big headache and a hangover. I didn't want to bring it up if I could find something some other way."

"And that man you were with last night? Is he involved in this search?"

"He's the son of the photographer who took the picture." Julia didn't explain that Alex was the one who had taken the picture.

"And he thinks it's you, too?"

"He thinks it's worth looking into."

"You're both nuts," Liz said flatly.

Julia sighed. Liz tended to have a closed mind and could be very judgmental. She was always the last one to try anything new, and she often refused to look at problems in her life. She hadn't been able to accept their mother was going to die until she'd actually died. Up until then, Liz had insisted that their mother would get well, that life would return to normal. Maybe it was her age. She was six years younger than Julia, and she still wanted and needed to be protected. Julia usually tried to do just that, but not this time.

"Don't you have to work this afternoon?" Julia asked, deciding to change the subject.

"Not for a while yet. I think you're taking a risk, Julia. You could lose Michael over this ridiculous search that will probably turn up nothing in the long run. Do you want to take that chance?"

A few months ago, make that a week ago, Julia would have said no, that she was happy with the way things were, but the photograph in the museum had opened up her eyes to the fact that the status quo had changed when her mother died. There was nothing to hold her back now. She could finally ask the questions and find the answers that she needed to fill out the missing part of her life. Michael should be able to understand that and so should Liz. "I'd rather look now than later," she said. "When I get married, I want to do it knowing everything I need to know about myself. If Michael can't give me a few days to figure that out, then he should be the one you're talking to, not me."

"Are you sure it will take only a few days?"

"I'm not sure about anything. I'm taking it one step at a time. And while I know you hate it when people don't do exactly what you want, you're going to have to let me do this, Liz, because I'm not willing to stop until I get some answers."

"Have you considered the fact that you might be better off not knowing, that maybe Mom had a good reason for never telling you about your past?"

She had considered that, more than once. "That might be true, but I think the not knowing is worse."

"I hope you're right about that."

"So do I."

"Have you found anything yet?" Liz looked around at the mess Julia had made. "You've certainly been thorough. I still can't believe this is all we have left of Mom's life. It doesn't seem like much."

"I know. I keep thinking there must be more. Although I haven't come across any paperwork, birth certificates, that kind of thing, so maybe there is more. I remember putting a lot of boxes in Dad's spare bedroom when he moved."

Liz frowned. "I can't believe he's happier living in an apartment. He should have stayed in the house. Mom loved that house. And I'm still pissed off at him for selling it."

"The house had too many memories. He couldn't stand it."

"It's going to be strange this Christmas. No tree in the corner of the living room, no Christmas dinner around the big table. It won't be the same at Aunt Lucia's house."

"No, it won't." Julia could see how much Liz hated that thought. "But we'll still make it a good holiday. We have each other. That's what matters."

"I guess. Are you done here?"

"Almost. I have one more box to go through."

Liz kneeled down next to Julia as she opened the last large box. Instead of their mother's clothes, they found children's clothes.

"I remember this outfit," Liz said, pulling out a pink jumper. "I used to love it."

"And I used to wear this sweater all the time," Julia added, pulling out a blue sweater with embroidered flowers on the front. "I wonder why Mom kept these clothes. She was always doing spring-cleaning. I rescued a few things from the garbage on more than one occasion."

"That's true, but these were our favorites." Liz dug farther into the pile. "I guess she had a sentimental soft spot after all. Who knew?"

"There's a lot we don't know about her, Liz. I spent all night thinking about what I don't know about her, like where she grew up and where she spent her summer vacations. Where she went to school, who her friends were, her first boyfriend. She never talked about herself, and we never asked. Why didn't we ask?"

"I guess I wasn't that interested," Liz admitted, the smile quickly disappearing from her face. "I thought we'd have more time."

"Me, too." Julia touched her sister's hand to comfort. She was still the big sister, and she'd promised her mother she'd always watch out for Liz. "Even though we knew the diagnosis, we couldn't stop hoping. And Mom never wanted to say good-bye. She never wanted to talk about the end, even though we all knew it was coming."

"You're right. She asked me two days before she died to take her out into the garden so she could decide what to plant in the fall." Liz blinked back a tear, then reached back into the box. "I see something. Hey, what's this?"

She pulled out a hand-painted wooden doll about ten inches tall. The artwork on the doll was intricate and detailed. A woman's face was painted on the round head, a wreath of white flowers on her dark hair. The larger, cylinder-like body of the doll showed the woman's costume, a white dress with three feathered tiers and a floral pattern that mixed red flowers and green leaves. Along the base of the doll was a circle of swans that glistened in the lacquer finish. Julia's heart skipped a beat. The swans matched the one on her necklace. And she knew this doll. She'd held it in her hands before. "It's stunning," she murmured.

"I don't remember seeing it before," Liz said.

Julia took it out of Liz's hand. She opened the top and found another doll inside, then another one, and another. "It's a nesting doll," she said. "It's called a matryoshka doll."

"What? How do you know that?"

"I don't know how I know that." Julia looked from the doll to her sister, feeling like she was about to fall over the edge of a cliff. "But I know what it is. It's a Russian doll. And it's mine."

CHAPTER FOUR

"I NEED to look through Dad's negatives," Alex said to his mother as she ushered him into the living room of her two-story house in Presidio Heights.

"And good morning to you, too," Kate Manning said sharply. She sat down on a spotlessly clean white couch that took up one wall of the large room, and crossed her arms in front of her. Dressed in a light blue silky pants outfit with a pair of impractical spike heels, she looked very sophisticated. Alex couldn't remember ever seeing her in sweats or tennis shoes, and certainly never without her makeup. She had always been very conscious of her appearance.

Alex sat down in the antique chair across from her, sensing this would not be the easy visit he'd hoped for. Time had not mellowed his mother's attitude, and he was reminded of why he rarely chose to visit her. If he wanted to get anywhere with her, he'd better backtrack and start over. "Sorry, Mother. How are you?"

"I'm fine, not that you care. It's been months since we've spoken."

"We saw each other last night."

"Before that. Don't get cute with me, Alex. You don't return my calls. You don't answer my e-mail, and you couldn't be bothered to remember my birthday."

"I sent you a card."

"Three weeks late."

"I was in a remote jungle in Africa. The mail service wasn't good."

"You always have an answer to everything," she said with a wave of her well-manicured hand. "Just like your father."

Alex sighed. How many times had he heard that phrase? Just like your father. Well, he was proud to be just like his father. But that wasn't an issue he intended to discuss with her. "Do you still have Dad's negatives?"

Her mouth drew into a tight frown. "I might. Why would you want them after all these years?"

"I'd like to take a look at something."

"At what? Are you here about that photo taken in Moscow? The one you were asking about last night?"

"Maybe." He saw something flicker in her eyes, and he couldn't help wondering what it was.

"Your father was very upset after that trip," she murmured. "Or maybe it was later—when the photo was published in the magazine. I overheard him yelling at Stan about it. He never told me what the problem was." She paused, a question in her eyes, a question he still couldn't answer. When he didn't speak, she added, "Then it was too late to ask. Your father was gone, and you were so angry with me, you wouldn't look at me—not even at the funeral." Her voice caught, and he saw an expression of pain in her eyes. "When you did speak to me, you told me I'd broken up the family. But that wasn't completely true, Alex. I didn't do it alone."

"I don't want to get into our family history," he said quickly.

"Then you shouldn't be digging up the past. Your father had a lot of secrets. That last year of his life—he was different. I didn't know what caused the change. Maybe it was his job. Maybe it was me. Maybe it was another woman," she said with a bitter edge to her voice.

"You don't have any proof there was ever another woman." He couldn't refrain from defending his father. He'd heard her make the comment a number of times, and it irritated the hell out of him.

"I may not have proof, but I know something was off. Charles used to get calls from a woman late at night. I heard her voice more than once. He said she was a business associate, but he was a freelancer, and there were no female editors working at any of the magazines."

"You can't be sure of that."

"Oh, I am. I checked." She paused, her mouth tightening in a hard line. "I'm not sure I ever told you this, but I spent most of my child-hood watching my mother turn a blind eye to my father's cheating. I swore that I would never do the same. I wouldn't allow your father to turn me into a pathetic, hopeless, helpless woman like my mother, who was suddenly shocked to realize the whole town knew her husband was cheating on her."

Alex had known his mother wasn't close to her parents, but he'd always thought it was because she was ashamed of their blue-collar roots. Her father had been a plumber, her mother a waitress. Appar-ently there had been more to the story.

Kate drew in a deep breath, a frown on her face now, as if she were sorry she'd said so much. "I just want you to leave the past alone, Alex."

"It's funny that you would say that. You're the one who is throwing a spotlight on Dad's work every chance you get. You hated his job, and you probably hated him, too, yet here you are acting like the tragic widow, and it's been twenty-five years and two marriages since you were with him."

"I'm not acting like a widow. That's what I am. You'll never under-stand the relationship I had with your father or how I felt about his work," she said hotly. "But I know what it was, and I have every right to make sure his photographs continue to be recognized. I'm even negotiating a possible book contract."

"Really." He studied her thoughtfully, not liking the way she avoided his gaze. "Why? Do you need the money?" Her home was beautifully decorated, her clothes expensive and well made. She didn't look like she was short of cash, but he had no idea where she stood with her personal finances. Her last two husbands had not been rich, but very comfortable. And if he knew his mother, she'd gotten her fair share in the divorces.

"I'm surprised you would ask, Alex. You've never shown any interest in my personal well-being."

"That's not an answer. But it's your business." He got to his feet. "Where do you have the negatives?"

"They're in a box in the hall closet. I want them back, though, Alex. I may need them for the book."

"Fine."

"Wait. Don't go like this," she said, holding up her hand in a plea for him to stay. "I don't want to fight with you."

"We've never done anything else," he said with a shrug.

"Because you've always seen your father as the hero and me as the villain. That's not the way it was."

"Mother, it's over. It was over a lifetime ago. I've moved on."

She shook her head. "If you've truly moved on, leave the negatives here."

"I can't do that."

She gave him a searching look. "Why do you care about that photo?"

He debated for a second, not wanting to confide in his mother, but he had to give her some explanation, so he said, "I want to know more about that girl."

"After all these years? Why now? Has something happened?"

"No, nothing has happened," he lied, preferring not to get into the subject of Julia. "I've always wondered whether that photo was cropped, if something important was left out of it when it was published in the magazine."

Her eyes narrowed. "Why on earth would you wonder that?"

"I'm curious, and I have some time before my next assignment."

"I don't believe you, Alex." Her eyes turned reflective. "You know something you're not telling me. Your father knew something about that picture, too. He was so upset when it was published. The night before he died, he stopped by here to give me a check, and I could see that he was afraid of something." She took a breath. "I've never said this to you, Alex, but I'm not sure that car crash was really an accident."

Her words hit him like a punch to the gut. He had to force some air into his chest so he could breathe. "What? What are you saying?"

She gazed straight into his eyes and said, "I think someone deliberately ran your father's car off that road."

His mother's words were still ringing through Alex's mind when he entered his apartment an hour later. His father's car hadn't been deliberately run off the road. The car crash was an accident. It had been raining. The roads were slick. The other car was simply going too fast when it sideswiped his father's car. His father lost control and drove off the edge of a cliff into the Pacific Ocean. That's what everyone had said and what he'd reminded his mother of a short while ago. But as he stared at the box now resting on his coffee table, he saw his father's face the day before his death, the fear in his eyes when he'd made Alex promise never to tell anyone about that photo or that girl. Were the two events somehow tied together?

They'd never recovered his father's body. The currents were too strong. He'd been swept out to sea.

Was that true... or a convenient explanation to cover up something more sinister?

His mother had no proof of her suspicions. She said she'd mentioned her doubts to Stan, and Stan had told her that the police report was clear that it was an accident.

They'd never found the other driver. There had been no witnesses.

Dammit. He hated all the doubts suddenly racing through his mind. Why had she brought it up now, after all these years? Just to throw him off? To create a mystery where there wasn't one? To make her widowhood even more dramatic? To get a bigger book deal?

His phone rang, and he reached for it, hoping it wasn't his mother calling him back with another bombshell. "Hello?"

"Alex, it's Julia. I found something in my mother's belongings. I want to show it to you."

"Where are you?"

"I'm at work right now. Can you meet me at my apartment in a half hour? It's in North Beach, 271 Lexington, Apartment 2C."

"What did you find?"

"I don't want to get into it over the phone, and I just have a minute before I have to go back on the air."

"On the air?" he echoed.

"I host a radio show on KCLM 86.5. I've got to run. I'll see you soon."

Julia was a disc jockey, Alex thought as he hung up the phone. That surprised him. He walked over to his stereo and turned on the radio, just in time to hear her beautiful, sexy voice.

"You're listening to '*World Journeys with Julia*,' " Julia said into the microphone. "Next up is Paolo Menendez, who brings us a delicious blend of reggae, calypso, and Caribbean rhythms from Cartagena on the Caribbean Coast." Julia flipped off the microphone and pushed the button on the computer to start the next set of songs.

She sat back in her chair, staring at the matryoshka doll. Since she'd discovered it in her mother's belongings, she'd been racking her brain trying to remember where it had come from. She remembered holding on to it really tightly, and for some odd reason she had the vague feeling that someone had tried to take it away from her and she'd started crying. She hadn't stopped until the person had given it back. Unfortunately, that person was just a dark shadow in her mind. It must have been her mother. It couldn't have been anyone else.

As she was putting the doll into her large brown leather handbag, the door to the control room opened, and Tracy Evanston walked into the room. A twenty-six-year-old African-American woman with dread-locks and a nose ring, Tracy hosted the three-to-five show featuring the best of jazz music.

"Hey," Tracy said. "I love this guy you have on now. Any chance we could get him to perform at the concert?"

"He wasn't available," Julia replied. "Believe me, I tried." It had been her job to book musicians for a special charity concert the station was sponsoring in the fall, and she'd been fortunate enough to get a good list of talent. They were hoping to raise enough money to fund music programs in the local schools, one of her pet projects.

"Too bad," Tracy replied. She tossed her keys down on the desk and picked up the schedule. "You are working too many hours, Julia. How are you going to do all this work and plan a wedding?"

Julia inwardly sighed at the mention of her wedding. "I don't know yet. I'll work it out."

"Why don't you take some time off? I'll happily take over some of your work. My little sis is off to college next year, and I want to help her if I can. So keep that in mind if you need to take off a few days. I can use the extra money."

"I will."

Tracy suddenly straightened, glancing out the glass window that led into the production room. "Oh, my. Who is that nice piece of work?" she asked.

"His name is Alex Manning," Julia replied, feeling unsettled by Alex's sudden appearance. She'd told him to meet her at her apartment, not here where she worked. She didn't want to bring up her past in front of Tracy, who wouldn't be shy about asking a lot of questions that Julia didn't want to answer.

"And how do you know him?" Tracy asked with a mischievous smile. "Is he the reason you've been stalling Michael on setting a wedding date?"

"Don't be ridiculous. I just met him yesterday."

"Well, he is fine. Don't tell me you haven't noticed."

Of course she'd noticed. But she wasn't interested in him on any sort of personal level, which meant her palms should not be sweating and there shouldn't be a shiver running down her spine, but there was, especially when Alex tapped on the window and smiled at her. She was definitely attracted. A normal response, she told herself. As Tracy had said, Alex was a good-looking man. Maybe she was just noticing because she was engaged, and she wasn't supposed to want anyone else.

What was she thinking? She did not want him. He was just the means to an end, a person to help in her search. That was it.

"Julia, ten seconds," Tracy said, motioning toward the microphone.

"Oh, right." She flicked on the microphone, watching the computer screen in front of her count down the seconds. "You've been listening to *'World Journeys with Julia.'* Join me again tomorrow from one to three when we'll take a musical tour through the Congo. Next up is jazz specialist Kenny Johnson." She punched the button to play the string of commercials that separated their segments. "Have a good show," she said to Tracy as she stood up.

"You have a good—whatever," Tracy said with a sly smile. "Don't do anything I wouldn't do."

"That leaves me a lot of options."

"Just remember you're not married yet. You can still change your mind."

"That won't happen." Julia picked up her bag and walked into the production room where Alex was waiting. "You were supposed to meet me at my apartment."

"I thought I'd check out where you work. I didn't picture you as a DJ," he added with a smile, "but you sound good on the radio. You have a great voice."

"Thanks." She wasn't surprised he didn't see her as a disc jockey. Most people thought DJs were wacky people, which might be true for some, but not all, especially not at KCLM, which played a wide variety of music. "I'm also a producer for some of our other shows. We're a small station. Everyone wears more than one hat." She waved her hand toward the massive collection of CDs in the room. "I'm a music fanatic, in case you were wondering."

"Then it sounds like you have the right job."

"It's perfect for me. Do you like music?"

"I play a little guitar," he admitted. "When I'm home, which isn't often. What about you?"

"I play the piano, the drums, and a little saxophone. I'm pretty much mediocre at them all," she said candidly. "I would have been a musician if I'd had any talent. Instead I play other people's masterpieces."

He grinned. "The next best thing."

"Exactly."

"I enjoyed hearing Paolo Menendez," Alex added. "I saw him perform in Cartagena. He played an acoustic guitar solo that was out of this world."

"You saw him play?" she echoed, feeling extremely envious. "It must have been amazing. I would kill to hear him in person, but he never travels to America."

"Maybe you should go to Cartagena."

"That's a thought," she replied, but she knew it was impossible. There was no way she'd ever get Michael to Cartagena.

"Does your fiancé share your passion for music?" Alex asked curiously.

She shook her head. "Not really. Michael likes pop and rock, but he listens mostly to sports radio. Anyway, I wanted to show you this." She reached into her handbag and pulled out the matryoshka doll.

"It's a Russian nesting doll. I found it in my mother's things. It's my doll. I remembered that as soon as I saw it."

She watched for his reaction, but Alex didn't give anything away. Instead he took the doll from her hand and studied the design.

"There are smaller dolls inside," she added.

He set the doll on the desk and took it apart, one piece after the other.

"What do you think?" she asked.

"I don't know. It's just a doll."

"It's a Russian doll."

"I bet they sell them here in the United States."

His pragmatic answer disappointed her. "Don't you think it's rather telling that I would have a Russian doll?" she persisted.

"Maybe, but it doesn't prove anything. The doll isn't in the photo. And there aren't any marks that identify this doll as being made in Russia."

"Look at the swans. They're just like the swan on the necklace."

"I saw that. Did you notice that there are dolls missing?" he asked her.

She sent him a blank look. "What do you mean?"

"The first two fit together perfectly, but there are gaps between the others. You have five dolls. I'm guessing that there were more."

"I can't imagine where they would be. I went through everything that belonged to my mother. This is all I came up with." She perched on the edge of the desk. "Damn, I thought I was onto something."

"You still might be," he conceded. "We can research this doll, see what we can find out. There might be some way to trace where it came from."

"That sounds like a good idea."

"I've been known to have a few."

"Where do we start? The Internet? I have a computer at home. We can go there."

"Why don't we get something to eat first?" he suggested. "I haven't had time to shop for food. Besides, we can kill two birds with one stone. There's a Russian deli near my apartment. The owner came over from Russia about ten years ago. Maybe she can tell us something about your doll."

"Another good idea," she said with a grin. "I'm impressed."

"I'm just getting started, Julia."

The smile on his face and the sparkle in his light green eyes took her breath away. Her body tingled and her heart began to race. She forced herself to look away, focusing on putting the doll back together and regaining her composure. She didn't know why Alex was having such an effect on her, but whatever the reason she had to get over it— and fast. She was engaged. She was committed. She was supposed to be in love.

"Ready?" Alex asked.

She nodded, still avoiding his gaze. As he headed for the door, she looked through the glass, catching Tracy's eye. The other woman gave her a thumbs-up sign. Julia wanted to tell Tracy it wasn't like that, that she wasn't interested in Alex, but she was afraid that would be a lie.

Dasha's Deli was located in the heart of the Haight, where parking was scarce, so they decided to leave their cars at Alex's apartment. The short walk to the deli took them past tattoo parlors, funky art galleries, jewelry stores and shops touting sixties souvenirs, flower children T-shirts, black lights, and beads. "This is a great neighborhood," she said to Alex as they stopped at a traffic light. "Have you lived here long?"

"About six years."

She sent him a sideways glance. Even though he'd cleaned up his act from the day before, his face was still bruised, his dark hair a little too long, his jeans faded, and his T-shirt a bit wrinkled. He was definitely not a nine-to-five business executive or a corporate worker bee. He was a photojournalist who roamed the world, a free spirit. No wonder he'd chosen to live here when he was in town. "This neighborhood fits you," she said.

He nodded in agreement. "It does. Freedom to be different is a luxury in many corners of the world. It's nice to be reminded that it still exists here in San Francisco."

The somber note in his voice reminded her that he'd probably seen some horrific sights in his travels. "Is it hard? Photographing how the rest of the world lives?"

"Sometimes."

"But you love it?"

"Most days I do. Lately, I don't know..." His voice dropped away. "Hey, we're here."

Julia was disappointed to see the deli sign. She wanted to hear what Alex had been about to say. "What do you mean, lately?" she prodded.

"It's a long story, and I'm hungry."

"Will you tell me the story while we eat?"

"Probably not," he said candidly. "It would kill your appetite."

"Alex. You can't start something and not finish it."

"We're here to solve the story of your life, not mine," he reminded her. "Let's keep our focus." He opened the door and waved her inside. "After you."

As Julia entered the restaurant, the delicious smells of fresh breads and cakes assailed her. The bakery counter was immediately to her left, the deli counter on the other side of the room, a crush of small tables in the middle. It was a little late for lunch, but there was still a good crowd, so they took a number and waited. As they did so, Julia searched her brain for some sense of familiarity with the Russian smells. They warmed her heart, made her mouth water, but was that just because they were so tantalizing or because she remembered them?

A short, round woman in her fifties with dark brown hair, black eyes, and a nurturing smile called their number, then greeted Alex by name when they stepped up to the counter.

"You have been a stranger," she said with a heavy accent. "Where have you been?"

"All over the world," he replied. "I brought a friend with me today. Julia, this is Dasha." Julia smiled and said hello as Alex went on to explain. "Julia has a Russian doll that she found in her mother's things. We're hoping, if you have a few minutes, you might talk to us about it."

"Of course," Dasha said. "I would be happy to look at your doll. But first you will eat. What do you like?"

"I'm not really sure," Julia said. "It all looks wonderful."

"Then we will give you a sampling. When you come back, you will order your favorites."

"That sounds perfect."

Dasha filled several plates with a variety of foods.

Julia couldn't imagine how they would get through it all. They sat down at a small table against the wall and unloaded their trays. "This is too much," Julia complained. "I'll never eat it all."

"That's what I said the first time, but I was wrong." Alex tipped his head toward the bowl of soup by her elbow. "Try the borscht first," he suggested. "It's the best."

Julia looked down in fascination at the deep purple soup, topped with a dollop of sour cream. "What's in it?" she asked.

"Cabbage, leeks, potatoes, and beets. That's what gives it the purple color."

She took a heaping spoonful, murmuring with appreciation at the delicious taste. "It's good. Hot and hearty."

"You're not a picky eater, are you, Julia?"

"Not at all. I love to try new food. You?"

"I'd starve otherwise. Where I go the food choices can be very exotic."

"What's the worst thing you've ever eaten?"

Alex thought for a moment. "A wormlike bug in the Amazon. They fry 'em up like French fries, but they still taste like worms."

"Why did you eat it?"

"I was hungry," he said with a laugh. "And I didn't want to offend my host. I was hoping to get his permission to take some photographs, so I ate what he ate."

She admired his determination. "Are there some lines you won't cross to get your shot?"

"Not that I can think of. It's my job to get the picture no one else can get. If that means eating worms, I eat worms." He pointed toward her plate. "Try the cabbage rolls next. They're stuffed with beef. Delicious. No worms, I promise," he added with a grin that was incredibly appealing—irresistible, in fact.

She found herself smiling back and thinking what an interesting man he was and how different from Michael. Alex was worldly, adventurous, and probably a little reckless, or a lot reckless. But she wasn't here to analyze him; she was here to get answers about her doll. Since Dasha still had a line of customers, Julia dug into her cabbage rolls, then a tomato and cucumber salad followed by piroshki, pastry puffs filled with chicken. When she pushed her plate away, she was completely stuffed. "I'm never eating again," she said.

"You haven't tried any of the desserts yet."

"Stop. You are a bad influence." As she finished speaking, Dasha came over to their table.

"Did you enjoy?" she asked, smiling at their empty plates.

"Very much," Julia replied. "It was all wonderful."

"Good. Now, you wanted to ask me something." She took a seat next to Alex and offered Julia an inquiring look.

Julia took the doll from her bag and set it on the table between them. "I found this doll among my mother's belongings and wondered if you could tell me anything about it."

"Oh, my, this is lovely," Dasha said. She slowly turned the doll around with an admiring gaze. "Beautiful. And very unique. The matryoshka doll is meant to be a symbol of motherhood and fertility. The smaller dolls inside are the babies." She paused for a moment. "The woman's face reminds me of someone. I can't think who. Oh, look at that." Dasha pointed to a tiny mark on the bottom corner of the doll. "There was a famous artist named Sergei Horkin, who used to sign his paintings with this S slash mark. I believe he did paint a few dolls. I can't remember whether it was the subject that was a famous person or if the famous person was the one who commissioned the doll. Either way, this doll could be very valuable if he was indeed the artist."

"Really?" Alex asked. "Is this Sergei still alive?"

"No, no, he died many, many years ago in the 1930s."

"The 1930s? Do you think the doll is that old?" Julia asked in surprise.

"I'm not an expert, but it might be."

"Do the swans or the art have any significance?" Alex inquired.

"Swans are often used in Russian stories," Dasha replied. "Swan Lake, for example:"

"A beautiful ballet," Julia said, glancing at Alex. "Have you seen it?"

"No, but I take it that the ballet has something to do with a swan."

"A sorcerer casts a spell that forces young women to live as swans unless they secure a man's undying devotion," Julia explained. "Siegfried, a prince, falls in love with the swan queen, Odette, but the sorcerer makes his evil daughter, Odile, pretend to be Odette and tricks the prince into promising his love to her. In the end, Siegfried and Odette realize they can only consummate their love by dying together."

"Very romantic," Alex said dryly. "You must die to get love. Hell of a choice."

"But their love was worth dying for," Julia reminded him. She could see that Alex was not at all touched by the story. She wondered if he'd ever been in love. He certainly had a cynical side to him. Was that because of a love gone wrong or no experience with the real thing?

Alex turned to Dasha. "Is there anything more you can tell us?"

"You should talk to my cousin, Svetlana. She runs a shop on Geary called Russian Treasures. She knows everything there is to know about these dolls."

"We'll go there now," Julia said, excited to have a lead.

Dasha quickly dashed her eagerness with a shake of her head. "Unfortunately, Svetlana is out of town until tomorrow night. The girl who runs the shop when she is gone doesn't know anything. She's an American teenager. If you go on Monday, Svetlana will be back then." Dasha stood up. "Now, I must return to work. Don't be a stranger, Alex. And you come back, too, Julia. You look good together."

"Oh, we're not together," Julia replied quickly. "I'm engaged to someone else. Alex and I are... We're practically strangers."

"Sometimes strangers end up lovers," Dasha said. "It happened to me when a stranger asked to share my umbrella in the rain." A soft look came into her eyes. "We were both supposed to be with other people. We'd made promises, but love doesn't always go as one plans, and sometimes promises have to be broken. We've been together forty-two years now, and we've been through many rough storms, but they're easier to bear when there's an umbrella to share and a stranger who has become a good friend." Dasha smiled and returned to the deli counter.

Julia felt a little awkward after that pointed story. She didn't want Alex to get any ideas.

"Relax, Julia," he said abruptly. "I'm not offering to share my umbrella with you."

"That's good. Because I'm engaged."

"You've mentioned that."

"You probably don't even carry an umbrella, do you?"

"It would only slow me down," he replied.

"And a woman would slow you down even more."

He met her gaze head-on. "I've never met one yet who could keep up with me. Are you ready to go?" he asked, getting to his feet.

She hesitated, battling the impulse to continue their personal conversation. Whether or not Alex had a woman in his life or wanted one was not her concern or her business. She was simply curious, but she could see by the determined look in his eyes that he was eager to move on. "Yes, I'm ready." She put the doll back into her bag. "I wish we could talk to Svetlana today. Do you think we should go by her shop anyway?"

"Why don't we look up Sergei Horkin on the Internet? Maybe we can find something about his paintings there. I'd like to get back to my apartment. I picked up a box of my father's photos at my mother's house earlier today. I still want to find that negative."

"Can I help you look?" she asked impulsively.

Alex hesitated. "Don't you have other things to do?"

"Nothing as important as this."

"Really?" he asked curiously. "Does your fiancé feel the same way?"

"Michael wants what's best for me. He'll understand." At least she hoped he would.

CHAPTER FIVE

LIZ FOUND Michael halfway up a ladder in front of the small two-bedroom house he'd bought near the Marina as a surprise for Julia. She smiled as he tried to keep his balance while dipping the roller into the paint tray on top of the ladder. He really was a good-looking guy, she thought, with his wind-tossed light brown hair, ruddy cheeks, and strong build. Even dressed in paint-spattered jeans and a T-shirt, he was handsome and sexy. Julia was crazy to think she could put this man on the back burner and not risk losing him. Or maybe Julia wasn't crazy; maybe she was just sure of their love. Michael had certainly been devoted to her the past year.

"You missed a spot," she said, pointing to the area above his right shoulder.

"Hey, Lizzie," he said with a wave. "Just in time. I could use a hand."

"You look like you could use more than a hand. Don't you need a crew to do this?"

"I can do it myself." He climbed down the ladder, wiping his hands on his jeans. "Or with a little help. What are you doing right now?"

"I wasn't planning on painting," she said, her hand itching to wipe the splash of paint from his face. She forced herself to put her hands in her pockets.

"My brother bailed out on me, and I want to get the front done today. I have charters to run tomorrow. I could really use your help."

"I don't have anything to wear."

He unbuttoned his shirt and shrugged his arms out, tossing it over to her. She caught her breath at the sight of his muscular chest covered with a nice spattering of black hair.

"You can wear mine over yours," he said.

"Are you sure?"

"Absolutely. I can work on my tan."

She didn't think he needed to do that. His body was already nicely browned. She put his shirt on over her tank top. It smelled like sweat and Michael, a heady scent. She was losing it. Michael was a friend, almost a brother, and soon to be her brother-in-law. She needed to get out more, have some dates, find herself another guy to get all hot and bothered about.

"Have you spoken to Julia today?" he asked.

She was glad he'd brought up Julia. It put a nice solid wall between them. "I saw her earlier."

"Is she still thinking about looking for her real father?"

"Yes. I tried to talk her out of it, Michael, but she's stuck on it. You know how she is when she gets curious about something. She can't stop until she figures it out. Remember that puzzle she worked on for three weeks straight until she finally put all the pieces together?"

"This isn't a puzzle. It's her life. And mine, too. I want her to focus on getting married."

"I understand."

"You don't think there's any possibility she's connected to that photo, do you?" he asked.

"No," Liz said. "That's a crazy thought. Julia is not Russian. She's just... Julia." She frowned, realizing that she didn't know Julia's ethnic background. But what did it matter? Julia had been happy with herself for twenty-eight years. Why did she have to suddenly change now?

"Maybe it's an excuse," Michael said, his lips tightening, a hurt look entering his eyes. "So she doesn't have to think about the wedding or move forward with our plans. She's stalling."

"I'm sure that's not true. It's probably the wedding that has brought it all to her mind. She's thinking about family, about changing her name, about having kids with you, and she wants to know about her past, so that there won't be any surprises later."

"There's nothing she could find out about her past that would change the way I feel about her. I wish she could understand that."

Once again Michael impressed her with his complete and total devotion to her sister. "You're an amazing man," she couldn't help saying. "Julia is lucky."

"You should tell her that."

"Believe me, I have."

Michael glanced back at the house. "Why don't I give you a tour before we start painting? You can tell me what you think of my surprise."

"Damn," Alex muttered, as they neared his apartment building. His mother was getting out of a silver-gray Mercedes parked at the curb. This couldn't possibly be good. He didn't want to talk to her again. And he especially didn't want to talk to her in front of Julia. But his mother had already seen them. She was waiting on the sidewalk for them.

"Who's that?" Julia asked.

"My mother," he said with a sigh.

"You don't sound happy to see her."

"I'm not," he muttered. "She's the devil."

"She can't be that bad."

"You don't know her. Why don't we keep it that way?" He paused in mid-stride. "I'll catch up to you later."

"You want me to leave?" she asked in surprise. "I thought we were going to look for the negative."

"I'll call you when I find it." He cast a quick glance at his mother, who was now frowning and tapping her foot impatiently on the sidewalk.

"Does your mother know something about the picture?" Julia asked, a suspicious note in her voice. "You seem awfully eager to get rid of me."

"Alex," his mother called. "I need to speak to you." She began walking toward them, and Alex had no choice but to meet her halfway.

"What's up?" he asked tersely.

"Aren't you going to introduce me to your friend?"

"Julia, this is my mother, Kate Manning."

"It's nice to meet you," Julia said.

"And lovely to meet you, too," Kate replied. "I rarely get a chance to even say hello to Alex's friends. He keeps them far away from me."

"What are you doing here, Mother?" Alex interrupted.

"I told you. I need to speak to you. Why don't we go upstairs into your apartment? You can offer me a drink while I get better acquainted with your friend."

"She's not my friend," Alex growled.

"Well, thanks a lot," Julia murmured.

"My mother's version of friend is not the same as yours. She thinks I'm dating every woman I'm seen with."

"Well, you must admit you do date a lot of them," Kate interjected.

Since it was quickly becoming apparent that he wouldn't be getting rid of either woman any time soon, Alex opened the door to his building, and the three of them walked up the stairs to his third-story apartment.

"You really should get a bigger place in a nicer building," his mother said, breathing a bit heavily from the climb. "One with an elevator. It's not like you can't afford it. Alex is very successful," she added to Julia. "One of the most sought-after photographers in the world today. Just like his father was."

"That's what I understand," Julia said, sending Alex an amused smile.

"*Celeb Magazine* wants to list him as one of their ten most eligible bachelors," his mother continued.

"Really?" Julia said. "That's very impressive."

"How long have you known each other?" Kate asked.

"About twenty-four hours."

Kate seemed taken aback by Julia's response. "Oh, I thought—"

"You didn't think. That's the problem," Alex interrupted. He opened the door to his apartment and ushered them inside. Tossing his keys down on the table, he put his hands on his hips and said, "Now, what do you want?"

His mother wasn't at all intimidated by his abruptness. She simply squared her shoulders and looked him straight in the eye. "I want your cooperation," she said. "I'm meeting with a reporter at the *Tribune* this afternoon. She does the People Watch section. Her name is Christine Delaney. You've probably heard of her."

"I don't read the gossip column."

"She wants to interview both of us in connection with the exhibit. I'd like you to come with me. It would be great publicity for your father's work and for you."

"I'm busy, and I'm sure you can handle it on your own."

"It's important that she speak to you as well as me," his mother persisted. "In fact, I'm not sure there will be a story if you don't come."

He saw the steel in her smile and heard the determination in her voice, but he did not intend to give in. "Like I said, I have things to do."

"Your father—"

"Don't play that card," he warned her. "You're the one who wants publicity, so go for it. I'm sure you can find some other angle to the story. I'm not interested."

His words created a long, tense silence between them. He could see the anger in his mother's eyes, but she obviously didn't want to create a scene in front of Julia. Maybe it was a good thing she'd stayed.

"Fine," his mother said finally. "If that's the way you want it." She turned to Julia and offered her a gracious smile. "I'm sorry if I interrupted. My apologies."

"It's no problem," Julia said, sending Alex a questioning look.

Julia obviously didn't understand why there was so much tension between him and his mother, but he didn't intend to explain it to her. He was relieved when his mother started to leave without further comment. His relief was short-lived, however, when she paused, then turned, giving Julia a thoughtful look.

"Have we met before?" his mother asked.

"I don't think so," Julia replied.

"You look very familiar. Your eyes... I feel as if I've seen you somewhere. I'm very good with faces, and yours..."

Alex moved quickly across the room, opening the door to his apartment, hoping to get his mother out of the room before she developed the picture in her mind. He was too late.

She snapped her fingers. "The photograph. The orphan girl behind the gates." She looked at Alex, a question in her eyes. "The one you wanted the negative for. Is she the reason you came looking for it?"

"Don't be silly."

"I don't think I'm being silly," his mother said, her sharp mind adding up the facts. She studied Julia for a thoughtful minute, then said, "What are you up to, Alex? Is it possible that Julia is the girl in the photo?"

"Don't you have an interview to get to?" he countered.

She hesitated, glancing down at her watch. "You're right. I have to go. But we definitely need to talk. We'll finish this later."

"There's nothing to finish."

"Oh, I think there is. It was nice to meet you, Julia—whoever you are," she added with a troublemaking smile.

Alex shut the door quickly behind his mother. "Great, just great," he muttered.

"Why didn't you tell your mother you think I'm that girl?" Julia asked.

"I don't want her involved. She's very manipulative, and she always has an agenda. You don't want to become an item on her agenda, trust me."

"You don't make her sound very nice."

Alex knew he was probably painting her more black than he needed to, but his feelings about his mother were complicated and prejudiced by past experience. "She's not important," he said. "Let's look for that negative."

"Of course she's important. She's your mother," Julia said, obviously not willing to drop the subject.

"I'm a little old to need a mother." He saw a shadow pass through her eyes, and he was reminded that she'd recently lost her mother, someone she'd obviously loved very much. "Let's stick to your life and your family."

"She's a beautiful woman," Julia said, ignoring his comment. "Is she married?"

Alex sighed, knowing he could give Julia some information now or spend the next hour dodging her questions. "Okay, I'll give you this much and that's it. My mother uses people to get what she wants, mostly men. She's never worked a day in her life, but she lives well, because she marries well, and she does it over and over again. She married my father because he was an up-and-coming photojournalist. She thought she'd get famous along with him. Unfortunately, he left her behind most of the time and preferred to have his photos printed anonymously. Two years after my father died, she married a doctor— he had money, a big house, and a really nice Porsche. He also liked to gamble. Eight years later, he lost thirty grand in Las Vegas, and she kicked him out. Three years later she married a successful lawyer, a city councilman. He was a great guy, until he had an affair with a high school girl and ruined his life and my mother's life in the process. That was three years ago. I'm not sure when husband number four will make his appearance, but I don't really care. She lives her life. I live mine. End of story. All right?"

"All right," Julia replied, without making further comment.

He was surprised by her restraint. He was also surprised that he'd told her as much as he had. But it was too late to take it back now. "The negatives are in that box," he said abruptly, moving toward the coffee table.

Julia followed him across the room and sat down on the couch. For some reason her silence really annoyed him. He told himself to forget about it, forget about her, and get down to business. Then he made the mistake of looking into her eyes, of seeing warmth, compassion, under-standing, and the ice around his heart cracked just a little. Damn her.

"Just say it," he ordered.

"Say what?"

"Whatever you're thinking, so we can get past it."

"I think we should look for that negative," she said.

"You don't want to talk about my mother or what I just told you?" He still couldn't quite believe it. Most women he knew were insanely curious when it came to his personal life.

"What's important is that you don't want to talk about it," she replied. "I can respect that."

"Good." He sat down on the edge of a chair and pulled the box over to him. His breath caught in his chest as he saw the photo lying on top of a pile of papers. It wasn't one of his father's famous historical pictures. It was a family portrait taken when they were still a family. At six years old he'd sat between his parents with a happy smile, believing that his life would always be wonderful. Why the hell was he doing this? He didn't want to go back into the past. There was nothing there for him. "I don't need this," he muttered, setting the photo on the table.

"What is it?" Julia asked, as she picked up the picture. She paused, then said, "You all look so happy."

"Sometimes pictures do lie, especially when the subjects know they're being photographed. That's why I always try to take candid shots where I can capture the real feelings, the real emotions. None of that phony smile crap."

"Maybe it wasn't phony at the time," she suggested.

"Two years after that photo was taken, my parents separated. They would have officially divorced if my father hadn't died in the meantime."

"I'm sorry, Alex."

"Yeah, well, it's not a big deal," he replied.

"I'm surprised you didn't grow closer to your mother after your father died," Julia said. "It was just the two of you."

"She's the one who split up the family. I was extremely pissed off at her. By the time I wasn't angry anymore, she was dating and planning her second wedding." Alex tossed her a pile of photos and negatives. "Start looking through those."

For the next hour there was nothing but blessed silence as they both went through the photos, prints, press clippings, negatives, and other assorted papers in the box. "It's not here," Alex said with annoyance. He'd been so sure they would find the negative. "I don't understand it. Everything else is here, including the other negatives from that trip."

"I guess it was a long shot. In twenty-five years anything could have happened to it." Julia picked up an envelope and her eyes narrowed. "This is weird. It's addressed to Sarah. That was my mother's name."

A chill ran through him as her gaze met his. Another coincidence? Or a clue?

"There's nothing in it, though. It's empty," Julia said, shaking out the envelope. "It couldn't have been addressed to my mother, could it?"

"Of course not."

"There are probably a million Sarahs in the world. Just like there are millions of matryoshka dolls and swan necklaces." The pitch of Julia's voice grew higher with each word. Finally, she threw the envelope down and stood up. "This is crazy. I have to go," she said shortly.

"Just like that?"

"I have things to do. I have a wedding to plan and a fiancé who needs me. And this is just ridiculous," she added, waving her hand in the air in frustration. "We can't find the negative. We can't find anything. And I know who I am. I don't need to do this."

"I thought you did. I thought you wanted the truth," he reminded her. But he could see the wheels spinning in her head and knew she was talking herself out of the whole idea.

"No, I don't. I'm just going to forget about it. I'm sorry I dragged you back into the past, Alex. Thanks for your help. But I'm done."

She grabbed her purse and was at the door before he could get to his feet. He thought about stopping her, but in the end he let her go, because she was running scared, and he couldn't blame her. Looking down at the envelope, he wondered if there was any possible way that his father and Julia's mother were somehow connected. If they were, it wasn't that far of a stretch to link Julia to the photograph. As he stared at the envelope, memories of a dark-haired woman meeting with his father in the square all those years ago flashed into his mind.

Had that woman been Sarah?

The next day Julia attended Sunday morning Mass surrounded by DeMarcos. They took up almost three rows at St. Mark's Catholic Church. This was her family. This was her place in the world, she thought, as the priest spoke about community. It was almost as if he were speaking directly to her, telling her that the most important thing in the world was to cherish the people around her. The sermon only reinforced her decision to let the matter of the photograph go.

Seeing her mother's name written on that blank envelope in Alex's apartment had terrified her. She didn't even know if it was the same Sarah, but she had suddenly realized exactly what she was about to do—dismantle everything she knew about herself, her mother, and her past. She couldn't do it, so she'd run. Alex must have thought she was completely nuts. She wondered if he'd continue to look into the photo. He seemed to have his own reasons for wanting to know if the girl was her.

Well, it didn't matter. She was done. And that was that.

So why couldn't she stop thinking about it all?

It wasn't just the picture that kept returning to her mind; it was Alex. She was intrigued by him, more than she should be. He'd told her only the beginning of his story, and she wanted to know the rest of it. She wanted to know more about his relationship with his mother and also with his father. She wanted to know what drove him now to roam the world in search of the perfect photograph, sometimes risking his life in the process.

But she wouldn't hear the rest of his story, because they had no reason to speak again.

Maybe it was better this way. She was engaged. Her attention was supposed to be solely on Michael. Even now, he was reaching for her hand, giving it a squeeze, as if he sensed she was drifting away from him and he wanted to pull her back. He was such a good man. She loved him. There was just a tiny, tiny part of her that wasn't sure she was in love with him the way she should be.

She stood up with the rest of the congregation as the Mass ended, waiting for the priest to walk down the aisle so they could file out of their pews. The solemn, reverent atmosphere immediately became more festive when the DeMarcos hit the sidewalk outside the church and began chatting about anything and everything as they walked the few blocks to her aunt Lucia's house, where they would share their traditional Sunday brunch.

Julia was happy not to have time for quiet or personal conversation. She knew she should tell Michael that she was giving up the search, but she wasn't quite ready to bring it all up, not with so many people around.

By the time they entered the house, Lucia's two-story home was already crowded with cousins, aunts, and uncles. A large buffet was set up on the dining room table. The men tended to gather in the living room, usually watching one of the televised football games, while the women put the food out and gossiped about their lives, and the kids played out in the yard or upstairs in the attic, where Lucia's grandchildren had set up a fort.

Liz grabbed her hand as they paused inside the front door. "Come help me in the kitchen," she said.

"I'll be back," Julia told Michael. He nodded, already drifting over to the big-screen television set.

"I haven't had a chance to talk to you since yesterday," Liz said as they walked down the hall to the kitchen. "You were asleep when I got home last night. What have you been doing? Did you find out anything about that doll?"

"Not really," Julia said evasively.

"Did you talk to that man again—the photographer's son? What's his name?"

"Alex Manning. I did speak to him, but—"

"There you are," Gino said, coming through the kitchen door. "My two girls."

Julia received a kiss on both cheeks from her father, watching with a smile as he did the same to Lizzie. Gino DeMarco had always been an affectionate and passionate man with a big personality. When he walked into a room, you knew he was there. Her mother had been much more restrained, quieter, sometimes overshadowed by Gino's light.

"I want to talk to you, Julia, about this wedding of yours," Gino said. "Lucia tells me that I have not been paying enough attention, so now I am paying mention," he declared. "What can I do to help? Besides write a check, which of course I am happy to do."

"Thanks for offering, but at the moment it's all under control."

"Under control?" Liz echoed. "You haven't done anything yet. And didn't you tell Michael you were postponing the wedding?"

Gino looked disturbed by that piece of information. "Is something wrong?"

"No, everything is fine. Can we talk about this later?" Julia asked. She stepped aside as another one of her aunts came out of the kitchen with a large tray of lasagne.

"I just want it to be the happiest day of your life, as my wedding to your mother was for me," Gino said, his eyes watering, his mouth trembling with emotion.

Julia blinked back her own tears. At least she knew one thing for sure. The marriage between her mother and this man had been one of love and passion. Whatever else was up in the air, she could hold on to that certainty. Lizzie was called away by their aunt Lucia to take some appetizers out to the living room, which she did reluctantly. Gino surprised Julia by pulling her into one of the bedrooms off the hall.

"Is something wrong?" she asked him.

"I know you went to the storage locker yesterday," Gino said, concern drawing lines around his eyes and mouth. "I didn't get a chance to ask you why."

Julia didn't want to tell him that he'd had the chance; he'd just been too hung over to take it. But she didn't have the energy to deal with his drinking today. For the moment he was sober, and he was waiting for an answer. She wasn't sure what to say. Her decision to leave the past alone began to waver. Maybe if she asked just one question or two...

"I was hoping to find something in Mom's belongings about the first couple years of my life," she said, not wanting Gino to think she was looking for her real father. That wasn't the case, and she didn't want to hurt him. He'd been the only father she'd ever known, and he'd been a good one. Even without the words, though, she saw shadows fill his eyes.

"Your mother wondered if the day would come when you would ask questions she didn't want to answer."

"You talked about it?" Julia asked in surprise.

"Yes, of course."

"What did she tell you?"

"Very little, I'm afraid. She said it was too painful to discuss."

"That's what she told me, too. But I feel a bit lost without any photos of myself as a baby or knowledge of not only who my biological father was, but who my grandparents were. I don't know where my mother grew up or anything about her life before you and me. I don't know what she looked like when she was a young girl. And I find myself really wanting to know."

"Because she's gone, and it's too late to ask her," Gino said with a touch of insight that she thought he'd lost in the past few months when he'd dulled his brain with alcohol.

"Maybe that's true," she said, deciding not to tell him about the photo for now. "Do you know anything about her life before she met you, or before she had me?"

He thought for a moment. "Let's see. I must know something."

"That's what I thought, too, but then I realized I didn't know much."

Gino frowned, his eyes reflective. "I know Sarah went to college at Northwestern near Chicago. She said she lived over a coffee shop on University Avenue. That's when she picked up her caffeine habit. She mentioned something about a roommate named..." He pursed his lips as he thought. "What was her name? Jackie? Yes, I think it was Jackie."

"I thought she went to college in New York," Julia said in surprise. "The only thing she ever told me about her past was that she was born in Buffalo and lived in upstate New York most of her life. She said she came to California after college to visit a friend and never went home."

"I don't believe it was after college, but much later. Sarah mentioned that she came here for a friend's wedding when you were three years old. She loved it so much she never left. And she said you did much better in the California climate. Something about allergies."

"I don't have allergies."

"I guess they improved when you got here."

"I thought I was born in Berkeley. She said we lived in Berkeley." Julia shook her head in confusion. Why were such simple facts so convoluted?

"You were living in Berkeley when I met you," Gino said. "That's true."

But how long had they been in Berkeley? Her mother had married Gino when Julia was four and a half years old. "Tell me again about your first meeting," she said, knowing the story, but wondering if she'd missed something in the details.

"Sarah brought you into the restaurant. She had met Lucia at a fabric store, in some workshop on draperies or something. They both loved to sew. Lucia told her about the restaurant, so Sarah brought you over one day to see the lobsters. You were a pretty little girl. I think I fell in love with both of you at the same time," he said with a warm, loving smile. "Lucia suggested that I let Sarah make up some new curtains and table-cloths for the cafe. I agreed. Three months later we were married. I thank God Lucia met Sarah and brought her to me. She was my angel." His voice caught, and he wiped his hand across his eyes. "I'd never met a woman who wanted to give up her whole life for me."

"What do you mean?" Julia asked, struck by his words. "What did she give up?"

"Well..." He thought for a moment. "She gave up her friends in Berkeley, and when I told her I wanted to have another child and have her stay home, she readily agreed. I don't know if I can explain it, Julia.

Sarah just became an integral part of my life. And selfishly I never questioned her devotion or her lack of friends and family away from me. I was happy that we never had any conflicts about where to spend the holidays." He paused, letting out a small sigh. "I know you want to ask me about your biological father."

"Not because I don't have a terrific father," she assured him. "And it's really not about him—whoever he is. It's about my mother, and my grandparents. I don't even know their names. I don't know if they're still alive or what they did for a living or if they ever wanted to see me. I feel like I should know that much."

"Henry and Susan Davis," he said abruptly. "Those are your grand-parents' names."

Her heart skipped a beat. "How do you know that?"

"Sarah told me. I don't really remember why or what we were discussing at the time."

"But Mom went by the last name of Gregory before she married you. How did she get from Davis to Gregory?"

Gino stared back at her, puzzlement in his eyes. "I don't know. I suppose I could be wrong. Maybe your grandparents' last name was Gregory and not Davis. I'm not sure, Julia. The important thing is that Sarah's parents disowned her when she got pregnant. That was the end of their relationship, and Sarah was adamant about not having any contact with them. I didn't feel it was my place to press her for more information, and frankly I didn't care who had come before me. As I said, I liked the fact that I had the two of you to myself, that you became DeMarcos in every sense of the word. But I guess that wasn't fair to you."

Julia didn't know what was fair anymore. But she did know that none of her questions had anything to do with Gino. "You don't have to apologize. I've had a great life. No complaints."

"Just questions," he said.

"Yes. Do you remember anything about where Mom and I lived in Berkeley? An address maybe? Or the name of one of her friends?"

"You lived in a little apartment over a garage. Sarah said she'd only lived there for a month or two. I went there once or twice. I think the street was Fremont or Fairmont. Does that help at all?"

"It might. At least I know the names of my grandparents. That's something. One last question: I found a Russian doll in the storage locker among Mom's things. Did she ever tell you if she'd traveled to Russia?"

His eyes widened and he laughed. "Russia? Are you kidding? Your mother hated to travel. I'm sure she never left the country."

"If she had left the country before she met you, she would have had a passport, right? Did you ever see a passport? I didn't find any of Mom's personal papers in the storage locker."

"I haven't gone through the office things, which are in boxes in my apartment. I don't remember seeing a passport. But your mother paid all the bills and kept track of the paperwork. I left all that to her, so I don't have any idea what's there."

"Could I take a look sometime?"

"Sure, whatever you want, Julia. Is that it?"

He hadn't told her much, but the few details he had shared with her teased at her mind, making her reconsider her plan to stop researching her past.

"I think we should have some wine, some food, and some good conversation," Gino said when she didn't reply. "Shall we join the others?"

"Sure."

As they left the bedroom, they went in opposite directions. Her father headed toward the makeshift bar in the kitchen, while Julia joined Michael at the end of the buffet line in the dining room.

"Everything okay?" Michael asked, putting his arm around her shoulders. "You disappeared for a while."

"I was talking to Dad."

"About his drinking?"

Julia felt a spark of guilt at the question. She probably should have been talking to him about his drinking, but she'd been too caught up in her own problems. "We didn't get to that," she muttered.

"He's still grieving over your mother. I'm sure he'll slow down soon."

"I hope so."

"I have an idea. How about a sail this afternoon?" Michael asked, an inviting smile on his face. "It's a beautiful day."

"I have to work. You know that. One to three every Sunday," she reminded him.

Irritation flashed through his eyes. "I wish you'd get rid of that shift. It would be nice to spend more time together on the weekends."

She'd heard him make that comment before. While she appreciated the fact that he wanted to spend time with her, he didn't seem to understand how important her job was to her. "I'm lucky I can host my own show on the weekends, Michael. I get bigger audience numbers than when I host the ten-to-midnight weekday shows. Besides, I thought you were running a charter today."

"Not until sunset. You could join me for that. You'll be done with your show by then."

"It's a possibility," she said tentatively. She didn't mind sailing, but it wasn't her first choice of things to do, especially when Michael was running a charter. She usually felt like the odd man out and spent most of her time wishing she'd stayed home and gotten caught up on her bills, her laundry, and the other details of her life.

"Julia," Liz interrupted, holding out Julia's cell phone. "I heard it ringing in your purse. He said it was important."

Julia took the phone from Liz, noting the frown on her sister's face. "Hello," she said, moving away from Michael as she did so.

"Julia, it's Alex. Something's come up. We need to talk."

"I told you I was done." She walked into the living room, casting a quick look behind her to make sure no one was close enough to overhear. Fortunately, Liz was talking to Michael, diverting his attention from her.

"I just got a call from a newspaper reporter," Alex continued. "Apparently my mother told her that I'd found the world's most famous orphan. And she gave her your name."

"What?" Julia asked in shock. "Are you kidding me? Why would she do that?"

"Obviously to generate publicity for the exhibit. The reporter just called me. I tried to persuade her that my mother was wrong, but this woman is very persistent. I'm sure she's going to track you down. And I wanted you to be ready."

"Great. What am I supposed to tell her?"

"That's up to you."

"Dammit, Alex, how could your mother do this to me?"

"It wasn't about you. It was about what she wanted. It's always about that. I told you she's manipulative."

Julia heard the bitter note in his voice, but at the moment she was too wound up to respond to it, too focused on what this meant for her and her family. "I'm not going to talk to a reporter about that photo."

"You may not have a choice."

Julia saw Michael waving at her from the dining room. "I can't talk right now. I'll call you later." She ended the call, forced a smile on her face and went back to join him.

"Who was that?"

She licked her lips, not wanting to lie to him, but liking the idea of telling him the truth even less. "Just a friend," she said evasively. "It wasn't important."

"Liz seemed to think it was." His eyes narrowed. "Was it the guy you were talking to Friday night outside the restaurant? The photographer?"

"Yes," she said.

A hard glint entered Michael's brown eyes. "He's not a wedding photographer, is he?"

She had no choice but to answer honestly. "No, he's the son of the man who took the photo that I saw at the museum."

"Julia." His voice was filled with disappointment. "I can't believe you're still thinking about that."

"I'm sorry. I was going to stop, Michael. I was planning to tell you that today, but Alex said that a reporter has gotten wind of it and wants to talk to me."

"A reporter? Are you out of your mind?" he asked in amazement. "You're taking this to the press? You're going to kill your sister and the rest of your family. Do you know that?"

"It was never my plan to take it to the press, but I have to figure out what to do now that it's already there. This reporter thinks I'm that girl in the picture."

Michael shook his head, a tense line to his lips. "You tell them you're not that girl and that's the end of the story."

"Do you think they'll believe me?"

"Why wouldn't they? It's as crazy an idea as I've ever heard. Do you honestly think you and your mother were living in Russia when you were a baby? Don't you think she would have told you about that? I know you have a big imagination, but even you must admit that this is absurd. You're grasping at straws, Julia, and I know why."

"Why?" she asked, almost scared to hear his answer.

"You want a reason to postpone the wedding. That's it, isn't it?"

CHAPTER SIX

"WHY DID YOU DO IT?" Alex asked as he faced his mother late Sunday afternoon. Unable to get her on the phone, he'd come to her house. He'd found her sitting calmly in her living room, sipping a glass of red wine and addressing invitations for a party she was hosting in a few weeks. "Why did you tell the reporter that Julia was the girl in the photograph?"

"You told me to find an angle, and I did," she said, no apology in her voice.

"You used an innocent woman to generate publicity for yourself."

"For the exhibit," she corrected. "For your father's work and for yours. If you'd come with me to the interview, I wouldn't have had to bring up Julia's name." She settled back against the white cushions of her couch. "Now, why don't you tell me where Julia DeMarco came from?"

"I'm not going to tell you anything. You obviously can't be trusted."

"Oh, please," she said with a careless wave of her hand. "I didn't do anything wrong. Maybe I jumped the gun a bit, but it's obvious you think Julia is that girl, or you wouldn't have come here looking for the negative to that picture."

Alex stared at his mother, amazed at her brash confidence, her belief that she could do no wrong. She was so focused on her own life, her own goals, that she couldn't see anyone else. Nor apparently could she see the potential consequences of her actions.

"You told me to drop this," he reminded her. "Just yesterday morning we had a discussion about whether or not I should be looking into anything connected with the Moscow trip. You even suggested the possibility that Dad's accident was not an accident." He paused, giving his words a moment to sink in. "So how do you explain why you suddenly decided to publicize a picture taken during that last trip? Did you consider the possibility that Dad's accident and that trip, maybe even that picture, were somehow connected?"

His mother's expression faltered at his question, and her hand was noticeably shaky as she set down her glass of wine on the coffee table. "I—I didn't think about your father's accident being tied to that photo. Why would I?"

"Because you suggested it yesterday," he said in angry frustration. "You're the one who put the idea in my head."

She stared at him for a long moment. "I don't know what I think about your father's accident. And I didn't plan on telling the reporter about Julia. It's just that Christine appeared so bored when you didn't show up. She kept checking her watch and didn't seem to be paying any attention to me. I wasn't sure she'd write even one line about the exhibit. I knew I needed to catch her interest, and Julia's face was fresh in my mind. It just came out."

"That's the problem, Mother. You never think before you speak."

"How would you know, Alex? You barely spend any time with me," she snapped. "And you act like I was trying to hurt you. I just wanted to get the most publicity I could get for the exhibit. It's not only for me, Alex. It's for you, too. Don't you want the world to know about your father's work?"

"You should have gone into politics. You always know how to spin things. But you shouldn't have done this," he said, seeing a flash of guilt in her eyes. "And you know it."

"I'm sorry if I spoke out of turn. But I'm sure you can fix it. Just set up a meeting with Christine Delaney. Convince her I was wrong and give her something else to write about. She was really interested in you, and she's a single, attractive woman. I'm sure you can charm her into another story."

"You don't have any moral boundaries, do you?"

"I didn't say sleep with her; I said charm her. Honestly, Alex, you make such a big deal out of nothing. You're so self-righteous and judgmental, just like your father. The rest of us aren't good enough for you." She picked up her wine and took another sip. "It's not as if you haven't broken the rules before. When it's what you want, like the perfect photograph, it's a different story. Then you'll do whatever it takes. When I ask you to bend a little, you act like I just told you to kill someone."

It bothered him that there was some truth in what she said. It wasn't as if he hadn't played fast and loose with the rules before. But this was different.

"What happened with the negative?" she asked, changing the subject. "Did you find it? Were you able to see the full picture?"

"I didn't find the negative. It must have been destroyed."

"What are you going to do next?"

"I'm going to check with Joe and Stan to see if the negative could still be at the magazine."

She nodded. "If there's anything I can do to make this better, I will. And I promise not to speak out of turn again. If you'd like me to call Christine, I will. I'll tell her I was wrong."

"No, I'll do it," he said. He didn't want his mother to get any more involved in the matter.

"Fine. Whatever you want."

He stood up, then paused, thinking about the envelope with the name Sarah on it. His instincts told him not to share any further information with his mother; then again, who else did he have to ask? "You mentioned something about another woman in Dad's life," he said slowly. "Did you ever have anything more concrete than a suspicion? Like a name?"

"Sarah," she said immediately, her mouth drawing into a tight line. "He used to talk to someone named Sarah on the phone late at night.

Whenever I came into the room, he'd hang up. But sometimes I'd listen outside the door, and I'd hear him laughing or whispering."

A wave of uneasiness swept through him at that piece of information. "Do you know Sarah's last name?"

She gave a quick shake of her head. "I asked Charles, but he never answered me. He said she was an old friend, and I was paranoid. He always said I was paranoid, but I wasn't, Alex. I knew something was off with him before we separated. I knew he was lying to me. He was too evasive, too distracted, too secretive. When I asked him to trust me enough to tell me the truth, he couldn't. That's when I told him I wanted a divorce. It wasn't because I didn't love him. It was because I loved him too much."

Alex didn't want to get into a discussion of his parents' marriage. His own memory was not one of love, but of bitter discord about everything and anything. They'd fought, yelled, screamed at each other. Then his father would slink into the shadows, and his mother would slam her bedroom door. He had often wondered how they'd ever gotten together in the first place. But he had to admit he'd put the blame on his mother more than his father. He'd heard her yelling, but he'd never seen evidence of his father's secrecy.

"There are always two sides, Alex," she said softly now. "To every story."

He looked into her eyes, searching for truth and honesty, but deep down inside he still didn't trust her not to be exaggerating or even lying about the past. "I've got to run," he said. "Just don't talk to anyone else about Julia or that photo, all right?"

"Does this mean you won't be leaving town anytime soon?"

"Not until I get to the bottom of this mystery."

"Are you personally interested in Julia?"

"I barely know her," he prevaricated.

"She's a beautiful woman."

She was beautiful, and he hadn't been able to stop thinking about her since she'd showed up at his door on Friday. But he didn't intend to share that with his mother.

"You always loved that photo," Kate said with a speculative glint in

her eye. "I caught you staring at it more than once after your father
died. That little girl—she called out to you in some way."

"Because I didn't know why she was so important. And I still don't.
But I'm going to find out."

The violin solo playing through her headphones was hauntingly
beautiful, meant to soothe and relax. The tension in Julia's neck and
shoulders had just begun to ease when the phone on her desk rang yet
again. Since she'd returned home from her afternoon radio show, the
phone had been ringing every fifteen minutes. It was always the same
person, Christine Delaney, a reporter with the *Tribune*, who asked her
to call back as soon as possible. She had no intention of calling her
back. What would she say?

Julia slipped off her headphones in time to hear Christine's voice
on the answering machine. She glanced away from the offending
phone to meet Liz's annoyed glare. Her sister, wearing yoga pants and
a sweatshirt, sat with her bare feet propped up on the coffee table, a
bowl of ice cream on her lap, the television blaring reruns of
Seinfeld.

"She's not going to stop calling until you call her back," Liz said, as
she muted the television. "This is really annoying."

"And I should tell her what?"

"That you're not that girl."

"I need proof."

"Is that what you're looking for on the Internet?"

Julia stared at the computer screen in front of her. That's exactly
what she was doing. She'd put in the few small clues her father had
given her, hoping that somewhere there might be some information she
could tie back to her mother.

Liz set her bowl down on the table, got up, and crossed the room to
peer over Julia's shoulder. "You're looking at obituaries?" she asked
with surprise. "Who do you think died?"

"My grandparents, maybe. I know they lived in Buffalo. And their
last name was Davis. Henry and Susan Davis."

"Have you found anything?"

"I think so. Maybe." Julia pointed to the screen, to the name Henry

Davidson. "It's not Davis, but it's close, and the first names are the same."

"Mom's maiden name was Gregory."

"I know that's what she told us, but Dad said he believed her parents' names were Henry and Susan Davis. He never asked why the names were different."

"What does the paper say?"

" 'Henry Davidson, age eighty-one, native of Buffalo, died after a long illness. He is survived by his wife, Susan.' It goes on to talk about his work as an engineer, his marriage of fifty-nine years, and his charity endeavors. There's nothing about a daughter."

"Then it can't be the same family."

Julia looked at Liz and saw nothing but skepticism in her brown eyes. "You think I'm making too big of a leap?"

"Yes. Susan and Henry aren't unusual names. Their last name was Davidson, not Davis, and there's no mention of a daughter named Sarah."

As Julia listened to Liz compute the facts, she was acutely aware of how different they were. Liz saw the negatives. Julia saw the possibilities. Even now, she had butterflies racing through her stomach at the thought of having located her grandparents. Maybe the facts didn't add up exactly right, but her instincts told her she was onto something. "You're overlooking some important points," she argued. "They live in Buffalo, same city, same names. The ages are right. I think it's worth looking into."

"What else did Dad tell you today?" Liz asked. She cleared a corner of the desk and sat down on it.

"He said Mom went to Northwestern University. He mentioned a roommate named Jackie. They lived on University Avenue, over a coffeehouse."

"Mom always did love her coffee," Liz said with a wistful note in her voice. "I never had to set my alarm. I woke up to the sound of the coffeemaker beeping every morning at seven a.m. She said she couldn't talk until she had her morning coffee." She let out a sigh, then said, "But I don't see how any of that information is going to help you."

"At least I know where she went to college. For some reason, I always thought she went to Berkeley—I guess because we were living there when she met Dad. He said he only went to our apartment twice. He couldn't remember the address, just the street name, Fairmont or Fremont. I found both streets in the city, but they're long, seven to ten blocks each. If I went house to house, it could take me months to find anyone who remembers a tenant from twenty-five years ago. I have nothing but crumbs to go on." As she finished speaking, Julia felt depressed. Liz was right. She had no useful information to go on, except maybe the obituary. If she tracked down Susan Davidson, she could at least close that door or find a new way into her mother's past. "I wonder if I could get Susan Davidson's address on the Internet," she muttered, her fingers flying across the keyboard.

"And if you find her, what will you say?" Liz asked.

"I'll deal with that moment when I get to it."

"Look, Julia, what's really going to change if you find your grandmother?" Liz asked. "Nothing, that's what. You'll still be you, and she'll still be the woman who turned her back on our mother. What on earth would you want to say to her?"

Julia stopped typing to look at her sister. "I don't know what I'd say to her. But she's not just my grandmother, Liz. She's yours, too."

Liz appeared taken aback, as if that thought had never occurred to her. "I—I guess you're right," she said slowly. "I think of Nonna as my grandma."

"Well, you may have another grandmother. Aren't you at all curious about Mom's background?"

A moment passed before Liz shook her head. "No, I'm not curious. I don't need another grandmother. We have a huge family, Julia, with more occasions and dinners and lunches than I even want to attend. I don't feel like I'm missing anything, and I don't understand why you do." She put up a hand as Julia started to answer. "I know, I know. You have a bigger hole to fill than I do, because you weren't raised by your biological father. But even if our positions were reversed, I don't think I'd feel the same way. We had a great life. And it seems wrong to do this now that Mom's gone and Dad's upset. It's like a slap in the face to him. Mom dies and you have to find your real father."

But that wasn't what she was doing. She wasn't looking for her father at all. She was looking for her mother, for their past, the one they'd shared in the four years before Sarah had married Gino. She wasn't trying to slap her father in the face or make him feel like he'd done a bad job, but she could certainly understand why Liz or even her father might see things differently.

"I spoke to Michael after you left for work today," Liz said, breaking the lengthening silence between them. "He's trying to be patient, but he waited through Mom's illness, the funeral, giving you time to grieve, and now this. How can you ask him to put your relationship on hold again?"

Julia didn't know how to answer. Everything Liz said was true. Michael had been patient. He had waited for her. But was it so unfair to take a couple of days to look into a picture that was bothering her? "Michael and I have the rest of our lives to be together. I'm only asking for a little time," she said. "I haven't even canceled our wedding date yet. It's been two days since I saw that photograph. Can I just have a few minutes to figure out if it should be important to me?"

Liz frowned. "I suppose that's not completely unreasonable. I just don't want you to lose Michael. And I don't want you to create any more problems for our family."

Before Julia could reassure Liz that that was not her intent, the doorbell rang. She got up to answer it, thinking it was Michael. It wasn't.

The flash went off in her face, the light momentarily blinding her.

"Miss DeMarco? I'm Christine Delaney."

Julia blinked as the tall, brunette woman standing in the hall came into focus.

"I must say, I can see the resemblance," Christine added, lowering the camera in her hand. "I've spent most of the day studying your photograph." She slipped the camera back into her bag and pulled out the catalogue from the photography exhibit. It was opened to the page featuring the orphan girl.

Julia swallowed hard, trying to get her wits about her.

"How did you get to this country?" Christine asked.

"I can't talk to you right now." Julia moved to shut the door, but Christine stuck her foot out.

"Wait, don't go. I promise not to bite. I just want to be the one to share your story with the world."

"There is no story."

"There must be. I did some research and found out there was quite a buzz when that photo was first published. A lot of people wanted to adopt you. I'm sure everyone will be interested in knowing what happened to you." Christine offered a warm, inviting smile that was meant to encourage Julia to confess.

"I'm sorry, I can't," she said abruptly. "Please just go away."

"Is that it?" Liz interrupted, grabbing the catalogue from Christine's hands. "Is this the famous picture?" She paused. "Oh, my God." Liz looked from Julia to the photo and back again. Her face turned white, her eyes wide in disbelief.

Very aware that the reporter was watching them with extreme interest, Julia grabbed Liz's arm and pulled her back into the apartment. She managed to shut the door in Christine's face, throwing the deadbolt into place to make sure she couldn't get back in.

"Call me when you want to talk," the reporter yelled. "I'm slipping my card under the door. I promise to tell your side of the story."

Julia put a hand to her racing heart as quiet returned to the apartment. Christine was gone for the moment, anyway.

"I get it now," Liz said as she met Julia's gaze. "This little girl..." She shook the catalogue in her hand. "She looks just like you when you were a kid."

Julia felt an immense relief that Liz finally understood why she was so unsettled. "Michael didn't see the resemblance."

"Maybe because he didn't know you back then. But I did." She glanced back down at the photograph. "I still don't understand how this child could be you, though. How could you have been in Moscow? And in an orphanage? Unless you're thinking that Mom adopted you?"

"I don't see how she could have," Julia replied. "It was the Cold

War. No one was adopting babies from Russia back then." She took the catalogue out of Liz's hand and looked at the photograph once more. "This girl is at least three years old."

"I agree," Liz said. "It's completely impossible that you're that girl."

"And I can't let myself think even for one second that I wasn't Mom's child," Julia continued. "Mom used to say how we had the same nose and the same long legs. I can't bear to think it's not true." She closed the catalogue, wishing she could put away her doubts just as easily.

"It is true," Liz said forcefully. "You're my sister and our mother's daughter. Maybe this girl is your double. They say everyone has one in the world. This is yours. It's just a coincidence."

"I agree, but I have to know for sure. If I can find something to prove I was here in the United States when this photo was taken and that girl was in Moscow, then I'll be able to let it go. Will you help me, Liz?" She saw the conflict run through her sister's eyes.

"I don't know, Julia. I'm afraid." Liz paused for a long second. "Maybe you want to know the truth, but I'm not sure I do. I don't want to lose you."

"That won't happen. We'll always be sisters, no matter what."

"You say that now, but—"

"But what? You can't think that our relationship would ever change. It won't. You have to believe me," she said, determined to convince Liz of that fact.

"I don't know what to believe. I hate that this is happening. It's too much. Mom died just a few months ago. Why can't things be normal for a while?"

Julia had always tried to give Liz what she needed. That was her job as the big sister. And right now her sister needed her to back off from searching for her past. But she couldn't do it. She'd taken care of Liz all her life, and she'd spent the past two years watching over her mother. This time she needed to put herself first.

Liz picked up her sandals and slipped them on. "I'm going for a walk."

"I'll go with you."

"No, I need to think. I'll take my phone. Don't worry about me. You have enough to worry about."

The apartment was quiet after Liz left, too quiet. Julia paced around the room, too restless to return to the computer. Liz, who certainly hadn't wanted to see any resemblance between the girl in the photo and Julia, hadn't been able to look away from the picture. That simple fact made Julia even more determined to find the truth. But she couldn't do it alone. She needed help. And there was only one person she could ask.

"Thanks for coming by," Alex said as he opened the door to Joe Carmichael. Joe was dressed in faded blue jeans and a bright orange T-shirt. A San Francisco Giants cap covered his balding head.

"Don't thank me yet. I've come empty-handed," Joe replied, holding up his hands in evidence. "I spoke to Ellie, who keeps track of everything at the magazine. She couldn't find any negatives belonging to your father. She said she looked everywhere."

Alex hadn't really expected a different answer, but it was still disappointing. "Thanks for checking."

"Want to tell me what this is about?"

"Not right now."

Joe gave him a speculative look. "Am I going to have to bail you out of jail again?"

"I never say never."

"Does this mean you're temporarily out of commission? Or should I give you your next assignment?"

Alex felt a familiar rush of adrenaline that came with the thought of a new assignment. He loved the anticipation of a new challenge, and he very much wanted to say yes, he was ready for his next job. Why shouldn't he leave? Julia had already bailed on him. Maybe it would be better to turn his back on the past and move on. But he hated leaving loose ends, unanswered questions.

"I think I have my answer," Joe said. "It never takes you this long to say yes."

"I'm in the middle of something," Alex admitted. "I need a few days to clear it up. Then I'll be back in business."

"Just let me know when you're ready or if you need my help."

"I will." Alex opened the door to his apartment, surprised to find Julia in the hall, her hand poised to knock.

"You're home," she said, her hand dropping to her side. "And I'm interrupting."

"No, you're not. I was just leaving," Joe said, giving Alex a grin. "No wonder you're not ready to leave. It's about time you thought of something other than work."

Alex didn't bother to explain Julia's presence. And she didn't seem inclined to explain it, either. He supposed he could have introduced them, but after an awkward minute, Joe cleared his throat and said, "I'll see you around."

"Who was that?" Julia asked, as Alex ushered her into his apartment.

"An editor I work with. What's up? I thought you were done with me, done with the photo, done with everything—despite the fact that we had a deal."

His harsh words brought a flush of red to her cheeks, and he saw guilt in her gaze. "I got scared when I saw my mother's name on the envelope. That's why I ran. I came back because that reporter you told me about has been calling me, and a short while ago, she showed up at my door and took my picture before I could stop her. She wants to tell my story, but I don't know what my story is." She paused. "I know I blew you off yesterday. I was wondering if I could have another chance."

Alex wanted to say no, to send her on her way, because his life would be much easier without her in it. But she was part of his unfinished business, at least until he knew for sure that she wasn't the girl in the photograph. He shut the door to his apartment. "Come in." He walked over to the couch and moved a stack of newspapers so she could sit down.

"You have a lot of papers," she commented.

"I like to keep up with what's going on in the world. And check out my competition."

"You take photos for newspapers, too?"

He nodded, taking a seat on the armchair across from her. He winced a bit as he moved. His rib was almost healed, but now and then he still got a twinge.

"Are you all right?" Julia asked, her sharp eyes not missing a thing.

"Fine."

"I couldn't help noticing the black eye and the bruises the other day. I looked you up on the Internet. I guess you got into some trouble in Colombia."

"The local police didn't care for some of my photographic choices. They threw me in jail for a few hours, and for fun a couple of guys beat the living crap out of me," he replied, leaning back in the chair. He put his feet on the coffee table between them, and added, "It wasn't a day in the park, but I lived."

"It sounds awful." She tilted her head thoughtfully. "Why do you do it? After experiences like that, why do you go back for more?"

"I haven't gone back yet."

"But you will."

It wasn't a question but a statement, and he had no choice but to agree. "I will. I like what I do. It's challenging, and I run my own life. As a freelancer, I go where the stories are and sell my photos to the highest bidder."

"Do you ever get tired of the traveling, the conditions that you have to live in?'

"Sometimes—when I haven't seen a shower in a few days or had a decent meal. But I've always had itchy feet. I can't stay too long in one place. I get restless." He paused, more than a little curious about her, although his instincts told him that getting to know her better wasn't in his best interest. Still, he couldn't stop the questions from coming out. "What about you? Are you a traveler?"

"I'd like to be, but I haven't been anywhere yet." She played with her hands, twisting the diamond engagement ring on her third finger.

He wondered again where her fiancé was and why he wasn't getting involved in her search for the truth. Not that Alex wanted him involved, but it seemed odd.

"I'm an armchair traveler," Julia continued. "I let the music sweep me around the world. But one day I'd like to go in person."

"What's stopping you from going right now?"

She shrugged. "I have responsibilities. Or I did, anyway. Every time I thought about going somewhere, there was always a reason why I couldn't. Especially during the last two years," she added. "My mom was sick for a long time. I didn't want to go far."

"And now?" he pressed her. "Do you have big honeymoon plans?"

"We haven't gotten that far, but Michael doesn't really like to travel. He's a homebody."

"He doesn't know what he's missing. There are places on this earth that you should definitely see."

"Like where?" she asked eagerly, leaning forward, her blue eyes lighting up with interest. "Tell me about some incredible place that you've been."

He thought for a moment. "The Iguazu Falls in South America are spectacular. They border Argentina, Brazil, and Paraguay. The power and the roar of the water thunders through your body. It feels like the earth is opening up." He saw the falls in his mind, but his memory didn't do them justice. His camera hadn't been able to capture their beauty, either. Maybe some things couldn't be frozen in time.

"They sound amazing," Julia said. "Where do you go next, Alex? Do you know?"

"Not yet. I just got back from a six-week trip through South America. It was long and hot, not to mention painfully sickening in..." His voice trailed away as he realized how much he was sharing with her. The more involved they got, the more complicated everything would become. And he preferred to keep his relationships simple.

"What do you mean, painfully sickening?" she asked, obviously not willing to let the conversation go.

"I don't want to talk about it."

"You can't just stop in the middle of a sentence."

"Sure I can. It's not pretty, Julia. It's not something a woman like you needs to hear about."

She stiffened at that. "What do you mean, a woman like me?"

"Beautiful, innocent, untouched by the grim reality of life."

"You're wrong, Alex. I just faced a very grim reality. I watched my mother die. Don't talk to me about being untouched by terrible pain."

"I'm sorry." He paused. "It's just that the poverty and violence some people in the world endure are beyond inhumane. Lately, I've begun to wonder what the hell good I'm doing taking someone's picture right before their head gets blown off."

He saw her shock and was glad. Maybe now she'd let the subject drop.

She didn't. "Did that really happen to you?" she asked quietly.

"Yes."

"When?"

"Last year."

"How did you deal with it?" she asked.

He had a hard time resisting the compassion in her eyes, and for the first time ever he found himself wanting to tell someone about one of the worst hours of his life. "I tell myself that at least I got the picture. At least her story will be told. Her death won't be hidden away like so many others, because I was there. Hell of a rationalization, but it keeps me sane."

She stared at him for a long moment, and he sensed she was reading his mind or maybe his heart. "But it doesn't make the pain go away, does it? Who was she?"

"Just a woman who wanted my help." He drew in a long, shaky breath as memories of that night filled his head. "Her eyes were black as midnight and absolutely terrified. She knew her husband was coming after her. He'd accused her of committing adultery. But she'd been raped by a man in the village." Alex shook his head, wanting to rid himself of the image that was printed indelibly on his brain. "I should have done something. I should have seen him coming, but I was looking at her, aiming my camera, and the next thing I knew, she'd been shot through the head. It was so clean, one small hole in her forehead, almost like a beauty mark. Her eyes were still open when she hit the ground. She was still looking at me, begging for my help, but it was too late." His stomach churned, and he battled back a wave of nausea. "But at least I got the picture, right?"

"That photo was important," Julia said slowly and deliberately. "You made her life and her death matter. Your work throws a spotlight on injustice in the world. That's a noble calling."

"Don't try to make me into some hero," he said harshly. "I was thinking only of myself. I should have helped her, not photographed her. I'll never forgive myself for making that choice. It made me realize how often I don't see the person, only the shot, only the award-winning photographic record."

"So she changed the way you think."

"Yeah, and I wish she hadn't. It was easier the other way." He rose. "I need a beer. Do you want one?"

"Sure," she said.

He used his time in the kitchen to regain his control. He was pissed off at himself for telling Julia so much, but in an odd way, it was a relief to share it with someone. He pulled two beers out of the refrigerator, popped the tops, and took the bottles back to the living room. Julia was on her feet, gazing at some of the framed photographs on his walls.

"This is your work, too?" she asked, taking a beer from his hand.

"Yes. Why do you sound surprised?"

She waved her hand toward the colorful garden landscape. "I didn't take you for a flower guy."

"I have my moments," he said with a smile. "I took those shots when I was in college. I was just figuring out how to use my cameras. When I moved in here, I needed to put something on the walls, and I figured the women I brought home would like 'em."

She smiled back at him, and the somber mood between them lightened. "So you ask women if they want to come home with you and see your pretty pictures?"

"I don't phrase it quite like that."

"I'll bet."

He took a swig of his beer. "Why don't we get back to you, Julia? Tell me again what happened with the reporter who came to your door."

"She wants to interview me. She's very persistent. I told her I have nothing to say, but I think I'm going to have to tell her something. The question is what?"

"What do you want to say?"

"I'm not sure. But I'm even more concerned about what I want to do next. I don't suppose you have any brilliant ideas?"

"Find out who you are. Before someone else does." He looked her straight in the eye. "I told you when we first met that you couldn't back out until this was over, and you can't. Not because I say so, but because when you came to me you set things in motion, and with a little help from my mother they're still in motion."

"You're right. I spoke to my father earlier. He gave me a few tips that I took to the Internet. It's a long shot, but I may have a lead on my grandmother."

"Really?"

She nodded. "The names are slightly different, but she may live in Buffalo, New York, where my mother said she was born. My father also told me my mother went to Northwestern, but I don't know—"

"Your mother went to Northwestern," he cut in. "My dad also went to Northwestern." Alex's nerves began to tingle the way they always did when his instincts told him he was onto something.

Her gaze filled with uncertainty. "It's a big school. Do you think there's a connection between them?"

"We did find that envelope with the name Sarah on it. How old was your mother?"

"She turned fifty-eight right before she died."

"And my father would be fifty-nine if he'd lived, so they would have been in college at the same time. My mother told me that a woman named Sarah used to call my dad late at night. He said she was an old friend." Alex thought for a moment, wondering where they could take this lead. "Old friends," he repeated. "That's it. I need to talk to Stan."

"Who's Stan?"

"He used to work at *World News Magazine*. He was my father's editor, but more importantly, he was one of his best friends. And I know that friendship dated back before my parents got married. Maybe he can tell us more about Sarah."

"Can you call him now?"

"Absolutely." He reached for the phone. A few minutes later he had an invitation from Stan to come by the house. "We can go now."

"We're really going to do this, aren't we?" Julia asked, her expression tense and uncertain.

"Second thoughts again?"

"I'm a little afraid of what we'll find out," she said, her beautiful blue eyes reflecting her every emotion. She would never be difficult to read. Everything she felt could be seen on her face.

"I'm more afraid of living the rest of my life not knowing why that photo was important to my father," he countered. "But I can go on my own."

"No, I said we were in this together, and that's the way it's going to be." She slipped her hand into his, and his entire body stiffened.

He had the irresistible urge to seal her promise with a kiss. How crazy was that?

Julia slipped into the passenger seat of Alex's car, her heart pounding and her stomach doing flip-flops. There had been a moment back there in Alex's apartment when she'd actually thought he was going to kiss her. The look in his eyes... She could see it now, that glitter of desire, want, need. Something inside of her had responded to that look. She'd started to lean forward; then Alex had stepped away, grabbing his keys, calling out orders to go into the hall while he turned out the lights and locked his apartment. He'd obviously thought better of whatever impulse had made him look at her like that. It was just as well. She was engaged. And they were just... She didn't know what their relationship was, but it certainly wasn't close enough to involve kissing.

She cast him a sideways glance. He seemed tense. She didn't know if he was thinking about what had passed between them or worrying about what would come next. And she certainly didn't feel brave enough to ask the question.

A few minutes later Alex drove into Presidio Heights, where stately homes and high-rent apartment buildings lined the ridge above Cow Hollow and bordered the historic Presidio Park. "Your father's friend certainly lives well," Julia commented. "These homes are beautiful."

"Stan moved here a couple of years after my father died. His wife had also passed on. I don't know if he inherited some money or what, but this house is quite a step up from the condo he used to live in. He's the kind of man who enjoys being surrounded by beauty, whether it be art, antique furniture, the perfect gold cuff link, or a woman."

"He didn't remarry?"

Alex shook his head. "He said he never would. I'm sure he has his reasons. Here we are."

Stan's home was located at the top of a very steep hill, a renovated Victorian at least three stories tall. It was impressive and a bit off-putting, Julia thought. She couldn't imagine why a single man, who had to be nearing sixty, would want to live alone in such a large house. Then again, she didn't understand why her own father had sold their spacious, comfortable family home and moved into a small apartment. To each his own, she supposed.

They were halfway down the walk when the front door opened. Stan must have been watching for them. He greeted them with a warm smile. "Hello, Alex."

"Thanks for agreeing to see us," Alex replied.

"No problem. You know you're always welcome."

"This is Julia DeMarco."

"Hello," Julia said, comforted by Stan's friendly handshake. He seemed like a nice man and hopefully was someone who could help them. She paused inside the house, struck by the spotless, sparkling beauty of the hardwood floor in the entry, the ornately carved staircase that led to the second floor, and the tall arched doorways leading into the living room and dining room. "Your home is stunning," she murmured.

"Thank you. Why don't we go into my study? It's more comfortable there. I've got a fire going. It's a bit chilly out tonight, and my old bones get colder these days."

Stan didn't appear old. He was very tall and thin, and dressed in well-tailored slacks and a black cashmere sweater. He was obviously a man who liked to dress well as much as he liked to live well. His study was just as impressive as the rest of the house, with dark red leather couches, a thick throw rug in front of the stone fireplace, and an antique desk and chair by a large bay window. She imagined he had an incredible view in the daytime. She sat down on the couch next to Stan while Alex took a chair across from them.

"Now, what can I do for you?" Stan asked.

Alex leaned forward, resting his arms on his knees. "I need some information about someone my father used to know. Her name was Sarah. I don't know her last name, but I'm hoping you do."

Surprise flashed through Stan's eyes. "I thought you wanted to talk to me about the photo of the Russian girl." As he finished speaking, his gaze moved to Julia's face.

She wondered what he saw when he looked at her, but his expression was difficult to read. "We'll get to that," Alex replied. "Right now, I'm more interested in Sarah. Do you know who I'm talking about?"

Stan sat back against the couch. "Your father had a friend named Sarah. Someone he went to school with at Northwestern. Is that who you mean?"

"What was her last name?" Julia asked sharply.

"It was Davis, I believe," Stan replied. "Sarah Davis. Why do you ask?"

"My mother's name was Sarah," Julia answered, the words spilling out in excitement. "But her maiden name was Gregory, or it might have been Davidson. Are you sure it was Davis, not Davidson?"

"I think so. Why?"

"Julia's mother also went to Northwestern," Alex interrupted. "We wondered if our parents knew each other."

"Why don't you ask your mother?" Stan inquired, directing his gaze toward Julia.

"She passed away six months ago."

Stan swallowed hard and a pulse jumped in his throat. "I'm sorry to hear that."

"Can you tell me about the Sarah you knew? What did she look like? Did she and Alex's father have some sort of romantic relationship? Did you know both of them?" Julia asked.

"Whoa, slow down," he said, putting up a hand in defense. "I'm not sure I have the right to discuss Charles's personal business."

"He's not here to protest," Alex said. "And I can't see why he'd care, unless you know something about him and Sarah that we don't?"

Stan thought for a moment, then said, "I met Sarah twice. She was a brunette, average height, dark brown eyes, very pretty, and quiet. She let Charles do the talking. Their friendship lasted after they graduated from college. He once told me that they had a lot in common."

"Like what?" Julia asked.

"He didn't say."

"Mom thinks he was having an affair with Sarah," Alex interjected. He saw Julia start and knew he'd taken her by surprise as well.

"You never told me that," she said.

"I didn't know the person my mother was referring to was your mother—although we still don't know that for sure since the last names are confusing." A sudden thought occurred to Alex. He was surprised it hadn't occurred to him before. "You don't happen to have a picture of Sarah, do you, Julia?"

"Actually, I think I do." She reached into her purse and pulled out her wallet. She flipped past the pictures of Liz and some other girlfriends. "This was taken at my college graduation." She handed Stan the photo. "Is she the woman you knew?"

"Yes, that's her," Stan said. "That's Sarah Davis."

"Damn," Alex swore.

"What?" Julia asked. She saw a new light in his eyes. "What did you just remember?"

CHAPTER SEVEN

ALEX TOOK the photograph from Stan and gave it a long, careful look. He finally had the proof they were looking for. But Julia wasn't going to like it.

"What is it?" Julia asked again, her eyes worried. "Tell me."

Alex pointed to the woman in the photograph. "I think I saw this woman talking to my father in Red Square that day in Moscow."

Julia started shaking her head even before he finished speaking. "My mother never went to Moscow. She didn't travel. She was afraid to fly. We never went anywhere that we couldn't get to by car. You're wrong. You have to be wrong."

"I don't think I am," he said gently.

She stared at him with pain and confusion. "But you don't know for sure, do you? You were just a little boy."

"That's true. It's possible that I'm mistaken." He didn't think he was wrong, but something inside of him wanted to get that look of betrayal out of her eyes.

Julia turned to Stan. "Do you know if my mother—if Sarah—was in Moscow when that photograph was taken?"

"I don't know," Stan replied. "Alex was there. I wasn't."

"What do you know about that trip?" Alex asked. "Was there some hidden agenda that I was unaware of?"

"You need to let this go, Alex," Stan said abruptly.

"Give me a reason to let it go."

"It could be dangerous to you, to your mother, maybe even to Julia."

"Be more specific."

Stan's gaze darted away in an evasive manner. Alex was surprised and disappointed. He'd always counted on Stan to be up front with him, tell him the truth no matter what it was. Now he had the distinct feeling that Stan was about to lie to him.

"Your father made several trips to Russia in the two years before he died," Stan said finally. "He was fascinated with the country and the people. He took any opportunity he could to get an assignment over there. He even got you into that theater group, so he could take you with him. He wanted you to see that part of the world, and he wanted you with him. I told him it was a mistake. I believed that Charles was sticking his camera into places where it didn't belong. He had a few run-ins with the government, but we were usually able to smooth things over. I wasn't sure that would always be the case. So I told him to be careful, to follow the rules and not take photographs of anything he wasn't cleared to shoot."

"Like the photo of the girl in the orphanage," Alex said. "What was in that picture that no one was supposed to see?"

"I don't know. Charles wouldn't tell me, but he was upset that the photo had been published. He hadn't realized it was on the roll he sent to the magazine."

Alex knew why, because he'd taken the photo. "What else did Dad say?"

"He asked me to look out for you and your mother if anything happened to him."

Alex felt the hairs on the back of his neck stand up at those strangely prophetic words. "My mother doesn't think Dad's death was an accident. Is that what you're saying, too?"

Stan's eyes filled with regret and guilt. "There were a lot of unexplained details. They couldn't find another car or your father's body. And—"

"They didn't find your father's body?" Julia interrupted, her blue eyes wide with shock. "You never told me that, Alex."

He swallowed hard. "I don't like to think about it." He paused, knowing that he had to explain, even though it made him sick to his stomach to go back to those memories. "They found his car, but everything inside of the car was ripped and washed away, the seat cushions, the steering wheel, the spare tire... It was a twisted shell of metal. I saw it when they pulled it up the side of the cliff. They were still trying to find my dad..." He drew in a much-needed breath. "They searched all the next day. Mom and I waited at the edge of the bluff. I thought I'd see him again. I thought they'd find him swimming or floating the way he'd taught me to float on my back when I got tired."

"Oh, Alex, I'm so sorry," she whispered.

Her words brought him back from the past, and he was grateful. Clearing his throat, he said, "Yeah, well, it's over. Or at least I thought it was over." He shot Stan an angry look. "I didn't know at the time there were so many unanswered questions. Why didn't you get those answers, Stan? You were one of my father's best friends. You should have raised hell if you had doubts. You should have made those detectives work overtime to get to the truth."

Stan's mouth drew into a hard line. "I was going to do just that, but I got a call from a man named Daniel Brady. He was a close friend of your father's, too. He worked for some government agency; I was never sure which one. He was very cagey about who he was and what he did. After your father's accident, Brady told me to back off. He said you and your mother would be in danger if there was further investigation."

"That's bullshit," Alex said, jumping to his feet. He couldn't believe what he was hearing. Stan had suspected that his father had been killed and hadn't done anything about it? That was completely out of character.

"Alex, calm down," Stan said, putting out a placating hand.

"The hell I will. You turned a blind eye because someone told you to? I don't buy it. And you shouldn't have bought it, either. What aren't you telling me, Stan? Because there has to be more."

Stan slowly stood up, so they were looking directly into each other's eyes. "I don't know any more. Frankly, I never wanted to know more. I wasn't like your father. I didn't care about people trapped by a government half a world away. He wanted to help them, but he couldn't, because he was only supposed to photograph them. He was frustrated. I think he decided to take some action that he shouldn't have taken. When Brady told me to mind my own business, I didn't see any point in going against him. I couldn't bring your father back, but I could do what he asked—I could look after you and your mother. And that's what I did."

"My father didn't take that picture. It was me. I took it." Alex paused, seeing surprise in Stan's eyes. "He never told you that?"

"No, he didn't."

Alex paced back and forth in front of the fireplace. Stan's comments raised so many questions in his mind. Even if his father had wanted to take action, he wouldn't have gotten involved in another country's politics... Or maybe he would have. Alex had certainly had similar thoughts in the past year—that taking a picture wasn't enough. There were times when he'd been able to get into places and see things he wasn't supposed to see because he had a press pass and a camera. Had the same thing happened to his dad? Had he seen an opportunity to help and taken it? Had he died because of it?

Or had he died because Alex had taken that picture?

God, how could he live with himself if that were the case? Knowing that he might be responsible for his father's death made his chest tighten and his breath come short and quick. He felt dizzy and had to sit down. Julia was suddenly beside him, her hand on his thigh.

"It's not your fault," she said urgently.

He looked into her blue eyes and saw that little girl again. Maybe it wasn't his fault. Maybe it was hers. He'd been drawn to her then, and he was certainly drawn to her now. If he'd walked away before, none of this would have happened.

"She's right," Stan said. "We don't know if your father's death had anything to do with that photograph."

"It's a hell of a coincidence then," Alex replied. "Let's examine the sequence of events. The photograph is published. My dad comes to me in a panic, making me swear not to tell anyone, and the next day he's dead. Some government agent tells you to back off. Even my mother thinks the accident is suspicious. We're developing a pretty clear picture of what went down. Now we need to figure out why. What was in that damn photo that was so disturbing? Do you have the negative? I asked Joe, and he couldn't find it in the magazine files."

"I assume your mother has it."

"She doesn't."

"Then it must have been destroyed." Stan paused. "It's not important, Alex. It all happened a long time ago. There's nothing to be gained by traveling back to the past. You won't be able to change anything that happened. You can't bring your father back. Sometimes you just have to let go."

"Like you did? You let go too damn fast," Alex said, fixing Stan with a hard glare. He saw Stan's face pale and knew he'd struck a nerve, but he didn't care. The man who'd been like a father to him for most of his life now seemed like a stranger. How could he have failed to push for an investigation into his best friend's death? It was unthinkable, inexcusable. "Tell me something, Stan," he continued when the older man remained silent. "Why did you encourage my mother to put my father's photos in the exhibit, especially the picture of the little girl?"

Stan shrugged. "It's been twenty-five years. There was so much publicity at the time of the photo—people searching for the girl, wanting to adopt her—I didn't think there was anything more to come of it now than had come of it before."

"What happened back then?" Julia interrupted. "When people were searching for the girl, what did they find out?"

"There were inquiries to adoption agencies," Stan answered, "about how the child might be adopted. Someone in the government contacted the orphanage and was told it had no record of the girl. We printed that in the magazine a few weeks later. Eventually the interest died down."

"Someone in the government?" Alex echoed. "Let me guess: Daniel Brady?" Stan didn't have to answer. The truth was written across his face. "Where is this Daniel Brady now?"

"I have no idea."

The answer was smooth, but Alex didn't buy it. "That's funny, because I would have thought that you might have called him as soon as I told you that Julia came knocking on my door last Friday."

A nerve twitched in Stan's neck, and his lips tightened. "What will it take to convince you to drop this search, Alex? The last thing your father would want is for you to keep digging into his personal matters. He wanted to protect you."

"I'm not a child. I don't need protection." He looked at Julia. She hadn't said much during their conversation, but he was sure she had taken in every word. "What do you think?"

"I think we should find out what happened," she replied in a firm, determined voice.

"I agree." Alex got to his feet. "I want to talk to Daniel Brady."

"I'll have him get in touch with you," Stan replied.

"Why don't you give me his number?" Alex countered.

"You can trust me, Alex. I'll let him know you want to talk to him." Stan took a breath. "Is there any way I can ask you not to involve your mother?"

Alex uttered a short, harsh laugh. "Believe me, that's not something I'm considering. She already talked to one reporter about Julia being that girl."

"She shouldn't have done that."

"Well, she did. And now this reporter is intent on finding out Julia's story. Why don't you tell Mr. Brady that?"

"I will."

"Good. Ready?" Alex asked Julia.

She nodded, offering Stan a soft good-bye and a thank-you. Alex didn't feel inclined to offer either. He was almost at the door when Stan called him back.

"Alex, don't go there."

"I have to."

Julia waited until they were in the car, seat belts fastened, engine running, before she asked, "So where are we going?"

"You'll see," he said.

Julia should have guessed where they were headed as soon as they left the city, but it wasn't until she saw the Pacific Ocean and Alex pulled off at a vista point on Highway 1 that she realized his full intention. Without a word, he turned off the car and stepped out onto the gravel-filled parking area. She hesitated for a moment, wondering if he'd rather be alone. But as she thought about exactly what had happened here, she knew he shouldn't be on his own. She got out of the car and walked over to the waist-high wood railing at the edge of the cliff. The air was colder here, with the wind blowing spray off the ocean.

Her pulse sped up as she looked over the railing. It was a clear night, and the stars and moonbeams lit up the scene below. It was at least a two-hundred-yard steep drop to a rugged beach filled with sharp rocks, boulders, and crashing waves that thundered in and roared out. The ocean took what it wanted... when it wanted. There was no escape, not if one got too close to those powerful waves.

Here, at night, in the dark, Julia could imagine all sorts of terrifying monsters in that black sea, waiting to claim another victim. Instinctively, she took a step back from the railing. She'd never particularly liked heights. She always felt that odd sensation of knowing how easy it would be to slip over the edge. Shivering now as her vivid imagination made her even colder, she wrapped her arms around her waist. She wanted to go back to the car. In fact, she wanted to go home, but she couldn't leave Alex here alone to picture the most terrifying night of his life.

She thought back to his earlier words, when he'd told her how he'd waited on this bluff for the search-and-rescue team to bring up the mangled car and, he'd hoped, to bring back his father, still alive, still in his life. How scared and lonely Alex must have felt. She wondered why his mother had brought him here. Why hadn't he been kept protected at home, surrounded by other loving relatives?

"This is where it happened," Alex said finally, his voice deep and husky, filled with emotion.

She glanced at his hard profile. His gaze was on the beach below, his thoughts obviously in the past. She remained silent, willing him to share whatever he needed to get out. Alex wasn't a man to confide his personal problems. She sensed that he carried most burdens alone, especially the heavy ones, the ones that touched his heart. The fact that he'd even brought her here told her that his defenses were weakening, that his need to find the truth about his father's death was overshadowing his need to stand solitary and strong.

"This is where my dad's car went over," he continued. "All these years I thought it was an accident. He was driving too fast. He liked speed. He always had. The roads were slick. It was raining, and he couldn't see. There were so many plausible reasons why he went over the side of this cliff."

"Those reasons could be true," she offered tentatively. "We don't know for sure that they're not."

"I know. I can feel the truth in my gut."

She didn't know what to say. No words could take away the pain he was feeling, especially now that he thought he was responsible for what had happened. He'd taken that photograph. With that one reckless, impulsive act, he'd put something in motion, something neither of them understood.

"Why were you so damn important?" he muttered, shooting a frustrated glance in her direction.

"I don't know. I wish I did."

"We have to find out."

"We will," she said with determination. Her doubts about her mother and her own past were bigger now, but her resolve was also stronger. She would know the truth, whatever it took. Which brought her back to her own part of the story. "Do you really believe you saw my mother in that square? And don't answer quickly," she added, putting up her hand. "Think about it. Because it's important that you get it right."

He turned to gaze at her, his face a mix of shadow and light. "I'm good with faces, Julia. I know that's not what you want to hear."

"How could my mother have been in Moscow that day?" The thought was inconceivable.

"It makes some sense—if she was friends with my father."

Julia considered that for a few moments. She didn't want to believe Alex was right. She preferred to think he was mistaken. He'd only glanced at the photograph of her mother and herself. And her mother was so average in looks—brown hair, brown eyes. There was nothing spectacular about her. She could have resembled a thousand women. But Julia was afraid to take the rationalization too far. If she were going to try to deny everything they discovered, she'd never get anywhere. So she forced herself to open her mind.

"Let's say she was there," Julia said aloud. "Maybe I was there, too. Maybe my mother put me in that orphanage while she was meeting with your father. She might have thought of it as a day-care center, a temporary babysitter."

"I suppose," he said slowly, but she could tell he wasn't buying her theory.

"It is possible," she persisted. "At least give me that."

"You couldn't have just been there on vacation, Julia. It wasn't easy to visit Russia at that time. Your mother would have had to have a good reason."

"What about that theater group? My mom and I could have been part of the group, too. We should look into that." The more she thought about it, the more that seemed like a possibility.

"Don't you think you would have remembered a trip like that?" he asked.

"I don't remember anything," she said in frustration. "The years before my mother's wedding to Gino are a complete blank. So why would I remember that?"

"Sorry." He paused. "It does seem odd that your memories don't begin until you're adopted by your stepfather. I wonder why you can't remember at least bits and pieces of your earlier years."

She could see where he was going, and she didn't like it. "You think I'm blocking something out, don't you?"

"It's just a thought."

"Fine. If you don't agree with my theory, what's yours?"

"About my father or your mother?"

"Both."

Alex rested his elbows on the railing. "It probably wouldn't have been unthinkable for my father to get caught up in some Moscow intrigue. I've been tempted a few times to step out from behind the camera. I just never knew he felt that way. He always told me that a good photographer stays detached, remains an observer. But if he saw something that bothered him, maybe that would have changed his mind."

"So you think he could have been spying for the government? Isn't that what Stan implied was going on?"

"I'm not willing to go that far. My dad loved photography. He was never without his camera. I don't believe it was just a front. It was a part of him. When he was shooting, he was in another world. I wanted to be a part of that world. I knew that from the time I was a little kid." Alex looked back down at the water and sighed heavily. "I thought I knew my father. All these years I thought I knew who he was. And now he seems like a stranger. How did that happen?"

She could hear the pain in his voice, and it touched her deeply. Alex had followed in his father's footsteps. Now those footsteps were taking him down a path he didn't want to go. He'd thought of his father in one way for so long, he couldn't think of him differently. Just as she couldn't think of her mother as anyone but the quiet, suburban mom she'd grown up with. Trying to picture her mother meeting a man in a Moscow square was impossible.

"At least I know one thing," Alex continued. "My dad's accident was no accident. I should have realized that years ago. One minute he was terrified. The next minute he was dead. That wasn't a coincidence. And it was all because of that damn picture."

A cold wind blew Julia's hair across her face. As she peeled the wet strands off her cheeks, she realized that the fog was coming in. The stars had disappeared. The moon was going into hiding, too, and they were being covered by an ice-cold blanket of mist. It was as if the universe were taunting them, telling them they would only see the truth when it was time, and not a second before. She moved closer to Alex, wanting his warmth, needing his strength. She felt suddenly afraid of what was coming.

She put a hand on his arm. She could feel the muscles bunched beneath his sleeve. He was as tense as she was, and angry, too, furious with himself. It wasn't a reasonable anger, but how could she convince him of that?

"You're not responsible," she told him again. "You were a little boy when you went to Moscow. You took a picture. That's all you did. You can't take the rest of it on."

"My dad told me not to play with his camera," he said, his voice rough and filled with contempt for his own actions. "I didn't listen. If I had, my father would still be alive."

"I know I can't make you feel better—"

"You can't," he said, cutting her off. "Don't even try, Julia. Just stop talking."

She stared at his hard profile. He looked so alone, so lost in his misery. She wanted to help him, but he wouldn't let her. He was a proud man who had high expectations for himself. He didn't tolerate failure or incompetence, and right now he was blaming himself for something he couldn't have prevented.

"It's a terrible feeling, isn't it? To suddenly realize that everything you thought you knew about yourself and your parent might be false."

"Hell of a feeling," he muttered.

"But you're not alone. I'm here. And I know what it's like to suddenly wonder if my life has been built on a lie."

He turned to look at her. She could barely see his face. The fog was thicker now. It surrounded them, dampening their clothes and their skin. She felt as if they were the only two people in the world, lost on an island of shifting truth.

She shivered. Alex opened his arms.

She didn't know who moved first, but suddenly her breasts were pressed against his chest and his mouth was on hers, and she wasn't cold anymore. She was warm, deliciously warm. She took in his heat like a dry sponge, letting it soak into every corner of her body from the top of her head to the tips of her toes. She didn't want to think anymore. She didn't want to try to remember. She wanted to forget... everything.

His lips were salty from the ocean air, his mouth hot, demanding, reckless. All the emotions they were feeling—the sadness, the anger, the need, the frustration—played into the dance of their tongues. Alex's hands tangled in her hair, trapping her in a kiss that went on and on. Everything else was vague and shadowy, but this moment was real, and Julia didn't want to let it go. Finally, they broke apart, their hot breath steaming up the cold air.

"Oh, my God," she said, putting a hand to her lips. "That wasn't supposed to happen."

Alex's gaze was locked on her face. "I'm not going to apologize."

"We need to go. Right now." She practically ran to the car. Alex moved more slowly. She had her seat belt fastened by the time he slid into the driver's seat. "Don't say anything," she warned. "Just take me back to your apartment, so I can get my car."

"It was just a kiss, Julia."

It was more than a kiss. She knew that deep in her heart, and she suspected he did, too.

CHAPTER EIGHT

AFTER MUTTERING a quick good-bye to Alex at his apartment building, Julia drove home, telling herself that everything was fine. So they'd kissed. It had been a brief, energy-charged moment, a simple release of tension, that hadn't meant a thing to Alex, and nothing really to her. It wasn't a big deal, and she had to stop thinking about it. She had more important matters to worry about: her mother, Alex's father, that damn trip to Russia that seemed to inexplicably connect Sarah to Charles. She still didn't want to believe that Alex had seen her mother in the square that day, but she had to be willing to look at the facts. Sarah and Charles had been friends. She'd start there and move forward. She wondered if Gino had ever heard Sarah mention Charles. It was worth asking.

As Julia paused outside her apartment door to locate her key, she heard laughter coming from inside, male and female laughter. Liz and Michael. She drew in a deep breath, fighting the urge to turn and run. She didn't feel up to dealing with either of them tonight. She felt so conflicted, so mixed up. And she knew they'd only tell her she was crazy and that she should drop the whole thing. But it was late, and they'd worry and probably wait up for her if she didn't show up. She might as well face them now.

Putting what she hoped was a casual smile on her face, she unlocked the door and stepped inside. Liz and Michael were sitting on the couch watching television. A bowl of popcorn was on the coffee table, as well as two glasses and a couple of soda cans.

"It's about time," Michael said, jumping to his feet when he saw her. He ambled over and gave her a kiss. She turned her face just slightly, so his lips caught the corner of her mouth. She moved away quickly, feeling guilty that she didn't want to kiss him, that another man's taste still lingered on her lips.

"What have you two been doing?" she asked him, as she put her handbag down on the small oak dining table by the kitchen.

"Watching Comedy Central. Your sister has a very odd sense of humor."

"It's the same as yours," Liz said from the couch where she stuffed a handful of popcorn into her mouth. "You laughed so hard you were crying."

"No, that was you," he retorted.

Julia smiled at their exchange. "I think I'll make some tea. It's cold outside. Winter is coming."

"The slow season," Michael said, following her into the kitchen; it was barely big enough for one, much less two. "I'll be happy if the rain stays away for another month or two," he added. "I can use the cash. I've been thinking about our honeymoon."

"You're not supposed to tell me," she said quickly, cutting him off. "It's traditionally a secret."

"I want to make sure you like the idea."

"I trust you," she replied. And she did trust Michael. It was herself she wasn't so sure about.

"So, where have you been, Julia?" Michael leaned against the kitchen counter, his arms folded across his chest, a speculative look in his eyes.

She filled the kettle with water and turned on the heat. "I've been trying to figure things out," she said vaguely.

"Liz told me about the reporter who showed up here earlier. Has anything else happened?"

"That's probably the worst of it," she lied. The worst of it was that she'd kissed another man. But she couldn't tell him that. He would only be hurt.

"I took another look at the photograph. Liz showed me the catalogue," he said. "I'll admit there's some resemblance between you and that girl, but there are millions of blue-eyed blondes in the world. And that photo was taken twenty-five years ago. I just don't think it's you, Julia. I think you're reading into it more than you should."

She heard the earnest conviction in his voice and knew he wanted desperately to convince her of that fact. But too much had happened that he didn't know about. "I'm afraid I do think it's me," she said.

"Why?"

"A lot of reasons. The girl's face, the necklace, the fact that my mother very carefully hid the details of my early life." She waved her hand in the air. "My mother was incredibly secretive. I'm only beginning to realize how much care she took to cover up her past. What I don't know yet is why she felt compelled to do that."

Michael let out a sigh that sounded like a mix of disappointment and frustration. She couldn't blame him. How could he understand when she couldn't?

"Are you sure you're not just latching onto some dramatic backstory to replace the emptiness in your own life?" Michael asked.

It was a fairly insightful comment coming from Michael, who was usually more pragmatic and not inclined to analyze anything. Was she doing that? Was she adding drama to a blank space to make it more interesting, more important? It would be better if she were doing that. Then in reality nothing about her life would be a lie, and there would be no mystery to solve.

"Julia, think about it. You got into this the second we set our wedding date. I think you panicked when you realized that we were finally moving ahead with our plans. You jumped onto the first passing ship, and that photograph was it." He moved suddenly, planting himself in front of her, tilting up her face with his finger so that she had to look at him. "It's okay," he said. "It's all right to admit to being nervous. Marriage is a big step. It's forever. You don't have to make up a reason to postpone the wedding. I'll call the Legion of Honor tomorrow and tell them to cancel the December date. We'll find somewhere else after the first of the year, when you're ready. All right?"

"Yes," she agreed, feeling a weight slip off her shoulders. "Because I can't think about getting married until I know who I really am."

His mouth drew into a taut line. "Julia—"

"I'm sorry, Michael, but my mind is made up. You may be right about some of my motivation, but there's something wrong about the background story my mother gave me, and I can't let it go until I know what that something is."

"No matter who you upset in the process?"

She stepped away from him as the kettle began to sing. She turned off the heat and pulled two cups out of the cupboard.

"Liz was upset earlier," Michael continued. "She was almost crying when she came to see me. She said she was afraid of losing you to your past. With your mother gone, it's tough on her to see you being pulled away."

"I understand. I don't want to hurt Liz, but this is something I have to do."

"You're pulling away from me, too," he said, his eyes troubled. "I thought it was because I was pressuring you too much about the wedding, but is there some other reason? Is it that man who's helping you? Were you with him tonight?"

She wished she didn't have to answer that question, but Michael was waiting. "Alex and I went to speak to a friend of his father's."

"Why?"

"Because apparently there's some connection between his father and my mother. They knew each other in college. We're still trying to figure out the rest."

Confusion ran through his eyes. "I don't understand. Now you're tied to this guy, too?"

"I don't know yet. I have only bits and pieces. Nothing makes sense. That's what I'm trying to tell you, Michael. It's not my imagination. There's something wrong with the story my mother told me about our past."

He considered that for a long moment. "Okay, so why don't you let me help you? I can do whatever he's doing. I can look on the Internet. I can go with you to talk to people."

She was surprised by his offer. "You would really help me, feeling as you do about the matter?"

"I want to be the guy you turn to, not this Alex," he said, with irritation.

"He's involved, Michael. He's my key to the past."

"And that's all he is to you?"

She hesitated for a split second too long. "Of course that's all he is," she said, but it was too late. She saw anger flare in his eyes. "Michael—"

He put up his hand, cutting her off. "No. You've said enough for now. It's clear to me we won't have a reasonable discussion about our future until you get the answers you're looking for, which won't be tonight, so I'm going home. I'm running a fishing charter at five o'clock in the morning. We'll talk tomorrow."

She was relieved to postpone the discussion. "All right."

"Come here." He opened his arms, and she moved into his embrace. He held her tight for a long moment, resting his chin on top of her head. "I don't want to lose you, Julia," he murmured. "I wish you could see that the future is more important than the past."

She didn't know what to say to that. Michael knew everything about himself. He could trace his ancestors back to a villa in Tuscany a hundred years ago. He didn't understand that her world kept shifting beneath her feet. That she had to find something solid to stand on.

He leaned in and kissed her long and hard. She kissed him back, because she really wanted to love him. But there must have been something missing, because when he pulled away he looked even more troubled than before. They had to talk. She had to tell him. They had to be honest with each other.

"Michael," she began again.

He shook his head. "No, not now. I don't want you to say anything until you're sure. I'll see you tomorrow."

Julia blew out a breath as he left. She had a feeling she was sure—

sure that she couldn't marry him. But she was so confused. She didn't want to hurt Michael. She didn't want to make a mistake in either direction. She needed time to think. But tonight her mind was too full to concentrate. Maybe tomorrow, in the cold light of day, everything would make more sense.

"I'd like to thank Guillermo Sandoval for being our guest today," Julia said, smiling at the slim, classically trained Brazilian musician whose group would be playing popular Latin American rhythms later that night at a San Francisco nightclub. "There are still tickets available for tonight's performance. Don't miss Guillermo's intriguing blend of samba, choro, and bossa nova, the music of his homeland. We'll be giving away two free tickets after this message from our sponsor." Julia hit the button to go to commercial and took off her headphones. "Thank you so much for coming," she said as Guillermo got to his feet. "I know eight o'clock in the morning is early for a musician."

He smiled. "I didn't mind. It was my pleasure. Your station has wonderful programs, important music that should be shared with the world."

"I completely agree." Julia escorted him out of the control room as the next on-air host arrived to take over at the microphone. In the lobby, the receptionist offered Guillermo coffee and pastries. Julia stopped by her cubicle to check her messages and found Tracy in her chair, reading the newspaper and eating a doughnut. With only four full-time employees at the station, they were very casual about sharing office space. "What's up?" she asked.

"Not much. Good interview." Tracy popped the rest of the doughnut into her mouth.

"Thanks. Anyone call while you were sitting at my desk?"

"Only about half a dozen people. How did you suddenly get so popular?" Tracy tossed a yellow pad in front of Julia, on which she had scribbled several messages. "Your sister called twice. Michael, your father, and some guy named Alex, who I'm betting is the hunk who came by to see you the other day, also called."

Julia stared down at the list of names. It was early in the morning. What on earth could have happened?

"That guy, Alex, said to call him before you call anyone else," Tracy continued.

That definitely didn't sound good.

"Is this all part of the wedding mania? Or is something else happening?" Tracy asked.

"It's a long story."

"If you need to talk, I'm here. Now I'll get out of your way. Let me clean this stuff up."

As Tracy picked up the newspaper, one of the sections slipped to the desk. Julia picked it up, her heart stopping at the headline and the photograph. "Oh, my God," she murmured. "I can't believe they printed this."

"Printed what?" Tracy grabbed the paper from Julia's hand, then whistled under her breath. "You're a celebrity, girl. Not the best picture of you I've ever seen, but... Wow." She looked at Julia with a question in her eyes. "Is this why everyone is calling?"

"I think so." Julia glanced back at the newspaper, reading the headline again: *FOUND! World's Most Famous Orphan.* How could they print such a thing without any proof? She took the paper back from Tracy, flipping to the page with the article, where there was another photo of Julia as well as one of Alex. The story focused on the exhibit and the fact that one of Charles Manning's most famous subjects was now living in San Francisco. They gave her name, spoke of DeMarco's Seafood Cafe, and finally admitted that, while the photographer's widow, Kate Manning, said they were almost convinced that Julia was the orphan girl, proof had not been clearly established.

"Is it true, Julia? Are you her?" Tracy asked.

"I don't know. What I do know that is no one should have printed this article without concrete evidence."

"They always print gossip in this section. It's what sells the newspaper."

"Well, they shouldn't print anything that isn't a fact. This story could hurt a lot of people—my father, my sister, Michael." She shook her head in frustration. She should have realized that once the reporter had a photo of her, she would probably print it. "Dammit, what am I going to do?"

Tracy offered her a compassionate smile. "I have no idea, but I think you're about to be rescued by the cavalry."

Julia looked up to see Alex stride through the front doors of the office, a grim, determined expression on his face.

She ran out to the lobby to meet him, the paper still in her hand. "I just saw this. I had no idea they would run a story based on nothing."

"I know. Are you all right?"

She shook her head, feeling completely overwhelmed. Her head was spinning so fast she was dizzy. She didn't know what to do first, where to turn. When Alex held out his arms, she moved into his embrace without a second thought. He pressed her head to his chest, and she closed her eyes, feeling for the moment that she was in exactly the right place.

Unfortunately, the moment ended far too soon. "I did some research this morning on your grandparents," Alex said, stepping away from her. "I found Susan Davidson, the surviving spouse of Henry Davidson. I called her on the phone and asked her if she had a daughter named Sarah."

Julia's eyes widened. She'd been thinking about contacting Susan Davidson, but hadn't quite found the nerve to take that step. "What did she say?"

"She said Sarah died twenty-five years ago in a fire."

"No!"

"She also said that Sarah attended Northwestern and not a day went by but that she didn't miss her daughter."

Her nerves began to tingle. "Did she know about me?"

He shook his head. "No. She said Sarah died single and alone. Then she started crying and had to hang up."

"That doesn't make sense," Julia murmured. "Twenty-five years ago I was three years old. And my mother said that her parents disowned her when she had me, so why would they have thought she was all alone? Wouldn't they have wondered what happened to the baby? To me? It must be a mistake. This Susan Davidson is not my grandmother."

"I think she is," Alex said, refusing to go along with her.

She met his gaze and saw nothing but confidence. "Why? We don't have any evidence."

"Sure we do. Don't start running scared again, Julia."

She bristled at his brisk tone. "I'm not doing that. I'm examining the facts."

"No, you're trying to twist the facts, undo the connections, but you can't. Your father gave you the names of your grandparents, Henry and Susan. They had a daughter named Sarah, and she went to Northwestern. It all matches."

Maybe it did. Maybe she was just scared to connect the dots. Thinking about vague, nebulous grandparents was different than actually speaking to them.

"But you're right," Alex continued. "We shouldn't jump to conclusions without further investigation. That's why I bought two plane tickets for Buffalo, New York. We're on the ten-forty-five flight, and if we're going to make that flight, we need to leave now."

Her jaw dropped in amazement. "Are you out of your mind? I can't go to Buffalo."

"Of course you can. Even with the time difference and a short layover in Chicago, we can be there by eight o'clock tonight."

"What about my family? I can't leave them to fend for themselves, especially with this article in the newspaper." She dreaded having to return calls to Liz and Michael, who would probably not be happy about this latest development.

"Without you the story will die down faster," Alex argued. "Tell them to say, 'No comment,' until you get back. This is the best lead we have, Julia. We have to take it."

"What about Daniel Brady?"

"Haven't heard from him. I left Stan another message. They both have my cell phone number. We'll be back tomorrow."

Julia hesitated for a long moment. It was one thing to move along in her daily life and do a little research, but flying across the country was a big step. Still, the sooner she got some answers, the better. And she was curious about whether or not this woman was her grandmother. "Did you tell her about me?" she asked. "Did you tell her we were coming?"

"I didn't get a chance. She hung up too fast. I can go on my own if you'd rather stay here. I thought you might—"

"Want to meet her," Julia finished. "I do. If she is my grandmother, she's probably the only person who can tell me about my mother. I need to stop by my apartment and pick up some clothes. And I'll bring the necklace and the matryoshka doll. Maybe she'll know where they came from."

"And some photographs of your mother," Alex said. "I want to make sure we have the right woman."

It was just after eight o'clock in the evening when they landed in Buffalo. Julia was glad she'd grabbed a coat before leaving San Francisco. The northeastern air was much colder, and the clouds were threatening rain, maybe even snow, and it was only September. She couldn't imagine her mother, who had shivered in sixty-degree weather, living on the East Coast with its long and brutal winters. Maybe that was one of the reasons why she'd never gone back. But deep down Julia suspected her mother's reasons had nothing to do with the weather.

Alex rented a car and put Julia in charge of the GPS as they made their way out of the airport. They'd decided against calling Mrs. Davidson in advance. Since Alex had spoken to her that morning, at least they knew she was in town, and hopefully she would be at home. Julia still couldn't quite believe that she'd jumped on a plane and flown across the country with barely an hour's notice. But she was already glad that she'd come. No matter what they learned, at least she could see the city where her mother had spent the early part of her life.

It turned out that her grandmother didn't live in Buffalo proper but in the nearby suburb of Amherst, an upscale neighborhood with gracious old homes set back from the street, lots of trees, and beautiful yards. Alex parked in front of a white two-story house with light blue shutters and colorful floral window boxes. Julia wondered if this idyllic place was where her mother had grown up. It was hard to believe she would have turned her back on such a home, or on her parents, for that matter.

Before they could get out of the car, a woman came through the front door. The light went on as she crossed the porch to pick up the newspaper. She was a small woman, barely five feet, with short, dark brown hair. She wore a burgundy velour warm-up suit, her feet in tennis shoes. Was this her grandmother?

Julia bit down on her bottom lip, feeling suddenly terrified to talk to the woman.

"Showtime," Alex said.

"Don't say it like that," she snapped at him. "This isn't funny. This is my life."

She could tell by his expression that he thought she was overreacting, but he was wise enough not to say so. "Are you ready?' he asked instead.

"No, but I don't think that will change in the next few minutes." Julia glanced out the window and saw the woman giving them a curious look. She probably wondered why they were parked in front of her house. Julia stepped out of the car and moved up the walkway. "Mrs. Davidson?" she said in what she hoped was a friendly voice.

"Yes. Who are you?" the woman asked warily. "I won't be buying anything."

"And we won't be selling anything," Alex said, flashing her a reassuring smile.

Julia saw Mrs. Davidson relax under that smile. The man could certainly put on the charm when he wanted to. "We'd just like to speak to you for a few moments," Julia told her.

"About what?"

Julia hesitated, not sure how to begin. "About your daughter," she said finally. "Sarah."

Mrs. Davidson gasped and put a shaky hand to her heart. "Sarah?" she echoed. "Why would you want to talk about Sarah?" She turned to Alex. "You're the man who called this morning, aren't you? I told you my daughter is dead, and I really don't care to talk about her with strangers. If you'll excuse me—"

"Wait." Julia drew in a deep breath, knowing there was no easy way to deliver the news. "I'm not a stranger. Sarah was my mother."

"No." The woman began to shake her head, her eyes wide in disbelief. "No, that's not possible. Sarah was killed in a fire. She didn't have any children. You're thinking of another Sarah."

"Show her the photo," Alex advised.

Julia reached into her purse and pulled out the photo of her mother and herself taken at her college graduation. She handed it to the older woman. Mrs. Davidson moved so she could look at it under the light. Alex and Julia followed, waiting for her reaction. It wasn't long in coming.

As she studied the photo, her breathing came short and fast. "That's her. That's Sarah, my baby girl." She lifted her head to stare at Julia in bewilderment. "She's older in this picture. I don't understand. She died twenty-five years ago."

Julia swallowed hard. "No, she didn't. That picture was taken seven years ago. I have others, some from last year and the year before."

"She's alive? Where is she? I want to see her."

Damn. She hadn't phrased that right. "I'm sorry, but I should have started by saying that my mother died six months ago."

A flood of emotions ran through the older woman's eyes. She opened her mouth to speak but no words came out. Then she began to sway. "I can't—breathe."

Alex grabbed the elderly woman just before she hit the ground. He swung her up into his arms and carried her into the house.

"Oh, my God!" Julia felt incredibly guilty. Had she caused her grandmother to have a heart attack or a stroke? She wasn't a young woman. She was thin and frail, and she'd lost her husband only a short time ago. Julia immediately regretted blurting out the news about her mother without any warning. "I shouldn't have said it like that," Julia murmured. "I should have softened the blow."

"There was no way to do that." Alex set Mrs. Davidson down on a floral-print sofa in the living room, pulling a pillow under her head. He put his finger against her pulse and bent his head to check her breathing. "I think she just fainted."

"Maybe I should get some water or a cold towel."

"Good idea."

"I hate to walk around her house, though. It's not like she invited us in."

"Well, we're in now," Alex said. "And since she identified Sarah as her daughter and your mother, then you're family."

"I can't believe it." Julia stared down at her grandmother. Her skin was pale, her face lined and wrinkled, especially around her eyes and mouth. Judging by her reaction, she'd obviously loved Sarah very much. But why on earth did she think Sarah had died in a fire? And why had Sarah said her parents disowned her because of her pregnancy? Julia had so many questions. She wanted her grandmother to wake up, to give them some answers. But they would have to go slow. The woman was probably in her early eighties. Who knew how strong she was? "Do you think we should call 911? What if something is really wrong with her?"

"She's coming around," Alex said.

Sure enough, her grandmother was moving her arms and legs. She blinked a few times, then opened her eyes, her expression more dazed than before. "What—what happened?"

"You fainted," Alex said gently, as he knelt beside the couch. "Right after we told you about Sarah."

Susan stared at them both, then struggled to sit up. "I don't understand any of this. Who are you people? Why are you here? Is this some kind of a cruel joke?" Anger entered her voice.

"It's not a joke." Julia sat down on the other end of the couch while Alex stood up and backed away, giving her grandmother some space. "My name is Julia DeMarco. My mother, Sarah, told me years ago that her parents disowned her when she got pregnant with me. I always believed that to be the truth until Alex called you this morning and you said that Sarah died twenty-five years ago."

"She died in a fire," Susan began, then stopped. "But that picture you showed me... Can I see it again?"

Julia handed her the photo and watched the myriad emotions cross Susan's face as she studied the picture. She traced Sarah's figure with a shaky finger.

"This is her, my baby, but she's so much older than when I last saw her."

"She was fifty-one then, fifty-eight when she died this year."

Susan started shaking her head again. "She was thirty-three when she died. I know, because it was right after her birthday. We got a call from Chicago," she said haltingly. "A woman we didn't know. She said she was Sarah's next-door neighbor and that she had horrible news. There had been a fire in their apartment building. Sarah didn't get out. There was nothing but ash when it was over." Her voice caught and she struggled for control. "I couldn't believe Sarah was dead. I thought it was a nightmare, and I would wake up, but I didn't." She turned to Julia, her brown eyes big, pleading, filled with pain. "Why? Why would anyone tell me that she was dead if she wasn't?"

Julia swallowed hard, her heart breaking at the agony on her grandmother's face as she relived the moment when she'd heard her daughter was dead. Only now she had to grapple with the fact that Sarah hadn't died then. She'd lived for another twenty-five years, but she'd never gotten in touch. Why not?

"My mother said that you turned her away when she got pregnant," Julia said again. "Do you know why she would have told me that?"

Susan's face was a portrait of confusion. "I don't know. Sarah was pregnant once, when she was twenty-seven years old. She had an ectopic pregnancy, in the tubes, you know. She had a lot of complications. The doctor said she'd never have children after that. She was devastated by the news. Her boyfriend left her. He couldn't bear the thought of marrying her and not having kids. It was a very sad time."

Julia couldn't believe what she was hearing. "But she had me, and

she had another child, too, my little sister, Elizabeth. She had two preg-
nancies after that one."

"How old are you?" Susan asked.

"I'm twenty-eight. My mother was thirty when she had me. How
could you have not known about me? That would have been three
years before she supposedly died in that fire."

Susan started to speak, then began to cough, choking on the
emotion, Julia thought, as her grandmother's cough turned to sobs.
Susan struggled to get up. "I have to..." She didn't finish her sentence,
but they could hear her crying all the way to the bathroom.

"This is awful. We're killing her," Julia whispered. "I don't know
what to do."

"You can't stop now," Alex said. "You're in the middle of it, and she
deserves to know the truth, too, don't you think?"

"Maybe she would have been happier not knowing. I'm ruining her
life. Her daughter lied to her and never visited her or spoke to her in
twenty-five years." Julia shook her head, not understanding how her
mother could have done such a thing. The woman who had raised her
had been kind, gentle, and compassionate. How could she have turned
her back on her family? Unless there was some misunderstanding...
That had to be the reason. Sarah had obviously believed the Davidsons
didn't want her. Why?

"I wish my grandfather was still alive," she said to Alex. "Maybe
he knew more than he shared with his wife."

"Somebody knew something," Alex said. "If we ask enough questions, maybe we'll get to the truth."

"This is hard."

"Just stay focused on what we're trying to accomplish."

She eyed Alex thoughtfully. "Is that what you do when you're in a
difficult situation—you simply put your heart on hold?"

"It's how I survive."

"I don't know if I'm made that way. I hate hurting people."

"In the long run you might be helping her. She may have lost her
daughter again, but she's gained two granddaughters. That should be
worth something."

She smiled at his attempt to make her feel better.

"That didn't work, but I appreciate the effort." She rose as Susan walked back into the room with a box of Kleenex. Her eyes were red and swollen now, and she appeared to have aged ten years since they'd arrived, but she wasn't crying anymore. That was something. "Are you all right?" Julia asked.

"I don't think so. But I want to hear the rest of your story."

"I'm glad," Julia said, offering her a thankful smile. "It means a lot to me."

"You're really my granddaughter?" There was a note of wonder in her voice, but no sign of anger or disappointment.

"I think so. Why don't we sit down? We can start at the beginning, wherever that is."

"Why don't we start with Sarah and her years at Northwestern," Alex suggested as Susan and Julia took seats on the couch.

Susan twisted a Kleenex between her fingers as she considered Alex's question. "Sarah was in Chicago a long time. After she got her bachelor's degree, she went to graduate school to get a master's degree. She wanted to work at the United Nations, something important like that. She always had big dreams of changing the world. She used to sit with my mother for hours, listening to her stories of life in the old country. I think that's where her passion for the language began. She would often call my mother on the phone just to practice her accent."

Julia's heart skipped a beat. She had the terrible feeling she knew what accent Sarah had been practicing. She looked to Alex and saw the same gleam in his eyes.

"What language did Sarah speak?" Alex asked.

"Didn't I say? I'm sorry. My mother was Russian. Sarah spoke fluent Russian."

CHAPTER NINE

JULIA COULDN'T STOP the gasp that slipped through her lips. "Your mother was Russian?"

"Yes, my mother came over to this country right before the revolution. She never lost her accent or her desire to speak her native language. I'm afraid I didn't share that desire. It embarrassed me that my mother spoke a foreign language, but Sarah was different. My mother came to live with us when Sarah was a teenager. They loved each other very much. They had a special bond." Another tear drifted down her cheek. "My mother died when Sarah was twenty-four. It was a very difficult time for her. They were so close." She wiped her face with her tissue.

It was too much to take in, Julia thought. She had so many questions, she didn't know which one to ask first. She got up and paced around the living room, too restless to sit. She walked over to the mantel and picked up a photograph of Susan and a man who was obviously her husband.

"That's Henry," Susan said. "He died last year."

Julia picked up another photograph, one of Sarah as a little girl, sitting at a piano—the same piano that was in the corner of the living room. "She told me she didn't know how to play the piano," Julia murmured.

"Really? Sarah was very good at it," Susan said.

"It's strange. I've seen the picture, but I don't feel as if we're talking about the same person."

"I don't, either," Julia replied.

"Tell us what happened after Sarah got her master's degree," Alex interrupted. "What kind of work did she get?"

"She got a job teaching Russian at a university," Susan replied. "She fell in love with a professor there. He was the father of the baby she lost. After he broke up with her, she quit her job, and I'm not sure what she did next. She told me she was traveling, taking time for herself. We didn't see her much, a handful of visits in three years. Then she was—gone."

"You never had a fight or disagreement that harmed your relationship?" Julia asked.

Susan shook her head. "Nothing. The last time we spoke she said she loved me very much."

"When was that conversation?" Alex asked.

"About two weeks before they told me she died."

Alex frowned at her answer. "Didn't you ask questions? Didn't you inquire into the circumstances of her death?"

"Alex, give her a chance to explain," Julia said quickly. Alex wasn't nearly as emotionally involved with Susan as Julia was, and she wanted him to take it easy on her grandmother.

"I'm sorry. I don't mean to push you. I just wonder how you came to believe Sarah was dead."

"Henry asked all the questions. He went to Chicago, and spoke to the police. They said the fire was due to a spark near a gas can. There was an explosion. By the time the fire department got there, the town house was engulfed in flames. Sarah was the only one at home. Her roommate was actually out of the country at the time. So she escaped..." Her voice broke, and tears began to stream down her face once again.

"It's okay. You don't have to say any more," Julia told her.

"When Henry asked to see her... they said there was nothing left to see." Susan drew in a deep, painful breath. "We buried her ashes in the cemetery down the road. I've gone there every year on her birthday. I pray for her and I talk to her and tell her about our family, our life." She sniffed as her mouth crumpled once again. "How could she have been alive and not let me know?"

Julia had no idea how Sarah could have let her mother suffer the way she had. For twenty-five years she'd kept her silence, allowing her mother to believe she was dead. Unless... was there another explanation? Had there been a third party involved in the deception? Had Sarah been told her parents didn't want her at the same time her parents were being told she was dead? Was that even remotely possible? There was a time discrepancy. And that time was what bothered her the most. Sarah had supposedly died when Julia was three years old, about the time that photograph was taken. But Sarah had always told Julia that her parents had disowned her when she became pregnant.

"I just can't understand why Sarah would have hurt me that way," Susan added, dabbing at her eyes. "I thought I'd cried out all my tears, but they just keep coming."

"I'm so sorry," Julia said, feeling helpless in the face of such terrible grief. "I shouldn't have come here and dropped these revelations on you."

"You said I have another granddaughter, too?"

Julia nodded. "Elizabeth. I call her Lizzie. She and I have different fathers. I don't actually know who my father is, but my mother married Gino DeMarco when I was four and a half, and nine months later Lizzie came into the world. She's twenty-two now. And she's beautiful. She looks a lot like our mother."

"You don't look anything like Sarah," Susan said.

Julia knew Susan didn't mean anything by her somewhat harsh words, but they still stung. "She used to say I had her nose and her long legs, but you're right. We really didn't look much alike."

"And she told you that we disowned her?"

"That's what she said."

Susan shook her head in disbelief once again. After a moment, she asked, "Where do you all live?"

"San Francisco."

"That's so far. How did Sarah end up in San Francisco?"

Julia could only shrug. "She never spoke of her past. She said it was too painful. And she kept her silence until the day she died."

"How did she pass?"

"She had breast cancer. She fought hard for two years before she lost the battle."

Susan's eyes teared up once again. "My mother had breast cancer. They shared that, too." She paused for a long moment. "I'm glad Sarah got to be a mother, that she found love." Her voice was heavy with sadness. "I'm sorry she didn't want her father and me to be a part of her life. That I'll never understand."

Julia looked to Alex for help. She didn't want to say any more. It seemed as if every word that came out of her mouth only brought her grandmother more pain.

"Maybe we should go," he suggested.

"No, don't go," Susan said suddenly. "Not yet. I have so many questions to ask. Do you have any other photos of your mother?"

Julia nodded. "Yes, I brought several with me. I was wondering if you had any pictures of her when she was a little girl."

"Upstairs." Susan stood up. "I'll show you everything I have, and you'll tell me about your life together. And maybe somewhere we'll find some answers."

It was after midnight by the time they left Susan's house and checked into the hotel near the airport. Julia was exhausted but also wired. She'd seen her mother's bedroom as well as dozens of photographs of Sarah as a little girl. She'd learned about her grandfather, grandmother, and assorted relatives. They'd shared stories and tears. Alex had been as patient as a saint through it all. She glanced at him now as they took the elevator to the third floor and walked down the hall to their adjoining rooms, wondering what he was thinking.

"Are you going to go to sleep right away?" she asked. "I feel like talking."

"That's all you've been doing for the last four hours." He unlocked his door and opened it. "Aren't you talked out yet?"

"Not really. We probably bored you to death, didn't we?"

He shrugged. "It wasn't too bad."

"I guess I'll see you in the morning." She checked her watch. "Which is in about five hours. Good night."

"Good night."

She walked into her room and set her purse and a small overnight bag on the table. Sitting down on the edge of the bed, she flipped on the television, but it was late and there was nothing on but infomercials. She turned off the set, knowing she should just go to bed, but her head was spinning with everything she'd learned. She smiled when she heard a knock on the connecting door. Opening it, she said, "Did you change your mind?"

"I can't sleep, either." Alex walked past her and sat down on her bed. He stretched out his legs, resting his back against the headboard and patted the mattress next to him. "Why don't you sit down?"

She hesitated, her instincts telling her that that could be a dangerous move. They'd been so caught up in the search, she'd been able to ignore her attraction to Alex. But now they were alone in a hotel room, and the kiss they'd shared the night before was back in her mind.

Had that been only last night? So much had happened since then.

"What's the matter, Julia? You look worried."

"I'm engaged."

"Yeah, you've mentioned that a few times."

She sat down on the side of the bed, deliberately putting some space between them. "I should call Michael and Liz, too. They're both probably wondering where I am. And I have so much to tell Liz."

"I thought you left messages for them."

"I didn't say where I was, just that I'd be home tomorrow."

"Sounds like a good message to me. Do you really want to tell them over the phone?"

She thought about her options. With the time difference, it would be only nine o'clock in San Francisco. Still, what would she say? That she was in New York with Alex, that she was at this moment sharing a bed with him? That didn't sound like a good idea. They would be back tomorrow. It would be easier to explain everything then.

"You're right. This information should be delivered in person. I'll talk to them both tomorrow." She didn't like his knowing smile. "What? Why are you grinning at me like that? Did I say something funny?"

"You keep making excuses not to talk to your fiancé. Don't you ever ask yourself why that is?"

"I've been a little busy lately. And what do you know about it anyway? Have you ever been in love? Ever been engaged, married, or shacked up with someone?"

"Do they still call it 'shacked up'?"

"You know what I mean. Don't be evasive."

"Have you heard the phrase 'it's none of your business'?"

"That doesn't apply to us. We're friends, and friends share."

"You don't have many male friends, do you?"

"What? Is your love life a secret?" She pulled her legs up beneath her, sitting cross-legged on the bed, so she could face him. "There must have been a serious girl at some point in your life. You're in your thirties, right?"

"Thirty-four," he said. "There have been a few women, one serious. We lived together for about a year when I was in my twenties. She wanted more than I could give her. End of story."

She eyed him with interest, pleased he was finally telling her something. "She wanted marriage?"

"A house, kids, the whole deal. But I was just starting my career. I knew I wasn't ready for any of that. I thought she might wait, but she didn't." His voice was dispassionate, cool, but there was something in the tightness of his expression that told Julia he wasn't as uncaring about the failed relationship as he pretended to be. "After that, I focused on work and put relationships on the back burner."

"It sounds kind of lonely, Alex."

"Believe me, it's not," he said, the grin back on his face.

"I'm not talking about sex. I'm talking about relationships."

"That's the difference between men and women. We want sex. You want a relationship. I realized a long time ago that I'm not cut out for the married life. I like to be free—just like my father."

"But your father married your mother," she pointed out.

"Yeah, and look how well that turned out," he said in a voice filled with sarcasm.

"You're not your father. Maybe things would be different for you now that you're older. You're established in your career. You're successful. Maybe it's time to try another relationship."

"Are you volunteering?"

"No." She immediately squashed that idea. "I'm—"

"Engaged. Yeah, I got that. You're on your way to a permanent address, what every woman wants."

His arrogance put her back up. "How do you know what every woman wants? That's a very generalized statement."

"That's what you want, isn't it?"

She started to answer yes, then stopped. Is that what she wanted—a permanent address? She'd been raised to want that. But did she? Did she really?

"It's not that difficult a question, Julia," he said dryly.

"I was going to say yes, but the truth is I'm not sure what I want anymore. Every girl grows up thinking about marriage, a home, and babies. I know I want children someday, but not anytime soon. I have things I want to do first."

"Like what?"

"Travel. I want to see some of the world. I'd also like to get my radio show nationally syndicated. And there's this charity that brings music to poor children in other countries. They provide musical instruments to those who can't afford them. I run a concert in San Francisco that helps out the charity, but I'd like to do more. I believe that music brings a peace and a harmony to people, that it inspires and heals and..." She paused at his smile. "Too much information?"

"Not at all. I like it when you get fired up about something. Your eyes sparkle."

"I'll admit I'm a fanatic about music. When I play a piece on the piano or bang out a rhythm on some drums or just listen to a song on the radio, it changes me. It makes me feel better, more powerful and capable, less stressed. It transforms my life for those brief moments. I want everyone to have a chance to feel that way. Is there something wrong with that?"

She didn't know when his opinion had become important to her, but it had, and she seemed to wait forever for him to respond. She licked her lips in nervous impatience and saw his gaze drop from her eyes to her mouth, and just like that the air between them became charged with electricity.

"Alex?" she prodded. "You were going to say?"

"I have no idea. You distracted me."

She swallowed hard at the desire flaring in his eyes. "Maybe you should go back to your room."

"Just when things are getting interesting? Weren't you the one complaining that I always stop in the middle of a conversation?"

"Which you just did. I was telling you about my passion, and you didn't even respond."

"Oh, I responded all right," he said. "Believe me."

She felt a warm flush wash over her cheeks. "That's not what I meant."

"You want to know what I think, Julia?"

She slowly nodded. "Yes."

"I think you're the most fascinating, beautiful woman I've run across in a long time. I like your passion for music. I like that your dreams are big and bold. And I like the way you lick your bottom lip when you feel things you shouldn't feel—the way you're doing now." He held out his hand to her. "Come here."

Her breath caught in her chest. She couldn't. It was tempting, but it was wrong. "I can't."

He swung his legs to the floor and moved so quickly she didn't realize his intention until his arms came around her shoulders and his face moved within inches of her own. "You know what an engagement period is for? To figure out if the person you're going to marry is the one you really want."

"I think it's just supposed to give you time to plan the wedding," she said somewhat desperately.

"I want you, Julia. I think you feel the same way, even though you're fighting it as hard as you can."

"Even if I did want you," she said breathlessly, as his mouth moved closer to hers, "it would be a fling for you, a one-night stand. You said yourself that's not what I'm about." But wasn't that exactly what she wanted right now? His hands were stroking her back, his breath hot on her face, his mouth so temptingly within reach. Every instinct she had was telling her to go for it.

Her cell phone rang, the sound hitting her like a splash of cold water in the face. She jumped back. Alex's hands fell to his sides.

"Saved by the bell," he mocked. "Are you going to answer it?"

She grabbed the phone out of her purse and saw it was Liz. "There's no way I can tell her where I am right now. She wouldn't understand. I don't understand." She stared at him, feeling as angry with him as she was with herself, because he was confusing her even more. "I'm supposed to be in love with Michael. I don't know why I want you so much," she said honestly, "but I think you need to go back to your room."

"What I need is you. One kiss."

"It won't stop there."

"It will—unless you don't want it to."

"You're the devil, you know that?"

"I've been called worse. Don't you want to be sure, Julia? If you're really supposed to marry your Michael, then this won't bother you at all."

Before she could answer, his mouth covered hers with a purpose and determination that cut through her defenses. She might have been able to fight him, but she couldn't fight herself, too. She wasn't that strong. One kiss, she thought. Then she could get him out of her system.

———

"Julia still isn't picking up her phone," Liz complained. Michael didn't answer. He was busy scraping wallpaper off what would be the master bedroom in his new house. His shirt was unbuttoned, and there was a fine layer of perspiration across his chest. She drew in a deep breath and forced herself to look away and focus on the matter at hand. She'd been calling Julia off and on all day, but aside from one brief message from her sister stating that she was onto a new lead, there had been nothing but silence. "I need to talk to her about the newspaper article. And a man called our apartment earlier. He had a heavy accent, and he asked for Julia. His voice made my skin crawl." Which is why she'd come running to Michael's house.

Michael paused, wiping the sweat off his forehead with the back of his hand. "What kind of an accent?"

"He sounded Russian. Just when I start believing that Julia is completely crazy to think she's that girl in the photograph, something happens to change my mind."

"I need a beer," Michael said. "You want one?"

"Absolutely." She followed Michael down the hall, into the family room/kitchen. "Hey, what's with the sleeping bag and pillows?" she asked, pointing to the pile in the corner.

"I've been sleeping here. That way I can work late and start early."

"On the floor?"

"It's not that bad," he said with a laugh. "Did anyone ever tell you you're a spoiled brat?"

"I think Julia has mentioned it a few times."

He opened a beer and handed it to her. "I don't have any glasses."

"This is fine."

Michael leaned against the counter as he sipped his beer. "Tell me more about the phone call. What did the guy say?"

"He asked for Julia. No, wait. He twisted her name. It sounded like

Yulia. I said she wasn't home. He asked me where she was, when she would come back, if she had a cell phone number he could contact her on. He said he had to speak to her immediately. I tried to put him off. He got agitated, started saying something in Russian, I guess. Then the line went dead." She shook her head, feeling edgy and restless. Too much was happening too fast, and she was in the dark about most of it. "I really need to talk to Julia."

Michael nodded. "I'm sure she'll call you back."

"She hasn't so far. This isn't fair, Michael. She stirs up a hornet's nest, then leaves me to fight off the stinging bees."

He smiled at that. "You do love to be dramatic."

"I'm not being dramatic. My life is spinning out of control. So is yours, in case you hadn't noticed."

"I've noticed," he said heavily. "But Julia is worth waiting for."

Liz wasn't so certain of that. The last few days seemed to be pulling Michael and Julia further and further apart. Michael was renovating a house and planning for the future. Julia was digging up skeletons and searching for her past with a man who wasn't her fiancé. She wondered why Michael wasn't more bothered by that fact.

"Why don't you help me scrape some wallpaper," Michael suggested. "It will take your mind off your problems, and I could use the help."

The last thing she wanted to do was scrape wallpaper. Then again, she didn't particularly want to go home, where the doorbell and the phone would keep ringing with mysterious strangers laying claim to her sister. "Fine," she said. "On one condition: We work for an hour, then play some cards."

Michael loved blackjack. In fact, he'd been the one to take her on her first casino trip to Lake Tahoe after her twenty-first birthday. Julia had stayed on the beach while Michael had shown Liz how to play craps, blackjack, and poker. She'd been hooked ever since. "I have cards in my purse," she said.

"You carry cards with you?"

"I have to admit I was hoping to talk you into a game. On your break, of course. I know you're obsessed with this house."

"I am obsessed with it," he admitted. "It's the first place that's mine. I've been living with my family my whole life. I've never had a place of my own. This is what I've always wanted."

"It's a great house."

"Julia will like it, don't you think?"

For the first time she heard some doubt in his voice. "Sure, she'll love it."

"You're just saying that, aren't you?"

"I don't think it's the house you have to worry about," she told him.

He frowned. "I know, but the house is the only thing I can control at the moment. Julia is the wild card."

CHAPTER TEN

"ENOUGH," Alex said, breaking off the kiss. He jumped off the bed, running a hand through his wavy brown hair.

Julia blinked, dazed by the last few minutes of passion and desire. "What?"

"This is..." He waved his hand in the air as if he couldn't come up with the word. "A mistake," he said finally. "I don't poach on another man's turf. What the hell am I doing? And what the hell were you doing—kissing me like that? How can you say you're going to marry a man, then kiss someone else like your heart is up for grabs—or at least your body."

She bristled at his accusatory tone. "You're the one who pushed me into a kiss. This wasn't my idea. You started it."

"You weren't fighting it. You were kissing me back."

"You took me by surprise."

"Yeah, well, the surprise ended more than a few minutes ago."

She stared at him, and then sighed. "You're right. I kissed you back. I couldn't stop myself. I'm a terrible person."

"Why don't you break up with this guy, Julia?"

"Because it's complicated. Michael stood by me through the worst months of my life. He held my hand while I watched my mother die. He comforted me. He did whatever I asked. He was a rock."

"So you say, 'Thank you.' You don't say, 'I do.' "

"My mother loved him. She was so happy the day we got engaged. She told me Michael was everything she'd always wanted for me. It was the first time she seemed proud of me. She didn't encourage my love of music. In fact, she discouraged it. She thought the radio station job was silly. She wanted me to get married, have kids, build a family of my own."

"So you said yes because of your mother?" he asked in amazement. "I still haven't heard a good reason. Do you love the guy at all?"

"Of course I love him. I just said that, didn't I?"

"Actually, you didn't. You said you owed him and it made your mother happy."

"I do love him. Michael is wonderful. He's probably too good for me."

He stared at her for a long minute. "So what's this about? You have a fling with the bad guy, then you marry the good guy, and everything works out great for you? What happens when you get tired of the good guy—are you going to have an affair?"

"I would never do that," she said, jumping to her feet in anger. "What kind of woman do you think I am?"

"I don't know. More importantly, I don't think you know. You are probably the most confused person I have ever met."

"You're the one who confused me because you took my damn picture twenty-five years ago." It felt good to yell at him, to let off some steam.

"And I am sorrier than I can ever say."

She sighed as he began to pace around the room. "What are we doing, Alex? We're both exhausted. We're not thinking rationally. We should call it a night and get some sleep."

"I'm not going to sleep. I'm too wired, even more now than I was before," he said. "You have a way of doing that to me, Julia."

She knew the feeling. She felt edgy and her stomach was churning. "Let's turn on the radio."

"Why?"

"Because there's probably some good music on. It always helps me relax." She knew she was probably about to make another mistake, but it seemed to be a night for mistakes. "I don't really want to be alone. Would you stay? Just hang out with me, no touching, no kissing."

His hesitation was obvious.

"It's a big bed." She sat down on one side of the bed and placed two pillows in the middle, building a little barrier. "I'll stay on my side. You stay on yours."

"You trust me to do that?"

She didn't even hesitate. "Yes."

He debated for another second. "Fine. I'll stay."

"Good." She turned on the radio, running through the stations until she heard a violin and viola playing Mozart's Duo in B-flat Major. "Isn't this beautiful?" she asked, leaning back against the bed. Already she was feeling better.

Alex stretched out on his side, resting his head on his elbow. He listened for a moment, then said, "It's nice."

"Nice? That's a lukewarm word. There's a perfect harmony between the two instruments, a pure, splendid tone. It's so powerful I can feel the music within me."

"It's nice," he said again with a small smile. "I prefer a saxophone or a trumpet, something announcing its entrance into the piece."

"I could find something else."

"No, this is fine. You like it. That's good enough for me."

She stared up at the ceiling, letting the music take the tension out of her shoulders, her neck, her entire body. She tried not to think about everything that had happened that day. There was too much to absorb, too many revelations to analyze.

"Julia?"

She turned her head to look at Alex. "Yes?"

"Beautiful."

"That's a better adjective for the music than nice."

"I wasn't talking about the music," he said, with a dangerous look in his eyes. "I was talking about you."

Oh, God. She had a feeling those pillows between them weren't going to be enough to keep them apart. She drew in a deep breath, then closed her eyes, conflicted over whether she wanted Alex to make a move or not. She heard him shift on the bed. Her body tensed, and then she realized he'd turned away from her. Was he angry? Should she say something?

"Relax, Julia," he said a moment later. "We don't have to figure out everything tonight. There's always tomorrow."

After an almost six-hour flight, they landed in San Francisco just after eleven o'clock Tuesday morning. Alex was used to traveling and sleeping very little, but he had to admit he was tired. They'd only had a few hours of sleep the night before. And that sleep had been more than a little restless. Lying next to Julia with just a few pillows between them had been quite a test of his self-control. It wasn't the right time— for either of them. He should never have kissed her, never given in to that impulse. But the more he got to know her, the more he liked her, and the more he found her irresistible.

At least their trip had been a success. Julia had found her grand-mother. They'd learned quite a bit about Sarah's past. Now they had to concentrate on unraveling the rest of the secrets.

His cell phone rang as they were walking out to the parking lot, and he didn't recognize the number. "Hello?" he asked warily, not sure whom to expect.

"Alex Manning?" a man asked.

"Yes."

"This is Daniel Brady, Alex. I saw the photo in the newspaper, and I spoke to Stan Harding. I think we need to talk."

"We certainly do."

"Can you meet me at the Cliff House in a half hour? I'll buy you a drink."

"All right. I'll be bringing Julia with me."

"I wouldn't have it any other way. See you then."

"Who was that?" Julia asked as he ended the call.

"Daniel Brady. He wants to meet us in thirty minutes."

Her eyes lit up. "That's great news. Finally, everything is clicking into place."

"Let's hope so."

A layer of fog hung over Ocean Beach, painting the sky a dull gray. Alex parked in the lot next to the Cliff House, a historic three-story restaurant overlooking the Pacific Ocean and Seal Rocks, where the sea lions came to play. Set at the most western edge of San Francisco, the Cliff House also offered a view of the large ships about to sail under the Golden Gate Bridge, into the harbor of San Francisco. Alex had visited the restaurant once before when he was a child. His father had told him stories about the restaurant and its once-famous neighbor, the Sutro Baths, an extravagant public bathhouse built in the 1800s that was later turned into a seaside amusement park. The baths and the amusement park were long gone, but the restaurant remained.

As soon as they got out of the car, an older man stepped from a charcoal gray sedan parked across from them. Dressed in casual tan slacks and a long-sleeved brown shirt, he appeared to be in his sixties. His light brown hair was thin on the top and cut short. His stomach had a bit of a paunch to it. He had a cigarette in his mouth, which he quickly stubbed out as he approached them.

"Alex, you look well."

He didn't know why he was surprised or unsettled by the fact that the other man had recognized him. "Daniel Brady?" he asked.

"That's me." Brady offered Alex a smile and removed the dark glasses that covered his brown eyes. "And you must be Julia. I saw your picture in the paper. It didn't do you justice." He paused. "I know I offered to buy you a drink, but something has come up, and I won't be able to stay. Why don't we take a walk and talk for a few minutes?"

Alex fell into step alongside Brady, with Julia following a step behind. "Why have I never heard of you?" he asked. "Stan said you were a good friend of my father's, but I don't recall your name ever being mentioned. And I know we've never met before."

"Your father and I saw each other when we were both on assignment, usually in another country."

"So you do work for the government?" Alex asked. "Do you happen to have any identification?"

Brady chuckled at that question. "I've got a driver's license. Will that do?" He paused and pulled his wallet out of his back pocket. "You're not as trusting as your father."

"Since he's dead now, I'll take that as a compliment," Alex said sharply. There was something about Brady—maybe his smug smile, or his knowing manner, that irritated him. He took the license from Brady's hand and gave it a quick glance. The face was the same. The address was in Maryland. "You're a long way from home."

"I always am."

"What about a government ID?"

"What I do doesn't require ID. I've been on the job for thirty-seven years now. I can get you a character reference if you feel you need one."

"What exactly do you do for the government?" Julia asked.

Alex watched Daniel closely, wondering how he'd react to such a pointed question.

Daniel simply smiled and said, "That's classified, I'm afraid." He slipped his license back into his wallet, then into his pocket.

"If you can't answer that question, maybe you can answer this one," Julia continued. "Am I that girl in the photograph?"

"I can see why you might think so," Daniel replied. "But even if you believe you're that girl, you must say you're not. You must call the newspaper and tell them they're mistaken. Any other reporters you speak to must get the same comment."

"Why?" Alex asked sharply. "Why should she lie?"

"For her own safety." Daniel's expression turned somber. "The photograph revealed something that was supposed to be hidden, but your father didn't know that. He made a mistake. He paid for it."

Alex felt his heart stop. Stan had implied that his father's accident had been a result of the photograph, but he wanted to hear Daniel Brady say it. "Are you telling me my father was killed because of that picture?"

Daniel hesitated for a long moment, then said, "His accident was highly suspicious. The only reason I'm telling you that is because Charles was my friend, and you're his son, and he wouldn't want the same thing to happen to you."

"That's not good enough. Who killed my father? Who ran him off the road? Tell me, dammit." Alex took a step closer to Daniel. He wanted to grab Brady by the collar and shake him until the truth came out. "I'm tired of vague innuendos. I want the facts. And I want them now."

"I've told you all I can tell you, Alex, without putting you in danger."

"To hell with that. I can take care of myself."

"And Miss DeMarco? Do you want to risk her life as well as your own?"

"I can take care of myself, too," Julia replied. She shot Alex a look that told him to keep going and not back down. He intended to do just that.

"If you won't tell me about my father's death, then tell me about the picture," Alex demanded. "What do you know about it that I don't?"

Daniel glanced around, as if he was worried about being overheard, but they'd moved a hundred yards away from the restaurant, and there was no one in this part of the parking lot. "I want to help you, Alex, but I'm caught between a rock and a hard place. I don't know if you know this, but your father saved my life once. I was a young agent. I got into some trouble in Germany. Your father came to my rescue. I owed him. And the day after that photograph was published in the magazine, he contacted me. He said he was calling in my debt. He wanted me to protect you. I promised him I would."

"In case you haven't noticed, I'm a grown man. Whatever promise you made ended a long time ago."

"I don't think so."

"Look, Julia's picture has been printed in the newspaper. This story is coming out whether any of us want it to. If you know something, you need to tell us, so that we're not stumbling around in the dark. I think my father would appreciate the need for you to be honest with me."

Daniel thought for a moment. He looked away from them, gazing out at the ocean. Alex wondered if he was thinking about Charles having met his end in that same ocean, just a few miles away. The sea was waiting for an answer, and so were they.

Finally Daniel looked back at them, his jaw tense, his eyes wary. "All right. I'll tell you this much. I believe Julia is the girl in the photograph."

Alex's heart fell to his stomach. He'd suspected that was the case ever since Julia had knocked on his door, but now someone was actually saying it out loud. He glanced at Julia and saw shock and fear on her face.

"Are you saying my mother was there?" Julia demanded. "Did you know her, Mr. Brady? Did you know my mother?"

"Yes, I knew her a long time ago," he admitted. "Sarah was in Russia with the theater group. She worked behind the scenes as a costumer."

"Oh, my God. She was there." Julia turned to Alex. "My mother was there. You did see her. I didn't want to believe you, but you were right."

Alex was surprised that Brady had told them about Sarah. "So Sarah's identity and the reason why she was in Russia aren't classified?" he challenged.

Brady shrugged. "I barely knew the woman. She was friends with Charles and Stan. Stan helped her get into the theater group."

"She must have taken me with her," Julia said. "I must have gotten a Russian visa or whatever as part of the tour, just like you did, Alex. And she must have put me in the orphanage so someone would watch me while she was meeting with your dad."

Alex still wasn't sure he bought Julia's scenario, but he looked to Brady for the answer. "Is that true? Did Sarah leave Julia at the orphanage for some reason?"

Brady hesitated. "That sounds right."

He was lying. Alex's gut instinct told him the man was lying. "Then why would anyone care that Julia's picture was taken? She was an American girl."

"She wasn't supposed to be there. Certain places were off-limits to foreigners. No one wanted to acknowledge that there were orphans in the Soviet Union, and they certainly didn't want photographs taken of such venues. That's why the government denied all knowledge of the girl." He paused. "Now, will you let this go? There's nothing more to know."

"Of course there is," Alex said harshly. "No one killed my father because there weren't supposed to be orphans in Moscow. What was the real reason? And who did it?"

"I don't know who did it. Whoever took him out was a pro."

"I don't understand," Julia said, interrupting them. "Why would anyone kill Alex's father after the picture was printed? What could they possibly gain from that? The deed was already done. What was revealed was revealed."

"That's an excellent point," Alex said slowly. "Why would anyone have gone after him then?"

"It was punishment. Payback. They'd given him access to their country. He'd abused their trust."

"Who the hell is *they*?"

"I've told you everything I can. Drop this line of inquiry, Alex, before someone else gets hurt."

"What about my mother?" Julia asked. "She was in Moscow, too, and if I was the girl in that photo, and she was connected to me, then she should have been in danger, too. But no one came after her. Did they?"

A pulse jumped in Brady's throat. "I don't know. She was lucky, I guess."

"Lucky?" Alex echoed. "That's your answer?"

"Sarah went into hiding after that picture was published. Her cover was good."

"Her cover was good?" Julia repeated, as if she couldn't believe what she was hearing. "You're talking about my life, my stepfather, my little sister, the past twenty-five years we lived with my mother, with Sarah. It was a cover?"

"It sounds like you had a good life, Miss DeMarco. Maybe you should leave it at that."

"I can't. Not until I know who my mother really was."

Brady glanced down at his watch. "I'm sorry, but I have to go."

"You can't leave yet," Julia protested. "I have more questions."

"They'll have to wait," he replied.

"What if we need to talk to you again? How do we get ahold of you?" Alex asked.

"Call Stan. He knows where to find me."

"How does he know?" Alex asked suspiciously. "How are you and Stan friends? Was Stan involved in whatever went on in Moscow, too? You said that he got Sarah into the theater group. What exactly was his role?"

"Stan was your father's editor."

"I know that, but what did he have to do with setting up cultural exchanges in Moscow?"

"Stan is a patron of the arts," Brady said with a secretive smile. "He worked behind the scenes of many cultural exchanges in Russia and other countries. Why don't you ask him about it?"

"I think I will," Alex said slowly. He thought back to his conversation with Stan and knew that the other man had definitely not shared any of his own involvement in that Russia trip. Why? Was he hiding something else?

"I do need to go," Brady said. "If you want to reach me, call Stan. I'll get back to you as soon as I can. I want to be of help to you and Julia—whatever you need. The most important thing is that you both back out of this, get rid of the press, and go on with your lives." That said, he turned and walked to the car.

"What do you think?" Julia asked when they were alone.

"He was lying at least some of the time."

"I agree, but which part of the time? The time when he was talking about my mother or your father... or about Stan?"

"Hell if I know." Alex dug his hands into his pockets and stared out at the ocean. "My father was murdered. That's what I know for sure."

"I'm sorry, Alex," she said quietly. "But it still wasn't your fault."

"It was someone's fault."

"Let's take a walk on the beach," Julia said. She kicked off her high-heeled sandals and rolled up the cuffs of her blue jeans.

"I don't want to walk on the beach. It's foggy, it's cold. And we should be doing something." Although he couldn't quite think of what that something was.

"It's not as cold as Buffalo. The sand will feel good between your toes. And we need to think before we act. Come on, Alex."

"Fine." Alex slipped off his tennis shoes and socks and followed her onto the sandy beach. For a while they just walked, absorbing the sounds of the waves crashing on the shore, the seagulls squealing as they dipped in and out of the water, and the low drone of a small airplane cruising along the coast. As the minutes passed, the fog began to lift, rays of sunshine peeking through. By afternoon it would probably be completely sunny, but for now Alex appreciated the fog. It mirrored the way he felt inside. There were sparks of light in his brain, but still a thick curtain wouldn't let him see all the way to the truth.

The cool, moist sand felt good beneath his feet. The sensation brought him back to reality, grounding him in the present, taking him away from the past. He couldn't remember the last time he'd walked on a beach. He'd always been too busy for such simple, time-wasting pleasures.

He paused as Julia bent over to pick up a shell. Her long, thick, wavy blond hair blew loosely about her shoulders, and he itched to put his hands through her hair again, the way he had the night before, trapping her face to his kiss. His gut tightened at the memory. Julia was a beautiful woman. It was no wonder he was attracted to her. Unfortunately, it wasn't just her body he found immensely appealing; it was her personality, her willing-to-try attitude, her determination to know the truth even if it hurt, her curiosity in the outside world, and her kindness, her compassion, her softness—a softness that would probably get her into trouble if she trusted the wrong people. He would have to make sure she didn't do that. He would have to protect her.

But first he had to figure out who the wrong people were. He walked down to the water's edge, thinking once again that the sea held the answers. His father had died in this ocean, his hopes and dreams for the future lost in the waves. All because of a photograph. How could he ever forgive himself? His father's death was all his fault. And there was no way to change any of it.

A sharp wind picked up off the ocean, spraying his face with water. For a split second he wondered if his father was trying to tell him something. Was he wrong? Was he buying into a story that someone was trying to sell him? Why should he believe Daniel Brady or Stan or even his mother? None of them had given him one ounce of proof.

"Help me," he muttered. "Help me figure out what to do next. Should I talk to Brady? Should I talk to Stan? Is there someone I'm not thinking about?"

A large wave took shape, growing in size and power as it rolled toward the beach. It crashed against the sand just a few feet away, the water coming all the way up to him, washing his feet and the bottom of his jeans in water. Was it some sort of answer?

"A little cold for wading, isn't it?" Julia asked, as she came over to him.

"I didn't move fast enough."

"You didn't move at all. What are you thinking, Alex?"

"Nothing."

"I don't believe you. I know you're hurting inside, and you're not the kind of man who admits that. You like to be big and strong and invincible. And you hate it when you're not."

She had that right. He hated feeling weak, powerless, the way he did right now. The hatred had begun a long time ago when his parents had told him that they were separating, that his father wouldn't live with them anymore, that he'd only see him occasionally. And those powerless feelings had grown after his dad died, after the funeral, after he was left alone. So he'd created a life for himself in which he was in control. He worked for himself. He called his own shots. He decided when to go and when to stay. Everything had worked fine... until now.

"It's hard to lose a parent," Julia continued. "When my mom died, I felt as if I'd lost my right arm. I didn't think I would ever feel whole again. I can't imagine what that would have felt like if I'd been a child, as you were when your dad died, especially since your mother isn't the warm and fuzzy type."

"I hated her," Alex admitted. "For a long time I wouldn't even talk to her. I blamed her for keeping me away from my dad, for the year I'd lost while they were battling for a divorce. I even thought she'd driven him out that night, on that wet, rain-slicked road. I believed they'd had a fight and he was driving too fast. I guess I was wrong."

"You don't sound sure."

He turned to her. "I'm not sure. Everyone lied before. Who's to say they're not lying now?"

She shook her head, understanding in her eyes. "I don't know. Do you think Brady was lying about my mother being in Russia?"

He knew she wanted a different answer than the one he could give, but he had to tell the truth, at least the way he saw it. "No, Julia. I'm sorry, but I think your mother was in Russia."

"I don't want to believe it."

"It makes sense that she was there. Think about it. She was friends with my father. Her grandmother was Russian. She was passionate about the country, fluent in the language. Of course she was there."

Julia frowned. "Then I must have been there, too."

"Yes."

She lifted her chin, a light of battle coming into her eyes. "Okay, then. She was there, and I was there. We have to find out why. What next?"

What to do next—that was a hell of a question. "You could do what Brady said—lie, tell everyone you were born and raised in Berkeley, and that you never left the country. Then you'll be free of this mess. You can marry your Michael and live happily ever after."

"With my past buried in a mystery? That's not me, Alex." She paused. "Actually, that was me. I never had the courage to look at myself in the mirror and question who I was. I let my mother die without asking her the questions I wanted to ask. I was too scared. And I'll tell you something: I'm still scared. But I'm not walking away this time. I'm going to follow this trail to the end of the road—even if that road leads me all the way to Russia."

CHAPTER ELEVEN

WHEN JULIA ENTERED her apartment she found Liz sitting at their kitchen table with the sewing machine out and a pile of fabric all around her.

"Hey," Julia said tentatively as she set her bag on the floor. She wasn't sure what to expect from Liz. She'd received a dozen messages on her cell phone begging her to call, but she'd kept putting it off, wanting to talk to Liz in person. Now she wished she'd done it over the phone. Her sister's attention was focused on the material she was stitching, and Liz gave no indication that she'd even heard Julia come in. She was obviously angry.

"What are you working on?" Julia asked, stalling with trivial conversation. Although she was a bit curious about what Liz was planning to do with the yards of floral fabric spread out in front of her.

"A project," Liz muttered. She stopped sewing and glanced at Julia. "So you finally decided to come home. What's the occasion?"

Julia sighed at the tone of Lizzie's voice. She was tired from her trip, confused about everything she'd learned. She didn't want to fight with Liz, but she had a feeling it was inevitable. "I left you a message that I was staying with a friend," she said.

"Does this friend have a name? Oh, wait, let me guess—Alex Manning."

"We were following a lead. In fact, I have some news to tell you."

"I'm not really interested, Julia. Since it's obvious you don't care what I'm doing, I don't care what you're doing."

Julia pulled out a chair and sat down across from her. "Don't be like that, Liz. Don't make this hard."

"Is that what I'm doing?" Liz asked, hurt in her big brown eyes. "How could I be making your life difficult when I haven't seen you in twenty-four hours? Did you ever consider that my life might have gotten harder when you disappeared and the press had no one to follow but me and Dad?" Liz began to pull the pins out of the fabric, her movements jerky and angry.

"Have they been bothering you?" Julia asked, feeling guilty. "I am sorry, Liz. I thought they'd wait until I surfaced again."

"Where did you go?"

"I went to Buffalo, New York."

Liz's jaw dropped. "You're kidding. You went all the way across the country yesterday and came back today?"

Julia nodded. "I found our grandmother."

Liz stabbed herself with a pin and yelped. She put her finger in her mouth, licking off the drop of blood.

"Are you okay?" Julia asked.

"What did you just say?"

"I found our grandmother, Susan Davidson, the woman I read about in the obituary."

Liz swallowed hard, then sat back in her chair, drawing in a deep breath of air. "I can't believe you went to see her without telling me."

"I wasn't sure you'd support me," Julia replied.

"You're right. I wouldn't have supported you. Dammit, Julia, it's one thing to screw up your own life.

Why do you have to mess up mine, too?" she asked. "I was finally feeling normal after a year of uncertainty, and now you're turning everything upside down."

Julia heard the pain in Liz's voice and wished she could make it better instead of worse. But there didn't seem to be any way to get to the truth about her own life without touching on Liz's life. She had to make Liz understand that there was a positive side. After all, they now had a grandmother they hadn't had before. That was something. She reached for her handbag and pulled out the photos Susan had sent back with her.

Before she showed the photos to Liz, she needed to tell her the rest. "There's something else you have to know. Mrs. Davidson thought that our mother died twenty-five years ago. She was told that Sarah perished in a fire."

Lizzie's face was a picture of confusion. "I don't get it."

"Mom let her parents believe she was dead." Julia didn't know how else to put it. She and Alex had run through a number of scenarios, including the fact that maybe someone else had intervened, making both Sarah and Susan Davidson believe the relationship was over for different reasons. But who that third person would have been was unexplainable. "I don't know exactly what happened," Julia said as Lizzie remained silent, obviously digesting the news. "Mom said that her parents disowned her. Mrs. Davidson told me that Sarah died in a fire. One of them lied, or someone else lied, but the bottom line is that Mrs. Davidson knew nothing about us or our life with Sarah."

"Stop calling her Sarah. She's Mom," Lizzie complained.

Julia nodded, but she knew that she was starting to think of her mother as Sarah more and more, maybe because it helped delineate the person that her mother was before she'd married Gino. "These are photographs of our grandparents and Mom when she was little." She set the stack down on the table in front of Liz. "You look a lot like Mom when she was younger."

Liz hesitated. She stared at the photos as if she were afraid they would jump up and bite her. "I don't think I want to look at them."

"They won't go away just because you don't look."

"Don't push me," Liz snapped. "You're the one who's always whining about feeling rushed. Can't you see you're doing the same thing to me?"

"I'm sorry. You're right. I've had more time to think about this than you have. If it helps at all, Mrs. Davidson is really nice, and it was clear to me that she adored Mom."

"Then why did she disown her?"

"She said she didn't do that," Julia repeated. "She didn't even know about me. The last she knew was that Mom was single and alone. She didn't even believe Mom could have kids because of an ectopic pregnancy she'd suffered a few years before I was born."

"She must be lying. Or maybe this Mrs. Davidson was hiding something. She and her husband could have done something horrible to Mom when she was a child. Maybe she was abused or something..." Liz waved her hand wildly in the air as she tried to come up with reasons for the confusion.

"I honestly don't think Mom was abused by our grandparents," Julia replied. "Mrs. Davidson couldn't stop crying when she found out who I was. She couldn't understand why Sarah would have wanted her to think she was dead. She loved her so much."

"Then why would Mom have lied to us? If you don't think Mrs. Davidson is lying, then you think Mom did."

"I'm afraid I do," Julia admitted, even though it hurt to say the words. "Mom must have had her reasons. She told Gino the same story, that her parents had told her she was dead to them after she got pregnant with me. She never veered from that story."

"So there's something we're missing," Liz said. "I don't think we should take this woman's word over Mom's word. We don't know Mrs. Davidson at all."

"She'd like to know us. She'd like to come out and meet you— when you're ready," Julia amended quickly when Liz began to shake her head.

"That's not going to happen. I don't need another grandmother, especially one I don't trust. Mom didn't want us to know them. That's good enough for me. I don't even care about her reasons. She always wanted to protect us. Whatever she did had to be for that purpose."

Julia wished she could have such blind faith in their mother, but there were too many details blurring the picture of the mother she'd known. "There's more, Liz."

Liz put up her hand. "Please, stop. I don't want to hear more."

"Mom majored in Russian in college," Julia said, ignoring her plea. "Her grandmother, our great-grandmother, was a Russian immigrant. Apparently they spoke fluent Russian together." Liz didn't want to believe her. Julia could see the denial in her eyes. "Don't you think that means something?"

"I don't know what it means. You're driving me crazy. You have so many questions about everything. Why can't you just love the things you have, the people with you, instead of always wanting more? Why can't you be satisfied for once in your life?" She jumped to her feet. "I have to go to work."

"Don't run out, Liz. We need to talk about everything."

"No, we don't. Here's what I think. You do what you want, and leave me out of it."

Liz grabbed her keys and purse and strode from the room. Julia stared after her, wondering how they had gotten so off track with each other. During the past year they'd been closer than close, sharing the work it took to keep their mother comfortable and happy. Now they were as far apart as they had ever been.

Liz would say it was Julia's fault. Maybe it was. Maybe she did want too much.

But unlike Liz, she couldn't turn a blind eye to the lies that had been told. She'd spent her whole life stopping herself from asking the questions that mattered, afraid she would hurt her mother. But her mother was gone now, and it was time she got the truth—the whole truth.

Stan didn't seem surprised to see Alex when he showed up at his front door. "I thought you might come by," he said, waving Alex into the house. "Did you meet with Brady?"

Alex nodded, following Stan once again into his study. "We did. He basically confirmed what you suggested, that my father was murdered."

"I'm sorry, Alex. Do you want to sit down? Can I get you something to drink?"

"No, thanks." Alex paused. "There's something that's been bothering me since I left Brady."

"What's that?"

"He said you were friends with Sarah, that you got her the job with the theater company, and that you, in fact, were one of the primary players in setting up the whole trip. He also said it wasn't the first time you were involved in a cultural exchange between our countries. Why didn't you mention that when Julia and I were here on Sunday?"

Stan frowned, his lips drawing into a tight, irritated line. "Brady shouldn't have told you that."

"Because it isn't true, or because you didn't want us to know? You told Julia and me that you'd only met Sarah twice. That was a lie."

"There weren't many more meetings than that," Stan said. "My involvement with Sarah was limited. Charles told me she was excellent with a needle and thread. The group needed several costumers, so she was recommended for the trip."

"What about the exchange itself?"

"I made a couple of calls."

Alex suspected it was more than a couple of calls. Stan was being far too evasive. "Were you in Russia with my father?"

Stan walked around the desk by the window and sat down, putting up a barrier between them. He pressed his fingertips together, then said, "No, of course not."

The words were delivered in a firm, steady tone, no hint of a lie. Alex had no reason not to believe Stan, but he couldn't shake the uneasy feeling that he hadn't asked exactly the right question. Still, Stan had been his father's closest friend, and even after his dad's death, he had kept in touch. He'd made the effort to come to Alex's games, his high school graduation. Stan had helped him get his first camera, his first job. Alex had never believed they had anything but a completely honest relationship. Now because of a few small details, he had doubts.

Alex sat down in the chair in front of the desk. He picked up a pen and twisted it between his fingers. "Tell me more about your connection to the theater group."

Stan tilted his head to one side. "I made a few calls with government officials that facilitated the exchange. I did it for Charles. He was the driving force behind the entire effort. He obviously had another agenda besides photographing the event."

"Which you must have known at the time."

"I suspected," Stan admitted, "but I didn't ask questions."

"You should have. What about Sarah?" he continued. "Did she have Julia with her when she went to Russia? Because it's becoming very clear that Julia is that girl in the photo."

Stan shrugged. "I didn't know anything about Julia. I have no idea why she was in that orphanage, if she is in fact that girl. I do know the photo was a problem for Charles. He didn't tell me why, except that he was furious it had been printed without his knowledge. I already told you that, Alex."

"How could you not know if Julia was with Sarah? Brady said you were friends with both of them. And you must have helped the performers acquire papers for their travel."

"That wasn't my job. And Brady is mistaken. I wasn't friends with Sarah. Charles was. Everything that involved her was done through him."

"What about this theater group? Can you put me in touch with anyone who was on that trip with my dad and Sarah?"

Stan's mouth turned down in a displeased frown. "Alex, please, just drop it already."

"That's not going to happen, especially now that I know my father was murdered to keep him silent about something. He might have lost his voice, but I haven't. And I'll speak for him when I know the truth."

"That kind of reckless behavior could get you silenced as well."

"I'll take that chance."

Stan shook his head. "You're just as crazy as your father. He always thought he could beat the odds, too, but look what happened to him."

"You should have found his killer twenty-five years ago, Stan. You should have looked harder."

Anger flared in Stan's eyes. Alex felt a momentary flash of guilt, but he quickly discarded it. He wouldn't take back his words. It was the truth. Stan should have made sure the investigation continued, instead of letting the government shut him up.

"I don't understand why you didn't," Alex added. He waited for Stan to offer an explanation, but he remained silent, so Alex came up with his own answer, an answer he didn't like at all. "Did they threaten you? Was that it?"

"Leave it alone."

"I can't, dammit," Alex said loudly, bringing his fist down on the edge of Stan's desk. "Why can't I get a straight answer from anyone?"

"The night your father died, I received a message on my answering machine. The voice was garbled, but the message was clear. If I asked any questions, my parents would be killed. I'd already lost my wife. And Charles was gone, too. There was nothing to be gained by pursuing the truth. It wouldn't have helped you or your mother. Charles wouldn't have wanted you to grow up thinking he'd been murdered. I know that for sure." He gazed into Alex's eyes. "Would you have made such a different decision?"

"Yes, I would have seen justice done for my friend," Alex said without hesitation. "Is that it—the whole truth?"

Stan hesitated for a split second too long. "That's it," he said. "Now will you let it go?"

"No, because unlike you, I don't have anything to lose."

"What about Julia? Are you willing to risk her life? And the lives of her family, her sister, her stepfather, her friends?"

Alex's eyes narrowed. "How do you know so much about her?"

"Brady filled me in."

"Of course." Alex stood up. "I want to talk to someone in that theater group who was in Moscow. Where do I look?"

A brief pause followed his question; then Stan said, "The Sullivan Theater Group out of Los Angeles. I'm sure you can find their number. A woman named Tanya Hillerman sits on their board now. She was an actress during the Moscow tour."

"You had that information on the tip of your tongue," Alex said, wondering why.

"I figured you'd be asking. You're stubborn as hell." Stan rose from his chair. "As you said, you're a grown man now and capable of making your own decisions, so I'll leave you to it. Just be careful. Don't underestimate the enemy."

"I wish I knew who the enemy was."

Alex made the call from his car after retrieving the number for the Sullivan Theater Group from Information. After working his way through a receptionist and a secretary, he was given a number for Tanya Hillerman. As he waited at a red light, he punched in her number. The phone rang three times before a woman's voice came over the line.

"Hello," she said.

"Tanya Hillerman?"

"This is she. May I help you?"

"I hope so. I'm interested in speaking to you about a cultural exchange that took place in Moscow twenty-five years ago."

"Who are you?' she asked, an edge to her voice now.

"Alex Manning." He heard her sharp intake of breath.

"The photographer? I thought you died."

"That was my father, Charles," he said. "Is that who you're thinking of?"

"Oh, yes, Charles. You're his son. The little boy who stood at the back of the stage and tried to blend in with the scenery."

"That's me," he said wryly. He had hated that brief stint on the stage. Even though he hadn't had a speaking part, he'd felt very self-conscious. He was much more comfortable behind the lights than under them.

"What did you want to ask me, Mr. Manning?"

"I assume by what you just said that you were there."

"You don't remember me? I was the star, you know. I actually played out a death scene on stage. It was my trademark. No one could die like me. It was very slow and painful to watch, but I enjoyed it."

Alex didn't know how to respond to that. He cleared his throat. "Can you tell me if you remember a costumer named Sarah Davidson or Gregory?"

"Sarah? Let me think. There were a few girls who worked behind the scenes. Was she the dark-haired girl with the big brown eyes?"

"You tell me."

"I do remember a woman like that. She was very quiet, and new to the company, but excellent with a needle and thread. That was the first and only trip she made with us. She didn't continue on with the company after that trip."

"Do you know if she had a child with her, a little girl?"

"There were some children in the company like yourself, Alex. I don't know if one of them belonged to this Sarah." She paused. "I'm surprised you're not asking me more questions about your father."

He stiffened. "What should I be asking?"

"Well, I always thought your father had other reasons for being in Russia—reasons that had nothing to do with our theater exchange. It was even rumored that he might be some sort of a spy. I thought it was very dangerous and sexy. I flirted with him madly, but he never flirted back."

"He wasn't a spy; he was a photographer. And he was married," Alex added pointedly. Defending his father came naturally, but as he did so, he wondered if he had the right. Tanya Hillerman was the third person to imply his father was a spy. Could they all be wrong?

"I think he said he was separated," Tanya continued. "It didn't matter. He wasn't interested in me. He had more important things to do. I knew it even if he didn't say it." She paused. "It was a different world back then. No one trusted anyone, especially over there. The KGB watched us like hawks, worried we would tempt some of their artists with our American ways. It was terrifying at times. Your father and I spoke about it once. He had such passion for the Russian people. I worried that it would get him into trouble. Up until that trip, I'd never not been free, but that week I felt trapped. I never wanted to go back there. And I never have. When did your father pass away?"

"A few weeks after that trip," Alex said shortly.

"He was so young, so vibrant. How did it happen?"

"A car accident."

"Oh, dear. That's terrible. Such a shame. He was a very talented photographer."

"Yes, he was."

"Are you still involved in the theater, Mr. Manning? If you grew up to look like your father, I imagine you'd make a wonderful leading man."

"No, I'm not in the theater. I'm a photographer, just like my dad." He hung up the phone, wondering if that was true. He'd always thought he'd followed in his father's footsteps. Maybe he hadn't. Because right now those footsteps seemed to be leading him far away from what he'd always believed to be true.

Christine Delaney, the reporter from the *Tribune*, was waiting in the lobby of the radio station when Julia finished her show Tuesday afternoon. As soon as she saw Julia, Christine put up a hand in apology. "I'm sorry about the hit-and-run photo the other day."

"I don't think you're sorry at all," Julia replied. "And I have nothing further to say to you." Julia tried to sidestep around her, but Christine got in her way.

"I've done some research, Miss DeMarco. I found someone who used to work at the orphanage in Moscow where your picture was taken."

Julia couldn't believe what she was hearing. "You contacted someone in Russia?"

Christine's smile was smug. "Actually, the woman lives in the United States now. She came over about six years ago. She was a cleaning woman at the orphanage. She didn't want to talk to me at first, but I assured her that I would keep her anonymous."

"Why would you do that?" Julia asked suspiciously.

"Because I want your story, not hers." Christine paused, giving her a speculative look. "She told me that everyone in the orphanage was instructed to say that you were never there. They were threatened with death if they spoke about your presence. She said you were there for only one day, and she believed your parents were in serious trouble with the government."

Julia tried hard not to react, not to reveal anything to Christine, but inside she was reeling. She had to say something. She had to buy some time. She fell back on what Alex had suggested earlier. "I'm not that girl. It's a mistake. I was born and raised in Berkeley, California. I have a birth certificate to prove it." She did have a birth certificate, something she hadn't considered before now.

"Birth certificates are not that difficult to obtain, not if you know the right people," Christine said.

"I don't know what you mean," Julia replied, even though she suspected Christine was right about fake birth certificates being easy enough to get. She had to find a way to convince Christine to move on to another story. "I don't think I look like that girl in the picture," she said with as much cool as she could muster. "In fact, I'm considering suing your newspaper for printing that photo and suggesting all kinds of lies." She hadn't been considering any such thing, but Christine didn't have to know that.

"And you just happened to be hanging out with Alex Manning the other day as his mother told me? Please, Miss DeMarco, don't insult my intelligence. You're that girl and I'm going to prove it."

"Why would you want to?"

"Because it's a great story, and the newspaper never lets me write about anything but celebrities. This is my big break. I can help you. I've already found someone who worked at the orphanage. If you really want to know who you are, you need me."

"I know who I am," Julia said flatly. "I don't need you for anything." She walked out of the station, hoping to leave Christine behind, but the woman followed her onto the sidewalk.

"You say that now, but you'll change your mind," Christine said. "I'm very persistent. I don't give up."

"And you won't change my mind," Julia retorted. She wondered if she could make a fast break for her car, which was parked just down the street. That's when she saw a man watching her. He was built like a linebacker with a square, muscular body. Dirty blond hair showed beneath a baseball cap. A pair of dark sunglasses hid his eyes, and he wore a tan jacket over slacks. She couldn't tell his age, but he was probably in his fifties. As Julia stared at him, she wondered why he didn't look away, why he was searching her face as carefully as she was searching his. Was he another reporter? He certainly didn't look like one, but she hadn't had that much experience with the press.

"Miss DeMarco," Christine said, drawing her attention back to her. "Please, let me tell your story. I really need this break."

Her smile was meant to be disarming, but Julia didn't buy it. "I'm not your break," she said, "and I'm busy."

Christine thrust her card in Julia's face. "Call me anytime, night or day."

Julia took the business card and stuffed it into her pocket. As Christine left, the man came toward her. He said something she didn't understand. It took her a moment to realize he was not speaking English. He repeated his comment in a more agitated, determined voice, his arms gesturing. She backed away, his tone making her nervous.

The door to the radio station opened behind her, and two of her coworkers came out. She latched onto them in relief. "Hey, where are you guys going?" she asked, feeling there was safety in numbers.

"Coffee. Want to come?" Tracy asked.

"Yes, sounds great." She cast a quick look over her shoulder. The man had moved down the street, but he was still watching her. She linked arms with Tracy and walked in the opposite direction. She was probably letting her imagination get the better of her, seeing danger where it didn't exist, but Brady's warning that her questions could get her into trouble was still fresh in her mind. She didn't want to suddenly disappear as Alex's father had. Until she knew which people in her life were telling the truth and which ones were lying, she'd trust no one.

A half hour later Julia was back in her car, driving across town to her apartment. Her coworkers had walked her to her car after she'd mentioned the strange guy who appeared to be watching her. Much to her relief, he'd disappeared. She pulled into a parking spot in front of her building and got out. As she did so, she saw Liz heading up the steps. When it appeared that Liz was planning to ignore her, Julia called out for her to wait. Liz made a face but did as she was asked, tapping her foot impatiently on the ground. "What?" she asked.

"I want to go up with you."

"Why? You haven't wanted to do anything else with me."

Julia sighed, wondering how long her sister's bad mood would last. "I'm getting really tired of your attitude, Lizzie."

"Likewise, sis," Liz said sarcastically. "By the way, the family— our family, if you still consider them family—wants to throw you an engagement party at DeMarco's in a couple of weeks. Aunt Lucia wants you to call her and pick a date."

"What did you tell her?"

"Nothing. I'm staying out of your so-called wedding plans."

Julia thought that was a good idea since she knew a conversation with Michael was long overdue. To her credit, she had tried to call him from the radio station, but he'd been out on his boat. She'd have to catch up with him later.

Julia and Liz walked up the stairs together. Liz seemed to have nothing to say, and Julia didn't know how to break the silence without drawing another sarcastic remark. "I wish we could be on the same side," she said as they reached their door.

"I'm on the DeMarco side. I don't know what side you're on."

Julia blew out a frustrated breath and opened the door. Her jaw dropped at the sight of their apartment. It looked as if a bomb had gone off. The room was in shambles. "Oh, my God!" She put a hand to her mouth, feeling like she was going to be sick.

"What's wrong now?" Liz demanded, pushing past her, only to stop abruptly and gape in amazement. "Someone broke in," she said, stating the obvious.

"I can't believe this," Julia said, dazed. Their home hadn't been just robbed, but ransacked. The drawers in their desk had been dumped on the floor. The CD cases were open and broken apart. The cushions on the couch and the upholstery on the kitchen chairs had been slashed. Fear swept through Julia at the violence of the burglary. She grabbed Liz by the arm. "They might still be here," she whispered. "We have to get out."

Julia looked toward the hallway and the closed bedroom door. They never closed the bedroom door. They turned and ran.

CHAPTER TWELVE

JULIA AND LIZ didn't stop running until they reached the sidewalk, where they drew in gulping breaths of air.

"We have to call the police." Liz reached for her cell phone with a shaky hand. "Oh, God, Julia, you don't think they're going to come after us, do you?"

"No, of course not." Her chest heaved as she struggled to calm her racing heart. "They're probably gone. I just didn't want to take a chance. Not after I saw what they'd done to the cushions on the couch and the chairs. They must have had knives."

Liz paled. "Let's get farther away," she suggested.

"Good idea."

When they reached the other side of the street, Liz made the call while Julia stared up at her bedroom window, which faced the street. She thought she saw the curtain move. Was someone in there watching them? She heard Liz talking to the police and knew she had to call Alex. She pulled out her cell phone and punched in his number, relieved when he answered right away.

"You have to come over," she told him, her lips trembling so hard it was difficult to get the words out. "Someone broke into my apartment. They might still be there."

"I'll be right over. Stay out of the apartment, Julia. In fact, you should get yourself to someplace safe."

"Liz and I are across the street. She's talking to the police. It's the middle of the day. Nothing will happen to us here," she said, hoping it was the truth.

"Keep your eyes open," he advised. "I have a feeling this burglary wasn't random."

"I don't think it was either, Alex. They didn't steal our stereo or our television, but they slashed the pillows on the couch like they were furiously angry or completely crazy."

"Or looking for something in particular," Alex said. "Do you have any idea what that could be?"

"I don't know. I can't think. I'm shaking."

"All right, relax. We'll figure it out."

"Maybe the swan necklace or the matryoshka doll," she said. "Maybe that's what they were looking for."

"Do you know if they were taken?"

"They're still in my purse from our trip to Buffalo." She put a hand on the strap looped over her shoulder.

"Hang on to that bag. I'll be there in five minutes."

Julia closed the phone and saw that Liz had finished her call. "What did the police say?"

"They're on their way." Liz gave Julia a worried look. "This has something to do with you and that photo, doesn't it?"

"I have the terrible feeling it does."

The police arrived at the same moment as Alex. They searched the apartment first, then let Julia, Liz, and Alex into the living room. The damage was as bad as Julia remembered. All the tiny pieces of their lives were strewn across the room: magazines, books, knickknacks, the fabric Liz had been working on, and Julia's CD collection. Even the pictures on the wall had been stripped down and thrown onto the floor. It didn't look as if the burglars had missed one inch of the room.

The police asked them to look around and see if anything was taken. It was impossible to tell with the mess, but obviously expensive items and even a twenty-dollar bill on the kitchen counter had been left untouched, which was even more worrisome. After a long discussion about whether they had any enemies or knew of anyone who might have wanted to hurt them, the police said they believed the apartment had been turned by a pro, someone who was looking for something in particular.

Julia glanced to Alex, wondering if she should mention the photo and the Russia connection, but saw by the almost imperceptible shake of his head that he thought it would be better to keep that information to themselves. But she could give the police something. "There was a man watching me when I left work today. He made me so nervous, I didn't go to my car; I went and got coffee with my friends. When I came back a half hour later, he was gone." She gave them the description of the man, although she could tell by their expressions that they believed it was a stretch to connect some man who might have been watching her to the vandalism done in her apartment.

"Are you going to tell them about the picture?" Liz whispered to Julia.

"There's nothing to tell yet," she murmured. "I don't think we want more media attention, do you?"

"No," Liz replied, a scowl on her face.

"We're done for now," one of the officers said. "You should both be careful. If they didn't find whatever they were looking for, they may be back. Stay with friends tonight, and if you think of anything that will help us investigate, give us a call." He handed Julia his card.

Julia slipped it into a pocket, her fingers coming into contact with the card Christine Delaney had given her earlier. She had a feeling she wouldn't be calling either one of them, but she said, "Thank you."

Michael arrived as the officers were leaving. His eyes widened in shock when he saw the state of their apartment. "What happened?" He looked from Julia to Liz, his gaze settling on Alex. "Who are you?"

"This is Alex Manning," Julia said, realizing they'd never actually met. "Michael Graffino."

The two men sized each other up, then connected for a brief, wary handshake.

"So, what's going on?" Michael asked again.

"Isn't it obvious?" Liz asked. "Julia's search has now put us in danger."

"Someone broke into your apartment because of the photograph?" Michael echoed in surprise. "Are you sure?"

"No, we're not sure," Julia replied. "We don't know."

"What we do know," Liz cut in, "is that nothing was taken, but everything was ripped apart by a big, sharp knife."

Michael's attention shifted to the cushions on the couch. His skin turned pale. "God! What if you'd been here when they came? You could have both been killed."

That thought had crossed Julia's mind as well. And she could see that his words had stirred Liz up even more.

"We're lucky that didn't happen," Julia said.

"Lucky? You call this lucky?" Michael asked sharply. He shot Alex a hard look. "What do you think about all this? You don't seem to be saying much."

"I think Julia has it covered."

"And I think Julia needs to stop this craziness before something worse happens."

"She can handle herself," Alex replied.

"And she can speak for herself, too," Julia interrupted, drawing their attention back to her. "We shouldn't jump to conclusions until the police finish their investigation." Actually, she was already jumping to conclusions, but she didn't want to share them with Michael or with Liz. She needed to talk to Alex alone. But Michael would have none of that.

"Why don't you leave?" Michael said to Alex. "I'll take care of Julia and Liz." He put a protective and proprietary arm around Julia's shoulders.

She could hardly knock it off, but she didn't like the way Michael was staking his claim, or the way Alex was looking at her, as if he couldn't believe she was standing there letting Michael take control.

She sensed the situation was on the verge of exploding into something even worse.

"Maybe you should go, Alex," she said quietly, silently pleading with him to understand.

Alex hesitated, an unreadable look in his eyes. Then he shrugged. "Sure. Call me later."

Julia had to fight the urge to run after him. She was far more interested in talking to him about what this break-in might mean than in dealing with Michael and Liz, who were both annoyed with her. But she knew she couldn't leave. She had to talk to them first. She owed them that much.

Liz walked over and shut the door behind Alex, then put her hands in the pockets of her jeans as she stared at Julia and the destruction surrounding them. "This is scary," Liz said. "What kind of people are you mixed up with?"

"I don't know," Julia muttered.

Michael pulled her around so he could gaze into her eyes. "Julia. Please. I'm asking you. Let this search of yours go. Call the newspaper. Tell them they were wrong. You're not that girl. And your family needs to be left alone."

"Don't you understand, Michael? It's too late. Everything is in motion. I told the reporter I wasn't that girl. She didn't believe me. And it's obvious that someone who saw my picture in the newspaper thinks I'm that girl. And it looks like that someone believes I have something that I'm not supposed to have."

"What? What do you have?" he asked impatiently. "Is there more you haven't told me?"

She couldn't even remember what she had told him. Her head was spinning with bits and pieces of information. "I don't know what I have that they want. Maybe it's the swan necklace. Maybe it's the matryoshka doll. It's possible that it's old and valuable. Your guess is as good as mine. I'm just glad they were in my bag, not the apartment."

"So they might come back looking for them, looking for you," Michael said.

"I hope not. And I'm just guessing that that's what they're looking for. I really don't know." She still needed to go to the Russian shop and talk to Dasha's cousin, Svetlana, about the doll. She'd forgotten all about that part of the story. Maybe that's what she would do next.

"Julia, this is too dangerous," Michael said. "If you come forward, if you make a public statement that you're turning over these items to the police, whoever did this might back away."

"Or they might not." She could see the disappointment in his eyes. "I'm sorry, Michael, but I don't want to turn over my necklace and that doll to the police. They're the only clues I have to my past. I have to finish my search."

"At what cost? You and Liz could have been killed. If you aren't thinking about yourself, what about your sister?"

"Yeah, what about your sister?" Liz echoed. "Listen to him, Julia. He's making good sense. Yesterday some man called here. He had a Russian accent. He kept calling you Yulia. And he seemed agitated when I couldn't put you on the phone. He scared me. There was something in his voice." She paused. "I wonder if he was the one who did this."

Julia wondered if he was the same man who'd been outside the radio station. Maybe she shouldn't have run from that man. Maybe she should have stayed and confronted him, instead of taking off like a scared child.

"You need to back off," Michael urged. "If you show complete disinterest in the story, perhaps the press will move on to something else."

"I think Michael has a point. Without you, the story has no teeth," Liz added.

How could she fight both of them? Julia wished Alex hadn't left. She could have used another person on her side. "I'm sorry," she repeated, with a helpless wave of her hand, "but I can't stop. The reporter told me today that she spoke to someone who worked at the orphanage in Russia. She's digging deep and digging fast. She's determined to solve the mystery of that little girl with or without me. Even if I do nothing, she's moving forward. I need to stay ahead of her, just in case..."

"In case what?" Liz asked.

She drew in a breath. "In case I have to protect Mom's reputation."

"What does that mean?"

"I'm not sure yet, but there's a good chance that Mom and I were in Russia when that picture was taken."

Liz's gaze darkened with some emotion. "How do you know that? Do you have proof?"

"I'm working on it."

"What did the person at the orphanage tell the reporter?" Liz asked. "Could she identify you?"

"No, apparently she just said that the employees were threatened with death if they spoke of the girl at the gates."

"Oh, come on. That's a little dramatic, isn't it?" Michael scoffed.

Julia tipped her head at the mess surrounding them.

"And this isn't dramatic? I think someone made a very powerful statement here today."

He couldn't argue with that. "All right. What are you going to do next?"

"Start cleaning, I suppose," Julia replied.

"You can't stay here. You'll have to come to my apartment. We'll go from there."

"There's no room at your place. You're living with your brother. And what about Liz?"

"Yeah, what about Liz?" her sister echoed again.

"You can stay with your father," Michael told Liz. He glanced back at Julia and shook his head. "And you—I guess I might as well tell you this now. I was going to wait until it was ready—until you were ready —but since you need a safe place to stay..."

"What are you talking about?" Julia asked, confused again.

"I'm going to start cleaning up the bedroom," Liz said, interrupting them. "I'll be in the other room if anyone needs me."

Her sister certainly seemed eager to be gone all of a sudden. "You don't have to leave," Julia said.

"Yes, I do," Liz said with a nod. "Believe me, I do." She hustled out of the room, making a point of closing the bedroom door behind her.

Julia turned back to Michael. "What is it? What do you want to tell me?"

He took a moment, then said, "I bought us a house, Julia—near the Marina. It has two bedrooms and a garden. You're going to love it."

His words came out in a rush. She blinked, sure she hadn't heard him correctly. "Excuse me? What did you just say?"

"I think you heard me."

"I don't think I could have," she said with a definite shake of her head. "You better say it again."

"All right." His chin lifted and his shoulders went back as he said, "I bought us a house, Julia, a place for us to raise our children and grow old together. It's what you've always wanted. It's your wedding present."

Stunned by his words, she didn't know what to say, how to react. It was all too much. The day had been one bad surprise after another.

"Say something," Michael instructed.

"What should I say? I can't believe it. You bought us a house?"

Michael's brown eyes lit up with eagerness as he grabbed her shoulders. "It's great, Julia. It's a fixer-upper, which is the only way I could afford to buy in that neighborhood. There's a school nearby, about three blocks away. You'll be able to walk with the kids. And the recreation center is close by. You can take your yoga classes there, and I can play in the basketball leagues. It's the perfect place for us to start our life together."

"I already go somewhere for yoga," she said, not sure why it seemed important to tell him that in the face of everything else he'd said.

"So maybe you'll change your mind, and switch to the rec center. I can't wait to show you the house. I wanted it to be completely done before I did. But this is better. You can help me fix it up the way you want it."

"Does it matter what I want?" she asked.

"Of course it does," he replied, the light dimming in his eyes. "I love you. I want you to be happy."

"Then why didn't you tell me about the house? Why didn't you show it to me before you bought it? Don't you think we should be making these decisions together? A house is a huge purchase."

"I'm the man. I want to provide for you and our children. It's the way I was raised."

"First of all, we don't have children yet. You make it sound like they're already here." And that little fact had drawn goose bumps down her arms. "Second of all, I want kids, but not yet, not really soon."

"You're almost thirty. How long do you want to wait?"

"I don't know—until I'm ready. My God, Michael! You bought us a house without telling me. Don't you think that's crazy? How did you even afford it?"

"I've been saving for years. I've always wanted a place of my own, real estate, my land, my house, something I can put my mark on. And no, I don't think that's crazy. I think it's smart. I think that kind of foresight makes me a good man."

"Except you just said 'my,' like, three times. What happened to 'our'? What happened to us making decisions together as partners?"

"And how the hell would I get you to make such a decision? You can't even focus on our wedding, much less the rest of our life," he snapped back.

"That's not an excuse for leaving me out of the loop. Not on something this big."

"I thought you'd be happy that I took care of it for you."

"Happy? How could I be happy? You didn't consider my feelings."

"And you've been considering mine? I've asked you to give up this search a half dozen times now, and your answer has been hell, no. You don't care what I think at all. And you're not even giving this house a chance. You might love it."

"It's not the house. It's the fact that you bought it without telling me, that you're planning our lives without my input. That's not right, Michael." She knew the moment of truth had finally come. She had to face their relationship head-on. "We're not right."

"Just stop there—"

"No." She shrugged out of his hold. "I can't stop. I have to tell you how I feel."

"It's that guy, Alex, isn't it?" he demanded furiously. "He's the reason you're pulling away from me. You're attracted to him, aren't you?"

"This isn't about him," she said, sidestepping the issue of attraction. "It's about you and me. Us. It's my fault, Michael. I let things go on for too long. And I'm sorry about that."

He shook his head. "Don't."

"You're one of the best men I've ever known. The way you took care of me and Liz during Mom's illness was unbelievably kind and generous. But I've known for a while now that you and I...that we're not right for each other."

"We're perfect for each other," he said desperately. "How can you say that?"

"Because it's true. Because you don't see me the way I am. I never said I wanted a house. I never said I wanted kids in the next five years. You just assumed I did. And I should have corrected you a long time ago."

"I know you want kids."

"But I want other things first," she said passionately. "I'm beginning to realize how narrow my life has been. Mom was so strict about things I could do or not do, who I could see, where I could go, and I let her control me. And I started letting you do the same thing."

"I love you," he said with genuine, heartbreaking sincerity.

"I love you, too," she whispered, "but not the way a woman loves a man she's going to marry." She knew she was hurting him, and she felt horrible. She'd never wanted to bring him pain.

"You're just confused because of your past and this mystery you're chasing," he said, not willing to let go of his dream. "You'll feel differently when it's over, when that guy is out of your life."

"I won't. It's true I'm confused. But the one thing I've come to realize in the past few days is that I want to live my life to the fullest. I don't want to have regrets. I don't want to stop myself from asking questions or stating my opinion because I'm afraid the person I'm talking to will get hurt. I want to be free, Michael. I want to travel. I want to work on my music, on my goals. And I don't want to cheat myself or you. That's what I'd be doing if I married you."

"You're making a mistake," he said flatly. "A big one this time. Has he offered to travel with you? To help you with your music? To show you the world?"

She shook her head. "Alex hasn't done any of those things."

"But if he asked you to go with him, you'd go."

"It's not about him," she said, refusing to let herself even consider that question.

"You can protest all you want, but I think you're lying." He paused, his jaw tight, his mouth set in a hard line. "I guess it's over then."

She glanced down at her left hand and slowly pulled off the engagement ring he'd given her almost a year ago. She handed it to him. "You're a great guy, Michael. I hope you find someone who really deserves you."

"Yeah, yeah, nice guys always finish last," he said bitterly. "I hope you find what you're looking for, Julia." He paused. "If you change your mind, I might still be around. Or I might not. You never know."

Julia blew out a sigh as Michael left the apartment. She felt drained of emotion but also relieved that she'd finally broken it off. She glanced down at the tan line on her third finger and knew she'd done the right thing. That ring had been feeling heavier and heavier the last few days.

"What happened?" Liz asked, returning to the room. "I heard yelling."

"We broke up," Julia said, steeling herself for more criticism from Liz, but for once her younger sister was silent. "Did you know about the house?"

Liz gave a sheepish nod. "Michael wanted it to be a surprise. I've been helping him fix it up. That's what I was sewing—curtains." She picked up the fabric on the floor and set it on the table.

"You should have told me, warned me."

"It wasn't my place. You're always telling me to stay out of your relationship, so I stayed out of it."

"You've been helping him fix up the house. How is that staying out of it?"

"I didn't tell him what to do. I just painted and scraped wallpaper. I knew you were going to be pissed."

"Of course I'm angry. What woman would want her fiancé to buy a house without her input?"

"A woman who saw it as a romantic, loving gesture," Liz suggested. "Didn't it please you at all to know that this man wanted to take care of you, protect you, make your life easier?"

Liz's words made Julia feel foolish and a little guilty. But she had to remind herself that she and Liz were very different women when it came to men and relationships. "It made me feel as if Michael had no regard for my opinion or my feelings," she said. "Maybe to some women it would have been a romantic gesture. That just proves we weren't right for each other."

"You should reconsider, Julia. See the house at least. You might love it. And perhaps if you talk things through, you'll be able to compromise, find a way to work things out. Unless you don't want to work things out? Did you break up with him because of the house—or because of something or someone else?"

Julia knew it would be smarter not to answer Liz's question, but she had the sudden reckless urge to confide in someone, and the words came out before she could stop them. "I kissed Alex last night."

Liz's eyes widened. "So that's it? You dumped an incredible man because you're attracted to a sexy bad-boy photographer? Is Alex really going to be in your life? Doesn't he spend most of the year traveling around the world?"

"I didn't dump Michael for Alex. He was just a small part of it, but a part I couldn't ignore. If I were really in love with Michael, I wouldn't have been so attracted to Alex. How could I marry one man knowing I had feelings for someone else? Michael is an incredible man, but he's not the man for me. And I should have figured that out a long time ago. But everyone loved him so much. I thought I should love him, too."

Liz stared at her for a moment, then shook her head in bewilderment. "You're right about one thing, Julia. Michael is an incredible man. I hope you won't regret this decision."

"I won't," Julia said, praying she was right about that. She glanced around the room, realizing she had other problems to address. "This place is really a mess. I can't believe how many things are broken." She felt sad and angry at the same time. "We have to find out who did this."

"It appears we have a lot to find out. We can't stay here," Liz added. "The lock is broken. My pullout couch is destroyed, and your bed isn't much better. Besides, the police said whoever did this might be back. So what do we do? Go to Dad's place? Aunt Lucia's?"

Julia suddenly realized that she couldn't go to any of those places, not when she might be bringing danger in her wake. "You go," she said. "I don't want to make anyone else a target. It's probably better if I stay away from the family right now."

"You might be right," Liz said with a sigh. "You're going to Alex's, aren't you?"

"He's already involved."

"Yeah, sure. I get it. Call me on my cell if you need me, and Julia... be careful. Not just with this search—with your heart. I may not know as much about life or men as you do, but even I recognize a heart-breaker when I see one, and Alex has that written all over him."

CHAPTER THIRTEEN

ALEX OPENED the door to Julia a little before six o'clock on Tuesday evening. He hadn't been sure she'd come to him. She might have gone home with Michael. Her fiancé had certainly made it clear that he wanted to take care of Julia and her sister. But here she was, wearing black pants, a light blue button-down blouse, and a short, trim black jacket. Her blond hair was done up in a ponytail, long hoop earrings dangling from her ears. She was pretty as a picture, he thought, then grimaced, reminded that their relationship had begun with a picture.

"Can I come in?" she asked.

He stepped back and waved her inside. "Where's your fiancé?"

"Probably at his new house—the house he bought for us without asking me," she said, a decided edge to her voice.

Alex let out a low whistle at that piece of information. There was a lot he didn't understand about women, but he did know that making a big purchase without talking to your soon-to-be wife was a huge mistake.

Julia paced around his living room in anger and frustration, but then she'd had a hell of a day—hell of a week, in fact.

"I couldn't believe it, Alex. Michael had our whole life mapped out without any input from me. He simply assumed we wanted the same things."

"Did you ever tell him differently? Most men aren't mind readers."

"You're taking his side?" she asked in surprise and obviously still in a fighting mood.

He put up a hand in defense. "Hey, I don't even know him. I'm just saying that maybe he assumed certain things because you didn't tell him he was wrong."

She put her hands on her hips and sent him an irritated look. "I have a job that I love, and I've told him about it numerous times. But Michael thought I would quit my job, stay home, and have children immediately."

Alex winced. "Ouch."

"And he asked me to quit searching for my past. In fact, he insisted. I said I couldn't. I explained that it's out of my hands now. My God, someone just trashed my apartment. I can't just disappear, even if I wanted to. So I told him that..." She paused, drawing in a long breath.

Damn. Alex had a feeling he didn't want to hear what she was about to say next. As much as he thought Julia needed to break off her engagement, he also liked the fact that there was a tangible barrier between them, a real reason not to get involved. He had a feeling that was about to disappear.

Julia held up her left hand and he saw the naked third finger. "I broke up with him. I told Michael I couldn't marry him. Not because of anything that I just told you, but because I'm not in love with him. I let our relationship drift along, because it was easy, and it was nice. That was wrong. I should have come clean a long time ago. I don't know why I didn't," she added with a shake of her head. "It wasn't fair to Michael. I feel bad about that. I never meant to hurt him, but I did, and that wasn't right."

He appreciated her honesty, her self-critical words.

Julia wasn't a woman to let others take the blame when it wasn't deserved. He liked that about her. He liked a lot about her. Clearing his throat, he said, "What now?"

"Now I have a mystery to solve. That's all I can think about for the moment."

He nodded. "Someone wants something that they think you have."

"Well, that narrows it down," she said with a hint of sarcasm. She took a seat on the couch, kicking up her feet on the coffee table. "We're not getting anywhere fast. By the way, I spoke to that reporter again. She cornered me at the radio station, and get this: She said she found a woman here in the United States who worked in that orphanage and who had seen me there. She said the woman told her they were under threat of death to talk about me. What do you think about that?"

He thought for a moment. "I'm not sure I buy it. Sounds vague and a little too convenient, maybe part of Christine's plan to make you trust her."

"I never thought about that. You think she made up the woman?"

"Did she give you a name?"

"No, that was based on my being willing to work with her. Apparently Christine thinks I'm her ticket to big-time news journalism."

"She might be right. Let's see what else she comes up with. I also did a little digging." He sat down next to her. "I had another conversation with Stan." He paused, still unable to shake the feeling that Stan hadn't been completely honest with him.

"And..." Julia prodded.

"He gave me the name of a woman who worked with the theater group and who was in Moscow with us."

Her eyes sparked with interest. "Really? That's great."

"Not so great. Tanya did remember my father quite clearly and also Sarah, but she had no idea if you were there or not."

"So she couldn't say I wasn't there?"

"No. She said there were a few children with the company. She didn't know who belonged to who."

"It's still possible, then, that my mother might have taken me to Russia with her."

He nodded, knowing that Julia needed to hang on to that fact, and for the moment they had no proof that it wasn't true. "Tanya also implied that my father was spying for the government," he added, "and I'm starting to believe it."

"It's difficult not to. I have the same question about my mother. Did she really go to Russia just to sew costumes?"

"Doubtful. I called a friend of mine in the State Department. I asked him to check out the key players—Brady, Stan, and your mother."

She flinched at the mention of her mother. "I guess you had to include her."

"Ryan said he'd get back to me as soon as he could." He took a breath, then continued. "I did press Stan on my father's death, on the fact that he didn't do anything to investigate it. He said he received a threat against his family if he didn't mind his own business. Apparently that was enough to make him look the other way." Alex couldn't hide the scorn in his voice. "Hell of a friend he was."

"Don't judge him too harshly. If they threatened his family, he was in a difficult spot."

"Yeah, well, he should have found a way out of the spot. I would have."

Julia gazed at him with her beautiful blue eyes, so full of emotion and concern for him that he had to fight not to put his arms around her. He clasped his hands tightly together and looked away.

She put a hand on his knee, and he stiffened.

"Are you hungry, Alex?"

The question was not the one he'd been expecting. He had to think for a moment. "I guess."

"I haven't eaten since that excuse for a breakfast we had on the plane."

He glanced back at her. "Do you want to go out?"

"Unless you're going to tell me you're a five-star chef?" she asked with a smile.

He laughed at that. "I never learned how to cook more than the basics, and I eat most of my meals on the run."

"Do you have a favorite restaurant you go to when you're in town?"

"No. Why don't you pick?"

She hesitated. "There's a new Moroccan restaurant on Union Street. It's supposed to be good, just like the real thing. Although you've probably eaten in a real restaurant in Morocco, haven't you?"

"Actually, that's one place I haven't been yet."

Her eyes sparkled. "Then it will be an adventure for both of us. Are you game?"

"I'm always game."

"I've been wanting to try it, but it never seemed to be the right time. And Michael isn't an adventurous eater. It will be my treat. It's the least I can do." She smiled as she stood up. "I kind of like this, picking the restaurant, paying for my guest. I think I'll even drive."

"Whoa, slow down. I'm driving."

"You don't think I can drive?"

"I like to be the driver."

"So do I, and I've been the passenger every time we've driven so far. Come on, Alex. You can trust me. I promise not to hurt you."

He sighed. "Fine, you drive. But I warn you, I am definitely a backseat driver, only you'll be hearing my comments from the front seat." As they left the apartment, Alex thought about what Julia had just promised. He didn't believe he was risking his life to ride in the car with her, but he had a distinct feeling that by spending more time together, he was definitely risking his heart. And the funny thing was that until Julia had entered his life, he'd almost forgotten he had a heart.

Julia entered the restaurant, feeling as if she'd just stepped into another world. The tented ceiling, the thick brocade tapestries on the walls, took them straight to Morocco. They sat down on low, soft cushions, the room lit only by candles. It was a lush, sensual atmosphere, and Julia felt a shiver run down her spine as she glanced over at Alex. He was as comfortable here as he was anywhere. She'd never met a man who could adapt to any environment as easily as Alex did. He made whatever room he was in his own.

A waiter came by to explain the menu and suggest drinks. As soon as he left, a beautiful woman entered and performed a belly dance for them. She seemed especially interested in drawing Alex's attention, and Alex seemed to enjoy every second of her performance. In fact, he looked as if he'd forgotten Julia was even present.

It didn't matter, she told herself. They weren't on a date. They weren't involved. They weren't committed to each other. Alex could flirt with the belly dancer. Heck, he could take her home and sleep with her, and Julia wouldn't have a thing to say about it, except that she really wouldn't like it.

Julia frowned at the turn of her thoughts. She took a sip of wine, relieved when the woman moved away. "She was pretty," she commented, feeling completely insincere.

"Beautiful," he said with a smile. "I'd like to see you in one of those costumes."

"I doubt that will ever happen. I'm far too inhibited." She licked her lips as his gaze roamed her face, as if he were searching for all her personal secrets. There were some things she didn't want to share with him.

"Are you inhibited?" he asked. "Or is that just the way you've been raised to be?"

"It's the same thing."

"It's not. I believe we're influenced by our environment, the people in our lives."

"I suppose that's true. My mother was very big on rules and doing the right thing, telling the truth, never going astray. She and my father made such a big, happy family life for us that it was easy to be content in it. It wasn't until she died that I started to look around and wonder what else I wanted. I must say it's difficult to believe she might have been the biggest liar of all." Every time Julia thought about the lies, her heart hurt.

"She didn't lie about her love for you," Alex said in a tender voice. "She obviously took care of you, protected you, tried to make you happy. That's the important stuff, Julia."

"I'm trying to focus on that, but it's not easy when I'm hit with a new problem every time I turn around."

"You have had a busy week."

"Tell me about it. I can't believe I just walked out and left my apartment in such horrible condition. I should have cleaned it up."

"It will be there when you get back. What's your sister up to?"

"I think she went to my dad's house." Julia sighed. "I don't want to talk about any of it right now. Do you think we could put a moratorium on the subject through dinner?"

"Absolutely," he said with so much relief she had to laugh.

"I'm glad you agree. You know, this is nice."

"It's a cool restaurant."

"I wasn't talking about the restaurant. I was talking about how good it feels to spend time with you—away from all the drama."

"For a few minutes anyway," he said lightly, lifting his wineglass to hers. "To you, Julia, whoever you are."

"Whoever I am," she echoed.

An hour later they'd stuffed themselves on stewed vegetables, slices of fried eggplant, and a melt-in-your-mouth lamb dish. They'd also shared a lot of conversation about anything and everything—books, politics, religion, and world events. There was no topic that was out of bounds. They argued, debated, and laughed. Julia didn't think she'd ever laughed so much in her life, which made her feel guilty when she stopped to think for a minute. She should be sad that her engagement was over and that she'd probably hurt a very nice guy. Instead, she felt free. That was wrong. Yet it was right, too, and feeling bad wouldn't make Michael feel better. Hopefully time would open his eyes to who she really was and why they never would have been happy together. With that rationalization, she was able to put Michael out of her mind, as well as the rest of the problems in her life. She would have so many things to deal with tomorrow—her apartment, her mother, her past— but for the moment, she wanted to be carefree. And she couldn't have picked a better partner for this outing than Alex.

She loved the way his mind worked. He was sharp, perceptive, interesting—a truly fascinating man. He lived a life that she wanted. Not the photography part, but the traveling part.

"Do you think you'll ever quit?" she asked, as they left the restaurant and headed toward the car. "Ever decide to stay in one place and just take pictures at the local mall?" she added with a teasing smile.

"I'd rather shoot myself than work at the mall." He shrugged his shoulders. "I'm used to my life. It works. It's challenging, too. I love being able to get the shot that no one else can get."

"And you really believe that your job is enough for you?"

"It has been so far."

"Even though I just broke off my engagement, I still want to get married—someday."

"Of course you do."

"Why do you say it like that?" she asked.

"I said it before. Most women want to be married."

"And most men—"

"Want to have a lot of sex."

"You can have a lot of sex in a marriage," she pointed out. She saw his teasing smile and had a feeling that no matter how hard she tried, she wasn't going to get a more serious answer out of him.

"I'll keep that in mind," he said. "So, Julia, are we sleeping together tonight?"

At his question, she almost tripped on the uneven sidewalk. "What?"

"You heard me. You need a place to stay, don't you? I'm offering my bed."

"And where are you going to sleep?"

"I'm waiting to hear my options. In the meantime, can I drive home?"

"No," she said, hoping she could bring the same definitive no to the bed question.

She walked around to her side of the car and reached into her purse for her keys. Suddenly a man appeared out of nowhere, tall, burly, and he was heading straight toward her. She didn't have a chance to move, but Alex did. One minute she was standing up; the next she was hitting the ground with her backside and Alex was chasing some guy down the street. Her heart pounded against her chest as she tried to get her bearings. Her handbag was still on her shoulder, although now that she thought about it, she had the distinct feeling that man had been trying to take it from her. If Alex hadn't moved so quickly, she would have lost the doll and her necklace.

She stood up, feeling nervous and abandoned. Alex and the man had disappeared. She was alone in the dark. Suddenly aware of how isolated she was, she searched hastily for the keys. They were at the bottom of her bag. With a shaky hand, she hit the open button, and slid inside. With the doors closed and locked, she felt a little better. But where the hell was Alex? God, she hoped he was all right.

What if the guy had a gun or a knife? Alex had no way to defend himself. He was on his own. And so was she.

Alex increased his pace, narrowing the gap between himself and the man who had tried to attack Julia. His heart was beating double time, his breath coming quick and fast as he followed the man around the corner of Union Street, up a short hill and into a small park. It was darker here. No streetlights. Plenty of shadows.

Alex could barely make out the man now. Only the light blue streak of his Windbreaker glittered in the moonlight as he dashed among the trees. Alex couldn't lose him. He had to find out who he was and what he wanted. This was his chance.

But that chance was elusive and fast.

One minute the man was in his sights. The next he was gone. Alex stopped, looked around. The park was empty but edged with a thick line of trees. There was no apparent way out of the park. The man would have to come back in his direction.

Was he hiding?

Alex tried to catch his breath, make his mind work. He had to think.

An eerie feeling of being watched crept down his spine. He turned slowly, sharpening his gaze on each flickering shadow. There were too many trees, too many bushes, all rustling in the whispering breeze. As he listened, the sounds of the night grew louder: the crickets, the faint honk of a distant horn, the rumble of traffic on a nearby road, the sound of laughter from one of the open apartment windows surrounding the park.

"Come out, dammit," he said aloud. "Talk to me. Tell me what you want."

Nothing but silence answered his call. Was the man waiting, watching? Or was he gone? Had he found a way out that wasn't obvious to Alex?

If he had...

Julia was alone in the car. And she was the one they wanted.

What the hell was he doing?

Turning, Alex ran back the way he'd come, desperately hoping Julia was all right.

CHAPTER FOURTEEN

JULIA FLINCHED at the sound of footsteps coming down the street behind her. She was almost afraid to look. What if it wasn't Alex? What if it was the man who had tried to grab her bag? What if he'd hurt Alex and had come back to get her?

She sank down into the seat, hoping he wouldn't see her.

The footsteps drew closer, then paused. Someone whistled. A shadow moved across the front seat, and the door handle on the passenger side was flipped. It was locked. It didn't open. The man stumbled as he tried the door again.

She couldn't breathe. She didn't know what to do. Should she start the car, try to pull out? What if Alex came back and she wasn't there?

Before she could come up with an answer, the man moved on.

It wasn't the same guy, she realized. This man was older, wearing a bulky coat and pants. His hair was long, and he wore a woolen cap on his head. He had a paper bag in his hand, and as she watched, he raised it to his lips and took a swig. He continued on, trying the door handle on every car parked along the street.

He was probably homeless and looking for somewhere to sleep, she realized. He wasn't after her. She forced herself to breathe again.

Until she heard the sound of someone running.

She'd never been as scared of the night as she was right now.

Please let it be Alex, she prayed. She closed her eyes, afraid to look. Someone tapped on the window. She tensed, then relaxed when she heard his voice.

"Julia, it's okay. Let me in."

She flipped the locks with a wave of relief, and Alex slid into the passenger seat. "Thank God, you're all right," she said, flinging herself into his arms. She hugged him tight, not wanting him to let her go. He didn't. He pressed her face into the curve of his neck, his hand cupping the back of her head. She could feel his pulse jumping beneath his skin, and she could smell the sweat of his desperate chase. But he was safe. So was she. And they were together.

Finally, Alex pushed away, his eyes glittering in the shadows. "I lost him. I was afraid he'd come back here, afraid—" He cut himself off. She could finish the sentence in her head. He'd been scared for her, and fear was a character flaw as far as Alex was concerned. But in her mind, fear was a normal reaction to a terrifying situation.

"I'm all right," she assured him. "I was worried about you. I thought he might have had a knife or some other weapon."

"He ran into a park and disappeared. I didn't even get a good look at him. All I know is that he was fast."

"Was he blond? Did he have a baseball cap on his head? A man came up to me at the radio station earlier today, and he made me really nervous."

Alex's eyes narrowed. "What are you talking about?"

"There was a guy watching me when I was talking to Christine Delaney. He came up to me when she left, and he said something I didn't understand. I think it might have been in Russian. My friends interrupted us, and he took off. Do you think it was the same guy?"

"Could have been. Why didn't you tell me about him before?"

"Didn't I?" she asked in confusion. "I guess I told Michael or Liz. I can't remember now. Did I also mention that Liz said a man with a thick, probably Russian accent called our apartment yesterday?"

"Goddammit, Julia," Alex swore. "What else don't I know?"

"I think that's it. I'm sorry, but everything is happening so fast, and

I don't know what goes together and what doesn't." Overwhelmed, she had the terrible feeling she might burst into tears at any moment.

Alex put his hand on her leg. "It's okay. It's fine. We'll deal with it all, Julia. Don't worry."

"The man who came at us just now... He was after my purse, don't you think?" She'd had a few minutes to think, and she distinctly remembered the man trying to rip her bag off her shoulder.

"Yes," Alex said, meeting her gaze. "I'd say it's a safe bet he couldn't find whatever he was looking for at your apartment, so he decided you have it on you."

"Should we call the police?"

"Let's go back to my apartment first and take another look at the doll and the necklace. Maybe we missed something."

She nodded and turned the key in the ignition. She didn't realize she was shaking until she flooded the engine with too much gas.

"Easy, Julia," he murmured.

"I was so scared," she whispered. She gripped the steering wheel so tightly her knuckles turned white and her hands stung, but she didn't care, because it felt good to have something solid to hang on to. "When you disappeared, I didn't know what was going to happen." She looked at him and saw nothing but understanding and support. "I just got back in the car and protected myself. I should have gone after you, but I was a chicken."

"Sh-sh," he said. He leaned forward, putting a finger against her lips. "You did exactly the right thing."

She blinked back a tear. "I was so worried that I was going to lose you, Alex, and I've lost so much lately that—"

Alex cut off her words with a tender kiss. "I'm not that easy to lose," he murmured against her mouth. "I'm fine, Julia. He ran. He wasn't looking for a confrontation."

"Maybe not this time. What about the next time?"

"Don't think about all the things that might happen. It will drive you crazy." He tucked a piece of her hair behind her ear.

"I'm already feeling crazy. Should I stop looking for answers? Should I try to go back to my normal life? How do I even do that?"

"You can't go back to normal, because it doesn't exist anymore."

"If it ever did. What I thought was normal was a fictional story my mother created for me to live in. Nothing about my life was based on anything real."

"That's not true. Your mother may have created a cover story, but she lived her life with you, your sister and your stepfather. I don't think she was spying for the government when she was taking you to Girl Scouts," he added lightly. "In fact, we don't know if she was spying for the government at all. Maybe she simply went on that trip to Moscow because she wanted an adventure, and my father gave her the opportunity."

"I'd sure like to believe that. But if that were the case, why would she have hidden it from me? Why would she have disappeared from her parents' lives? Why would she have changed her name? Lived a lie?"

She wanted Alex to give her the answers, but she knew she was asking for too much. "She might have been spying the whole time I was growing up. How would I have known? Apparently she was very clever."

"I think your mother got out of the spy business, if she was ever in it, after that trip to Moscow, or maybe when she married your stepfather. From what you've told me about your idyllic childhood, I can't believe Sarah was anything but a devoted homemaker."

"I don't know what she was anymore, and that scares me, too," Julia confessed. "We were so close. We shared so many conversations. All the best moments of my life were with my mother. And now I can barely remember those times. My memory is blurred by all the terrible lies that continue to be revealed. Now when I close my eyes, I see Susan Davidson's face crumpled in pain when she realized Sarah had been alive. I hear Brady telling me that Sarah was in Moscow. Even your voice echoes through my head—your words, 'I saw your mother in the square that day.' What's real? What's not real? Why don't I know?"

"Your brain is too full," Alex replied, a smile spreading across his lips. "You've had a lot of shocks tonight. Give yourself a break. You don't have to figure everything out in the next five minutes."

"Maybe I do," she countered. "Who knows what the next five minutes will bring?"

"Nothing bad, I promise. Even the bad guys need to rest."

"How can you joke?"

"Because worrying is a waste of energy. Let's go home." He paused, his eyes suddenly sparkling. "I have an idea. Why don't you let me drive?"

His obvious attempt to regain control of the car made her smile back at him. "No way. I drove us here. I'll drive us back."

His sigh was long and dramatic, and eased the tension of the moment. "If you must."

"I must," she replied, her hands steadier now as she pulled away from the curb.

"I'll sleep on the couch," Julia said as they climbed the stairs to Alex's apartment a short while later. "I don't want to completely disrupt your life."

"A little late for that sentiment. You're the one who knocked on my door last week and started this ball rolling."

"It's not all my fault. You took the picture. You started this twenty-five years ago."

"Thanks for the reminder." He paused as he took out his key. "You know we slept together last night, and it was just fine."

It hadn't been just fine. She'd spent most of the night fighting an urge to roll into his arms and make love to him. And last night she'd had a barrier, an engagement ring and a fiancé. Now she had neither. But she still had a brain, and right now it was telling her that getting further involved with Alex would not be a good idea. She might not have wanted the steady, suffocating relationship Michael had offered, but she also didn't want to get her heart trounced by a *love 'em and leave 'em* type, no matter how sexy he was.

"The couch works for me," she said lightly. "Unless you'd rather I go to my dad's apartment and get out of your hair. I just don't want to put him in danger."

"No, you can stay here." Alex opened the door and flipped on the light.

Julia gasped at the sight that greeted them. Whoever had ransacked her apartment had done the same to Alex's, with just as much brutality and violence. Every piece of furniture had been upended, flipped over, ripped, cut, trashed. Even Alex's photographs had been snatched from the walls, the tables, the bookcase. Shattered glass lay on the floor where some of the picture frames had been thrown in ruthless abandon. The fury of the search seemed even worse here, as if the person had grown more frustrated and angry with each passing second.

"Dammit," Alex swore. "I should have seen this coming."

She should have seen it coming, too. Why hadn't she considered the fact that someone might follow her to Alex's apartment?

"I swear, if they broke my camera equipment..." Alex disappeared into the bedroom before Julia could tell him to be careful. She could hear him opening the closet door, slamming a dresser, muttering to himself. She was afraid to move, worried she'd step on something important, do even more damage.

Alex finally returned, looking marginally calmer. "The bedroom isn't as bad as this room," he said. "The cameras are okay. Nothing was broken as far as I can tell."

"I'm sorry," she said, knowing the words weren't enough to cover the destruction. "They must have followed me here. They must have been watching me. That man outside the restaurant... He probably did this, knowing we were there. When he didn't find what he was looking for here, he came after us. I can't believe how much I'm ruining your life."

"It's okay, Julia. It's just stuff. And you're not the one who's ruining my life."

"Of course I am. If I'd never seen that picture, never come here, never started asking questions—"

"Well, you did, and it's done. We can't start second-guessing now."

"So, what's next? Who's next? Are they going to go to my dad's apartment, to my aunt and uncle's home?" she asked. "They're probably watching me right now. And I hate that I don't even know who I'm fighting. It could be one person or two or three—who knows?"

"I certainly don't. It's possible there were two—one here, one at the restaurant watching us."

"Should we call the police?"

"In a minute. Let's take another look at the doll and the necklace. They're the only things you have that might have come from Russia."

They set two of the dining room chairs upright and sat down at the table. Julia opened her bag and pulled out the doll and the necklace. Alex immediately began to take the doll apart. "I know we're missing some dolls," he said. "I wonder if that's important." He examined each doll closely, his brows knitting into a frown as he peered particularly closely at the inside of one doll. "I think there's a number scratched here. It looks like a four to me. What do you think?"

She took the doll from his hand and saw the mark he was referring to. It did look like a four. "I think you're right," she said.

He picked up another doll. "And this one is a seven."

Julia took each doll as he discarded it. In the end they had five dolls and five numbers. "What do you think the numbers mean?"

Alex met her questioning gaze with a shrug of his shoulders. "I have no idea. The problem is, I don't think we have all the numbers, because we don't have all the dolls."

"We should go to that shop, Russian Treasures. Maybe that woman can tell us what the numbers mean. They could just be a production code."

"They could be, but there's nothing uniform about the way they look. It's as if someone scratched the numbers with a sharp knife."

His words sent a chill through her, and something stirred in her mind. A distant memory? She struggled to bring it into focus, but her brain wouldn't cooperate.

Alex sat back in his chair, a frown on his face now. "What's wrong?"

"I thought I was remembering something, but it won't come back."

"Something about the doll?"

"I don't know," she said in frustration.

"Julia, don't force it. The memories will come back when they're supposed to."

"How can you be so patient?" she asked. "I thought you were a man of action."

"When it's called for. But I also know how to wait for the perfect light, the right angle, and the clearest view. Your mind takes photographs of everything you see just the way a camera does. Eventually it will develop those early pictures for you."

"Hopefully before I'm dead," she said, her words a mix of sarcasm and real fear.

"Hopefully," he agreed with a small smile. "We'll check out that Russian store tomorrow. Now, are you sure there isn't anything else your mother might have had that could link you to the doll or that trip to Russia?"

"I went through everything in the storage locker, but my father did say that their business and personal papers are at his apartment. I haven't had a chance to look through them yet." She glanced down at her watch and saw it was after ten. "It's too late to go there tonight. I'm a little afraid to go at all. What if they follow me there, too?" She sat up straight, a terrible idea crossing her mind. "Or perhaps they've already been to my dad's apartment. It wouldn't be difficult to find his address. He's listed in the phone book. I have to call him, make sure he's all right." She rifled through her handbag for her cell phone. "At least he lives in a security building. That's something."

"So far they've struck when no one has been home," Alex said reassuringly. "There's no reason to think that will change."

"There's no reason to think it won't, either. We don't know who we're dealing with. I'm calling my dad."

"And I'll call the police. I think it's time we brought them in on the whole story."

It was almost eleven o'clock at night when Alex ushered two detectives from the San Francisco Police Department out of his apartment. Julia remained in the living room, her heart still racing. The last hour of questions had done nothing to reassure her that she was safe. After telling the police the story of the orphan girl photograph and Julia's recent picture in the Tribune, it had become clear to all of them that the latter event had triggered the break-ins.

Someone had seen Julia's picture, believed her to be that girl, and come looking for something. The detectives had examined the necklace and the matryoshka doll but had been unable to find a reason why the two tourist-type souvenirs would be important. Even if the doll was worth a couple thousand dollars, it wouldn't be enough to trigger the kind of vandalism and burglary that had taken place here tonight or at her apartment earlier that day. There had to be something else.

In the meantime, Julia had called her father and discovered that he was fine. She told him to be careful and alert to anyone lurking around his apartment building or near the restaurant. She'd left a message for Liz on her cell phone, wishing that her sister had picked up, so that Julia could know she was all right. It had occurred to her that Liz might have gone to Michael's house, so she'd even forced herself to call his apartment, but he hadn't answered, either, and she'd gotten the same voice mail on his cell phone. She had to trust they'd be okay as long as they weren't with her. She was the target, not them.

Alex shut the front door and headed for the kitchen. "How about a drink?" he suggested.

"Anything cold would be great."

"You got it." He returned a moment later with two bottles of mineral water.

Julia took a long draught, feeling a renewed sense of energy as the carbonation tickled her throat. Then she looked around the room, and her energy faded as quickly as it had come. They both had a lot of cleaning to do, not to mention major repairs. A lot of the furniture would have to be replaced or fixed before their apartments would really be livable again.

"I wish I'd never gone to the Legion of Honor," she murmured. "Look at the trouble I've brought myself, you, my family."

Alex shrugged, kicking off his shoes. "Never look back," he advised. "It doesn't do any good."

"Do you think the police will be able to find who did this?"

"Doubtful."

"You can't even try to be optimistic?"

"Sorry, but I think whoever broke in here knew what they were doing. It has a feel of professionalism about it. I don't think they left one fingerprint behind."

Julia traced her finger along a particularly ugly gash in the sofa cushion. "This is nasty. And I don't get it. What would I be hiding in a sofa cushion?"

"Something small," he replied, a thoughtful look on his face. "Which would rule out the matryoshka doll, don't you think? It's almost a foot long."

"Exactly. The necklace?"

"It sure doesn't look like anything special. I don't get it."

"Then there's something else at stake, something else they think I have, but I don't. Or I have it, and I don't know it."

He smiled. "That narrows it down."

She blew out a sigh, which turned into a yawn. It had certainly been a long day. She could hardly believe they'd flown back from New York earlier that morning. "We should talk to Mr. Brady again," she said. "Tell him about the break-ins. Maybe he can get someone in his intelligence agency to figure out what's happening."

"I'll call Stan first thing in the morning," he promised. Finishing his bottle of water, he set it down on the table.

For a moment there was silence between them. Julia's mind drifted from the problems of the day to Alex. He was sitting so close, their thighs were practically touching. She could hear him breathing, and the scent of his aftershave washed over her like a warm, inviting breeze— like a call to move closer, to run her lips across his jaw, the corner of his mouth...

Her nerves began to tingle in anticipation. She licked her lips as her pulse quickened.

Should she do it? Should she cross the few inches that separated them, run her hand through his hair, trap his handsome face with her suddenly impatient hands?

Alex cleared his throat. He shot her a hard look, then said, "You should go to bed. I'll take the couch."

Disappointment hit her like a cold shower. He obviously wasn't feeling what she was feeling. "I don't want to put you out of your bed. Besides, this sofa is pretty short, and you're a lot taller than I am." Taller, stronger, sexier... God, why was she so charged up? It must be the extra adrenaline in her body that was making her feel like she wanted to jump on him and not let him up for a long, long time.

"Just take the bed and don't argue. I can sleep anywhere." He quickly got to his feet.

She stared at him, surprised by the harsh tone of his voice. "What's wrong?"

"Nothing. It's been a hell of a day."

"That's it?"

"That's it. Let's call it a night. I'll get the bed made up."

"You don't have to do it. I'll take care of it."

"It's my bed. I'll do it," he snapped.

"Okay." She followed him into the bedroom, watching his sharp, impatient movements as he stripped the tumbled covers and began to remake the bed. "I'll help," she said. "Toss me a corner of the sheet."

"I can do it."

"It will go faster if I help you," she repeated as she moved to the other side of the bed.

"And I said I'd do it."

"Don't be ridiculous." She didn't know why he was being so stubborn. Leaning over, she grabbed the sheet. Alex yanked his end back so quickly that she fell halfway across the bed. Pushing her hair out of her face and feeling extremely irritated now, she tugged on her end of the sheet.

Alex had more strength, but she had a lot of determination. She pulled again, refusing to give up until she'd taken the sheet completely out of his hands. He dove for it. She tried to scramble out of the way, but he landed on top of her, pinning her hands over her head.

She pushed against his chest. He didn't budge. Nor did he appear to have any intention of moving. In fact, his dark eyes glittered with desire as he gazed down on her, and her breath caught in her chest. She was completely at his mercy.

"What is your problem?" she demanded, trying to focus on anger and not desire.

"You. You're my problem. I don't want you in my bed."

"You just said you did. In fact, you insisted."

"I don't want you alone in my bed," he corrected. "You're driving me crazy."

"I am?" she asked, somewhat bemused by that fact.

"I want to make love to you, Julia."

Hearing his intention stated so firmly and clearly made her tremble with anticipation. When he reached out and stroked her cheek with his hand, her whole body tingled. She swallowed hard, trying to think. She'd just broken up with Michael. She couldn't do this.

"You're an amazing woman," Alex murmured, his fingers now tracing her mouth. "So soft, yet so strong when you need to be." She held her breath as he leaned over and replaced his fingers with the tip of his tongue, which he ran lightly across her lips. "Hmm, I want more," he murmured.

So did she, but she couldn't ask, couldn't speak. She could only wait for his mouth to cover hers completely. Despite his words, he didn't immediately deepen the kiss. His mouth hovered just an inch above hers, teasing, taunting, until her nerves began to scream.

Finally, he moved. Or maybe she did.

Their mouths met in a deep, passionate kiss that went on and on. He released her hands, and she immediately flung them around his neck, pulling him closer, running her hands through his hair, enjoying the textures of his mouth, his skin, his hair. His palms skimmed up her sides until his hand covered one breast, his thumb playing the nipple into a tight point. She felt as if she were on fire, losing control with each passing second.

This wasn't her, was it?

She didn't have casual sex, did she?

Not that kissing Alex felt even close to casual.

"Stop thinking," he muttered against her mouth. "I can hear the wheels turning in your brain." He lifted his head to look at her.

"I'm not sure," she whispered. "I just got out of a relationship. I'm not certain I want to dive right into another one." She saw something flicker in his eyes and realized that he didn't want a relationship; he just wanted sex. She felt incredibly disappointed. "Oh," she said. "You're not looking for anything more than tonight or maybe just the next fifteen minutes."

"I think I can do better than fifteen minutes," he said lightly as he sat back. "It doesn't always have to mean something, Julia."

"I think it does—to me." She paused. "I know that sounds like a real girl thing to say, but that's what I am. If we make love tonight, Alex, I'm afraid I might fall in love with you. I don't think you want that."

She wanted him to refute her statement, tell her that's exactly what he wanted, because in truth she was already halfway in love with him, maybe more.

Alex didn't answer for a long tense moment. Then he said, "I'll leave you to make up the bed."

"You're not going to say anything else?"

"I don't make promises I can't keep." He got up and walked to the doorway, then turned back to her. "I don't know what real love is supposed to look like or feel like, Julia. And since you thought you were in love with someone else about eight hours ago, I'm not sure you do, either." On that note he left, closing the door quietly behind him.

She flopped back onto the bed, wondering if she'd made a huge mistake. As she stared up at the ceiling, she considered what he'd just said. He was wrong about one thing: She hadn't been in love with Michael eight hours ago. In fact, she'd probably never been in love with him, not the way she should have been. His kisses had never made her feel so dizzy, so off balance. Michael had been nice, comfortable, caring. Alex was hot, reckless, passionate.

She knew she wanted more in her life than what she'd had with Michael, but Alex was like a stick of dynamite. When it came right down to it, did she really have the courage to go after everything she wanted? She could stay here and play it safe, or she could march out into the living room and take the biggest risk of her life.

Her brain battled her body. Finally logic and caution won out. She couldn't make love with Alex tonight. It was too soon. She was too confused. It wouldn't be right.

But tomorrow was another day.

CHAPTER FIFTEEN

Liz sat in her father's kitchen early Wednesday morning, watching him pour two glasses of orange juice. He topped off his drink with a discreet shot of vodka. She knew she should say something, but she wasn't in the mood to argue with him. She hadn't slept well on his couch, and her nerves were strung tight after the break-in at her apartment. She still had to face going back there and trying to put her belongings back together.

Everything was changing, she thought with a small sigh. Her life felt wrong in every way. Just seeing her father padding around the kitchen in mismatched pajamas with his hair standing on end and an air of fragility about him reminded her how different everything was. Breakfast in her family had always been a big, happy affair. Her mother had loved cooking up plates of eggs, bacon, and potatoes, topped off with fruit, pastries and juice. She'd insisted they all come dressed to the table, their hair brushed, their faces washed, ready to face the day

The man in front of her wasn't the father she remembered from those days. He hadn't bothered to wash his face or brush his hair. She wasn't even sure when he'd last taken a shower or gone in to work. She certainly hadn't seen him at the cafe in days. What on earth was he doing with his time? As she watched him drink his orange juice, she knew she had her answer.

Clearing her throat, she said, "Why don't I make us some breakfast? Would you like scrambled eggs, an omelet, maybe some pancakes?"

He leaned against the counter and gave her a bleary smile. "Your mother used to make pancakes, blueberry pancakes. Those were her favorite."

"I know," she said gently.

He sipped his juice halfway down the glass, licking his lips at the end. She should say something, but the words didn't want to come. Instead, she said, "I could try to make blueberry pancakes. I might have to run down to the store and get some berries, though." She got up from her chair and looked through his cabinets. She was shocked to see how empty they were. "Dad, you don't have any food in the house. What have you been eating?"

"Your aunts take care of me," he said with a shrug. "I don't feel like cooking anymore."

Which meant a lot coming from a man who made his living running a restaurant and prided himself on turning out good, quality food. "Is that why you haven't been down at the restaurant lately?"

"I'm tired of working," he said heavily. "Tired of so many things." He walked over to the table and sat down.

"Is there anything I can do to help?"

He shook his head. "I'll be all right. I'm worried about you and Julia. I think she should stay here, too, although I'm sure Michael wants to take care of her."

Liz saw the question in his eyes and damned Julia for once again not being here to do her own dirty work. She returned to her chair, trying to think of what to say. In the end, she just gave it to him straight. "Michael and Julia broke up last night."

Her father appeared truly shocked by the news. "What?" he stuttered. "How? Why?"

She didn't know which question to answer first. "I'm not sure why, but certainly Julia's push to find the missing pieces of her past didn't help. After Michael saw our apartment last night, he begged her to give up the search. She said she couldn't. She's obsessed, Dad, determined to find the truth. The past twenty-something years don't matter to her as much as the first three or four years of her life that she can't remember. And she seems to have forgotten how good Michael was to her through Mom's illness and how perfect Mom thought Michael was for her." Liz blew out a breath of frustration. "I don't get it. I can't understand why she'd let him go. Maybe he was rushing her a bit, but good grief, they've been together over a year. It's not exactly lightning speed."

"Your mother would be disappointed," Gino said. "And not just in Julia, but in me. I've let my daughter down."

"How do you figure that?"

"I should have paid more attention to what Julia was doing. I should have guided her more."

"It's not your fault. It's Julia's. She's the one making these foolish decisions. She really hurt Michael. I went to his house last night. He was drinking himself into oblivion." As she said the words, Liz wondered if her father would see the parallel between Michael and himself. They were both choosing to dull their pain with alcohol. The problem was that once the alcohol wore off, the pain came back.

Gino didn't appear to make the connection. He finished his juice and got up to make another drink. She should say something, she told herself again. But right now her dad was the only one she had to talk to, and that would end if she attacked his drinking.

"Julia is changing right before my eyes," Liz continued. "Can't you make her stop, Dad? I think she'd listen to you."

He put up a hand. "I can't make her stop. I don't know who her biological father is, but if she is determined to find him, then she should be allowed to do so."

"It's disrespectful to you. You raised her. You treated her like your own daughter."

"And that's the way I think of her. She's my daughter, and I want her to be happy. I'm sorry about Michael, though. He's a good man."

"It's not just her biological father she's interested in," Liz continued. "It's Mom's past as well. Julia is convinced that she's that girl in the picture, which means she had to be in Russia when she was three years old. That means Mom would have had to be there, too. How could that have happened?"

Gino gave a helpless shake of his head. "I can't imagine..."

Liz hesitated to voice her next thought, but she couldn't seem to stop it from coming out. "Do you think Mom could have adopted Julia?"

Gino sent her an angry glare. "No," he said firmly. "Absolutely not. It's impossible. They were close, like two peas in a pod, when I met them. And Sarah would have told me if she'd adopted Julia. She was always honest. She never lied about anything. Don't you remember her telling you over and over that the truth would never get you into trouble—only a lie would do that?"

Liz nodded. She remembered that well. Now she couldn't help wondering if different rules had applied to her mother. "There has to be some reason why Julia looks like that girl."

"It's a coincidence," he said, pouring more orange juice. "Julia was four years old when I met her. I would have noticed if she was speaking Russian."

"That's true," Liz said, relieved. "If she was a Russian orphan, she would have been speaking Russian."

"Of course. Why didn't I think of that? I feel so much better now."

"Julia did have her own little odd way of talking, though," he said with a fond smile. "And she had an imaginary friend she was always whispering to."

Liz's good mood dimmed. "What do you mean, her own way of talking?"

"She'd jumble up words so sometimes they didn't make sense. It was just a phase she went through. It passed. I'm sure you did the same thing. You know how kids talk."

"Yeah, you're probably right." She stiffened as the buzzer rang in the apartment. "I'll get it." She walked over to the intercom. "Yes?"

"It's Julia. Can you let me up?"

Liz pushed the button and glanced over at her father in time to see him pour more vodka into his glass. She drew in a breath and walked out to the living room to answer the door. She wasn't surprised to see Alex standing behind Julia. The two seemed to be joined at the hip these days.

"Hi," Julia said, offering her a tentative smile. "How are you, Lizzie? I called you a couple of times last night, but you never answered your phone."

"I was busy. I do have a life, too, you know."

"How's Dad?" Julia asked, as she and Alex entered the apartment. "I want to talk to him."

"You better talk to him soon. He's in the kitchen sipping vodka and orange juice."

"It's nine o'clock in the morning."

Liz shrugged. "He's a little bothered by all the turmoil. You know, break-ins, pictures in the newspaper, his oldest daughter searching for her past in Russia, of all places."

Julia's mouth tightened. "You don't have to be sarcastic, Liz. I know this is very upsetting for everyone, especially you and Dad."

"And Michael. He was also drinking last night." Liz sent Alex a sharp look. "You better watch yourself. Julia has a way of driving all the men in her life to drink."

"Liz!"

"I'm sorry, but it's true." Liz felt a twinge of remorse for her harsh words, but she didn't intend to apologize to Julia. Her sister was the one who had stirred up their perfectly happy lives. "What are you doing here, anyway? I thought you didn't want to bring trouble to Dad."

"I don't, but I need to look through Mom's papers."

"Julia, is that you?" Gino asked, as he stumbled into the living room. "Are you all right? I've been so worried."

"I'm fine, Dad." Julia gave him a kiss on the cheek. "Is everything all right here?"

"Life goes on," he said with a fatalistic shrug of his shoulders. His eyes narrowed in on Alex. "Who's your friend?"

"I'm sorry. This is Alex Manning," Julia replied. "His father took the photo of the orphan girl. He's helping me find the truth."

Gino stuck out his hand, and Alex shook it. Liz couldn't believe her father was acting so welcoming. She didn't feel nearly as charitable. As far as she was concerned, Alex Manning was egging Julia on. Maybe if he hadn't been in the picture, Julia would have backed off a lot sooner.

"Do you mind if I take a look through Mom's papers?" Julia asked her father. "It's a long shot, but maybe there's something in there."

"Of course," he said. "I have nothing to hide. I don't think your mother did, either. She adored you. You were her baby."

Liz was relieved to hear her father tell Julia that. Someone needed to shake up her sister, remind her of the way life used to be.

"I know she loved me," Julia said, a troubled expression in her eyes. "But some things don't add up. I just want to make them add up."

"I don't want your curiosity to lead you into more danger," Gino said. "You should stay here. I thought Michael was protecting you, but Liz tells me that you've split up."

"Yes. It just wasn't working out. I know you liked him very much. But I feel sure it was the right decision for both of us."

Gino nodded. "It's your life to live, Julia, but Michael is a good man. Your mother loved him."

"I know she did, but I... I didn't. Not enough to marry him. That wouldn't have been fair."

Gino sent Alex a speculative look. Her father was probably wondering the same thing she was, Liz thought—if Julia's feelings about Michael had changed with the introduction of Alex into her life.

"I don't want to stay here," Julia added. "I don't want to put you in danger."

"But you don't mind putting this man in danger? It's not appropriate that you're staying with him." His voice took on a sharp edge. For all his kindness, their father was traditional in his views toward men and women sleeping together before marriage.

"Alex's apartment was broken into yesterday, too," Julia said.

"Are you serious?" Liz asked, stunned.

Julia nodded. "Yes, I think I was followed there."

Liz gazed into her sister's eyes and saw regret, but Julia obviously wasn't sorry enough. "So they could be outside right now," she said, "waiting to do the same thing to this apartment. How could you come here and put Dad in danger?"

"We weren't followed," Alex interrupted. "I'm sure of it. We took separate cars. We changed over to a friend's car in a crowded parking lot before we came here."

Liz sniffed, determined not to let on that she was at all impressed by their cloak-and-dagger maneuvering.

"I also told the police everything," Julia said. "They're going to be watching this apartment, too, just in case."

"You need to stop asking questions," Liz said. "Then we'll all be safe again."

"We won't be safe until we find what they're looking for." Julia turned back to Gino. "Are the papers in the second bedroom?"

"Yes. The room is in chaos. I'm sorry. I haven't had the energy to clean it up. I'll let you get to it, then." He meandered down the hall to the kitchen, probably to refill his glass, Liz thought. When he was gone, she turned on Julia, her anger and resentment coming to the fore. "Dad is drinking himself to death, Julia. Don't you even care?"

Julia took a step back in defense. "Of course I care, but I'm a little busy at the moment."

"Too busy for your own father? That's great."

"Liz, please."

"Please what? He's been drinking orange juice and vodka since he got up. He hasn't been to work. He hasn't gotten dressed in days. Did you even notice?"

"Well, you're here," Julia retorted. "Why don't you stop him, Liz? As far as I can tell, you're doing nothing. In fact, that's pretty much all you've been doing the last few months."

Liz didn't like the way Julia had turned the tables on her. "What are you talking about?"

"You keep waiting for everyone else to do something. You want me to stop looking for my past. You want Dad to stop drinking. You want me to intervene in that. What about you? What do you want? Ever since Mom got sick, you've been drifting along, whining about how everyone else is disappointing you. Are you going to finish college or just work at the cafe for the rest of your life? Don't you have any dreams of your own?"

"I—I don't know." Liz felt overwhelmed by the hard-hitting questions. A flood of tears pressed against her eyes, and she forced herself to hold them back. She did not want to cry in front of Julia and Alex. But suddenly she couldn't contain her emotions, so she ran.

She didn't stop running until she was halfway down the street. She was furious. She was hurt. Most of all she was stunned to realize that Julia was right. She stopped walking to wipe away the tears that were streaming down her face. God! Julia was right. She'd put her life on hold the second her mother had been diagnosed with cancer. She hadn't been able to see the future—because the future would be without her mother. And that was too painful to consider. In the months that had followed, she'd never taken her life off hold. She had no plan, no purpose, no nothing.

And as she looked around, she also realized she had absolutely nowhere to go.

"I can't believe I just said that. I should go after her." Julia stared at the door Liz had recently slammed, feeling incredibly guilty that she'd taken out her frustration on her sister.

"It sounded like you needed to say it."

"I hurt her feelings."

"Probably," Alex agreed.

She shot him a dark look. "You're supposed to say, 'No, you didn't. Don't worry about it'."

He shrugged his shoulders. "I don't have a sister or a sibling. I don't know the protocol."

Frustrated, Julia waved a hand in the air. "Liz has been on me so much the past few days. She wants to run my life, and she criticizes every decision I make. I guess I got tired of it. You're lucky you're an only child."

"I agree." He paused. "Are you going after her, or are we looking for the papers?"

She debated for a long moment. She seemed to be doing that a lot lately. Making decisions had once been easy for her, probably because she'd never had anything really important to decide. Now, every day there seemed to be new, compelling, distracting choices. She'd spent most of the night before weighing the risks and benefits of inviting Alex back into his own bedroom. In the end, she'd taken the safe route and done nothing. She'd slept alone in the bed, with Alex on the couch in the living room. She was still mad at herself for that.

One of these days she would have to do something bold, something completely out of character. Maybe she'd start with letting Liz stew awhile instead of immediately trying to be the peacemaker, as she usually did.

"We're here. Let's search," she said decisively. "I'll talk to Liz later. Maybe if I find out something, it will be easier to make up with her."

"Don't count on it," he said pessimistically. "I have a feeling we've just hit the tip of the iceberg. This situation is going to get worse before it gets better."

"Thanks for that sunny thought," she said as she led him down the hall to the second bedroom.

"I'm a realist. In my job I have to be. The camera doesn't lie."

"But people do. And that's what we have to figure out now. Who was lying and what were they lying about?" She paused in the doorway, not surprised to see the clutter of boxes, books, and clothes. "This will take some time. At least with two of us, it will go faster."

Alex glanced around the room. "What is all this stuff?"

"I'm not sure. My dad sold our family home right after my mom died, and the market was so hot, the house sold in a day. We put some things in storage, because we weren't up to going through it all. I guess the office stuff and my parents' bedroom things are what's in here. Where should we start?"

"Let's work our way into the room."

She knelt down and opened the first box. "It's weird how in the end our lives boil down to things."

"Some really ugly things." Alex held up a statue of a deformed man. "Don't tell me this was on your coffee table."

She laughed. "My mom made that in a sculpting class. It was the first thing she ever made. We took the class together at the recreation center. I wanted to do something artistic, and she wanted to do some-thing with me." Her smile faded as she thought about how much time they'd spent together with all the lies between them.

"Don't do that," Alex said. "Don't replace all the good memories with doubts."

She gave him a curious look. "How did you know I was doing that?"

"Experience. It's a waste of energy. It won't get you anywhere."

"I guess you're right, but it's hard."

"Look at this," Alex said, holding up a manila file folder. He pulled out a piece of paper. "Your birth certificate."

She took the paper out of his hand. She'd seen it before when she'd gotten her driver's license and on other occasions. But now she read it more closely. There was no father's name listed, just her mother's and hers, and the hospital, St. Claire's, Berkeley, California. "It sure looks like I was born here. It has an official State of California stamp."

"It looks authentic," Alex agreed, "but papers can be bought and paid for, especially if a governmental agency is involved."

"That's what the reporter told me. I didn't know it was so easy to make up an identity for someone."

"If your mother did that, she had help."

Julia dug into her own box, which consisted mostly of scarves, gloves, and other accessories. Nothing there. She turned to the next one.

A moment later, Alex whistled. "You were a chubby little girl."

She frowned, slipping the photo from his hand. It had been taken at her eleventh birthday party, and she was definitely bulging. "They fed me a lot of Italian food," she complained. "My family thinks the more you eat, the happier you are, and I hadn't lost my baby fat yet."

"You're carrying more than a baby there," he teased. "And look at those railroad tracks on your teeth."

"Oh, shut up. I'm sure you weren't always this attractive."

"So you think I'm attractive?" he said with a charming wink.

"I think you're full of yourself, that's what I think."

"You like me."

"I don't." But she was still smiling when she tossed the photo back into the box. "Concentrate on what you're doing."

Slowly but surely she progressed through the boxes and moved across the room, finally landing on a box of costumes. Now that she knew her mother had traveled to Russia as a seamstress, the costumes took on new meaning. She pulled out the red cape she'd worn when she'd played Little Red Riding Hood in the third grade, then the angel costume she'd sported one Halloween. "We always had homemade costumes," she said. "My mother loved to sew. She never said she'd done it professionally, though."

"Of course she didn't," Alex replied. "She obviously wanted to hide her past in every possible way."

"Which means we probably won't find anything here."

"Keep digging. Sometimes people get careless."

With a sigh, Julia set back to work. The next box held Christmas cards and letters and an address book. The floral-patterned address book had been by her mother's bed the day she died. Her mother had wanted to let people know she was sick and was thinking of them, so she'd spent most of the last month writing brief notes. When she was too tired to hold the pen, Julia and sometimes Liz had written them for her. Unlike most of the other items in the room, which were from happier times, the address book reminded Julia of how bad that last week had been, watching her mother fade away before her very eyes. She was glad that she had been with her, but sometimes she was sad, too, because the image of death occasionally overpowered the other memories. She didn't want to remember her mother sick; she wanted to think of her happy and healthy.

Sitting cross-legged on the floor, she opened the address book and skimmed through the pages. There were three letters stuck in the back of the book, addressed and stamped and ready to go. Liz was supposed to have mailed them the day they were written, but she must have forgotten. The first one was to Pamela Hunt, the mother of a close friend of Julia's. The second was addressed to Grace Barrington, one of the waitresses who had worked at DeMarco's for at least a decade. And the third... Julia held the envelope up to the light, realizing that the writing was definitely her mother's, the letters weak and somewhat messy, making the name almost illegible. It took her a moment to decipher the writing.

"This is odd. It's addressed to Rick Sanders. I've never heard of anyone by that name."

Alex came to her side, squatting down next to her. "Why don't you open it?"

"Do you think I should? It's my mom's personal letter. She meant to mail it the day before she died. I remember watching her struggle to write it, but she said she had something important to say."

"Maybe a confession," Alex suggested. "Go on, open it."

"Why would she confess to someone named Rick Sanders?" At his pointed glance, she slid a finger under the flap and opened the envelope. There was one piece of notepaper inside. Julia took a breath and began to read. *'Dear Rick. I know we agreed not to speak, but I must let you know that I'm very sick. I don't think I'll make it another month..."* Julia's voice faltered as she realized she was reading some of her mother's very last words. "I can't." She held the paper out to Alex.

He took over. *"I'll think of you fondly always. I know you were angry with me for what I did, but it worked out the best for all of us. Julia is a beautiful woman now. And I have another daughter as well. My life turned out to be very happy. I hope that you, too, were able to find some happiness. I know you made the ultimate sacrifice, but I was never surprised by your actions. You were and are the most heroic man I've ever known. Love, Sarah."*

Alex lifted his head, his gaze meeting hers. "Who do you think it is?" she asked. "Who is Rick Sanders?"

"Maybe we should ask your father."

"I don't think so. I don't believe he would want to read a letter like this from my mother to another man, one signed with love."

Alex turned over the envelope. "The address is in St. Helena. That's about an hour and a half from here, isn't it?"

"Just north of Napa. You're not thinking of going there, are you?"

"Why not? You said your mother wrote this letter just before she died, and that it was important. I think we should deliver it personally."

"It's odd how she spoke of me by name, as if the person would know me, but not Liz," Julia mused. "You're right. We need to go there."

"What about work? Do you have a show tonight?"

"That was the call I made earlier. I've already arranged to cover my job for a few days so I can devote my time to figuring out what's going on." She paused. "We haven't completely finished here."

"It doesn't look like these boxes are going anywhere."

"You're right about that. I'm sure my dad hasn't set foot in this room since he moved in." She hesitated. "I should say good-bye to him. And I should probably talk to him about the drinking he's doing. Liz is right. I have been shirking my responsibilities in that regard."

"That sounds like too long a conversation to have right now. And one you should probably have when your father is one hundred percent sober," he pointed out.

"True. I guess it can wait. I just hope my mother wasn't having an affair with Rick Sanders. My father would be devastated—" She stopped abruptly, clapping a hand to her mouth. "Oh, my God. You don't think Rick Sanders is my real father, do you?"

Julia had two hours to ponder that question on the drive to St. Helena, a small town in the wine country north of San Francisco. She'd been focusing so much on her mother that she hadn't thought about her biological father, but it made sense that her mother would have written to him just before she died. What didn't make sense was that she'd kept him a secret, never told Julia who he was or where he lived, which wasn't all that far from where she'd grown up.

As Alex turned off the freeway, Julia rolled down the window and let the fresh air blow against her face and through her hair. It really was a beautiful area, she thought, as they passed apple orchards and fields of grapevines from which were made some of the best wines in the world. Growing up in an Italian family, she'd certainly tasted her fair share of red wine, but she'd never actually toured the wine country. Her father and uncle had gone a few times, but her mother had never been interested.

Why? Because the wine country was too close to someone of significance in her life?

"You haven't said a word in about an hour," Alex commented. "What's on your mind?"

"I keep wondering if I'm going to see my father in a few minutes. What will I say? What will I do?"

"You don't know that Rick Sanders is your father."

"I know my mom mentioned me specifically and then added that she'd had another daughter. He has to be someone she knew before she married Gino."

"That still doesn't make him your father."

"I need to be ready just in case. I used to think about meeting my dad, especially when I was a teenager. I'd look in the mirror, and I wouldn't see my mother in my features. I kept thinking that there was someone else in the world who looked like me. Of course, I didn't imagine that it was a little girl in a Russian orphanage," she said with a halfhearted smile,

He grinned back at her. "Good. You still have your sense of humor. That's important."

"Why is that important?"

"Laughter can get you through life. I've spent a lot of time in Africa, in villages where half the parents are gone, dead from HIV and other diseases. I couldn't believe these people could find anything to smile about, but every time I took out my camera, that's just what they did. They smiled in the face of unspeakable poverty."

Julia turned in her seat to look at him. His eyes were on the road, but she could tell his thoughts were in the past.

"I gave this one little boy a pen and a piece of paper," Alex continued. "You would have thought I'd just handed him a million dollars. He couldn't stop smiling. He played and drew all day long until there wasn't a centimeter of empty space on that piece of paper."

"Did you ever see him again? Do you ever see anyone again—the people whose pictures you take?"

He shook his head. "Most of the time I don't go back to the same location. Occasionally I do. I did return to that village about a year later."

"Please don't tell me he was dead." She hated to think of such a sad thing.

"I don't know what happened to him. The whole village was gone, wiped out by a flood. They said some people got out, but they had scattered to other villages. No one knew about that particular boy."

"So maybe he's still there playing with your pen and smiling."

He offered her a tender smile. "You have a soft heart, Julia. That could get you into trouble."

"I suspect it already has."

"Is that why you let things drag on with Michael? You didn't want to hurt his feelings?"

"Partly. I do care for him, and he treated me well. I never wanted to hurt him." She paused. "But I wasn't referring to Michael. I was thinking about my mom, how I never had the guts to ask her the questions I'm asking now. I let her put me off, because I didn't want to make her mad or upset her. And look where that got me."

"You said you had a good relationship with her, so your silence bought you that."

"I suppose. We talked all the time, even when I moved out of the house. She always knew what I was up to. She just couldn't stop checking up on me."

"How long was she sick?"

"About two years from start to finish. The last six months were particularly bad. It was difficult to watch. At least we had time to say our good-byes. I thought we had taken care of everything important. But I know now that my mom concentrated on things in the present or the future. She never spoke of the past in all the time she was sick. She only wanted to discuss what we would do later, after she was gone. Up until the very end of her life, she kept her secrets. I wonder if I'll ever know why."

"There's a good possibility you will know why, but you may wish you didn't before this is over."

"At this point, I'd take any truth over the uncertainty."

Alex shot her a speculative look. "Easy to say now. You don't know how bad it could be."

"Are you trying to prepare me for something? Do you have some suspicion you haven't shared?"

"I know what you know," he replied. "But I've seen some crazy shit in this world. You never know what people are capable of doing."

She probably didn't know. She'd led a sheltered life, protected from the harsh side of reality, protected by her mother. She sighed as she glanced out the window. The sign for St. Helena came into view. "Ready or not, here we come," she muttered.

"Are you talking about Rick Sanders or us?"

"Both. I don't have a good feeling about this, Alex."

"I haven't had a good feeling since you knocked on my door last Friday."

For a while they drove along a rural frontage road dotted by farms, horses, a couple of cows, and small homes. Julia breathed in the scent of freshly cut grass. It was a beautiful day, with a royal blue sky and a bright sun, the kind of day that reminded her summer was not far behind them and winter was still a ways off. It was also the kind of day that seemed too bright for anything bad to happen. She hoped that would be the case.

Alex asked her to check the map. She told him to turn right at the next intersection. Gradually the landscape grew more crowded with homes, businesses, gas stations, and strip malls. Rick Sanders lived on a street called Caribbean Court. Julia didn't think the area at all resembled the Caribbean. The address they were seeking matched a modest one-story, ranch-style home. There was a beat-up Chevy, at least twenty years old, in the driveway. The grass in the front yard was sparse, dry, with big areas of dirt. The flowers were wilted, weeds growing between rosebushes planted along the front of the house.

Julia's nervousness intensified as they parked the car and got out.

Was she actually going to meet her father? On this day? At this moment?

Would she know instinctively when she saw him? Or would he seem like a stranger?

She put her hand on Alex's arm as he started down the walk. "Wait. I don't think I'm ready."

"You don't have to say or do anything, Julia. I'll handle it. I'll mention your mother's name. We'll see how he responds. You can just watch, listen."

"What if he says something to me when he sees me? What if he recognizes me? What if I don't want him to be my father?" He smiled at her, and she knew she was flipping out. "Too many questions?"

"One step at a time."

"I like to be prepared for any possibility."

"Sometimes the best things come when you least expect them."

"Or the worst."

"Who's the pessimist now?"

"All right." She drew in a deep breath. "Let's go. I hope he's home."

As soon as Alex rang the bell, they heard the sound of a dog barking and a man's voice, telling the dog to quiet down. A moment later the door opened. Julia blinked. The sun streaming in behind them put the man in shadow. All she could see was his blue shirt and white shorts. His features were completely indistinguishable.

Alex grabbed her arm and squeezed tight.

"Ow," she said, but he didn't appear to hear her. He was staring at the man with shock and horror.

The man stepped onto the porch, and finally Julia could see him. His hair was dark, his eyes a light green.

"Rick Sanders?" she queried.

Silence met her question. Then the man drew in a deep breath and said, "Not exactly. Do you want to tell her, Alex?"

"You know him?" Julia asked in amazement.

Alex's mouth tightened. "Goddammit, Julia. He's my father."

CHAPTER SIXTEEN

ALEX COULDN'T BELIEVE what he was seeing. The man in front of him could not possibly be his father. His father was dead!

But the brown hair, the green eyes, the long, thin face looked so familiar.

Alex blinked once, twice, three times. The image in front of him didn't change. He still saw his father's face. He was older, definitely. There were lines around his eyes, some gray in his hair, slack in his skin. But he hadn't changed that much. He was still the man who'd supposedly died twenty-five years ago, the man who had driven his car off the edge of a cliff, the man who Alex believed had been murdered.

How could this be? It was impossible. It was unbelievable.

His father—Charles Manning—was alive.

Alex put a hand on his gut, feeling like he was about to throw up. His breath came fast, his heart pounding against his chest. He couldn't think.

"Alex." Charles held out a tentative hand.

Alex jumped back, knocking his hand away. "What the hell is going on? Who are you?"

"You know who I am. You just said so." Charles stared at him through eyes dark with pain and guilt. "How did you find me?"

The question went through his head twice before it made sense. "I wasn't even looking for you," Alex said finally, feeling a deep and bitter anger rising through his body. "I came here looking for Rick Sanders."

"Why?"

Alex couldn't remember why now. His mind was spinning.

"Because my mother wrote you a letter that she never mailed," Julia interjected. "My mother's name was Sarah. I believe you knew her."

His father drew in a quick, hard breath. "Sarah? She sent you?"

"No. She's dead," Julia said bluntly.

Alex saw the surprise flare in his father's eyes. Whatever else he knew, he hadn't known that.

"When did it happen?" Charles asked.

"Six months ago." Julia handed him the letter. "She wrote you the day before she died. I didn't find the letter until today. I thought I'd personally deliver it. I didn't know that you..." Her voice trailed away.

Charles Manning stared down at the letter in his hand but made no attempt to read it. Then he glanced back at Alex. "Will you come in, so we can talk?" He stepped aside so they could enter the house.

Alex hesitated. Did he want to go in? Did he want to listen to anything this man had to say? He was still reeling. His father had let him believe he was dead for years and years. How could he possibly explain that?

"Let's go inside," Julia said quietly, her hand on his arm.

He'd forgotten she was there. He looked down at her and saw compassion in her eyes. "Looks like you weren't the one who had to worry," he said sharply.

"We need to hear what your father has to say."

"What could he say? How could he possibly explain the fact that he's alive and living under another name?"

She didn't try to answer his question. Neither did his father. They both just stared at him. Alex knew he needed to go inside. He needed to talk to his father. But this was wrong. It was all wrong. They had come here to find Julia's father, unlock the secret of her past. He was supposed to be the observer, not the participant. Dammit.

He wasn't ready for this confrontation. He'd never be ready.

This was his father.

The last time they'd spoken, Alex had been nine years old. And right now he felt about nine, overwhelmed with emotions that normally had no place in his life.

Julia tried to take his hand, but he pulled away. He couldn't stand to touch her. Couldn't stand to feel anything more than he was feeling. He walked into the house, looking around the dingy room. There was a green couch along one wall, a ripped, taped armchair in a corner in front of an old television set. A dog barked from behind a gate in the kitchen.

"Noah, quiet," Charles said sharply.

The dog barked once in reply, then sank to the ground.

Alex stared at the black lab with the white streak down its nose. His father had a dog—the pet he'd never been allowed to have. His mother had always said dogs were too messy, too much work, and his father was always on the road, so that was that. But now his dad had a dog. Unbelievable.

"Alex, let's sit down," Julia suggested.

He shook his head, his gazed fixed on his father's face. "You want to talk—talk."

Charles cleared his throat. "I don't know what to say. I wondered if this day would ever come."

"You did? You wondered?" Alex tasted bile in the back of his throat. "When did you wonder? The day we buried an empty box in the ground, or was it later? Were you at your own funeral? Did you watch us grieving over you? Was it a big joke?"

"No, of course not."

"How could you do that to us? How could you let us believe you were dead?"

Charles stared back at him with apology in his eyes. "I'm sorry, Alex. I'm sorry you had to find out like this."

"No, you're just sorry I found out."

"It's a long, complicated story."

"So start explaining. Not that I have any reason to believe a word you say."

"I deserved that," Charles said.

"I don't know what you deserve. Why don't you start with why you faked your own death to your wife and child?"

"To protect you," Charles answered.

"From what?" Alex's hands clenched into fists. He was so angry he wanted to hit someone or something. It was all he could do not to give in to the impulse.

"From the people who were after me because of the photo you'd taken."

Alex hated being reminded that the photo was his fault. He'd blamed himself for his father's death even before this past week. He'd always felt that somehow he'd been responsible. Then when Stan and later Brady told him his father had been murdered... He shook his head as anger raced through him once again. "I can't believe I blamed myself for your fake death."

"Why would you blame yourself for my accident?" Charles asked sharply.

"Let's see—maybe it was because Daniel Brady told me yesterday that you were killed because of that picture I took."

"Brady told you that? Did he tell you I was alive?"

"No, he didn't mention that little fact." Alex's stomach burned once again as he remembered that Daniel Brady had told them Charles was probably murdered, and he'd said it with a straight face. "That bastard," he murmured. "He knew all along you were alive."

"He helped me set up the crash," Charles admitted. "Brady was never supposed to tell you it was anything but an accident." He paused, his eyes serious. "He must have wanted to scare you off. Why were you talking to him?"

Alex ignored that. "Does Mom know that you're alive?"

Charles shook his head. "No."

That was a small consolation. At least he hadn't been the only one duped.

"After the photo was published, I received a death threat," his father said. "I knew you and your mother were in danger. The only way I could protect you was to die. If I were dead, you would be free."

"You're going to have to give me more than that," Alex said, pacing back and forth across the room, adrenaline rushing through his bloodstream. He couldn't handle the emotions ripping through him—anger, frustration, disappointment, sadness, bewilderment...

"It's too dangerous to tell you more," his father replied. "I've protected you all these years. I won't stop now just because you're grown."

"How dare you tell me that you've protected me! You left me fatherless and alone. You let me grow up thinking you were dead. Do you have any idea what that was like?" Twenty-five years of grief and rage for all that he'd lost with his dad drove him over the edge. Alex picked up the glass vase on top of the television console and heaved it toward the fireplace. The glass shattered into a million pieces. He felt only marginally better.

"Alex, calm down," Julia said, worry in her eyes.

"Why should I? He broke up my life."

"I know you're upset," Charles began.

"That doesn't even touch what I'm feeling. How the hell can you stand there and talk about protecting me when you walked out on me? I wanted to be just like you. God! I can't believe I ever thought that way." He bit down on his bottom lip so hard he tasted blood. "I'm not doing this," he said. He headed for the door, his only thought to get as far away from his father as possible.

"Wait, don't go," Charles said. "We need to talk this out."

Alex paused in the doorway. "How are we going to talk when you won't tell me anything? I'm done. You can keep your secrets. I don't give a damn anymore. I'm out of here." Alex slammed out of the door, striding down to the sidewalk so fast he barely felt his feet hit the pavement. He was so mad. His head was pounding, and his nerves felt as if they were on fire.

"Hang on, Alex," Julia yelled. She caught up with him at the car. "I'm driving."

"No, you're not."

"Yes, I am. You're in no condition to drive. You'd probably run us off the road."

"You must be mistaking me for my father. He's the one who runs off roads and pretends to be dead." He slammed his fist down on the hood of the car, relishing the pain that shot through his fingers and up his arm. He could handle that pain. He could handle what was real, what made sense.

"Give me the keys," Julia said, blocking his way into the car.

"I am fine."

"You're nowhere close to fine. And you know it."

He didn't want to waste time arguing with her. He tossed her the keys. "Drive fast," he ordered. "I want to get the hell away from here."

They should have stayed and talked it out, Julia thought as she drove Alex back to San Francisco.

There were questions that should have been asked—about the photograph, about Sarah, about herself. Those questions would have to wait. When Alex had time to think, to recover, maybe he'd be more receptive to another discussion. If not, she'd do it on her own. But she wouldn't leave him now. For the first time since she'd met him, he seemed completely overwhelmed and out of control. Every muscle in his body was clenched. There was a nervous, reckless, angry energy about him as he tapped his fingers on his leg, then the armrest, shifting every few minutes as if he couldn't possibly get comfortable. She doubted he would feel comfortable for a very long time.

His father was alive. She couldn't imagine what Alex must have felt when his father stepped onto that porch. She knew how much Alex had idolized his father and how much he loved him. In fact, up until this moment she might have said that Charles Manning was the only person Alex had ever loved with any kind of depth. He certainly didn't seem to possess the same emotion for his mother or for any other woman in his life.

She shot him a sideways glance, wondering what he would tell his mother. But she wouldn't ask. She couldn't push him right now. He was a spark ready to explode.

"Can't you drive any faster?" Alex asked as they crossed the Bay Bridge to San Francisco. "Why don't you change lanes?"

"Alex, chill. Do you want me to turn on some music?"

"No." Alex tugged on the seat belt restraining him and shifted in his seat once more. He breathed out a heavy sigh, then said, "He's not dead, Julia."

She cast him a quick glance, but he was staring straight ahead. "I know," she said.

"I watched them put an empty casket into the ground. I didn't know it was empty at the time. No one explained that to me when I was nine, but I figured it out later. I don't even have to close my eyes to remember the cemetery staff throwing big chunks of dirt onto the casket after they'd put it into the ground. My mother didn't want me to watch, but I couldn't look away." He turned to her. "Where do you think he was? Hiding behind some tree or statue in the cemetery? Was he watching us cry for him? How could he let us think he was dead? What kind of man does that to his child and his wife?"

"I'm sorry, Alex."

He didn't seem to hear her. He was too lost in his thoughts, his memories. "I went into my parents' bedroom during the reception after the funeral. I didn't understand why people were laughing and talking as if nothing had happened. I wanted to feel closer to my father, so I went into the room my parents shared when they'd been living together. He hadn't been there in months, but I thought I could still smell his aftershave. I went into the closet where he had left some clothes hanging in the back. I stayed in that closet for over an hour."

Her heart broke at the image of the lonely, terrified little boy he described. "Did your mother find you?" she asked softly, hoping that Kate Manning had had enough tenderness at that point to pull a nine-year-old Alex into her arms and hold him.

"No, she didn't come looking for me. Eventually, I came out on my own and put myself to bed. He was gone and I had to accept it. So I did." Alex rubbed his forehead with his fingers as if he had a pounding headache.

"I have some aspirin in my purse," she offered.

"I don't need it. I'm fine."

"Yeah, you already told me that."

A few minutes later she exited the bridge and drove straight to Alex's apartment building, hoping she wouldn't find any more surprises. They'd have to pick up their cars later and return the car they were driving to Alex's friend. But at the moment all she wanted to do was get Alex home.

When they entered the apartment, it was just as they'd left it—complete and total devastation. Maybe it was a good time to clean up. It would give them something else to focus on besides the horrible truth they'd just uncovered.

She followed Alex into the bedroom, surprised when he pulled out an overnight bag from the closet and tossed it onto the bed. "What are you doing?" she asked.

"I'm leaving."

She was shocked. Those were the last words she'd expected him to say. "What do you mean?"

"I'm getting out of here. I don't need this," he said, running his hand through his hair. His eyes were wild, filled with reckless anger. "A good photographer doesn't get involved with his subjects. He stays on the right side of the lens," he added. "I never should have gotten involved with you."

"But you did get involved, and you can't leave. We're not finished. We don't know everything."

"I know more than enough. You can talk to my father on your own. I'm sure he can help you figure out the rest. Maybe he'll tell you more if I'm not there, if he doesn't have to protect me," he said with bitterness.

"I know you're hurt—"

"You don't know anything."

"Yes, I do," she argued. "Your father lied to you. My mother lied to me. I know how it feels to have the rug pulled out from under your feet."

"Your mother didn't pretend she was dead."

"She did to her own parents." She paused, letting that sink in. "Don't you think it's another odd coincidence that both of our parents chose to do that to the people they loved? Doesn't that make you wonder exactly what they were involved in? It had to be big, Alex. These aren't tiny white lies, little secrets. Don't you want to know exactly what happened?"

He hesitated, a flicker of uncertainty flashing through his eyes; then he shook his head, his mouth drawing once again into a taut, resolute line. "I don't care about any of it. My father left my life twenty-five years ago. I've gotten along fine without him and without knowing anything else. I can go another twenty-five years the same way."

"No, you can't."

"Watch me." He zipped up his bag and went to the closet to get his camera case.

Julia wished she could find the right words to stop him from leaving, but he seemed hell-bent on doing just that. "Is there anything I can say to make you change your mind?"

"No. You should stay with your father. Don't hang out on your own," he advised.

"What do you care? You'll be gone." She wanted him to reply, but he just continued packing. She walked out of the bedroom, into the living room, hoping with every step that he'd call her back. There was nothing but silence.

Julia took a cab to where she'd left her car, then decided to return home and figure out her next step. She could drive back to St. Helena on her own, but it was late afternoon and the traffic would be bad. Besides, she needed time to process everything they'd learned.

When she entered her apartment, she found Liz, dressed in blue jeans and a skimpy T-shirt, doing her own packing. She had two suitcases on Julia's bed and was quickly filling them up.

"What are you doing?" Julia asked, unable to believe she would have to play out the same scene again—this time with her sister.

"I'm moving out," Liz announced.

"Why?"

Liz paused and stared at her as if she couldn't believe the question. "Why do you think? I don't want to be a part of your search. It's obviously dangerous. Not that you care about risking my life."

"Of course I care, Liz."

"But it's not even about that. It's what you said earlier."

Julia felt a wave of guilt. "I'm sorry if I came down too hard on you. I just can't keep fighting you and everyone else at the same time."

"No, you were right. I've been drifting aimlessly for too long. I moved in here because I didn't know where else to go. And I wanted you to get married to Michael so I'd have a wedding to plan, even if it wasn't my own. I urged you to talk to Dad about his drinking so he wouldn't get mad at me. I even wanted Michael to let me help him with his new house so I'd have something else to do besides work at a place where I ladle soup into bread bowls and wait tables."

Julia couldn't believe what she was hearing, but she didn't intend to argue. Instead she said, "It's understandable that you've been drifting, Liz. Mom just died. It was a long illness. I drifted, too. That's why I let Michael and me go on for so long. In fact, I think that's why I started dating him in the first place. Mom had just gotten sick, and I thought how fast life was going and how I was almost thirty and I wasn't close to getting married. I latched onto Michael like he was a buoy and I was drowning." She walked farther into the room. "Don't move out. Let's just start over."

Liz put up a hand in defense. "No. We can't start over, because you're still involved in searching for your past, and I can't be part of that. I'm afraid of where that search will take you and what our relationship will be when you're done."

"We'll always be sisters."

"You say that now, but your feelings might change."

"They won't. I know they won't."

Liz shrugged. "All right. I'll believe you for the moment, but I'm still moving out. I don't want to live here with some madman running around after you, and I also need to take a step forward for myself. This seems like a good time to do that."

"Where are you going? To Dad's?"

"That would be easy, but no. Mary down at the cafe told me that her sister is in Europe for two weeks. I'm going to stay at her place while I look for something more permanent." Liz paused. "I don't think you should stay here alone. Maybe you should move in with Alex."

Julia shook her head. "I can't do that. Alex is leaving."

Liz's eyes widened in surprise. "Where's he going?"

"Back to work," she said simply, not having the energy to get into a lengthier discussion.

"Just like that he takes off? Nice guy. So what will you do now? I thought you needed his help to figure out your secret past."

"I'll do it on my own. I can handle it." She wasn't nearly as confident as her words.

"Maybe I should stay here after all," Liz said halfheartedly. "I don't want you to be alone."

Julia hesitated. She didn't want to be alone, either, but she also didn't want Liz in danger. And she knew that Liz needed to make this move for herself. "I'll be fine. I'll probably find somewhere else to stay, a friend's house or something. Don't worry about me."

"I can't help it." Liz gave her a disgusted smile. "You're my sister." She walked over to Julia and put her arms around her, giving her a quick hug. "Be careful, okay?"

"I will. I promise."

As Liz left, Julia sat down on her bed and gazed around the room, which was in the same state she'd left it in yesterday. She might as well start cleaning, throwing away the broken pieces of her life. It would give her something to do while she considered her next move. And tomorrow she would go back to St. Helena and talk to Charles Manning. He was her only link to the past. Maybe Alex was right. Maybe his father would tell her more if she were on her own. She just hoped she was ready to hear it.

It was almost midnight when the knock came at her door. Julia started at the sound. She set down the broom she'd been sweeping with in the kitchen and moved cautiously to the front door. She didn't live in a security building, so anyone could come right up to her door. But she did have the deadbolt on as well as a chain. She peered through the peephole and was shocked to see Alex on the other side. She'd thought he'd be on a plane to some other continent by now.

"You came back," she said as she opened the door. Alex still wore the blue jeans and black polo shirt he'd had on earlier, but there was no sign of the overnight bag he'd been packing when she'd left his apartment. "What are you doing here?"

"Hell if I know," he said cryptically, as he walked into her apartment. "I see you've cleaned up."

"As much as I could. Some of the furniture I'll have to replace."

"Where's your sister?"

"She moved out earlier. She's going to get her own place."

His eyes narrowed. "That was sudden."

"Not really. We haven't been living together all that well the past few months. She only intended to stay here temporarily after my mom died and my dad sold the house. One day just ran into the next." She stopped abruptly. "You didn't come here to talk about Liz. So, why did you come? You couldn't get a flight out tonight?"

He crossed his arms in front of his chest. "I went to the airport. I bought a ticket, stood in the security line, waited at the gate. When they called my seat number, I couldn't make myself get on the plane. My bags are on their way to Peru right now, and I'm probably on some FBI flight watch for bailing at the last minute." He looked into her eyes and sighed. "I kept thinking about you, Julia, and the deal we made to find the truth together. You should have called me on that earlier."

"How could I after what you learned today?"

His expression turned grim. "I don't want to talk about that."

"How can we not? Your father—"

"Don't call him my father. Call him Rick Sanders. That's who he is now." Alex looked away from her, but she could tell he was battling his emotions.

She walked over to him and put a hand on his arm, but he shrugged it off.

"Don't feel sorry for me. I don't want your pity," he said.

"What do you want from me?"

A long silence followed her question. Finally, he gazed back at her. "I don't think you're going to give me what I want." He put his hands on her waist and pulled her up hard against his body. "Are you?"

Her breath caught in her throat at the look of intense desire in his eyes. No man had ever looked at her like that. A shiver ran down her spine as he shifted, grazing her breasts with his hard chest.

"I don't know what's true anymore," he said. "There have been so many lies, secrets, inconsistencies in my life. But I know this: I want you, and I think you want me. Is that enough?"

A week ago Julia would have said it wasn't nearly enough, that she needed romance and candlelight, soft words, proper dating, promises. But none of those things had ever made her feel as alive as she felt right now. Alex was right. She didn't know what was true anymore, either. The only person who wasn't lying to her was Alex.

She answered him the only way she could—with a kiss. He gave her a second to lead, then took over, his mouth moving hungrily over hers, demanding entry so his tongue could take possession. She'd never been feasted upon, but that's exactly the way she felt now. His kiss was demanding, consuming, overwhelming, and she didn't want it to end. She gave a small cry of disappointment when he pulled away to kiss a path across her cheek. Then her stomach clenched again when his tongue swirled around her earlobe and he licked a delicious path down the side of her neck.

Conscious thought deserted her as his hands moved up her sides, his fingers flirting lightly with her breasts. She wanted her clothes off and his hands on her—all over her. Then she wanted to return the favor. In fact, she wanted to start right now. She ran her hands under his shirt, touching his hard, muscle-bound chest. He moved closer to her, pressing his groin into her belly. He was hot and hard, and she was melting fast.

He yanked her shirt up and over her head so quickly that a strand of her hair caught in one of the buttons, and she yelped with pain.

"Sorry, sorry," he muttered, pulling her hair free with impatient hands.

"You'll have to kiss it better."

"I intend to," he said, his gaze burning into hers. "I intend to taste every inch of you."

"Oh." Her chest tightened at the promise in his eyes, in his voice.

He pressed her back against the wall, one hand in her hair, the other playing with the light blue lace trim on her bra. He ran his finger back and forth along the edge, his eyes following the path until she wanted to scream. She caught his hand with hers.

"Wait," she said.

"Second thoughts?"

She didn't answer. She simply flipped open the front clasp on her bra. The edges clung to her breasts. She wondered if she had the nerve to peel them away. He didn't give her the chance as he pushed the bra all the way off. His hands covered her breasts as his mouth returned to hers. She didn't know how they got the rest of their clothes off, but somewhere between the living room and the bedroom, they managed to strip themselves naked. By the time they reached the bed, there was nothing but skin and heat.

Love, lust, sex—whatever it was—had never been so hot, so impatient, so demanding. And not just on Alex's part, but on hers, too. Julia found herself making impulsive, bold moves she'd never made before. There were no rules with this man, no boundaries, nothing to hold her back. Every touch, every taste was a risk, but for once she met the risk head-on. She didn't know where they would be tomorrow, but tonight Alex was in her arms, and she was in his, and when their bodies came together, everything was right with the world.

CHAPTER SEVENTEEN

JULIA WOKE up to the sun streaming through her bedroom window and Alex shifting restlessly beneath her. She lifted her head from his chest and saw that his eyes were wide open and he was watching her. She self-consciously patted down her hair, sure it must be flying in a hundred different directions. They'd had quite a workout the night before. She felt tired but wonderfully loved.

"Good morning," she said, feeling a little shy now that it was daylight. She pulled the sheet up over her shoulders.

He smiled at her, pushing the sheet back down. "You look beautiful in the morning."

"Oh, please, that can't be true."

"It's your eyes. They're so clear, so blue. They're like a window into your heart. You show all your emotions."

She wondered what emotions she was showing right now and was tempted to look away, but there had been nothing except honesty between them until now, and she didn't want to change that. "Your eyes hide everything. I'm never completely sure what you're thinking."

"I like it that way."

"I'm sure you do." She traced his jaw with her finger and saw his eyes darken and his lips part. They'd made love twice already and it still wasn't enough. "We should get up," she said.

"I'm already there," he replied with a grin.

She laughed. "I can see that. Actually, I can feel that." She pressed her thigh into his groin and his arms came around her back. "What are we going to do about it?"

"I have a few ideas."

"Really? You haven't used them all up?"

"I haven't even come close." He rolled her onto her back, pinning her beneath him. His hands cupped her face, and the smile faded from his lips as his expression turned serious.

She wondered what he was thinking. She was afraid to ask.

"Julia," he said, then stopped.

She waited for him to finish. He didn't.

"What?" she asked.

He shook his head, then kissed her, long, slow, and tender, like he was never going to let her go. She ran her hands up and down his back, loving the weight of him in her arms, the way he moved and touched her, the way he made her feel wanted and loved. Not that they'd spoken of love. Maybe for Alex it was just desire, chemistry, physical attraction, but she liked him. She liked him a lot. Probably too much. He'd never promised to stay or to love her. And one day he would go, and she'd probably find herself with a broken heart.

But he wasn't leaving today, and if today was all she was going to have, she'd take it.

Hours later, Julia was dressed and back in the car, this time with Alex behind the wheel. She'd thought it would take a huge argument to convince him to go back to St. Helena to see his father, but he'd brought it up himself. He said he knew they had unfinished business.

Despite his resolute determination to get to the bottom of things, she could feel his tension as they drove north on the freeway. The closeness they'd shared the night before evaporated with each passing mile. She knew Alex wasn't thinking about her, but about his father and what he would say next.

"Are you okay?" she asked.

"I'm fine," he said briefly.

"Are we back to fine again?"

"All right. I'm not looking forward to this meeting. In fact, I keep thinking about taking the next exit and making a U-turn."

"If you want to, you can."

He shook his head. "No, I don't run away. I never run away."

She didn't remind him that just yesterday he'd done exactly that.

"Okay, maybe I retreat," he amended, giving her a sideways glance. "Then I go back and do what needs to be done."

"You're not doing it alone."

He patted her thigh. "I know, and I appreciate that fact."

She smiled at him. "I'm really glad you didn't leave, Alex. It means a lot to me that you came back last night." She saw his face stiffen and realized she was treading into dangerous territory regarding their personal relationship. "Don't worry. I'm not asking you for anything," she said quickly.

"Dammit," he swore.

"What? Jeez, don't you think you're overreacting a little?"

"There's someone following us." He tipped his head toward the rearview mirror. "Since we left the city, a black Explorer has been on our tail. I'm going to change lanes. Take a look through the side mirror and tell me what you see."

Julia saw the car immediately and her pulse quickened. "I see two men. I don't recognize them." The Explorer moved behind them, staying three cars back.

"Let's see if they're serious," Alex said.

She didn't like the sound of that, but she didn't have a chance to voice her concern.

Alex waited until the last second to take the next exit, veering across four lanes to do so. The black Explorer attempted to move over but was cut off by a truck and a loud booming horn. Once off the freeway, Alex drove under the overpass, making several twists and turns until they were a few miles from the freeway in some part of Napa that Julia had never seen before. Alex pulled the car into the parking lot of a supermarket, ducking in between a minivan and a truck, then turned off the engine.

They had a good view of the only entrance into the parking lot, and they sat for several minutes without speaking, waiting to see if the Explorer had managed to catch up with them.

"You must have lost them." Julia finally released the breath she'd been holding. "Who do you think they were?"

"I have no idea, but they were definitely following us."

"One of them could have been the guy you chased down Union Street. Although I didn't see a baseball cap on anyone's head. What do we do now?"

Alex thought for a moment, then reached behind him to grab the map. "Let's see if we can find a back way to St. Helena that doesn't take us on the freeway."

After reviewing the map, Alex drove back roads to their destination. It was slower going, but they arrived at Caribbean Court without any sign of the black Explorer.

"I wonder if anyone followed us here yesterday," Julia mused.

"I was just thinking the same thing."

"I hope we didn't put your father in any danger."

Alex pulled up in front of his father's house. He threw the car into park so fast, Julia almost hit the windshield. She put out a hand to brace herself. "What's wrong?"

"Look," he said.

She wasn't sure she wanted to look. Slowly, she turned her head, licking her lips, praying she wasn't going to see the men they'd just tried to outrun, or something even more horrible.

It was a sign that had caught Alex's attention. The For Rent sign planted on the front lawn hadn't been there yesterday. Her gaze darted to the driveway. The beat-up Chevy was gone. The garage door was closed; the only sign that a car had ever been there was a puddle of black oil on the driveway. She glanced back at the house. The curtains and windows were closed up as if someone had left and was never coming back.

She swallowed hard. What had happened here after they'd left yesterday? Had someone gone after Charles?

"God, Alex," she murmured. "What if they...?" She couldn't say it. She didn't even want to think it. She reminded herself that their apartments had been broken into when they weren't home. No one had been hurt—yet.

"Let's go," Alex said decisively.

She shot him a quick look, but he was already moving out of the car. She caught up to him on the front porch. The screen door was slightly ajar and crooked. Had it been like that yesterday? Or was it evidence of violence? She wasn't sure she wanted to go with him, but Alex was already ringing the bell, pounding on the door, shouting his father's name.

No one answered. She could feel Alex's tension, his fear. She grabbed his arm when he reached for the doorknob.

"Wait," she said. "Maybe we don't want to go in there."

"Believe me, I don't want to go in there," he replied, "but we have to try."

It was too easy. The knob turned in his hand.

Alex entered the room first. Julia clung to his back, peering around him as he stopped in the living room. She'd expected to see chaos, destruction. Instead, she saw nothing. Everything was gone. There wasn't one stick of furniture left in the room, no evidence of the vase Alex had broken, no sign of the television or the couch. A fine layer of dust covered the hardwood floor, dust that appeared to be untouched, as if no one had ever been in the house. But Charles Manning had stood in this room only yesterday. His belongings, his life, his dog, for God's sake, had all been real. Hadn't they? She blinked, wondering if she was somehow dreaming.

Alex stepped away from her.

"Where are you going?" she asked quickly, reluctant to be alone.

"To check the bedroom. Wait here." He returned a moment later, his expression grim. "He's gone, not a trace of him left. He disappeared into thin air just like he did before."

"How? How does someone leave that fast? It was yesterday afternoon, barely twenty-four hours ago." She felt incredibly disappointed and also unnerved. There was something about the empty house, the fact that someone had gone to a lot of trouble to wipe Charles Manning off the face of the earth again, that was frightening. She hoped nothing had happened to him.

"My father must have had help. Damn him."

"Do you think he did this?"

"He disappeared once before."

She heard the bitterness in his voice and knew he was hurting again. He'd taken a huge personal risk to come here and face his father, and he'd been deserted again. The sound of a car drew her toward the window. She pulled the curtain aside to see a silver Honda Civic park in front of Alex's car.

"Who do we have here?" Alex muttered, as he peered over her shoulder.

Daniel Brady got out of the car. It wasn't the same car he'd driven to the beach. She idly wondered how many he had. Brady looked around him before making his way up to the front of the house. He wore a navy blue suit today with a white shirt and a conservative tie. He looked like a corporate businessman more than a government agent —or whatever he was. Alex's friend in the State Department had never called back with that information. Julia still wasn't sure exactly what Brady's job entailed. Maybe it was time to find out.

Brady opened the front door without bothering to knock. He didn't appear surprised to see them standing in the living room.

"Where is he?" Alex asked.

"I'm sorry. That's classified," Daniel said smoothly.

"Then why are you here?"

"He thought you'd come back. He wanted you to know he's all right, but that your visit yesterday compromised his safety and yours. He had to leave."

"How did our visit compromise anyone's safety?" Julia asked. "Were we followed?"

"It's possible."

"So nothing specific happened," Alex said. "This was just a preemptive strike."

"Exactly. I told you to drop it, Alex. You don't know who you're dealing with."

"Because you won't tell us," Julia snapped. "If you don't, Alex and I may keep stumbling into trouble. Maybe you should explain what's going on."

Brady withdrew an envelope from his inside jacket pocket. "We're providing you with a background, Miss DeMarco."

"Excuse me?"

"Everything you need is in here. Addresses where you lived with your mother before she married your stepfather. We've also listed a job where your mother worked and character references who can testify to her presence in Berkeley during the time in question. We have photographs of you as a toddler playing in the park in Berkeley, long before that picture in Russia was ever taken."

Julia stared at him in amazement. "How can you do that? How can you have pictures of me when I don't have pictures of me?"

"Technology is amazing."

"So it's all fake, and you expect me to use it? Why would I do that?"

"Because you're in danger. And not just you, but your family, your sister, your stepfather, and everyone attached to you. The break-in at your apartment was only the first step."

"How do you know about the break-in?" she asked.

"We have contacts in the police department."

"Do you know what they were looking for?"

"I assume something that you acquired in Russia."

"What do you mean, the first step?" Alex interrupted. "What do you foresee happening next?"

"A direct confrontation. Julia has something they want."

Brady's voice was so deadly serious, it sent chills down her spine.

"But I don't know what that something is. You have to give me more information," she pleaded.

"Believe me, I'd like to help you, but I can't. My hands are tied. I'm sorry."

"You're not sorry," Alex cut in. "If you were, you'd help us."

"This is above my level. And I am sorry, because your father was a good friend of mine."

"Don't you mean *is* a good friend?" Alex asked.

"The last time we spoke, you neglected to mention that my father was alive. How could you make me think I was responsible for his death?"

Daniel tipped his head in apology. "I wanted you to realize this was serious business. It was a miscalculation."

Julia couldn't believe the coolness of his tone or his words. "A miscalculation? Don't you have any feelings at all?"

"In my business, feelings get you killed."

"Apparently it's not all that difficult to be reborn again," Alex said sarcastically. "My father did it. Sarah did it. Did you set up her death, too? Were you the one who called her parents and told them she'd died in a fire?"

"I had nothing to do with Sarah."

Brady sounded sincere, but Julia wasn't sure she could believe him. He obviously made a living with his lies and his secrets.

"Take the envelope," Brady said, holding it out to Julia. "Take yourself out of the line of fire."

Julia thought about doing exactly what he asked. Wouldn't it be easier to end it now before someone else got hurt, maybe someone she loved? Then again, she'd lived her whole life looking the other way and not asking questions. She didn't want to spend the rest of her days doing the same thing. "I can't," she said.

"You're making a mistake."

"At least it will be mine to make. Everyone else has had their turn."

Brady turned to Alex. "Can't you talk some sense into her?"

"I think she's making perfect sense."

Brady held up his hands in surrender. "All right. But if you change your mind, you'll have this. Take it."

He pushed the envelope into her hand, and she thought about what it contained. She glanced at Alex, having second thoughts. "Do you think I'm putting my family in danger?"

He met her gaze with clear, honest eyes. "You might be, but it's your call."

"I guess I should think about it."

"We've got a long drive home."

"Where did he go?" Julia asked, suddenly aware that Brady had disappeared from the house.

"I have no idea. He truly is a spook." Alex took one last look around the house. "I wonder how long my dad lived here."

"I hope someday you can ask him."

"I'm not counting on it."

As they left the house, there was no sign of the Explorer or Brady as they got into Alex's car. Alex started the engine, then moved to release the emergency brake between them.

"What's this?" he muttered. He pulled out a folded slip of paper that had been tucked under the brake and opened it. "Meet me at Pirate's Cove Cafe, Marine World, four o'clock," he read aloud.

"Meet who?" Julia asked.

"It doesn't say." Alex's gaze met hers. "It couldn't be Brady. He was just here. I think he said everything he had to say."

"Who else could it be?"

"I'd say it's a fifty-fifty chance it's either the men in the Explorer or my father. I'm not sure who I'd rather see."

"Why would someone want to meet at Marine World?" Julia asked as they pulled into the parking lot of the amusement park near Napa.

Alex considered her question as he surveyed the parking lot, which was crowded even for a Thursday. "Lots of people, neutral location, good place to blend into a crowd, and even if someone is following us right now, they wouldn't expect we'd be meeting someone here."

Julia appeared impressed by his deductive reasoning. "You sound like you've been involved in clandestine meetings before."

"Believe me, I've never done anything like this," he said dryly. And that included getting personally and emotionally involved with a woman he'd spent the night with. He'd managed to keep sex casual and easy the past decade, but there was nothing casual or easy about his relationship with Julia, and it was getting more complicated by the second.

"Do you like roller coasters?" Julia asked as they approached the main entrance. A monster roller coaster with three wild, curving loops was just off to the right, and they could hear the screams coming from the cars hurtling down the first drop.

"I haven't been on one in years. What about you?"

"I love them," she said with a smile, "and I haven't been on one in years, either. We should take a ride while we're here. I could use a good scream right about now. Get out all my frustration." She cast him a quick look. "I really thought your dad would be at the house and he'd tell us everything we wanted to know."

"It's my fault. We shouldn't have left yesterday. I was just so pissed off, I couldn't think straight."

"I know, and I completely understood why you had to get out of there."

Alex bought their admission tickets, and they strolled into the park, stopping at an information sign to check the location of the Pirate's Cove Cafe. When he saw the skull and crossbones next to the name, a funny feeling swept over him, a vague, distant memory teasing the back of his brain. He'd been only five or six, and his dad had taken him to Disneyland for his birthday. They'd ridden on Pirates of the Caribbean, and he'd loved the waterfall drops. He'd made his dad take him on the ride three times in a row. He hadn't wanted that day to end, but it had. And the next day his father had left for another business trip. It was a month before they saw each other again.

It had been hard, he realized, all the times apart, and even more difficult for his mother. She used to cry when his dad left. He'd forgotten that—until now.

"I think it's this way," Julia said, tugging his arm. "Is something wrong?"

He shrugged off the memories. "No, everything is—"

"Fine," she finished with a smile. "Your favorite word and always a lie."

"Hey, a little while ago you said I was the most honest man you knew."

"Not when it comes to yourself. You never let on how you're feeling."

He flashed her a smile. "I think you figured me out pretty well last night and this morning."

A warm blush spread across her cheeks, and it made his smile widen. She was so beautiful and sexy, and yet there was also an appealing innocence about her. It was a potent combination and one he probably should have resisted.

"Let's keep our minds on the present," Julia said.

"That's fine with me."

"Yeah, I know," she said with a laugh. "Pirate's Cove is over there."

Alex let her lead the way, enjoying the view from behind. Julia wore tight blue jeans and a clingy camisole top that left her shoulders bare. Her blond hair danced around her shoulders with each step. He had to stick his hands into his pockets to stop himself from reaching for her. He had the insane desire to hold her hand or put his arm around her, and that kind of casual affection had never been part of his life.

"There it is," she said, pointing to a wooden shack with a skull and crossbones painted across the front and a dozen tables with umbrellas set amidst thick green plants and a dark pool of water that was probably supposed to be the cove part of Pirate's Cove.

Only a few of the tables were taken, and those were occupied by families and small children. Alex glanced down at his watch. It was only three thirty. They had a good half hour to wait. "We're early," he said. "Or else they're watching us from somewhere else."

"That's a creepy thought." She took a step closer to him as she looked around the area. "I don't see anyone suspicious."

"Neither do I." He paused. "I have an idea. While we're waiting, why don't we take one of those scream-inducing rides you love?"

Her eyes sparkled. "Really? Do you think we should?"

"Why not? Why should we sit here and wait? Let 'em wait for us."

"Okay. Which coaster do you want to ride?"

"How about that one?" he said, tipping his head toward a square box that rose about six stories, then dropped at breath-stopping speed to the ground.

"That looks fairly terrifying," she said, adding with a teasing smile, "You won't be scared, will you?"

"Not if you hold my hand," he joked.

She pulled his hand out of his pocket and gave it a squeeze. "I'd be happy to."

Her warm touch gave him chills, and suddenly he wasn't afraid of falling six stories, but of falling in love. There was no way he could let that happen. He didn't know what love was really all about, and he didn't believe he would be good at it. Just like his father, he'd always be leaving, always be saying good-bye. It wouldn't be fair to put any woman or kid through that. But right now they were just taking a ride. He could handle a ride. It had a beginning, a middle, and an end. When it was over, it was over.

They waited in line for fifteen minutes before they were strapped into the elevator car that would rise to the top, then shoot to the ground. Alex felt a tingle of nerves as they rose, the ground getting smaller, the view getting bigger. He glanced over at Julia, who stood next to him, her fingers white as she gripped the poles holding her in. She looked scared but brave, which was pretty much the way he'd seen her every day this week; only this time the fear was simple and specific, not vague and complicated.

The car hit the top with a jarring thud, probably designed to give their hearts a jump start on the thrill ride. A second later they were diving toward the ground. Julia's scream rang through his ears, and he found himself joining in. They landed with a soft, gentle thud that seemed completely out of sync with the breath-stealing pace of the ride.

"Oh, my God," Julia said. "I think my stomach is still up there."

"Mine, too," he admitted with a laugh as they exited the car. "But that was great."

"Did you love it?"

"I did." And before he could analyze his thoughts or his actions, he leaned over and claimed her mouth with his, tasting her excitement.

"What was that for?" she asked, looking a bit dazed when they broke apart.

"No reason. Except you look like a bottle of sparkling champagne right now, and I wanted to take a sip." She licked her lips, and he shook his head. "Don't be doing that or I won't be held responsible for my actions."

"Maybe I don't want you to be responsible."

He raised an eyebrow. "That sounds like an invitation. Too bad we're in the middle of an amusement park."

She tossed her hair with a laugh. "I know. Now you have something to look forward to."

Her words made him think about the coming night, and the next day, and the one after, but he didn't want to plan that far into the future. "Yeah, that's great," he said. "We better go back to the Pirate's Cove."

"What did I say?" She grabbed his arm, stopping him in his tracks.

"Nothing."

"No, I said something that made you freak out a little."

"I have a lot on my mind," he said. "Don't be so sensitive."

"Yeah, I was going to say the same thing to you." She paused, tilting her head as she looked at him. "I get it, you know, Alex. Last night was not the beginning of something for you. It was just a night. Maybe that's all we'll have together, maybe not. I'm not going to tie you down, make you promise to stand by me forever, just because we slept together. But I'm also not going to watch everything I say."

"I am not freaking out. I am calm. I am fine." He heard her sigh at the word. "Well, I am. So let's get on with it."

"Fine," she said, the smile returning to her face. She waved her hand toward the cove. "After you."

Alex's nerves began to tighten as they neared Pirate's Cove. He wondered who would be waiting for them. Would it be his father or someone else?

A man sat at a far table near a thick line of bushes, sipping a soda. He wore a fishing hat, sunglasses, and a short-sleeve shirt over a pair of shorts. He was in his sixties. And he was Alex's father.

Julia looked at Alex. He was paler now than when they'd exited the thrill ride. She had a feeling it took every last ounce of courage he had to sit down at the table.

"Thank you for coming," Charles said quietly.

"Does Brady know you left us the note?" Alex asked.

Charles shook his head. "I wasn't supposed to have any contact with you. It was part of the deal I made twenty-five years ago. As soon as you left yesterday, a moving truck arrived, as well as a package of papers for a new identity. I had no choice but to leave. However, I had a feeling you'd come back, and I didn't want to disappear on you again. So I watched the house and left the note in your car. I hoped you'd come here after you finished with Brady." He paused. "What did he tell you?"

"That we'd compromised your safety," Alex said.

"Mr. Brady also wants to provide me with a background I can show to the press," Julia added. "I told him I wasn't interested. I can't live a lie." She saw Charles flinch at her words, and she almost wished she could take them back, but she didn't. Maybe he and her mother had been able to live their lives pretending to be someone they weren't, but she couldn't do it.

"You should reconsider," Charles said. "It would make your life easier."

"My life has been nothing but easy," she replied. "My mother made sure of that." She deliberately brought her mother into the conversation. "There are things I want to ask you about her. Did you read her letter?"

Charles slowly nodded, a gleam of understanding in his eyes. "Yes, and I imagine you have a lot of questions."

"Questions my mother should have answered, but she didn't, and you're the only one who seems to know anything about her," Julia continued. "I know she was in Moscow working as a costumer with the theater group. What I don't know is what I was doing over there and how I got into that orphanage." She watched Charles closely for a reaction, but he was staring down at the tabletop now. "Please, you have to tell me. I can't go on not knowing."

When he raised his gaze to hers, she saw nothing but trouble in his expression, and she had a feeling she was going to be very sorry she'd asked.

"I don't know how to tell you this," he began.

"Just spit it out," Alex ordered.

"Sarah didn't take you to Russia with her. You were already there," Charles said.

It took a moment for his words to sink in. Then Julia's heart stopped. "Are you saying... ?" She couldn't bring herself to finish the question. "Oh, God!" She put a hand to her mouth, terrified to say more. She couldn't take a breath. She felt as if an elephant had landed on her chest.

Alex put an arm around her shoulders, which was probably the only reason she didn't keel over. "Breathe," he said.

"I'm trying." She took several gulps of much-needed air.

"Tell her the rest," Alex said to his father.

"Sarah is the one who took you out of the orphanage and brought you to America," Charles continued. "She was a government agent. It was her job to get you out of Russia."

"No." Julia couldn't believe it. "Then who am I? Who are my parents? Why would she pretend I was her daughter? I don't understand."

"Your parents were Russian."

"Were? You make it sound like they're dead. God, are they dead?"

Julia pressed her fingers to her temple, feeling a pain racing through her head.

"Julia, slow down," Alex said.

Charles looked around, obviously concerned about their conversation being overheard.

She lowered her voice, then said, "I want to know everything you know. Are my real parents dead?" It felt odd to even use the term real parents, but what else could she call them?

"Yes, they are. I'm sorry."

"Really dead or just pretend dead like you and my mother—I mean, Sarah?"

"They died in an explosion at their home."

"No," she whispered, grieving for the parents she'd never known and never would know.

"You were supposed to be in the house with them," Charles continued.

It took a minute for his words to make sense. "I was supposed to die, too?"

His gaze didn't waver. "Yes."

"Why wasn't I there?"

"You had been taken from the house and hidden in the orphanage until we could get you out of the country. No one was supposed to know you were ever there."

"But I took a picture of her," Alex said sharply. "I made sure everyone knew she was there."

Charles looked at his son, his expression one of a deep, aching regret. "I'm sorry you got involved, Alex. I never should have taken you to the square that day. I shouldn't have brought you to Moscow at all. That was selfish of me."

Alex glanced away. "Let's focus on Julia."

Charles turned back to her. "What else do you want to know?"

"How did I get to the United States?" she asked.

"Sarah brought you out with fake papers. She was supposed to put you in an established home that was set up for you, but she didn't. On the trip over, she fell in love with you, and there were other extenuating circumstances."

"Like what?"

He drew in a breath before continuing. "Sarah always had wanted a child, but she'd had a bad pregnancy, ending in miscarriage, and she thought it was doubtful she'd ever have a baby of her own. That fact ate away at her, making her reckless, making her want to take chances. She thought you might be her only opportunity to have a daughter. And she rationalized that she could raise you as well as any other foster home. So why not her? She knew the agency wouldn't agree. They didn't want her connected to you in any way. It would compromise other activities Sarah and I had been involved in while we were in Moscow."

Julia was beginning to understand. "So my mother—Sarah... I have to stop calling her my mother, don't I?"

Charles shook his head. "She was your mother. She loved you so much. Don't doubt that."

"How can I not? Sarah faked her death, just as you did. She let her parents believe she was gone so that she could take me and disappear. She obviously had no moral boundaries. Her life was a lie. And so was mine."

"She faked her death to protect her parents."

"Did you cook up that reason together?" Alex asked scornfully. "Sounds like you were following the same script. Were you also having an affair? Mom certainly thought you were."

"No. Sarah and I were just friends—always. We met in college at Northwestern. We both had an interest in the world. Sarah wanted to go to Russia because her grandmother was Russian. She actually joined the agency before I did. She was the one who suggested I might be able to help with the cover of my photography. Originally I was just supposed to take pictures, but gradually I felt compelled to do more. I met people over there who wanted to be free, and I wanted to help them," Charles said with passion in his voice. "I know you two can't understand. You've never seen what we saw. Back then, there was no freedom. People disappeared. They died on a whim. No one was held accountable."

"And you were going to make them accountable?" Alex demanded. "Who did you think you were, God?"

"No, I was just one person who wanted to make a difference."

"I thought you liked being a photographer. I thought that was your life, your sole ambition. You told me it meant everything to you. Over and over again, you told me that," Alex said. "I grew up thinking it was the most honorable profession in the world, shedding light on the injustices in the world."

"It was honorable, and it still is. It just wasn't enough for me." Charles took a breath, his eyes offering up an apology. "I never thought my decisions would affect you or your mother. I thought I could keep my second line of work separate. I believed I could leave the danger on the other side of the ocean. I was wrong."

"What I don't understand," Julia said, drawing the men's attention back to her, "is why you and Sarah were in danger after the picture was published. What could be gained by going after either one of you then?"

"The people who killed your parents now knew you were alive. They believed I had seen you because I took the picture. If they could find me, they could find you. Since Sarah had you, they could have gone through her as well, or used her parents as leverage. We had to disappear. Without us, there was no trail back to you."

Julia thought about that. It made sense in a strange way. "All right. Let's say that's true. What about now? Why has someone broken into my apartment as well as Alex's place? Why would they want me dead now? It's been twenty-five years, and I don't even know who I am, much less who they are."

Charles clasped his hands together as he rested his elbows on the table. "Your parents made their plans very carefully. For two years they plotted how to leave Russia. It was rumored that they had something valuable to sell, something priceless that would provide them with enough money to live on once they were granted asylum here."

"What was that something?"

"I wasn't cleared for that kind of classified information, so I don't know."

"How could my parents have had something priceless in communist Russia during the Cold War?" Julia tried to remember what she'd learned in world history in high school. "Who were they?"

"Your mother, Natalia—"

"Natalia? That was her name?" A distant memory flashed in Julia's head, a man calling impatiently for Natalia.

"Yes, Natalia Markov. And your father's name was Sergei." Charles paused. "Natalia was a featured ballerina at the Bolshoi Ballet. She was the third generation ballet dancer in the family. Natalia's grandmother, Tamara Slovinsky, danced for the Imperial Court before the revolution. She was in so much favor that she received many valuable presents—jewels, paintings, antiques. It was believed that Tamara managed to hang on to some of those presents, secreting them away or perhaps getting them out of the country. Tamara's husband was Ivan Slovinsky, a famous composer who fled to France during the revolution."

"Oh, my God! Are you serious?" Julia asked in amazement. "I've studied Ivan Slovinsky. He wrote an incredible number of operas and ballets at the turn of the century. His music was powerful, awe-inspiring. He was truly gifted, and he was my..." She had to think for a moment to calculate the relationship. "He was my great-grandfather?"

"Yes."

"I can't believe it." She turned to Alex in excitement. "Maybe that's where I got my love of music. I've always wondered why I feel such passion for any kind of melody when no one else in my family cares even a little about it."

Alex smiled at her. "It makes sense now."

"What about my father?" she asked Charles, impatient to hear the rest. "Was he also in music or ballet?"

"No, your father, Sergei Markov, was a high-ranking party member and a loyal communist until he fell in love with Natalia. Then he became disenchanted with the government. He could see that Natalia's career could be so much greater if she went to America. Apparently he had information that he was willing to share with our government if he and Natalia were granted asylum here."

"So the Russians killed them before they could leave," Julia said slowly. "That's what happened, isn't it? Did anyone investigate?"

"The Russian government blamed the explosion on faulty wiring. It was considered a tragic accident. They had the last word."

"This is just mind-boggling. I can't wrap my brain around it all." She thought for a moment, trying to make sense of everything Charles had told her. "My mother was a ballerina. I thought about taking ballet once, but Mom—Sarah—wouldn't let me. She always had a reason why she couldn't sign me up."

"Sarah didn't want you to dance," Charles interjected. "She was afraid you might grow up to be like your mother, that someone would eventually make the connection between you."

"Which is probably why she also discouraged me from pursuing my passion for music," Julia finished.

Sarah certainly had a lot to answer for. Only it was too late for her to give any of those answers.

"You can't tell anyone about any of this," Charles said. "If the people who killed your parents find out you know the truth, it will be even more dangerous for you."

"They think I have this priceless object, is that right?"

"I suspect so."

"This is unbelievable." Her head felt heavy with the amount of information she'd received, and she pressed a hand to her temple, feeling the ache spread across her cheekbones and around her eyes. "I don't know what to think. How am I supposed to feel? I know who my parents are, but they're dead. I can't meet them. I can't talk to them." The finality of that made her feel terribly sad. "I almost wish I'd never seen that picture of myself. I could have gone on believing I was just Julia DeMarco and not the orphan girl at the gates."

"You're not the girl in the picture," Charles said abruptly.

Her gaze flew to his. Her stomach did a somersault. "What do you mean? Of course I am." She silently begged him not to spin her around in another direction.

"Of course she is," Alex echoed in surprise. "I saw her. I took her picture. I was there."

Charles looked from Julia to Alex, then back to Julia again. His silence drew her nerves into a tight, screaming knot.

"Just say it—whatever it is," she begged.

"All right. I've told you this much. I might as well tell you the rest. You aren't the girl in the photograph, Julia."

"Then who is?" she demanded.

CHAPTER EIGHTEEN

"YOU HAVE A SISTER," Charles said, his voice slow and deliberate. "A twin sister. She was the one standing at the gate that day. You were inside the building." Shocked silence met his words. Julia didn't know what to say. It was clear Alex couldn't find words, either. The surprises just kept coming, each one bigger than the last.

"That's impossible," she said, finally finding her voice. "Why wouldn't that have come out before, when the picture was published?"

"No one in the general public ever connected the girl at the gates with the twin girls of Natalia and Sergei Markov, who died in an explosion. In fact, it was printed in the Russian newspaper that everyone in the house was dead, including the servants. No one ever came forward when the picture was printed to state your true identity. So if anyone recognized you, they kept it to themselves."

She could barely comprehend his explanation. She was still thinking about the fact that she had a sister. "I would remember," she said, racking her brain for any hint of a memory, but her mind was blank. She didn't remember a sister or parents or Russia, or anything that happened before she was in the United States. Yet something teased at the back of her mind. Why couldn't she bring it forward, let it out?

"Where is she?" Alex asked. "Where is this sister? Why didn't Sarah keep her and Julia together? Did something happen to her?"

Julia caught her breath at his question, silently pleading that her sister wasn't dead, too.

"It was too dangerous to keep the girls together," Charles explained. "They were taken out of the country separately."

"Who took my sister?" She stumbled over the word sister, realizing it no longer applied just to Liz, but to another woman as well.

"Another agent. Before you ask, I didn't know his name or anything about him. I wasn't supposed to be involved in that aspect of the operation. Stan made it clear that my job was to make the cultural exchange look authentic. Divert suspicion and attention by creating media opportunities for the theater group. The Russians wanted positive press."

"Wait," Alex said, putting up a hand. "Stan? Did you say Stan made it clear? I thought he was just an editor."

Charles smiled at that. "Stan was never just an editor. He was a friend. A crazy, wild friend."

Julia didn't understand the gleam in Charles's eye. Nor had Stan Harding given her the impression of being crazy or wild. Alex appeared confused, too.

"Are you saying Stan was involved in the operation to get the Markovs out of Russia?"

"He was a ballet fanatic. He'd met Natalia a few times when she came to the States. She confided in him. He set up the defection."

"So he lied, too," Alex said bitterly. "Big surprise."

"Let's go back to my sister. I want to know where she went after she left Russia, and why we weren't reunited," Julia said.

"Sarah wanted to get you back together," Charles replied. "But she had to keep you under wraps once the photo came out. Your sister had already been placed in a temporary foster home on the other side of the country. When things died down, Sarah wanted to find your sister, but she couldn't ask anyone for help. She broke all the rules when she took you. She was in hiding from everyone, including the agency. No one knew where she was. She had grown up in New York State and went to school in Chicago. Everyone was looking for her in those places. No one was looking for her here. I didn't even know she had you or where she was for over ten years. Then I saw her one day by accident down on the Wharf. I couldn't believe my eyes."

"So she kept me from my sister, the only blood relative I had left? And she deprived me of my grandparents? What gave her the right to do any of that? I should have known about my heritage. I should have known everything," Julia declared, feeling angry and betrayed and sad all at the same time.

"You were never supposed to know any of it. The people who killed your parents wanted the whole family dead. The only way to protect you was to keep you hidden away. If you knew who you were, Sarah was afraid you'd do what you're doing now: go looking for answers that could get you killed."

"That should have been my choice, especially when I became an adult. I can't believe I sat by her bedside talking to her about our life together, our hopes and dreams, and none of this ever came out."

"Don't judge her too harshly," Charles said. "She loved you very much."

"What kind of love is filled with lies?"

"Sarah gave up her life for you, Julia," Charles said. "She walked away from her parents, her home, her community, her identity just so she could raise you. That wasn't cowardly; that was brave."

His words touched her. How could they not? But Sarah's sacrifices didn't make up for the lies. "I don't think I can forgive her."

"Give yourself some time," Charles advised. "Remember, love isn't always simple."

"People like you and Sarah are the ones who make it complicated." She sat back in her chair, the noise from the roller coasters penetrating her brain. She'd been so caught up in Charles's story, she'd lost track of time. Only now did she realize that the shadows were longer and deeper. It was getting late. They'd been talking for a long time.

She glanced at Alex, wondering if he wanted to take the lead now, ask his father some pointed, personal questions. She was surprised by the speculative look in his eyes as he stared at her. "What are you thinking?" she asked.

"That your sister looks just like you."

"Obviously, if she's my twin." She didn't understand his point.

"If that photo of you in the Tribune got picked up nationally, or if Christine Delaney continues her quest to publicize you, your sister might see your picture in the paper and wonder why she has a twin she never met."

"And whoever is after me might go after her," Julia finished, suddenly realizing where his thoughts were headed. "We have to find her and fast." She turned back to Charles. "Do you think Mr. Brady knows where my sister is now? He knew where I was, right?"

Charles shook his head. "Brady didn't know where you were until Stan called him last week. As I said, Sarah disappeared off the face of the earth. Even when we reconnected, she made me promise to stay silent."

"What about my sister? Does she know who she really is?"

"The original foster family was paid handsomely not to ask questions. It's my understanding that that family broke up and your sister went into the system like any other American orphan."

"What's her name? Wait." Julia squeezed her eyes tight as an image popped into her head. *She was playing with a doll. She was looking in the mirror, and she called the doll...* On second thought, maybe she hadn't been looking in the mirror. Maybe she'd been looking at her sister. Yes, that was it. Her sister held the doll she wanted. Julia asked for it back, and she called her... "Elena," she whispered, her eyes flying open. "Her name was Elena."

"You remember her?" Alex asked.

"Just that. I think I've dreamed about her, but I always thought I was dreaming about me. That's weird, isn't it?"

"You'll probably remember more now," Alex told her. "You suffered a huge trauma, being ripped from your home, your parents, your country. It's no wonder you blocked it out."

She directed her attention back to Charles. "You said Brady doesn't know where Elena is. Do you? Or does Stan know?"

"It could be dangerous for you to find her."

"According to you, I'm already in danger just by virtue of being alive."

He tipped his head in acknowledgement. "True. All right. I know that your sister goes by the name Elaine Harrigan. At one point she was a ballet dancer with a Washington DC ballet company. Maybe that will help you find her."

"How do you know that?"

"Sarah found her about ten years ago. I don't know how or what she ever intended to do with the information. She only said she was worried because Elaine was in ballet and someone might connect her to her famous mother."

Her sister was a ballet dancer. Another surprise, and yet it seemed right. She studied Charles, wondering why he'd decided to come clean. "Why?" she asked. "Why tell me now?"

"Alex is a grown man. You're a grown woman. It's your turn to make your own decisions." Charles's gaze focused on Alex. "Will you tell your mother about me?"

"I have to," Alex replied. "She deserves to know the truth."

Charles pulled a piece of paper out of his pocket and pushed it across the table. "This is where I'll be if you want to talk to me, or if your mother does."

"I thought you were supposed to disappear again."

"I was. Brady won't be happy that we met, but I couldn't desert you a second time, Alex. I understand that you may never forgive me for what I did. But I know in my heart that I did what I believed was right. And I still believe it. You might have grown up without a father, but you lived, and you have a good life now. I've read a lot about you, everything I could get my hands on. You've made me proud."

"You should have come to me sometime in the last twenty-something years," Alex said harshly. "You should have found a way to tell me you were alive."

"I didn't think I had the right. You'd moved on. If you or your mother want to talk now, that's where I'll be. I'll leave it up to you."

"Mom will probably come after you with a gun," Alex said, but he put the piece of paper in his pocket.

"How is she?" Charles asked.

"She's divorced again, her third. She seems to have developed a fondness for her memories of you. She's been publicizing your photos all over town. In fact, your work is part of an exhibit at the Legion of Honor. But you probably already know that. You've been so close to us all these years."

"I started out across the country, but I eventually made my way back to San Francisco. In the beginning I wanted to watch over you."

"You watched me?" Alex asked, a rough edge to his voice.

"A few times. Enough to know you were all right."

"Yeah, I was fine. Just fine." Alex rose. "I think we're done here. Julia?"

"Just one last question," she said. "Did Sarah ever consider telling me the truth?"

"No." Charles looked her straight in the eye. "Sarah was afraid you would hate her for what she'd done. She told me she'd do everything she could to make sure you were happy and that you never lacked for anything, especially a family. She would make certain you were surrounded by love."

"I was," Julia said quietly. And now she had to wonder if Sarah had ever loved Gino, or if he'd just provided the family she so desperately needed to make the illusion complete.

An hour later Alex pulled off at the exit just before the Bay Bridge and turned into a hotel parking lot. He didn't stop driving until they had gone to the far side of the building, completely hidden from the freeway.

"What are you doing?" Julia took a quick look over her shoulder. "Is someone following us again?"

"No, but we can't go back to our apartments. They know where we live. I don't want someone trying to grab you or your purse. In fact, I don't want them getting anywhere near you.

His protectiveness touched her. She liked that he cared enough to worry about her. "What do you suggest we do?"

"Get a hotel room, call the airport, book a flight for DC first thing in the morning."

She turned sideways in her seat, amazed that she could still feel surprised after everything she'd learned. "You really think we should hop on a plane to Washington DC, with nothing more than a name and a ballet company?"

"It's a good start. We'll have better luck tracking your sister there than here."

"If she's still in DC. Your father said the information was at least ten years old."

"But she was there, and she probably had friends in the ballet company. Someone might know where she is now," he pointed out.

"It's so spontaneous. I'm not the kind of person who jumps on planes every other day. It will be expensive, won't it, this close to departure?"

"I have lots of Frequent Flyer miles. It won't cost us a dime. I think of air travel like car travel. Going to DC is like going to St. Helena, except the trip is a few hours longer."

"So speaks the world traveler," she said with a smile.

"Is that a yes or a no?"

"It's a yes. I want to find my sister. I still can't believe I have a sister." Her smile dimmed. "Oh, no," she muttered.

"What now?" he asked warily.

"Liz. She won't like this at all. How will I tell her I have a twin sister who shares my blood, especially now that I know she doesn't? She won't understand. She was worried that she would lose me to my biological father. How on earth am I going to make her understand it doesn't change things?"

"It does change things. How could it not?"

"I love Liz. She'll always be my sister."

"But she won't be your only sister. That will take some adjustment, especially since Elaine or Elena looks just like you."

"Liz will definitely feel like the odd girl out," she agreed.

"Don't tell her yet. It will be easier to present the whole picture when it makes sense. If you give her this much, it will only be confusing and disturbing."

"Which describes my feelings exactly."

He ran his finger down the side of her face. "It's been a rough day for you. And here I thought it would be all about me and seeing my dad again, listening to his lies."

"Yeah, well, I didn't want you to have all the fun," she said lightly, trying to stay on the surface of her emotions. She was afraid if she didn't, she would have a complete meltdown, and it wasn't the time for that. "How was it, seeing your dad again?"

He shrugged. "I don't know."

"I think you do."

"If I do, I don't want to talk about it."

"Are you going to wait to tell your mother about your dad?"

"Yes," he said, without a hint of doubt in his voice. "I want to know everything first."

"We're getting closer," Julia said. "We finally know who my parents are—and that Sarah isn't my mother." She let out a sigh of weariness. "I don't want to talk about this right now, either. I have a headache."

"You need a break, time to let everything sink in."

"I feel like there's a thick curtain in my brain and I can't see past it. How could I have forgotten my twin sister for even a moment? Shouldn't there have been a connection between us? Shouldn't I have felt as if a part of me was missing?"

Alex's eyes filled with compassion. "Don't be so hard on yourself. You were three years old. You were a baby. Your whole life changed in an instant. I'm sure you missed your sister when you were first sepa-rated. But you had to bury that pain to survive. Then your life was filled with other people."

"That's true. My mother—Sarah—did manage to get pregnant, despite what everyone else told us. I was there for that part. I wonder if she regretted taking me then. After all, she had her own child. She could have given me away and still had her own family." Julia thought about all that had transpired, how many lives had been touched by her mother's one reckless decision. And up until today, she'd never thought of her mother as reckless. "My mother feels like a stranger to me now. How could I live with her for twenty-five years and not know her at all?"

"I know you're probably mad as hell at her, Julia, but I have to say, who knows what would have happened to you if Sarah had left you in foster care as she was supposed to? It's highly likely that you ended up having a much better life with her. It wasn't as if she stole you from your parents. They were already gone."

Alex was right. Her parents had been killed before Sarah decided to keep her. "I hadn't thought of it like that."

"That's because you haven't had time to think."

She smiled at him. "Thanks for sticking by me. I appreciate it."

"We made a deal to see this through."

"And I couldn't do it without you. You're a rock."

"A rock, huh? I think you can do better than that," he said, moving his hand down to her knee, where he let his fingers stray up her thigh.

She grinned as she put her hand over his, stopping his exploration. "Are you looking for compliments?"

"I'm looking for something," he said with a laugh.

"Behave yourself."

"I'm tired of behaving. I've been good all day." He leaned forward and stole a quick kiss.

That's all it took to send a wave of heat through her body. She was really in over her head, she thought. Far too involved, far too attracted, far too tempted.

Alex leaned in and pressed his mouth against hers, lingering a little longer this time, making her remember the way he'd kissed a path down her body the night before. She tried to get closer to him, but she ran into the gearshift, reminding her that she was making out in a public parking lot.

She pushed Alex away with an embarrassed laugh. "Not like this," she said.

"Good point. There's a hotel room just a few feet away." There was a question in his eyes as he finished his sentence, a question she could easily answer.

"Let's get a king-size bed," she said.

His eyes darkened. "Now you're talking."

"Actually, I don't feel like talking. That's all we've done today. I don't want to think anymore," she replied.

"Neither do I."

"Aren't you worried that I might be using you?" she teased.

"Use away," he said with a crooked grin. "I'm all yours. Come on."

She laughed as he jumped out of the car. She had to jog to keep up with him. She tried to act nonchalant as Alex asked for a room, not that it mattered. The desk clerk wasn't even remotely interested in who they were or whether or not they had any luggage.

They kissed all the way to their room on the fourth floor, laughing like reckless teenagers when Alex fumbled with the key card and couldn't get the door open. She took it out of his hand and did the honors. Finally, they were inside.

Julia didn't have time to see the room, because Alex pressed her back against the door, his lips on her mouth, his hands on her breasts. He was hot and hard, and she was on fire. All the tension of the day blew up in one explosive kiss. They made short work of their clothes, falling on the bed, naked and eager to get as close as possible.

"We should slow down," Alex said with a groan as his hands roamed restlessly on her body.

"Next time," she said, pulling him into the cradle of her hips. She wanted him inside of her, on top of her, surrounding her with his body, his heart, and his soul. She needed to hold on to something real, and he was beautifully real. She trusted him more than she trusted herself, so she stopped thinking and directed all of her crazy, mixed-up emotions toward him until they both found a blessed release.

It was a while later before either one of them moved; then Alex rolled off her onto his side. He pulled her into his body, spoon fashion, putting his arm across her waist. She blew out a breath and closed her eyes. Maybe she'd just take a little nap. There would be plenty of time to think and worry and analyze when she woke up.

Alex fell asleep before she did, his deep, contented breathing providing a comforting rhythm. Julia let her mind drift, trying to think of something nice, pretty, uncomplicated—a field of wildflowers or a running stream... Instead, her sister's face floated through her mind.

Elena sat next to her on the couch. They were both too short for their legs to reach the ground, so they were kicking their feet up in the air, sometimes kicking each other by accident. Only she didn't always do it by accident; sometimes she did it on purpose, because she was tired of waiting. But Elena sent her a cross look, so she stopped.

Julia looked around the room. It was dark and a little scary. The furniture was big and really old. The pictures on the wall were of people she didn't recognize. They looked mean. The only pretty things in the room were the vases of flowers that her mother received almost every day from her fans.

Everyone loved her mother. Wherever they went, people came up to kiss her hand, to tell her she was beautiful, magical, like a princess. Julia wanted to be a princess like her mother. But Elena would probably make a better one. Everyone said Elena was just like their mother, so graceful, so sweet, and already learning how to dance. Julia didn't want to dance. She wanted to play one of the big instruments that made lots of noise. She thought that would be more fun.

The door opened and a woman came into the room. She wore a beautiful red dress, and her hair fell down to her waist in pretty blond waves. She smiled at them both and kneeled in front of them, putting a hand on each of them.

She was talking again about leaving. They would be parted for a short time, she said. Only a few days. They would have to be brave little girls.

Julia felt tears gathering in her eyes and fear knotting her stomach. She didn't want to be brave. She didn't want her mother and father to leave. She wanted them all to be together. Her mother was sad, too. A tear dripped out of her eye and down her cheek. Julia put out her hand and caught the tear with her fingertip. As she stared at it, she felt terribly afraid.

Her mother stood up. She blew them a kiss, telling them to have courage and faith, that love was worth the risk.

Then she was gone. Olga helped them put on their hats and their coats, and whisked them away from the house. Once outside, Julia pressed her fingers against the cold pane of the car window, watching her house fade away. She wanted to go home. She began to cry and pound on the window, but they kept getting farther and farther away... and she couldn't stop screaming.

"Julia, wake up. Wake up," Alex said loudly.

She felt someone shaking her, and Alex's voice finally reached her subconscious. Her eyes flew open. It took her a moment to remember where she was—in a hotel room with Alex. She was an adult now, not that scared little girl, but she was still trembling.

Alex ran his hand up and down her arm. "Are you okay?" he asked with concern.

She realized her cheeks were wet and her throat felt hoarse. Had she been shouting? "I was dreaming," she said, rolling over to face him.

He wiped away her tears with gentle fingers. "Bad dream?"

"Bad and good. I remembered the day my mother sent us away. She told us to be brave. She said love was worth the risk. I didn't know what she meant. I was so scared. I felt like I was choking on the fear. I knew I wasn't going to see her again. I could feel it."

He stroked her hair. "At least the memories are coming back now."

"I don't want them back," she said. "They hurt."

"How about some water?"

She nodded. As Alex got up, she slipped under the blanket, not quite as comfortable with her nudity now that they weren't making love. Alex pulled on his briefs and jeans, then returned to the bed with a bottled water from the minibar. He handed it to her, then picked up the room service menu from the nightstand. "What do you think about some food? It's after seven."

It was such a practical question, she had to smile. "I am hungry."

"They look like they have a pretty good menu. Steak, fish, salad. What's your pleasure?"

"Cheeseburger, French fries, and a chocolate milk shake. Oh, and maybe a salad, too, so I don't feel totally guilty."

He gave her a knowing grin. "That's exactly what I order every time I come home. It always makes me feel like my life is back to normal."

"I have a feeling it will take more than a cheeseburger to make me feel that way, but at least it's a start."

While Alex was ordering, Julia rose from the bed and got dressed.

"I liked you better naked," Alex said as he hung up the phone.

His wicked grin was completely lethal. She almost felt like stripping down for him again—almost. After a day of shocking revelations, her brain was beginning to work again. And she needed to start thinking about her current situation and what she was going to do about it.

"Back to work, huh?" Alex asked, obviously reading her mind.

"Is your laptop still in the car?"

Alex glanced around the room. "It must be. You distracted me so much, I forgot to bring it in."

"We need to make plane reservations for tomorrow, and we should try to find the location of the ballet companies in Washington DC. Maybe we can get a head start on tracking down Elena. We can also look up information on my mother and father."

"Thank God for the Internet," he said. "I'll get the computer out of the car." He slipped on his shirt and buttoned it up. "Don't let anyone in while I'm gone."

"I'm sure no one knows we're here."

"I still want the deadbolt on as soon as I leave. We can't be too careful, Julia. My dad made it clear that whoever killed your parents had connections on this side of the world. And we know firsthand those connections still exist."

"Are you deliberately trying to scare me? I just got my heart back to its normal rhythm."

"I..." His expression turned serious. "I don't want anything to happen to you."

"I already slept with you. You don't have to sweet-talk me," she said lightly.

"I mean it, Julia. Lock the door."

"I will." She followed him to the door, prepared to throw the dead-bolt as soon as he left. Alex put his hand around the back of her neck and kissed her as if he were leaving forever, instead of just going to the car. Then he was gone.

Shaken, she slid the deadbolt into place, hoping to God he really was coming back. That would always be the problem with Alex, she realized. She'd never be sure how long he would stay or if he'd return. But how could she complain? If she'd wanted a man who never left, she wouldn't have broken up with Michael.

CHAPTER NINETEEN

LIZ WAITED on the dock as Michael helped the last of his passengers off the fifty-foot yacht he used for charter services. The Annabelle was one of two boats owned by Michael's family. She knew he preferred the sailboat over the yacht, but his older brother had seniority in deciding which boat to run. She waved as he saw her. "Hey," she called.

He looked as if he wished he hadn't seen her and that she'd go away, but she was determined to talk to him. "Can I come up?" Without waiting for a reply, she boarded the yacht.

Michael wore his sailing clothes: jeans, a sweater, and a thick jacket. His face was red from the wind, his light brown hair ruffled and damp.

"What do you want?" he asked, a grumpy note to his voice.

"That's a nice greeting. I came to see how you were."

"I'm working. That's how I am."

"You're done working," she pointed out. "And I think you owe me more than attitude. I did help you with your house, not to mention a few dozen other things over the last year."

"Fine. But if you came here to talk about Julia, I'm not interested."

"I didn't come here to talk about Julia. I came here to talk about me.

You probably don't care about any of this, but I want you to know anyway. I quit my job at the cafe. I signed up for some classes at San Francisco State. I'm going to finish my education."

"What brought this on?"

"Julia gave me a kick in the butt. She pointed out to me recently that I've been sitting on the sidelines watching everyone else play. And she was right." Liz paused. "I'm still pissed off at her, but what she said about me was true. I have been drifting aimlessly for over a year now. I kept thinking something great would fall in my lap, but I guess it doesn't happen that way." She watched him closely for his reaction, knowing his opinion was extremely important to her. "What do you think?"

He didn't answer right away, and each passing second made her more anxious.

"I think you're on the right track, Lizzie," he said at last, his scowl replaced by the warm smile she loved so much.

"Really?" She felt so relieved. "That means a lot to me. You're important to me, Michael. Not just because of what you were to Julia. I thought we were friends, too."

"We are friends." He patted her on the shoulder. "Don't ever think we're not."

"I won't. How's the house coming along?"

"It's not. I haven't felt like working on it since—"

"But you have to finish it. It's your house. It's your dream."

"A dream is something you share with someone."

"I don't believe that," she said with a toss of her head. "A dream is personal. That house means something to you. I should know. I saw the way you lovingly caressed the walls."

"I didn't do that."

She grinned. "You were close. Anyway, want some help? I have some free time tonight. I can scrape wallpaper, paint, or do whatever you need."

"That's a nice offer, but—"

She cut him off. "I'd really like to help, and if you're smart, you won't turn me down."

"I don't even know if I'm going to keep the house. It's too big for a single guy. Unless you think Julia will change her mind?"

Liz wished she could give him a different answer, but she couldn't. "I'm sorry, but I don't. I think Julia has a lot of plans that don't include you. She's on a quest to change her life. She's like a bird sprung from a cage, and she wants to fly everywhere, see everything."

"You're right. I've been thinking a lot about the relationship we had. Julia started pulling away from me the day of your mother's funeral. I was just hanging on so tight she couldn't get loose." He dug his hands into his pockets and walked to the side of the boat, staring out at the bay. "If it hadn't been this search of hers, it would have been something else that broke us up. I was just so ready to get married. I couldn't see that she wasn't."

Liz didn't say anything. Michael was lost in his thoughts, and she didn't want to intrude. Getting over Julia would be difficult for him, but she believed now that they would both find a better future on their own.

"I never should have bought that house without talking to her," Michael added. "I told my sister about it, and she said she couldn't believe I'd made such a bonehead move. Apparently it's not romantic to surprise a woman with a house."

"I think it's really romantic. If it had been me, I would have been very happy, but that's just me. I still think you should finish remodeling it. It's a great place, and you love it. Someday you'll find a woman who loves it, too. Then it will be ready."

Michael turned back to her. "Maybe I'll paint the back bedroom today. If you want to help, I won't say no."

"I'm your girl," she said, "as long as you buy me a pizza. I'm starving."

"Okay, but we're getting plain cheese pizza. I hate all that fancy—" Michael stopped. "Do you know that guy?" he asked, tipping his head toward a man on the pier. "He's been staring at you since you got here."

As Liz turned her head, the man pulled his baseball cap down over his eyes and walked away. "I don't know him." She licked her lips, feeling a little nervous. "I hope he's not the man who broke into our apartment. Julia said he was following her around. What if he's following me now?"

"The police haven't found out who ransacked your place?"

"No. I'm scared, Michael."

He stepped closer to her, putting his arm about her shoulders. "Don't worry. I'm here. I'll take care of you."

"Thanks."

"I hope Julia has someone watching her back."

Liz had a feeling that someone's name was Alex.

"It's me," Alex said as he knocked on the hotel room door, his laptop under his arm.

Julia flung the door open, her beautiful blue eyes worried. "Thank God, you're back."

"Why? Did something happen?" He searched her face for a clue to her distress.

"I just had a little panic attack, imagining that someone was waiting for you by the car or something crazy like that. I'm losing my mind, aren't I?"

"Not even close, but you don't have to worry about me. I can take care of myself."

"I know. I'm still glad you're back." She took the computer from his hands and set it on the table, then wrapped her arms around his waist and gave him a long, loving hug. "You don't mind if we stay like this for a while, do you?"

His hands slipped under her camisole top, caressing her back. "Hey, you left your bra off."

"I didn't think I needed it," she murmured.

"You don't," he said with pleasure. "In fact, we could get rid of this shirt, too."

Before she could answer, a knock came at the door.

"Don't answer it," she said, the fear back in her voice.

"Room service," a voice called out.

"It could be a trick," she warned him.

"Julia, we just ordered food," Alex said calmly. He set her aside, looked through the peephole, then opened the door. As the waiter set up the table, the delicious aroma of burgers and fries filled the room. Alex was reminded of how long it had been since they'd eaten. Julia must have realized the same thing. Her panic gone for the moment, she was already into the fries before he finished tipping the waiter.

"Hmm, this is good," she said when they were alone. "I'm starving. I haven't had a big cheeseburger in a long time. I feel so decadent."

He grinned at that. "I can show you more decadence than a cheeseburger."

"Save it for later," she said with a laugh.

Alex pulled over a chair, and for the next few moments they ate in companionable silence. He finished first, but Julia was a close second. She sat back with her milk shake in hand and a satisfied sigh.

"I think I inhaled that," she said. "And you still beat me."

"I'm used to eating on the run."

"Sleeping on the run, working on the run, pretty much everything else on the run," she said with a knowing glint in her eyes.

"What? You have me all figured out now?"

"Not even close. You're a man of mystery."

"Good. That's the way I like it."

"That's not the way I like it." A frown drew her brows together. "Tell me something I don't know about you. Like a juicy secret."

"You want to know more secrets? Haven't you had your fill?"

She made a face at him. "A personal secret, Alex, nothing that involves foreign governments or spies."

He grinned. "I don't have any."

"You must."

He thought about it and realized that he truly did not have any secrets from her. She knew more about him and his family than anyone. In fact, he'd let her get closer to him than any other person on earth. How had he let that happen? And how was he going to put an end to it?

He'd tried to walk away once before, but he hadn't been able to leave her, not in the middle of everything. He would go when it was over, when they knew everything there was to know. Then he'd leave, wouldn't he?

Of course he would go. He had jobs waiting for him. One call to the magazine, and he'd be on his way to some distant country on the other side of the globe. Just the way he liked it.

Julia would go on with her life. And he'd go on with his.

She'd be a good memory, one of the best. But that's all she would be. Their affair would end like all of his other relationships. He didn't know how to do long term. He'd never wanted to learn. Until now... He drew in a sharp breath, determined to put that ridiculous thought out of his mind.

"It's okay, Alex," Julia said gently. "You don't have to worry I'll tell your secrets."

"I wasn't worrying about that."

"Then what's making you so uptight? You have your stone face on right now, and that usually means something is bothering you."

"I don't have a stone face."

"Yes, you do. Your skin tightens over your cheekbones, and your jaw gets really set, and even your eyes look cold. They have that 'don't ask me any questions' look in them right now."

"Then maybe you should stop asking me questions," he pointed out.

She stuck out her tongue, breaking the tension, and he felt his face relax. He had been tightening up. He just hadn't realized it until she'd pointed it out.

"You know, we're even on the secrets issue," she told him. "I may know yours, but you also know mine." She paused. "Except maybe one."

He waited for her to elaborate, but she simply set down her milk shake and stood up.

"We should get to work," she said. "We need to make plane reservations for tomorrow, and—"

"What's the one thing?" he asked, extremely curious.

"I'm not going to tell you."

"Why not?"

"Because it's personal, and..." She paused for a long moment. "It would probably scare you to death."

He gazed into her eyes and saw a question there, a question he was terrified to answer. "I guess everyone is entitled to one secret," he said lightly. He got up from his chair and retrieved the laptop. He sat down on the bed with his back against the headboard and opened the computer, hitting the button to boot up.

Julia sat down on the bed next to him. "I'll tell you if you really want to know," she said.

"I don't think I do."

"Okay, but fair warning... before you leave for good, I'm going to tell you."

"I'll keep that in mind. Now, I think we should take the first flight out tomorrow." In fact, if they could get on a flight right now, he would. Because another night with Julia wasn't going to make the leaving any easier.

"Let's see what you can get," Julia said.

His fingers flew across the keyboard. Within five minutes they had reservations on a seven a.m. flight to Dulles. "Now what?" he asked.

"Look up my mother's name, Natalia Markov."

"Here she is," he said a moment later, pulling up a page on Russian ballet dancers. There was a grainy black-and-white photograph of the ballerina. He adjusted the screen so Julia could see it better. He heard her sharp intake of breath and knew that she'd remembered something.

"I know her," she said softly. "That's my mother. She's beautiful."

Natalia was stunning, Alex thought. She looked a bit like Julia, but she had a lighter, more ethereal quality to her face and figure. As he studied her picture, he remembered something his father had said earlier, something that had gotten lost in his head until now. "Stan knew your mother," he said aloud.

"That's right," Julia said. "Your father told us that Stan helped them set up the defection. Why didn't he tell us that? He made it sound like he knew nothing."

"He said he was too scared for his family to look into my father's death. I bet he knew the death was fake all along." He thought back to their meetings. "And you—you must have reminded him of your mother. Yet, he gave nothing away. Hmm."

"What are you thinking?"

"I wonder if Stan hired someone to break into our apartments."

"That's ridiculous."

"Is it?" he queried. "Think about it. We went to Stan first. He knew about you before anyone else would have time to find you."

"He's a dignified, respected, older man. I can't see him breaking and entering."

"What about manipulating? Directing? Calling the shots—like he did when your parents tried to defect?"

"You really believe that's possible? What about the guy in the cap? Or the men who followed us to Napa?"

Alex shrugged. "They could all be working together, or different parties could be coming at us from different directions."

"Great. I feel much better now," she said dryly.

"I'm going to call Stan, confront him, see what he has to say." Alex set the laptop aside and grabbed his cell phone off the table. He waited impatiently for Stan to answer. A message machine came on instead. "Call me immediately," Alex said. "It's extremely important. Don't let me down." As he hung up, Alex realized Stan had already let him down, just like everyone else in his life.

"He'll call back. He cares about you," Julia said, putting her hand over his. "I saw the way he looked at you, as if you were his son."

"Yeah, well, I'm not his son."

"Don't judge him until you have all the facts."

"Fine." He tipped his head toward the computer screen. "Did you learn anything else?"

"I can't seem to focus on reading the article. I can't look away from my mother." She smiled sadly. "How could I have forgotten her until just this second? How could I have forgotten them all? My sister, my father, my mother?"

He put his arm around her, pulling her close. "You suffered a trauma. Everything you knew was ripped away from you when you were too small to understand what was happening. Sarah gave you love and comforted you. She took care of you and became your entire world."

"And she surrounded me with people. First Gino and all his relatives, then Lizzie."

"Exactly. There were so many good people in your life who loved you that there was no reason for you to search your brain for anything else. It was probably too painful to try to remember, so you didn't."

"You're being too easy on me," she said.

"No, you're being too hard on yourself."

"I feel like I betrayed my mom and dad by forgetting who they were, and my sister, too. What am I going to say when I see Elena? How am I going to tell her that for the past twenty-five years I never gave her one thought?"

"You'll say what's right," he assured her. "I'm curious as to whether or not she ever remembered you or your parents."

"I just hope we can find her. What if she's no longer in DC?"

"Then it will take longer."

Julia kissed him on the cheek. "I like your confidence. You make me believe in the impossible. Thanks."

"No problem." He returned his gaze to the computer, but he wasn't thinking about the information on the screen; he was thinking about Julia. She was making him believe in the impossible, too.

It was a cool, crisp September day in Washington DC. The cab ride from the airport was long and nerve-racking after an equally long and nerve-racking flight. They'd hit lots of turbulence, which had done nothing to calm Julia's upset stomach. But at least they were here, and they had come armed with one address, that of the DC Ballet Company, located near the John F. Kennedy Center of Performing Arts. On the Internet, they'd discovered her sister's name, Elaine Harrigan, listed among the former stars of the company. Unfortunately, there had been no photo. Not that Julia needed to know what her twin sister looked like. All she had to do was gaze in the mirror.

"You're missing all the sights—the White House, the Washington Monument, the Capitol," Alex told her. "What's so fascinating about your hands?"

Julia realized she was still staring down at her tightly clasped fingers. "I was just thinking." She lifted her head. "And worrying about what's coming next."

"Hopefully a reunion with your sister."

"I want that—I think. I'm nervous. What will I say? What will she say? Then I worry that we won't find her at all."

He took her hand and gave it a squeeze. "Stop trying to predict the future."

It was good advice, and she wanted to take it. She looked out the window just as the Kennedy Center came into view. It was a beautiful, magnificent building set on the banks of the Potomac River. Her sister had probably danced there, Julia thought. Just like their mother, she'd taken to the stage, danced her heart out, and probably drawn the applause of thousands.

The cab passed by the center and a few blocks later stopped in front of a two-story building with white columns and a fountain in front of it. A sign over the door read DC BALLET COMPANY. Alex gave the driver money to wait for them. Julia kept her large handbag with her. She had a tight grip on it, knowing that even though they'd flown across the country, someone might still be on their tail.

They entered the building and stopped at the information desk in the lobby.

"Can I help you?" a young woman asked.

"We'd like to speak to whoever is in charge." Alex offered her a charming smile, and the woman responded immediately.

"That would be Mrs. Kay," she said. "Can I tell her what this is regarding?"

"Elaine Harrigan," Alex said. "She danced here several years ago. We're relatives of hers, and we're trying to find her. Do you think Mrs. Kay could give us a few minutes of her time? It's very important."

"I'll see if she's available." The receptionist made a brief call, then put down the phone. "You're in luck. She'll see you. Down the hall, second door on the left."

"Thank you," Alex said.

Julia felt herself growing more tense as they walked down the hall. She paused at the first door, glancing in at a large studio with hardwood floors and wall-to-wall mirrors. A group of six women in black leotards was going through a routine. She could hear music in the background and the sharp voice of an instructor. The dancers were all thin but strong, and their faces showed the same resolute determination, reminding Julia that professional ballet was not for the faint of heart. An old memory came back as she saw one girl unlace her ballet slipper. In her mind, she saw her mother taking off her slipper to reveal a bloody big toe. She'd simply wiped it off, bandaged it up, and put the slipper back on.

"Come on," Alex urged, pulling her away. "Let's find Mrs. Kay."

The door to the next room was half-open. A woman stood with her back to them. She was looking out the window behind her desk and talking on the phone. Alex knocked. She turned around and waved them in with an impatient hand.

With the woman still focused on her phone call, Julia had a chance to study Mrs. Kay. She had to be in her sixties. Her hair, a beautiful, vibrant white, was cut short, just past her ears. She was very thin, showing all of her fine bones. Her body was lanky, her legs long. She was probably a dancer, too, or had been. Finally, she set the phone down.

She smiled and said, "Elaine, I haven't seen you in awhile. I thought Judy said some of your relatives were here. She must have gotten confused."

Julia gulped. This woman thought she was Elaine, which meant Mrs. Kay knew her sister.

"Your hair is so short," Mrs. Kay said. "I thought you told me you'd never cut it."

"I'm not Elaine," Julia finally managed to get out. "I'm her sister, Julia."

"What?" Her eyes narrowed in disbelief. "Is this some sort of joke?"

"I'm Elaine's twin sister."

"That's not possible. You don't have any family."

Julia drew in a deep breath. "I'm telling you the truth. I'm Julia DeMarco. I was separated from my twin sister Elena—Elaine—many years ago. Now I'm trying to find her. And I hope you can help me."

Mrs. Kay came around her desk, her gaze never leaving Julia's face. "Come over here," she said, "and shake my hand."

It seemed like an odd request, but after a moment's hesitation, Julia moved across the room and did as she was asked.

"You aren't Elaine," the older woman said, still holding Julia's hand, "but you're the spitting image, except for your hair."

"She's my identical twin sister."

"Well, that explains it." Mrs. Kay cocked her head to one side, a confused expression lingering on her face.

"Do you know my sister well?" Julia asked.

"Of course. She lived with me for several years. I should introduce myself. I'm Victoria Kay. I run this dance company. You said your name was Julia and—" She gazed at Alex inquiringly.

"Alex Manning," he said.

"Nice to meet you."

"Does Elaine still dance for you?" Julia asked.

"No. You even sound like her. It's amazing." Victoria shook her head. "I'm sorry. I'm just so bemused by your appearance. Elaine told me everyone in her family was dead. I know she grew up in foster homes.

I actually became her foster parent when she was fifteen. She was such a gifted dancer, I knew I had to find a way for her to dance. She had a rare talent."

"Why isn't she still dancing? Is it just age? Did she get too old?"

"Heavens, no. She stopped right before the peak of her career. It was five years ago. She was crossing the street, running to meet a date. She was late, and she didn't look where she was going. A car hit her, and she broke both her legs. One was beyond complete repair. She never danced again. In fact, she still walks with a limp." Victoria's eyes filled with regret. "That's how I knew you weren't her—the way you walked. It was so tragic, what happened to her. Elaine was truly special. She didn't just dance to the music. She lived it. And her career was over in the blink of an eye."

Julia felt her heart break at the story. "What happened to her after that?"

"She recovered as best she could. She had to start over, find a new life for herself."

"Do you know where she is now?"

"She runs an antique shop on Carlmont Street in Georgetown. You can probably find her there. I don't think she ever leaves. I'll write down the address for you." Victoria moved toward the desk. "Please tell her I'm thinking about her. You know, she once told me that a piece of her heart was missing. I didn't know what that meant. Now perhaps I do. You're the missing piece."

Julia was still thinking about Victoria's words when they took a taxi to Georgetown. "If Elena told Victoria that her parents and sister were dead, then she must have remembered us," Julia said, looking to Alex for confirmation. "But why did she think I was dead?"

"Maybe the agents told her that. They didn't want her to look for you."

"That makes sense. It sounds like she grew up alone, though."

"It does," Alex agreed. "I wonder what happened to her foster family."

"Maybe it wasn't a good one. God, I hope she wasn't mistreated or abused. That would be so wrong, so unfair."

"Just remember that whatever happened to Elena, it wasn't your fault, Julia. You were a child, too. You couldn't choose your surroundings any more than she could pick hers."

"I know you're right, but I still feel guilty that I've had such a happy life. And that accident she had sounds horrible."

"Life can deal out some bad cards," Alex said. "She had to play them out. So did you."

"Now we have the chance to start over, don't you think?" Alex didn't respond to her hopeful smile, his face grim. "What are you thinking?"

"That you could get hurt. Elena may not welcome you with open arms."

"She thinks I'm dead, Alex. When she realizes I'm alive, she'll be happy, won't she?"

"I guess we'll find out," he replied.

Julia looked out the window, taking a moment to appreciate the beauty of the neighborhood: the brownstones, the shops, galleries and restaurants. At least her sister lived in a wonderful area. She must be reasonably successful. Maybe her life hadn't turned out all bad.

The taxi pulled up in front of a store called River View Antiques. As Julia got out of the cab, she forced herself to breathe deeply. She was about to come face-to-face with her past. She didn't know if she was ready, but it was too late to have second thoughts. Alex put a hand on her back and gave her a gentle push.

As they entered the store, a bell jangled. On first glance all Julia could see was stuff. Large pieces of furniture, bookcases, dressers, tables, and antique desks lined the walls. On every available tabletop were knickknacks from decades past: silver teapots, antique jewelry, old picture frames, and ceramic dishes. The room smelled like dust, incense, potpourri, and history. All of these items had once belonged to someone. They probably had fascinating stories to tell. But she wasn't here to browse. She was here to see her sister. "Hello," she called out.

"Be right there," a woman replied.

The voice sounded familiar, or was Julia imagining it?

A moment later, a woman came through a beaded curtain to greet them. She wore black capri pants and a light blue silk button-down blouse. She walked with a slight limp. Her blond hair was pulled back in a barrette at the base of her neck, but it drifted down to her waist, reminding Julia of her mother's hair.

"Hello—" The woman stopped abruptly as she looked straight at

Julia. Her blue eyes grew big and scared. "Oh, my God! It can't be you."

Julia couldn't find her voice. All she could do was stand there and stare.

Elena stared back at her. She blinked once, twice, as if she could make Julia disappear.

They were mirror images of each other, the same height, the same build, the same blue eyes, the same nose, the same chin. Only the length of their hair was different. Julia swallowed hard. Even though she had known what was coming, she still felt shocked by the reality.

"I don't understand," Elena said. "You're supposed to be dead. Everyone is dead—Mama, Papa, and you. I'm the only one left. They told me so, over and over again. This is crazy. I must be dreaming. You can't be real, Yulia."

Hearing the Russian version of her name spoken in Elena's soft voice, which was so similar to her own, made Julia's stomach turn over. This was her sister. Her blood. And she remembered her now in vivid detail.

"I'm alive," Julia said. "And I'm real. This isn't a dream." She hesitated, then opened her arms and held her breath, hoping that Elena wouldn't reject her. She really needed to touch her sister, to know with her heart what she could see with her eyes.

CHAPTER TWENTY

ELENA MOVED SLOWLY, uncertainly, finally putting her arms around Julia and giving her a tentative, brief hug. Julia would have liked to hold on, but Elena was already stepping away. They stared at each other again. It would probably take days for reality to sink in, but as the seconds ticked away, memories that had been buried deep within Julia came rushing to the front of her mind. She'd shared a bedroom with Elena, sometimes a bed when one of them had been too scared to sleep alone. They'd played together, fought together, laughed together, and cried together. How could she have ever forgotten Elena? They weren't just sisters, but twins. They were a part of each other, born together, meant to be together forever. Instead, they'd been torn apart, and twenty-five years was a long time.

"Where—where have you been all these years?" Elena asked finally.

Julia didn't know where to start. It was such a long, complicated story. "San Francisco," she said. "I was taken there after we left Russia."

"That's a long way from here. Why were you taken there, and I was brought here? Did they tell you I was dead?"

How could Julia say she hadn't been told anything and she hadn't remembered anyone? It sounded wrong. But she had to say something. Elena was waiting. "I was raised by a woman named Sarah. She told me I was her daughter, and I guess at some point I bought into the story. I don't know when it happened. Until yesterday, I couldn't think of a time when Sarah and I weren't together. She married a man and had another daughter, and we were a family."

"I don't understand. You didn't remember me?"

Julia felt another wave of guilt. She wanted to lie, if only to save Elena from being hurt by her words, but she couldn't let another falsehood be told. "I didn't remember anything until I heard your name yesterday. Then it all came back. I remembered the day Mama told us we were going to be apart. I remember how scared we were."

Elena stared back at her. "I don't remember that. I don't remember our parents at all. I just have blurry images of people whose faces never become clear enough for me to recognize. But your face was always clear. I never forgot about you. Are our parents really dead? If you're not, then—"

"No, that part is true. They died before we left Russia."

"Are you sure? They told me they died when we got here." Elena stopped, her eyes troubled. "Do you know about them? I asked and asked, but no one would tell me anything, not even their names. I just think of them as Mama and Papa."

"We have a lot to talk about." Julia saw Elena dart a quick look at Alex and realized she'd forgotten he was standing there. "I'm sorry. This is Alex Manning," she said. "He helped me find you. Do you go by Elaine now, instead of Elena?"

"I thought I'd always been Elaine, but now that you mention it..."

"You used to be Elena, and I was Yulia, but now I'm Julia with a *J*. I guess they wanted us to have more American names."

"I guess so," Elena said slowly. "It's nice to meet you, Mr. Manning."

"It's even nicer to meet you," he replied. "Is there anywhere we could talk?"

Before she could answer, the bell behind them jangled, and a curly-haired young man in his early twenties wearing baggy jeans and an extra-large T-shirt walked through the door. "What's up?" he said to Elena, then did a double take when he saw Julia. "What the—"

"This is my sister," Elena said quickly.

"I thought you didn't have any family."

"We've been separated for a long time. I need to take a break. Can you watch the store, Colin?"

Colin couldn't take his eyes off Julia. "She looks exactly like you, except your hair is longer."

"I know. I'll explain later. And I'll be upstairs if you need me." She turned to Julia. "My apartment is on the second floor. We can talk there."

Julia nodded. As Elena mounted the stairs, her limp became more pronounced, reminding Julia that Elena had suffered more than one loss in her life. They had so much to discover about each other, and Julia wanted to know everything.

Elena's apartment was not as stuffed with items as her shop, but it was still warm and cluttered, with knickknacks and colorful but mismatched furniture.

"I wasn't expecting anyone." Elena grabbed a basket of laundry off the couch. "Just sit down somewhere," she said as she headed toward the bedroom.

Julia glanced at Alex. "Well, what do you think?"

"I would have recognized her anywhere," he said with a smile. "It's hard to believe there really are two of you. Double the fun."

She sighed at that. "Let me know when we start having fun. I feel so unsettled. My stomach is churning. I don't even know how to explain it all to Elena."

"You'll find a way."

Julia hoped he was right.

When Elena returned, they sat down together in the large room that seemed to serve as living room and dining room, with a small kitchenette off to the side. After a moment, Julia said, "Why don't you start first, Elena. Tell me what happened to you when you got to the States."

Elena stared down at her hands, clasped tightly together in her lap. "I went to a foster home, the O'Rourkes." I lived there for three years, I think. Then they got divorced and couldn't be foster parents anymore, so I was sent to another home. That's pretty much the way it went for the rest of my childhood. I was moved every couple of years for one reason or another. It was not a happy time for me. The only place I loved was ballet class. No matter where I lived, I always managed to talk my way into a class by either trading chores for the teacher or begging a lot. When I was fifteen, I got into a bad situation at one home, and I ran away. I hid out at the ballet academy where I had taken some lessons. Mrs. Kay found me. She took me in, became my foster parent, and helped me become a dancer." She paused, a dark shadow crossing her face. "Now I run an antique store. Your turn."

Julia knew Elena had left out a lot of her life, but it was enough for a start. "I was raised as Julia DeMarco. My mother Sarah never told me I was adopted, and as I said before, I didn't remember anything but the story she constructed for us. She married an Italian man, Gino DeMarco, when I was five. They had a baby girl named Elizabeth. We grew up together. I never thought I was anything but a member of the family until I saw a photograph of a famous Russian orphan girl. I thought it was a picture of me. It was taken by Alex. I started researching the photo, and it turns out it wasn't me at all. It was you."

"I was in a famous picture?" Elena asked, her eyes wide and surprised once again.

"It was at an orphanage," Julia explained. "I guess we were put there until we could be smuggled out of the country."

"An orphanage?" Elena echoed.

"Yes. Your hands were on the gates, and—"

"Wait." Elena suddenly straightened. "The day was cold and gray. I wanted to go home. I didn't know where you were. I asked everyone I saw, even a boy who came over and took my picture," she finished. "I remember that now. That was you, Alex?"

He nodded. "You said something to me, but I didn't understand. I just knew there was a look in your eyes I wanted to capture."

"I was scared. I didn't know where I was or what I was doing there." She turned to Julia. "What was I doing there? And where were you?"

"I think I was there, too," Julia replied. "We were both there because our parents were important Russians, and they were planning to defect."

"Who were our parents?"

"Natalia and Sergei Markov."

"Natalia Markov, the ballerina? She was our mother? That can't be right. You must be mistaken."

"I'm not," Julia said. "You really didn't know? No one ever told you that you resembled her in any way?"

Lost in thought, Elena didn't say anything for a long moment. "I can't believe it. Natalia Markov. No one ever put the two of us together. But then, why would they?"

"You must have inherited her talent," Julia suggested. "I don't know if I did. I never had an opportunity to dance, but it never really spoke to me, either. I've always loved music more than dance."

"What happened to her? And to our father? How did they die?" Elena asked.

"In an explosion at the house. Our father worked for the Russian government. Apparently he offered to exchange information for freedom."

"Who took us out of the country if our parents were dead? And why didn't they leave us with our grandparents? Didn't we have grandparents?"

Julia hadn't thought that far back. "I don't know about our grandparents. I know our great-grandparents were tied to ballet and music, but they were probably dead before we were born. I was told that U.S. agents smuggled us out of the country somehow; the details have yet to be explained to me."

"They couldn't leave you there after your parents died," Alex interjected. "You probably would have been killed. In fact, I hate to speed up this reunion, but you both may be in danger. And we need to discuss how we're going to address that possibility."

"What do you mean?" Elena asked. "How could we be in danger?"

"My photo was published in the newspaper in San Francisco, with an article announcing that I was the orphan girl," Julia explained.

"Then both my apartment and Alex's were ransacked. Someone tried to mug me, and we've been followed. It's all very disturbing. It appears that someone, whoever killed our parents, thinks I have something of value, some sort of family treasure that was going to support our parents and their new life here."

"What kind of a treasure?" Elena inquired with a bemused shake of her head. "This is such an amazing story."

"No one seems to know exactly what the treasure is. When I found out about you, I knew I had to warn you. Since they know I'm alive, it stands to reason they know or suspect you are, too."

"I certainly don't have a treasure," Elena said. "I don't have much of anything."

"I have two things from our past." Julia reached into her handbag and pulled out the necklace. "We each had one of these, remember? You were wearing yours in the picture."

"Yes, of course," Elena said. "I still have it."

"I also found this matryoshka doll." Julia set the doll on the coffee table. "Some of the pieces are missing. Do you have them?"

A light sparked in Elena's eyes. "I do. I'll get them." She went into her bedroom and returned a moment later with the necklace and the doll. "One of my foster parents tried to take these away from me once. I had to fight to get them back. They were all I had left of my family. I wasn't going to give them up. Sometimes I slept with them under my pillow just in case one of the other kids tried to steal them."

Julia frowned. It didn't sound as if Elena had had a very good life.

Elena opened the largest doll, which belonged to Julia, and said, "I want to put them together so they fit right."

As she did so, Julia flashed back to a similar scene. Her mother had taken the dolls apart on her bed. She'd said she wanted them each to have some dolls to take with them on their trip. So she'd divided them, every other one, then handed each of them a set of the dolls. She'd told them a story... What was that story?

"Our mother told us about these dolls," Julia said slowly. "Do you remember?"

Elena thought for a long moment. "She said the doll had been painted for her grandmother."

"She was a dancer, too," Julia said. "Tamara Slovinsky. You followed in their footsteps, Elena. You lived their legacy." Elena blinked quickly, and Julia realized too late the pain her words had created. "I'm sorry. I forgot."

"No, it's all right. I had an accident. I was careless. It's my fault that I can no longer dance."

"I bet you were great when you did."

"I was all right," she said modestly. "I didn't really care about being great. I just wanted to dance. I loved the way it felt to be on the stage, to be lost in a world of make-believe, where the girls were pretty and the boys were handsome and the music lifted you up as if you were flying."

Julia was touched by her sister's words. She felt the same passion for the music that made the dancer soar. They were truly two halves of the same whole.

"Do you mind if I take a look at the doll?" Alex interrupted. "There were some numbers on Julia's set. I wonder if there are any on yours. Do you have a piece of paper?"

"Sure," Elena said, retrieving a notepad from a nearby table.

Alex took the dolls apart again, one at a time, jotting down a number after each one, until they had a string.

"Ten numbers," he mused.

"Maybe it's a serial number for the doll," Elena suggested.

"The numbers are scratched lightly into the surface of the wood. I think someone put them there after the dolls were made."

"Maybe our mother did," Julia said slowly, remembering the sharp knife by her mother's side the day she'd had the dolls open on the bed. "What could they possibly mean?"

"I don't know," Alex replied. "But we should try to find out. I can't believe I'm going to say this," he added heavily. "I'll call my father. He might know something."

Julia knew what a huge step that was for him, and she nodded gratefully. "Thank you."

Alex started to put the dolls back together, then paused. He shook the smallest one. "This is interesting. I hear a rattle." He shook it again. Julia leaned in, hearing the same small noise. The doll was one that had belonged to Elena's set.

"Did you ever notice that before?" Julia asked her sister.

"I haven't taken that doll apart in probably fifteen years. And the smallest one never opened."

"It looks like it was glued shut. There's a fine line," Alex said. He looked at Elena. "Do you mind if I try to open it, see what's inside? It could be important."

Elena shrugged her shoulders. "It's fine with me. I can't imagine what would be in there. What do you need? A knife? A screwdriver?"

"Either would be great." He pressed on the middle of the doll with his fingers.

"Do you really think there's something in there?" Julia asked.

"We know someone has been looking for something and that it's small." He took a paring knife from Elena's hand and ran the tip around the middle of the doll where there should have been an opening. After a moment, he was able to pull the two pieces apart.

Julia held her breath as he produced a silver key.

"Look at this," Alex murmured.

"Why would a key be in there?" Elena asked.

"I wonder what it goes to." Julia took the key from Alex's hand and twirled it around in her fingers. There's a number on it—423."

"I have a safe-deposit box key that looks a lot like that," Alex commented.

She met his eyes. "You think this goes to a safe-deposit box?"

"Perhaps that ten-digit number on the dolls is for a bank account." Alex rose. "I'm going to call my father now. Do you mind if I use the bedroom?"

"Go ahead," Elena said with a wave of her hand. "I don't think I made my bed, though. Neatness isn't one of my strengths."

"Mine, either," Alex said with a smile. "I'll feel right at home."

As he left the room, Julia handed Elena the key. "What do you think? Any other ideas?"

"I feel like I'm two steps behind you and Alex. I don't know what we're looking for."

"We don't know, either. We're just winging it."

An awkward silence fell between them. "This is weird, huh?" Julia said, understating the obvious. "You and me, after all these years."

"Really strange," Elena agreed. "I can't stop looking at you. I'm sorry if I'm staring."

"I feel the same way. I know you, and yet I don't."

"We were babies the last time we saw each other, three years old. It's no wonder it feels uncomfortable now."

"But it feels good, too," Julia said.

"Yes, it does. I've really missed having family," Elena confessed.

Julia wanted to say the same thing, but in all fairness she couldn't. She'd had a good family to grow up in. And another sister as well. She still didn't know how she would tell Liz about Elena. That wasn't a conversation she was looking forward to.

"Is he your boyfriend?" Elena asked, nodding toward the bedroom.

"What? You mean Alex?"

Elena smiled. "Of course I mean Alex. Who else would I mean?"

"Actually, I was engaged to someone else until a few days ago. My fiancé didn't want me to search for my real family. It turned out to be the last straw between us, and I'm glad now. I realized he wasn't the one for me."

"Because of Alex?"

"I didn't break up with him because of Alex," Julia prevaricated. "What about you? Any men in your life?"

"Not recently. I was engaged, too, a couple years ago, before my accident. He was a choreographer, a good one. He couldn't bear the thought that I'd never dance for him again. So he left. It hurt, but life goes on. I learned that lesson a long time ago."

Julia scooted forward on the couch, clasping her hands together. "I'm so sorry that your childhood wasn't happy. I wish we could have been together. It isn't fair that I grew up in a loving home and you didn't. I feel so guilty."

"It wasn't your fault. We should have been kept together, not hidden away from the world."

"For our protection, they say," Julia reminded her. Although she wasn't quite sure if that was the true reason or the convenient one. They'd become baggage, children no one wanted to be associated with. That's why they'd stuck Elena in a foster home. Julia was lucky, very lucky. Sarah had wanted her desperately enough to change her entire life and her past just to be able to take care of her. For the first time, she felt a lessening of her anger toward Sarah. At least she had been loved and taken care of. She needed to remember that and be thankful.

Alex returned to the room. "I reached my father. He'll have Brady trace the number. He thinks it's a bank account. He knew your parents made plans before the defection. Your mother had come to the U.S. a number of times with her ballet company. My father believes that she may have stashed away a great deal of money during those visits."

"So the treasure might be cash," Julia said.

"Might be," Alex agreed. "He'll call me back. I told him where we were. He said to stay put. Apparently your parents were planning to live here in DC, because your father was going to work with our intelligence agencies. That's how Elena ended up here. It was the initial drop point."

"You make me sound like a bottle of milk or a newspaper," Elena said with a touch of annoyance.

"Sorry. Those were his words, not mine."

"It would make sense that they'd come here so our father could work with the government," Julia interjected. "Does your dad think the account might be here in the city?"

"That's his guess. Or possibly New York," Alex replied. "Your mother made several trips there as well."

Julia's cell phone began to ring. She slipped it out of her purse and saw Liz's number. "It's my sister," she said, feeling awkward when she said it. "My other sister." She cleared her throat and answered the phone. "Hello."

"Hey, it's Liz. What's going on? I haven't heard from you in a while. Have you found out anything?"

"A couple of things," Julia said. "I don't want to get into it on the phone, though. I promise to tell you everything as soon as I get back."

"Get back? Where exactly are you, Julia?"

She hesitated, then said, "I'm in Washington DC."

"Why? What's there?"

"It's a long story."

"And you don't want to tell me. I get it. I just wanted to let you know that some guy was watching me on the docks this afternoon."

"What did he look like?" Julia asked, her pulse quickening.

"He was big and stocky, and he wore a baseball cap. He left as soon as he realized I'd seen him. Do you think he's the guy who burglarized our apartment?"

"I think he might be. Don't go back to our place, Liz, especially alone."

"I won't. Believe me, I'm not looking for trouble."

"I'll call you when I get home," Julia said. "In the meantime, be careful, Liz. I don't want anything to happen to you."

"I will. Is Alex still with you?"

"Yes."

Liz sighed. "You're crazy, Julia, but I guess everyone deserves to fall for a bad boy once in her life."

Julia wanted to say it wasn't like that, but how could she? She glanced at Alex, who was talking to Elena with a warm, interested look on his face. She wasn't falling in love with him. She was already there. After saying good-bye, she hung up the phone.

"Everything okay?" Alex asked.

"Liz said some guy was watching her. It sounded like the same man who was watching me at the radio station. I feel bad. I'm here. She's there. I don't want her to get hurt."

"Liz is your... sister?" Elena asked, tripping over the word *sister*.

"Yes. She's younger than me, just twenty-two. I've always taken care of her. She's really angry with me for getting involved in all this."

"Does she know about me?"

"I wanted to make sure I could find you first, so I haven't said anything yet."

Elena nodded, understanding in her eyes. "That will be difficult for you, won't it?"

"Probably."

Elena cleared her throat. "I need to go downstairs and check on Colin. You're welcome to stay here and wait for that call."

"Actually, I was thinking about food," Alex said. "And it will probably be hours before my father calls back."

"I'd love to see more of your shop," Julia put in. She exchanged a look with Alex and knew they were once again on the same page. She needed some time alone with her sister, and he was more than willing to give it to her.

"I'll get some takeout and bring it back," he said. "Any suggestions?"

Elena thought for a moment. "If you're adventurous, there's a great Thai restaurant around the corner."

"Oh, my God. You are my sister, " Julia said with a huge smile. "I love exotic food."

Elena grinned back at her. "So do I."

For the first time since they'd arrived, Julia felt optimistic and back on balance. "This is going to be good," she said, and she wasn't talking about the food.

It was almost midnight when Julia and Elena finally talked themselves out. While Elena went into the bedroom to undress, Julia helped Alex make up a bed on the couch. "Will you be all right out here?" she asked.

"I'd be better if you were with me." He gave her an intimate smile that reminded her how long it had been since she'd kissed him or touched him. "Come here," he said softly.

She cast a quick look over her shoulder. "Elena might see us."

"One kiss."

"It's never enough," she said with a sigh as she moved into his arms. His hands spanned her waist as he kissed her gently, tenderly, with only a hint of the passion they'd shared the night before. "That was awfully restrained," she complained.

"Believe me, if it wasn't, you'd be on your back right now and we'd give your sister the second shock of her life."

"Promises, promises," she said with a smile. She pressed another kiss on his lips. "Thanks for being so great today."

"I didn't do anything."

"Yes, you did. You supported me, and you didn't try to take over. You did good. I owe you."

"And I will collect," he promised. "I just hope my father calls tomorrow. I'd like to get that number resolved."

"I think he will. He wants to help you."

"To absolve his guilt, maybe. Whatever the reason, I'll take it. The sooner we figure out the ending to this mystery, the better."

A twinge of pain ran through her at his words. As soon as the mystery was over, they would be over. To be fair, he probably hadn't meant it like that, but it was still true.

"Hey, what's that frown for?" He tipped up her chin with his finger.

"Nothing. I was just thinking about all the secrets, the lies, the constant surprises. I never know what will happen next."

"But that doesn't stop you from fighting on," Alex said, a note of admiration in his voice. "A lot of people would have quit or backed away by now, not wanting to risk losing everything they believed in. You're something else, Julia." He ran his fingers through her hair. "Beautiful, smart, and gutsy. Hell of a combination."

"Are you scared?" she asked, half-teasing, half-serious.

"Terrified," he said lightly. He kissed her again, then released her. "Go to bed, Julia, before I can't let you go."

"I'd stay, but—"

"But you two women need to bond. I get it. And believe me, I've had enough girl talk to last me awhile. I'm going to watch something macho on television and not think about anything else until tomorrow morning.

"Good night." Julia stole one last quick kiss before leaving. When she entered the bedroom, Elena was wearing a long T-shirt and sitting on the side of her queen-size bed. She was brushing out her hair, and Julia was struck once again by the resemblance between them.

"If you want to sleep with Alex, it's fine with me," Elena said, setting down her brush. She gave Julia a curious look. "I still don't understand exactly what your relationship is."

"I'm not sure, either," Julia admitted. "I'm afraid to analyze it too much, especially in the middle of everything else."

"But you like him."

"Oh, yeah, more than a little. But that seems crazy, too, because a few weeks ago I thought I was in love with someone else."

"What happened to the other guy? I know you said he was upset that you were searching for your family, but was that all of it?"

Julia sat down on the bed. "No. I told you that my mother, Sarah, died six months ago. Well, Michael was so great through her illness. For two years he was supportive, kind, caring—everything a woman could want. After my mom died, he wanted to get married, and we'd been engaged for so long, I knew I had to say yes. I owed him. Deep in my heart, I knew that Michael wasn't the one for me. He was just taking up where my mom left off. Sarah raised me in a controlled little bubble. She protected me and hid me away from the world. I guess she was always looking over her shoulder, afraid she would be found out. Michael wanted a wife who would stay in his world, who wouldn't make waves, wouldn't want to travel or have a big job or do anything different. That's fine for him, but I would have suffocated."

"Alex certainly doesn't seem the type to put you in a bubble," Elena observed.

"I'm not sure he wants to put me anywhere. He's an admitted loner. He likes to travel light, and he told me that he's never met a woman who made him want more than a casual affair."

"I hope he didn't say that after you slept together."

"No, before. I'm a fool, huh?"

Elena smiled. "He's a good-looking man, Julia. He's smart, success-ful, exciting—the last thing I would call you is a fool. Just don't let him break your heart."

"I'm trying to keep that in mind."

Elena tossed her a T-shirt. "You can sleep in this."

"Thanks."

Julia took off her jeans and top and slipped on the T-shirt. She climbed into the bed next to Elena, feeling both awkward and strangely comfortable. A moment later Elena switched off the light.

"Was it hard losing your boyfriend when you had your accident?" Julia asked.

For a long minute, there was silence; then Elena said, "His leaving didn't hurt as much as the fact that I couldn't dance anymore, but it was very painful. I really loved him. I made a huge mistake. He only wanted the successful dancer who could bring his choreography to life. He didn't really want me, all of me. He was an ass."

"And there hasn't been anyone since?"

"I've been busy. I had to restart my life, get a new career going. Victoria—Mrs. Kay—she helped me get the shop. She actually owns this building, and I pay nominal rent. There's no way I could afford this area if I didn't have connections."

"The shop is great. I'm so impressed by how many beautiful pieces you have."

"I love knowing that each piece in my shop has a history. I don't love it as much as dance, I'll admit, but I like seeing things find their rightful home. Probably something subliminal about that, huh?"

Because they'd never been able to go home. "Probably," Julia agreed.

"Well, good night," Elena said.

Julia smiled as a long-ago memory flashed through her head. "Good night," she said. "Sweet dreams."

"You, too."

"Don't let the bedbugs bite."

"Julia."

"Elena," she echoed. "You know I hate to go to sleep first."

Elena's soft laugh floated through the shadowy darkness. "I remember that now. You never wanted me to go to sleep before you. Every time I said good night, you said something else, so you'd always have the last word."

"And so I'd keep you awake." Julia stared at the ceiling, watching the moonbeams play across the room. They had once been best friends, as close as two sisters could be. Twenty-five years had separated them, but the connection between them was already back. "I missed you," Julia whispered into the darkness.

"I missed you, too," Elena said softly.

Julia closed her eyes, content now to let Elena have the last word.

CHAPTER TWENTY-ONE

JULIA CREPT out of bed just after eight o'clock. Elena was still sleeping, and the apartment was quiet. She walked into the living room and saw Alex sprawled across the narrow couch. He'd kicked off his blanket and wore only a pair of navy blue boxers. Her breath caught at the sight of him. He really was an attractive man, and she felt a stirring of desire at his tousled hair and whisker-laden cheeks, the sweep of his dark lashes against his olive-skinned face. She wanted to touch him, wanted to run her hands down his strong arms and across his sculpted abs. She wanted to wrap herself around him until they were touching in every possible way.

Kneeling next to the couch, she leaned over and traced his lips with her tongue. He responded immediately, his hand catching the back of her head and pulling her in for a deeper, longer, more passionate kiss.

"You were awake," she accused breathlessly when she opened her eyes and saw him watching her. "Why didn't you say something?"

"I wanted to see what you would do," he said with a grin.

He had no idea what she'd wanted to do... or maybe he did.

"Did you sleep well?" she asked.

"Not bad. I had a good dream. Want to know what it was about? You were the star."

"What was I wearing?"

His grin widened. "Nothing."

She couldn't help smiling back. "You are bad."

"In my dream you were bad." He pulled her to him, his hands brushing the sides of her breasts.

She would have liked to strip off her T-shirt and join him on the couch, but she could hear her sister moving around in the bedroom. "Elena will be out here any second," she said, gently pushing him away.

"Kill-joy." He sat up on the couch, running a hand through his hair. "How are you two getting along?"

"Good." She sat next to him. "I keep thinking it should be more uncomfortable, that twenty-five years should have made us strangers, but there's still a connection between us. We know each other on a very basic level." She felt a little self-conscious at her words. "Maybe there is some sort of twin thing going on."

A cell phone rang from the vicinity of Alex's pants. Julia tossed him his jeans, and he pulled out the phone. "Hello." He glanced over at Julia and mouthed, Brady. "A bank account number, huh? Where's the bank?" He listened for a few more minutes, then said, "Yes, we found Julia's twin sister, the one you neglected to mention. I know, isn't that amazing? Those two should never have been separated or lost in the system. If you guys hadn't screwed up, they wouldn't have spent the past twenty-five years apart." Alex paused for another moment. "Yes, we do have a key, and I have a feeling it will fit. All right. We'll meet you in an hour, as soon as the bank opens." He grabbed a pen off the coffee table and jotted down an address on the back of a magazine. "Got it. What about protection? Julia and I have been followed more than once." He listened, then said, "Fine, see you then."

"What did he say?" Julia asked as soon as Alex had ended the call.

"The numbers scratched in the dolls are for a bank account here in DC. Brady wants all three of us to meet him at the bank when it opens. He also said there's a safe-deposit box, and I have a feeling the key we found in the doll fits right into that box."

Julia felt a rush of excitement. "Good news for a change. But when did Mr. Brady come to DC?"

"Probably as soon as my father called him and told him where we were. Brady said there's a good deal of money in the account. And who knows what's in that safe-deposit box?"

"I can't believe it's right here in DC. We're finally at the end of the trail," Julia said.

"And at your parents' intended destination. This is where they were coming. It would make sense that whatever they'd stashed away was here. And I believe your mother also performed here."

"At the Kennedy Center, probably." Julia smiled. "And Elena danced there twenty-something years later. That's nice, isn't it?"

"It is nice. Your mother wanted you both to have the life she couldn't have."

"Hopefully, somewhere in the universe she's smiling down on us because we're finally back together."

"Apparently the bank account is in both your names, with your Russian surname. Brady says he can get past the red tape. He has paperwork to prove that you and Elena are the heirs to Natalia and Sergei Markov. That will allow the bank to release the money as well as the contents of the safe-deposit box to you."

"I wonder what's in the box," she mused. "It must be valuable enough to still be of interest to the Russian government. Why else would they have people following us?"

"Only one way to find out."

She stood up. "I'll tell Elena to get dressed."

Julia felt nervous and edgy as they drove into the three-story parking garage next to the downtown bank where Brady had told them to meet. She couldn't believe they were finally nearing the end of their search. Soon she would know exactly why someone was after her. She glanced over her shoulder as they entered the garage, wondering if anyone had followed them here to the nation's capital. But there was no one behind them.

Alex parked the car, and they took a moment to glance around. The parking garage was shadowy and half-full, probably because it was Saturday. A car pulled in next to them. Julia stiffened, then relaxed when she saw Brady get out of the car.

"You must be Elena," he said as they gathered together.

"Yes," she said tentatively. "And you're?"

"Daniel Brady." He turned to Julia. "Did you bring the key?"

"I have it," Julia said.

"Good. The bank account was set up in your names," Brady added as they walked toward the bank. "Yulia and Elena Markov. I've already spoken to the bank manager and circumvented some red tape to get into the account."

"How did you do that?" Alex asked sharply.

"Let's just say I have friends in high places. At any rate, there is five hundred and twenty-seven thousand dollars in cash in the account."

Julia's jaw dropped. "How did my parents get that much money?"

Brady shrugged. "I'm sure they had their ways. The bank account has been paying off the rent on the safe-deposit box, which is why it wasn't closed in the past twenty-five years."

"What's in the box?" Elena asked.

"I'm hoping there might be something in there to tell us who killed your parents," Brady replied.

His answer surprised Julia. She hadn't considered that possibility. "Do you think our parents knew who set that bomb in their house?"

Brady's eyes narrowed. "I see Charles gave you the whole story."

"He thought I deserved to know." Julia lifted her chin, looking Brady straight in the eye. "And he was right. So I'll ask you again: Do you think our parents knew who killed them?"

"Your father certainly knew he had enemies in his own party. They were watching him. Love can make a man stupid. They suspected he was softening because of his love for your mother. He had to leave Russia, and we wanted to get him out. But they got there first. With any luck, your father may have left us a clue as to who set that bomb." Brady opened the door to the bank. "After you."

Julia stepped into the cool quiet of the bank. There were only a few people working: two tellers, a loan officer, and the manager, who came out of her office when she saw them.

After preliminary introductions, she said, "I've arranged for a cashier's check as you directed, Mr. Brady. It will be ready momentarily."

"Good. Now we'd like to take a look at the safe-deposit box," Brady said.

The manager took them over to the vault area where the boxes were located. She asked both Elena and Julia to sign in, then escorted them all into the room where Julia inserted the key into the lock. Her anxiety made her fumble, but eventually the lock turned.

The manager pulled out the box and set it on the table. "I'll leave you to it."

Julia looked to Elena for guidance. "Do you want to—"

"Go ahead," Elena said. "You know more about this than I do."

Julia drew in a deep breath and looked into the open box. There was a white business-size envelope with their names, Yulia and Elena, scrawled across the top. She didn't stop to open it, setting it aside for the moment. A large manila envelope came next. It was filled with scraps of paper that were yellowed with age and scribbled upon with blue and black ink. It took Julia a moment to realize that the notations were musical scores. She wondered if they had been composed by her great-grandfather. She wanted to linger, but everyone was waiting.

"Keep going," Alex urged. "You can figure out the music later."

The final object in the box was a Russian icon, a framed picture of St. George about five by seven inches in size. Julia remembered it hanging over the doorway in her parents' bedroom. In fact, they'd had icons all over the house. For good luck, her mother had told her. Some luck the icons had brought them.

"That's it," she said. "A letter, musical scores, and a picture." She felt disappointed. "I don't know what I was expecting, but..." She glanced down at the musical scores again. "Wait. If these scores were written by our great-grandfather before the revolution, they could be worth a fortune."

"Really?" Elena asked. "Who was our great-grandfather?"

"A famous composer, Ivan Slovinsky. He ran to Paris during the revolution. He lived in exile there for the rest of his life," Julia explained. "Our parents must have believed the scores would be worth enough to set them up in a new life." She looked down at the letter. "I guess we should read this."

"Save it for later," Brady suggested. "Let's get your check and get out of here."

Julia picked up the envelopes and the picture, and they left the room. The bank manager asked Brady to sign a form, then handed them a check closing the account.

"Why are we withdrawing the money?" Alex asked, as they made their way toward the front door. "This is a bank. Seems like a good place to keep it."

"I assume the girls will want to split it up," Brady replied. "If they tried to get the money on their own, they'd need a lot of forms and new identification. I thought I'd make it easier for them. It's the least I can do." He paused, turning his gaze on Julia. "I do want to take a look at that letter just in case there's anything in there to lead us to the people who killed your parents. May I suggest that we go to one of our safe houses so that we can all feel comfortable and secure? It's not far from here."

Julia glanced at Alex, who shrugged in agreement. She turned to Elena. "Is that okay with you?"

"Whatever you think is best," Elena replied. "I'll leave it up to you."

"We'll follow you," Alex said, as they entered the parking lot.

"I think the girls should come with me," Brady said. "So I can protect them."

"I can do that, too." The air between Brady and Alex suddenly sizzled as the two men seemed immensely irritated with each other. "I'll take Elena and Julia. We'll follow you to the safe house," Alex repeated, "and we'll keep the letter and everything else with us."

Brady looked as if he wanted to argue, then forced a tight smile. "All right. We'll play it your way... for now."

Julia didn't like the tone of Brady's voice. Was there something else he hadn't told them? She'd thought it was over. They'd found the safe-deposit box. She had the contents in her bag. Everything that had belonged to her parents was now in her possession. She should be feeling happy, not tense or worried, but she couldn't stop the uneasiness sweeping through her. The tiny hairs at the back of her neck prickled as they walked farther into the dark shadows of the garage, which seemed more menacing now than before.

She wished someone else would come into the garage or a car would drive by. It was too quiet—eerily quiet. The only sounds came from their feet hitting the pavement—four pairs of feet. Or was that five?

Julia took a quick glance behind her. She sensed someone was watching them.

She must have paused, because Brady put his hand under her elbow. "Keep walking," he said in a low voice.

She wanted to pull her arm away from him, but he had a tight grip on her. "Hey," she protested.

"I want to get out of here fast," he muttered. His tension seemed as palpable as her own, and that made her more fearful.

"Alex." She didn't know what she wanted to ask him, but she needed him closer to her. But Alex was on the other side of Brady, a good five feet away.

Suddenly, a man came out from between two cars. It was the same man Julia had seen at the radio station and probably the same man who had tried to grab her purse on Union Street. Up close, he was even bigger than she remembered, with a square, angry face and wild eyes. He began to move forward. She tried to back up, but Brady still had a hold on her arm.

"Get in my car," Brady said to Julia, flipping the locks open on his vehicle, which was closer than Elena's car.

"Don't move," the man said in a thick Russian accent. He reached into his coat pocket.

"He's got a gun!" Brady yelled.

Julia gasped in horror as Alex tackled the man around the knees and toppled him to the ground. "Do something!" she cried.

"Get in the car," Brady repeated, shoving her onto the front seat. He grabbed Elena next and pushed her into the back, then jumped behind the wheel and gunned the engine. He peeled out of the parking lot, leaving Alex and the Russian fighting for the weapon.

"Stop!" Julia yelled. "We can't leave Alex on his own."

"He's already got the gun," Brady said, looking in the rearview mirror. "Don't worry, Julia. Alex can handle it. I've got to get you out of here." He pulled out his cell phone, punched in a number, and barked into the phone that he needed backup at the Hastings Street Garage.

Julia's stomach churned. She looked back at Elena, whose face was white with fear. God, she hoped Alex was okay. She knew he was tough and fearless, but how could he fight a gun? They shouldn't have run. They should have stayed to help. "We have to go back," she said again. "We need to make sure Alex is all right. Please, turn the car around."

"Alex would want me to get you to safety," Brady said. "He knows help is on the way. He'll be fine. Trust me."

"If help is on the way, then we'll be safe there, too," she argued.

"I don't know how many more men are in the garage."

Julia thought about the two men who'd followed them to St. Helena. Maybe there were more people involved. But who were they? And if there were more of them in the garage, then Alex was definitely in trouble.

"I demand that you turn this car around."

He ignored her.

"Please," Elena muttered from the backseat. "Please, do what she asks."

Brady tossed Julia a look that told her he was going to do exactly what he wanted. "I know what I'm doing. I've been in these situations many times before."

She supposed that was true, but it still didn't make her feel better.

Her instincts were screaming in protest, her gut telling her something was terribly wrong.

"We need to look at that letter," Brady continued. "You may have incriminating evidence in your bag. We can't allow it to fall into the wrong hands. It might threaten not only your own security, but that of others in our government as well."

His serious words reminded Julia that this mystery had begun a world away. She wondered if the letter from her parents would finally answer all of her questions.

"We're almost there," Brady said as she began to open her purse. "Hang on." He spun around a corner on two wheels, the tires squealing in protest.

Julia's heart leapt into her throat as Brady dodged in and out of traffic. She hoped Brady wouldn't kill them on the way to saving their lives. Five minutes later they were heading out of the city, across the Potomac and into a residential neighborhood. In fact, the area was almost rural, with lots of space and land, with a house every quarter mile. Julia had no idea where they were. Finally, Brady pulled into the driveway of a modest one-story home that was set apart from its neighbors by tall trees on each side of the property. "Inside," he said, looking around as he escorted them into the house. Julia barely had time to see the living room before Brady pushed them into a back bedroom. "Safest place in the house," he said.

When they were all in the bedroom, Julia finally let herself breathe. They were safe, at least for the moment. That security hadn't registered with Elena, whose blue eyes were dark and worried. Her skin was pale, and beads of sweat lined her forehead. Elena was probably even more confused than Julia. Her sister hadn't spent the past week running from some sinister force the way Julia had.

She turned to Brady, suddenly aware that he had taken the contents of the safe-deposit box out of her bag. The letter he'd expressed interest in had been tossed onto the bed. Brady was now fiddling with the frame on the Icon.

"What are you doing?" she asked.

He didn't answer her. Instead, he produced a small screwdriver and took the frame apart. His eyes lit up as he pulled out a dark red stone that caught the sunlight. A ruby?

Julia had the sudden feeling the surprises weren't over yet. "Oh, my God! Is that real?"

"Oh, yeah," he muttered.

The ruby was followed by another huge stone, then another, until there were six in all: an opal, a diamond, two sapphires, two rubies—a fortune in jewels.

"I knew it," he said in satisfaction. "I knew they were in there."

"What do you mean, you knew they were there? Where did they come from?" Julia demanded.

For a moment it didn't appear that he would answer her; then he shrugged. "I guess it doesn't matter if you know. The jewels belonged to your great-grandmother. She was a favorite with the Imperial Court. She received one perfect stone after each performance and had them sewn into her costumes. Then the revolution swept across Russia. The costumes disappeared. Tamara claimed they'd been stolen, but it was rumored that she'd hidden them away." His smile grew smug as he faced Julia. "Your mother told me about them one night. She said they could be used to buy her family's freedom. How could I resist an offer like that?" He glanced down at the stones. "I've waited twenty-five years to hold these babies," he muttered, closing his fist around the stones. "They're finally mine."

"Yours? They're ours," Julia corrected.

"I don't think so."

Julia looked into his cold, dark eyes and saw the truth. Brady had been in Russia at the time of the defection. He knew about her parents. He knew about the jewels. He'd probably worked both sides. He hadn't wanted to help her parents defect; he'd wanted to get the treasure. She swallowed hard, realizing where her thoughts were taking her. She was probably staring at the man who'd set a trap for her parents. "It was you, wasn't it?" she asked, the words escaping from her lips before she could consider the wisdom of saying them. "You're the one who killed my parents."

"They double-crossed me," he said flatly. "They set me up to think

I already had the jewels in my possession. It was their ticket to freedom, but they gave me fakes. They deserved what they got."

"They didn't deserve to die," she protested, pain and anger filling her soul at his callous disregard for their lives.

He shrugged. "It had to be done. I couldn't let them leave the country with the jewels."

His coldness, his complete lack of conscience, was now starkly evident. How could Julia have missed it before? How could she and Alex have been taken in by his offers to help? That answer was obvious now, too. They'd trusted Brady because Charles and Stan trusted him. Did the other two know of his duplicity, or had they been conned as well?

"Did anyone ever suspect you?" she asked.

"Of course not," he said in a cocky tone. "I was too clever. The Russians thought the Americans had done it. The Americans believed the Russians had done it. No one ever knew it was me. And no one ever will." He pulled a gun out of his jacket and pointed it at her.

Elena gasped. "No!"

Julia began to shake. She'd never been this close to a real gun before. It was terrifying, but if she was going to die, she had to know the rest. "Why?" she asked. "Why did you kill them? Why didn't you just steal the jewels and disappear?"

"I couldn't take the chance that I would be discovered," he said smoothly. "I told them it was the perfect plan. They give me the jewels. I get them out of the country. Only the real plan was they give me the jewels; then they die." His expression turned ugly, his mouth curving with anger and disgust. "But they tricked me. They gave me fakes. I didn't find out until after they were dead. I thought you were all dead. I thought the game was over. Then a little photograph appeared in a magazine, and I knew there was still a chance the jewels had gotten out with you and your sister. It just took until now to find them, but they're mine now. And it's over. It's all over."

"Why didn't you come after us before?" Julia asked. "Why wait until now?"

"You were hidden away by the time I got to the States. I found

Elena." He tipped his head toward her sister, who was shivering so hard Julia could hear her teeth rattling. "I went through her stuff. I saw the dolls, the necklace, but she had nothing else. I thought that you must have it all—that Sarah had taken the treasure, that she was the one who'd outsmarted me. But she'd covered her tracks so well, I couldn't find her."

So her mother had saved her life.

"Sarah didn't know what she had, did she?" he asked.

"I have no idea what she knew," Julia retorted. "But she had me. That's all she wanted."

"She always did think small."

"Don't say that," Julia told him angrily. "You don't know anything about her."

"And I don't care," Brady replied. "This conversation is done. I'm going to finish what I started. Give me your purses. You won't be calling anyone for help. Put them on the ground and push 'em over here."

Julia didn't want to obey, but he had a gun, and she couldn't think what else to do. She put her handbag on the ground and kicked it toward him, wondering how on earth they could get out of this situation alive. She tried to reassure Elena with her eyes, but Elena wasn't stupid. She knew they were in big trouble. Now Julia was glad that Alex wasn't with them. Maybe he'd survive if she didn't. The thought was terrifying. She didn't want to die, not now, not when she finally knew who she was and what she wanted.

Brady tossed their purses through the open door, his eyes focused on the two women as he backed away. "Think of it like this—at least you'll go together, and it will be quick. Over in a flash," he said with a cruel smile.

Julia's heart began to beat double-time. Her parents had been killed by a bomb going off in their house. Was that what Brady had planned for them? Was he going to blow up this house with them in it?

"You must listen," the man pleaded.

Alex didn't want to listen, but since he had the Russian pinned up against the garage wall, one arm against the man's windpipe and no backup in sight, he could either knock him out or give him a chance to say his piece. "Talk then."

"Brady. He's the one who killed Natalia and Sergei."

There was a spark of truth in his blue eyes, eyes that looked remarkably similar to Julia's, Alex thought. Not that he trusted this guy, but it suddenly occurred to him that Brady was gone, as were Julia and Elena. "How do you know?"

"I'm Roland Markov. Sergei's half brother," he said breathlessly. "I have a driver's license. In my pocket," he added. "I was going to show it to you."

Alex sent him a skeptical look, but he had to admit that despite the fact that Brady had yelled, "Gun," there was no actual evidence of a weapon. "Where is it?"

"In my inside jacket pocket."

"Don't move," Alex ordered, holding the man with one hand as he reached into the pocket. He pulled out a brown billfold and flipped it open. The driver's license photo was accurate. So was the name. The address was in Los Angeles. "You're a long way from home," he said. "And you were in San Francisco. Julia saw you several times. You broke into her apartment and mine."

Roland shook his head. "No, that wasn't me. I saw Julia at the radio station, yes. I spoke to her in Russian. I wanted to see if she understood. She got scared and ran. But I didn't break into her apartment. That was Brady. I saw him and another man enter her building one day. I wasn't sure if it was him. It had been many years since I'd seen him."

Alex didn't know what to believe. "I chased you through the park. You tried to grab Julia's bag."

"No, that wasn't me. I don't run fast. If you chased me, you would have caught me."

Alex had to admit the man was big and a little slow, which was why he'd been able to pin him against the wall.

"I saw the photograph of Elena in the LA newspaper," Roland

continued. "I read the story, and my wife said I must go to San Francisco and see if it is really her."

The fact that Roland correctly identified the girl in the photo as Elena made Alex believe he was telling the truth. He slowly released him, but stayed close.

"So why didn't you just introduce yourself?"

Roland's tongue darted out, sweeping his bottom lip in nervousness. "I realized the girl in San Francisco is Yulia. When I saw others watching her, I became afraid. I didn't know who killed Sergei for sure. Could be secret police, could be friend, could be anyone. I think they come back now to kill Yulia. Or to get what they hadn't gotten before. I decide it is best to wait and watch."

Alex stared at Roland. "Get what?"

"Natalia had several precious stones from a century ago. She and Sergei told me they would use them to start a new life. And they would send for me when they could. When they died, I didn't know what happened to the jewels until I saw the picture of Elena. If she was alive, perhaps she had the jewels, too."

The treasure, Alex thought. He finally knew what it was. "Wait. Why do you think Brady killed Sergei and Natalia? How could he get the treasure if they were dead?"

"Sergei was worried about betrayal," Roland said heavily. "He told me he had made elaborate plans for the defection to work. Brady must have thought he had the jewels or that he could get them once Natalia and Sergei were dead." He paused, his eyes sad. "They were so careful, but they still trusted the wrong man."

"And Brady let everyone think that the Russians had done in their own people," Alex said slowly, as the pieces of the puzzle came together. "Very clever. So where are the jewels?"

"I believe they were hidden in the frame of a picture."

Alex's heart sped up. The Russian icon. "Dammit. We have to find Brady."

"I've been following him since yesterday," Roland said. "He went to a house this morning. It's not far from here."

"Let's go." Alex ran for Elena's car. Fortunately, he still had the keys in his pocket.

"We should hurry," Roland said. "Once Brady has the stones, he'll have no reason to keep Elena or Yulia alive."

Alex's heart jumped into overdrive. He gunned the motor and tore out of the parking lot, following Roland's directions to the highway and praying he wouldn't be too late. "Maybe Brady doesn't know the jewels are in the icon," he said hopefully.

Roland didn't answer him. Alex shot him a questioning look.

Roland met his gaze, then shrugged. "He knows."

There was something in that fatalistic shrug that disturbed Alex. "Tell me something, Roland. Did you come here to save the girls or to get the jewels?"

"Perhaps the girls give me small token of gratitude."

Alex was disappointed, but also relieved to get an honest answer for a change. "I won't let you hurt Julia or Elena," he warned.

"I don't want to hurt them. They are family."

"Rich family now," Alex commented. He didn't know if he trusted Roland or not, but he'd deal with him later. First he had to find Julia before Brady found those stones.

Julia saw Brady backing toward the door and knew they had only one chance to escape, and it was now. No time to plan, think or analyze. She drew in a big gulp of air, praying she was making the right decision; then she let her instincts and her anger take over. This man had killed her parents without remorse. She would not let him kill her and Elena, too.

She threw her body at the arm that held the gun, hoping to knock it out of his hand. Instead she heard a gunshot, and they both tumbled to the ground. She waited for a searing pain somewhere in her body, but she could feel nothing but an intense desire to stop him from shooting again.

Adrenaline gave her strength and determination as she wrestled for the gun. Brady was bigger than she was, stronger. He knocked her across the face with the back of his hand. Stars exploded behind her eyes. She'd never taken a punch before, and the pain was shocking. But she couldn't let it stop her. He was scrambling to get to his feet. She jumped on him again, knocking him down on the dusty hardwood floor.

He reared back in fury, throwing her against the bed. Her head bounced off the corner of the bedpost, and another shot of pain screamed through her body. She struggled to get her breath, to move. She had to move!

But Brady was getting away.

He stumbled toward the door.

Julia watched in horror, unable to do anything but wait for her breath to come back and her muscles to follow her command.

Suddenly Elena moved. She picked up the only other piece of furniture in the room—a simple wooden desk chair. Brady was so intent on reaching the door, he didn't see her coming. Elena whacked him over the head. The sound of the wood cracking against his skull was something Julia would never forget, but her relief when he landed on the ground with a dull thud was even better.

For a split second she and Elena simply stared at him, unable to believe he wasn't moving, wasn't getting up, wasn't waving the gun in their faces.

The gun... Julia finally got her feet back under her. She grabbed the gun near his hand and tossed it across the room.

"We've got to get out of here," Elena cried, grabbing the envelopes off the bed. "Hurry. The house is going to explode."

"Not without the stones," Julia replied. She forced herself to open Brady's clenched fist, terrified that at any moment he would wake up and grab her arm.

"We don't have time. Please," Elena begged. "The bomb could go off at any second."

"Go without me. I'll be right there."

"No, I can't leave you behind."

"And we can't leave the jewels behind. They belonged to our great-grandmother." Julia peeled Brady's fingers apart. Even unconscious he seemed determined to hang on to those stones. Finally, she got his hand open enough to take the jewels. She grabbed their purses on the way out of the bedroom, and they dashed toward the front door, hoping against hope they'd get out in time.

As they hit the porch, the cool air struck Julia like a welcoming hug. They were out. They were free.

A car came screaming down the street. Alex.

Her heart sang again as he jumped out and came running toward them. He was alive. He was all right. Thank God!

"Brady?" Alex asked, meeting her halfway up the walk. "Where is he?"

"Inside." She grabbed his arm as he headed toward the house. "There's a bomb," she yelled. "There's no time." She pulled him back toward the car, shocked to see the Russian get out of the vehicle. "What is he doing here?"

"Long story," Alex shouted. "But he's family."

His words were cut off by an enormous explosion. A roaring, thundering sound was followed by blazing heat and a tornado of flames that threw them to the sidewalk. Alex's body came over Julia's as debris and fiery ash rained down on their heads. After the initial blast, Alex got up, and they scrambled toward the other side of the car, collapsing onto the ground. Julia saw Elena and the Russian hiding there, too, their bodies paralyzed with fear and shock as they gazed back at the inferno that had once been a simple house.

"You're all right?" Alex asked, his worried gaze searching Julia's face while his hands ran up and down her arms. "He didn't hurt you?"

She shook her head, swallowed, tried to speak. Finally, she tipped her head toward the Russian. "Who?"

"Uncle," Alex said. He gave Elena a reassuring nod. "He's your uncle Roland. I don't know what his story is yet, so don't get too close."

Elena was staring at the man as if she'd seen him before. "I remember you. You always gave us chocolate."

Roland smiled. "Yes, that was me. Your mother used to scold me. She said I was spoiling you."

"Why didn't you tell me who you were when you came to the radio station?" Julia asked. "Why did you speak to me in Russian?"

"I wasn't sure it was you. I wanted to know if you could understand me. But you had forgotten everything. Then your friends came. I knew the time wasn't right. But you're safe now. You're both safe."

While Elena and Roland tentatively embraced, Julia moved into Alex's arms. "Thanks for coming to save me," she said.

"I thought I was going to be too late," he said tightly. "But you saved yourself."

"With Elena's help. She knocked Brady out with a chair while I was trying to get the gun."

"You went after Brady?" he asked in amazement.

"It was our only chance. It was probably stupid."

"Probably," Alex agreed. "And amazingly brave."

"You were brave, too. You went after Roland before you knew he was a friend. When Brady left the two of you fighting, I was so afraid you were going to be hurt or killed. I begged him to turn back, but he wouldn't. He said he called for backup, but that must have been a lie, part of his plan. He needed us to get the jewels and the money. That's all he wanted." She paused, seeing the truth in his eyes, but still she had to say it. "Brady told us that he killed our parents. He thought he already had the stones. They set him up. I guess in the end they didn't trust him as much as we did."

"Maybe they knew him better. Don't beat yourself up, Julia. Hindsight is always crystal clear."

"I know." She touched the swelling around his right eye. "I think you're going to have another black eye."

"It was worth it." He paused, his lips tightening. "God, Julia. I thought I might lose you today."

She blinked back a tear at the raw emotion in his voice. She didn't know if she could call it love, but it was something. She pressed her mouth to his, kissing him with everything she had. It ended all too soon as the sound of sirens intruded and grew louder and louder.

"I think we have company," Alex said. Fire engines and police converged on the block.

"We're going to have a lot to explain." She opened her hand and showed him the stones. "These were hidden in the icon."

"That's what Roland thought. Put them away for now," Alex advised. He reached for his cell phone. "This time I'm going to call for backup."

"Who?"

"My father. I think it's time he came all the way out of hiding."

"Brady fooled him, too. He played everyone. He was very clever." She looked at the burning house and said with a degree of vengeful satisfaction, "And now he's dead."

CHAPTER TWENTY-TWO

IT WAS after midnight before Julia, Elena, Alex, and Roland returned to Elena's apartment to regroup. They'd spent the entire day and evening being questioned by local police and numerous government agencies. The entire story had finally become clear. What had once been thought to be a politically motivated murder had in fact been precipitated by simple, old-fashioned greed, a greed that had nothing to do with nationality.

Once Brady had learned of the existence of the jewels, he had become obsessed with having them for himself. In talking to various government agents, Julia and Alex had learned more about Brady's background. He'd grown up poor and found his ticket out of a Detroit slum at an army recruitment office. While in the army he'd become an expert with explosives. He'd later worked his way up to Intelligence and eventually a career as a spy.

For Brady it had never been about ideals or political freedom or national security; it had been about adventure, excitement, and fortune. On more than one occasion various valuable objects had disappeared under Brady's watch, but no one had ever suspected the career spy of working more than one side until they raided his apartment in New York City and found a stash of priceless art, jewelry, and cash. Brady had apparently lived well away from the spotlight, and he'd covered his tracks until now. His obsession with the jewels that had once eluded him had made him reckless and careless. Today Brady had been caught in a trap of his own making. Julia supposed there was some justice in that.

"I must say you brought a great deal of excitement with you," Elena said to Julia as she slipped off her shoes and stretched out her legs. "I've never had a day like this one."

"I hope you're not sorry I found you." Julia sat down across from her. Alex was outside talking to Roland, and for the first time since they'd been trapped in the house with Brady, she and Elena were alone.

"Of course not," Elena said with a definitive shake of her head.

Julia was relieved to see the color back in her sister's face and the sparkle in her eyes. "You know, I wouldn't have made it out of there alive if it hadn't been for you."

"Likewise. If you hadn't jumped on Brady, he would have locked us in that room. Are you always that impulsive?"

"I'm afraid so," Julia replied with a sheepish grin. "One of my many bad habits. But you were pretty impulsive yourself, grabbing that chair and knocking him out. I was impressed."

"Desperation breeds courage and creative ideas." Elena gave Julia a thoughtful look. "What's next, Julia?"

"I haven't had time to think about the future. I've been a little busy."

"You have a life to get back to, family who love you, friends who are probably worried about you, a job..." Her voice trailed away as she picked at an errant thread on the sofa cushion. "And I have my life to continue here. I guess there's always the phone and e-mail."

"Oh, Elena, please come to San Francisco with me," Julia said. "I want you to meet my family. They'll be your family, too."

"You really are impulsive," Elena said with a small smile. "You should think about that some more, Julia. Your family is not my family. They would surely consider me an outsider, probably even a threat to their relationship with you, especially your sister Liz. I've been the outsider before, the one people had to tolerate. I'm done with that."

The sadness in her voice broke Julia's heart. She frowned, wishing once again that Elena hadn't had to suffer so much. "You're wrong, Elena. My father Gino is wonderful and kind and generous. All the DeMarcos are like that. They adopted me, and they always made me feel welcome. I know that once they understand the story, they'll do the same for you." She paused. "And I really need another blonde in the family. Everyone else has dark hair, and I've always stood out. Please just don't say no," she added hastily when Elena began to interrupt. "Think about it. If you want, I'll go home first and fill everyone in; then you can come and visit, at least."

"I have the shop to run. And—"

"And you can still take a few days off. I'm sure of that."

"You don't know how busy I am, and I only have a handful of part-time employees."

"You can do it if you want to," Julia said firmly. "And you should want to, because we're sisters. And this is important to me."

Elena rolled her eyes. "You're trying to make me feel guilty."

"Is it working?" Julia asked with a grin. "I really want you to meet Liz. She might be restrained at first, but she will love having another sister."

"Impulsive and optimistic," Elena said. "I will think about it, but not tonight. My mind is too tired." She paused, her gaze moving to Julia's handbag. "You know, we never read that letter."

"You're right. I'll get it." Julia jumped to her feet. They'd retained the letter, but the music scores and the jewels, as well as the check, had been placed in another safe-deposit box at a different bank, just in case Brady had any other associates looking for a shot at the treasure. "I know one of the government agents read it," Julia said as she took the letter out of her purse. "He told me it was personal, with no evidence against Brady." She stared down at it, hesitating. "I'm a little scared. I think we know everything now, but maybe there's more."

"Let's hope the worst is over," Elena said. "If it isn't, at least we're together."

Julia smiled at her sister, then pulled the single piece of paper out of the envelope. Her heart skipped a beat when she realized the letter was written in Russian. "I can't read it," she said with extreme disappointment. "We'll have to get it translated."

"I can read it," Elena replied.

Julia raised an eyebrow. "You remember Russian?"

"No. I took some classes a while ago. It made me feel closer to the family I'd lost." She took the paper from Julia's hand. After a moment, she began to read:

"My dearest girls, if you are reading this letter, then your father and I are probably gone. Perhaps we are wrong to risk everything for freedom, but it is love that drives us—our love for you, and our love for each other. We are counting on our friends to deliver us safely to America. If that doesn't happen, we pray that you both will grow up in a world that allows you to express yourselves and be who you will be, without restriction. Please don't be sad. Don't grieve for us. Be happy. Find love and joy in your lives. That is everything we wish for you. You will forever be in our hearts. Love, Mama and Papa."

Julia blinked back tears and saw that Elena's cheeks were wet as well. "Our parents were willing to risk their lives for freedom and love, and Brady betrayed them for a fortune," she said.

"I wonder if there was any one moment when they knew the truth," Elena murmured.

"It probably happened too fast. At least Brady died the same way. There's some justice in that. That sounds cold, doesn't it? But I'm not sorry he's dead."

"I'm not, either."

Julia leaned back in her chair, thinking about the note and her parents. Her mother's face was beginning to come into her mind more and more. She could even hear her voice. The memories were finally returning. "Mama was beautiful," she said, looking over at Elena. "And so brave. I've never had that much courage."

"You did today."

"Because I had to be brave. I was backed into a corner."

"So were our parents."

"I think Mama would have been happy to know that you became a dancer and followed in her footsteps."

"For a while, anyway."

"Both of your careers were cut too short."

Elena nodded. "Life is never fair or easy."

They both turned as the front door opened and Alex came in. His right eye was purple and swollen, his clothes wrinkled and smelling of smoke. "I'm going to take off," he said, surprising Julia with his words.

She got to her feet. "What do you mean? Where are you going?"

"To find a hotel room and get some sleep. Roland will give me a ride. He has a rental car."

"You can stay here," Julia said quickly, not wanting him to leave. She hadn't had two minutes alone with him all day...

He offered her a weary smile. "I'll pass on another night on the couch. I'll come by in the morning and we'll go to the airport together —unless you're going to stay here for a few days?"

"No, I need to get home and tell everyone what I've learned."

"Then we'll leave tomorrow. There's a flight at noon. Will that be all right?"

"Sure." She followed him to the door and out into the hall, put off by his cool tone. "Alex, do you want me to come with you tonight?" She held her breath, waiting for his answer. Because she would go with him in a second. She just couldn't read him right now. She didn't know what he wanted from her. Was he pulling away because he wanted to give her more time with her sister... or was he just pulling away?

"No, you should stay with Elena," he said briskly. "We'll catch up tomorrow."

"Are you all right?"

"I'm fine."

She frowned, wondering if he'd ever give her a different answer than that. She had no choice but to accept it. "Okay." She leaned forward and tried to kiss him on the mouth, but he moved, and she caught the side of his cheek. Then he was gone.

Was he just tired and looking for a good night's sleep? Was that the reason for his distance? Or was this the beginning of the end?

Alex pretended to sleep on the flight back to San Francisco. He knew Julia wanted to talk, but he didn't. There was too much to say, and yet there was nothing to say. It was over. She finally had her answers, and he had his. There was no more left to do. He could return to work, and he was looking forward to that.

He hadn't picked up his camera since Julia had come knocking on his door a week ago. So much had happened in the past nine days. His entire life story had changed, and so had hers. They were both different people now.

The flight attendant came on with the announcement that they were preparing to land in San Francisco. Julia put her seat back up and gave him a speculative, serious look. "Where are you going when we leave the airport?"

"Home, then to my mother's house. After that I'm going to find Stan." He'd been thinking about his father's friend all way the home. It had occurred to him that nowhere in their discussions the day before had Stan's name come up. Why was that? Why hadn't any of the government agents they'd spoken to known of Stan's role in the defection?

"I'd forgotten about Stan," Julia murmured, her gaze catching his. "Your father said he set the defection plans in motion, yet no one mentioned him yesterday."

It scared Alex that he and Julia had begun to think exactly the same. They'd gotten so close. He almost didn't know where he left off and she began.

"Do you think Stan knew about Brady's double cross?" she continued. "I mean, he was the one who contacted Brady about us. He could have been working with him, setting us up to lead them to the jewels." She blew out a sigh. "I thought this was over, but maybe it's not. Maybe I'll always be looking over my shoulder, wondering who's going to come after me next."

"It won't be Stan. I'll make sure of that. If he's guilty of anything, I will see that he pays for what he did. I can promise you that."

"That's a lot of I's.' What happened to 'we'?"

He shrugged. "You have your life, your twin sister, your other sister, your gazillion relatives, your music. I'm sure you'll be busy. I can take care of Stan on my own."

"Where are you going next?"

"Wherever my next assignment is," he said flatly, trying to ignore the hurt look in her eyes.

"We're not going to talk about us, are we?" she asked.

He didn't answer. What could he say? They were sitting in the middle of a crowded airplane, people all around them. It was hardly the moment for that kind of talk. Not that he intended to find that moment. "I don't do good-byes."

"So I wasn't going to get one?"

"Julia, this isn't the time or the place."

"I don't know about that. You're trapped in your seat. You can't escape. It seems to me the best chance I have for getting a straight answer."

He was glad to hear the lighter note in her voice, even if it was forced. He liked emotional scenes even less than good-byes. "I think your life will be very full when Elena comes out to visit you and your family."

"She's coming only for a few days. Then she'll go back to her life in Washington DC."

"And you'll return to your life. You can pursue your music passion with that extra bit of cash you inherited. And I'm sure the jewels and the musical scores are quite valuable."

"I won't sell them. I'll keep them in the family. That's where they belong, although I might see if I can get an orchestra to play my great-grandfather's music. It should be heard." She paused. "What about your dad?"

Alex shrugged. "I'm sure he'll go on doing whatever he was doing." It occurred to Alex that he didn't even know what that was. Maybe someday he'd take the time to find out, but not any day soon. Julia gave him a long stare that told him she wasn't happy with his answer. "Hey, he chose to be separate. Don't try to make me feel guilty."

"He did that to protect you."

"Does that mean you've forgiven Sarah for doing the same thing to you? For lying about everything in your past?"

She nodded slowly. "I'm going to try. Sarah gave me a wonderful life. And my parents were already gone. Who knows what would have happened to me without her? I think Sarah hurt her parents more than she hurt me. Like you, they had to believe someone they loved was dead. Which reminds me. Susan isn't my biological grandmother. I hate to take that away from her, too."

"At least she has Liz."

"That's my next goal—to persuade Liz to see her. I'm going to blend these families together if it's the last thing I do."

He smiled at her determination. "I don't have any doubts that you'll succeed. You're a strong woman, Julia."

"Stronger now, I think. You helped, you know. I couldn't have survived this past week without you."

The wheels of the plane touched down on the ground, and within minutes they were parked at the gate.

"I'll catch a cab home," Julia said as she released her seat belt.

He was surprised by her words, having been sure he would face the inevitable good-bye at her apartment.

"I can give you a ride," he said halfheartedly. "My car is here. It's no problem."

"That's all right. I can see that you want to be on your way."

She looked at him with her beautiful blue eyes, and it took every ounce of strength he possessed not to weaken. "All right," he said. "If that's the way you want it."

"Thanks again, Alex."

"I don't need your thanks."

Her smile grew sad. "I know. You don't need anything from me. You made that really clear. And it's okay. I don't have any regrets." She got up and joined the crowd of people leaving the plane.

Alex sat in his seat until everyone was gone. She might not have regrets, but he certainly did.

When Alex pulled up in front of his mother's house an hour later, he was stunned to see a man walking up the steps. Damn him!

Alex jumped out of the car and caught up to his father before he rang the bell. "What are you doing here?"

"I came to tell your mother the truth," Charles said, his words heavy and filled with emotion.

His father had cleaned up a bit and was wearing slacks and a brown sport coat over a white shirt, but Alex knew that his appearance would still scare the life out of his mother. "You can't just show up at her door," he told him. "You might give her a heart attack. Let me prepare her."

"It's my lie, not yours. I thought you were still in Washington."

"I just got back," Alex said. His father had been part of several conference calls the day before, so he was completely up to speed on everything that had gone down. "By the way, have you spoken to Stan?"

"No. I haven't been able to reach him."

"How come no one talked about him yesterday?"

His father appeared taken aback at his question. "I don't know. I never thought about it."

"Maybe you should. Stan's the one who connected me to Brady in the first place."

"If you think they were working together, you're wrong," Charles said. "Stan would never have gone along with stealing my life and yours and your mother's. Nor would he have ever killed in the first place, not for jewels or money. He's not that kind of person."

"You didn't think Brady was that kind of person, either."

His father's face paled and his jaw tightened. "You're right. He conned me. I just wish he wasn't dead. I would have enjoyed killing him myself."

He'd never thought his father capable of murder, but Alex was beginning to realize that he hadn't known Charles Manning at all, not the real man, not the man who'd gotten involved in a Russian defection plot or the man who had gone underground and lived his whole life in the shadow of the family he'd left behind. The question was—did he want to know him?

"There is something else I've been wondering about," Alex said. "Why did Brady force you to go underground and fake your death? He was the one who killed the Markovs. And he knew you didn't know anything about the girls or about the treasure. I don't get it. How were you a threat to him?"

"It was part of the plot. Brady had to continue to make our government believe that the Russians had killed Natalia and Sergei, that I was in danger. He faked the threats to me to lend credence to the idea that the Russians had long arms. He certainly convinced me that was the case. I honestly believed I was in danger." Charles paused, clearing his throat. "But in retrospect, I think the real reason Brady had me die was to try to flush out Sarah and Julia. He thought Sarah cared for me. He thought if anything would draw her out of hiding, it would be my funeral. She'd come to the service; then he would find out if Julia had the stones."

Alex had never considered that possibility. It made sense. "And later? He never told you anything over the years? What about the other day? Why did Brady make you disappear again?"

"He didn't want me to tell you the story. He tried to convince me I needed to keep silent for your protection, but I knew you wouldn't stop looking. And I couldn't stand the thought of you searching for answers that might risk your life, so I wanted to help you. In the end, I almost got you killed. You found the treasure, and Brady followed you to it."

"So the whole government moving you out of your house again, that was all engineered by Brady? He had a hell of a lot of power."

"Yes," Charles agreed. "Too much. No one ever suspected he was a double agent. Now I believe we may find out other terrible crimes he committed over the years."

"So there was never a time in the last twenty-five years when you didn't think you could come out of hiding?" Alex queried again. "You must have wondered if the danger still existed."

"I know you can't understand, but for at least the first five or six years, I did still believe in the danger. Brady would occasionally catch up to me, relay information that I now know was false. He would question me about Sarah, ask me if I'd heard from her. He kept saying he wanted her to come in, to stop hiding, to be able to live her own life. They were more lies, but I believed him. And then there came a time when I just didn't think I had the right to go back and interrupt your life. Your mother had remarried. You seemed to be doing well."

"And how would you know that?"

"I told you. I watched you sometimes, at school or at one of your games."

It gave Alex the chills to think his father had been that close to him, and he'd never known.

The front door suddenly opened. "Alex, is that you?" his mother asked. "Who are you talking to?"

Fortunately, his father had his back to the front door. Charles was staring straight at Alex, and there was suddenly fear in his eyes. Alex didn't know what to do, how to make this easier for everyone involved. As soon as his father turned around, she'd get the shock of her life.

"Mom," he said tentatively, "I want you to take a deep breath and try to stay calm."

Her eyes narrowed. "What's going on?"

"It's Dad," Alex said. He nodded to Charles. "Turn around."

His father turned so slowly, Alex felt like he was watching a movie. His mother's eyes grew wider and wider until she let out a small cry, putting a hand to her heart.

"No," she said, shaking her head, backing toward the front door.

Alex jogged around his father and up the steps to his mother, putting his arm around her trembling shoulders.

"Who is he?" she whispered.

"It's Dad," Alex said. "He's alive. He's been alive all these years."

His father put up a hand in entreaty. "Kate," he murmured. "I'm sorry."

She put up her own hand as he took a step forward. "This isn't possible. I must be dreaming. This is a nightmare and you're both in it."

"It's real, Mom." Alex's hand tightened on her shoulder. "You always thought his death was suspicious. That's because it never happened."

"I don't understand."

"He's—"

"Let me explain," Charles said firmly. "I need to do this, not you, Alex. Can I come in, Kate? Can I tell you what happened and why?"

Kate turned to look at Alex, her eyes seeking confirmation. "Is it really him?"

"Yes."

For a moment, she looked lost, panicked, completely unlike the mother he'd known. But ever so slowly, she regained her composure. Her back stiffened. Her head went up. Her jaw tightened.

"Then I guess you should come in," she said, a steel edge to her voice now. She led them into the house and took a seat on the white couch in the living room.

Alex and his father took chairs opposite her. Silence surrounded them like a thick, thorny, uncomfortable coat. The only thing breaking the quiet was the ticking of the grandfather clock in the entryway, the same clock Charles had bought for Kate on their fifth wedding anniversary. Alex doubted either of them heard the clock. They were too caught up in staring at each other, although neither gave anything away. He waited for the explosion. He knew one was coming. Maybe his father was right. Maybe he didn't need to be here for this. It wasn't his lie.

But it was his family. And this was the last loose end. He needed to tie it off so he could leave and never look back.

"Well, you said you were going to explain," Kate said briskly. "Do it."

Charles leaned forward, his gaze focused and determined. "I believed that the Russians were after me because of a photograph I took in Moscow. I received death threats toward you and Alex. The government, a man named Brady whom I had worked with for many years, told me that I needed to disappear. I was their only link to the—"

"Orphan girl at the gates," she said. "I get it."

"Exactly. So Brady helped me fake my death. He said you and

Alex would be safer if I was gone. The trail would end with my death. In the Soviet Union, I had seen firsthand how brutally people could be killed. I had those images in my mind when I made my decision. It was not an easy one to make." He shot Alex a quick look, probably sensing his disgust, Alex thought. "But I knew it was far more difficult for the two of you to live with that decision than it was for me to make it."

His mother stared at his father for what seemed like hours. Finally she said, "So that's it? You disappeared, and we went on, and you never looked back."

"I looked back every day. I've told Alex that. I'm sure neither of you will believe me when I say this, but I loved both of you very much. And each day that went by I thought of you. I prayed you were well, that I had done the right thing."

"Then why come out now?" she demanded. "Why didn't you just stay dead?"

"I found him," Alex interjected. "Julia and I were looking for her father, but we found him instead."

"Julia," she echoed. "I knew she was that girl in the picture."

"Actually, that's her sister," Alex replied. "An identical twin. Both girls were part of a planned defection that didn't occur because the parents were killed."

"It was my job to help get the girls out of the country through the cover of the theater," Charles added. "It was one of many jobs I had in those years that involved undercover work for the U.S. government. I had gained the trust of certain people in the Russian government. It was easier for me to get around because of that trust."

"So it was your selfishness that left Alex without a father," Kate said pointedly. "Now, that's the first thing you've said today that hasn't surprised me." Trust his mother to turn the story her way, Alex thought. Not that he could blame her. He wasn't too thrilled with his father, either.

"You can go now," she told him with a regal wave of her hand. "I think you've said enough."

"I will go." Charles stood up. "But if you need anything—"

"Why would I need anything? I've made my own way the past twenty-five years. I don't need you for anything."

"I guess you don't. Although you seem to be awfully interested in my pictures these days."

His mother tossed her head. "I had every right to make money off your work and to keep your reputation alive. It was for Alex. He was so proud of you and your accomplishments. I never wanted him to lose that. I was doing it for you and your legacy."

Alex had to admit she had a beautiful way of spinning the truth. It had never been about him, but he didn't intend to get in the middle of this fight. It was between the two of them.

"You're welcome to do what you want with the photos," Charles said. "They served their purpose. They did what I wanted them to do at the time. They showed something important to the world. That's all I ever cared about. That's why you were always angry with me. I wasn't ambitious enough. I didn't want the fame or the celebrity. I wanted to stay in the background."

"Because you were spying on the Russians," she said, "not because you wanted obscurity. And you know, I wasn't stupid. I knew something was going on. And that woman—Sarah—were you sleeping with her?"

"Sarah was always just a friend. She was also working for the government," he added. "We both wanted to do something for the people over there."

"So altruistic," she sneered. "Worry about people you don't even know, but to hell with your family. What kind of heroism is that?"

She had a good point, Alex thought. And his father took the hit hard, his face aging before their eyes.

There were deep, grooved lines around his eyes, across his forehead, and at the corners of his mouth. He'd spent twenty-five years living a lie and feeling guilty. They'd all paid a price, Alex realized.

"I can't defend what I did to you and Alex," Charles said. "I can only tell you that my intentions were to keep you safe, and at least in that effort I succeeded. I'll go now. And I am sorry, Kate, for whatever that's worth. Do what you want with my pictures. I gave up photography the day I died."

Alex was surprised to hear that. "What have you been doing?"

"Working as an auto mechanic. My father was one. He taught me how to work on cars. I never thought I'd want to have that job, but in the end it became my life. I've been able to make enough to survive."

"Did you marry again?" Kate asked sharply. "Not that I care."

"I never remarried," he said quietly. "I never tried to re-create my family. I knew that would be impossible." He drew in a long breath and slowly let it out. "I want you both to be happy. That's all. I'm sorry for everything I've done that hurt you. Not just for faking my death, but for choosing to involve myself in something I knew could bring danger to both of you. That's what I truly regret. I was selfish. I couldn't see past what I thought was so important. I was a shortsighted photographer. I should have turned that camera on myself; then I would have seen the truth." He gave a regretful shake of his head. "Good-bye."

Alex wanted to say something, but he didn't know what.

His mother didn't seem to have the same problem. "You owe me, Charles," she said.

"Whatever you want, Kate."

She hesitated. "I want you to stay dead."

Alex's breath stuck in his chest as he waited for his father's answer.

"I can do that," Charles said. And with that, he walked out of the living room, out of the house, and out of their lives... again.

"I hate him," Kate said a moment later, but there was more pain in her voice now than anger. "You hate him, too, don't you, Alex?" Her eyes pleaded with him to agree.

He wished he could give her what she wanted, but the truth was he didn't know how he felt about his father anymore.

Julia stared at the house Michael had bought to surprise her. She still couldn't believe he'd made the purchase without asking her first. But she wasn't here about the house or about their relationship; she was here to find Liz. She needed to tell her sister the entire story. Maybe Michael needed to hear it, too. She owed him that much.

She walked up the front steps and saw that the door was ajar. She knocked, then pushed it open, hearing laughter in the kitchen. She walked through the doorway and saw Liz on a short ladder, using a roller on the ceiling, while Michael was on his knees doing the baseboard, complaining that Liz was once again spattering him with paint. He was right. They both wore as much paint as the walls, and they looked surprisingly at ease with each other.

Julia had always known they were good friends, but now she couldn't help wondering if Liz and Michael should have been the couple all along. She cleared her throat, drawing Liz's attention. Her sister almost dropped the roller when she saw her.

"Julia!" Liz squealed.

"Hi," she said. "Michael."

Michael slowly rose. "What are you doing here?"

"I wanted to talk to Liz. My aunt told me she was helping you with the house. It's nice," she added somewhat awkwardly. "This room is really bright."

Liz got off the ladder. "So, tell us—did you find what you were looking for? Did you find your real father?"

Her question made Julia realize how little Liz knew about all the events that had happened in the past few days. "I did. I found out a lot of things about my father... and my mother."

A glint of fear flashed through Liz's eyes. "I don't want to hear this, do I?"

"You have to hear it."

"I'm not your real sister. Mom adopted you, didn't she?"

Julia saw the worry in Liz's eyes and knew she had to put an end to that right now. "You will always be my sister, no matter what, so don't even think about trying to end our relationship. I'm not giving you up."

The tension in Liz's face eased at her words. "But we don't share the same blood, do we? Come on, Julia, tell me the truth. I can take it."

"We don't share the same blood."

"So you are that Russian girl in the photo?"

"Actually, I'm not. That was my sister."

Liz's jaw dropped. "What?"

"There are two of you?" Michael echoed, shock in his voice.

"Yes, there are two of us. We're identical twins." She paused, letting her words sink in. "Her name is Elena. I think I used to call an imaginary friend Elena, but she wasn't a friend, she was my sister, and I didn't know what had happened to her."

"Dad told me about your imaginary friend and your made-up language," Liz muttered. "That was Russian, wasn't it?"

"I think so." She swallowed hard, trying to figure out the best way to tell the story. "My parents were important Russians. They were trying to defect. We were separated to make it easier to get us out of the country, and they were killed before that could happen. Elena and I were brought to the U.S. by different government agents, and Sarah, who was one of those agents, decided to keep me and raise me as her own."

"No," Liz said in disbelief. "Mom was not an agent. You're not going to tell me that."

"She was. I know it sounds incredible, but it's the truth. Oh, Liz, it's a long story, and I want to tell you everything. But I need to tell Dad, too, and I was hoping maybe we could do it all at once. Will you come with me to see him?"

Liz hesitated, glancing over at Michael. He gave her a small nod of encouragement.

"All right," Liz said, "I'll come with you." She set the roller down in the tray. "Just let me wash my hands." She walked out of the kitchen into the adjacent laundry room and turned on the faucet in the big sink.

Julia stared at Michael, feeling more than a little uncomfortable being alone with him. She didn't know what to say, so she settled for, "I'm sorry about everything."

"So am I," he replied. "But I'm glad you found your past. No more missing pieces."

"It feels good knowing who I am, why I never felt like I quite fit with my parents, why my mom tried to steer me away from things that I loved. She didn't want to lose me. She gave up her whole life to keep me, and she couldn't take a chance that I would ever slip away, so she trapped me with her love. I didn't see it until she was gone."

"And then you thought I was trapping you, too."

"Not exactly—"

He cut her off with a wave of his hand. "No, I think that is exactly what I was doing, although I didn't realize it. I had this image of you that I couldn't let go." He smiled sadly, with enormous regret. "I'm just sorry that I wasted so much of your time."

"You didn't. You were great. It was me. All me. I couldn't commit to you because I knew deep down I wasn't happy with the way my life was going."

"I can't believe I bought this house for you without telling you. Pretty stupid, huh?"

"It's going to be a great family home for you and the right person."

"I hope so."

Liz returned to the room, looking from one to the other. "Are we done here?"

"We're done," Michael said, meeting Julia's gaze. "We're definitely done."

Two hours and several cups of coffee later, Julia finished telling her story to Liz and Gino as they sat in her father's kitchen. Both had been stunned by the revelations she'd shared, especially in regard to Sarah. She'd tried to soften the blows by emphasizing how much Sarah had sacrificed to build their family, but she knew that Gino and Liz would have to find their own way to acceptance of the woman they'd all loved.

Gino hadn't said anything in almost twenty minutes, Julia realized. And he'd been staring down at his black coffee for at least the last five. "Are you all right, Dad?" she asked, covering his hand with hers.

There was pain in his eyes when he looked at her. "Do you still want to call me *Dad*?"

"Of course I do. You're the only father I've ever known. I love you. I love Lizzie, too. You're my family."

"But we're not," Liz said.

"Yes, you are. Blood doesn't matter more than love, and we love each other," Julia said.

"If blood didn't matter, why did you need to know your real parents?" Liz asked.

It was a good question. Julia tried to explain. "Because I needed to know myself as much as I needed the history. I've always felt a bit out of step with everyone. I couldn't figure out where I got my love for music or even my looks. I know Mom used to joke that I had her nose and her legs, but I think she just said that to make me feel like I fit in. She did everything to make me happy. I'm angry in some ways, but in other ways I know I've had a good life because of her."

"She should have told me," Gino said heavily. "I should have asked more questions about you and your father."

"She left that life behind. The only truth Sarah lived was with the three of us. The lies ended when she married you, Dad. You have to remember that."

"You think you know a person, but you don't," he said.

"But you did know her. You knew the little things," she said. "You knew the way she liked her coffee, the way she cried at romantic movies. You knew the way she read the newspaper from back to front, and the way she laughed—half giggle, half snort." She smiled at the memory. "We all knew her. We did."

"What about your other sister?" Liz asked. "What are you going to do about her?"

Julia took a breath. "She's flying out here next weekend. I want you all to meet her. I'm hoping..." She paused, waiting for them both to look at her. "I'm hoping that you'll accept her. She's had a tough life. She grew up in foster homes. She has no family, except for me—no father, no sister, no nothing."

"I'm kind of jealous of her," Liz confessed. "She shares your blood. And you're twins. You're going to get closer to her and forget about me. I just know it."

"I have room in my heart for two sisters. What about you?" Julia challenged. "And what about you, Dad? Do the DeMarcos have room for another person at next weekend's Sunday brunch?"

"Yes," he said, a smile crossing his lips for the very first time. "Of course. We will make room for your sister at our table whenever she comes."

"You are a very generous man," she said, leaning over to kiss him on the cheek, "and I'm lucky to have you. Which reminds me, we need to talk about your drinking, Dad. I know I've been distracted, but not too distracted to notice that you've been drowning your sorrows in alcohol. I don't want to lose you. And I think you should stop. I'll help you, whatever it takes."

He patted her hand. "I feel better when I drink. The pain is not so sharp."

"But Dad—"

"I know," he cut in. "Your sister already talked to me about it."

Julia looked at Liz in surprise. "You did?"

"You told me it was my turn to take action," Liz replied. "Dive in, take charge, stop being a spectator, you said. So I did. Dad and I had a long talk last night."

"I'm glad." Things were going so well, Julia wondered if she should push her luck; then she decided to go for it. "There's one other person I'd like to invite for next weekend's Sunday brunch."

"Alex?" Liz asked with a wry smile on her lips. "I should have figured."

Her heart flip-flopped at the sound of his name, but she shook her head. "No, not Alex. I was thinking about Susan Davidson, Sarah's mother, and your grandmother. I'd like the two of you to meet."

Gino glanced at Liz. "What do you think, honey?"

"I think it's a good idea," Liz said slowly. "If Julia is getting another sister, I might as well get another grandmother, if you don't think Nonna will mind," she said to Gino, referring to his mother.

"She'll be all right with it," Gino replied. "There's always room for one more."

"Good," Julia said with a smile. "You're both being really generous, and I appreciate it more than you know."

"What about Alex?" Liz persisted. "Why don't you invite him, too?"

"Because he's leaving. In fact, he's probably already gone. He couldn't wait to get back to his job." She blinked back a tear. She wasn't going to cry over Alex. She'd had a good time with him. And he'd been great. She'd known all along that what they had was only temporary.

"You love him, don't you?" Lizzie said quietly, with compassion in her brown eyes.

"I wish I didn't, but I think I do." She paused. "There's something else I need to tell you."

"There's more?" Liz queried. "I thought we knew everything."

"About the past, yes, but I want to talk to you about the future. I'm planning a little trip..."

CHAPTER TWENTY-THREE

TWO WEEKS later Julia could barely believe she was traveling by taxi through the streets of Moscow with Elena by her side. She smiled at her sister. "We're here," she said.

"I keep pinching myself to make sure I'm not dreaming. Two weeks ago I didn't know you existed, and here I am in Russia with the sister I thought was dead. Life takes some very mysterious turns just when you least expect it," Elena replied.

"I'm so glad you were willing to come with me. I know it was kind of an impulsive thing to do. And you're more into planning than I am. But I was afraid if we waited too long, we'd never do it."

"Fortunately, the Russian government was willing to extend us visas," Elena replied. "That expedited matters."

"I guess the Russians were happy to discover an American end to an old Russian crime. It certainly released any lingering doubts about who killed our parents."

"It's too bad Mama and Papa told Brady about those jewels. They might have lived otherwise."

"I'm sure they did the best they could with the information they had. They didn't know who to trust, and they took a chance."

"And it got them killed." Elena turned sideways in her seat. "I wasn't sure about this trip, you know. I kept thinking we should let this part of our lives stay in the past, but now that we're here, I'm excited." She paused. "I keep thinking I should remember something, but I don't. Do you?"

"Not at all," Julia said with a sigh. "Maybe when we start walking the streets something will come back. I hope so, anyway."

"Me, too. But whatever happens, I'm glad we came. I'm also glad I met your family. They were really nice to me. I'm grateful for that."

Julia sat back in her seat, watching the sights go by, and thinking about the last ten days. As Elena had said, the DeMarcos had graciously accepted her into their midst, including Liz, who after some initial awkwardness had opened her heart. Liz had also been willing to spend time with her newly discovered grandmother, Susan Davidson, who had finally been filled in on the whole story. It would take some time to blend the families, but Julia was convinced it would happen in the end.

There were still a lot of things they had to figure out, especially about the money, the jewels, and the music scores, but she and Elena had both agreed to do nothing until they'd made this special trip back to the past. They needed to shut that last door before they could completely move on with their lives.

Ten minutes later, the cab pulled up in front of the Hotel Metropole, located across the street from the Bolshoi Theater. Her mother had danced there, so had her great-grandmother, and it was as good a place as any from which to retrace their steps.

Once they were checked in, they proceeded to their room, which was nicely decorated with sketches on the walls, two double beds, a desk, and a chair. While Elena made a stop in the restroom, Julia headed toward the window. The Bolshoi Theater was directly in view. It was a beautiful building, with eight strong columns and the Chariot of Apollo sculpture on top. There was so much history to the building, so much history that was important to her family of dancers and musicians.

"What are you staring at?" Elena asked, joining her at the window.

"The Bolshoi."

"It's stunning," Elena said with a sigh. "I dreamed of dancing there one day. But it wasn't meant to be."

Julia put her arm around her sister's shoulders. They had spoken of many things, but not about the accident that had taken away Elena's ability to dance. Someday she hoped Elena would confide in her the rest of her life story.

"I remember watching Mama from the wings," Elena continued. "I thought she was so beautiful, and I wanted to fly like she did."

Julia had brief flashbacks to the inside of the theater as well, but she hadn't enjoyed watching her mother as much as she'd enjoyed hearing the power of the orchestra. "We should go there second," she said.

Elena raised an eyebrow. "Where are we going first?"

"To the orphanage where Alex took your picture. That's how this long journey began. We would never have found each other without that photo. Are you ready?"

"I suppose."

Julia didn't like the sound of hesitancy in her sister's voice. "What's wrong?"

"I'm a little afraid of the memories," she confessed. "Aren't you?"

"No," Julia said, feeling nothing but excitement. "I know it will be sad to see where our parents died and go to their graves, but I feel for the first time in a while that the future is wide open for me. And I'm ready to make peace with the past."

Elena smiled. "Then lead on."

They left the hotel and walked through Red Square, known as Krasnaya Ploschad in Russian. It was a much bigger space than Julia had imagined. At one end was the Kremlin, a medieval walled city on a hill above the Moscow River. At the other end were the colorful domes and spires of St. Basil's Cathedral. The rest of the area was rife with history, according to the guidebook Julia had read on the plane trip. North of the cathedral was Lobnoye Mesto, or "Place of Skulls," a circular raised platform on which public executions were carried out in the days of the tsars. Beyond that, across from the Lenin Mausoleum, was the GUM department store, Russia's version of a shopping mall.

Julia wanted to personally visit each site, but first they were on a mission to find the orphanage. After discussing her goal with several government agents, she'd been given an address, and now they were nearing the place where it had all begun.

In fact, it came out of nowhere, the unpretentious stone building with a fence and steel gates protecting its inhabitants. She had no idea if it was still an orphanage.

Julia stopped abruptly. Elena did the same. She tried to remember ever being in that yard, by that gate, but she came up blank. Maybe she'd never been out there. But Elena had. Julia moved closer to her, until they were shoulder to shoulder.

"I remember standing there," Elena whispered. "I was so scared, so terrified. I knew something had happened to our parents, something beyond bad. I could feel it in my heart. Then a man and a woman came. They took me away. I cried for you, but they covered my mouth, and then we were gone." She put a hand to her stomach. "I feel like I'm going to be sick."

"Maybe you should sit down. There's a bench over there."

"No, I'm going back to the hotel."

"I'll go with you."

Elena put up her hand and took a step away. "I need a little time, Julia. Okay?"

"Are you sure?" Julia didn't want to let her go on her own.

"I'm certain. I'm not as good as you are at sharing feelings. It's going to take me time to feel comfortable with it all."

"I understand. We can leave. We can do something fun."

"Later. I'm tired. I just need a break. Besides, there are some things we need to do on our own." She gave Julia an odd little smile, then walked away.

Julia frowned. She had wanted to do everything together, but she was beginning to understand how much harder it was for Elena to be part of a twosome. She'd grown up alone, forced to keep everything inside. It was the only way she knew how to cope. Maybe with time, that would change.

Julia walked over to the gate and put her hands on the steel. There was no one in the yard. In fact, the building looked vacant. There were no signs, just a sense of bleakness about it, as if nothing happy or good had ever happened there.

"Would you mind if I took your picture?" a man asked.

She whirled around in surprise. "Alex?" She couldn't believe it was him, but there he stood, dressed in jeans, a black shirt, and a black leather jacket. A camera case hung over one shoulder. His brown hair was ruffled by the breeze, his green eyes alight with excitement. He looked impossibly handsome. Her palms began to sweat and her spine tingled. "What are you doing here?" she asked, finally finding her voice.

"I realized I didn't have a picture of you. All that time we spent together, and I never took a photo. What kind of a photographer am I?"

"So you came all the way to Moscow to get one?"

He grinned. "I do what I have to do to get the shot. You know that. I called your apartment a couple of days ago. I spoke to Elena. She told me you were on your way here."

"Is that why she ran off so suddenly?" Julia asked, suddenly making sense of Elena's odd comment that there were some things they needed to do on their own.

He nodded. A moment passed; then he said, "I have something to give you." He set down the camera and pulled an envelope out of his jacket pocket.

For some reason the sight of another envelope made her nervous. "What is it?"

"It's from Stan. I finally tracked him down. He told me everything, how he helped set up the defection, how much he wanted your mother to dance in the United States."

"Did he know about Brady's plan to kill them?"

Alex shook his head. "No, not at all. You see, Julia, Stan had a huge crush on your mother, Natalia. He met her a few times, and he wanted very much to help her. I guess they became friends on a few of her trips to the United States. He was devastated when she was killed. And he told me he was sorry that he hadn't been honest with us. He believed he was protecting me and you. Like my father, Stan thought that the Russians killed your parents. As an apology, he sent you this. Open it."

"I'm afraid. I don't want any more bad surprises."

"This is a good one."

She took the envelope out of his hand and pulled out a photograph. Her heart stopped beating as she realized what she was seeing. It was a black-and-white family picture of Natalia, Sergei, Elena, and herself. She pressed it to her heart as she blinked back a tear. "It's all of us together," she whispered.

He smiled at her. "Stan thought you would like it. He said Natalia gave it to him a long, long time ago."

"I love it. I'll have to thank him when I get back. I'm glad he wasn't involved, Alex. I know you care about him." Julia blew out a breath, seeing a new light sparkle in Alex's eyes. He obviously wasn't finished. "Was there something else?"

"Elena told me that she thinks you're in love with me."

"I can't imagine why she'd say that," Julia replied, her heart racing as he took a step forward.

"Maybe because I told her I was in love with you," he said.

"What?" She couldn't possibly have heard him say the words.

"You heard me." He moved closer until he was just inches away. "I missed you, Julia."

"You did?" she whispered, gazing into his eyes and seeing the love he was talking about.

"Yeah, I missed your smile and your beautiful blue eyes, the way you lick your fingers after you eat something really delicious, how excited you get when you try something new, the light that shines out of you when you talk about music and changing the world one melody at a time."

"Oh, Alex," she murmured, incredibly touched by his words.

"I tried to forget you. I buried myself in work, thinking it would fill me up the way it used to, but it didn't. There was still a hole in my heart. I didn't actually know I had a heart until I met you. You see, I put it on ice about twenty-five years ago, just a few weeks after I left this very square."

She put her hands on his shoulders. "It must be hard for you to come back here."

"No, it's easy, because you're here, and because now I know what I want. Which, in case you haven't figured it out yet, is you. I want to be with you, Julia."

"Even if that means a permanent address?"

He nodded. "Wherever you are is where I want to be. I've lived most of my life thinking I was just like my father, that photography was my sole passion, that the world was my backyard, that it was more important to show what was happening in the world than to live my own life. But my father gave it up for love. He gave it up for me." He put his hands on her waist. "And I'm willing to give it up for you."

She bit down on her lip, her eyes tearing. "Really?"

He smiled. "Absolutely. You're an incredible woman, Julia—smart, sexy, brave—and you never quit. You inspire me."

"I feel the same way about you, Alex. Your courage, your sense of adventure, the way you embrace new things constantly amaze me. And you're really good in bed, too," she added with a smile.

"It's about time you mentioned that," he said with a sexy growl. "I think I'm the luckiest man on earth right now." He leaned over and placed a tender, passionate kiss on her lips.

"And I'm the luckiest woman," Julia murmured against his mouth. "Do you know why I came here?" she asked him, pulling away for just a moment.

"Tell me."

"I wanted to connect with my parents. The letter my mother wrote to us made me realize that my parents lived their lives with purpose and passion. They were willing to risk everything for love and family.

That's the way I want to live. I don't want to play it safe. I want to follow my heart—wherever it leads. This trip was the first step."

"Where are you going next?"

She moved deeper into his embrace. "Right here. I love you, Alex. I was going to come and find you after this trip." She paused. "I don't want you to stay in one place for me. I want to go with you wherever life takes us. I have some thoughts of my own about spreading music around the world. I could use a partner for that."

"You've got one. And if the last few weeks are any indication, I think you and I are going to have a very exciting life."

She gazed into his eyes and saw a future filled with promise. Now she knew not only where she'd come from... but where she was going.

# # #

I hope you enjoyed these three novels! If you'd like more summer reads, grab the Summer Reads Series:

SUMMER READS - Books 1-3, Vol. 1
Summer Secrets
Golden Lies
Don't Say A Word

SUMMER READS - Books 4-6, Vol. 2
One True Love
Just The Way You Are
All She Ever Wanted

SUMMER READS - Books 7-9, Vol. 3
Almost Home
Some Kind of Wonderful
Love Will Find A Way

SUMMER READS - Books 10-12, Vol. 4

Daniel's Gift
Ryan's Return
Ask Mariah
The Sweetest Thing

For a complete list of my books, visit my website!